Cry Jerusalem

Book Four: 69-70 CE

Final Siege

Ward Sanford

Published by Stadia Books LLC

www.CryForJerusalem.com

Cry For Jerusalem

Book Four: 69-70 CE

Final Siege

Ward Sanford

CRY FOR JERUSALEM
BOOK FOUR: 69–70 CE
FINAL SIEGE
WARD SANFORD

Copyright © 2023. All rights reserved. No part of this book may be reproduced or transmitted in any form or by any means, electronic or mechanical, including photocopying, recording, or by any information storage and retrieval system, without written permission from the author, except for brief quotations as used in a review.

978-1-950645-07-7

Front cover artwork created by ADDUCENTCREATIVE.COM.

PUBLISHED BY STADIA BOOKS LLC

WWW.CRYFORJERUSALEM.COM

CRY FOR JERUSALEM is a work of fiction inspired by eyewitness records of historical events. Some characters, many scenes, and most of the dialogue have been fictionalized for dramatic purposes.

What Professionals & Reviewers Are Saying About Cry For Jerusalem Book One, Two, and Three

"The story sweeps across a first-century world that's diverse, gritty, and laced with tension. Majestic and colorful landscapes such as Jerusalem, Rome, and the many places in between, both on land and sea, are richly detailed. I loved the maps that are included at the beginning. Sanford uses his characters well. Men and women have strong influence on the plot, including women who interacted with and changed their circumstances despite social constraints. Everything is supported by an incredibly well-researched foundation. The time period and social customs are delightfully developed... there is political and religious strife, moments of ancient beauty, and well-developed characters to carry the plot forward. Sanford is a talented author with an exciting new series to get lost in."

--Historical Novels Review Issue 91

"In this first installment of a series, Yosef comes to realize what a tinderbox the political situation has become. As Roman leaders become increasingly authoritarian and hungry for tax proceeds, Jewish militancy increases, setting the stage for a brutal confrontation, a historical predicament vividly and intelligently depicted by Sanford. And Nero, looking for an excuse to rebuild Rome, raise taxes, and consolidate his power, takes Florus' advice to burn the city to the ground, starting the "most extensive and destructive fire that Rome had ever experienced." The plot is as gripping as it is historically edifying, remarkably authentic, and rigorously researched. At its conclusion, readers will be left impatient for the book's sequel. An impressive blend of historical portrayal and dramatic fiction."

--Kirkus Reviews

In this historical novel set in the first century, the lives of four unlikely friends are threatened by the gathering war between Emperor Nero's Roman Empire and the Jewish population in Jerusalem. Nero has nearly bankrupted Rome as a consequence of relentless prodigality, diminishing the empire's power and sending many of its provinces into mutinous discontent. His devious plan is to manufacture a war with the restive Jewish population—especially in Jerusalem—in order to plunder its treasury, and he's prepared to deceive his own generals in order to accomplish this.

In this second installment of a four-volume series, Sanford deftly depicts the historical conflict by chronicling four intersecting lives. All of these characters meet by sheer happenstance but form a potent bond: Cleopatra; Nicanor, a Roman centurion; Sayid, a Roman soldier in Nicanor's legion; and Yosef, the military commander in charge of Galilee. Nicanor participates in a major loss against the rebels at Beth Horon under the leadership of Cestius Gallus, who entrusts the centurion with a packet of documents substantiating his suspicions that his campaign was purposely sabotaged by his own advisers. Meanwhile, Yosef tries to unite Galilee to oppose the inevitable Roman invasion but is despondent that his own people visit so much violence upon themselves, an inner conflict subtly portrayed by the author: "Yosef did not know who he hated more for what had happened—the Romans that had pushed the situation in Judea to this point or his own people who, for selfish reasons, had killed the innocent or let them be killed. They were driving them all toward inevitable death and destruction."

Sanford's historical rigor is impressive, and his account of the age's troubles, nimbly nuanced, unburdened by any calcified moral strictures. One caveat: For readers unfamiliar with the series opener, this will be a difficult (though not impossible) novel to follow. But the sequel is a captivating treat for those who enjoyed the book's predecessor.

A thrilling blend of powerful emotional drama and meticulous historical scholarship.

--Kirkus Reviews

"It's such a beautifully structured piece of writing. It has that quality of surprising you while feeling inevitable. The series is one of the highlights of each year for me."

--Simon de Deney, actor, audiobook narrator, University of Oxford Master of Arts (M.A.)

About Cry For Jerusalem

A four-novel—historical fiction—series based on the writings of Yosef ben Matityahu (Titus Flavius Josephus). Yosef's (Josephus's) work as a historian provides valuable insight into first-century Judaism and the background of early Christianity. He has specific details on the First Jewish–Roman War, which he witnessed and took part in at a high level. The story takes place from late 63 to 70 CE, a little over one-third of the way into 200 years of increased and sustained internal peace and stability for Rome, though not without lesser wars, conflicts of expansion, and revolts. This *Pax Romana* was first broken by the Jewish (Judean) first war of rebellion. First-century Judea was a time of new belief systems, persecution, and economic upheaval. Ruled by Rome's puppet-King Agrippa, the Judeans had fragmented into three factions under the Romans: the status-quo pro-Roman Moderates; the nationalists, Zealots who wanted Judean and Jewish independence; and the Sicarii, a violent splinter group who not only wanted freedom from Rome but also had a goal to kill all pro-Roman collaborators.

Two thousand years ago, men and women were driven to act—as they are today—by the same emotions, needs, and wants. In CRY FOR JERUSALEM, we experience how such actions forever changed the world for Jews and Christians through our main cast of characters: In Book One, we meet Yosef, a Jewish scholar, sent from Jerusalem to free priests imprisoned in Rome; Nicanor, a Roman centurion; Lady Cleo, a Roman noblewoman whose marriage is arranged to Gessius Florus, a man who becomes the new Judean Procurator; and Sayid, a legion auxiliary, serving in the lady's escort.

Synopsis of Book One: Resisting Tyranny

Yosef, Nicanor, Sayid, and Lady Cleopatra's (Cleo's) shared experience forms an unlikely bond of friendship tested throughout the four novels in the series. Was it fate, destiny, or some divine plan that brought these four very different travelers together to survive a shipwreck while traveling to Rome?

In Rome, the reader meets Emperor Nero and is introduced to the intrigue that permeates the empire. At the suggestion of Gessius Florus and to serve his own purpose, Nero sets Rome afire while shifting the blame onto the Christians. This sets events in motion to replenish Rome's depleted treasury by igniting a war in Judea to steal the vast treasure believed held in the Jewish Temple in Jerusalem.

Yosef, Nicanor, Cleo, and Sayid experience the Great Fire of Rome and its aftermath. Then each separately returns to Judea, where their fates further converge: Yosef to report the release of the Jewish prisoners and to attempt to stave off the increasing militancy of the anti-Roman factions, hoping to find a peaceful resolution with Rome; Nicanor—having avoided the Praetorian Guard duty he did not want—to return to his beloved legion duties in Antioch; Cleo, now married and accompanied by her husband; Gessius Florus, who is to become the new Procurator of Judea; and Sayid, glad to return to auxiliary duty in a land where he feels at home, is assigned to Lady Cleo and often thinks of Yosef and Nicanor.

In Jerusalem, the reader meets Miriam, Yosef's sister, who survives a tragic attack by Roman soldiers that changes her forever, turning her into something and someone she could never have imagined, which becomes a dark secret she must hide from her family.

In Judea, Gessius Florus shows his true colors. His oppressive actions were designed solely to squeeze more tax revenue and heighten tensions between Jerusalem's factions and Rome. He creates situations and events—including a massacre in Jerusalem shortly after Passover—that lead to chaos and the birthing of a full-blown war. All were intended to justify stealing the Jewish Temple treasure and to further his plan to keep a large part of it for himself and send the rest to Nero.

In Antioch, the reader meets Cestius Gallus, governor and commander of the 12th Legion. Circumstances and the rebels' actions forced him to lead his legion and allied forces into Judea for an ill-fated—ultimately aborted—attack on Jerusalem and one of the worst defeats of any Roman legion during their retreat through the pass at Beth Horon.

Yosef, Nicanor, Cleo, Sayid, and their family and friends play critical roles at a focal point in the history of Western civilization. As the winds helped to spread the great fire in Rome, they also carried embers to Judea, where they threatened to ignite a conflict that would forever change the world for Jews and Christians.

About Cry For Jerusalem

Synopsis of Book Two: Against All Odds

The epic saga continues its sweeping arc from Rome to Jerusalem, Antioch to Galilee. Ancient history comes to life—and events become plausibly explained that history has left unanswered—through the actions of historical figures in the aftermath of the 12th Legion's retreat from Jerusalem and defeat at Beth Horon. The Romans: Nero, Gessius Florus, and Tigellinus, each had agendas. Cestius Gallus, former commander of the 12th Legion, bears the ultimate burden... and the fate of his actions. And we meet Vespasian, who has taken over the campaign against the Judean rebels at Nero's order.

Cleo suffers at the hands of Gessius Florus while continuing her secret attempts to let other Romans know her husband's role in inciting a war that could have been prevented. Nicanor and Sayid, meanwhile, find themselves reluctant messengers drawn into the intrigues of powerful Romans whose sole purpose is the self-enrichment only found in the chaos of war. The Jews: Yosef ben Mathias (Josephus), who becomes the military commander in Galilee, commits to lead and fight in a war he knows his country can never win. A rebel leader, Yohanan ben Levi (John of Gischala)—seeking power among the Jews—confronts and obstructs Yosef in Galilee. While in Jerusalem, Yosef's sister Miriam descends deeper on her dark path of revenge and retribution.

The reader witnesses the Siege of Yotapta (Jotapata), where thousands of Jews died fighting Roman legions—against all odds—in one of the bloodiest battles in Jewish history. All of these were experienced and chronicled by the famous Jewish historian Josephus.

The story behind the legendary (but real) Copper Scroll further develops. Considered "the most unique, the most important, and the least understood" of the Dead Sea Scrolls, it describes the locations of the Temple treasure moved from Jerusalem to be hidden—assumingly—from the Romans. But the treasure has never been found.

The factions and dissension grow and weaken Jerusalem, while the intrigues within the Roman Empire lead to the Year of Four Emperors and the civil war that shaped the empire for decades.

SYNOPSIS OF BOOK THREE: GROWING ANARCHY

Yosef—defeated and captured at Yotapta—remains Roman General Vespasian's prisoner, as many of his countrymen consider him a traitor. Nicanor travels to the empire's western provinces to help Cleo by enlisting the aid of Marcus Otho, her brother and governor of Hispania Lusitania Nero, facing execution, commits suicide, and Lord Galba, who is close to Marcus Otho, becomes the new emperor. Cleo, unable to flee to Rome with Nicanor, has been hiding in Jerusalem with Yosef's family. Sayid returns to the Roman army and finds his father. Miriam rekindles feelings for Ehud, a former love who has returned to Jerusalem, but the Sicarii believe him a Roman collaborator. In Jerusalem, the effort to save the Temple treasure begins as factions within bring the city to anarchy. In Rome, discord and forces within threatened to fracture the empire and set the stage for what became known as Rome's Year of the Four Emperors. Galba is assassinated, Otho becomes emperor, and events move Jerusalem inexorably closer to its siege and destruction.

Contents

Dramatis Personae I
Historical Background VII
Map 1 – The Western Part of the Roman empire IX
Map 2 – The Seven Hills of Rome and Its 14 Regions X
Map 3 – The Center of Rome XI
Map 4 – Judean Provinces XII
Map 5 – Jerusalem XIII
Map 6 – The Temple Complex XIV
ACT I ....
I (1) Februarius 69 CE Rome 1
II (2) Februarius 69 CE Rome 4
III (3) Februarius 69 CE Jerusalem 10
IV (4) Februarius 69 CE Jerusalem 12
V (5) Februarius 69 CE Jerusalem 18
VI (6) Martius 69 CE Caesarea 22
VII (7) Martius 69 CE Rome 26
VIII (8) Martius 69 CE Jerusalem 31
IX (9) Martius 69 CE Jerusalem 35
X (10) Martius 69 CE Caesarea 39
XI (11) Aprilus 69 CE Near Placentia 43
XII (12) Aprilus 69 CE Jerusalem 46
XIII (13) Aprilus 69 CE Caphera 50
XIV (14) Aprilus 69 CE Caesarea 56
XV (15) Aprilus 69 CE Caesarea 59
XVI (16) Aprilus 69 CE Brixellum 62
XVII (17) Aprilus 69 CE Brixellum 66

XVIII (18) Aprilus 69 CE Brixellum 69

XIX (19) Aprilus 69 CE Jerusalem 74

XX (20) Aprilus 69 CE Caesarea 78

XXI (21) Maius 69 CE Near Aternum 82

XXII (22) Maius 69 CE Jerusalem 87

XXIII (23) Maius 69 CE Jerusalem 90

XXIV (24) Maius 69 CE Caesarea 93

XXV (25) Junius 69 CE Tibur 96

XXVI (26) Junius 69 CE Rome 99

XXVII (27 Junius 69 CE Rome 101

XXVIII (28) Junius 69 CE Jerusalem 106

XXIX (29) Junius 69 CE Hebron 110

XXX (30) Junius 69 CE Caesarea 113

XXXI (31) Julius 69 CE Puteoli 115

XXXII (32) Julius 69 CE Jerusalem 118

XXXIII (33) Julius 69 CE Caesarea 123

XXXIV (34) Julius 69 CE Har haKarmel / Mount Carmel 126

XXXV (35) Julius/Augustus 69 CE At Sea to Caesarea 131

XXXVI (36) Augustus 69 CE Jerusalem 136

XXXVII (37) Augustus 69 CE Jerusalem 139

XXXVIII (38) Augustus 69 CE Caesarea 142

XXXIX (39) Augustus 69 CE Caesarea 147

XL (40) Augustus 69 CE Caesarea 150

XLI (41) September 69 CE Jerusalem 154

XLII (42) September 69 CE Jerusalem 159

XLIII (43) September 69 CE Caesarea 164

XLIV (44) September 69 CE Caesarea 167

XLV (45) October 69 CE Verona 171

ACT II ....

XLVI (46) October 69 CE Jerusalem................................176

XLVII (47) October 69 CE Caesarea...............................180

XLVIII (48) October 69 CE Alexandria............................184

XLIX (49) October 69 CE Alexandria 188

L (50) November 69 CE Jerusalem 192

LI (51) November 69 CE Jerusalem 197

LII (52) November 69 CE Mevania 201

LIII (53) November 69 CE Alexandria............................204

LIV (54) November 69 CE Alexandria 208

LV (55) December 69 CE Rome...................................... 212

LVI (56) December 69 CE Sycaminum 216

LVII (57) December 69 CE Caesarea............................... 221

LVIII (58) December 69 CE Caesarea 223

LIX (59) December 69 CE Jerusalem..............................228

LX (60) December 69 CE Jerusalem 233

LXI (61) December 69 CE Jerusalem.............................. 237

LXII (62) December 69 CE Near Bousbastis 241

LXIII (63) December 69 CE Bousbastis.......................... 245

LXIV (64) Januarius 70 CE Caesarea..............................249

LXV (65) Januarius 70 CE Caesarea 252

LXVI (66) Januarius 70 CE Jerusalem 254

LXVII (67) Januarius 70 CE Jerusalem 257

LXVIII (68) Januarius 70 CE Caesarea........................... 261

LXIX (69) Februarius 70 CE Jerusalem 265

LXX (70) Februarius 70 CE Jerusalem 269

LXXI (71) Februarius 70 CE Jerusalem 272

LXXII (72) Februarius 70 CE Caesarea.......................... 276

LXXIII (73) Februarius 70 CE Caesarea 283

LXXIV (74) Februarius 70 CE Sycaminum............................. 287

LXXV (75) Martius 70 CE Jerusalem...................................... 291

LXXVI (76) Martius 70 CE Jerusalem 294

LXXVII (77) Martius 70 CE Jerusalem 298

LXXVIII (78) Martius 70 CE Caesarea 301

LXXIX (79) Martius 70 CE Caesarea 305

LXXX (80) Martius 70 CE Qumran 309

LXXXI (81) Martius 70 CE Qumran 312

LXXXII (82) Martius 70 CE Qumran 315

LXXXIII (83) Martius 70 CE Qumran 320

LXXXIV (84) Aprilus 70 CE Caesarea 323

LXXXV (85) Aprilus 70 CE Caesarea 326

LXXXVI (86) Aprilus 70 CE Caesarea 330

LXXXVII (87) Aprilus 70 CE Jerusalem.................................. 334

LXXXVIII (88) Aprilus 70 CE Jerusalem 337

LXXXIX (89) Aprilus 70 CE Gophna....................................... 343

ACT III..

XC (90) Aprilus 70 CE Near Jerusalem 347

XCI (91) Aprilus 70 CE Jerusalem 351

XCII (92) Aprilus 70 CE Near the Modi'in Valley 354

XCIII (93) Aprilus 70 CE Jerusalem 359

XCIV (94) Maius 70 CE Jerusalem 364

XCV (95) Maius 70 CE Jerusalem... 367

XCVI (96) Maius 70 CE Jerusalem 370

XCVII (97) Maius 70 CE Jerusalem 374

XCVIII (98) Maius 70 CE Jerusalem 376

XCIX (99) Maius 70 CE Jerusalem..382

C (100) Maius 70 CE Jerusalem 386
CI (101) Maius 70 CE Jerusalem 391
CII (102) Maius 70 CE Northwest of Jerusalem 397
CIII (103) Maius 70 CE Jerusalem 399
CIV (104) Junius 70 CE Jerusalem 402
CV (105) Junius 70 CE Jerusalem 406
CVI (106) Junius 70 CE Jerusalem 410
CVII (107) Junius 70 CE Jerusalem 413
CVIII (108) Junius 70 CE Jerusalem 416
CIX (109) Junius 70 CE Jerusalem 421
CX (110) Junius 70 CE Jerusalem 427
CXI (111) Junius 70 CE Jerusalem 430
CXII (112) Junius 70 CE Jerusalem 435
CXIII (113) Junius 70 CE Jerusalem 440
CXIV (114) Junius 70 CE Jerusalem 443
CXV (115) Junius 70 CE Jerusalem 446
CXVI (116) Julius 70 CE Jerusalem..449
CXVII (117) Julius 70 CE Jerusalem 452
CXVIII (118) Julius 70 CE Jerusalem... 456
CXIX (119) Julius 70 CE Jerusalem 460
CXX (120) Julius 70 CE Northwest of Jerusalem.................... 463
CXXI (121) Julius 70 CE Jerusalem 466
CXXII (122) Julius 70 CE Jerusalem 470
CXXIII (123) Julius 70 CE Jerusalem 474
CXXIV (124) Julius 70 CE Jerusalem 477
CXXV (125) Julius 70 CE Jerusalem 482
CXXVI (126) Julius 70 CE Jerusalem 484
CXXVII (127) Julius 70 CE Jerusalem 488

CXXVIII (128) Julius 70 CE Jerusalem 491

CXXIX (129) Julius 70 CE Jerusalem 494

CXXX (130) Julius 70 CE Jerusalem 497

CXXXI (131) Augustus 70 CE Jerusalem 500

CXXXII (132) Augustus 70 CE Jerusalem 503

CXXXIII (133) Augustus 70 CE Jerusalem............................. 507

CXXXIV (134) Augustus 70 CE Jerusalem 510

CXXXV (135) Augustus 70 CE Jerusalem...............................513

CXXXVI (136) Augustus 70 CE Jerusalem 515

CXXXVII (137) Augustus 70 CE Jerusalem 517

CXXXVIII (138) Augustus 70 CE Jerusalem 520

CXXXIX (139) Augustus 70 CE Jerusalem 522

CXL (140) Augustus 70 CE Jerusalem 524

CXLI (141) Augustus 70 CE Jerusalem 527

CXLII (142) Augustus 70 CE Jerusalem 532

CXLIII (143) Augustus 70 CE Jerusalem................................. 535

CXLIV (144) Augustus 70 CE Jerusalem 537

CXLV (145) Augustus 70 CE Jerusalem....................................541

CXLVI (146) Augustus 70 CE Jerusalem 543

CXLVII (147) Augustus 70 CE Jerusalem 547

CXLVIII (148) Augustus 70 CE Jerusalem 550

CXLIX (149) Augustus 70 CE Jerusalem 553

CL (150) Augustus 70 CE Jerusalem..557

CLI (151) Augustus 70 CE Jerusalem 559

CLII (152) Augustus 70 CE Jerusalem 563

CLIII (153) Augustus 70 CE Jerusalem.................................... 567

CLIV (154) Augustus 70 CE Jerusalem 570

CLV (155) Augustus 70 CE Jerusalem...................................... 573

CLVI (156) Augustus 70 CE Jerusalem 576
CLVII (157) Augustus 70 CE Jerusalem 578
CLVIII (158) Augustus 70 CE Jerusalem 582
CLIX (159) Augustus 70 CE Jerusalem 588
CLX (160) Augustus 70 CE Jerusalem 591
CLXI (161) Augustus 70 CE Jerusalem 596
CLXII (162) Augustus 70 CE Jerusalem 599
CLXIII (163) Augustus 70 CE Jerusalem 603
CLXIV (164) Augustus 70 CE Jerusalem 608
CLXV (165) Augustus 70 CE Jerusalem 612
CLXVI (166) Augustus 70 CE Jerusalem 616
CLXVII (167) Augustus 70 CE Jerusalem 619
CLXVIII (168) Augustus 70 CE Northeast of Jerusalem 622
CLXIX (169) Augustus 70 CE Jerusalem 625
CLXX (170) Augustus 70 CE Jerusalem 628
CLXXI (171) Augustus 70 CE Jerusalem 632
CLXII 172) September 70 CE Caesarea 634
CLXXIII (173) September/October 70 CE At Sea/Rome 639
CLXXIV (174) Junius 71 CE Rome 646
About the Author 654
More From the Author 655

Dramatis Personae

Yosef ben Mathias
A young, upper-class, educated Jew sent—in Book 1—to Rome as an envoy to free imprisoned priests. Returning to Judea, when the war begins, he is assigned to become the military commander of Galilee. Captured by the Romans at the fall of Yotapta, a personal prisoner of General Vespasian and then his son Titus, Yosef tries to stop the war.

Rebecca
Yosef's mother who has a lineage of Jewish royalty from the Hasmonean dynasty.

Mathias
Yosef's father and a leader in the Sanhedrin, the governing body of the Jews in Judea.

Matthew ben Mathias
Yosef's older brother, an officer in the Jewish Temple Guard, who tries to save the Temple treasure from the Romans by hiding it.

Miriam
Yosef's younger sister, whose personal tragedy has transformed her into the Sicarii assassin known as 'The Hand.'

Ehud
Miriam's former crush. His family had left Jerusalem years before and had business connections with the Romans in Alexandria. Gessius Florus forces him to become another spy or his family will be killed. Events lead to his tragic death by Miriam's hand in Book Three.

Leah
Yosef's cousin was mutually attracted to Yosef at age sixteen and afterward... but married an abusive man.

Rachel
Leah's younger sister, who has also fallen in love with Yosef.

Dramatis Personae

YOHANAN BEN ZACCAI
Member of the Sanhedrin and Yosef's father's oldest friend.

ELEASAR BEN ANANIAS
Captain of the Jewish Temple Guard, a rebel leader, though not an extremist. He is Matthew's key partner in hiding the Temple treasure.

ZECHARIAH
A blind craftsman and a skilled warrior who befriended Miriam, teaching her the martial arts she uses as The Hand. Killed saving her a second time; he remains in Miriam's heart and mind.

HANANIAH
A master bladesmith and killer-for-hire who hates Jerusalem. Gessius Florus has brought him from Alexandria to serve as his spymaster and to hunt down and kill the Sicarii assassin, The Hand and get details on the hidden locations for the Temple treasure.

ARINS
A mercenary assassin from the Balearic Islands used by Gessius Florus's family for years and hired by him to enter Jerusalem and accomplish what Hananiah, his other embedded killer, had yet to do.

ELAZAR BEN YAIR
Leader of the Sicarii, who have taken refuge in Masada.

YOHANAN BEN LEVI (OF GISCHALA)
A rebel leader from Galilee, often at odds with leadership in Jerusalem. His refusal to accept Yosef's appointment as commander in Galilee resulted in death and disruption in the region. Abandoning his city, Gischala, to the Romans, he fled to Jerusalem, where he incites more dissension and tries to gain control of the city.

SIMON BAR GIORA
The rebel leader who led the force that defeated the 12th Legion and took their *aquila*, battle standard, at Beth Horon. He vies for control over Jerusalem with Yohanan ben Levi of Gischala.

Dramatis Personae

Yonatan bar Hilel
Leah's husband, a Zealot, who hates Yosef and his family. He becomes a chief lieutenant for Yohanan ben Levi.

Esau ben Beor
Once a leader of the Judean province of Idumea whose secret hatred of Jerusalem enabled Florus to leverage him to become his spy within the Sanhedrin. As The Hand, Miriam killed him, leading to her first encounter with Hananiah, Gessius Florus's killer in Jerusalem.

Nicanor
A Roman centurion and friend of Yosef. His father was a Roman legionary, and his mother was Greek. He's become entangled in the intrigues and agendas of powerful men in Rome. He returns to Judea from his mission for Vespasian and to enlist Lord Otho's help to save Cleo from Gessius Florus. He hopes to still somehow save her.

Graius
Lady Cleo's retired former major domus, who Nicanor discovered was once a renowned gladiator in Rome. He joined Nicanor on his journey to meet with Marcus Otho, governor of Hispania Lusitania, to seek his help in saving Lady Cleo. He died, saving Nicanor's life.

Cleopatra (Cleo/Ya'el)
A young Roman noblewoman and an admirer of Jewish culture, who had toured the eastern Roman provinces before wedding Gessius Florus, the man primarily responsible for inciting the rebellion. Married to a man she fears and hates, with Sayid's help, she escapes Gessius Florus. Now she's stranded in a country at war with Rome, hiding among its enemies under the Jewish name Ya'el.

Sayid
A young Syrian volunteer army auxiliary whose father was a Roman soldier of African descent who fell in love with his mother, a Syrian. Once assigned to Lady Cleo's retinue after her marriage, he's attached to the 12th Legion. And—like Nicanor—finds himself drawn into helping the legion commander, Cestius Gallus, and then his friend, Lady Cleo. After saving her from Gessius Florus, he returns to the army and fulfills his desire to find his father.

Dramatis Personae

ELIAN
A young slave boy who had been a servant in Lady Cleo's household in Ptolemais. When she flees Gessius Florus, Cleo can't leave him behind. He hides with her in Jerusalem.

ANTONIA CAENIS
Joined with General Vespasian in a *conturbernium*, a civil union and not a marriage, Antonia Caenis is a politically savvy advisor. She has connections throughout the empire and helped Nicanor in Rome.

GNAEUS BATIATUS
Owner of a gladiator training school, and a friend to Antonia Caenis, he provided a safe place for Nicanor in Rome during his mission for Vespasian.

MARCUS ATTILIUS
A freedman, a Christian, and a skilled fighter. He becomes a close friend to Nicanor in Rome.

FLORIN
A legion auxiliary was Nicanor's clerk and messenger when Nicanor was previously assigned as a watch captain at a prison in Rome. He served as Nicanor's personal aide.

CELSUS EVANDER
A legion quartermaster commander and friend of Nicanor.

MARCUS SABINUS
Sayid's father, who serves in the 15th Legion, Apollinaris. Badly wounded fighting Judean rebels at Gamala, he recovers and though now hampered by his healed injuries, joins the 15th Legion in the assault on Jerusalem.

CESTIUS GALLUS
Once the Roman legate (governor) of the eastern Roman provinces, including Syria and Judea, and commander of the 12th Legion. His attempts to alert Emperor Nero about how the war was provoked and his suspicions of Gessius Florus led to his death.

Dramatis Personae

Vespasian
The general Emperor Nero chose to command the Judean campaign to crush the rebels. He becomes the 4th new ruler in the Year of Four Emperors.

Titus
Vespasian's son and field commander of the legions in his father's campaign against the Judean rebels. Ultimately, he commands the final assault that leads to Jerusalem's destruction.

Gessius Florus
A Roman tax collector who married Cleo to become the Judean Procurator, then Nero's Imperial Tax Collector, while planning to steal the Jewish Temple treasure. He abuses Cleo until her escape and is a deadly enemy to anyone in his way.

Drusus
Hired by Gessius Florus as a courier of messages to and from his spies in Jerusalem, he is also an abnormally strong and cruel man. Gessius Florus finds more uses for him better suited to his brutality.

Krateros
A merciless killer and leader of the Thracian mercenaries hired by Gessius Florus. He becomes one of Florus's chief henchmen.

Galerius Senna
Senior Military Tribune of the 12th Legion. Becomes its commander when Cestius Gallus is relieved of his duties by Nero. Gessius Florus controls him.

Ophonius Tigellinus
The publicly prominent co-Prefect of the Praetorian Guard, who had been closely aligned with Nero, was equally intent on self-enrichment. He has a vested interest in the success of Gessius Florus in Judea. He, too, will be enriched by the theft of the Jewish Temple treasure.

Dramatis Personae

NERO
The despotic Roman emperor who brought the empire to the verge of bankruptcy. Under his reign, Rome was nearly destroyed by a great fire. He pursued Gessius Florus's plan to replenish the Roman treasury by stealing from Judea under the guise of war. His death launches the Year of the Four Emperors.

SERVIUS GALBA
The governor of Hispania Tarraconensis when Nero is finally held accountable for his misrule of the empire and forced to commit suicide. With support from northern province legions, Galba becomes the new emperor. Only to anger those who once supported him. He becomes the 1st new ruler in the Year of Four Emperors.

MARCUS OTHO
The brother of Lady Cleo, governor or Hispania Lusitania, and an early supporter of Galba. As the outcry against Galba grows, and the new emperor—an old man—chose another as his successor, Marcus Otho recruited enough support from within the empire to instigate Galba's assassination. He became the 2nd new emperor in the Year of Four Emperors, only to lose in battle to Vitellius, who also wished to rule.

AULUS VITELLIUS
As commander of the legions in Germania, a former consul, and governor of Africa Proconsularis, Vitellius contended first with Galba and then Otho for the legions' allegiance and support to become emperor. Upon Galba's assassination, he moved quickly to position himself to rule, only for Otho to be named emperor. After Otho's defeat and death, Vitellius reigned for eight months—the 3rd new ruler in the Year of Four Emperors—until Vespasian's forces drove him from the throne.

HISTORICAL BACKGROUND

By the fall of Jerusalem in 70 CE, the culmination of ***Cry For Jerusalem***, Rome had much of the known world under its control. The empire reached its largest expanse in 117 CE under Emperor Trajan.

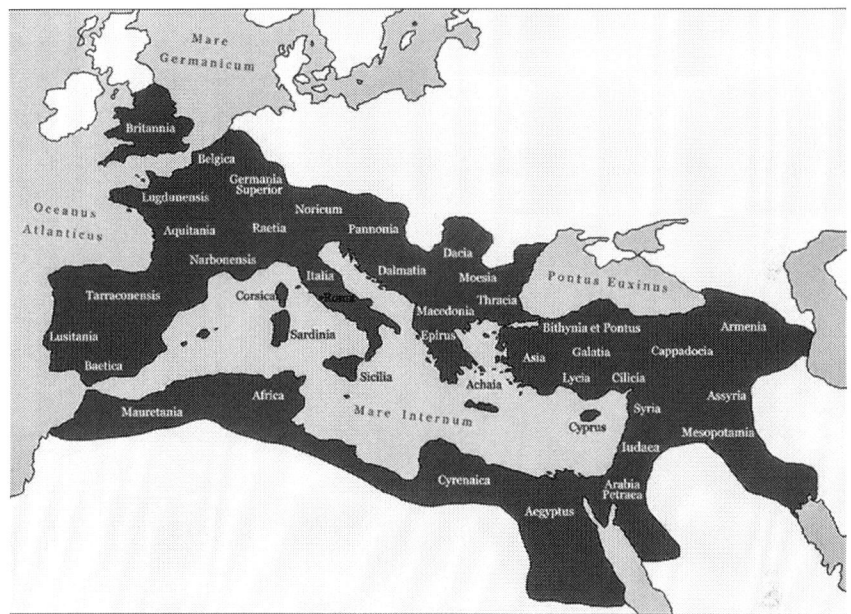

THE ROMAN EMPIRE CIRCA 117 CE

The empire encompassed an area of three million square miles. It stretched from the British Isles across western, central, and southern Europe, northern Africa, and western Asia. Its estimated 60 million inhabitants would have accounted for between one-sixth and one-fourth of the world's population. It was the largest unified political entity in the West until the mid-19th century. More recent demographic studies suggest the population could have risen to 100 million at its peak. The three largest cities in the empire—Rome, Alexandria, and Antioch—were almost twice the size of any European city before the 17th century.

The Romans had occupied greater Judea since the invasion of General Pompey in 63 BCE. Many large buildings and a grand

Temple complex in Jerusalem were constructed by King Herod the Great from circa 20 BCE until well after he died in 4 BCE. After Herod's death, the greater province was divided into four tetrarchs ruled by Herod's descendants, who functioned as Roman-controlled governors.

Map 1 – The Western Part of the Roman Empire

THE WESTERN PART OF THE ROMAN EMPIRE
IN THE FIRST CENTURY CE

Map 2 – The Seven Hills of Rome and its 14 Regions

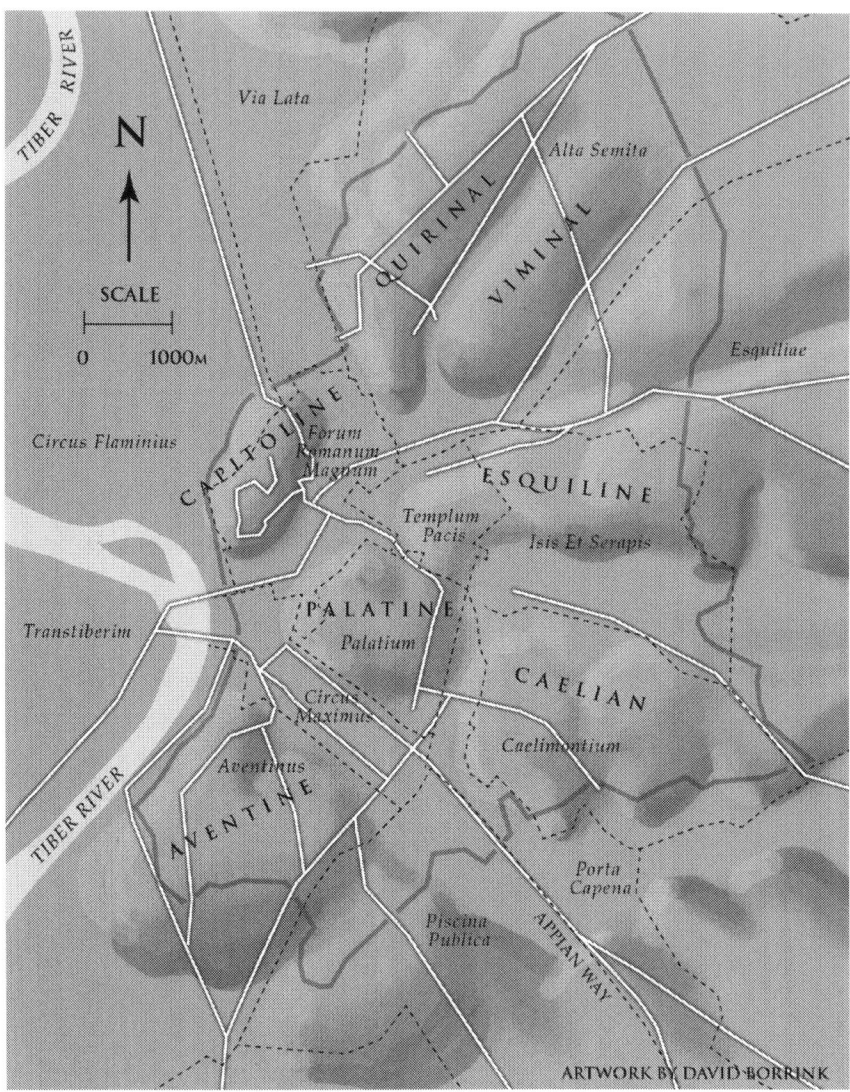

THE WALLS (SOLID LINE) AND ROADS (OPEN LINES)

Map 3 – The Center of Rome

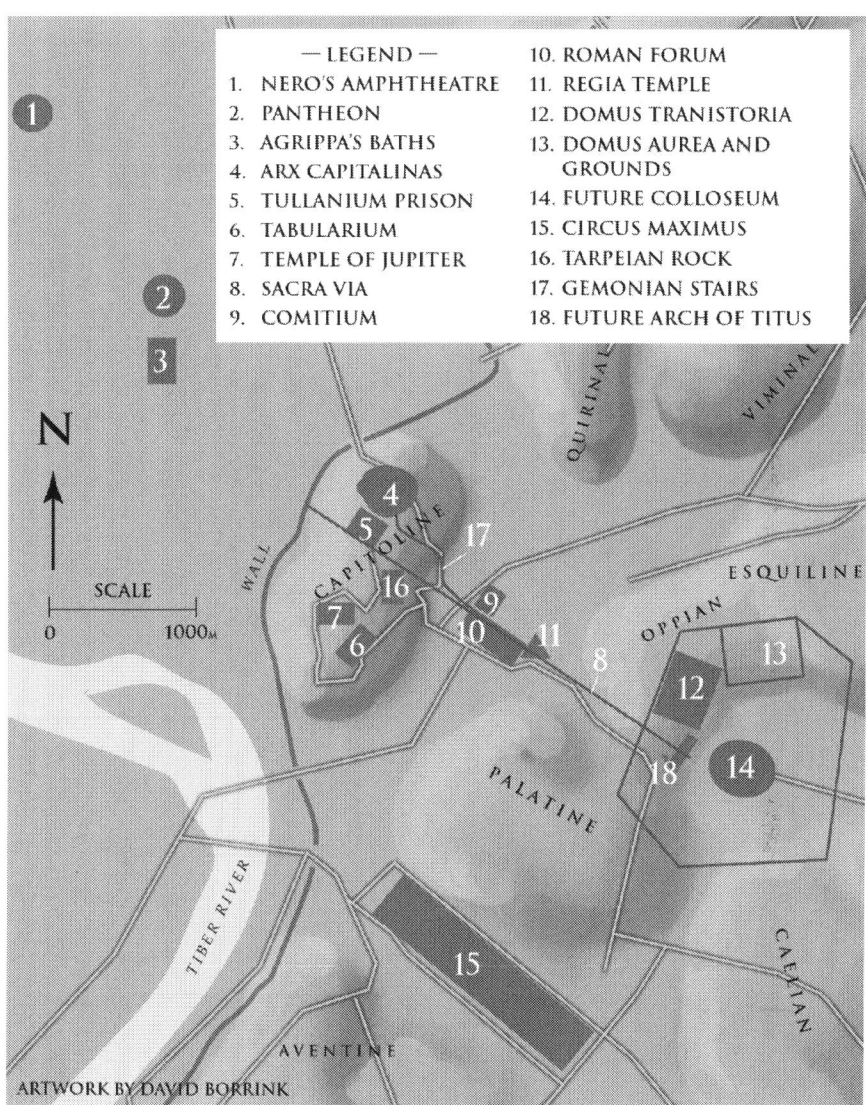

MAJOR FEATURES IN THE FIRST CENTURY CE

MAP 4 – JUDEAN PROVINCES

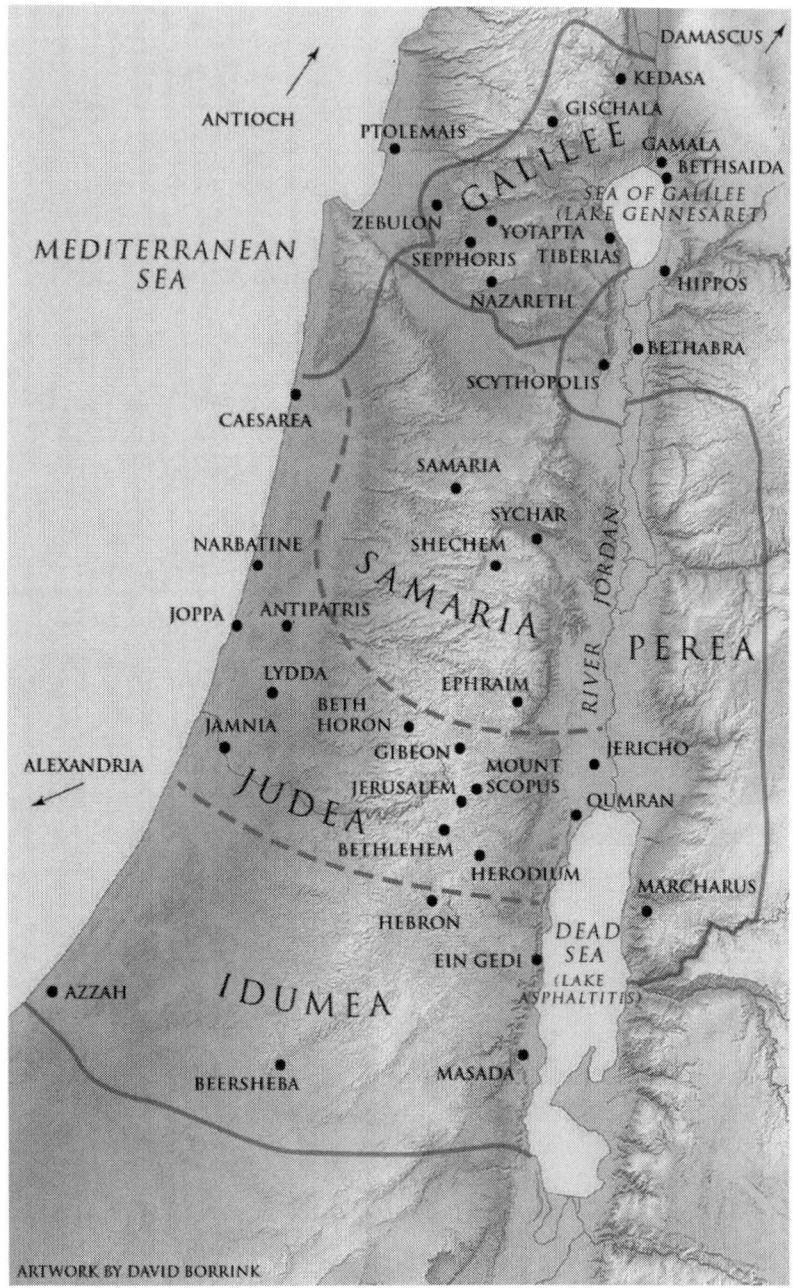

THE JUDEAN PROVINCES IN THE FIRST CENTURY CE

Map 5 – Jerusalem

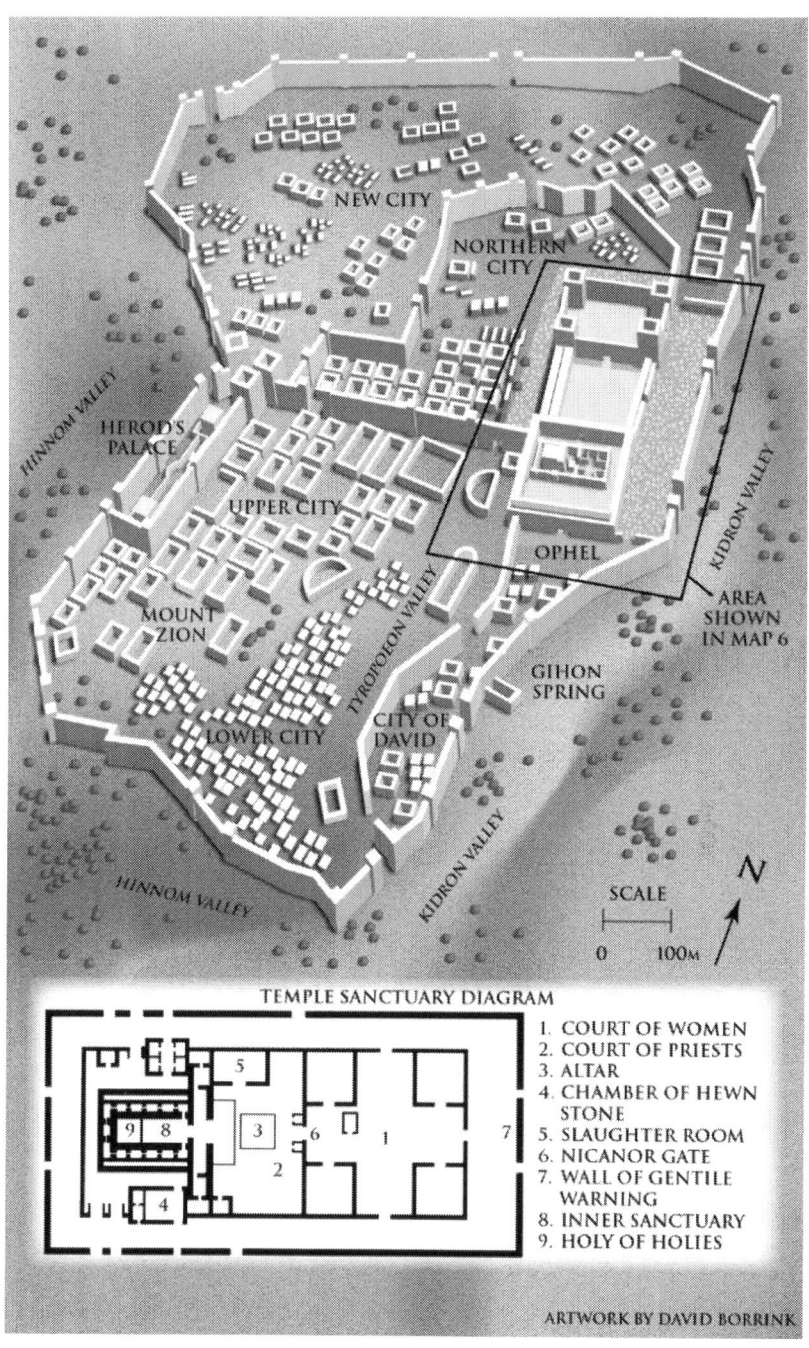

XIII

Map 6 – The Temple Complex

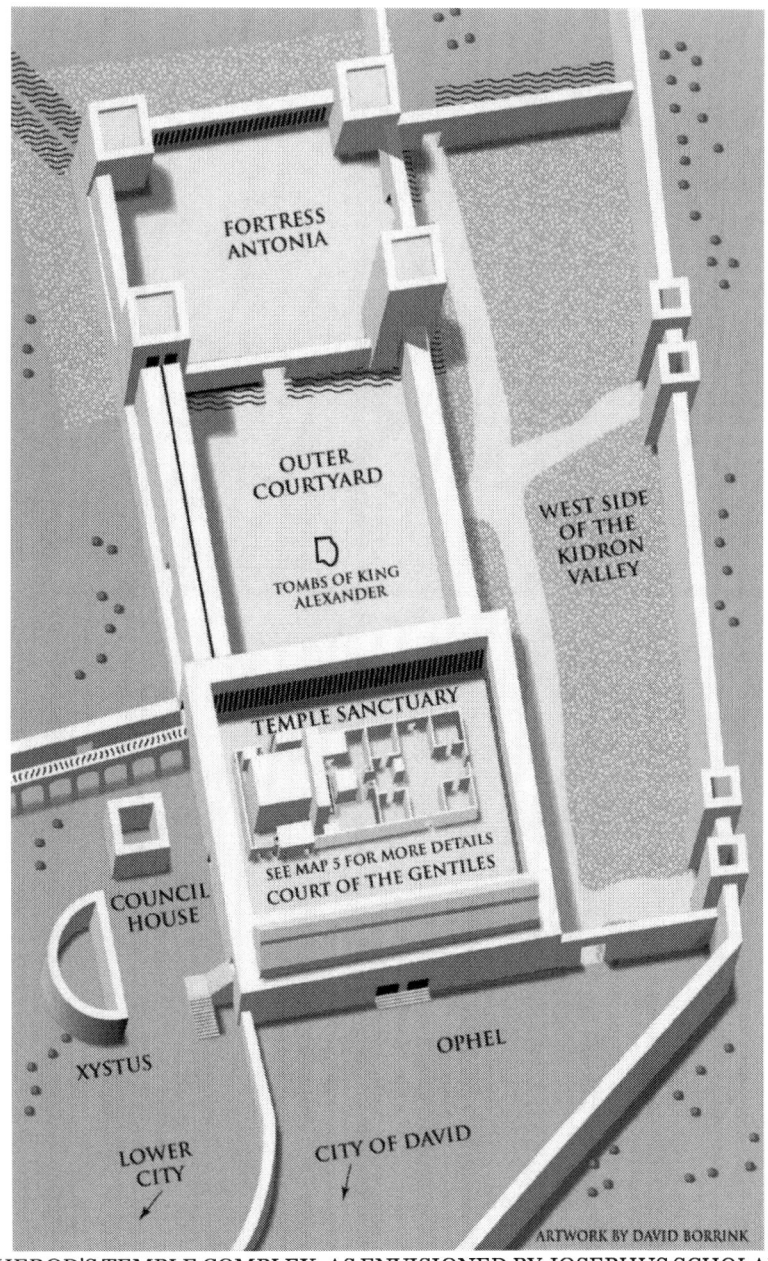

HEROD'S TEMPLE COMPLEX, AS ENVISIONED BY JOSEPHUS SCHOLAR THOMAS LEWIN

"But when you see Jerusalem surrounded by armies, then know that its desolation is near."

Yeshua ish Natzrat, 33 CE

ACT I

I

Februarius 69 CE

Rome

Circus Maximus

Nicanor had often heard the screams of wounded and dying horses in battle. Once the cacophony of combat had faded, that accompanying sound of suffering lingered, often for days. But it never haunted him as much as now, as the echoes in the massive arena seemed louder. What bothered him most was the roaring above the piercing shrill cries—the wild cheering of a hundred thousand men and women. The people of Rome, he thought, shaking his head, my countrymen.

The charioteers belonged to *factiones*, teams owned by affluent Romans, even the emperors. Each factione was marked by its own color and had its own followers. The commoners who cheered on the teams often fought the followers of opposing teams in the streets and the stands of the arena. Most charioteers were slaves but professionals with real incentives—if a driver often won, a share of the winnings could buy his freedom.

Every race had at least one crash of chariots, resulting in broken legs and jagged wounds where splintered wood had ripped into chests and bellies. But more animals than humans were injured, though the charioteers were often hurt and some killed.

After the third race, attendants did little more than drag the debris and thrashing bodies to the side. The most severely wounded animals were dispatched to still them with a thrust or slash. Nicanor was thankful for the end of their suffering. There was so much blood on the track they no longer bothered to cast dirt on the course between the races. Man and beast plowed on, churning up and splashing bloody mud.

Maybe today, Nicanor thought, the recommencing of the Games was *intended* to be brutal. To slake the bloodlust of crowds that had been denied that form of entertainment under Emperor Galba's cost-saving measures. But he did not want to return to compare the races of another day. This day was ending badly enough.

He looked away from the action on the track, ignoring the clamor, and his eyes went to what he had touched only hours before. He had stood upon the spina at the center of the arena—where a red granite obelisk rose over eighty feet into a cloudless, crystalline blue sky marked only by the fierce blaze of the sun. Shading his eyes, Nicanor followed the tremendous height of the monument into the sky. He shivered, despite the warmth of the sun that revealed the obelisk carvings. Or maybe the gusting northern wind swirling through the valley formed by the Palatine and Aventine hills stole the sun's heat. He had tucked the *focale* inside his *paenula* and drawn the hooded cloak closer so the shawl around his neck did not flare like a legion cavalry pennant in the wind.

Part of him wished he had refused Gnaeus Batiatus. But he could not deny the owner of the gladiatorial school he had met through Antonia Caenis, General Vespasian's companion and shrewd advisor—a wife in all but name—who had helped him on his return to Rome. His invitation to the Games and races—newly restarted by Emperor Otho—had included the rare privilege of access to the floor and track of the Circus Maximus. Rebuilt with stone to replace the wood destroyed in the great fire and expanded to hold even more spectators, the arena was even grander. Thanks to Gnaeus, he now stood on the centerpiece of the arena, an oval nearly 2000 feet long and 1500 feet wide. The spina, over 1100 feet long, lay within the circuit of the surrounding track and contained objects and structures that served the races. Seven metal dolphins were used for counting the seven laps of a race. Each would be tilted forward, tail up and head down, after a lap. But the most impressive to Nicanor was this obelisk.

His first time in Rome, a friend had told him of it. He smiled to think of Yosef, a Jew he had met on board the *Salacia* sailing to Rome from Judea and survived a shipwreck. But before they could come to see the obelisk from the stands, the great fire had swept the city. With his love of history, Yosef would have prized being close enough to touch it. The monolith was inscribed with Aegyptian markings several centuries old. It had been brought from Heliopolis, Aegypt, by Emperor Augustus 79 years before. Yosef had told him how the monument had first been erected in that foreign land by Ramses II over a millennium ago. Only to be taken far away to become a marker of the Roman conquest. But as much as he admired Rome, Yosef had ended up back in Judea, leading Galilean rebel forces against the empire as the smoldering unrest in the Judean province flared into open rebellion.

Nicanor had seen chariot races in the provinces, but none like those of this enormous arena. Gnaeus Batiatus had used his influence to get prized lower-tier seating—just above the rows for the senatorial ranks. Nicanor was glad to be closer to the track but wondered if his new status, conferred by Emperor Otho, influenced how others treated him. He'd become increasingly aware of the good and bad of that—the reward and risk—and he was worried.

His concern outweighed his pleasure with his privilege. Though he was here in Rome now, he mostly wished he had boarded that ship in Ostia with Lord Titus and sailed for Judea. A land of war, and the conflicts were likely to escalate soon after this lull in the storm they were enjoying—the delay of Roman retaliation—ended. Many expected that Otho's rule would stabilize the empire. Events long-stalled would now take their course. He wished he could be there, but not for the fighting. He wanted to be close to help Lady Cleo, another friend from the wreck of the *Salacia*. If the rumor spread throughout Rome was true, she was in Jerusalem, at the heart of the storm. His former aide, Sayid, a Syrian auxiliary, was resolute in his conviction that she was. It must be.

"Nicanor," Marcus Attilius called, "the races will begin soon. We must take our seats."

Nicanor laid his hand upon the ancient monolith for the last time, thinking of Yosef and how insignificant they were. The obelisk, the Circus Maximus, the looming hills, and the surrounding city made him feel small. Insignificant in Roman gods' eyes. But the words of the Christian Paul, words about his belief, gave the centurion a moment's pause. He wondered if the Christian god was not as hardhearted as a Roman deity. Maybe the Christian god looked down from their heaven—not from Olympus—and saw him trying to be a good man in bad times.

"Go ahead," Nicanor told his freedman friend, who was also a friend of Gnaeus. Marcus and Florin, his young clerk-messenger when he had served as a Praetorian Guard watch captain, were his closest companions in the vast city of Rome. "I'll follow you...." He looked back at the obelisk as he stepped down from the spina, crossed the track, and passed through an access tunnel to steps leading up to the stands. It stood tall but also alone. He felt a pang he did not understand at first. Then it came to him as he settled next to Marcus and Florin, and the arena filled. The jutting stone spire had made him think of Cleo, Yosef, and Sayid in Judea. He prayed they were still alive, standing firm... but not alone.

II

Februarius 69 CE

Rome

An Insula near the Tabularium

Marcus Attilius strode into Nicanor's apartment and paced the room, stopping near the shuttered window. He grumbled; it was too chilly outside to open it yet, though he wanted fresh air. "It smells much better at Gnaeus Batiatus's villa, and the rooms are warmer."

Nicanor grunted. The five-story *insula* east of the Tiber River was close enough to the *cloaca maxima* sewage effluence that he suffered when the wind carried the odor to him. This apartment building was newly built on a site cleared of the rubble from the great fire nearly four years before. It was better than the others he had looked at in the area; the odor was tolerable here. Some wealthy landowners and landlords of Rome, taking advantage of governmental distractions, did not feel accountable to the new construction laws when they raised their new buildings. But this structure seemed sound, and he preferred this small measure of independence over continuing to live with his friend. He trusted and even liked Gnaeus Batiatus, but being someone's 'guest' had worn thin long ago. His new duty required being nearer the city center.

"The emperor wishes me to be close to the Praetorian Prefect's office in the *Tabularium*," he replied as Marcus opened the shutter and let in a chilly gust. Nicanor could see through the window the large, many-sided structure he had been assigned to. Built in the late Republic, the magnificent building commanded the saddle between the Capitoline Hill's two summits. Its high colonnaded galleries overlooked the west end of the *Forum Romanum*.

Hearing a clatter in the passageway outside, Nicanor stepped to the door and opened it. Florin stood there, his arms wrapped around six legionary shields that hid him from just below his knees to mid-chest. The large *scuta* were newly painted and unscarred, their metal center bosses without nicks or gouges. "In the corner," he directed the young auxiliary.

Nicanor had grown almost as fond of the boy as he had of Sayid. But other than sharing the leanness of youth, they were quite different. Sayid had dark curls and dusky skin, with the look of the southern and eastern provinces. Florin was fair, with straight, light brown hair and the pale skin of many born in the empire's northern regions.

Since that moment at the Circus Maximus, Nicanor's musings often turned to Sayid and Yosef, wondering how they fared. But one thought, a constant worry, was always with him—Cleo. He remembered the night two years before. When Sayid sneaked into the Roman encampment at Ptolemais to tell him he had saved Cleo from the beatings of her husband, Gessius Floris. Sayid showed much bravery in saving Cleo and getting her safely away. He explained the noblewoman hid in the darkness beyond the camp perimeter fence. Nicanor ordered that she be brought in to him.

Once in the camp's shelter and Nicanor's care, Cleo explained she needed help to get out of Judea and away from Gessius Florus, the former Roman Procurator there. Nicanor already despised the man. He accepted Cleo's word that Florus had played a role in starting and escalating the war with the Judean rebels.

After telling Nicanor all of this, she asked to see Yosef, who had been imprisoned in Ptolemais after the fall of Yotapta in Galilee. Nicanor knew of the ill-fated feelings between Cleo and Yosef. Sparked during the shipwreck of the *Salacia* that they had all survived. Though he knew a Roman lady should not consort with even a highborn Jew, he reluctantly let them spend a brief time together.

Yosef had proposed that Cleo go to his family in Jerusalem, which Nicanor knew would be dangerous. At some point, that city would become the focus of a siege by the Romans, and Rome would win. The plan then became for Nicanor to take Cleo to Rome—ordered there by General Vespasian, the new commander of all the legions brought against the Judean rebels.

But Cleo and Sayid had failed to meet him at the port of Ptolemais as planned. He had had to sail for Rome without her.

Afterward, Nicanor heard more about Sayid's exploits and believed them. Sayid somehow got Cleo to Jerusalem despite the armed and angry rebels and many Roman patrols between Ptolemais and that city. As Nicanor worried about his friends in war-torn Judea, he realized that he, like Yosef, had feelings for Lady Cleo. Those feelings spurred his desire to reach her brother, Marcus Otho, then the governor of Hispania Lusitania. *He* might be able to protect her.

Nicanor had traveled with Cleo's retired *major domus*, a former gladiator named Graius. The two had met in Rome and then traveled to Hispania to reach Marcus Otho. Graius had been killed in the effort. Nero had recently died, and Galba became emperor, supported by Marcus Otho, who then changed his loyalty, and his supporters assassinated Galba. Marcus Otho had become emperor and had issued a decree to protect his sister. Nicanor hoped the decree had arrived in Judea in time to save Cleo, but it might be too late. Rebels in that city there would hunt for Cleo to use her as leverage with Emperor Otho. She would not be safe anywhere in Judea.

Nicanor shook away his fears and arranged the shields three by three along the adjacent walls near the window. He placed a charcoal-filled brazier in front of them and lit the charcoal. Wafts of smoke soon twined and drifted toward the window.

"That's a clever use of the shields," said Marcus, who had arrived only minutes ahead of Florin, moved closer, and held his hands over the small fire to warm them.

Nicanor shrugged. "Helps to reflect the heat... something I learned from many winters in cold field camps."

Florin squatted and set more charcoal onto the brazier, happy that Nicanor had requested him to be his aide. This duty was better than his former work in the prison, where only Nicanor's leadership eased the depressing surroundings of the Tullianum.

"So," Marcus said as he turned to Nicanor, "you avoided becoming one of Otho's personal bodyguards?"

"Yes. But I'm to help select them. The Batavians, who previously guarded the emperors, have become a problem; their province is restless under Roman rule. So, just before he died, Galba disbanded the soldiers who formerly served in Germania, removing them from the Praetorians. I told Lord Otho I would work with his new Praetorian Prefect, Plotius Firmus, to select men from the Praetorian ranks he could trust as his new personal guards. Florin and I know those men well," he nodded toward the young man, "we'll begin tomorrow."

"What other duties does Otho have for you?"

"I'm to be a *tribunus* on his personal staff, to serve as needed."

"That does not sound too troublesome but watch your back. There are still many who prefer a different emperor."

"The two times I've served here, some Romans always wanted someone else to rule. Are the people or the Senate ever content, or is there someone always stirring up unrest?"

"There are highborn and even bare-footed street philosophers who might answer you," Marcus said with a shrug, "but I cannot. I know commoners and nobles alike will be as they have always been.

Little changes." He unslung a pouch from his shoulder and took out a flat square of parchment with a blob of wax sealing the four corners folded to its center. "A rider brought this to Gnaeus's villa for you this morning. You should look at it now, and I'll take your reply to the rider. He told me he'd wait."

Breaking the seal so that the crumbled wax fell to the floor, Nicanor read the message and shook his head. "Push and pull me... come here... go there." He sighed and looked up. "Tell him to tell *her* I'll be there three days from now."

* * *

Tibur, Northeast of Rome

The Aniene Valley

A few hours on the road put Rome far behind Nicanor, and the smells and sounds of the city had long faded. The chilly breeze brought the fresh scent of the forests and hills ahead. Nicanor had finally lost the vestiges of his irritation at being summoned. The horse Carmenta—a gift from Antonia Caenis in thanks for Nicanor saving her Lord Vespasian's life at Yotapta—breathed deeply and evenly. Her good mood cheered him. She was always tense in the city and seemed to lose her edginess as they traveled farther into the countryside.

Nicanor had accepted that until all was done—his duty, the war in Judea, the turmoil in Rome, and Cleo safe—he would have to "go and do" as was needed, often at the direction of others. He was sure Antonia Caenis had a sound reason for asking him to come to her, but it likely meant something he would prefer not to do.

The valley, formed by the confluence of the Aniene and Tiber rivers, and the horse and rider were now surrounded by the Sabine hills, where temples and buildings had been built upon the heights. He was chilled to the bone, and he reached down to stroke Carmenta's neck. Their mouths streamed clouds of breath, and ahead of them, nestled on the hills and in the folds where the slopes joined, pillars of smoke rose from nearby villas and homes. "We're nearly there, girl. Then warm oats and a fresh blanket for you." Carmenta nickered and tossed her head. Nicanor relished that joyful sound. He thought of the ghost echoes of the horses at the Circus Maximus and their fate. To run at the lash of a whip, to die on the track, or, if lamed, to be dispatched without a care. He leaned to stroke Carmenta's neck. He had so many horses throughout his legion service. And that reminded him of years past and all that had happened to him... and his friends. He thought about what he'd said to Yosef after the shipwreck of the *Salacia* and after they survived the great fire in Rome and an attack by men he thought had set it. He patted Carmenta again, leaning over her neck to whisper, "We live."

But would he ever have what he now wanted most in life?

* * *

ANTONIA CAENIS'S VILLA

"I just looked in on Carmenta," Antonia Caenis said to Nicanor as she joined him at the kitchen table after he had washed up to meet her. "She has some scars... but you've taken good care of her." They sat near the broad stone fireplace where a cauldron of slow-cooking stew hung from an iron rod over the flames. Nicanor was enjoying the warmth of the fire and his cups of heated, mulled wine. While waiting for her, he watched a young servant clean and quarter a brace of rabbits for the pot, cut up vegetables to add, and then pour in barley to thicken it. The beginnings of a savory aroma wafted through the room.

"She has taken good care of me," he said. "Carmenta is the equal of any horse I've had." Nicanor thought of Abigieus, lost in the battle at Beth Horon on the retreat from Jerusalem. He had given the big warhorse to a wounded Sayid to carry him to safety. While he stayed behind in that cursed valley in command of a decoy cohort so the 12th Legion could escape during the night. The next dawn, he had watched his men die around him as they fought, and he'd nearly been killed. Afterward, as one of few survivors, he had made his way to the legion's rally point camp far from Beth Horon. Sayid had told him Abigieus had saved him but died from his wounds. Then there was Tempestas, with him throughout the siege of Yotapta, and he'd had to leave him behind in Judea. And now, Carmenta had saved his life and Graius's more than once. First, she swam them ashore from the shipwreck of the *Faustitas* off Gallicum Fretum. Then she had done her part in the stable fight in Hispania when they were on their road to meet with Cleo's brother, Marcus Otho. Her scars were from that journey. She was a warrior, as much as Abigieus and Tempestas.

"Thank you for coming. I don't dare to come to Rome. Things happen that might make—" Antonia stopped and shook her head. "There are too many eyes and ears in Rome, and I should stay away from the city."

"Because some are still unhappy... even before Marcus Otho has a chance to show he can be a good emperor?" Nicanor asked.

"Yes. But mostly—it's less about Otho and more about those who would benefit more under another emperor. Those men stir up disaffection so they or their allies can claim a 'better' choice to lead the empire. The whispers have grown louder for that man to be Aulus Vitellius."

"I've heard the name among the talk in the *tabernae* and streets of Rome, but I know little of him," Nicanor said. "Governor of Germania, right?"

"Yes. A greedy, self-indulgent man, a fat glutton. But he appeals to some. Two legions in Germania refused Galba, refused Otho, and demanded Vitellius as emperor. I've heard legions in Britannia, Gaul, and Raetia—southwest of Gaul—will also rally to Vitellius."

"Does that mean fighting for Otho against Vitellius? I mean *real* fighting, not fighting against something like Nero's bastard legion that Galba destroyed."

"Yes. It'll be against experienced, hardened frontier legions."

"*Futuo*," Nicanor swore under his breath.

"Yes," Antonia Caenis agreed. "You must warn Otho."

III

Februarius 69 CE

Jerusalem

The Upper City

"Miriam...."

The sound of her name and a touch on her shoulder woke her. She blinked as her eyes adjusted in the gray dawn light slanting in through the slats in the shutters above her. The room was almost warm from the corner brazier, now heaped with burning charcoal. She had not meant to sleep, expecting the cold to keep her awake until sunrise. Though she had sat and worried through many hours of the night, no one came home—not her father, mother, or brother Matthew.

"Father... Mother?"

"It's me, Miriam," Matthew said as he stooped over her. "Yohanan ben Levi's men have taken them into custody—Mother, Father, and many other Moderates and their families. Ya'el and Elian are gone, too—they must be with them."

"No... they..." Miriam stopped, shaking the sleep from her mind. In the hours of waiting and thinking, she realized her parents' absence meant something terrible was happening in the city besides what Ya'el and Elian had suffered. She would not tell Matthew that someone had taken them and demanded a ransom—the gold she had found in King David's Tomb. Matthew must focus on finding their mother and father. She would handle getting Ya'el, the former Lady Cleo, and Elian, the boy servant who had escaped with her to Jerusalem, freed.

"They what?" Matthew asked, yawning and stretching as if he had not slept himself.

"Nothing..." Miriam shook her head, her hands moving to check the sheaths of the daggers strapped to her forearms. A blanket fell from her as she sat up—and she knew she had not covered herself. She looked at him carefully. "Did you...?"

Matthew held up a hand to keep her from finishing the question. "I came in, found you asleep, and tried to make you more comfortable. Eleasar ben Ananias and I were late returning from Motza. We've learned that the treasure is at risk."

"What do you mean?" Miriam rose from the divan and rubbed her face with her hands.

"Last evening, several men returned who had been tasked with taking the Temple treasure shipments to their pre-selected hiding spots. Some of them were wounded and needed care. They reported that another of the wagon loads had been taken by men who were not Romans or Judean rebels. Bad as that was, though, we found something worse. When Eleasar and I returned to the city and came up from the tunnel by the Temple Enclosure, we saw Yohanan ben Levi's men rounding up unarmed Moderates and their families. Those who had protested against the Zealots. We hid until they had left the streets, and then I came home, found you asleep, and discovered everyone else was gone.

"Shortly, I must join Eleasar to try to make Shimon ben Gamliel get the Sanhedrin to stop Yohanan ben Levi. I'd like to see him thrown from the city walls, myself. Maybe that would force him to return home to Galilee and fight for Gischala."

"Would they take him in?" Miriam asked, not caring, for she was worried about her parents and Ya'el and Elian. "We know it is true... what Yosef said about the man in his letters from Galilee. And we heard the stories, too—he abandoned Gischala to the Romans."

Matthew added, "Yosef did more fighting against the Romans even though he thought we should never have started a war with them. He did more than that Gischalan coward ever did or ever will do. The man's charisma sways people to his side, but I think he reveals his true intent through his actions, not just words. He fled Gischala—not to help Jerusalem but to help himself."

Matthew cinched his robe tighter, donned a heavy cloak, and reached for the sword he had leaned against the divan. "No matter what is done with him, or if nothing is done at all... I must get our loved ones freed. I want you to stay here. We must be thankful you were not taken, too." Matthew shook his head as if to dispel the image. "Please wait here and let me worry only about them, not you."

"Do not worry about me; I can protect myself." Miriam saw his eyes go to her daggers and knew he remembered when she had saved him, and he had discovered her secret. Miriam surprised herself when she stood and astonished him when she gave him a tight hug that she quickly released. "Bring them home, Matthew."

"You'll stay here?" Matthew asked his hands on her shoulders.

"Yes." The word and Miriam's nod were a lie.

IV

Februarius 69 CE

Jerusalem

The Lower City

Miriam lowered her head and peered from beneath the cowl at the dull sky. Above her, the solid blanket of clouds was the color of dirty sheep, all laden with what looked like more rain, and a cold wind cut through the streets. She felt it through the cloak and other layers of clothing she had taken from Matthew's room. She had used a wrap to flatten her breasts, bound her lengthy hair, and smeared on some coal dust to darken her face so that she seemed a lean young man in an ill-fitting robe. She would move with purpose and—she hoped—not linger in anyone's mind if they paid her any heed.

Despite the chatter she had heard in the Upper City agora about Yohanan ben Levi and his arrest of Moderates, many people were on the streets seemingly without a care. Several she saw professed friendship with her parents but never spoke out against the Zealots. They were the kind of people who spoke loudly when with a few friends but not at all in public. Miriam found such people disgusting and did not understand how her parents could bear to be around them. Those people probably disavowed knowing her family now, for their obeisance was to whoever claimed leadership of the city. Now—as they walked the streets toward the Temple—they proclaimed that all should prepare their annual offering to the Temple treasury.

That made Miriam realize the date—the first of Adar. Her father and mother, too, would proclaim their tithe to the treasury. Tradition called for that to be spoken of aloud. But they never would have done it stridently, fearfully, to publicly show their compliance. Had her father been with the family that morning, he would have greeted all at breakfast sincerely: "When Adar comes, joy is increased." It had been years—since before Yosef returned home only to leave again for Rome—since that saying had proved true.

As she left the sloped path from the Upper City, passing under the viaduct that connected it with the Temple Enclosure, the threat of storm still hung ominous above. The keen wind did not seem able to budge the brooding mass of clouds. They frowned down upon the city as if in judgment. Yosef had often told her of his dreams and glimpses of what he saw in the sky over Jerusalem. They were things that many others saw, too, and all wondered at their meaning. The first time he had spoken of it was the same day she had killed for the first time, nearly three years before. It seemed a lifetime.

The memory of that day made her shudder more than did the chill wind twining its way through the streets of Jerusalem. That morning three years ago, her cousin, Rachel, had run to pound on their door and warn them, gasping as she told them the news: "The Romans are killing people in the agora! They're pulling the shopkeepers from the market, slaughtering them, and stealing their goods. Soldiers are entering houses now. I saw them cut down a young boy and his mother where the market ends at our street." Miriam had taken Rachel into their home and called to her mother: "We must hide, now!"

The women concealed themselves in the corner of the basement, behind a set of movable panels depicting plants along the shore of Lake Gennesaret. Still, they had hoped its flimsiness would help it be overlooked. They heard the front door and its frame splinter and give way with a crash. Her mother had held Rachel, trying to quiet her sobbing. The heavy footsteps above gave them an idea of where the intruder was, and Miriam knew they would soon be found by the marauders. She had risen, and her mother had whispered frantically, "Where are you going?"

Back then, she could not tell her mother why she must leave them and what she must do. It had not been long since she had been raped, and she could not sit in the darkness with Romans so close and sure to find them. Miriam had been unable to breathe at the unthinkable violence that could be done to Rachel, her mother, and again to her.

"I'm going to lead them away," she had told them, slipping off her sandals to sneak upstairs, where she had last heard someone moving around.

From the stairs to the bedrooms, she heard the man stomp from her parent's room to hers. She had sneaked up to the door, now ajar, and, staying low, she had opened it wider. There, framed by the daylight through her window, a burly Roman stood with his back to her. His legs were like tree trunks, each as thick as her waist, and he had a barrel chest. Silver flashed from one of her mother's necklaces the Roman held in one hand. In the other, he held Zechariah's lamp, the old man's gift to Miriam for when the darkness threatened to overwhelm her.

That was all it took.

She had stepped into the room. The soldier spun around, pulling a short sword from the scabbard at his hip. He had smiled, showing a mouthful of gaps where teeth should be. Miriam was shaking, but not from fear. Then, for the first time, she shook from a wave of cold anger. Miriam did not recall what the man said when she pleaded with him to take anything he wanted and leave. But what happened next, she would never forget.

She had known there would come a time when she would use the skills Zechariah was teaching her. Still, Miriam thought that would happen in the future, for she had had only one training session with him. Instead, she faced what had hurt her most since the dark day in the tunnel. She took a deep breath and saw the man's eyes drop to her full bosom as it expanded. Slipping her right hand into her left sleeve while he was distracted, she had felt for the haft of the dagger strapped to her forearm in a thin sheath. She had settled her grip with a deep breath.

She remembered that the man had reached out a massive, coarse-haired hand and grabbed her breast while whispering, "Don't run, little one."

"I won't," she had told him, then done precisely what Zechariah had begun to teach her.

Hold the knife handle in a firm fist grip, draw it from the sheath, and punch straight ahead and up under the chin in a smooth motion.

The blade had gone in as if she had stabbed it into a block of goat cheese. The Roman's mouth filled with blood as she stepped closer and shoved harder. The man shuddered, stunned, as his body sagged and dropped, pulling the dagger free from her hand. She knelt to retrieve it and looked into his eyes as he died, telling him again, "I won't run." The breeze through the window carried the coppery scent of blood from the streets of the Upper City. That same odor of death soon filled her bedroom—she would never forget the stench.

That same morning, Yosef and her father had carried a protest to Gessius Florus, the current Roman Procurator of Judea, who had claimed more taxes were owed. To enforce the collection and impose punishment on those who balked, he had unleashed his soldiers on the city, and they were killing and looting wantonly. Yosef believed Florus was retaliating brutally against those who had protested his heavy-handedness and made fun of him. Whatever the reason, the taxes and punishment were paid in blood.

As Yosef reported later, the procurator had held the two Jews all day. They had witnessed the massacre of thousands of their countrymen, women, and children who were not even responsible for paying taxes.

That night Miriam and Yosef tried to find the peace they had earlier enjoyed watching the evening stars from the rooftop terrace. "Earlier today," Yosef had told her, "the sky was full of red clouds, and among them, a vision of war chariots and men in battle above and encircling the city. People are talking of a new star in the sky, its tail shaped like a curved blade... a scythe in the firmament above Jerusalem."

Consumed with her first killing that very day, Miriam had not replied. Still, she had taken in Yosef's worry about the significance of the vision.

Miriam glanced up again at the clouds. Were Yosef here, he would agree they formed another portent. The people of Jerusalem—of all Judea—had done wrong. They had abandoned the tenets of their faith for self-serving reasons, which would lead to destruction.

She cast away that contemplation as she entered the main street of craftsmen's booths and other shops in the Lower City, where many people were beginning their day. Yet among them were haughty idlers in groups of two or more... men who followed Yohanan ben Levi.

Since the bird Cicero delivered the message demanding gold in exchange for Ya'el and Elian, Miriam had puzzled over who would have taken them. Who knew about that treasure, and how? She had decided to take no gold with her, which would require going into King David's Tomb again, possibly revealing its location to a spy. And then whoever had Ya'el and Elian might kill them all just for the gold in hand. If she had to, Miriam would barter the gold's location in exchange for the lives of the woman and boy. She could perhaps force their release by putting herself in the captors' hands, promising to lead them to the gold. Once Ya'el and Elian were safely away, she would kill as many of them as possible, even if she perished.

The morning light waned as the darkening clouds overcame the sun climbing behind them, and shopkeepers relit their lanterns and torches as if it were dusk. The breeze that reached the streets now carried the taste of rain.

"Please... no!" A woman's cry came from the narrow cross street just before Zechariah's shop. Miriam looked that way just in time to see that two men gripped the arms of a middle-aged woman—she was dressed in better-quality robes than were most in the Lower City. A spilled basket of goods was at her feet, and in a moment, Miriam knew it was likely the shopping she had done early to escape the rain for her master in the Upper City. The men dragged her deeper into the alley where the street torchlight did not reach. Those nearby, startled at the cry, returned to their shopping or hurried along the street. Nowadays, more people choose not to see what happened in Jerusalem's darkened areas.

Miriam entered the alley, and the brawnier man shouted, "Run along, boy! This is no concern of yours." The man's tone had the disdain common to Yohanan ben Levi's Galileans, who sneered at the people of Jerusalem. The slighter man with him laughed and tugged at the woman's clothing. The other growled, "If she doesn't take it off for us... we'll cut it off *for* her"—he raised the knife in his other hand.

Miriam was on them quickly, and her dagger sank into the base of the big man's skull. He roared, grabbing the back of his neck and twisting the blade out of Miriam's hand. His flailing fist caught her flush on the jaw, knocking her to the ground as he spun around. On her knees, she punched the man in the crotch, and as he sagged, grabbing at himself, her other hand came up with the second blade, biting into his throat and tearing it out.

At that, the smaller man let go of the woman, who fled the alley, but he faltered before running himself. As the big man went down, his massive hand reached out to support himself, and he grabbed a fist full of the smaller man's tunic and dragged him to the ground. He squirmed to get free of the larger man's death grip. His eyes bulged below the band of a wool cap pulled low on his forehead, his mouth gaping as Miriam yanked her dagger free and thrust it under *his* chin. The long blade transfixed his mouth, closing it with a snap so violent that it broke some of his teeth.

Just as she had done to the Roman in her bedroom. Miriam straightened up, breathing heavily, rearranged her clothing, and watched the man choke on his blood.

She turned toward the main street, where a handful of men and women were gathered, looking into the alley. She quickly sheathed her blades—inadvertently smearing blood on her arms and sleeves—and they flinched away as she pushed through them. As she did, one man stared at her, and she caught his eye.

Kefa! she cursed. Elazar ben Yair's spy in the Lower City was the messenger between her and the Sicarii leader. She did not need the complication of the Sicarii. Her contact with them had died with Ehud, whose death they had long sought. It would not have mattered to the Sicarii that Ehud had been forced to spy to save his family in Alexandria. Since Miriam had finally disclosed her secrets to her family, she had wanted no part in killing more of her countrymen.

She was determined to put violence behind her until the Romans came. But that just was not to be.

She felt tears pool in the corners of her eyes and wiped them away with the back of her hand. Before the Romans attacked, it seemed more men would try to harm her family, and those men deserved to die. She must save Ya'el and Elian. And if Matthew could not free their mother and father, she would also take a hand in that.

V

Februarius 69 CE

Jerusalem

The Lower City

"What is that you have, boy?" Hananiah asked Elian, who was sitting on the floor of the glassworks, spinning the two coins he had found beneath the bench near where he had slept.

Elian stopped and looked up at Ya'el for reassurance. She had told him not to be afraid, that all would work out, but she could see he feared the man. In the night, he had whispered to her that he wished Sayid were there to help. They both missed the Syrian auxiliary who had saved her more than once.

"Go ahead, Elian," Ya'el said with a nod. "He won't hurt you. This will soon be over." She had not slept, though she had pretended to until sunrise had stirred people on the streets outside. She sat between Hananiah and the boy and silently prayed Miriam had returned home from her exile hiding in King David's Tomb and that Cicero had reached her. If Miriam had received the message tied to the bird's leg, she would come to save them.

The boy hesitated, pointedly looking at the knife in the man's hand and rubbing the dried blood from the man's grisly touch the evening before. Ya'el had shuddered then, and Elian had remained frightened. The man slid his knife into its sheath and walked over to Elian, who handed him the coins.

Elian had shown Ya'el the coins when he found them. One was silver and one bronze. The silver bore the words "Jerusalem the Holy," and the bronze, "Freedom of Zion." Miriam's brother, Matthew, had told Ya'el they had been minted two years earlier by the new Judean government to replace the Roman bronze *sesterce*. The Judean coins Elian found were already being replaced with a new bronze coin that seemed to her to presage the city's coming defeat. The older statement of a desire for freedom had been changed to "Redemption of Zion," the hope for atonement. That felt deadly—an admission of guilt. She glared at the knifemaker as he took the coins from Elian.

"Go sit down and be still, boy." Hananiah pointed to the bench and, tossing the coins in his hand, turned back to watch the front door. The night before, Ya'el had seen him secure the rear exit into the alley behind the building, so the front was the only entrance.

Ya'el knew the man's unblinking eyes also watched her, looking toward her while he kept his head toward the door. They had spoken little since she sent Cicero with the message. She had soothed Elian to sleep but had remained awake herself. The knifemaker had lighted a lantern illuminating her and Elian, but then he had receded into the darkness. She could not see him, but she did not think he had slept... she had felt those eyes on her. Now he looked at her directly.

"Your bird will have delivered the message by now, right?"

Ya'el nodded, and Hananiah clearly assessed her. "Tell more about the man I saw you with," he said.

She met his stare and ignored the question as she had before. "I thought you were Miriam's friend?" she had said in a challenge, but he had disregarded *her* question. "Are you so greedy you would threaten her family?"

"She has nothing to do with this. The man you met with is a Sicarii... an assassin." Hananiah set the coins on a work table and pulled his long dagger from its sheath. Turning it as if admiring the gleam of the blade's etched metal in the lantern light, he glared at her from beneath dark brows. "*I* am Miriam's friend," he said as he thumbed the blade's edge. "But are you? You claim to be her cousin but spy on her brother for payment in gold. And you think *me* greedy...."

Ya'el chose silence. She would not refute the lies she had told Hananiah, for they protected Miriam. He did not know Miriam herself was the Sicarii killer he thought was a man.

"I followed you from Miriam's home to here," Hananiah said. "The man Ehud, who owned this"—he swept his arm around the expanse of the glassworks—"also a spy?"

Ya'el heard the shift in Hananiah's tone; his comments about Ehud became more slighting of the man.

"That is the talk I've heard," he commented. "I've heard that he and his family in Alexandria were—or still are—Roman collaborators. Are you one, too? Does this Sicarii, 'The Hand,' only *pretend* to be a Jewish patriot? I could see that the Sicarii might want to create more dissension to steal gold from wherever your *mina* came from."

He tapped the bar of gold he had set on the table and laughed. "The leaders of this city create their own chaos without help." He swept the two coins and the heavy bar into his pouch. Ya'el watched him retrieve a sealed square of parchment tucked into the sash at his waist. He pulled it out as if he would open and read it.

* * *

Miriam sensed she was trailed but would not slow her pace to confirm it. Likely it was Kefa, but it was dangerous to ignore the Sicarii. She would soon have to seek him out if only to see if his leader, Elazar ben Yair, had some message for her—hopefully a final one.

Zechariah had taught Miriam to use her speed and strike fast. She had hoped to catch the captor unaware at the glassworks. Miriam should have been there before daybreak but had been exhausted. Her guilt over her words to her family made sleep difficult. Her father had been justified when he cast her out for refusing to explain herself, her actions, and the time spent away from home. *Don't cry about what's done,* Zechariah had also told her. *The past is past. Now affects tomorrow.* She turned into the next alley, following it to another that ran behind a row of storehouses, one of which Ehud had used as his glassworks.

Miriam checked the door of the building next door. Once, when Ehud brought her, Ya'el, and Elian to his manufactory, Elian had pulled aside a canvas to reveal an interior door, asking where it led. Ehud had said it connected to the next building, which he used for storage. She would try that door before resorting to the front or rear—those were surely being watched. Ehud had commented that he had no need to secure the storage area: "Who would steal heavy barrels of silica and the natron we use to make glass?" He explained to Elian that the silica quartz sand came from his family's property in Sycaminum, and the natron—salt from dry lake beds—came from Alexandria. When Ehud had returned from Alexandria to open a Jerusalem glassworks, his father, Meshulam, had sent a caravan of supplies, more than he immediately needed.

After rechecking the alley, Miriam forced the stiff door open. She could see rows of barrels and other containers in the dim light, wondering sadly whether anyone would ever use their contents. When Ehud died, his workers disappeared within days. The landlord would probably see to it.

Miriam went deeper into the murk, and her eyes quickly adjusted. She spotted what must be this side of the door Elian had asked about. It would swing open from her side into the glasswork behind that canvas if it was still there. She put an ear to the door and heard voices—a man's and a woman's. She snugged the wrap around her chest, pulled the too-long men's tunic between her legs, and tucked the tail into the drawstring belt at her waist. Now her legs were free beneath the cloak. She put her hands on the door, took a deep breath, and heard Zechariah's voice in her head... *Slip in, move, and strike fast.*

* * *

Ya'el jerked when the canvas on the wall collapsed over Elian as the door behind it opened and struck the bench he had moved in front of it. The boy cried out, startled, as someone pushed through the door.

Hananiah's attention had been drawn to a group of armed men who had just stopped outside the front entrance of the glassworks. He spun around at the noise inside the room. He watched in surprise as a dirty-faced young man in a cowled gray cloak fell atop Elian in a tangle of canvas.

"Who are you?" Hananiah demanded, still holding the square of parchment in one hand as he raised his long-bladed dagger and stepped toward them.

Throughout the night, Ya'el's worry had been replaced by anger; she was again threatened by a man. As Hananiah swept past her toward Elian and the gray-cloaked figure who must be Miriam, she stood and swung her stool with all her might, crashing it into the back of his head.

VI

Martius 69 CE

Caesarea

A Portside Taberna

The taberna was full of wet or half-dry men and smelled of them and the brackish water of a busy seaport. The driest were the drunkest, having been out of the wind-lashed rain that swept the quay for two days. Sayid's cloak still clung damply to him, but it was drying quickly while he sat on the stool he had been fortunate to find in the corner nearest the hearth. Most men drank and ate with their friends at the crowded tables.

Sayid was alone and exhausted after a week of helping to move over 700 artillery pieces as they were checked for maintenance or repair. The hundreds of *ballistae* and *scorpio* torsion *catapulta* were like large, heavy crossbows in design, with wooden frames, winches, and bases. The power of these machines was in two coils of *nervi torti*, rope made from animal hair or sinew and enclosed in a metal-plated box under tension. They were wound up by handspikes turning the gears, pulleys, or windlasses so that the springs, when released, gave the device's arms, the *bracchia*, their tremendous power. The catapulta could hurl heavy stones or massive iron-tipped bolts for incredible distances. They required ongoing maintenance to be ready for the siege of Jerusalem when it began. If it began.

No new orders the soldiers knew of had yet come from Emperor Galba to General Vespasian about recommencing action against the rebels and Jerusalem. But rumors had sprouted that Galba had been assassinated, so the emperor might now be dead. Still, the rumors had come with official news of the *donativa*, the bonuses granted by a new emperor. The tradition had begun with Emperor Tiberius over 30 years before. Some said it was a reward for loyalty; others believed it was a bribe to secure it. It was reported that Galba promised the Praetorian Guard 7,500 denarii per man and that legionaries, even in the provinces, would receive a lesser bonus.

The men in the taberna seemed to be celebrating and spending money they had yet to receive. Sayid shrugged. It mattered little to him since auxiliaries did not receive a *donativum*. But Celsus

Evander, his commanding officer, had told him he had been promoted to *auxilia tesserarius*, which increased his pay by half. He raised a cup to that.

"You drink alone?" was the question asked by the tall, older man who appeared at his small table. His *sagum*—a cloak treated with *lanaoleum*, animal wax—had shed most of the rainwater, but the wind had found openings to drive the rain in. The cloak dripped, and beneath it, the man's tunic and *braccae* were soaked, the pants sodden.

Sayid looked up and said, "Yes... Father...." He slid his stool away from the fire so Marcus Sabinus could pull over a vacated bench. The older man groaned as he settled down and stretched his bad leg before him. That grunt of pain Sayid knew would be his father's only acknowledgment of his wounding at Gamla, a battle in Galilee against the Judean rebels who had lamed him.

The five words exchanged between them hung orphaned as the silence grew. Sayid had become comfortable with that, realizing it was his father's way. It was better than their heated, angry conversations when Sayid appeared in Lydda, where he had learned his father was stationed. Sayid had joined the legion to fulfill his childhood goals—he wanted to find his father and prove himself worthy of being his son. He had found the man but failed to impress him in his clumsy attempts at connection.

Sayid's mother had told him of her sporadic contact with the legionary who fathered her child but could not wed her. Even now, that rule still applied to Roman army soldiers. Sayid did not fault his father for that, but he felt mixed anger and shame when his father learned he served as a quartermaster's clerk. Marcus Sabinus, whose status as a soldier was his identity and the source of all his pride, could not be proud of a son who was not a soldier.

Sayid had not told his father about his combat at Beth Horon when he had been wounded in that humiliating defeat for the 12th Legion. The embarrassment still defamed the legionaries who had survived that battle. He had also fought and been injured by Judean rebels while on a mission given to him by Cestius Gallus, former Governor of Syria and then-commander of the ill-fated legion. And in an incident, he could never speak of to anyone but Cleo, Nicanor, or Yosef, he had been wounded when he killed Capito, the former Roman Procurator. Sayid had slain Gessius Florus's military aide and chief henchman to save Lady Cleo and a young slave boy named Elian. He had helped her disguise herself as a half-Greek Jewish woman named Ya'el, then got her to Jerusalem to hide.

Yes, Sayid thought, *I've felt the bite of an arrow and the stab of a sword. I know I am what my father thinks I'm not.*

Still, since the 15th Legion, *Apollinaris's* relocation to Caesarea, Sayid's father had visited him a few times. Though they spoke little on those occasions.

"Celsus Evander, my commander, told me of your promotion to *centurio princeps*," Sayid commented.

Marcus grunted and waved over an attendant carrying a brimful pitcher of beer, trying not to spill it as he moved through the room. Marcus took the mug the attendant filled for him, sipped, and set it beside him on the bench. Rubbing his hip and thigh, he started to speak again and stopped. He bent for the mug to drink again. Then he spoke: "You must wonder why I've reached only a low rank after so many years. After all, I joined the army before you were born."

"I don't *judge*, father," Sayid replied. But he thought... *you do.*

"Hmmph," Marcus snorted through a mouthful of beer at Sayid's emphasis on the word "judge." He wiped his lips with his hand and said, "I requested *commeatus* from the legion and was given that leave when I received word your mother would soon give birth. Did she ever tell you how hard it was to bring you into the world?"

Sayid shook his head, surprised—not that his birth had been difficult but that his father had spoken of it.

"Tahir almost died. I was with her—I held you, heard your first cries. And I stayed with your mother until your Aunt Yara could care for her. But she could not come until I had stayed past the leave granted me, and when I returned to my legion, I was punished. That mark on my service has dragged on me for years." Marcus used his good leg to push up off the bench and get his bad leg under him, and he drained the mug. He leaned forward, favoring his leg, set the vessel on the bench, and looked at Sayid.

"I've never regretted it," he said, resettling the damp cloak around his shoulders. "I've been assigned to General Sextus Cerealis's 5th Legion, *Macedonia*, soon to deploy into Idumea. We go to secure the troublesome areas for General Vespasian." With a curt nod, he turned and left.

Sayid understood the circumstances of his birth and the resulting consequences. It wasn't even the reminder about how close the son himself had come to disaster. If not for Cestius Gallus's written orders and Nicanor's confirmation and request that General Vespasian honor the orders of a disgraced commander, Sayid would have been punished for being absent from duty. And executed if caught and treated as a deserter. And it wasn't even the important news of his father's orders to serve under General Cerealis. It was the handful of words in between... *He did not regret—*

"Are you leaving?"

"What?" Sayid blinked out of his reverie to see a large man scratching his chin. The back of his scarred hand bore a tattoo—a green-scaled, fierce-toothed creature with a long tail. He had the look of a soldier but not a Roman one.

The man waved at the bench where his father had sat. "I'm taking this..."

"Go ahead." Sayid stood and pushed past him as the man sat on the bench, lifted the empty mug in the air, and shouted for the barkeep to bring wine.

At the door, Sayid glanced back, and the man raised the mug with his eyes on Sayid. Sayid stepped out into the weather, thinking about his father.

VII

Martius 69 CE

Rome

Domus Aurea

The palace grounds built by Nero spread over 300 acres and were lavish even by Rome's standards. There were structures for varied purposes, groves of trees, pastures with flocks, and private vineyards. The grounds covered parts of the slopes of the Palatine, Esquiline, Oppian, and Caelian hills. And now it belonged to Emperor Otho.

Nicanor wondered again at the great cost as he was escorted into an antechamber with a circular table supported by three columns of carved Carrera marble. Around it were several *solium*, high-backed chairs with arms, and smaller chairs—three each—at either side. On the table was a swath of purple cloth with two coins and a parchment page with drawings depicting the front and back of another coin. He picked up the coins: one with Nero's features and one with Galba's. The drawings of a proposed coin, he gathered, showed on one side a right profile of Marcus Otho with "IMP M OTHO CAESAR AVG TR P" around the perimeter. The image of the back had a figure he believed was the goddess Pax. She stood draped in a robe and held a raised branch in her right hand and a lowered caduceus in the left. Arcing around her was "PAX ORBIS TERRARVM. His thick finger traced the words. *So many who gain power through bloodshed claim they want peace in the world,* he thought, and held in the snort he did not want to echo in these vast halls.

"I've just sent that to the mint at Lugdunum," said Marcus Otho as he entered the chamber, followed by his elder brother, Titianus.

Nicanor set the drawing down, not asking why getting the new imperial coin was a priority. He probably did not understand some fine point of political necessity. *Still*, he thought. But said, "Sire, I asked to see you about Lord Vitellius, who has the support of Generals Caecina Alienus and Fabius Valens, who command two legions in Germania."

The two brothers exchanged looks as Marcus Otho sat in the high-backed chair and Titianus to his right. "I've just finished reading through Galba's papers," the emperor said. "Vitellius wrote that the

Germania legions were angered by his failure to reward them as promised. They helped put down the revolt of Gaius Julius Vindex, governor of Gallia Lugdunensis, a year ago—a rebellion against Nero. Yet Galba never paid them."

"Sire, Vitellius's generals have moved within 150 miles north of Rome. They're at the mountains of the southern border of Noricum, the Alps," Nicanor said.

Another look was exchanged between the Othos, and the emperor said, "Antonia Caenis told you this?"

Nicanor had felt eyes upon him since he'd assumed his position under Marcus Otho as emperor. The watchers surely knew he had visited her. "Yes," he admitted.

"How does she know, and is she sure?"

"General Quintus Petillius Cerealis reported it to her. He and some of his men, veterans who defeated Boudica in Britannia, recently returned to their homes in the Sabine hills. They crossed the northern provinces and encountered patrols from the Germanian legions ranging far from home and recruiting locals across Gaul."

"Who is this general?" Titianus asked.

"He's the husband of General Vespasian's only daughter, Domitilla the Younger, and Antonia Caenis trusts him."

"Vitellius has no military experience, so we'll plan to deal with his generals," Titianus spoke without consulting his brother, but the emperor nodded. "To aid in that," Titianus added, "we must eliminate remnants of support for Nero and Galba, for they might align with Vitellius."

Marcus Otho wrapped the coins and drawing in the cloth and set the bundle aside. "Nicanor, you told me of the scheming of Ophonius Tigellinus, Nero's former Praetorian Guard co-prefect. How he and Gessius Florus acted to prevent you from reaching me in Emerita Augusta to get help for my sister. We'll speak of the former Judean Procurator another time. But Tigellinus is hated by many here in Rome while still having information and contacts that could aid Vitellius. He has remained at his estate in Sinuessa since he feigned illness and abandoned Nero. We don't know if he only bides his time or has decided to become inactive. In either case, he no longer has a large retinue. I want you to take a unit of Praetorian Guards and bring him to me."

* * *

SINUESSA

Nicanor and his men were about an hour's ride north of the mouth of the Vulturnus River, where the Via Appia ended near the seacoast. From there, they took a winding road that bent directly toward the sea and toward Tigellinus's secluded estate. The ten *Evocati Augusti* were men who had served their time in the legions outside of Rome and had retired with *honesta missio*. After his honorable discharge, each had been invited to serve again as an imperial Praetorian. Emperor Otho had deemed these men too old for his personal guard. Still, they were more than capable of bringing Lord Tigellinus to Rome.

"You five," Nicanor pointed at them, "close off this road to the estate. There is no other." He studied the villa beyond the broad courtyard where they'd hitched their horses. The villa was perched precariously, it seemed to Nicanor, on an escarpment over the Tyrrhenian Sea. He waved to the remaining five men to follow him. He angled Carmenta toward where the courtyard's flagstones led to a porticoed path and a terraced overlook. He could see, far below, a rough dock carved from stone at the base of the cliff at the foot of a series of stone steps. Moored to it, a ship bobbed on the waves.

He assigned two men—one each—to watch the wings of the villa for anyone leaving from the back and two more outside the front entrance. He took the last *evocati* with him and met a man he presumed was Tigellinus's major domus. "I bring orders from Emperor Otho for Lord Tigellinus," Nicanor called out.

The man nodded and went into the villa, and soon returned. "Follow me, centurion," he said, and the men dismounted. Without comment or question, the servant took them through a great hall with black and white mosaic floor tiles depicting dolphins and fish. Nicanor was surprised to see so few staff as they approached a balconied terrace facing the sea.

Tigellinus stood framed by the bright sunshine, his back to them and his hands on the balustrade. He did not look away from the water below or turn to them as he spoke, "Join me out here, centurion... just you."

Nicanor signaled the Praetorian to stay and stepped out onto the terrace. "Lord Tigellinus..." When the former Praetorian Prefect half-turned to face him, Nicanor was surprised the man had not changed since last he saw him, the year before, and that he did not seem alarmed.

Noting Nicanor's scrutiny, Tigellinus smirked. "You've aged, centurion, but then you've had such a journey."

Nicanor was not bothered by the truth. He knew his scars were more visible, his hair was flecked, and his beard threaded with gray. The events of the last five years had worn him down. What offended him was the man's attitude. But he did not pause. He took out the scroll with its imperial seal and held it out, saying, "Emperor Otho invites you to accompany me to Rome, where you will meet him. Here's the order."

Tigellinus took it without reading it. "Come closer, centurion," he said, beckoning with a hand.

Nicanor—a hand on his *pugio* at his belt—warily moved to stand beside the former prefect.

"See that ship down there." Tigellinus pointed with the scroll at the water and rocks far below. "I can give you more riches—in gold and jewels—than you have ever earned in the army... or ever will. And I can order that ship's captain to take you anywhere you wish to go. Think of where you could live a peaceful life with all you want. Just do as I ask."

"Why don't you do that yourself?" Nicanor asked. "Take that money and go? Why are you still here?"

"Because I know people with power and influence interested in who rules the empire. They want me to be their intermediary with whoever is the emperor, and they will reward me with much more than I have now."

"Otho or Vitellius?"

"They prefer Vitellius, but Otho's string can be plucked to their tune in the interim without his knowledge."

Nicanor steadied his voice. "What do you ask of me?"

"Send your men away. Tell them I insist on speaking with you privately."

"And then?"

"You wait a while, then go to them and say I chose to kill myself here instead of the emperor having me killed when I return to Rome. Report to Emperor Otho that I killed myself—threw myself into the sea. That way, no one will come for me. That gives me time to finish my arrangements. Return here in three days, and the money and that ship will be here for you."

"How do I know you'll do as you say?"

"Because if I don't, you would go to the emperor and tell him you were mistaken, and I survived the plunge. The Othos must already think I plan to aid Vitellius or any who wish Marcus to be replaced as emperor. They'll turn out more Praetorians and informants to find me. So, either I lose everything by abandoning my plans just so I can survive... or I'm found and killed."

Nicanor shook his head. "I could just take you now and deliver you to Otho. Then I'd be done with you."

"You could, but I think he'll let me live once he hears what I can tell him. Perhaps he'll let me live long enough to finish what I've already initiated, and that would free me." The sneer played upon Tigellinus's lips.

Nicanor studied the man for a moment. "I've decided." He left the terrace and entered the great hall, returning shortly to say, "I've ordered my men to wait for me in the courtyard."

"Good," said Ophonius Tigellinus with a smile and tossed the imperial order over the balustrade. The wind caught and carried it until it dropped into the sea. He turned to Nicanor. "Well, centurion, let's—"

Nicanor had pulled out his pugio and slashed the former Praetorian Prefect's throat before he could finish his sentence.

"For Graius and Cleo," Nicanor said as the man fell, clutching at the wound as if his fingers could stop the gush of blood. Nicanor knelt, took the ceremonial dagger Tigellinus wore in an elaborate sheath at his waist, and put it in the man's hand. Leaning close, he whispered, "I'll do as you asked. I'll tell the emperor you killed yourself."

VIII

Martius 69 CE

Jerusalem

The Lower City, King David's Tomb

"Elian, do not run off!" Ya'el warned the boy as they left the tunnel passage and entered an antechamber to King David's Tomb. "No exploring!"

The boy was full of curiosity over a new adventure underground, having forgotten his fear of Hananiah at Ehud's glassworks. Miriam had told them the wall they crouched behind was one of the oldest boundaries of early Jerusalem, in the area known as the City of David. And nearby, they'd enter a hidden tunnel. Ya'el had been in other tunnels with Miriam and in this very tunnel with Matthew. She trusted Miriam's uncanny sense and eyesight to lead them in the almost pitch-black passage. But she kept Elian ahead of her for his safety. Still, she had let out a sigh of relief when Miriam found and ignited a torch kept far within the passage. Ya'el felt better when they left the tunnel and entered the antechamber. Miriam lighted a large lantern that filled the space with a welcome glow.

"Miriam, you're covered in blood! Your arms!" Ya'el cried, seeing her friend fully for the first time since they'd rushed from the glassworks. They hadn't known whether Hananiah was truly unconscious, but they did know armed men were out front, so they had run out the back. "Are you wounded?"

"It's not my blood," Miriam said with a shake of her head as she passed a waterskin to Ya'el. "It's from two of Yohanan ben Levi's men. They had attacked a woman and were about to—"

Ya'el, pouring water over her own arms to cleanse them, cocked her head toward Elian to stop Miriam mid-sentence. But the boy did not seem to be listening—he stared wide-eyed at the sheathed daggers on Miriam's forearms.

Miriam changed the course of her words. "I know Hananiah has no love for Jerusalem... and he spoke of leaving before the Romans arrive. But why would he take you and Elian hostage?"

"He saw you in your disguise," Ya'el replied, "when you passed that bar of gold to me. I had to lie and tell him 'The Hand' had paid me to spy on Matthew. He took the gold from me and wanted more." Ya'el turned to watch Elian scuff his sandaled foot on the stained stones where Miriam told them she had found the two long-dead Romans. She had been lost, Ya'el recalled, in a tunnel she entered from Solomon's Quarry, Zedekiah's Cave northwest of the Temple. She had traveled underground far south and found herself in this tomb. Miriam said the Romans had killed each other over the treasure they'd found deeper inside the tomb.

"Elian, come here," Ya'el said, handing him the waterskin. "Wash your face." She turned back to Miriam. "But I could tell by how he asked questions that there was something else. He knew more than just gossip and tales told of The Hand." She recalled the square of parchment Hananiah had dropped when Miriam struck him. Unthinkingly, Ya'el had snatched it up. Now she took it from within her robe and turned it over in her hands.

Miriam dried her arms and hands on a clean portion of her robe. She went to an alcove off the chamber and returned with clean clothing draped over one arm and a staff in the other hand.

"What's that?" Elian asked, pointing at the scarred wooden staff with a sharp metal ferrule at its end.

"It belonged to my friend, Zechariah," Miriam said. "He was blind and used this to help him find his way around. But Zechariah was also a mighty warrior. He used this staff also to fight; I kept it when he died."

Elian's eyes darted to Miriam's stained sleeves, covering the blades, then back to the staff.

Ya'el remembered when she and Matthew had come here to convince Miriam to return home, and she had reluctantly left the staff in this tomb. Miriam had said that with that act, she hoped to put the memories it evoked behind her.

Ya'el looked down at the sealed sheet in her hands, broke the wax, and unfolded the parchment.

"I've seen Ya'el use her bow," said Elian, pointing again at the staff. "Do you know how to use that... to fight?"

Miriam set her feet, brought the staff up, and gripped its middle. Twirling the shaft to align with her right forearm, she spun and extended the staff—ferrule lashing out—to cut the air over the lantern, making it flicker. The arc continued its sweep as Miriam continued her spin and brought the staff back to where it began. Her weight was evenly balanced on her feet, and the staff was aligned along her forearm. With a quick movement to bring the staff vertically, she planted it before her, hands grasping it above midway its length. "Yes, Elian, I can fight with it."

The boy's smile was as wide as his eyes in the lantern light.

"Miriam!" Ya'el had only partly watched the spectacle, for her eyes had stopped at the first lines when she recognized the sender's handwriting. "This is from Gessius Florus... to Hananiah!" She shuddered and went cold at the same time.

"What? Your husband?" Miriam carried the staff to look with Ya'el at the message.

"Yes," she said with regret that that man was still connected to her. "It confirms that he received a message from Hananiah about following someone who could help locate the Temple treasure—to find where it was being moved and hidden." Ya'el lowered the note, not reading the rest of it aloud. "I know Florus has used spies in Jerusalem—the knifemaker must be one of them."

"Yehudah ish Krioth," Miriam muttered the name, but Ya'el heard.

"Who?"

"One of the men I've killed. Yehudah was a member of the Sanhedrin. He met with your husband."

Ya'el gave a sharp intake of breath, and Miriam spoke again. "He met with... Gessius Florus in the tunnel where the two Roman soldiers—"

"Miriam..." Ya'el touched her arm in sympathy over that old attack that had changed Miriam's life. She did not want to add to her distress, but she must. "This message mentions Ehud. He, too, was spying for Florus, it seems." Silence surrounded them as she watched Miriam stiffen in shock.

* * *

Miriam had told herself that her heart was numb and that no memory of Ehud could hurt anymore. But the jagged stab of pain proved the lie. Her breaths shortened and shallowed as that handful of words struck her chest like flints from a sling, flints that then grew very heavy and pulled at her soul. She tried to do as Zechariah had taught her. *Find your heartbeat*, she heard him tell her. His voice was a beacon in the dark. *Count it and still your mind... then breathe deep and do what you must. Take the next step... then another.* Letting go of her deep breath, Miriam shook off Ya'el's arm and headed toward the exit passage.

"Where are you going?" Ya'el called, hurrying after her, waving Elian to stay where he was.

"To find Hananiah and confront him."

"You mean kill him?"

"I don't know."

Ya'el moved between Miriam and the passage opening. "Hananiah doesn't know you're 'The Hand'... but he knew Ehud and likely controlled him for Florus. You can't go face him now."

"Hananiah kept Ehud in a position where he had to do as Florus ordered," Miriam said. "Ehud died because of that. I killed him, but Hananiah set it up. So, I'm going to kill Hananiah."

"Wait!" Ya'el shifted in front of Miriam to block her way. "Isn't it better to watch Hananiah and see if he reveals any others working for Florus? There must be more. And we must find how Florus gets messages to and from Jerusalem. *Then* you can tell *Matthew*, and he can deal with Hananiah."

Miriam knew she would never let Matthew, or anyone else, do that... Hananiah was her responsibility, but Ya'el was right. And Zechariah had also told her... *Plan when calm so you can safely strike in anger. Anger is strength and can sustain you if you use it wisely.* In the shadows and flickering torchlight of that tunnel years ago, she had seen Zechariah, a blind man, kill the Romans who had attacked her. Later, when she knew more of him, of the death of his wife and daughter... she realized he had been killing—again—the men who had murdered his wife and child. His anger had sustained him. Ya'el was right, and Miriam must hold her anger for now.

"But Hananiah and maybe others will now search for *you*, Ya'el. You must hide here for now." Miriam could see from Ya'el's expression that she did not relish the thought of hiding. And were it not for Elian, she would not consider it, to be sure.

"Then you must watch him," Ya'el said. "Hananiah doesn't know you're 'The Hand.' But he will protect *you*. I think you're the only one he cares for..." Then Ya'el put up a fist to show her strength and said, "I think I felled him before he got close enough to recognize you." She offered a little smile. "Yes, we can hide here for a while." Ya'el glanced at Elian, who was finally obeying, for he had settled to the floor and was washing his face.

Ya'el continued. "Gessius Florus is responsible for Ehud's death and the deaths of thousands of others. His greed and desire for your Temple treasure drove him to instigate this war. It may come down to confronting Hananiah, but I pray to the gods that someday Gessius Florus pays for what he's done."

IX

Martius 69 CE

Jerusalem

City of David, Ophel

Miriam had chosen a way to her home in the Upper City that she usually avoided. The steps to the Huldah Gates in the southern wall of the Temple Enclosure were more crowded than those at the southwest corner, which climbed more steeply than the sloped path that passed under the viaduct. Today, or perhaps every day now, each overflowed with people going to or coming from the Temple.

Already populous Jerusalem was now bursting with refugees and early arrivals for *Pesach*, pilgrims who perhaps intended to remain in the city after celebrating Passover. The river of humanity moved slowly, but the crowd helped to hide her from anyone following. The buzzing of the talk around her was all about Yohanan ben Levi's men roaming Jerusalem and doing shocking things. No one seemed to pay attention to the one of many modestly dressed Jewish women who happened to carry a wooden staff as if she were an elderly man or patriarch.

Miriam patiently crossed the Court of the Gentiles, passed the Temple Sanctuary, and finally crossed the viaduct.

* * *

The Upper City

Miriam worried as she straightened furniture, returned things to their usual place, and filled each room brazier with charcoal. She relighted the largest in the family room that fronted the inner courtyard. No one was home, but she prepared everything as if they would be, as her mother had taught her. On the table were fruits, cheese, and earthenware pitchers of fresh water from the cistern. Unlike many affluent families in Jerusalem, her parents had no permanent servants. They believed it essential for their children to be involved in the everyday duties of the household and family. Though it had sometimes caused dissension, it had mainly created a stronger family bond, and Miriam was coming to realize how important that was.

After leaving Ya'el and Elian with enough food for a few days, she returned to the Lower City. She found Kefa at his leatherworks across from Zechariah's shop that the Sicarii also used as a meeting place and watch post.

"I saw you earlier," he said, his eyes sweeping over her maidenly attire, pausing at the incongruous—Zechariah's staff in her hand. "I have a message from Elazar ben Yair." He had handed it to her and said, "You should go home, get off the streets. What happened earlier with the woman you saved—attacks like that will only increase."

Miriam unfolded the Sicarii leader's message, unaddressed as they had always been, and reread:

> Simon bar Giora and his followers have been welcomed at my invitation. His men are needed against the Romans who will come to take Masada. He has successfully raided only in Idumea, where he fights the locals, not the Romans, who have increased their presence. He has told me he leaves soon with all his followers for Jerusalem. I do not think that will aid Jerusalem and may worsen things. With his men gone, we are fewer than 1,000. In Masada, we are diverse in our beliefs, but we stand as one people... together, unlike Jerusalem. I need fighters; you are welcome to join us. —Elazar ben Yair.

She refolded the parchment and tucked it into her robe. Taking a heavy cloak from a peg on the wall, she wrapped it around herself, filled a large cup with water, and climbed the stairs to the rooftop. Lighting a fire between two divans, she sat and drank deeply from her cup. Over the terrace rails were three tall shadows in the distance—the highest towers—barely discernible in twilight turning into night.

The southernmost, Phaesel, soared nearly 150 feet high. The northernmost, Hippicus, was most decorative, and Mariamne between them was half the height of Phaesel. All protected the city's western side, the easiest approach for any enemy until the city expanded to the north. There, King Agrippa's father, Herod, had strengthened the wall to be nearly impenetrable.

She looked up at a sky that had cleared enough to see the stars in the clear patches. She pushed aside her thoughts of dealing with Hananiah, Ya'el, and Elian, returning to what concerned her the most. Where was Matthew, her mother, and her father? And was Yosef still alive? If he lived and the rumors proved true that he had aided the Roman general, Vespasian, she wondered if she could forgive him or understand his purpose.

Yosef had been fascinated by the night sky—the *Shamayim*—Heaven's blanket over the Earth, covering it as a tent covers people of the deserts. She remembered Yosef telling her how the Greeks, in their philosophies, separate the two. But Hebrews believe the sky and Heaven are one and the same. "We don't wonder what's beyond the *Shamayim*," Yosef had told her, "but the Greeks do. They ponder the unknown." And that had made her consider her own "unknowns."

Would she ever feel remorse over the countrymen she had killed? How could she, when she seemed fated to kill more? Would each death increase the weight upon her? Or would each death add to the bitterness that had poured into her soul's abyss? The Romans had torn away a vital piece of her, and she was still wounded. Would the pain ever stop?

"I feel so alone," Miriam told the night.

A voice came from behind her, at the top of the stairs to the rooftop: "*Aht lo leh vahd...* you are not a stick, Miriam, separated from the tree."

"Mother!" Miriam cried, rising so quickly that she spilled water on the terrace matting. She rushed to embrace her.

"You remember the story?" Rebecca asked, hugging her daughter. "You are not alone."

"A family is like a tree..." Miriam whispered, seeing Matthew over her mother's shoulder. "Where's Father?" she asked, feeling her mother's grasp tighten.

"He is still held with hundreds of others," Matthew said. "Yohanan ben Zaccai, with the help of Shimon ben Gamliel, got Mother released. The Sanhedrin is also working to help Father." Matthew's face was haggard, drawn with exhaustion. "But I could find out nothing of Ya'el or Elian." He rubbed his eyes with the heels of his hands.

"They are safe and hiding," Miriam said.

Matthew sat then, his body drooping, bracing himself with his forearms on his knees. "Good," he said, his face relaxing and tightening again. "But news has come from Caesarea. The Romans believe an important Roman noblewoman hides here… and there's an offer of a large reward. Bounty hunters will be searching for her."

X

Martius 69 CE

Caesarea

The Roman Encampment, Vespasian's Praetorium

Yosef settled into the chair before the general's campaign desk, clanking his chains as he shifted to ease the bite of the cuffs on each wrist, ankle, and waist. *At least*, Yosef thought, *the neck collar is gone.*

Vespasian was infuriated at the assassination attempt against himself and had resumed restrictions on the personnel allowed in his presence. Yosef understood the anger since he, too, had suffered an attempt on his life—by the Gischalan Yohanan ben Levi.

Yosef and Vespasian had barely spoken since that attack, so he was glad to be in his presence again. Since Vespasian's son, Lord Titus, had gone to Rome months before, Yosef had had no one to converse with. He hoped to have an opportunity to ask about Sayid and to learn that his Syrian auxiliary friend was still safe and well.

"Do the Idumeans consider themselves allied with Judea?" asked Vespasian, his thick brows contracting with concern. The Roman general's head was squared off, the same shape as his stocky body.

Yosef blinked at the question but answered, "They are General… but there are issues between Idumeans and Judeans."

"A difference in beliefs? I'm told that some time ago, the Idumeans were forced to adopt yours."

"Yes. That assimilation created the issues, and some still exist."

Vespasian grunted. "It would seem so. Months ago, thousands of Idumean soldiers entered your Jerusalem to aid one of your leaders. A Yohanan ben Levi, I think, who seems to control that city. Prisoners taken since then—our scouts confirm it—report thousands were killed before the Idumeans left and returned to their home."

Yosef closed his eyes; he knew too well his people were often their own worst enemies. Yohanan ben Levi pretended to be a leader, stoking people's fear, claiming he was their defender against what frightened them and the solution to their problems. A craven narcissist, the Gischalan was a man of loud voice and false promises.

And he now controlled Jerusalem—Yosef was saddened and feared for his family.

"Now, your rebel general, Simon bar Giora, attacks Idumean towns and villages." Vespasian leaned back in his chair. He slapped the bronze-tipped vinewood rod he habitually carried rhythmically in his open palm. "Whose side are those two Judean leaders on? Whose side are the Idumeans on? I'm curious." He tapped the desk.

"But it doesn't matter," he said. "I've sent a legion into upper Idumea to deal with this Simon bar Giora, who brandishes the *aquila* taken at Beth Horon. The 12th Legion's standard will be returned where it belongs—and its taker destroyed."

Yosef shook his head at Vespasian's rhetorical questions. If Simon bar Giora led enough men to ravage Idumea, at some point, he would have to retreat from the Romans and fight from behind Jerusalem's walls. He prayed he and Yohanan ben Levi would join forces and not tear the city apart.

Jerusalem's leaders and factions had been a topic of discussion with Vespasian in the past. Yosef was careful not to reveal anything to hurt his people. Still, he did acknowledge a truth known by the Romans. "Rome also has leaders who work and conspire against each other to claim the city, the throne, and to rule its empire," Yosef replied. "I've heard my guards whisper gossip about Emperor Galba."

Vespasian nodded and replied, "Yes, but that's the only thing in common."

He does not acknowledge my mention of Galba, Yosef thought.

"No, General, it's not the only thing in common," Yosef said as he straightened and clanked his chains again. "We center our cultures on two cities: Rome and Jerusalem. Each is proud of their empire. Rome's present. Jerusalem's past. You wish to keep yours. We wish to regain ours... or at least be left to rule ourselves."

Vespasian leaned forward to rest his thick forearms on the desk. "Rome has never enforced its beliefs on you; your people can worship as you wish. And we've granted you a certain amount of self-governance."

"But Rome also taxes us heavily—driving many into poverty—and exerts strict control over the destiny of my people. One example is when your Emperor Gaius Augustus Germanicus sent his general, Petronius, from Syria into Judea three decades ago. He forced my people to erect a statue of Emperor Gaius in the Temple in Jerusalem. The attempt was an inexcusable act against our people and an affront to our god. More recently were the transgressions of the last two

Roman Judean Procurators. Especially the brutality of Gessius Florus, whose orders led to the murder of thousands of my people."

"Excuse me, General," came a voice from the entry. Gaheris Clineas announced, "General Titus has arrived."

Vespasian beckoned with his rod toward his personal aide, who stepped aside to clear the doorway. A cloaked man strode in, his billowing bright scarlet *paludamentum* attached by a gold clasp at his right shoulder. The man, a younger version of the man behind the campaign desk, stopped and smiled. "It's good to see you, General."

Vespasian rose quickly and clasped the man. "And you, my son. It's been too long."

Titus nodded to Yosef, who returned the greeting. "I'd like to report... there's news you should hear now," he said to his father, his eyes flicking back to Yosef. "Privately."

"Now is fine," said Vespasian. "The rumors have arrived ahead of you. It seems Yosef has heard them. Is any of it true? What of Emperor Galba?"

"He is dead, and Marcus Otho is now emperor." Titus took a packet of waxed vellum from his pouch. "Letters from Antonia Caenis include details. I'm told an official courier with orders from Emperor Otho should arrive soon. Their vessel was on our heels for a while, but the weather separated and delayed us."

"Where's Nicanor? I expected he would return with you." Vespasian glanced at Yosef, who had asked about his friend in their last conversation.

"No, General. Emperor Otho has the centurion, I mean... *tribunus*, now serving on his personal staff. That's also in the letters, along with a message from Nicanor explaining how that came to be. But," Titus removed a scroll with an elaborate wax seal, "I believe the new emperor expected Nicanor to serve on his staff in exchange for this." He handed the scroll to Vespasian.

The general broke the seal and scanned the unrolled page. He read aloud: "An imperial decree protecting his sister, Lady Cleo, who is hiding in Jerusalem or elsewhere in Judea." He set the curling sheet on his desk. "So, that rumor is true, too."

"What?" Yosef cried out, stunned. Cleo was in Jerusalem!

* * *

Legion Quartermaster Commander's Office

Centurion Celsus Evander studied Sayid, the chief clerk who had made his job much more manageable. "Are you sure?" he asked.

"Yes, sir," said Sayid, who had cleared the last of his records neatly stacked on his desk, warehouse inventories, and the current equipment manifest listing what was going to Caphatabria. "I'll go with the delivery of siege equipment and supplies and remain to serve in the unit. Thank you for arranging that with your friend and securing these orders." Sayid tapped the square of folded parchment on his desk that officially relieved him of his current duties and allowed him to join a combat unit.

"Your father will be sent there?"

"Yes, sir. The latest report to General Vespasian is that they are engaged at Capethra. Once that town's subdued, General Cerealis's 5th Legion, *Macedonia,* will march on Caphatabira, whose walls require siege machines."

Celsus did not ask how Sayid had gotten that information from a courier who should not have shared it. "Does your father know you join him there?"

Sayid shook his head and tucked his orders into his tunic.

"Don't die there, Sayid." Celsus had saved Sayid in Ptolemais, the return of a debt he owed his friend Nicanor. But he liked the Syrian, a capable young man determined to prove himself, even if to a father he had never known.

XI

Aprilus 69 CE

Near Placentia

310 miles northwest of Rome

Nicanor reined in Carmenta as the legion halted at a clearing just south of the banks of the Eridanus River.

"What happens now?" Florin asked as he stopped his own horse beside the tribunus.

Nicanor knew the auxiliary had never served outside Rome in the field or for any duty. The youth's face was flushed with his first experience of the army's primary purpose: to defend Rome and its emperor.

"This is where the advance scouts and engineers have identified the most defensible ground," Nicanor explained. "With good access to water and wood and building stone nearby to erect the *castra*, it will become the legion's encampment as long as we're here. See there," Nicanor pointed at men and horses moving beyond them. "Two cohorts—one heavy infantry, one cavalry—will provide security around the camp while others work. First, they will dig a trench around the perimeter and then erect basic defenses—a wooden palisade with small watchtowers twice the height of a man."

Florin gestured toward the men unloading wagons, careful in how they lifted and carried the contents of the carts. "What do those men do?"

"They carry caltrops and ball spikes made up of two or more sharp, sometimes barbed, long nails—arranged to point upward. They'll place them on either side of the ditch, and the ugly things will slow advancing soldiers or cavalry before they reach the camp wall."

They watched as the first fortifications rose around the emperor and his retinue. The defensive wall with an opening left for a gate is yet to be constructed. A dozen Praetorians from the emperor's personal guard spanned that gap in a double row of six. From the legion's main body, other detachments headed off.

"Those go to forage afield," Nicanor pointed to them. "They seek game and additional water sources. Others will cut wood and gather fuel for our fires." Nicanor turned in his saddle to see the wagons and supply train working closer to the camp. After them would come the rearguard cohort of heavy infantry and cavalry. "Now, Florin," he said, "go see the quartermasters about tents, camp stools, and provisions for us. Soon they will have distribution points for the men in the camp—I want you there first. For I don't want tents with holes or stools with weak legs. Also, though I haven't any men to command, locate the carpentry and blacksmithing areas and the medical tents. If you ever serve in combat, always find where the medics' tent is located. Getting a wounded man or yourself there quickly can save lives—maybe even your own."

He watched the nervous young auxiliary ride away and felt Carmenta's taut shoulder muscles twitch. He patted her neck and thought, *Maybe I should have left you behind.* A legion mount was accustomed to moving as a component within a formation and undisturbed by the sounds and hectic activity within a legion camp, but Carmenta was unsettled. Since they were part of the emperor's contingent, horse and rider had more room on the nearly nine-day march than the regular legionaries on the often-narrow road. Carmenta was a warrior, but she did not have the experience of a warhorse.

Nicanor had returned to Rome from Sinuessa, bringing Tigellinus's body. The emperor had merely looked at the corpse and nodded to accept Nicanor's story. Then the emperor had explained that his offer to co-rule with Vitellius or split the empire had been rejected just that same morning. He had little choice but to be ready for war.

Afterward, Nicanor had learned from Florin that Marcus Otho, fearing his hold on the city was precarious, had ordered an Ostia legion to Rome. That had proved nearly disastrous.

The Praetorian Tribune, Varinus Crispinus, detailed to greet the incoming legion, had opened the armory to draw out additional gear. But he had unwisely done it after sundown, thinking it would be less busy, easier to work through each cohort. The Praetorians on watch, some clearly drunk, mistook it as an attempted coup against the emperor and slew many of the incoming legion's officers. The watch captain had sent a runner to the emperor's palace to sound an alarm.

The emperor was hosting a banquet and quickly directed his two Praetorian prefects to settle the situation at the armory. Plotius Firmus and Licinius Proculus were admired by the Praetorian rank and file. They exercised newfound power in their support of Marcus Otho. The emperor had tried to soothe his guests, but some fled in a panic that spread through the city. More than anything, the citizens of Rome feared the empire's legion showing up at their gates, arrayed against the people.

The following morning, things worsened as Vitellius's rejection arrived, and the emperor had wisely not hesitated to react. Orders went out that he would lead men north to intercept any encroachment by Vitellius's forces. Nicanor had thought it a keen tactical and political decision, though politics was beyond his experience. He was less pleased that the orders included that he would accompany the emperor. It was a small comfort that the emperor would never go near any battle. Nicanor was no coward, as was attested by his scars earned in battle, but he no longer had the heart for combat. His spirit had dulled—he no longer felt the sharp eagerness to fight.

Before leaving Rome, Nicanor had asked Marcus Attilius to carry a message to Antonia Caenis in Tibur, requesting she forward it to General Vespasian. In it, he asked if Emperor Otho's decree had been delivered and if there had been any word of Lady Cleo. And he had also visited the Temple of Hercules to ask the gods to let Graius know he had completed part of his vow to the old gladiator who had saved his life. Tigellinus was dead, and additional efforts were being made to protect Cleo. He prayed he could soon be released from the emperor's service so he could return to Judea to help Cleo. And, if the gods granted him an opportunity... to kill Gessius Florus.

The pounding of approaching hoofbeats caught his attention, and he looked to the road leading from the nearest river crossing. The rider, breathing as heavily as his mount, stopped before the emperor's personal guard and called out to the general, "Sire, they're a half-day north of here! I spotted their standard, the *signum* of 1st Legion, *Germanica.*"

Nicanor scratched Carmenta between the ears, and her head lifted in pleasure. He leaned forward and said to her with resignation, "There'll be fighting tomorrow."

XII

APRILUS 69 CE

JERUSALEM

CITY OF DAVID

Though Miriam had left Yeshua ben Ananias behind her in the Upper City, his cries of doom echoed—perhaps only in her thoughts—as she passed into the City of David. She was disguised as a slender young man, and over one shoulder was slung a bag of provisions and a vessel of lamp oil for Ya'el and Elian. She gripped Zechariah's staff in her right hand, ready. When Matthew heard she intended to take food to Ya'el and Elian, he acknowledged she handled the staff well. Good enough to crack the skull of anyone who might confront her. Surprisingly, her mother had agreed, saying, "No matter how I feel, you'll do it anyway. So, you should appear to be an armed man, not a young woman." Matthew added, "I don't like you doing this, but you must appear capable. The craven men who follow Yohanan ben Levi seem to torment only the weak."

As they had stood at the rear gate of their courtyard, through the dawn stillness came haunting cries of "Woe... Woe..."

"Yet they leave the crazed alone, it seems," Matthew muttered as she passed through the gate.

Yohanan ben Levi's men continued to patrol the streets, mocking and shocking the native citizens of the city. Many were dressed as women, with braided hair and drenched in perfume, but they had no qualms about pulling a dagger. They would cut down anyone who crossed their path or did not submit to their demands.

Matthew had told her that those who fled the city found no safety outside the walls. Just as Elazar ben Yair's message to her had mentioned, Simon bar Giora had left Masada for Jerusalem, and his army now sealed the city. Those who left were killed or had their hands or feet cut off. Then they were sent back into the city as Simon's messengers with these words from him: "I swear by the God of the Universe I will break these walls and punish everyone within. Children and the old will not be spared... the innocent and guilty treated the same."

Matthew and Yohanan ben Zaccai said the threat was sent to the Sanhedrin. Still, it was meant for Yohanan ben Levi, instructing him to yield the city. Simon bar Giora was just as cruel and self-centered as the Gischalan but despised him. Simon saw himself as the rightful ruler of Jerusalem.

As she neared the old wall marking near the tomb entrance, Miriam tested the still air for the lingering scent she had learned often meant the Gischalan's men were about. More than once, the heavy scent had warned her just in time. She thought again of the doom prophet's call: "Woe to Jerusalem...." The city's fate was shaped by the hands of its would-be leaders as much as by the Romans. And it seemed to be upon them, whether inside the walls or outside.

* * *

KING DAVID'S TOMB

"It's difficult to stay here... I mean, I probably could tolerate it. But he," Ya'el gestured toward Elian, who sat glumly gnawing a piece of fresh bread from Miriam's bag, "I worry about him." The boy's first joy at seeing Miriam faded when she told him he and Ya'el must stay hidden longer. When she did not answer his question, "How long?" he grew sullen.

"I know, but it's still not safe. Now, all Yohanan ben Levi's men talk about is 'finding the Roman woman.'"

"Have you seen Hananiah?" Ya'el asked tentatively. As much as she wanted to live, she wanted more to see her husband suffer for all he had done. Hananiah's connection to Gessius Florus was the only means to that end if they could manipulate it. She knew Miriam wanted to kill Hananiah for the part he had played in Ehud's death, but they had talked about why she shouldn't. Not yet. But it was a dangerous game Miriam must play with Florus's spymaster and killer.

"Matthew, my mother and I have just come up with a way to explain your absence. I'll change at Zechariah's when I leave here and see Hananiah."

"You'll do as we decided?"

"Elian..." Miriam did not answer Ya'el. The boy stood and walked to her. He looked up at Miriam, disappointment still on his face. "Next time I come," she told him, "we'll explore one of the tunnels."

"Really?" The boy's eyes widened and brightened in the lantern's light. "Can I carry a torch?"

"Yes. I promise." Miriam patted Elian's shoulder. "Now go eat."

Ya'el watched as the boy, in a better mood, sat on a stone bench and chewed chunks of bread and cheese with more appetite. She turned to Miriam, who still had not answered. On her last visit bringing food, Miriam had told her of her mother's silent tears at night: "I see the remnants each morning." There had been no success in freeing her father, and where Yohanan ben Zaccai's pleading did not seem to work, perhaps gold would. Miriam planned to bring out more *minae* from the tomb's inner treasure chamber, believing Matthew could figure out how to use the gold bars to buy their father's freedom. Picking up a small lighted hand lamp, Ya'el followed a silent Miriam through the passage and stopped where daylight from the narrow entrance lessened the dark. She didn't ask again what Miriam would tell Hananiah—or do with him.

* * *

THE LOWER CITY

Hananiah looked up at the sound of someone entering the shop. When he saw it was Miriam, he pushed aside the sheet of parchment he wrote upon a note intended for Gessius Florus. His unconscious hand went to smooth his hair and passed over the soreness of a still-swollen lump on his skull. Icy anger had consumed him for days as, dizzy and with head throbbing, he searched the city for the woman Ya'el and the boy. But now that melted away at the sight of her.

"Hello, Hananiah...."

He could see she was upset. "Are you well, Miriam?" Hananiah's first thought was he would have to finish his work on Yonatan bar Hilel. "Has that man returned to trouble you... and your family?"

"No," she said as she stepped closer to his work counter, her face pale and taut. "My cousin and her son have left the city. I'm sad and worried about them—it's dangerous out there."

"Where did they go?"

"My mother received a message that they've gone to Masada. They feel it's safer there." Miriam rested her fists on the counter. He did not see a need to hide the parchment from her; she had other worries. Taking a breath, she seemed to relax and flattened her fingers. "I did not even get to tell them goodbye."

Ahhh, Hananiah thought, *'The Hand' has taken them to the Sicarii stronghold.* He'd never reach them there. "Perhaps it is safer," he replied. "I've seen your unhappiness here. Would you think of fleeing Jerusalem yourself... to find someplace where you can be safe? Before the Romans... make it impossible."

48

"It may already be," Miriam shook her head. "Now Simon bar Giora is here, outside the city, and he's killing or maiming any who leave."

"The Sicarii are at Masada," Hananiah said as he leaned toward her, "and I've heard it was a Sicarii who killed your friend, Ehud. But I also heard he was a Roman collaborator and deserved it." He had enjoyed spinning the lie about Ehud to Ya'el and the boy. But that man and his family *deserved* to suffer. Ehud's father, Meshulam, was like the wealthy Jewish builder who overworked his poor father until an accident killed him. And all the evil that had fallen upon Hananiah in Alexandria afterward was a rich man's fault, too. He set aside that bitter memory to study Miriam's face. Her expression was grimmer still, so he faked contrition. "I'm sorry... Ehud was your close friend, and I'm sorry about your cousin leaving."

He shifted his hand to rest on hers, and she stiffened with a flash from her eyes that seemed to carry a familiar glint. Then a tremor passed through her, and her features relaxed.

"I'm sorry if their loss makes you lonely," he said. "Are you... lonely?" His fingers stroked the back of her hand. He felt her tremble at the touch, but she did not withdraw her hand.

* * *

Miriam peeked again at the square of parchment on the counter. She recognized Hananiah's handwriting—the same as the warning message Ehud had discovered in the glassworks the night she had tried to talk to him. Miriam struggled to resist the urge to pull a dagger from her sleeve and plunge it into Hananiah's throat.

XIII

Aprilus 69 CE

Caphera

Sayid had traveled into Idumea only once before, briefly. Then he had been one of Lady Cleo's escorts when she toured Judea before returning to Rome to wed Gessius Florus. She had visited the central shore of Lake Asphaltitis, which some referred to as a 'dead sea,' and then the few major cities west and south of Jerusalem. Sayid's father had told him of his assignment to General Cerealis's legion, to be deployed to subdue those few cities still resisting Roman rule. So, Sayid studied copies of the maps the legion surveyors had made.

Nicanor had shown Sayid how to use maps to visualize where battles would occur and understand relative locations and distances. From the southern end of Lake Asphaltitis, a trip west from the valley and plain into the mountains required an ascent of nearly 4,000 feet. The arid range had many almost-inaccessible peaks separated by deep gorges. But there were also extensive areas of fertile farmland at the northern end. Irrigated from the Jordan, the fields grew plentiful wheat, grapes, figs, pomegranates, and olives for the region. Vespasian had ordered General Cerealis to secure that food for the legions in Judea—just one of many orders. What was left of the town of Caphera sat on a hill in a range only 22 miles southwest of Jerusalem. Its once-formidable defensive walls of massive stones were now rubble, and the citizens were dead or captured. Sayid could see the slave dealers the legion commander had retained. They shepherded a long line of captured men, women, and children shackled together on the road to Caesarea's newly burgeoning slave market.

Sayid, now a *pedes*, a simple foot soldier, was one of the hundreds in his cohort marching past the ruins of Caphera. The 5th Legion, Macedonia, had moved on to Caphatabira, where a bigger fight was expected. That city's walls were more formidable, and the city defenses more difficult to overcome. But its defeat was inevitable.

Sayid was the only man of the hundreds of sweat-soaked infantrymen who regretted the march halting for the night. They were all suffering in the heat, though summer was still two months away. He wanted to press on to Caphatabira, to be there for the start of the fighting. His cohort would reinforce the units under his father's command. But they also escorted vital support personnel for the legion prepared to be dug in for some time. The *fabri* and *fabrica carpentarii* took care of blacksmithing and repairs. And the wound dressers, the *caspari,* were as vital in the field as the medicus and surgeon they also brought with them.

The echoes of the *buccinator's* trumpet signal to halt and pitch camp for the night had barely ended when men hurriedly dropped their packs. They began clearing the surrounding ground and setting stakes for their tents. With a sigh, Sayid did the same.

* * *

A day later...

Outside Caphatabira

As the sun set, men were still completing the back side of the perimeter wall of the *castrum* as Sayid's cohort passed its boundary. The cavalry already patrolled the city-facing fortifications of the encampment, with more on the vulnerable flanks and fewer at the rear. Sayid's cohort now peeled off to augment the rearguard.

Though he'd been eager to arrive, Sayid only half-watched for his father's standard. The news he had heard at Caphera occupied the rest of his thoughts. His tent had been close to that of the medical unit. The other infantrymen—all veterans who had served together for two years at least—had not warmed to him. They formed their own conclusions about him when they learned he had been demoted from a comfortable legion headquarters job to serve in a front-line combat unit. Sayid was not welcome around their campfires. He had not attempted to correct their thinking. They wouldn't have believed his new assignment was voluntary; that would make them see him as a liar or crazy. So, Sayid ate alone at his own small fire. It was quiet enough there that he could hear the loud talk from the medicus and his men.

"The bounty just says that the lady—a noblewoman—is connected somehow to the emperor, and she's in Jerusalem. It doesn't say *how* they're connected."

Those words struck Sayid, and he did not hear the rest of their chatter—something about a wealthy nobleman. He knew Gessius Florus offered the reward and prayed to the gods Cleo was still safe. But with this bounty set on her, how long could that last?

***

The next dawn...

Not since Jerusalem, when he was there with the 12th Legion, had Sayid seen siege equipment arrayed before a city and thousands of Roman soldiers intending to conquer it. He could not help trembling with awe and pride at being part of the legion. A flash of regret shot through him that the people behind those walls were Yosef's countrymen, but he had chosen his duty.

Sayid had finally seen his father in formation in front of his cohort. His men were queued behind the line of siege machines, weapons servers, and *scutari*—the ranks of shield men protecting them. Once enough rocks and heavy bolts had weakened the ramparts and driven defenders from them, his father would order his men in... led and flanked by heavy infantry.

The signal came, and with precision, each siege weapon launched its first projectiles. The next few fired nearly simultaneously and then settled into the rhythm specific to each weapon and its crew. The second group of resupply wagons laden with bolts and stones for the dozens of *scorpio* and *ballistae* had reached the front line as two colossal siege towers trundled into place. Then something happened that Sayid and none of the Romans expected.

The massive city gates swung open. After a moment, another Roman salvo crashed several heavy stones into the large posts and beams, splintering the frame that supported the gate doors. The quick shift in targeting left the huge doors sagging and digging into the ground. They would not easily close until they were repaired.

Another barrage landed within the opening, and flights of heavy arrows kept the two towers and parapet on either side of the entrance clear of defenders. Another call from the Roman bugler rang out. A cohort of heavy infantry moved forward, armor glinting in the morning sun now spilling over the hill to the east. The formation centered before the gates but not close enough to foul the now-silent siege weapons should an order come to begin firing again.

Sayid shifted around to see better and heard the ripple of talk pass through the front ranks: "Someone comes from within the city... General Cerealis is sending one of his staff to talk with them."

The sun climbed higher, and the cool morning breeze was long gone before he heard more. At first, it was the sound of men relaxing, easing their muscles and weapons, the movement of men no longer poised for combat.

Then the word was passed: "Stand down... the rebels surrender."

The Jews wished to save their city from destruction and their citizens from death, Sayid thought. "The city is ours," he said aloud.

* * *

Sayid was more exhausted by *not* fighting than he had felt after the battle at Beth Horon. He did not expect to survive combat again, but every bit of his being had been ready to do what he must to prove himself as a soldier... to his father.

After the order to cease firing, he had seen his father moving through the ranks, checking his men and their equipment. He was ever the leader expecting readiness, Sayid thought. When he reached the last echelon, their gazes met at the end of the row. His father's eyes had flashed up to check the unit standard Sayid stood beneath, and then he had turned away.

* * *

Sayid sat gazing into his little campfire that night when he heard a familiar voice behind him. "I'm not surprised to see you awake. Do you worry?"

Sayid turned to look into the shadows, his eyes accustomed to the bright flames. "Hello, father," he said as the man entered the glow of the fire.

"General Cerealis is leaving two cohorts of infantry here as a garrison to make sure this city remains in our control."

Sayid was surprised at his father's tone as if they were peers discussing the army's movements.

"At dawn," the older man went on, "the rest of the legion and auxiliaries move on to Hebron to capture it." He limped toward the fire, set down the folding camp stool he carried, and slowly lowered his lanky frame to sit, stretching out his bad leg beside the fire.

"Hebron won't surrender," Sayid said and shook his head.

"I thought fear of facing them had kept you from sleep, but you seem to look forward to it. Why do you think they won't surrender as Caphatabira did today?"

"I've been there," Sayid replied, "when I served in the escort for a Roman noblewoman touring Judea. Hebron is one of the Jews' holiest cities. Three Jewish patriarchs are buried there: Ibrahim, Yitzhak, and Yakov, together with their wives. The Judean client-king, Herod, built a massive structure with six-foot-thick walls around the burial site. They call it 'The Cave of the Patriarchs,' and I've seen it."

"Wouldn't the Jews there surrender to save it?"

"I think they will die trying to keep it from capture."

"You want to fight them?" his father asked.

"Don't you? Being a soldier is everything to you, isn't it?"

"Doing my *duty* as a soldier is," his father said. "I fight when I'm ordered to, against the ones I'm ordered to fight." His voice had lost its mocking tone.

"Then why do you question whether I want to fight? It's *my* duty, too."

"So, you left being a clerk… for that."

"I must prove I can."

"To yourself?"

Sayid kept scorn in his voice. "I don't doubt myself. I've fought before and been wounded while doing my duty. But you must *see* me do it before you respect me."

"That's how I've measured myself since I became a man—in battle." His father reached inside his tunic, his hand pausing over his heart, then brought out a stained sheet of parchment. It had been unfolded and refolded so many times the frayed seams were beginning to separate.

"Your mother had this written and sent to me many years ago," he said. He handed the page to Sayid.

A chunk of wood burned through and settled into the bed of embers, sending up a dance of sparks. Holding the parchment near the light, Sayid read and reread the letter. "She asked you to not encourage me to join the legion as you did. She did not want me to follow your path."

"Tahir wanted you to grow up and become what I could not: a husband to a loving wife… a father to children. I have always loved your mother as she has loved me. Soon—if I survive this campaign, as is likely since now I can only *order* men into battle, not join them—I will retire and join her in Laodicea. As her husband."

"Do you think then you will see me as your son?" Sayid shook the letter in his hand. "Did you answer her?"

His father's eyes narrowed. "Careful with that." He gestured at the parchment sheet. "I told her I would not encourage you to join the legion."

"You kept that letter for all these years. But you have had nothing to do with my life." Sayid remarked, not able to keep the bitterness from his words.

The hardness in his father's face eased. "I felt it was not my right since I could not be with you and your mother and share the responsibility of raising you."

"Yet now you have judged me—and still you judge me. I've fallen short in your eyes." Sayid's sharp tone brought the stern expression back.

"I also told her," he said, "that a man—a boy who becomes a man—must do what he must." He nodded and studied his son. "If you are doing what you must, I respect that."

He rose stiffly and picked up the stool. "I'll leave you now." He stepped from the light of the fire but stopped in the shadow. "I will not expect to see you in Hebron."

XIV

Aprilus 69 CE

Caesarea

The Roman Encampment, Vespasian's Praetorium

Yosef recognized the ledgers spread open on the desk before Vespasian. He had asked about the legion's paymaster records before and had been present a few times as the general reviewed them. Vespasian frowned as he tapped rows of new entries, then looked up at Yosef and signaled for the guards to leave them. "What did you want to see me about?" he said.

"Would it be possible to see my Syrian friend, Sayid?"

"You asked me that the last time."

Since he had been captured in Yotapta, Yosef had been in the presence of the Roman general dozens of times and found the man steady and focused, a thoughtful leader. Vespasian was not reactionary nor driven by emotion. Still, a thinly veiled anger now simmered behind his bunched and lowered brows.

Yosef did not mention that Vespasian had not responded to his previous request but repeated his supposed reason for it. "I ask for someone I know to occasionally visit with me, General." He lifted his hands and dropped them back to his sides with the jangling of his chains. "Time weighs heavily on me."

Vespasian rubbed his chin with his knuckles and said, "*We* talk, and now that General Titus is back, I know you meet with him, too."

"And I appreciate our talks... I mean, I want to have time to speak with someone, general, who does not see me as their prisoner but as a friend." This was true, but Yosef needed to talk to Sayid about Cleo most. He needed to know how things had gone when Sayid left her in Jerusalem.

Vespasian still frowned. "I have sent for him to ask just that about the emperor's sister. But I was told Sayid had volunteered for a combat unit. Your friend is in Idumea now with General Cerealis's legion."

Yosef lowered his head and kept the worry from his voice. Sayid's desire to prove himself in battle could be deadly. "I see you're busy, general. Thank you for seeing me." He turned to go.

"Do you still dream, Yosef?"

Vespasian's question stopped him in his tracks. The Roman general was asking for portents of things to come. But Yosef also dreamed of the past now—especially since the death of his forced bride, Ariella. He had felt flashes so vivid it seemed the events had just occurred. He saw Cleo as they floated on a piece of the *Salacia's* wreckage, thinking they would die. Their tongues had been loosened by looming death, which gave them a kind of perverse freedom, and they shared things about themselves they shouldn't have. One flash had been when he realized she was the woman in his dream before he left Jerusalem for the *Salacia's* voyage to Rome. He'd also vividly remembered finding Miriam's *hamsa* in the tunnel beneath the Temple Enclosure. Another of the deaths of Dov and Levi at Yotapta. And he had a dark and close memory of the hatred on Ariella's face when she unveiled herself after the mockery of their marriage.

But Yosef could not speak of those dreams. He studied the brooding general and nodded before he turned away, saying, "I still see that you will become ruler of Rome, General Vespasian."

* * *

As Yosef left the room and was flanked by his guards for the walk back to his cell, Gaheris Clineas entered and gestured toward the ledgers. "Are you done with those, general?"

"Yes," said Vespasian, closing them and pushing them aside. He knew the men who received the bonus of the dead Emperor Galba would enjoy it—or had already. But he wondered how the empire could afford those sums spread out among all the legions. Antonia's letter mentioned how imperial officials whispered and worried about the empire's emptying coffers. As news of Marcus Otho's ascension was confirmed, Vespasian—as commander of all the legions in Judea—would have to do what he could to manage any expectations that another new emperor would issue his own 'loyalty' reward. A prudent emperor would not... but who knew what kind of emperor Marcus Otho would prove to be?

He watched as his aide took up the ledgers and stopped after tucking them under his arm. He turned to look at the general.

"What is it, Gaheris?"

"Have you reconsidered what I suggested, sir?"

"I'm not adding more men to my personal guard," Vespasian said simply. "The attack was my own fault. I no longer walk alone and am armed whenever I leave the praetorium." He saw the concern on the man's face and gentled his tone. "You've served with me a long time, Gaheris."

"Since you became legate of the 2nd Legion in Germania 28 years ago. And as your personal aide since the invasion of Britannia."

"Have you ever known me to be imprudent?"

The two men were the same age but had followed far different paths. They had mutual respect—and honesty. "Not in years, sir," he said with a smile. "Still, I wish you'd—"

"Any word of Governor Mucianus's ship?" Vespasian said before he could finish.

Gaheris sighed, "No, sir, but if he left as he mentioned in his last letter to you, he should arrive tomorrow unless he stops at Tyrus. There has been news that the city leaders wish to speak with him, as governor, about their *civitas foederati* payments to Rome—to ensure they remain a free city."

"Let me know when you hear any news of him."

Vespasian looked out the window as he considered his position. He had still received no definitive imperial orders from Otho other than the decree protecting Lady Cleo. Before he acted on it, he wanted to learn more about her from the Syrian auxiliary. When he did, he would likely elicit a visit and questions from Gessius Florus. Thankfully, the man had left him alone lately.

He wondered again about the message from Mucianus—he must speak to him face to face. Did the message mean he bore orders like those delivered to Gnaeus Domitius Corbulo two years before? That victorious general, a man he knew well, had been ordered away from his command to meet Nero. That emperor feared the man because of his reputation, the loyalty of the men he commanded, and his popularity with the citizens of Rome. Through his messengers, Nero had ordered the general to kill himself. The witnesses said that Corbulo had done so, exclaiming, "*Axios...* I'm worthy!" as he fell on his sword.

Antonia Caenis's long letter included her comprehensive assessment of current affairs in Rome. Marcus Otho was better liked than Galba but had only a tenuous hold. And Vitellius, the emperor's strongest opponent, was consolidating power for his own move to take the throne. Would Otho consider him a threat, too? *I do not think I will fall on my sword if so ordered*, Vespasian thought.

XV

Aprilus 69 CE

Caesarea

Gessius Florus's Villa

Gessius Florus studied, without interest, his copy of the letter that had also been sent to Gaius Licinius Mucianus, the provincial governor. Though Florus still held the position of an imperial tax collector, given him by Nero, he cared little about those duties. Let cities like Tyrus deal with Mucianus about their taxes and fees to the empire.

Still, he thought as he set the letter aside and drew a sheet of vellum toward him, then the pen and inkpot, *I should reply and offer to meet with them.* Then there would be no question that he was not serving the empire as he should.

Then he stopped, pen nib raised—the echo of heavy footsteps approached. While the exterior of the domus and surrounding walls had been strengthened and fortified, the inner halls were bare, and the rooms were empty other than his office and private chambers. So the sound carried. He did not look up at the entry of his office when the footsteps stopped there.

"Lord Florus..." The Thracian's voice was identifiable by its lesser deference... something that rankled Florus. Still, he needed the man and his men for now.

"Yes, Krateros."

"Your dog Drusus is here with the women you sent for. He got them from the markets at Ptolemais and has taken them to the quarters you set up."

"Good," Florus said, keeping the smile from his face. He felt a hunger stir inside him to hear their cries. That hunger would build until the evening when he could satisfy it. The Jewish women had been captured at Yotapta—under the command of that Jew, Yosef. And that made Florus's anticipation of entertainment with them much sweeter.

He frowned at the man who stood waiting. "Tell me why I've not heard that the Syrian auxiliary is dead yet."

Krateros shrugged his broad shoulders. "I should have taken him the night I saw him in the taberna. But inside, he was with a rangy, scarred legionary... and when he left, this Sayid must have followed him out. I would have had to kill them both... at night in a downpour. The big soldier would have been a handful on a clear night in good light. So, I waited. And now the Syrian is not at the encampment any longer. My man inside the camp says he checked with Celsus Evander, his former commanding officer. The information is that this Sayid is now with Cerealis's legion, fighting in Idumea."

"If he does not die in battle with the Idumeans, and if he returns here," said Florus, "I expect you to kill him. I don't care who he's with, as long as you can do it with no trace to me. That is... if you want to earn what I offered."

"I'll see to it," said Krateros, whose tone had lost some arrogance.

Florus waved a jeweled hand to dismiss the man, then stopped him. "You," he ordered. "Stop referring to Drusus as my dog or 'a little man on a big horse.'" He knew Krateros resented that Florus treated Drusus as Krateros's equal. "I don't think you want him to learn of it. If he does, you might not earn what I pay you... and certainly not the additional reward promised."

The man smirked but then nodded and left. Florus needed them both, as they served as a check and balance on each other. But he doubted he could stop the squat, powerful former legionary from killing the mercenary leader if they fought. Coin motivated—and to a degree controlled—Krateros. But Drusus would not let any slight go unpunished.

I've said what I must, he thought and left the two men to fate. Other matters required his focus. He called out for Irad, who always lurked nearby. When the major domus appeared, he asked, "Is your merchant brother expected soon from Jerusalem?"

The man nodded with a fleeting expression of wariness as he replied, "Tomorrow, lord."

"Good. Bring Boaz here when he arrives. Now, send Drusus to me."

* * *

"I know the women are here," Florus said when Drusus showed in the doorway. "But first, you saw to the second wagonload of treasure?"

"Yes, lord. It's secure with the other one in the warehouse, behind a new false wall."

"I want you to return to Sycaminum right now," said Florus. "A dozen men will arrive late tomorrow or the next day, and they will come to the warehouse. Half of them have instructions to remain there and guard the place, replacing the men there now—you will pay those off and discharge them. Bring the others here. Ask them no questions."

The short, stout man nodded once, turned, and left.

Florus did not trust the mercenaries to guard what was hidden within the warehouse—and what he hoped to add to the stash—so he had sent for men he trusted. They were violent men, mostly family, from his birthplace of Clazomenae. The deadliest was coming to Caesarea a different way, for another purpose.

Lord Vitellius had reported Galba's death and said that Marcus Otho had been declared emperor. Vitellius had said he was moving his legions closer to Rome. So Florus would please him and aid his cause by removing one potential obstacle in his path to the empire. It seemed Vespasian had received a decree from Marcus Otho to protect Cleo. But that imperial order would negate his own bounty for his errant wife, and he could not have Cleo fall into the hands of someone who would keep her alive.

What Florus had planned would render meaningless the decree, perhaps even lead to the end of it. Florus hoped most of all for a slinger's delight, the killing of two with one stone.

XVI

Aprilus 69 CE

Brixellum, Northern Italia

Imperial Encampment

Nicanor understood that Marcus Otho's imperial headquarters at Brixellum would serve as the base for the campaign against the legions of Vitellius. But the headquarters would not be close to the fighting. Brixellum was about 40 miles from Placentia and spread across hills that offered excellent views of the surrounding terrain—and the battle would take place on the flat plains. They had luxuries—temples, baths, and a forum. Perhaps those conveniences had dictated the choice. Still, a leader—even an emperor—should be closer to the men, accompanying them into combat. Marcus Otho had brought an entourage of magistrates and senior statesmen from Rome, and Nicanor did not understand the choice. Those men had no military experience and nothing to offer to a military campaign—and most had been reluctant to come. He was rendered uneasy when he witnessed, as part of the emperor's personal staff, their involvement in important decisions.

It was clear the battle would be to the north near the center of the vast plain of the *val padana,* the Po Valley, over 30 miles away. Lord Vitellius's General Aulus Caecina Alienus and his legions 11th, *Rapax,* and 5th, *Alaudae,* and auxiliaries were encamped astride the *Via Postumia* near Cremona. A second army commanded by General Fabius Valens would—by all reports—join them within a day.

"Why did we leave Rome and move so fast," asked Florin, "with only parts of the legions and their auxiliaries?"

The puzzled look on the young man's face echoed the nagging questions Nicanor had kept inside for days. Reports came in at the camp near Placentia that Caecina's army was nearing the town. Despite a successful skirmish against Caecina's advance units, the emperor had replaced his senior commander, Annius Gallus. He sent to Rome for his brother, Titianus Otho. Afterward, Nicanor heard the muttering of two senior officers exiting a supply tent, thinking they were alone. He caught part of it before they saw him. "The emperor fears good advice. What's been said about him is true—he panics even with success and makes poor decisions." As the two men went quiet and continued toward one of the command tents, Nicanor considered what had happened upon the arrival of Titianus.

As the new overall commander, Titianus had disregarded the advice of Annius Gallus and Suetonius Paulinus to wait for the rest of the legions to join them before engaging Vitellius's two armies. But the force of three Praetorian cohorts, 1000 legion infantry, and a small cavalry contingent that had remained in Placentia led by Vestricius Spurinna had been ordered to sortie. They were to lure Vitellius's army back to them instead of staying behind the city's reinforced walls and new parapets and towers. Marius Celsus had been ordered to move his 1st Legion to support Spurrina.

Nicanor had been in that first morning's meeting with Titianus when one of the Numidian riders who served as constant couriers between the field commanders and the emperor had brought Spurinna's latest report. They had repulsed an attack by Caecina, and Vitellius's general had pulled his force back to Cremona. In overall command at the time, Suetonius Paulinus had given Spurrina standing orders to not pursue any retreating enemy.

Titianus had then issued orders and sent a courier on a fresh mount to carry them to General Celsus. The general was to hold at Bedriacum, a small village east of Cremona. Nicanor assumed Titianus wanted Celsus's larger force to become greater bait to draw out the enemy. But that thinking went against all he had learned in decades of combat. Why not continue on to Placentia and add to its defense? Why not wait for the rest of the legions that could outflank and envelope any enemy laying siege to that city? They did not have the men nor equipment to confront a sizable enemy in the field until reinforcements arrived.

The emperor's army had not left Rome at full strength—another decision Nicanor questioned, as had Suetonius Paulinus. That general had, eight years before, as governor of Britannia, quelled the rebellion led by the warrior queen, Boudica, and he had led legions and had military campaign experience. The emperor privately asked Nicanor his opinion, and he told him he agreed with General Paulinus. But Nicanor also told the emperor that letting Aulus Caecina fall back unharried to Cremona had been a mistake. With Celsus's legion in support, they matched Caecina's force evenly. Still, since the legion was retreating, they could have done more damage to it, reducing its threat. Now, Fabius Valens would have time to join his army with Caecina's.

Multiple reports confirmed that Vitellius's generals led a combined force of 70,000 men, outmanning Otho's force of only elements of the 7th, 11th, and 13th Legions. Nicanor had once served under the commander Vedius Aquila, and he knew him as a good combat leader. But the balance of those legions and the entire 14th, the victors against Boudica, were still days away from joining them.

After long minutes of contemplation, Nicanor turned from his view of the nearby temple to answer his aide's question. The temple was alight with torches and bonfires, where Marcus Otho and his retinue of Rome's leaders were gathering as twilight darkened into night. "The rush to leave Rome," he said, "and not to wait for all legions available makes no sense to me. But politicians and nobles have a different perspective than men like us, Florin. If it were them doing the dying—a man skewered on the point of another man's blade—so tired he could not raise his own sword to block that fatal thrust, sweat, and blood in his eyes, grit in his teeth...." He shook his head at the contemplation, then went on. "Then maybe they'd listen and do what would put the battle in their—our—favor. I think the emperor fears being judged harshly—maybe perceived as cowardly—if he does not commit to battle now." He did not add, *And I think he feels Rome is slipping from his grasp. So Antonia Caenis believes.*

"What of the gladiators?" Florin asked. "What are they doing serving with the legions? When we left Placentia, half of them came here with us."

Nicanor, too, had questioned the spectacle of 2,000 gladiators led by a general, Martius Macer, whom he had never heard of, joining the formation queuing on the road outside Rome. Marcus Attilius, who had accompanied Nicanor to the rally point, had spotted them before returning to Rome and remarked, "The emperor has offered freedom and citizenship to them. Gnaeus Batiatus was unhappy that imperial recruiters had come to his *ludis* to make the offer. That is until he learned he would be paid for more than their worth."

Hearing that, Nicanor had thought of Graius. He wondered what the old fighter would say about it. "Why use them when he has legions to draw upon?" Nicanor asked, and the answer fit with something Nicanor had realized on the march to Placentia. He repeated that answer to Florin. "The emperor has brought five cohorts of Praetorians as his personal guard, but most have never been in a battle like what we—our men—face. And many of them have served only in the city. Martius Macer proposed the emperor add a force of selected gladiators to serve next to the Praetorians. Those hardened men—who had the prospect of freedom—served as inspiration for the softer city soldiers. He also intends to use the gladiators as a frontline assault unit to strike fast and with fury. The ones here are—I think—for his personal safety. His offer to them should secure their allegiance if others prove disloyal."

"And now we attack..." Florin said dully, his tone mirroring Nicanor's thoughts. "Why do men with little or no military experience not listen to men who have fought battles, who can back their advice with experience and reason?"

Nicanor shook his head and studied the clusters of men atop the nearby hill. In the dancing, firelight flashed the bright togas of the highborn wealthy and the new emperor's rich, deep purple and white cloak. All those men feared losing their position and power. He weighed their motivation against the soldiers who had neither position nor power but risked—life and limb—their only value to the empire. He found the highborn wanting.

He looked away, desiring nothing more than to return to Judea and find some way to help Cleo. "Two hours from here on a strong horse," he gestured to the north, "men will soon die for their leaders. And we will wait here to learn whether we're winning or losing."

XVII

Aprilus 69 CE

Brixellum

Imperial Encampment

Nicanor heard the bugler's call rise shrilly from the bottom of the hill. An imperial messenger had just passed through the main gate of the base encampment that encircled the hill. Nicanor headed toward the central command tent with Florin on his heels.

As they reached the tent flying the emperor's banner, the courier jerked his mount to a staggering stop. The horse's heaving sides were caked with sweat-mud covering its hocks, belly, and chest. The animal sagged, knees buckling, as the rider leaped away and dropped the reins, and he looked as exhausted as the horse. He tugged free the sweat-soaked, mud-splattered tunic and leggings that had bunched up with the ride without concern for whether a handler could see to the horse. Then he approached, ashen-faced, the six Praetorians outside the tent, whose presence confirmed the emperor was inside.

Nicanor knew better than to follow. Though they knew he served the emperor directly, the guards would stop him unless the emperor called a staff meeting. He turned to Florin and said, "Gather our things, prepare packs and provisions for the road... just enough for us. Bring our mounts from the corral."

"Is the emperor leaving?" Florin asked. "Is the battle over?"

"I don't like how that rider looks," Nicanor said. "He shows me the news is not good."

"How?"

"Did you smell the man?"

Florin blinked. "What? No, sir... why would I smell him?"

"He reeks of more than the sourness of a man who has spent hours on a hard-ridden animal. He has fouled himself—not stopping even to clean himself of the filth before reporting to the emperor—and that's not a good sign. Now, go. We must be ready."

Nicanor turned from his aide and saw the 12-foot pole outside the command tent, previously barren of any signal flags, suddenly flourishing one he recognized. A call for the imperial staff. He walked to the tent, and the Praetorians let him pass. Just inside, where the tent flaps were pinned back and secured, were six more enormous men, gladiators, three to each side. They were in full armor with unsheathed swords gripped at their sides. Nicanor thought he recognized two from the gladiator training school in Rome, where he'd spent time with the trainer and owner, Gnaeus Batiatus. One man, the bigger of the two, gave him a curt nod. The other scowled at him.

The stench of the rider was more potent within the tent, where the air was still. Marcus Otho, Licinius Proculus, and Suetonius Paulinus stood close to the man as he delivered his report in a quaking voice that steadied as he went on.

"General Celsus's men met them between the river and the road, sire. The Vitellians—there were so many more of them than of us—were spread wider than our ranks and three times deeper. And more—the legions led by Fabius Valens were coming from the west down the Via Postumia to reinforce Aulus Caecina's force. I was with General Celsus, and a rider came at a gallop and shouted to the general that hundreds, maybe thousands of Batavians, were crossing the river to strike at our exposed flank. General Macer's gladiators had turned to meet them, but the Batavians cut through. Some of Macer's men had retreated, but most went down—dead or terribly wounded. The man reported, and General Celsus acknowledged it. Then the man wheeled his mount back the way he came... into the fight."

The messenger stopped to breathe and gather his thoughts. "Without any opposition, the Batavians tore into us, rolling our flank up. They folded us back into the center of the line, like a wedge splitting wood." The quiver returned to the man's voice. "Our center could not hold, and the Vitellians tore us asunder. Spurinna's men, who had come from Placentia earlier, thrust at the Vitellians' rear. But that did not slow them at all. The men were overwhelmed, and they fell as our line broke. The battlefield became a spread of our men—some alone, sometimes two or three, but not more—against dozens of Vitellians surrounding them. Men tried to retreat toward the road, but those who broke free found it choked with the dead and dying."

Halted by the contemplation of what he reported, the messenger had to steady himself. "For most," he said, "there was nowhere to go. Some made it away. And as they fled past, they told me the Vitellian and Batavian foot soldiers slaughtered those few who faced them and killed the wounded. General Celsus ordered me to get here fast to tell you, sire."

The man stopped as more of the imperial staff entered the tent. Then he said, "That's when I knew all was lost, sire." The man's head dropped to his chest.

Nicanor moved back, letting the more senior men near the emperor and positioning himself closer to the opening. He would listen to everything said and reported, but he did not plan to linger. The look in Marcus Otho's eyes had alarmed him as the man gave his report. Though the emperor's pallid face seemed calm, his eyes were too wide open. And they jittered as he darted glances toward the advisers closest to him. Nicanor thought of his experience with the man. *Steady now*, he thought, willing it so. *We must have clear thinking and a firm hand now*. The feeling he got from the group of men now surrounding the emperor did not reassure him.

XVIII

Aprilus 69 CE

Brixellum

Imperial Encampment

The moon had risen but was hidden behind clouds, peeking out only as the night winds pushed the clouds around in the sky. Nicanor gave the moon a last glance before he entered the tent. Carmina, tethered alongside Florin's mount at the rear of the tent, snorted to acknowledge his return and mirror the anxiety of the men in the camp.

"What did the emperor say, Nicanor?" Florin asked from where he sat on the floor in their shared tent, surrounded by their packs and gear. "The talk through the camp is that the battle was lost, and all wait to hear what will happen next."

Florin told him the news had spread in a rustling of huddled speech, mostly whispers but some loud and angry. Such talk, Nicanor knew, would spread like an icy wind seeking every opening to steal the warmth from within—among soldiers absorbing a defeat and unsure of what was ahead for them. He shrugged off his cloak and draped it over his pack.

"After the messenger had been dismissed," Nicanor said, "more reports came in. Tens of thousands are dead and more sorely wounded. We cannot tend to them. They lie dying on the field." Nicanor had fought in many battles, where many had died. But he never dreamed he would be so close to a battle on *Italia*'s soil and where most of the dead on both sides were men of the empire. Nicanor did not add that, as the meeting continued, it became clear Marcus Otho's mishandling of the chain of command and the ensuing confusion had created chaos and distrust among the ranks. He had watched as the white-faced emperor received each report and thanked each deliverer before dismissing him.

The resolve the emperor had shown as he listened to the worst news possible cracked toward the end. He had then turned to his staff, and his expression was firm—but with resignation, it seemed to Nicanor. Plotius Firmus, the Praetorian Prefect, had appealed to

Otho to regroup, await the coming reinforcements, and reengage Vitellus's armies. Others agreed.

"The emperor said, I'll try to get this right, Florin, but I do not speak as well as Marcus Otho: 'This courage of yours exposes more to further danger. That would be too high a price to pay for my life. The civil war began with Vitellius, who is responsible for this armed struggle for supremacy. I, too, can set an example by preventing its repetition. It is not for me to allow all these young Romans, all these fine armies, to be trampled underfoot a second time to their country's loss. Let your devotion accompany me, just as if you had, in fact, died for my sake. But live on after me. I must not impede your chances of survival, nor you... my resolution. To waste further words on death smacks of cowardice. Here is your best proof that my decision is irrevocable: I complain about no one. Denouncing gods or men is a task for one who is in love with life.'"

Florin waited, listening, his mouth agape and eyes wide with fear. Nicanor patted his arm to settle the young man.

"Several men, understanding what his words meant, pleaded with him to take the night to reconsider. After a moment, the emperor agreed and sent for the statesmen and magistrates. He told them they must leave immediately to return to Rome. He sent riders to the nearest ports with orders for ships to be readied to carry them to safety. Suetonius Paulinus offered to join them, with one of the remaining cohorts to escort them. The emperor said he would do what he must to signal a surrender to Vitellius."

Nicanor stopped as a louder snort came from outside, accompanied by a tug of the side canvas of the tent.

"I'll check them..." Florin said and stood.

"No, I'll go." Nicanor bent to the small bag Florin had prepared and took two carrots from it for the horses. At the front of the tent, Nicanor sensed a large man in the shadows outside. His hand went to the pugio at his hip, bringing it up as he raised the flap.

"I would rather you stabbed me with those," said the man, pointing at the carrots in Nicanor's left hand. "I don't want your blade, Nicanor." He stepped forward into the light arc from Florin's lantern.

"General Aquila... what are you doing here?" Nicanor said, backing up Florin to wave the 13th Legion commander inside. The officer's tent, big enough for two men, one standing, was suddenly too small.

The general doffed his helmet and looked like he wished to remove his dented, nicked, and blood-smeared cuirass. He rubbed his haggard face with a hand that showed the rough stitching of a field *medicus* across its back. Blood encrusted the hand and wrist. The other hand was wrapped in a reddened mass of what had once been white linen. He saw Nicanor glance at it. "I lost three fingers to a crazed Batavian. Cleaved my shield from me and took them with it."

"I'm glad you're alive, sir." Nicanor motioned for the general to sit.

"We're a long way from Antioch, aren't we, centur—" He stopped and studied Nicanor, then said, "I mean, tribunus... a well-deserved promotion."

Nicanor nodded his thanks for his former commanding officer's words. "Toward the end of the meeting, I saw you arrive to speak with the emperor."

"With what men I have left. Those loyal to me fought with me, and we made our way off the Via Postumia; then, we caught some mounts and raced away. We would never have reached Bedriacum. And even if we had, that's a poor place to stand and fight." As the general settled onto a cot, he continued. "I've just reported to the emperor."

The expression that flitted across his face told Nicanor that Aquila felt as he did, that there was senselessness to the emperor's actions. "I reported on my piece of this loss," the general said, "my part in the death of so many. I also told him a messenger came to me last night from Sudeius Clemens, the emperor's commanders, ordered to secure the coast and towns inland. One of Aulus Caecina's patrols had wounded him, and he could go no farther."

The general stopped and seemed to consider his words. "I do not know others on the emperor's staff. I came to command the 13th Legion on the recommendation of Gaius Marinus, Governor of Syria, whom I had served with before. I know he is now aligned with General Vespasian... as I assume you are. I understand from Governor Mucianus that you served on Vespasian's staff recently. That man would not have made the mistakes we now suffer from."

Aquila took a small leather flask from his belt and shook it. "Empty," he muttered tiredly.

"Florin—" Nicanor reached for the full waterskin his aide had already taken from their packs. He handed it to the general.

"Since the battle, I can't seem to drink my fill," Aquila said. After slaking his thirst, the general passed the waterskin back to Florin. "You question what I'm doing here. Why am I not with the other generals and the leaders of Rome who are now feverishly readying to flee back to the city? Vitellius has won this battle and may soon become yet *another* new emperor before Nero has been dead a year. But he will not be the ruler who heals Rome's self-inflicted wounds."

Aquila gingerly massaged his jaw. As he turned his head, the lantern light revealed a large abrasion where the skin had been scraped away to leave a reddened swath with patches of clotted scabs of blood.

"A shield to the face?" Nicanor asked.

"Yes, and I recall you have experience with that, too."

"Yes," Nicanor grinned ruefully and rubbed his jaw. "That's why I grew this beard. Protection."

The slimmest curve of a smile flickered on the general's face. "Clemens's messenger carried a report that I just gave the emperor. It was yet another blow on top of the battle lost today. As I said, Vitellius is not the emperor we need. Gaius Murcianus believes Vespasian *could* be." He waited quietly for Nicanor to consider this thought, then said: "I'll repeat for you what I remember because after what's happened and what is soon to come, I want to serve Vespasian. Perhaps you can help."

The general stood and said, "Our allies against Vitellius within Italia have treated our mother country as if they were invading a foreign shore. They've burned villages, towns, and cities with savagery all the more frightful because the locals were unprepared for an onslaught. So many... men, their wives, children... are victims of war within what they thought was their country at peace." He paused for a breath. "So, now we face hostility from those frightened of *us*. The discord has affected many within the legions. There are reports of mutiny—I shared those with the emperor. Soldiers refuse to follow the officers... the men the emperor has placed in command. Even within my 13th Legion, I sensed resentment from many of the men. The emperor's actions have led to a loss of control, which is dangerous."

The general walked to the entrance and raised the flap. "When you return to Vespasian, tell him I wish to serve him and the Rome that could be... Antonia Caenis will know how to reach me."

"I will, sir." Nicanor nodded and watched the general cross pools of torchlight until he was out of sight among the other tents. The legion commander had said something that bothered him more than did news of the region's civil unrest, of anger now directed at Marcus Otho—the instigator of the conflict. Aquila had said "those loyal to me" of his men had fought alongside him to survive a lost battle. Nicanor thought about that long into the night.

***

The next morning...

"Florin, get up... we must go now."

"With the emperor?" Florin rubbed his eyes with the heels of his hands.

"Marcus Otho has decided; he took his own life at dawn. Emissaries are now on their way to plead with Vitellius... to tell him Rome is his."

Nicanor knew what he must do next. One thing Vedius Aquila had said was sure to prove true. His duty and obligation to Marcus Otho were over. Vitellius would, without fail, purge Rome of Marcus Otho's followers and closest advisers. Though a minor one, Nicanor would be at risk, so he would seek the help of Antonia Caenis to get away. He would return to Judea, to Vespasian. Marcus Otho's decree of protection for Cleo ended with his death. So in Judea, Nicanor would do what he could to save Cleo.

XIX

Aprilus 69 CE

Jerusalem

The Upper City

"I wanted Ya'el and Elian here for the *seder* of *Pesach*," Rebecca said, the taut cords of her neck showing the strain and her increasing frailty. "The seder is the most important."

Miriam knew her mother had slept little and eaten little since her father had been taken by Yohanan ben Levi's men. Even before that, her smile had become infrequent; only Elian had brought a light to her eyes and a smile to her lips. But now the boy, too, was gone from their home. *And home and family meant everything to her*, Miriam thought as she watched Matthew embrace their mother to comfort her.

Miriam gasped without thinking at that sight, feeling her chest press against her linen tunic, tightening the fabric against her. Her family had—once again—come to mean everything to her, as well. She had recovered some of the space within her. Where love had been in earlier days until hate and fear had pushed that love out and driven Miriam away from them.

"Mother, it was too risky," Miriam said, setting down the rag she'd used to clean. She went to hug her mother, too, leaving unsaid that the real danger was from Hananiah. It was not just men seeking the reward of finding any woman new to Jerusalem who might be the Roman noblewoman. Miriam had thought Hananiah believed her story of Ya'el and Elian leaving Jerusalem for Masada. But then she had spotted him loitering near her home as if watching for them. Or for her. Miriam shuddered at the memory of his hand stroking hers. She had made sure he did not see her through a window, and she had made sure he was gone when she checked mid-evening two nights running.

"At our sabbath meal together tomorrow night," Miriam said, "we can repeat some of our Pesach traditions with Ya'el and Elian." She squeezed her mother tight and then stepped back to study her face. "At midnight, Mathew and I will sneak out, get Ya'el and Elian, and bring them back. They'll stay inside all day, share a meal with us, and then tomorrow at midnight, we'll take them back."

Her mother's face eased, and Miriam embraced her again and saw Matthew's stern look as he mouthed the word 'No' and shook his head. She understood his concern—she had concerns, too, but glared back with a mouthed 'Yes.' Her mother needed this, but so did Ya'el and Elian. She prayed she was right about Hananiah not watching late at night.

* * *

The next evening...

Yohanan ben Zaccai was nearly through his reading aloud again from the *Haggadah*, the story of the exodus from Aegypt, fulfilling the *mitzvah* to teach all Jewish children that story. A wave of sorrow washed over Miriam, and she saw it on her mother's face and Matthew's, too. Her father had always done the reading. Matthew had expected to do the reading since their father was imprisoned. They had been surprised and worried when Yohanan ben Zaccai arrived at sundown to join them. Their mother had said, "I invited him. He knows about Ya'el and Elian, so there's no harm." Miriam had doubts. Matthew's furrowed brow showed he had them, too.

* * *

The *Kadeish, Ur'chatz, Karpas, Yachatz, Magid,* and *Ha Lachma Anya*, were done. Yohanan had reached the *Ma Nishtanah*, the Four Questions. Miriam, morose and missing her father, took a moment to realize the old rabbi had stopped. She looked up to find him, her mother, and Matthew looking at her expectantly. Wiping her eyes, Miriam nodded to her mother—she understood. The youngest child in the family was to ask the questions, so she must. The memories clutched at her heart. Her early stumbling and stuttering of the recitation had vanished as she grew older and found her voice. She could still hear her father's teaching: "Even if you are alone, you must ask and answer the questions." The flood of tears on her cheeks was matched by her mother's. Still, she straightened her back. It was her responsibility.

Across from Miriam sat Elian next to Ya'el, who had Cicero on her shoulder. The bird was surprisingly calm, perhaps partly because her mother was beside him, too, for she had cared for the parrot in Ya'el's absence. Ya'el and Elian sat quietly, happy to be out of the confines of a dark and lonely antechamber within King David's Tomb. Miriam thought *they're family now* and beckoned to Elian to sit next to her. "Do this with me... repeat what I say." The boy's smile brightened the room as he carefully followed her recital. Miriam looked at her mother, whose smile was, at that moment, as bright as Elian's.

The joy lasted until Yohanan reached the Haggadah part, which speaks of the Four Sons. Silent sobs shook her mother—she knew those tears were for her father and Yosef—as her father's oldest friend finished. Then came the *Rachtzah*, the washing of hands for the *Schulchan Orech*, the meal. When her mother had begun to cry quietly, Elian had risen to sit beside her and hold her hand. Then the opened dishes of food brought back his smile and the vestige of a smile on Rebecca's face.

It was late by the time Miriam began the *Chad Gadya*, One Kid, in her clear sweet voice. Her father had taught her and her brothers the young goat's song. He explained that it was really about the retribution Yahweh would levy over the enemies of the Jewish people at the end of days. At the end of the meal, Yohanan ben Zaccai stood.

"Thank you for inviting me, Rebecca," he said. "I hope to see you again soon with news about Mathias." He gripped Matthew's shoulder and said, "I must speak with you for a moment." The old rabbi led Matthew to the door, their heads bowed together as they stepped out.

Ya'el rose and called to Elian, "Come, let's clean up before we must go."

Elian tugged Rebecca to her feet. "You can help us!" he said with a laugh.

Miriam sat and watched them, enjoying their chatter and her mother's lightness as she teased the boy. When Matthew returned, his face was creased with thought.

"What is it, Matthew?" Miriam asked, and her question brought the others into the room.

"Simon bar Giora has been allowed to enter the city with his men. He carries before them the standard he took from the Romans at Beth Horon. Yohanan believes he intends to take control of the city from Yohanan ben Levi and his followers." Matthew turned to Ya'el. "There's also news of Rome that confirms a rumor we heard is true. Emperor Galba is dead, and Lord Marcus Otho is now emperor."

Ya'el gasped. Rebecca put a hand on her arm. "Do you know him?" she asked.

"He is my *brother*!"

Rebecca's hand went to her mouth in surprise, and Matthew's eyes widened. In the stunned silence, he leaned toward Miriam and whispered, "When I went out, Rachel was on the street, headed here to see you, but I stopped her." He glanced at Ya'el, who still seemed in shock. "I told her you weren't feeling well. She said to tell you Ya'akov has returned, and she believes he plans to see you."

XX

Aprilus 69 CE

Caesarea

The Port, Near the Temple of Augustus

Vespasian looked up the broad stairs that rose 40 feet from dockside to the west-facing temple platform that extended over 300 feet, comprising twelve vast warehouses of goods shipping into and out of the city. Columned porticos on the three sides marked the *termenos*. The sacred area, where, on a high podium, rose the temple Herod had dedicated to the goddess Roma, the embodiment of imperial Rome, and the god-king Augustus. Stairs from the other side descended into the city's center to the south.

"Why not meet Governor Mucianus at his ship?" Vespasian asked his aide.

Gaheris Clineas inclined his head toward Vespasian's son, Titus, who answered the question.

"General," he said to his father, "it's too busy with sailors and warehousemen unloading and loading vessels. Some of the area is narrow, bounded by water on one side and buildings on the other. Unless we stop the work to clear the docks, there's no room for an adequate guard for you or our men to patrol."

Vespasian eyed his son and then the steps rising to the temple. His wounding at Yotapta had left him with an aching foot. The pain was sharp enough today that he had decided to forego his evening walk on the promenade near his praetorium. A late messenger had announced Governor Mucianus's arrival and suggested meeting near the port so he could reboard quickly to sail. Gaheris Clineas had replied to set the meeting at the temple instead. Vespasian took the first step up with a barbed sideways squint at his aide.

* * *

The rangy, long-limbed man moved with a litheness that belied his years, and only the close-cropped iron-gray hair, white-streaked beard, and seamed face showed he had passed middle age. His hands, corded with sinew, toyed with the braided cord about his waist as he watched the handful of men around Governor Gaius Mucianus. A

Balearic Islander, he had long served in the eastern provinces and learned the faces of influential men. At some point, someone with money would want them killed or threatened, or these men themselves would seek to hire him. The reasons did not matter... only the money did.

It had been easy for him to join the crew of the governor's ship once he had disposed of the rope and rigging maker the evening before. Then he had reported to the ship's master at the last minute before sailing, asking for work. The captain had hurried him aboard, glad not to delay the sailing any longer. The islander had sailed the *mare nostrum* long enough to learn the craft. He blended in from port to port, and thence where he could practice his actual trade, he'd learned it from birth in his employer's household.

He was pleased that Gaius Mucianus had gone to an open area near the port. As he followed, he watched the two men with the governor shift around but never quite block his line of sight. One man pointed down the steps just as two groups of six armored men came up to separate and fan out inside the temple. The gaps were large enough for him to sight through. Once he had finished his attack, he would be close to the low balustrade where he had strung a line into an alley leading to the port or the city's chief marketplace.

The man knew the soldiers would instinctively move toward the man they were to protect, leaving the area behind them unwatched. It would be for only a moment, but that was all he needed. He shifted his pack, which contained the fine coat of a well-to-do merchant—it would cover his sailor's garb once he was in the alley. Then he would be just one of many going to and from the port. The Roman war on the Jews had made many merchants wealthy, from slaves or from commodities. They were busy men, and he would fit in with them. Still, he did not have too far to go for his employer to take him in.

He palmed one of the three lead bullets and touched the cord around his head, unneeded for his short hair—but the range was too great for that shorter sling, so he left it there. Instead, he loosened the longer cord and unwound it from his waist. He ran it through his hands, finding the cup formed by a webbing of six narrow leather strips. His eyes never moved from his aim, even as his peripheral vision confirmed that no one was near who could obstruct his movements.

Three bullets and 30 seconds are all I need, he thought, pulling the slashed old purse from his belt and dropping it at his feet. Then he nestled the first missile in place.

* * *

Vespasian had made the last step up to the temple floor and saw Mucianius and his two men moving toward him when a stab of pain shot through his foot, and he stumbled. Gaheris Clineas had reached to steady him, and just then, something struck the aide in the brow with the sharp crack of snapping bone. The man's left eye bulged from its socket as a second crack came from the same direction, ripped through his skin, and pulped the eye as the lead missile sank deep into his head.

Gaheris cried out and dropped to his knees, and a third shot whistled past Mucianus but caught his ear, tearing the lobe and then grazing Titus, scoring a bloody furrow on his cheek.

* * *

That evening...

VESPASIAN'S PRAETORIUM

"I'm sorry about Gaheris, general," said Titus. "He was a good man."

Vespasian gestured for his son to sit down and waved away the legion's chief quartermaster, just appropriated as a temporary aide. "Yes, he was," he grunted and hunched forward, resting his forearms on the desk. "Did you catch the man?"

"No, sir, but we found these." Titus set down a torn purse, a gold coin, a semicircle of broken wax, and two lead bullets with pointed ends.

Vespasian picked up the gold coin and turned the new Aureus to glint in the lamplight. He rubbed a thumb across the face of the man depicted on it. "Emperor Otho..." He set it down and carefully lifted the crumbling red wax, part of an imperial seal. He crushed it between his forefinger and thumb, then poked at the coin. "Not Galba as before..."

"Do you think Emperor Otho would try to kill you?" Titus asked.

"I hear he fears disloyal legion commanders, and he'll likely do what he can to remove any he judges doubtful. I wish I'd seen this before Governor Mucianus sailed. I would have warned him to be watchful."

"I'm sure he will be, anyway. What did he have to say when you finally talked with him?"

"From here, he sails to Perinthus, Thracia, where he'll join with men he sent from Antioch. He hopes to meet with and gain the support of legion commanders from Moesia, Pannonia, and Illyricum."

"For Otho?" Titus picked up the coin from the desk and squinted at it. "Will you continue to support him?"

"I'll decide once I have more word from Rome and Governor Mucianus. If Otho falls, he thinks Vitellius unacceptable as emperor."

"If not Vitellius, then who?"

"We'll have to see." Vespasian leaned back, and his features sagged. "Is there anything else?"

"What about Emperor Otho's decree regarding Lady Cleo?"

"Do not act on it until we know Otho's intentions. I will not help the sister of a man who might have tried to kill me and who killed my closest comrade."

XXI

Maius 69 CE

Near Aternum, on the Adriatica

A barkeep at the taberna told Nicanor and Florin the bridge was the equal of any in Rome. Emperor Tiberius had ordered its construction to span the Aternus, connecting the city's two parts. When they crossed the bridge, sheets of seaborne rain lashed them with the wind from the east coming from over the Adriatica. Carmenta, her ears laid back, grunted her displeasure, and Nicanor felt for her. The far-too-many days it had taken to get here from Brixellum had been hard. Days were spent in a frenzy of fighting through patrols sent out from the victorious Vitellian armies to secure all east-west roads to the coasts and south toward Rome. The patrols swept up the remnants of Marcus Otho's men who had yet to surrender, and they were loath to let any get away.

Nicanor turned in his saddle to check on Florin. The young man, amazingly unwounded though he was no fighter, had been frightened and dispirited even before the rain. With his head down, his wet, lank hair hanging in his face, Florin swayed on his mount. They had had little rest between their sporadic encounters with the patrols and clashes with large groups of armed and angry locals, who turned them away from even the smallest village.

Nicanor questioned whether they had been wise to let the four gladiators join them south of Brixellum. Just he and Florin might not have been seen as a threat—but six men, four heavily armed and armored, would be. But the two of them could not have broken through Vitellian ranks alone. The men's horses, taken from the imperial corral at Brixellum, were as swift as Carmenta. They'd all be able to outrace the patrols they could not fight, though Florin's mount was floundering badly when they reached Bononia.

There, Nicanor had decided his plan and route. The plans did not include the four gladiators, who included Pricus and Verus, the two he'd recognized in the imperial command tent. They had been slave-gladiators with Gnaeus Batiatus's troop of fighters. Though he had not learned the names of the other two, Nicanor knew they had also been imperial sentries or extra bodyguards for Marcus Otho.

When they reached Bononia, the gladiators intended to continue south, reversing the route on the Via Flaminia that Marcus Otho had led them on from Rome. Nicanor had told them, "My duty is done, and we go on to Ravenna to find a ship."

He had ignored Pricus's inquiry about where they sailed. He waited long enough to see the four well on their way before he and Florin stripped their clothing of any rank or insignia. Then they continued on the Via Aemilia toward Ravenna. But that was not their destination. They avoided the direct road to Rome and what would likely be heavier patrols and the movements of Vitellius's forces. Instead, they went south along the coast to reach the Via Tiburtina, just ahead of them in Aternum.

Nicanor slowed Carmenta to ride alongside Florin. "We'll stop for the night on the other side of the city," he said, "but close enough to the road west to Tibur for early tomorrow."

Florin's head bobbed in agreement or exhaustion, and then he raised it to look at Nicanor. "Will Antonia Caenis be there?"

"It's likely, but if not, we can still rest there, and I'll be able to get a message to her."

Nicanor studied Florin's face. The rain had stopped, and the late afternoon sun broke through the clouds, bringing a little cheer. "What is it, Florin? Do you wish you had gone with the gladiators?"

"No, you told me your plan before you told them. I serve you, sir. But..." Florin's voice trailed off without finishing.

"But what, Florin?"

"With the emperor dead, whom do you serve?"

"General Vespasian. And I need Antonia Caenis's help to get passage to Judea—to Caesarea." Since Marcus Otho's death, though, Nicanor felt Cleo was the only person he owed any duty to.

"Will I go to Judea with you?"

"Do you want to?"

"I'm under your command, so I must go."

Florin had once been excited to serve a legion in the field, but since Brixellum, the aide had been silent, anxious, and now he seemed doubtful. He had changed much since serving as a clerk-messenger at the Tullianum. *Death and defeat can do that*, Nicanor thought. But Florin was—or would become—a good man if given a chance.

"I will not force you, Florin. It's for you to decide."

"I'm a soldier, sir. Not a warrior like you, yet I'm still part of the army. If you go and I stay, where will I serve, and whom?"

"We'll work that out," Nicanor said, thinking Antonia Caenis could get the young man assigned to General Marcus Antonius Primus's command in some capacity. "You just think of what you want."

* * *

ATERNUM

A TABERNA NEAR THE PORT

Nicanor thought of the sailors' saying he had heard several times at sea. *The red skies last night promised a beautiful morning.* And it was. Aternum was built upon a sprawl of hills surrounding the mouth of the river that flowed into the Adriatica. The inn he had selected sat above the sea, atop one of the highest hills overlooking the port below. Where he stood now on an outcrop offered a splendid view. The sunrise colors of orange and saffron had shaded to blue when he heard the steps on the stone walkway behind him. He turned to see Florin looking much better after a hot meal, a night's rest, and dry clothing. "Are they ready?" Nicanor asked.

"Saddled and waiting, sir."

"Are *you* ready?"

"Yes, *sir*."

Nicanor remained a moment, staring at the Adriatica. The water beyond the harbor was rich indigo, with currents of a lighter blue-green catching the sun's rays, topped by a froth of whitecaps from a stiff breeze that lifted the brims of the waves. He pointed southeast and said, "I was born several days' sail from here, in Patras. I yearned to join the legion and leave my birthplace when I was barely a teen. Now I wish to find a place as peaceful as the one I longed to leave."

"Still, you plan to sail to Judea to return to serve General Vespasian, who fights a war against the Jewish rebels?" Florin sounded confused.

"Yes. My last duty. When that is done... when what I must do is done, then I am done."

"And you'll find a place like Patras?"

"I pray so." Nicanor turned, his cloak catching the wind and swirling around his legs. "Let's get to Tibur so that I may start."

* * *

3 days later...

Tibur

Antonia Caenis's Villa

Antonia Caenis greeted Nicanor: "After the *Parilia* festival ended last week, a relay of riders brought the news of Marcus Otho's death. It' ironic the celebration of the founding of Rome come's this year when Rome's unstable. Otho left no successor, and his brother Titianus disappeared. He's not been seen since he left Rome to join the emperor at Brixellum. When we learned here of the outcome at Bedriacum, we no longer wanted even the remnants of pastoral joy worshipping the shepherds' goddess. *Pales* should understand.

"When the Senate declared Vitellius emperor, he was in Colonia. I'm told he went to consult a Chattian seeress, someone he knew when he was governor of Germania. He has announced that she foretold his secure and long rule."

"Do you believe soothsayers and seeresses?" Nicanor said with a snort. His own experience with them had given him doubts.

After the great fire, Nero consulted the books of *Libri Sibyllini*, the oracle. But men with influence can use the words of prophets and soothsayers, manipulated as foretelling, to suit their needs. Heraclitus, the Greek, wrote centuries ago that an oracle had a 'frenzied mouth' uttering 'things not to be laughed at.' I agree with his writing. Shared with concocted passion, the words will be believed by some."

"And is that what Vitellius has done? Make use of the oracles?"

"Publicly, he only uses the part that serves him. The people want to hear that their ruler has the blessings of the gods."

Nicanor wondered but did not ask how she knew that. "What does Vitellius leave out?"

"His secure and lengthy rule would only come if his mother, Sextilla, died before him."

"That's likely; she's surely old."

"Vitellius is a glutton. He's tall, but his big belly is the only thing imposing about him. His face is always flushed crimson from overeating and too much drink. He limps from an old injury to his thigh where a four-horse chariot struck him. His health is not good; his mother might outlive him. Still, he wants to rule for as long as he has to live... longer still if the prophecy is true. So, he had her killed to fulfill it. The people of Rome do not know that yet, but they will."

"I'm glad to be away from there," Nicanor said as he paced the room. "I hope to never set foot in that city again." *Enough chatter about things that no longer matter to me*, he thought and stopped before her. "Can you arrange a ship to take me to Caesarea?"

"Yes, but I must ask you to do something for me... for Lord Vespasian."

"I'll do anything I can to help."

"I need you to go to Rome one last time before you leave for Judea. Domitian is there now. He's only 18, and I need you to see that the general's youngest son is safe. Rome is crawling with men seeking Vitellius's favor or leverage to use against any who might oppose him. But many secretly work against this newest emperor. Only the Senate and Vitellius's four or five legions back him as emperor. An effort has begun to find someone better who will have the support of more of the empire. You can help by seeing that Domitian is safe with someone who cannot be swayed to Vitellius's side. Will you go to Rome and do this for me, for General Vespasian?"

Nicanor felt the knot in his stomach tighten, and he glanced at Florin, who quietly listened.

Nicanor nodded and said, "Yes."

XXII

Maius 69 CE

Jerusalem

The Lower City, The Cenacle, Upper Room

Matthew looked around the room where his father had told him Yeshua ish Natzrat had eaten a last seder with some of his followers. Before the Romans took him over 30 years before. It was said some of those closest to him denied Yeshua that same night. He thought... *They've always been with us. Those who turn on each other to save themselves or to gain an advantage.* Men like Yohanan ben Levi and Simon bar Giora.

 He studied Yohanan ben Zaccai, who was sitting across from him. At Yeshua ish Natzrat's arrest, he would have been a young man—as his father was then. Matthew had once asked Yohanan if he, like others, believed Yeshua could have been the Messiah. The old rabbi had replied, "If you're holding a sapling and someone tells you, 'Come quickly, the Messiah is here!' first, finish planting the tree. Then go greet the Messiah. In the years since Yeshua's crucifixion, until this war, I have been too busy planting trees. And there have been too many Messiah claimants to get drawn into that debate."

 Matthew smiled, recalling those words. Yohanan was ever a teacher who believed in the youth of Judea. Next to him sat Nahum, the Essene leader from Qumran, who had just shared the news that another wagon load of treasure had been taken. He cautioned that much had been successfully hidden, but no more should leave Jerusalem. Many of Simon bar Giora's men were encamped outside the walls, patrolling all the city's roads and footpaths. "Whether they take the treasure to enrich themselves or raise an alarm that someone within Jerusalem is stealing it," Nahum said, looking around at the other men. "Either would be disastrous."

 "The Sanhedrin should not have invited Simon bar Giora into the city to stop Yohan ben Levi," said the old rabbi with a shake of his head. "The Gischalan was already losing men who were shocked at his brutality. Even Idumeans, who had remained his allies, now break away, and some have since tried to kill him. He was forced to defend himself at the palace he has taken for himself—he has fortified it."

"Little good that did," Eleasar commented. "The Idumeans quickly breached it—they are the better fighters—and Yohanan, his Galileans, and the Zealots with them have fled to the Temple. The Idumeans then ransacked the Gischalan's palace. They looted all the treasure stolen from the people of Jerusalem—all that he had hoarded there. Had the Sanhedrin not let Simon into the city, Yohanan ben Levi would have fallen further from his followers and soon had only his fellow Gischalans stand at his side. Now, those who detest Giora will remain with him."

"Now he boasts how Jerusalem's leaders asked for his 'benevolent protection,'" Matthew said with a sneer of distaste. "They welcome him as their deliverer, just as they had once embraced the Gischalan. And my father remains imprisoned."

Eleasar ben Ananias nodded. "Simon now treats the Sanhedrin leaders as his enemies--to be ousted just as they wanted the Gischalan ousted. Yohanan ben Levi and Simon bar Giora are carving the city into pieces, fighting for control. It won't take long for what was one city to become two, each side at the other's throat. All the while, a much larger threat than both of them together will *surely* come."

"Yohanan ben Levi tried to recruit all of us Essenes here and outside Jerusalem," said Nahum, "to join him and the Zealots to help them keep control of the Temple."

Matthew eased the scabbard of his sword and stretched his legs beneath the table. "I'm not surprised," he said. "The Gischalan needs to replace the men he's lost. Giora has far more than he does."

"The Gischalan called us the *Osei ha Torah*... the Doers of the Law, as the Torah describes the Essenes." Nahum tugged at his beard, making Matthew think of his father. "I refused him. I would never call for an Essene to join him. He warned me to reconsider, or I'd suffer the consequences. I believe he plans for his men to kill me."

"Is that why you asked Yohanan to set the meeting in this Essene area of the city for security?" asked Matthew.

"Yes. They're watching for any men who search for me and will tell them I've left the city. And I soon will. But I needed to speak to you about the Temple treasure and explain how we're rebuilding Qumran. When I return there, we'll create a durable scroll recording the other treasure locations across Judea. We will keep it safe. But you must hide the guide—the secret key. Only the two together will lead to the treasure."

A sound of footsteps on the stairs brought Matthew and Eleasar to their feet, swords drawn. Matthew waved the two older men behind them and ordered, "Stay behind the table...."

"Nahum... Nahum...." A voice called. A slender man with a sparse fringe of beard bristling with stiff spikes appeared from below. Flushed from running, he stumbled to a stop as he entered the room, and his eyes went first to the blades angled toward him... then to the man he sought. He swallowed the lump in his throat. "Elam, my father, sent me. An angry man named Yonatan bar Hilel leads men searching for you. He says it's for a meeting with Yohanan ben Levi. As you asked, my father told him you'd left the city. But this man did not believe him, and they tore our house apart. Half his men are searching house to house, and the others, with men they've recruited, are now at the Gate of the Essenes, stopping *everyone*."

"Go home," the Essene leader said as he stood. "Don't run—walk. And thank your father for me." Nahum turned as the youth scampered down the steps. "What should I do?"

"The Giscalan will have sealed the Lower City," Eleasar said as he sheathed his sword and reached for his cloak draped over the table.

"I've nowhere to hide, then." Nahum paced the room.

"I have an idea," said Matthew. "Yohanan... change robes and cloaks with Nahum." The two men stood puzzled for a moment, staring at Matthew. "Hurry, just do it," Matthew snapped. Shortly, Yohanan ben Zaccai wore the white linen robe and light gray cloak favored by Essenes. And Nahum was clad in the brown and darker gray of the old rabbi.

"Good," Matthew said. "Nahum, you'll come with me, and Yohanan and Eleasar will head toward the Upper City." He beckoned to the Essene. "We must move fast... but carefully."

XXIII

Maius 69 CE

Jerusalem

The City of David, King David's tomb

"As emperor, my brother will stop this war," declared Ya'el. "And when he does, he'll hear of my husband's involvement at its beginning. Lady Octavia knows and will tell him, too. She has Cestius Gallus's reports, letters, and copies of mine, and what I found when my husband was the Judean Procurator. Marcus will ask about me, and when Gessius Florus tells my brother I've left him, he'll connect that with the rumor. I'm the Roman noblewoman hiding in Jerusalem. If Sayid and Nicanor still serve under General Vespasian, they will also tell Marcus what Gessius Florus has done."

"Done to you?" Miriam asked, wiping sweat from her face with a small cloth.

"Done to your people... *and* to me."

Miriam had heard that the news of yet another Roman emperors' death had made many feel there would now be no attack. Some even thought it a sign that Rome would not continue their war against Jews. Even her mother had hugged Ya'el tightly, crying, "Your brother could order Yosef freed and returned to us!"

"I don't know, Ya'el," Miriam said, and she kept repeating it. "We should be careful," she said now... and not grow careless. Others may discover your connection and think you should be taken hostage for leverage." Miriam had persuaded Ya'el to remain in hiding until some action from her brother was certain. But she did not know how long Ya'el's promise would hold.

"Are you not happy, Miriam?"

Miriam had heard the implication of that question several times in her talks with Ya'el since the seder. The news about Marcus Otho had buoyed Ya'el's spirits. Elian now eagerly expected to leave the underground chamber for good. He had even told them his plans for taking Cicero exploring. *If Marcus Otho sends for her,* Miriam wondered, *to return to Rome, will Elian go with her?* The thought of losing the two of them—and even the bird—saddened her as she could never have imagined a short time ago. *But maybe Yossi can come home!* That thought had brightened her prospects. Then Ya'el pressed her on something she did not want to think of.

"Will you see this Ya'akov—the one Matthew mentioned, who has returned to Jerusalem?"

Miriam ignored Ya'el as she pulled blades free from the training figure she had set up here after wrestling it down the alleys and passages from Zechariah's shop in the dark of night. The two blades from its torso returned to their forearm sheaths, and she plucked a third from the figure's throat to hand to Ya'el. She had begun teaching her how to attack with a knife. And in return, Ya'el had promised to teach her how to use a bow. But first, Ya'el needed shafts for arrows to train with.

As Ya'el took the dagger from her to awkwardly slide it into the new sheath strapped to her own left forearm, Miriam readied for the question again. She knew Ya'el had only good intentions and wanted Miriam to feel the bliss she felt at being freed from Gessius Florus. Ya'akov had loved her and been heartbroken when she had not married him. But Miriam had loved him enough to spare him learning about the attack that made her break their engagement. Going back to him now, returning to that love, meant reliving a part of her past she must put behind her.

As she stood straight after picking up her staff, Miriam felt Ehud's father's ring on the cord around her neck settle back on the arc of her left breast. She rested a palm over it, pressing it closer to her. *That* part of her past would never leave; it could never be forgotten or hidden away. That weight rested on her heart.

The rattling of stones and scuffling of feet warned them of someone in the passageway. Miriam hurried to where the passage entered the antechamber, freed a dagger, and brought her staff up for a thrust or strike. Over her shoulder, she saw Ya'el move behind her, holding the new blade.

"Matthew!" Miriam was surprised to see her brother. "And Yohanan?" She recognized the dun-colored cloak and dark tunic habitually worn by her father's oldest friend. She and Ya'el sheathed their blades and backed away to give them room to come farther in. Now the light of the corner lamp showed their faces. She stared at the man with a long black beard with twists of gray that matched his grizzled brows over dark eyes.

"Who are you?" Miriam asked as she raised her staff.

* * *

The Upper City

Dawn streaked the sky as Miriam turned into the lane that led to the rear gate of her home. Patrols of men had filled the streets until long past midnight, so she and Matthew had remained in hiding. They were exhausted, but he had nevertheless headed toward a meeting with Eleasar ben Ananias.

After Matthew had explained who the man, Nahum, was, she recalled Yosef's letters from his time with the Essenes. Nahum was a good friend of her brother and Yohanan ben Zaccai... and he was in trouble.

"Do you know of any clear tunnels to get outside the city and not be seen by any of Yohanan ben Levi's or Simon bar Giora's men?" Matthew had asked. "And it must be near here... I don't think we can sneak him too far anywhere within the city."

There was one tunnel she thought of, but she'd need to check it out first. According to Zechariah's maps, an old Canaanite dry tunnel started in the City of David, near Gihon Spring, and ran past the Water Gate and beyond the wall. It ended somewhere in the Kidron Valley. But she would explore that later—their mother was surely worried when she and Matthew had not returned during the night.

Nahum was safe with Ya'el and Elian in King David's Tomb, and Matthew would meet her there at sundown, and they'd take Nahum through the tunnel. *If it's not blocked,* she thought.

"Miriam?" The voice was deep, sonorous... she had told him once that it seemed to come from the bottom of a well. The sound of its questioning tone added greatly to the weight on her heart. Her hand went to the ring against her bosom. She felt awkward being found dressed as a young man and carrying an old man's staff. A gust of wind lifted the hood of her cloak as she turned to face him.

"Ya'akov."

XXIV

Maius 69 CE

Caesarea

The Roman Encampment, Vespasian's Praetorium

The cut on Lord Titus's cheek had nearly healed. It was a reminder of how many days it had been since Yosef had last been brought before General Vespasian. That day the general had been brusque, rude in a way he had never been before. He had gestured toward his son... at the bandage on Titus's cheek with spots of blood seeping through the cloth. Vespasian had then ordered Yosef, "Tell me of this other dream you had that you spoke of with General Titus. About other scrolls at...." He had glanced down at a map spread across his desk. "At Qumran."

Yosef had barely started when an out-of-breath man appeared in the doorway with a roll of vellum strapped in leather and sealed with wax.

"What is it, Junius?" Vespasian had asked.

"An important message, general. I apologize for interrupting, but it cannot wait."

Titus had gone to the door, leaned past the man, and called the guards into the antechamber. "Return the prisoner to his cell," he had said.

Yosef had since heard the muttering of his guards about the happenings of the day before that meeting. There had been a second attempt to kill General Vespasian, and that was how Titus had been wounded. Twice, a man alone had nearly done what an army could not.

Yosef told Lord Titus how glad he was that they had survived the attack. And he was. Yosef respected both men and feared what would happen to him if a less reasonable general took command.

This day, a large unfurled map showing most of Judea again covered General Vespasian's desk. The metal ferrule tip of his vinewood staff pointed at a spot southwest of Jerusalem.

"Yes, general?" Yosef asked as he stood before the desk, manacled hands clasped before him and short-chained to his waist cuff. Since his last visit, the slack had been removed because of the attack on

Vespasian, making it impossible for him to write. That was perhaps the harshest punishment. Writing in his journals was the one thing that fully occupied his mind and kept him distracted from regrets and recriminations.

"You've heard of what happened?" Vespasian asked as he laid down the stained sheet of parchment he had been reading.

"Yes, lord... I'm glad the man failed."

"He failed only in part... he took from me a good man. Gaheris Clineas was a trusted comrade. And I have too few of those I can rely upon—none with anything close to the years Gaheris had with me."

Yosef stood silently, waiting. Vespasian's fallen aide had meant a lot to the old general, and he better understood his anger the last time he was in this office. He watched the general poke the map with an index finger.

"My legions now control all the areas I want to have secured in your country." Vespasian thumped the field report he'd laid on the map. "Your city of Hebron has fallen, but it took longer than expected. The reports I've received say the fighting was fierce." He glanced up at Yosef. "You know this city?"

Yosef knew Hebron and its importance to his people. With a vision of Yotapta's destruction burned into his memory, he knew how it must be now in Hebron. The wailing of the wounded... the dying. And then the silence of the dead. The sky would be dirtied with smoke and the air foul with the stench of corpses.

"Long ago, in Hebron," he said, "there lived a race of giants so large... so terrible to see and hear. And they were formidable fighters. Stories are still told of them... and their bones are still there."

"No giants were defending the town this time," Vespasian said, "but they put up a fight." Vespasian pinned the city's location and traced a line north to Jerusalem with his finger. "Cerealis and his legion will be reinforced, resupplied, and then they are only a day... a day and a half's march from—"

"Jerusalem," Yosef finished for him. "Is that where you attack next, general?" Yosef quickly clamped down the shudder that threatened to shake him. *Is it now that my family... my city faces destruction?*

"You've told Titus of another dream," Vespasian said, "about other scrolls in Qumran." Vespasian's hand swept east of Jerusalem on the map to stop at the northern shore of Lake Asphaltitis. "You've said they hold portents of your city's fate."

Yosef nodded. "Yes, lord."

"I'll think about whether I want to see them before...." The general's big hand clenched into a fist and thudded down on Jerusalem.

"I could go with Lord Titus," Yosef said, "and show him where I saw the scrolls." *Perhaps I can come up with something to delay the inevitable.*

"Perhaps. But I must wait first."

Vespasian's words surprised him, and Yosef knew that what he must ask would risk the general's anger. But since hearing that Cleo's brother had become emperor, he had fostered hope, and he must ask. "Do you think Emperor Otho has changed his mind about this war? Is that why you wait, general?"

Vespasian stood, and his expression hardened. "Make no mistake. I will march on your city, Yosef. But Emperor Otho is dead. On the day of our last meeting, I learned he had been defeated in battle and surrendered. A new emperor assumes power, and I await decisions on what that means... for many things." He motioned to Titus and inclined his head toward Yosef, signaling his son to escort the prisoner out of the office. "Now, leave me."

Back in his cell, and long into the night, Yosef could think about nothing but that Vespasian was resolved to take Jerusalem. *It might be delayed... but it will come,* he thought. His family was doomed, as was Cleo if she were still in Jerusalem. What of his other friends? He knew Nicanor had somehow ended up in the service of Marcus Otho. Had he fallen with the emperor? And Sayid, what of him at Hebron?

For the first time, Yosef felt his survival would not help his city or family. Ariella was right... and the thought of her death was another guilty burden. His life should have ended in Yotapta. As the guard removed his lamps, leaving him in the dark, Yosef prayed for a dream. Anything that would rekindle hope that as long as he was alive, he might somehow save his family... save Cleo... and Jerusalem.

XXV

Junius 69 CE

Tibur

Antonia Caenis's Villa

Nicanor studied the barrel-chested administrator of Antonia Caenis's property in Tibur. General Vespasian's lady seemed to prefer former legionaries—ex-centurions, to be exact—and not the more polished men groomed for households among Rome's nobility. But then, Nicanor reconsidered. The general had told him his family was not of the old aristocracy dying out. His family was now in only the third generation with some affluence and influence, fourth if his sons Titus and Domitian were counted. But that prosperity had weakened in recent years.

Florin had offhandedly commented the day before that Crispus looked like how Nicanor might appear in ten years. That had made Nicanor smile... at first. But later, he had had unpleasant thoughts. The man's short-cut bristling hair was more gray than black, and his beard was iron-gray. And as with all old soldiers, his hands were crisscrossed with the scars of harrowing legion service. But Crispus had a dignified bearing and looked still strong enough to wield a sword. At their meeting over the crude map they'd fashioned together, with the help of the rider from Rome, the old former centurion had squinted at Nicanor. At first, Nicanor thought he was suspicious or angry, but then he'd learned Crispus's eyesight was failing.

"From Aternum," Nicanor said, "Florin and I encountered hundreds of Vitellian soldiers or men who had switched to the new emperor's side at Corfinium and Alba Fucens. But we saw none between there and Tibur." Nicanor had known that good fortune would not last.

"You're getting closer to Rome," the old centurion said with a grimace. "Vitellius is not there yet, but he'll soon come that way, and they want the city secure." He looked up at the rider to confirm his information. "So, here at Ponte Lucano, where it crosses the Aniene...." Crispus pointed at the straight line Nicanor had drawn with seven half-circles—arches—beneath that crossed the wavy line of the river. "How many men did you see?"

"Some were afoot," the man said, "but most mounted. I counted twelve midways on the bridge. But there were twice that on each bank and at the head and foot of the bridge."

"And you say archers are positioned here." Nicanor touched the circle symbol he'd placed on the south bank. It was a tower he recalled from his previous use of the Tiburtina when he'd traveled to and from Rome.

"Yes, sir." The man kept glancing out the window toward the stables. Nicanor knew the rider gauged the afternoon sun that had dropped lower as they discussed what Nicanor and Florin could expect between Tibur and Rome. The rider wanted to be with the group of men from the Aniene Valley who had, just that morning, headed north to join Marcus Antonius Primus's 7th Legion, *Galbiana*. But instead, he was ordered to remain with the small force General Primus had sent to Tibur two months before. The men in civilian clothing had arrived with cartloads of legion weapons and armor. Ready to take action if Antonia Caenis was forced to protect the control of the three main aqueducts—the Aquia Vetus, Novus, and Claudia—that supplied water to Rome.

Crispus scratched his chin. "How many archers?"

The rider shrugged. "Many, sir... some with regular bows... others had crossbows. Once they let me on the bridge... I couldn't slow down to look long enough to get a good count."

"Sounds like they're thick as the fleas on Verro here." The grizzled major domus reached to scratch between the ears of the dog sleeping at his feet. His fingers adjusted the dog's thick studded collar, the *melium* designed to protect the animal's vulnerable neck.

Nicanor glanced at the *vertragus*, a gray hound that looked much like the dog he had had as a child in Patras. He still felt a twinge of sadness at leaving his constant companion behind when he departed for the legions. When Crispus straightened, Nicanor rubbed between Varro's ears, too, and the dog stretched his neck so Nicanor could get to the best spot.

Nicanor straightened up. "If it seems too chancy, we'll shed the fleas by fording the river to the north. From that point, it's only fourteen miles to Rome." Nicanor stood and smiled at his young aide. "You can swim, can't you, Florin?"

At the younger man's nod, Crispus said, "We'll get you fresh clothing and make you seem like somewhat prosperous merchants. Not too much to draw brigands, but enough to be treated decently.

You shouldn't carry much in the way of weapons, though. Just the simple blades merchants carry."

Nicanor nodded. In Rome, Gnaeus Batiatus would better equip them, though he hated the thought of not being armed to the teeth if they had to fight on the way there. But then, if they did... just the two of them... they'd probably die. He glanced at Florin, who still looked drawn and tired from the fast pace since Brixellum. He thought... *I'll not do something foolish and get this young man killed now.*

He gave Crispus and the rider another nod. "Thanks for your help. We'll see Lady Antonia and give her our farewells now." Nicanor knew it would be brief, for she was anxious for him to get Domitian somewhere safe. She had promised to have details ready for him as soon as he finished the other meeting.

Best get on the last road there. Nicanor shook his head, ready for whatever he must do to help secure Domitian and then leave Rome and get to Judea.

XXVI

Junius 69 CE

Rome

Gnaeus Batiatus's Villa

"My man just left with the message from Antonia Caenis for Titus Flavius Sabinus," said Gnaeus Batiatus at dawn. He had cheerfully welcomed Nicanor and Florin to his villa the night before. He now sat with Nicanor and Marcus Attilius, where they had once watched morning training in the arena. But now it was quiet. "He'll stay outside the *secretarium tellurense* until the city prefect arrives at his office."

Nicanor had not known before the previous evening that Titus Sabinus was General Vespasian's older brother. Antonia Caenis's letter had explained the details that required the help of the city prefect. "Are you sure he'll be able to get the message to him?" he asked.

"My man knows Titus, and Titus knows him; the prefect will have it in his hand within the hour."

That familiarity told Nicanor even more about the man who commanded the urban cohorts. At Aternum, he had heard that Rome's prefect had directed the city's legionaries to swear allegiance to Vitellius. He had assumed most city officials would do that in their own self-interest. Now he wondered if the prefect was merely bowing to the inevitable and attempting to prevent bloodshed in the city. If so, he could continue to be one of Antonia Caenis and Vespasian's primary sources of information within Rome.

"My man will return with a confirmation of the meeting time and place," continued Gnaeus.

Nicanor nodded and gestured at the arena where patches of scrub grass had overtaken the worn-down packed dirt. He remembered what it had once been from seeing it many times and his combat within. "Your new arena near the Circus Maximus must be ready."

"Yes, it was. But then Marcus Otho's recruiter took my best fighters. Now I must find new men to train for the Games."

"And Sextus, your former *lanista,* works against you," Marcus Attilius said. He had shown pleasure at seeing Nicanor again but was now curiously silent. He rose, stretched, and added, "He hints that you supported Marcus Otho and are now against Vitellius."

"I've found another trainer, a better one, and a better manager. And I'm not for or against anyone… I care little about who rules. I care only about—"

"Profit," Marcus laughed and nudged Nicanor. "We know. But Sextus has spread the truth that you are also friends with Nicanor here." The freedman clasped his friend on the shoulder. "And Nicanor is known to have served Marcus Otho. I've seen two men we know, Pricus and Verrus, who have returned to Rome and fallen in again with Sextus. They came to see me, saying they told Sextus you were alive and did not believe the story you and Florin told them. I told them I had not seen or heard from you. But now Sextus gathers other men, freedman gladiators, to serve Vitellian loyalists as bounty hunters. I'm sure he has you on his list."

"I've heard from my financial backers that Sextus and men like him—those who have found reward in serving the allies of Vitellius—don't just kill," said Gnaeus. "They've found that the art of *surripio praeripio* is more lucrative than killing. Kidnapping for hire can earn them even more than murder. The right hostage can give influential men even more power… or prevent someone from rising to take it from them. That's what Titus Sabinus fears most. He can't hide, but his nephew Domitian must; he's not safe with him." Gnaeus Batiatus stood. "Does your aide still sleep? You're an easy soldier to serve under, Nicanor. Now, let's go eat. By the time we finish, we should hear back from Titus."

Nicanor thought the man cared about more than profit, or Antonia Caenis would not trust him. He smiled at the thought that, like Graius, Gnaeus Batiatus, and Marcus Attilius were not what they had first seemed to him. He thought fondly of the old gladiator who had once been Cleo's guardian—Graius had saved his life in Hispania Lusitania. As he followed Gnaeus and Marcus to the villa, he pondered, *these past few years… so much has happened, and it's changed me.*

XXVII

Junius 69 CE

Rome

The Pantheon

Nicanor had not walked the Pantheon since he had done it with Yosef ben Mathias years before, the first time in Rome for both of them. But he had seen it often since, from the Arx Capitolina and the Tullianum, where he had served as a watch captain in the Praetorian Guards two years before.

Yosef—who knew so much more than he about the history of Rome—had told him the Pantheon was a part of the complex created by the Roman general and architect Marcus Agrippa. Built on Agrippa's property in the Campus Martius nearly 90 years before, it included three buildings aligned south to north. The Baths of Agrippa, the Basilica of Neptune, and where he stood now... the Pantheon. The latter two were Agrippa's *sacra privata*, his private temples, not *aedes publicae*. Yosef had also told him Diogenes of Athens had crafted the Caryatides. The figures from the Greek term that meant 'maidens of Karyai,' a town on the Peloponnese. These sculpted female figures formed the temple columns. As a man born on the Peloponnese, Nicanor was proud of that. The capitals of the pillars were made of Syracusan bronze that gleamed in the late afternoon sun.

"You have some color back," Nicanor told Florin as they watched the sun sink behind Campus Martius. The once broad and empty plain was now covered with buildings and monuments, many still scarred from the great fire five years before. Titus Sabinus's choice of a meeting place was curious, Nicanor thought, because the area had become one of the most crowded in Rome. *That could be good or bad.*

"I slept well, sir," said Florin. "Thank you for letting me have the night and most of the day. I feel better."

"Have you decided what you'll do? Go with me or return to Tibur to join Primus's men left with Antonia Caenis? But at some point, they'll join that general and his legion."

"Must I decide now, here?"

"Not here, not now. But as soon as I see Domitian safely with Quintilian, the teacher Antonia Caenis spoke of, I go to Puteoli, where Lady Antonia has arranged a ship for me. The *Egeria* awaits me."

"There's Marcus," Florin said, pointing at the freedman climbing the steps from where their horses were tethered.

"And there's Domitian." Nicanor recognized the tall young man approaching the terrace they stood upon. Next to him was a shorter stout man who could only be General Vespasian's brother.

The freedman, youth, and city prefect reached them simultaneously.

Domitian spoke first. "I go with you only because my father trusts you, and you take me to Quintilian, whom my father knows. His teachings of rhetoric appeal to us both. My uncle here feels I'm no longer safe with him."

"You are not, nephew," said Titus Sabinus, whose glower matched his brother's, Nicanor observed. "Your father trusts this man and his... and Antonia Caenis. She has arranged this with Quintilian. I must go now; there's a risk if we're seen." He gripped Domitian's shoulders and, with a nod to Nicanor, turned and left.

"We must go, too," Nicanor said. "We have a horse for you... and it's not far to the domus Antonia Caenis asked Quintillian to rent outside the city."

* * *

THE PONS NERONIANUS

Nicanor disliked that they moved north, opposite the direction of Puteoli. But he had no choice. After delivering Domitian to Quintilian, he would have to pass through the city again to the Via Appia, taking him south. But he was glad to have now crossed Nero's bridge and to see the Via Triumphalis's intersection. They would follow it only a few miles northwest to the small villa. Carmenta's silver-gray gleamed a ruddy tinge in the day's last sunlight.

A cart with two men stopped so they could light the large lanterns at the crossroad and then move quickly and steadily to the others. A similar team would illuminate the bridge now behind them. Carmenta's ears twitched and angled toward Nicanor, a sign that something disturbed her. He glanced over his shoulder at the glow of light blooming along the bridge. "Florin," he said quietly, "watch behind us and let me know if you see anyone."

As their horses stepped onto the Via Triumphalis, Florin reported, "There are men on the bridge."

Final Siege

Nicanor shifted to see Florin half-turned in his saddle, facing the bridge they had just left. Carmenta snorted and shook her head, returning his eyes to search the road ahead. "How many, Florin?"

"I count eight."

"Let's move off to the side and let them pass." Nicanor pointed at a thin cluster of trees separate from the dense thicket at the road's shoulder. In the deepening twilight, the shadows of the trees should be just enough to hide them.

Nicanor glanced back and could tell the eight mounted men were armed and armored. Too much metal caught torch and lantern light for them to be merchants or locals about their usual business. But that did not concern Nicanor. Men so equipped were common, especially in these times, and when traveling at night. But he was alarmed when the eight reached the point on the road where they had just left it and slowed. Carmenta sensed it, too, and tensed.

"Be ready if they don't move on," Nicanor whispered, and then the eight turned toward them, searching for them among the trees.

"Futuo," Nicanor swore as Marcus Attilius moved his mount beside Carmenta, and the freedman pulled his sword. "Florin," he ordered, "stay behind us with Domitian. Directly behind us. Do not veer off if Marcus and I move fast to run through them."

Nicanor felt the thicket at Carmenta's haunches, and there was no easy path that way, though the sparse patch of trees was no defense, either. They must break through to the road and then outrun the eight.

As Nicanor heeled Carmenta with the command to brace, a flicker of thought flashed through him that he wished he had asked Antonia Caenis to give Florin a better mount. The riders fanned out abreast of one another instead of bunched together. Nicanor kneed Carmenta again, forward this time, calling out, "Charge them!"

They crashed into the horsemen at the edge of the road. The nearest road post's lantern cast a glow that revealed Sextus, Gnaeus Batiatus's former *lanista*, as Nicanor drove Carmenta at him. The man's blade was out, and a sneer twisted his face. From the corner of his eye, he saw Pricus and Verrus in the lead, closing in and slashing at Marcus, who wheeled his horse and wove a glittering defense of metal with his sword. The freeman deflected and beat down Pricus's blade to stab deep into the opening between the gladiator's breastplate and his throat. That slowed its withdrawal, and while he was still pulling, Verrus swung his sword at Marcus's neck, and another man crowded to strike at the freedman's legs.

Nicanor did not see the fatal blow fall on his friend, for Sextus was upon him with a scream, now wielding two swords, as the four with him lowered their spears to drive them at Nicanor. The five riders had farther split him and Marcus, and Nicanor lamented the increasing distance between them.

Carmenta lashed out with a flailing kick that unseated one of them. The second raked his blade across Nicanor's ribs as he and the two others went for Florin and Domitian. He heard a horse scream as it bolted past him with a blood-frothed muzzle and a spear through its neck, Domitian clinging to it. A rider wielding a long sword hacked at Domitian, and his mighty swing tore the blade from the boy's hand.

Florin raced alongside, defending Domitian, and Nicanor saw a deep slash in his aide's back. In the deepening twilight and dim lamplight, the blood was a wet blackness that poured from him.

Nicanor pulled Carmenta around, feeling his side now sticky with his own blood, and he gasped as the slash widened with his twist. Now Sextus closed in on him. Nicanor shifted his gladius to his left hand and pulled his pugio with his right. Raising his right arm sent a tearing pain through his side, but he clamped his elbow and forearm against it, gripping the dagger in his fist. He kneed Carmenta into a counter-turn as Sextus charged by him toward Florin and Domitian.

Vespasian's son was down, the dead horse pinning one leg. As the boy tried to pull free, Florin stood before him, sagging to the ground with the mortal weight of the spear transfixing his chest. Bloodied to its hilt, his short sword fell from his hand to land upon the man he had just killed.

Nicanor signaled Carmenta, and she reared, front hooves striking and missing. Sextus, who had leaped from his horse, landed near Domitian and kicked the boy in the head. Beside him, Florin lay still.

Nicanor's bloody hand had dropped the gladius to grip the saddle's pommel as Carmenta came up, but he could not hold. He tumbled backward from his saddle and struggled to find his feet.

Seeing Domitian lying still and pinned down, Sextus smiled and strode toward Nicanor, who had risen and stood waiting.

Nicanor's gladius was gone, and he had only the pugio in his left hand as he pressed the right to his side. "Come on, bastard," he snarled.

Sextus picked up Florin's short sword and raised his own *spatha*. The long sword arced at Nicanor's head as the gladius readied to stab into his stomach. Heart pounding, its drumming filling his head, Nicanor felt a torrid rush of bile flooding his throat. He had not noticed the thud of hooves as a horse crashed into Sextus and stomped as he fell under its feet.

Reining to a stop, Marcus dropped to the ground and ran his sword through Sextus's mouth as the man opened it to scream at the pain of his splintered legs. Several inches showed through the back of the former lanista's neck. Not waiting to watch the man choke on his blood, Marcus went to Domitian, who was feebly moving, to free him from the dead horse.

Nicanor cut a length from his cloak to bind his wound, and with a grimace, he knelt beside Florin and was surprised to find he still breathed. His eyes fluttered open as Nicanor touched him and said, "You did well. As good as any legionary I've ever served with, Florin. I'm proud of you."

Florin smiled. "I had decided to go with you, Nicanor... but now," he gasped, "I must remain here." He went slack in Nicanor's arms.

Nicanor felt the same despair that had swept over him as his men died around him at the defeat at Beth Horon in Judea. And more recently, at Graius's death on the road when they had gone to seek Marcus Otho's help to save Cleo. This pain was much greater than the wound in his side.

Marcus shoved Domitian onto Carmenta since his mount had drifted several feet away. The boy swayed. Marcus tried to steady him while calling to Nicanor, "Move, Nicanor—grab my horse's reins and mount. There are at least two men out there I did not kill."

The closest lanterns were knocked from their road posts, and darkness grew around them. The sound of more horses and the clatter of more armored men came from the bridge and onto the road toward them.

XXVIII

Junius 69 CE

Jerusalem

The Upper City

Miriam moved through the house, lighting lamps and lanterns. Out in the courtyard, she did what had once been Elian's chore he delighted in. She sheltered the lighting taper with a cupped hand against the twilight breeze so welcome after a warm day's heavy, still air. She heard her mother behind her in the courtyard, opening the large shutters that screened the family room from that space.

"We'll eat out here," Rebecca called into the house.

Matthew came out, followed by Yohanan ben Zaccai, who each took their customary seats. As usual, Rebecca had set her husband's place at the head of the table as if he could be with them. The old rabbi's head nodded toward where his friend should be sitting and leaned toward Rebecca to pat her on the hand.

"I have news about Mathias," the old rabbi said with a smile. "Tomorrow, Matthew and I will be able to see him."

After the happy murmurs at that news, Miriam commented, pouring water from the clay pitcher. "You've been asking and asking. Why did they decide now?" Then she caught Matthew's sharp glance... a warning. She realized without being told that some of the gold from King David's Tomb had been put to use. It seemed to have helped, though he had likely used only an amount plausible for their family. It would not be good to raise questions about a greater source. Zechariah had once told her that greed grew proportionate to the amount of gold it was believed one had that could be taken from them.

Miriam nodded to Matthew that she would ask nothing more, and she basked in the remarkable new light in their mother's eyes.

"Will they free him, Yohanan?" asked Rebecca.

The old rabbi shook his head. "I don't know. But at least we'll see him and tell him we are working for his release. But still good news." He turned to Matthew. "Now, do you have some way to get Nahum safely out of the city?"

"Miriam knows of a tunnel from the City of David that runs into the Kidron Valley. But it was partially blocked, I guess, by earthquakes. Eleasar ben Ananias and I, with a few Levites we trust, have almost cleared it."

"Then he'll soon be able to leave, and I must see him before he goes. Who knows when or whether I'll ever get another chance?"

"He's safe where he is, Yohanan... I can't bring him here." Matthew shook his head.

"Then take me to him...."

Matthew's and Miriam's eyes locked. Yohanan was their father's oldest friend, and they had known him all their life. But the fewer people who knew where Ya'el hid, the better. She already worried about the Essene knowing. They would just have to trust that Nahum would not speak of her.

The wind lulled, and they heard, faintly from the northeast, the harsh grating of stone on stone and the echoes of stoneworkers hammering wedges. Their curses were louder than the work sounds. "Again!" cried Rebecca, a frown creasing her face. "Why must they work into the night?"

"Yohan ben Levi is repairing Antonia Fortress... with men and material meant to reinforce the outer walls and gates." Matthew's disgust was evident in his voice.

"Why?" Rebecca asked.

Yohanan ben Zaccai answered. "The Gischalan plans to make the fortress his own. So, he takes from what should protect the city... as if he were drawing battle lines within—to prepare against Simon bar Giora." He sighed and pulled a bowl of pressed date cakes to himself, then hesitated to take one of the few. He raised a hand to forestall Rebecca's apologies for the sparsely laden table. "This is plenty...." He broke the cake in two, leaving half in the bowl, and put the other half on his plate. Then a stern look came over his face. "When we're done eating. It will be dark enough for Matthew to take me to where he's hidden Nahum."

* * *

THE CITY OF DAVID

"There's no place to safely hide here," Yohanan whispered to Matthew as they paused beside the oldest wall of the city. They had come through the Temple Enclosure from the Upper City, across the Court of the Gentiles, and through the Huldah Gates. They could still see the glow from the brace of giant lanterns at the head and foot of the steps that led down from the gates. "Did you hide him in some building?" The old rabbi gestured over the wall toward several nearby.

Matthew and Miriam had put off telling him as long as they could. Miriam squinted at her brother, prodding him to answer. Yohanan looked from brother to sister. He had already asked why she had come with them, and Miriam had responded that she must. With a frown at Matthew, she answered Yohanan now. "No, he's underground... near here."

"What... where?" The old man looked puzzled, and his eyes went from Matthew to Miriam again.

* * *

KING DAVID'S TOMB

"You should not be here... and you cannot stay!" Yohanan ben Zaccai sputtered as he paced the antechamber, his glare sweeping over Ya'el and Elian to rake Miriam and Matthew. He turned to Nahum... "They should have hidden you somewhere else."

"There was no time for delay and no place to take him, Yohanan," Matthew repeated.

"How did you find it... this tomb?" the old rabbi asked Matthew, who could not prevent his eyes from shifting to his sister. "Miriam?" The rabbi frowned at her.

"It was an accident," Miriam said, seeing no need to tell him she had been running for her life from a killer. "You know who Ya'el is... where she came from. Her bounty proved true the rumor about a Roman noblewoman hiding in Jerusalem. Many in the city have searched for her. This was the only safe place to bring her and Elian. And Matthew was right to bring Nahum here, too. Would you rather Ya'el and Elian be held as hostages or executed? Or Nahum be put in Yohanan ben Levi's hands, likely to suffer that same fate?"

Nahum put a hand on the rabbi's shoulder. "They did what they had to, old friend." He looked at Ya'el. "When the way is clear, you and Elian can still leave with me. You will be safe among the Essenes—we'll protect you and the boy."

Miriam felt a pang, but it made sense. Matthew seemed relieved and nodded.

Ya'el crossed her arms, and Miriam almost smiled as Elian did the same. Ya'el's tone was polite but firm. "Thank you, Nahum. But I must stay in Jerusalem."

"You've told me that... but not why."

"My brother, Marcus, will not pursue this war... Once I speak with him, there will be a truce and talks to resolve the wrongs done on both sides."

"Who is this Marcus she speaks of?" Nahum asked, puzzled.

"The new emperor of Rome," Miriam answered him.

"I'm sorry, Ya'el... have you not heard the latest news?" They all turned toward Yohanan ben Zaccai to see what more he would say. "My friend, the trader Boaz, arrived at noon from Caesarea. He had heard from the Romans that the latest emperor, Marcus Otho, had tried to assassinate General Vespasian but failed. And that Emperor Otho is now dead, defeated by Lord Vitellius, who has become emperor."

XXIX

Junius 69 CE

Hebron

The Tomb of the Patriarchs

The stench clung to the Hebron though it sat at 3000 feet, and winds coursed above the valley and plain below. The smell of the burning dead and the rotting bodies unretrievable beneath the collapsed walls shrouded Hebron. The city had been destroyed, save for Herod's building over the tomb of the Jewish patriarchs.

Sayid stood in the shadow of the eastern wall of the tomb, His eyes swept its length and height, and he remembered when he had last stood here with Lady Cleo on her tour of the provinces before the shipwreck of the *Salacia*. Before they had become friends when his duty to the noblewoman had mostly involved carrying and doing things for Camilla, her personal maidservant who had drowned.

The building he studied remained only because there were no rebels within it to kill or capture, so there had been no call to break its walls. No Jews had hidden behind them as a last defense. Instead, hundreds, maybe over a thousand men, lay heaped before the walls where they had made their last stand. The building over the cave tomb of the Jewish patriarchs remained, with far, far more dead outside it than within.

A sound of scuffing feet on loose stone reached him as a voice spoke.

"You were right...."

"About what?" Sayid asked his father. He had not seen him since Caphatabira, where his father had fought at the walls. While Sayid had been assigned to the *musculi* and *vinea*—the wheeled protective covers for the men working on tunneling under the walls or wielding rams to batter the city gates. His father's men had moved and manned the siege towers once the artillery had forced defenders from the walls. It had taken weeks before they finally breached the city.

"As you said they would, the last time we spoke... the rebels fought hard to keep us out of this city." His father's gaze swept over the surrounding devastation. "How is your wound?" He gestured at the linen dressing that wrapped Sayid's right bicep to wind under his tunic over and across his shoulder. "I saw you leave the medicus's tent... and a man seemed to follow you. I would have paid him no attention, but he had a curious tattoo. It was a crocodile—on his hand. I've not seen one since I served in Alexandria. After a bit, he turned from the street and away. I continued to see how you were."

"Were you injured, too, or did you worsen your—?"

"No," Marcus interrupted. "Actually, my leg strengthens... but," a sullenness crept into his voice. "I still only *order* men into the fighting, though I could fight almost as well as I once did." He pointed at Sayid's bandage. "Did that happen during the undermining?"

Sayid nodded, surprised his father knew his assignment in the siege. "We had finished under the wall base and had the tunnel supports in place. Just before we oiled them to set them on fire on General Cerealis's signal, fire arrows hit the man above me carrying the oil. He went down, and the oil spilled on him and on me. More arrows struck him, and the flames raced over him and caught me as he fell upon me. It's nothing."

Sayid moved past his father onto the rubble-strewn street and turned toward what had once been the city's main gate. He stopped— thinking he shouldn't—when he didn't hear steps following him. He looked back at his father, watching him, and asked. "Join me for dinner?"

* * *

ROMAN ASSAULT CAMP

The sun had long since set, and Sayid stared into the darkness. The upper section of the encampment was on a level area of the lower slope below the city. Before him, under the black blanket of a moonless night, he knew an expanse of untouched greenery spread over the lower heights and the plain below, beautiful in the daylight. Vineyards, olives, apricots, figs, and pomegranates would constitute a sizable food source now secured for the legions.

General Vespasian will be pleased, Sayid thought. He wondered if orders would soon come for some of the legion cohorts to return to Caesarea or if they would all hold here until the assault on Jerusalem.

As they ate, his father had told him of the news of Marcus Otho's death and that some provincial governor named Vitellius was now the newest emperor. That had shoved a dagger of fear through Sayid, as it surely had through Yosef, too, if his friend knew. Celsus Evander had sent a message via one driver of the resupply wagons to tell Sayid of Marcus Otho's decree protecting Lady Cleo. Hearing that, he had been sure the attack on Jerusalem might never happen and that he could save his friend. Now things were as they had been—Cleo was trapped in the Judean city next scheduled to fall, and Jerusalem would end as Hebron had... only on a far grander scale.

Sayid turned toward his tent. When they arrived at the camp, his father had asked him: "Why is yours set apart from the other men?" Sayid thought momentarily and told him, "They still don't accept me. They know I left, and some think I was forced from a duty most of them would love to have." He could not keep the mockery from his voice. "Clerk duty at the legion's headquarters camp. Easy work and beer at the local *taberna* at the end of the day." He could not restrain the stony glower he had given his father, whose opinion of his son's former duty had been clear. "They once thought me soft and that I would fail. Now they think me just stupid."

His father had accepted the glare and only nodded. Sayid noted he barely favored his bad leg as he stood, but his hand pressed at his hip as if to be ready for a spasm of pain. His father's expression hinted at something other than what he said next.

"General Cerealis has ordered supply caravans loaded tomorrow from local storehouses to set on a route between here and Caesarea. My men will be one of the escort units. Perhaps yours will, too." And then he had left.

Sayid crawled into his tent, grimacing at his arm and shoulder pain. Sitting on the pallet, he tugged his tunic to loosen it where it had bunched tight over the bandage wrappings. With a sigh, he lay back, willing himself to stop thinking. But a thought snapped him back from the edge of sleep. The man his father had thought was following him... with the crocodile tattoo on his hand. He must be the man from the taberna who had oddly raised his cup to him as if acknowledging their meeting. *What is he doing here?*

XXX

Junius 69 CE

Caesarea

Vespasian's Praetorium, the Promenade

Vespasian looked in both directions along the walkway, where he stood at a newly widened section. Just off the path sat a small *loggia* upon a manmade mound. From that slight height, even from one of the couches of wood and bronze within the structure, he could see through the columns out to sea.

He checked the flat cushions of the *lecti*, though he knew they were dry, having been placed for him just before his routine walk. Beneath, the latticework of leather straps had also been wiped down, and he nodded his approval. Attention to detail was one of his values, and he judged those who served him by theirs. He reclined on a couch, but it was uncomfortable after a while, and he wanted no distractions from his thoughts. There was much to think about. He settled into one of the *sella curule*, a foldable, bronzed-legged chair facing the sea, and rested his feet on the low table before him.

The sounds of the cooling breeze and the surf were one pleasure of Vespasian's morning and evening walks. Still, over them, he could hear the armored men marching two abreast at 50-foot intervals along the promenade. The soldiers were stationed there since the latest attempt on his life and Gaheris Clineas's death. He watched as his son strode toward him, nodding to each pair of soldiers he passed as he approached.

Vespasian waved his son into one chair and said, "Governor Murcianus is already on his way here by now." He rattled two vellum sheets in his hand, frowning. "Vitellius will soon be in Rome, though, according to Mucianus's man traveling with him, the debauchery celebrating the new emperor seems to have slowed him. Vespasian studied his son, noting the weariness around his eyes. "Ask me the question that's been gnawing at you."

"I've heard from all the legion officers and senior legionaries here and in Antioch," Titus said. "They support you, sir." Titus leaned forward, forearms on his knees. He waited, but Vespasian did not comment, so he straightened up and sat back with a sigh. "What does Governor Mucianus say of the eastern legions?"

Vespasian rested his vinewood rod across his knees. "Only that he comes with news I must hear in person." He did not add that only one thing would make Gaius Mucianus act again as a messenger and return so soon to Judea. Seeing his son's crestfallen face, he almost told him the news he believed Mucianus brought. But he held that close, just as he kept to himself the contents of Antonia Caenis's latest letter about Domitian—no need to worry him about his younger brother. For now, he would do enough worrying for both of them. And he must trust that Antonia's plan was sound and that Nicanor would see to its completion.

The crunch of steps on the gravel path broke both men's reveries. Vespasian looked over his shoulder to see who approached them. "Leave him with me, Junius," he called out to his aide escorting the Jewish prisoner. "You need not have come with him." He waved away the new man, who did not deserve Vespasian's coldness and harshness born of the grief he felt about the killing of Gaheris. Another wave dismissed the four guards who had stopped about a dozen feet from him, two on either side of the man they escorted.

He pointed at the chair next to Titus. "Come... join us." Vespasian scrutinized the man whose premonitions about him now might actually come true.

XXXI

Julius 69 CE

Puteoli

The Port, Inn, and Taberna

"So, now you owe me not only for saving your life... again. But also for this room and my medical services." Marcus tightened the last stitch with those words and tied it off as Nicanor grunted.

"You wouldn't have to restitch me if you'd done it right at Quintilian's," Nicanor said. He took the roll of what he hoped was clean linen from the table beside the cot. The healer woman Marcus had found earlier that morning said it had been boiled twice. She wouldn't know that unless she'd stolen it from a nearby *aesculpia* where serious injuries were treated. The bandage reeked of vinegar, which he knew helped keep wounds from rotting. He wrapped the swath of linen around his torso, with more layers over the wound in his side. Another grunt escaped him.

Marcus shook his head and replied, "I've not done much sewing up of wounds, and you didn't give me much time."

"Domitian couldn't ride any longer with that hurt leg. We had to hurry and leave him. But as I'd hoped, the men followed us."

"Then why did you leave Carmenta behind? The only thing I heard on the way here was you cursing that nag of Quintilian's. Those men could have caught up with us if not for the weight of their armor."

"If the boy was forced to run, despite the bad leg, he needed the best horse, Carmenta. I swore to Lady Antonia I would do all I could to help Domitian. And I cannot report to Vespasian and tell him I failed to see his son safe."

Still, Nicanor worried about the uncertainty of that protection. He grimaced as he pulled over his head another of Marcus's purchases that morning—the tunic he tugged down to cover the bandages. "We couldn't fight, so running... hoping they'd follow... that was all I could think of." He pressed a hand to his side and took a deep breath.

Marcus went to the water bowl on the table and washed the blood from his hands. "The woman didn't have any poppy but offered black henbane seeds to help you with the pain."

"Those make you see things, and you get all weak-kneed... I'll bear the pain." He was familiar with the discomfort of torn flesh... but leaving Carmenta stung more. Then something occurred to him, and he said, "I thought you were still in debt. How did you pay for the room and all this?" Nicanor held his hands out to indicate his tunic, all the scraps of linen, and the suturing things.

"Before the Games were interrupted, while you were away serving Otho, I defeated a gladiator who was once a champion of Nero—Hilarus had thirteen wreaths to his name. Then I beat Lucius Raecius Felix, victorious in a dozen fights. The odds were heavily in their favor." Marcus smiled. "So, I paid Gnaeus Batiatus back, and I still had some left for me."

Nicanor went to the window and cracked the shutter to spill late morning light into the room. When he and Marcus had arrived the night before, reeling from too many hours in the saddle, he was glad he could still find the inn he recalled from years back. Where there had been another time for recovery. He, Sayid, and Cleo had left Yosef there to recuperate from a fever, further delaying his journey to Rome behind them.

"Let's find the *Egeria*," Nicanor said. "Then you must take my message to Lady Antonia... I doubt hiding with Quintilian will protect the boy for very long." He grabbed the *sarcina* he usually strapped to Carmenta, now full of the new clothes and a cloak Marcus had bought him.

As he descended the stairs from their room, Nicanor winced and cursed at every step, hating that the second floor had had the only vacancy the night before. He felt the stitches pull and hoped they'd hold; he doubted the ship he planned to board had a *medicus* worth trusting.

"What is it?" he said as he bumped into Marcus, who had stopped at the bottom of the steps into the taberna's common room.

Road-stained, grim-faced, a grizzled centurion stood eye-to-eye with Marcus, who wore Domitian's fine robe, though it was now much the worse for wear. The centurion fingered the shoulder of the garment. "You're not General Vespasian's son... but you," he pointed at Nicanor above and behind the freedman, "are surely, Nicanor, the other man we seek."

"Futuo," Nicanor muttered, seeing the dozen armored cavalrymen behind the centurion. "Move aside, Marcus. Let them take me." He thought of Graius, a man too old to fight but with enough honor and skill to save his life. And Florin... denied all the years ahead of him... too young to die. He thought of all the men under his command that he had left on the valley floor at Beth Horon. He leaned forward to whisper in Marcus's ear, "No more will die for me. Return to Rome, check on Domitian, and get Carmenta from him. Take her and my message to Antonia Caenis."

The freedman did not move. He widened his stance, swept the cloak back, and gripped the sword at his hip.

"Nicanor...." A voice came from behind the dozen cavalrymen, who parted to let a shorter man come forward. "Let me tell you about another little port on the Peloponnese," he said. "Ahh... the women there ... you'd never think to find such as them in a quiet town. And I returned with the sweetest maiden, the best I ever had."

"Who is this?" Marcus asked over his shoulder.

Nicanor closed his eyes and let go of the breath he'd held. "For once... it's a friend."

XXXII

Julius 69 CE

Jerusalem

The Upper City

"We finally got to see Mathias," Yohanan ben Zaccai said to Rebecca as he settled on the divan with a sigh and creaking knees. Behind him, the hot midday sun shone through the open window. Matthew stood beside him, hands on his hips, ready to interrupt the old rabbi if he mentioned that Yohanan ben Levi's man had demanded more money at the last minute.

Matthew's gaze traveled the room. He still did not approve of his mother inviting Ya'akov to their home so often. But there he was again, his eyes cutting toward Miriam, who sat as far from him as possible while still remaining in the room. Their mother's eyes also shifted between the two until Yohanan spoke.

"He's weak but fine, Rebecca," the rabbi continued. "At least 300 men are being held with him in the grand city hall near the Temple."

Years before, Mathias had shown his sons every room and space within the magnificent building with its two splendid chambers and a massive, ornate fountain separating them. In one section was a stepped pool, a giant *mikveh*, for ritual bathing. Sculpted cornice-bearing pillars topped with Corinthian capitals supported the ceiling. The place was as light as the brightest day from the many lanterns and lamps that filled the rooms. The largest lamp was mounted on the wall high above. Beyond that, a series of ventilation holes reached outside. The place had been built for the city's leading men to entertain guests and where foreign dignitaries were received before entering the Temple Enclosure.

Now the once-vast building was dark and crowded, and when Matthew and Yohanan had entered, they soon stepped through pools of sludge and filth, and the chambers reeked of it. Soiled men lay on cushionless wooden sofas once used with luxurious pillows for dining. The building now held some of the same men who had once fêted their visitors within its walls.

Seeing his father in such circumstances had turned Matthew's stomach... then the site of the man's condition enraged him. The anger had replaced the churning in his belly with hot coals of passion for finding Yohanan ben Levi and cutting him down. But too many still followed the Gischalan, and the man went nowhere without a handful as his bodyguards. Matthew would be struck down soon after he killed the man... if he could manage it. Then who would be here for his mother and sister? And he must take more gold to the greedy Galilean jailkeeper or, as the man put it, "something might befall" his father.

"Can I see him?" Rebecca asked.

"No, but Matthew and I will see him again. He was overjoyed to see us and sends his love to you and Miriam."

Matthew saw slight relief on his mother's face while Miriam stiffened, her fists clenching until the knuckles were white. Her eyes went briefly to Ya'akov, who sat next to their mother. He knew his mother had liked Ya'akov greatly and had been saddened when Miriam demanded their betrothal be broken. And now Miriam's family understood why.

Rebecca had explained to Matthew that Ya'akov was a chance for Miriam to get over Ehud. But she did not know Miriam as well as she thought. Each day after Ehud's killing, his sister changed even more. That event had broken something in her that was never to be fixed. And that fact hurt him more than anything.

**

THE TEMPLE ENCLOSURE

Matthew had warned her away from the sloped path into the Lower City. "Yohanan ben Levi's and Simon bar Giora's men frequently clash there. When they are not fighting each other, they prey on the citizens. It's not safe."

Once through the Upper City agora, where she had hurried past Hananiah's new knife stall, they had crossed the viaduct to enter the Temple Enclosure, then toward the southwest corner and the imposing steps that descended to the Lower City. It was a well-lighted route, and they were less likely to encounter the rougher followers of the two factions there. But nowhere was safe from violence—she looked up at the fortified tower manned by slingers and archers. Matthew had told her about the four new towers everyone had seen Yohanan ben Levi and the Zealots erecting. The first was at the northeast corner of the Court of the Gentiles, a second above the Xystus, whose overlook they had just passed. The third stood at the corner over the Lower City. The fourth rose above the Pastophoria they had just passed under—The Place of Trumpeting. A priest with a shofar stood there every seventh day at twilight to trumpet the start of Shabbat and its end.

"Eleasar and I were passing here when another skirmish broke out," said Matthew. "Though Yohanan and his Zealots were far outnumbered, they had the four towers ready with archers and the Roman war engines arrayed along the length of the parapets of the cloisters. They stood off Giora's men, but not before they had plundered their stores. After Simon lost many men, he pulled back." Matthew shook his head. "The Gischalan turns upon our own people the weapons he found in Antonia Fortress. He has turned the area around our most sacred place into a battlefield." He grew quiet as they reached the steps.

"But it drew many people away from the Lower City and the City of David," Matthew continued. "No one was around to see us get Nahum into the tunnel and away. When we returned.... they were still here... some stripping the dead." A look of disgust twisted his face. "I'm glad Father could not see such as that. And Yosef... if he knew, it would crush his heart."

Miriam did not break the following silence. Matthew rarely mentioned their brother anymore, but she knew he often thought about him. Her own thoughts were conflicted. She loved Yossi. But the longer he seemed a privileged prisoner of that Roman general, Vespasian, the more credence was given to the belief he betrayed his people.

* * *

KING DAVID'S TOMB

"So, Yohanan ben Zaccai thinks he has a place where you'll be safe and someone you'll be safe with," Matthew finished.

Miriam had said nothing as Matthew explained what Yohanan had come up with, ignoring Ya'el darting glances at her. She did not like the idea. But Yohanan felt strongly that no one should be in King David's Tomb. She had not told him, or anyone, that she would still use it once Ya'el and Elian left. There were many passages and branch tunnels she had yet to explore.

"And this man, Shammai, is a... a what?" Ya'el asked.

Matthew answered, "A collier, a charcoal maker."

"He needs help to do that work?"

"Yes. Summer is his busiest time—hauling wood, tending the fires, and creating charcoal for winter. And now the city is far more crowded than usual, with many more people to keep warm in the coming winter. Many have fled the Romans, who take slaves whenever they ransack the countryside. They would rather risk being here at the hands of the Zealots than in the 'care' of the Romans. Shammai doesn't mind taking in a woman and a young boy to help him."

"He doesn't know who I am"—Ya'el looked at Elian, who sat on a nearby bench listening. "Or who *we* are?"

"You're just someone Yohanan is trying to help."

"What do you think?" Ya'el asked Miriam.

"It's hard work... for both of you," Miriam had to answer. "And many eyes will be upon you. Shammai lives and works in the newer city up north, just inside the third wall."

Elian was bouncing on the bench, eager for some change. But the boy was pale, and dark half-circles now discolored the flesh under his eyes. Ya'el had them, too... "But it's out of the way of most people. Still, Elian," he looked up, "you'll have to be very careful."

Miriam was just as worried about Ya'el. The news of her brother's death had shaken her, ripping from Ya'el the promise of escape that imperial power had offered. She had cherished the prospect of deliverance, holding it close since she'd heard he had become emperor. Miriam intuitively knew the woman she no longer considered a Roman needed some hope. After hiding inside a tomb without sunlight... more a dungeon or prison than a haven, Ya'el needed what Shammai offered to give her some desire to live.

Ya'el forced a smile and nodded. "Let's do it...."

"Good," Matthew nodded. "I'll tell Yohanan tonight, and he'll see Shammai about the timing. Come on, Miriam, let's go...."

"I'll stay awhile." Miriam could tell by his look that her brother knew she wanted to avoid returning home. Ya'akov was likely there for dinner, at their mother's invitation, hoping to see her.

Ya'el waited until Matthew was gone and turned to Elian to say, "Go play now...."

Elian shot from the bench to hug Ya'el. "I'm glad we're leaving this place," he said, his voice muffled in the fabric on her shoulder. The boy then smiled at Miriam, who was startled when he ran to hug her, too. Then he grabbed the bag of spinning tops Ehud and Matthew had made for him and went to the alcove where he had swept the stone floor clean for playing.

"Even with this move to stay with... this man, Shammai," Ya'el said, "we must work on Hananiah to use his connection to my husband. Perhaps if we feed him lies to pass to Gessius... we can thwart his plans or at least hinder them."

"I've seen and talked with Hananiah a few times. He has set up a shop in the agora... I fear it is so he can be closer to my home. Each time I see him, he tries to touch me." Miriam shuddered with pent-up hate, though her revulsion was almost as strong,

"What of Ya'akov?"

Miriam blew out a little puff of air at Ya'el's effort to switch to a happier topic. She deserved an answer. "He consoles my mother... though she and I know he wishes to comfort me instead. I've kept him at a distance... but that must change." She looked up to see the flash of surprise and happiness on Ya'el's face.

"I'm glad for you! You need someone to love who loves you back."

Miriam heard the wistfulness in Ya'el's voice and knew the woman had given up on her own hopes for love but still wished it for her friend. "I'll have to become closer to him," Miriam said. Then paused, decided, then murmured softly, "Hananiah asked me about him... asked why Ya'akov is at my home so much. He had a look in his eyes. Hananiah plans to kill him... but I won't let that happen."

XXXIII

Julius 69 CE

Caesarea

Roman Encampment, Vespasian's Praetorium

"If we delay longer, the Senate may choose another to replace Vitellius," said Gaius Mucianus, his lined face drawn tight as he paced the room before the old general. "He is already drawing the ire of the people and many senators. He has brought so many foreigners into Rome that the encampments cannot hold them all. He has ordered citizens to take them into their homes. These men from the northern provinces have never seen the riches of Rome's citizenry. Your brother's office is flooded with reports of theft and threats against those who try to stop them. They urge the city prefect to use the urban cohorts to keep peace. Also, the *areani* we've placed with Vitellius report that when he is secure in Rome, he'll order Germanian legions to replace those in Syria and Judea to reward their loyalty."

"That's a persuasive reward," Titus commented. "Winter duty is harsh for the northern legions. They'll follow anyone who can send them to more pleasant regions."

Surprised he'd been invited to this gathering, Yosef watched to see what was unfolding before him, for Rome and for Judea.

"So," said Vespasian, his own heavy brow creased with concern, "the Syrian and my Judean legions will be punished by being sent to Germania. Are your spies sure?"

"Yes, general." Mucianus nodded and added, "The rumor of it has reached them, and they are angry. They've become accustomed to serving there, and many have attachments in the communities around their encampments. The prospect of having it all taken from them by a man they have no respect for—even one presumed to be their emperor... they clamor against what might come to pass."

Mucianus stepped over to the table behind the desk. The governor touched the base of the *clepsydra*, the water clock. "Time does not wait. It passes for good men and bad." He looked at Vespasian. "These things I report are only a few reasons you must accept the principate. You are more worthy to rule than is Vitellius. You are more worthy than any man a Roman can put forth. The people and the Senate will not tolerate an emperor such as Vitellius—not when they compare him to the man you are. You've told me Antonia also says this in her letters. So, we cannot delay."

Yosef watched as Vespasian turned the rod in his hands, his thick fingers tapping the bronze ferrule as his gaze remained on the governor, who had looked askance at Yosef more than once at him since the governor had entered the room.

"And there's this, general," Mucianus continued glancing at Titus and then back to Vespasian. "Having a childless emperor does not help the empire. Nero, Galba, and Marcus Otho... are all recent proof. Though any offspring of those men might have brought difficulties upon the empire. And surely they would not be able to solve our problems. Vitellius is old, but his young son cannot effectively rule. Many men will curry favor to become the heir's adviser or maneuver close enough to kill him. They'll position themselves to become chosen or to buy or kill another to turn the choice their way. No. The empire needs a man with children able to rule. That succession is the greatest security an emperor can provide the empire, especially when the man who could become emperor has years of experience and has raised capable sons. You, Lord Vespasian."

The governor turned to Titus. "This, your oldest son, has become battle-tested and strong, a proven leader. And I've heard your youngest, Domitian, now has the ear and fellowship of many young men in Rome. They are the sons of powerful fathers who will support you over someone else, but only if you declare your intentions now."

Yosef watched emotions play on General Vespasian's ordinarily stoic face, the rod bending in his grip. *He thinks of what he talked about as we sat within the loggia on the promenade.* There the old general had spoken of what seemed newly defined as if he wished to discuss his deliberations with Yosef and Titus.

He had told them, "When a country is divided, loyalty is precious. Cohorts and cavalry cannot stop one or two men who choose to earn power and money—a great deal—by murdering influential men. Men with powerful positions and those who do not serve or prevent their agenda. It is easier to set whole armies in motion than to prevent a single killer."

Yosef now watched the general closely. There was much, too, for him that hinged on his answer.

Vespasian's eyes went to his son, who nodded. Yosef was surprised when the general's eyes then locked with his. *My only hope to save my people is to sway this man,* raced through his mind. He ventured a reply to Vespasian's look. "It is indeed what I have seen, Lord Vespasian."

Vespasian slapped the vinewood hard into his palm, then stood, walked to the governor, and gripped his shoulder. "Call a council of my supporters in the region," he said, "and we'll make it known that I accept the principate."

XXXIV

Julius 69 CE

Har haKarmel/Mount Carmel

The Altar

Below them, Yosef could see the port of Sycaminum, where the Roman galley from Caesarea awaited their return to carry them on to Berytus—Vespasian's next destination. Ptolemais, a place of bitter memories for Yosef, where he had been brought on the heels of the destruction of Yotapta, was across the bay from the jutting point of land Sycaminum sat upon. While chained to a post across that bay, imprisoned at the Roman encampment, he had last seen Cleo and Nicanor. Two friends he did not ever expect to see again. He prayed they still lived as he followed Vespasian and Titus from the overlook toward the clearing above them.

    Yosef had seen it in Rome, too. Temples or places of divination were often perched upon hills, as with the important Temple of Jupiter Optimus Maximus atop the Capitoline in the center of Rome. His eyes swept over the clearing, which seemed smaller now with so many armed and armored men spread across it, and then he returned to his view from the mountain. Unlike in Jerusalem, on this mountain, there was no elaborate temple or edifice built by man. Still, it was a place his people thought sacred to Jehovah, with a simple, natural stone altar. The Essenes, who prized its plainness, often frequented the site, which had been hallowed ground, a refuge for his people, for centuries.

    The mountain's name, *Har haKarmel*, meant Yahweh's vineyard, a garden land. Its southwest slope was lush, covered in oak, laurel, pine, and olive trees. The air was rich with the scents of the season. *Tammuz* was when olives, figs, and grapes ripened. As their group climbed a winding path from the port, they passed many small oil and wine presses scattered across the mountain. The men and women working them fled as the armed Romans appeared.

    Yosef was several feet behind Vespasian and Titus. These two Roman generals now stood before the altar at the edge of the clearing. Old stumps showed where trees had been cut down to create more space around the stone jutting from the earth. Just beyond it, Yosef knew, the mountain transitioned from a verdant, fertile slope to a steep ridge and the northeastern face of bare limestone and flint, pockmarked with caves. Yosef drew in deep breaths of the fragrant air. Despite the shackles he still wore, he felt freer than he had since his early days at Yotapta before the Romans arrived. That was a lull before the storm broke upon them... when the Romans pounded, eventually destroyed the city, and slaughtered almost all the men and women he led, enslaving those few who had survived.

The moment passed, and Yosef felt the weight of his chains again. Still, he was thankful Vespasian had brought him here and that he would travel with him to Berytus. He had not asked the Roman general how he had heard of this place or why he came here because that did not matter. He knew Vespasian's intent. Yosef sensed he had become symbolic, in some fashion, to the general. As a Jew, he was a token figure who affirmed the Roman general's future. Vespasian wanted him here to witness what a Jewish oracle would have to say about his destiny. Would it corroborate Yosef's visions? Or would it refute them... or be silent? The latter two outcomes would weaken his position with Vespasian, for the general seemed to have embraced Yosef's foretelling. But freedom might remain only a fleeting and distant memory if his visions meant less to Vespasian because no one else foretold a similar destiny for the Roman. And because Vespasian was not yet emperor, his defeat would undoubtedly lead to their deaths.

The gray-bearded man near the flat stone was flanked by two legionaries with their short swords drawn. Though frightened, he spoke: "What do you wish from me?" he said, his eyes sliding to the armed men on either side before he added, "lord?"

"What's your name?" Vespasian demanded.

"Basilides."

"You're the keeper of this," Vespasian pointed at the cluster of rocks, "altar?"

"I have that duty... lord."

"I come to make a sacrifice and to hear what you see within the animal, what it tells you."

"Your gods are not here... lord."

Vespasian turned and beckoned to the guards to bring Yosef to him. "Your visions," Vespasian said, "the voice you hear that spoke of me and the future... do they come from your god?"

Yosef felt the priest's glare as he answered. "That is the only voice I would hear, lord. That of the god my people worship."

Vespasian turned back to the priest. "This is your land, where your god dwells. I would hear from him what he thinks lies before me."

The priest paused, his gaze switching between Vespasian and Yosef. "You have an offering?"

Titus signaled, and a soldier came from the rear of the formation holding a struggling young goat in his arms. He set it on a broad flat stone, stepped aside, and the two legionaries flanking the priest held it down. Yosef suddenly recalled the prophet Elijah's famous visit here. He wondered momentarily if fire would again fall from the sky here and consume the offering. Perhaps it was a well-timed bolt of lightning that lit the fire.

The priest reached under the lip of the stone that formed a table before him and took out a bowl and a bag of cured animal hide. Stretching down again, he picked up and set a larger bowl before him. He poured water from the skin into the smaller bowl, rinsed his hands, and dried them on the front of his tunic. He stooped again and brought out a curved blade.

Yosef watched as the legionaries tensed at seeing the knife and almost lost their grip on the goat. Ignoring them, darting another glower at Yosef, the priest slit the animal's throat. Its blood flowed through a runnel carved into the stone to divert it off the edge and onto the ground, or Yosef thought, *a container to carry it away*. Within a minute of becoming still, the goat was cut open, and its entrails removed, rinsed, and placed in the empty bowl. The priest lifted and shifted the slick mass, studying it.

"What do you see, priest?" Vespasian strode closer, his hand gripping the hilt of the gladius at his hip.

The priest of the altar turned from his examination. His eyes noted the Roman general's hand on his sword. "Whatever your plan... lord. Be it building to add to your estate or engaging more servants, you shall have a great mansion, far-flung boundaries, and many people who support you."

The priest's divination, though phrased oddly, seemed to please Vespasian. He turned with a grim smile to face Titus. In the quiet of the sheltered clearing, Yosef heard his four guards a dozen feet away as they shifted their stance, becoming alert to orders from either general. Father and son exchanged nods but no words as Vespasian walked to stand before Yosef. "What do you think of these words here at a place your people feel is sacred?"

"His words," Yosef gestured at Basilides, "are eloquent. And in concord with the meaning of my vision and my belief in your destiny, Lord Vespasian."

* * *

BERYTUS

Yosef stepped off the galley onto the quay. His four-man guard had been reduced to two, one on either side. He glanced toward the gangplank as Vespasian and Titus followed, accompanied by their more sizable escort. The two Roman generals studied the city crowded around three sides of the port. Yosef saw the tension leave Vespasian's face and an expression of expectation, almost eagerness, shine from Titus. Two chariots gleamed in the sun where the dock broadened into a pier-side street. One had a team of two black horses, the other white. The four horses' hooves echoed on the stone with a bit of prancing that rattled their harnesses.

Vespasian and his aide, Junius, stepped into the chariot pulled by the white. Titus took the reins of the black and gestured for Yosef to step up to join him. Their escort formed lines on either side of the chariot as they moved off at a walk.

"Have you been here before?" Titus asked.

"No." Yosef looked around at this city, which surprised him. It was an impressive, albeit a much smaller, version of Rome in a setting 100 miles north of Ptolemais. The metal cladding of the chariot wheels scraped and then rang with their turn onto the *cardo maximus*. The broad central street ran north-south through the city, lined with extensive bath complexes and red-and-gray granite colonnades. The vast hippodrome loomed over the port, and Yosef speculated that inside, its high walls probably supported tiered seating as did the Circus Maximus in Rome. It was the largest he had seen outside of that city. He was amused to pass it in his first ride in a chariot—it seemed fitting and reminded him of the race he had attended with Nicanor in Rome.

"Fifty thousand or more people live here," Titus said. "Two-thirds are descended from the legions established here more than a century ago." They passed throngs of people lining the streets to greet Vespasian and others going about their daily lives. Many smiled, and Yosef heard laughter as they entered a market area and rolled toward what must be the city forum.

"They seem… happy," Yosef said aloud, wondering why it felt so peculiar. Then he realized he had not seen many joyful, relaxed people in years.

"Berytus is the only town in the eastern provinces with full *ius italicum*." The reins gripped in one hand, Titus squinted at Yosef to see if he understood. "That means they are exempt from all imperial taxation."

Yosef nodded. Now he understood the reason for this choice for Vespasian's council meeting. It was a town unburdened by imperial demands, devoid of the resentment often accompanying them. Yet Berytus benefited from its favored status within the empire as long as the empire remained stable.

Titus slowed to let his father's chariot draw farther ahead. In minutes it had stopped outside the city forum, and Yosef saw Governor Mucianus with a group of other men greeting Vespasian. Two of the regally garbed men he did not recognize… and a third he did. He had not seen Rome's Client-King Herod Agrippa the Second since before leaving Jerusalem for Galilee. Next to him was his sister, Queen Berenice, in a robe of gold silk trimmed in purple. He had last seen her at Jerusalem pleading with Florus to spare the innocents in Jerusalem three years earlier.

The woman's features were expectant when Vespasian stepped from the chariot, then crestfallen as she saw he was accompanied by his aide. She turned her sad countenance toward Titus's chariot, and Yosef saw her eyes light up with joy when she saw them.

Puzzled, Yosef turned to Titus, who was searching the crowd and then seemed to find what he was looking for, for he smiled. Yosef looked back at Berenice and then at Titus again. The two had eyes only for each other.

XXXV

Julius/Augustus 69 CE

At Sea to Caesarea

The Egeria

"Your fever's down," Marinus said when Nicanor left his cabin at the stern. "Anyte says the flesh around the wound is less swollen and cooler to the touch."

"I do feel better," Nicanor said, pointing at the fang of land to his right and then opposite it, at the rounded headland of cliffs to their left. "Is Messana just ahead... already?"

"Have you become a seaman and know these waters?"

"I remember maps you have shown me and those of another captain I've sailed with through here before. I recognize the two points that mark the northern end of the straits." He rubbed his chin, wiping away the drops of water still clinging there from his washing up. "So, I slept two days?"

"Almost. The morning after you boarded, you came not from your room, so I went there and found you feverish. I had Anyte tend to you."

"I remember a little of that. Is she the woman you mentioned at the taberna in Puteoli? You're my age, Marinus," Nicanor said as he shook his head, "and she is but a girl."

"She's my daughter. I see that surprises you!" Marinus said with a laugh. "The lady I spoke of is this ship, the *Egeria,* named for the goddess of sea nymphs. I had her built in Lechaion, Corinth's western port."

"So you've discovered a daughter in the year since I've seen you? Is she from one of your many ports?"

"Anyte is from Tegea, in the middle of the Peloponnese."

"A mountain girl?"

Marinus nodded. "She wanted to sail—at least once—upon the sea. She accompanies me to take you to Caesarea, and then we return home."

"I thought you called no port home?" Nicanor said. The shipowner seemed changed, different.

"There are some places I've lingered. One is Cenchreae, east of Corinth on the Saronic Gulf, west of Athens. I hope to show it to you one day. When I saw it, I thought of your talk about your birthplace and that one day you hoped to retire someplace like Patras. I'm of an age and now have the means." He glanced at the young woman who had come out and stood near the mainmast. "I have the means to retire near a daughter I can get to know as I grow older."

Nicanor blinked at the wistful expression on Marinus's face, then turned to study the ship and stepped over to a large metal grate inset into the deck. Holding his side though he felt only a slight ache, he knelt to see what was below. "Your other ships did not have oars," he said.

Laughter came from the rowers below as they slid the long oars from the brackets, securing them, and men opened the slots for them to be run out. The rasp of wood and grunts of the men taking positions on the benches was expected. But Nicanor was surprised that many smiled and jested with each other. "No slaves?"

Marinus shook his head. "I do what the navy does; I rely on freedmen. These are all Greeks and paid a wage." He beckoned with his hand. "Come with me."

Nicanor followed him to the bow, which seemed narrower and higher than others he had seen.

"I built her to cleave the waves at a better angle." Marinus slapped the railing where it arced into the base of the jutting spar of the bow, and he gestured behind them. "And the stern is higher to buffer the surge of waves when we run before a storm. Now, look"—he pointed ahead at a churning section of the sea. "We'll give her an excellent test, though I already think she handles better than any ship I own."

Beneath his feet, Nicanor felt the ship's mass tugged forward, a shuddering of the hull along the beam. The main mast shivered as some current working against the wind took the ship's body.

"Four times daily, the surface and deep-water currents switch and swirl north to south, south to the north." A gust spilling around the headland caught them, and the mainsail snapped above. "And there are crosswinds," Marinus pointed up.

Nicanor heard the lines and rigging above them thrum and tighten. He felt the *Egeria* sliding sideways and heard, though faintly and almost lost in the wind, the shouted orders of the shipmaster to deck sailors and the oarsmen below. A lurching memory of the *Salacia* and the *Faustitas* in the Strait of Gallicum Fretum made his stomach spasm. He saw the rocks just beyond the whirlpool but still reached by its pull. Any vessel unable to free from that drag risked being split open there. The ship's bow swung away from the water vortex as he watched, and the wind shear lessened as they passed into the lee of the bluffs of the eastern land mass. He now heard the rhythmic sound of the rowers charting in unison as the *Egeria* separated from the rogue currents. His stomach settled. "I did not experience this before...."

"Shipmasters have to be lucky or very smart. I timed our entry to when the cross-currents and pull were weakest and when rowers could overcome the danger. But even then... if the gods wish to play despite the timing... if they choose to strengthen the currents... they'll break you on the rocks and drag you down. Like the monsters Scylla and Charybdis in the Greek stories."

* * *

5 days from Caesarea...

"Thanks for tending to me," Nicanor said, "to my wound. You're gifted, Anyte—it's almost completely healed." He raised his arms over his head, pleased that there was no pain, just some stiffness on that side.

Marinus nodded his approval and said, "Her mother's ancestor in Epidaurus once dreamed she met the Asclepius, the god of medicine. Since then, the family have been healers. And Anyte's namesake was also a poet famed throughout Greece."

"So, she inherited all good things from her mother... nothing from you?" Nicanor smiled, teasing the shipowner.

"There is at least one thing," Anyte said. "I have his love of the sea." She smiled and arranged the drape of her *peplos* as she joined them at the table. More like a long tunic with a sash at the waist than a robe or gown, her garment was yellow with red trim.

Nicanor had noted her variety of garments, each day a different color. He turned to Marinus and said, "You must do well. A new ship... a new daughter with fine clothing."

Marinus beamed at the girl. "Anyte's mother is the woman I should have married, should never have left. But my family was from the mountains, and I went to the sea to establish myself as a successful trader." He sighed with a seriousness Nicanor had not seen in the man before. "That didn't go well for years, and I did not want to return to her as a failure."

"You don't seem to have failed."

"There's a saying... from some wise man or philosopher whose name I don't know: *'Pecunia nervus belli.'*" Marinus drank from his cup and then continued. "Money is like the blood in the veins of war. There's another... more to my liking because it's practical: '*Bellum facit mercatores divites.*'"

"Who said that one?" Nicanor asked. That saying was true. Some of Rome's wealthiest men—not just the merchants—had made their fortunes from war and conquest. Many in the provinces, too.

"I did...." Marinus smiled. "But I had help to succeed. Three years ago, I met Antonia Caenis, who helped arrange the army contracts that gave me a stable ongoing business to expand. That friendship continues to benefit us both."

Ahhhh, Nicanor thought, that explains how Lady Antonia gets letters to and from General Vespasian without relying on official couriers. And gathers information from around the empire. Marinus has ships coming and going between key ports, including Caesarea.

"So, you went back... finally returned to Anyte's mother?"

"I went to apologize," Marinus said, his smile slipping, "and to ask her forgiveness."

"Did she forgive you?"

"My mother died two years ago," Anyte said when her father did not answer. She had spoken little to him besides a few questions when changing his bandage. She seemed to spend much of her time writing and watching the sea. He had noticed the wax tablet she carried everywhere and seen the sheaves of scribbled-upon parchment in the cabin next to her father's.

"When I learned of her death and that I had a daughter, I found Anyte and explained that I took too long to return to her mother." Marinus shook his head. "No, I admitted I had hidden my failure from her mother by staying away. I benefited from the army contacts, ashamed of the years passing when I had promised to return. I wasted more time in the ports where commerce took me. And with women that I knew I never had to explain anything to... women I knew I'd never love. Still, after a time... Anyte forgave me."

The moment stretched into a minute of silence.

"Who is Cleo?" Anyte asked.

The question startled Nicanor from his musing on how what had once been his own routine life had shifted, how chance meetings and events had changed everything for him. He thought about it more often of late, reflecting on the past, present, and future. He was surprised that Marinus had experienced something similar. He looked at Anyte. "I'm sorry... you asked me something?"

"You said the name Cleo several times in your fevered sleep. Is she your wife?"

"No... no... she's someone I know."

"That's the woman you told me you waited for in Ptolemais when we first met," Marinus said. "You seemed to leave something of yourself behind when you took my ship from there to Rome two years ago. Is she why you return to Judea?"

"Yes," Nicanor said simply, but his mind ran on. He wondered if Antonia Caenis had communicated anything about Cleo to Marinus. She, too, had asked him about Cleo, and he had told her the truth. While he returned officially to serve General Vespasian, he hoped to help Cleo escape Judea and her husband, Gessius Florus.

"You want to find her and take her away?" Marinus asked.

"Yes, if I'm not too late."

A flicker of emotion flashed across the shipowner's face. "Tell me what I can do to help you."

XXXVI

Augustus 69 CE

Jerusalem

Bezetha, The New City

The sun was still broiling low in the west, the heat stifling the city as Miriam and Rebecca passed the Antonia Fortress and approached the *Struthius*, lying at the foot of the rock scarp. The reservoir collected the winter and spring rainwater from the rooftops. Miriam smiled, remembering how she and her brothers had played by its coolness as children. Late summer afternoons like this one, they had enjoyed the shade it offered three children tired from their explorations. She wished she could return to that innocence.

Built by Herod the Great, when the fortress was constructed, the giant cistern extended northwest to southeast. It was over 150 feet long and a third as wide, 13 feet deep at its northwest end and, where the pool's long walls dropped steadily toward the southeast, 18 feet deep. They climbed the rock-cut steps Yosef had told her were coated with a mortar made from chalk and ashes so that water could run off, improving the footing. At the small landing at the top of the steps, she and her mother paused, and Miriam hoped for a breath of wind to pass over the water. Just a breath would offer brief relief from the heat and dispel the thick, soot-choked air that enveloped them. But no wind came, and they turned from the water to look beyond.

Most of the structures in Bezetha, the city's northern section, had been destroyed by Cestius Gallus's 12th Legion in the assault on Jerusalem three years before. The devastation would have spread across the city had that legion not retreated. Miriam knew Ya'el had helped convince the legion commander to stop the attack and pull back from Jerusalem.

The outer wall of three, the section breached by the Romans, had been rebuilt, as had the other structures of Bezetha. The wall was thicker and stronger than the others. Space that had once been empty now held rough shelters for many who saw the city as a safe haven. Before them were hundreds of tents and crude mudbrick and wood houses. The dwellings thinned past the Struthius and the approach to Solomon's Quarry. And there they could see—and smell—Shammai's works.

Large mounds of dirt covered fire pits across the field, and the central chimneys filled the air with smoke and soot. In several days of burning, the fires would turn the wood in the holes into *pecham*, charcoal. With no wind to dissipate the smoke, it settled over Bezetha, even along the slope upward to Solomon's Quarry and Zechariah's Cave. Lower to the ground, the burning created fumes that seeped from the mounds, the vapor slowly spreading to the base of the city's outer wall, the far boundary of the charcoal works.

Leaving the Struthius, Miriam and Rebecca continued to the edge of Shammai's field. They could see two figures working in the smokiest area, the central fire pits. The taller person—a woman—coughed almost continually as she went from mound to mound, tamping down dirt anywhere the smoke plumed out. Miriam realized the water-dampened cloths covering the woman's lower face probably helped only for a while. But they would soon dry out. The boy clambered over logs and stacks of wood next to the burning mounds, a small hatchet in his hand. He lopped off branches and trimmed twigs and small limbs from the straightest of them. When he had an armful, he took them to a large wicker basket near a small building at a distance from the mounds.

"Mother, you know that sometimes you do what you must," Miriam said. "And this," she swept her hand to encompass Shammai's works, "is what must be done for them to be safe." Still, Miriam missed both Ya'el and Elian.

Ya'el walked with familiar dignity to the basket and lowered her face cloth. She raised a small cured-skin bag draped on a cord over her shoulder, poured water on another long cloth tied at her waist, and wiped her sooty face, revealing a weary smile. Elian ran to her and dropped another armful of wood into the basket, and Ya'el poured more water on the cloth and swept his sweat-tangled hair back from his brow. The boy's soot-streaked grin matched the woman's now somewhat cleaner one. He watched her take a lengthy straight shaft from the basket and run her fingers along its surface, nodding her approval.

"They seem to be doing well," said Rebecca. "But that a lady should have to do such work..." Rebecca shook her head. "I wish we could speak with them."

Miriam knew *she* must speak with Ya'el, but nothing her mother could hear. Though her mother knew her secret life as a fighter, she could not talk to her about what she'd done... and what Miriam knew she had to do. Matthew was especially busy with Eleasar ben Ananias gone to Masada to convince Elazar ben Yair to bring his people back to Jerusalem to aid its defense. Matthew and Yohanan ben Zaccai also dealt with Alvon, Mathias's jailkeeper. Who was becoming suspicious about the source of the gold he demanded from Matthew to keep their father safe. Miriam would have to do what Matthew could not without bringing suspicion to himself. Alvon must die. Soon. But she must first speak with Ya'el.

Miriam unwound the scarlet scarf from her upper arm. The small pouch sewn inside contained a message only Ya'el would understand—a place and time to meet. Checking to be sure no one was near, she raised two fingers to her mouth and, for a moment, was glad for the stillness in the air. The sharp whistle startled her mother.

"Miriam, what's gotten into you!" Rebecca jerked her head to look around them.

Miriam did not pay heed to her mother; she was watching Elian. When his eyes came up and toward her, she shook the red fabric and dropped it to the ground. Then Miriam took her mother's arm. "Let's go home," she said. Over her shoulder, she saw the boy's quick wave as he began trotting toward the scarf.

XXXVII

Augustus 69 CE

Jerusalem

The Upper City

Lately, the only thing that lightened her mother's spirit was the parrot Cicero's odd mutterings—almost human. So, Miriam was pleased to see her happy, even if only for the span of a dinner meal though it was overcast by the shadow of her father's absence. But she regretted the lie she had told to make it happen and the pretense she must continue to protect Ya'akov.

She watched her mother, still smiling, as she returned from walking Ya'akov out. So many norms and traditions had been set aside in these times. It was strange for her former betrothed to eat with just her and her mother. Miriam added to the strangeness by talking to him throughout the sparse meal. He had seemed pleasantly surprised.

Miriam shook her head sadly. Then donned one of Matthew's light cloaks and raced toward the rear courtyard, leaving her mother's dismayed question unanswered: "Where are you going now?"

A minute later, sweating and breathing heavily after running from behind her home, Miriam watched as Ya'akov entered the agora, busy on this sultry evening. A tease of wind stirred a little, and she turned her face into it, relishing the temporary coolness. As Miriam did, she saw Hananiah glide by without seeing her. He was stalking Ya'akov, who had stopped at a fruit stall and then moved toward the street she knew led to his family's house carrying his costly purchase. His parents had died in the Idumean slaughter Yohanan ben Levi had instigated a year before. The home had been vacant until his return, and he now lived there alone.

Hananiah's hands were tucked into his sleeves, and Miriam was alarmed since it probably meant he held a bared blade in one hand. The tall, lean knifemaker was much slighter than the heavier-built Ya'akov. Hananiah's rough tunic was dark red as he followed Ya'akov's broad back covered in white linen, only two arms lengths from the killer.

Miriam hurried to catch up to the two men as quietly as possible. Afraid to speak too loudly and draw Ya'akov's attention, she reached for Hananiah's shoulder just before the turn onto Ya'akov's street. The man spun with a hiss that quickly faded when he recognized her. The gleam of the dagger in his hand disappeared into his sleeve.

"Miriam...." Hananiah almost sounded pleased. But his head pivoted toward where Ya'akov had been in the street ahead. His eyes were those of a distracted predator, not wanting to lose sight of his prey.

"I saw you... and was glad of it." She managed the lie, for she wished to kill him even if she died. "I've been meaning to come to see you." That brought the killer's attention fully to her. She darted a look to make sure Ya'akov was gone. She knew Hananiah wouldn't kill Ya'akov on the street, but he might take the opportunity to sneak into his home. Then he would kill or perhaps wound him—as a warning. A vision of a bloodied Ya'akov shot a shudder through her.

"Can I talk with you?" Miriam asked as she drew him away under the canopy of one of the merchant stalls at the edge of the agora.

"Of course," Hananiah said, motioning her to a nearby table. His eyes seemed solid black in the swaying lantern hung from the overhead struts, the arcing glints the only thing that gave depth to his flat stare.

"You know my father is imprisoned," Miriam began, "but not for wrongdoing. Only because his beliefs do not match those of Yohanan ben Levi, and he—my whole family—does not like the Gischalan."

Hananiah nodded, his eyes bored into her as she continued.

"I overheard my brother Matthew speaking with someone about a treasure hidden in the city. Matthew is a Temple guard officer and won't look deeper into it. If he did, he'd be suspected of being involved... but we need the money for my father. If I look into it and find something more about any treasure, could you help me? My family must pay Yohanan ben Levi's jail keeper to keep my father safe... Of course, you would still have a large share of any treasure."

Hananiah leaned toward Miriam so suddenly and quickly that she almost flinched away. His lips brushed her cheek as he whispered, "I'll help you... but we must talk about afterward...."

Miriam closed her eyes, disgusted at the lies she must tell, even though this one also distracted Hananiah from Ya'akov for a short while. Ya'el was sure there was no hope of thwarting the legions assaulting Jerusalem since her brother's death. Nor could that now-dead emperor hold Gessius Florus accountable for his abuse. But the hint of treasure could be the lure needed—to allow them to send false information to Gessius Florus. Stoking his greed and leading him to a misstep could draw Roman authorities to his manipulations and perhaps even his punishment.

Miriam had no idea how they would ever know of that happening, but—for Ya'el's sake—Hananiah needed to live long enough to help it happen.

But as soon as she could... Miriam would kill Hananiah.

XXXVIII

Augustus 69 CE

Caesarea

The Port

"The last ship is in!" called the wharfmaster down the quay as the two dockmen tied off the bow and stern lines of the *Egeria*. Nicanor watched as Marinus checked the brow four sailors had just dragged into position. They lifted it onto two bladeless oar shafts that reached the dock. Attaching a line to their end, they slid it to the pier, where the two dockmen secured it to two iron rings inset in the stone surface. The sailors on the *Egeria* then pulled the shafts from beneath the gangway and anchored the ship's end of the brow to similar iron rings set into the ship's deck.

Marinus waved to Nicanor to follow him onto the dock, and Nicanor bent to lift his pack and shoulder it. He had one foot on the brow when he saw Anyte, robed in blue-bordered white, leave the cabin and cross the deck toward him, a tablet tucked under her arm. She stopped at the brow and smiled up at him.

"I did not wish to disturb you," Nicanor said in greeting. "I knew you were writing." He gestured at the stylus she still held. "I mean... I'm glad to get to see you before I leave. Thank you again for treating my wound. It healed quickly under your care."

"I hope your other wound heals as well."

"What other wound?" Nicanor shifted the pack containing clothes. He now wore a complete uniform for the first time since Brixellum. Marinus had known the quartermaster of the *legatus praetorians* at Paphos, who had provided him with the trappings of a senior centurion. Though he could officially wear the garb of a tribunus, a rank above a centurion, he didn't know if that rank a dead emperor had given him was still valid. Besides, he was more comfortable dressed as a centurion, strictly a soldier. He squinted at the young lady, wondering again what she meant as her smile gave way to an appraising look.

"I hope you find the woman you love."

Nicanor's face warmed, and he shook his head. "She's a friend in need of help. That's all."

"Still, I hope you find her and the place you seek to call your home." Anyte nodded toward her father, who stood on the dock, hands on his hips, checking the ship's dockside hull. "Troubled but good men deserve a home." She looked back up at him and reached to touch the leather cuff on his forearm. "I hope one day you'll come to visit us in Cenchrae. If she—your friend, this woman—is with you, bring her, too. My father is right... it's a place that can soothe the soul."

"Maybe one day I," he hesitated at the flash of her smile again, "maybe one day...." Nicanor bowed his head, and Anyte dipped hers in return.

On the dock, Nicanor joined Marinus, who now stood near the stern. "When you're in an eastern or southern port and need a ship, check the sterns for this." Marinus pointed an arm's length above his head at a deep-cut mark in a wood block. Nicanor could see the deep V shape with a vertical line rising even in the twilight. Halfway up its length, a rectangle contained the letter M within it. "All my ships now have one. Speak to the shipmaster or captain and show him this...." Marinus lifted his other hand. A metal circle from a leather cord dangled, within which the same symbol was carved into the wood. "Unless it's impossible, he'll carry you where you want to go or as close as he can get you." He held out the pendant to Nicanor.

Nicanor draped the cord around his neck, tucking the pendant inside his padded undertunic. "Thank you, Marinus." He looked up again at Anyte, still at the brow watching them. He returned her wave and smile. The dock was now empty. The workers had quickly dispersed as soon as they learned the *Egeria* was empty. It was a fact that had surprised Nicanor, but he was glad it allowed for better speed. He half-turned as a sailor came down the brow to mount a large lantern to one of its end posts. The man lighted it and returned to the ship with a nod to Nicanor.

"I hope you find her and can help her—your friend." Marinus's eyes twinkled in the lantern light. "I'll keep ships along this coast as often as possible and have ships regularly in Alexandria and Antioch." He smiled. "Remember what I said about making money...."

Nicanor almost admired the ship owner's profit-making from work done for the legions, even those in the war he was about to rejoin. That change in his perspective had surprised him at first. But he had learned too much to begrudge the man.

"Why not stay on board tonight?" Marinus asked.

"Because you sail on the early morning tide, it's better that I report in now. I might see General Vespasian this evening."

Marinus nodded. "I'd stay longer, but I have letters to deliver to Alexandria and, from there, replies to Rome."

Nicanor didn't ask about the letters... who they were to or from. He had left the intrigues of Rome behind him. The *imperium in imperio*, Antonia Caenis was knowledgeable about; the intrigues of the political realm within the physical. He looked forward to the legion structure that made sense to him and called for him simply to follow orders. *Can I still follow orders?* He felt he could, as long as the orders did not keep him from helping Cleo. If they did, he'd do what he must.

* * *

THE ENCAMPMENT

Nicanor, missing Carmenta even more, had passed up the offer of a cart ride to the camp, thinking he wanted to stretch his legs after nearly three weeks at sea. But now, drenched in sweat, he was fatigued from the day's heat that had continued into the evening. *Next time,* he thought, *accept the ride.* He approached the main gate and was passed through to report to the duty officer. After an hour of waiting, Nicanor—with the briefest regret—considered that an arriving *tribunus* might have been more speedily attended to. He followed a camp clerk to his temporary quarters.

Nicanor's tent was one of the dozens situated along a broad space between rows of other tents, the area lighted by campfires about 100 feet apart. He noticed a man-shaped target had been set at the far end of the space. And at his end, a group of men with bows and bundles of arrows argued and wagered. He watched for a moment, then turned inside and closed the flap of his tent. Shedding his uniform, hanging it from the center post peg, he drank from the wineskin Marinus had put in his pack. He wiped his lips with his hand and lay back on the cot. Nicanor heard the familiar sounds of soldiers at leisure outside, with the *thwang, hiss,* and *thunk* as nocked arrows flew to strike their target.

A memory of his first time in Rome brought a smile. Empress Poppaea had coaxed her friend Cleo into showing her archery prowess by besting Nicanor in a small contest. He and Yosef had thought it a joke until Cleo had done just that. He had seen how confidently she handled the bow, the surprising ease with which she drew it. Her steady arms, hands, eyes... and the arrow flying true to the center of its mark. A flush of pleasure and pride had flashed on her face, quickly replaced by a nod to herself that the result was what she expected. That moment—her action and reaction—was fixed in his mind. That impressed him perhaps even more than her resilience when they were adrift at sea after the *Salacia* went down when death seemed inevitable.

Cleo, with her bow, was clear in his mind. As he drifted to sleep, the smile remained as he thought, *green-feathered arrows*....

* * *

The next morning...

Vespasian's Praetorium

"Nicanor!" a voice behind him called. He turned to see a tall centurion walking quickly toward him. "When did you return?" Celsus Evander asked, gripping his friend's hand.

"Last night. I was just reporting to General Vespasian but learned he's—"

"Not back from Berytus yet." Celsus leaned closer. "He and General Titus have been meeting there with allies. The eastern legions and their commanders have declared support for him to become emperor."

Nicanor was not surprised. All he had heard from Antonia Caenis and the hints from Marinus had seemed to point to that eventuality. He wondered how Vespasian had reached that decision. The general seemed reluctant to become involved in what he disliked most: ambitious men's maneuverings. "And so, change continues for the empire…. he said.

"But, for the good of the empire, a better man must rule," Celsus replied.

"Agreed." Nicanor clasped his friend's shoulder. "Tell me… is Sayid with the 12th in Ptolemais? I think I'll go see him while I can."

"He's with the 5th Legion, *Macedonia*, one of General Cerealis's auxiliary units at Hebron. But the fighting is over now."

"Have you seen him since?"

"Yes, with the caravans carrying food from that region to supply the legions here." Celsus shook his head, a bemused look on his face.

"What about it?"

"You were right about needing help when he returned to the 12th. He was mistreated in Ptolemais. And someone tried to kill him. I stopped it and arranged to have him come here as my aide-clerk.

Then he talked with his father and insisted I help him get assigned to combat." Celsus shook his head again. "I know it had something to do with his father disrespecting him... but to fight when he did not have to..."

Nicanor blinked at hearing someone had tried to kill Sayid and that he had finally found and talked with his father. But that explained the young Syrian's actions.

"I must go now," Celsus said, waving a sheaf of parchment, "but come to the legion quartermaster's office at sundown, and we'll go to taberna to sit and talk."

* * *

That evening...

THE TRADERS TABERNA

The taberna was on the city's eastern end, on the main avenue but away from the port and brothels. "I come here since it's quieter—mostly locals, merchants, and traders," Celsus told Nicanor as they drank at a table near the front. "But we can find one livelier."

"This one suits me." Nicanor drained his second mug of beer. "Finish yours, and I'll get us another."

Minutes later, handling mugs filled to the brim, Nicanor turned from the barman's counter and bumped into a squat, powerfully built man who had just entered. The man jostled him aside as if clearing a path for the man who followed him. Cursing, Nicanor stooped to pick up the spilled mugs. He heard someone say, "Drusus, wait," as he grasped them and straightened up, and before him was a pair of legs, bared by the man lifting his robe to enter. Nicanor noticed old burn scars and the richness of the robe as he straightened to face the nobleman. The short, thickset man was now at his side. The nobleman's look of disdain vanished as he leaned forward and peered at the centurion in surprise.

Nicanor gritted his teeth as the man, still with that look, turned to the group of what seemed to be merchants and said, "Go ahead; the room should be ready. I'll join you shortly."

He peered again at Nicanor, and a smile that did not reach his cold eyes spread over his face. "Well, centurion... it's been so long," said Gessius Florus. "How interesting it is to see you again... here."

XXXIX

Augustus 69 CE

Caesarea

Gessius Florus's Villa

Gessius Florus shoved aside the message from Krateros that reported that the Thracian captain had still been unable to kill the Syrian auxiliary. The legion units at Hebron were alert to attacks on anyone. The few insurgent incidents from surviving rebels hiding nearby had been dealt with harshly. The Thracians could not get to him without reprisal as long as Sayid was surrounded by other soldiers in the field. Florus let Krateros and the two men he had taken with him watch the Syrian. The man was unimportant, though Florus would find it very satisfying to question him about Cleo... and then kill him.

He put down the reading crystal and rubbed his eyes. The device still helped him, but only for a while, and then anything he tried to read blurred over. The Pompeian craftsman had told him that his clients sometimes returned to him to craft a more potent lens as their sight worsened. He would send for a new lens, but he feared the inevitable. After years of diminishing eyesight, his mother and several of her ancestors had become *caecus*. He could expect complete blindness if he lived much longer.

He was on the verge of accomplishing his plan of six years before, the plan both his father and his uncle had doubted would succeed. His arrival in Clazomenae with one wagonload of Jewish treasure the month before had quieted them and given him the pleasure of seeing their expressions. He had done as he promised to make up for his financial missteps. The first taste of the Jewish treasure had whetted their appetite, and he wanted to see their faces when he brought home their portion of the treasure still to be taken.

Just as he had initially planned for himself within his agreement with Nero, he was hiding at least half of all he took from the Jews—it was his. Nero was dead, and now he had only Vitellius to string along. The new emperor served his purpose and offered imperial protection in exchange for funneling a large share of the treasure to him. And now, it seemed Vitellius was being replaced by yet another new emperor who knew nothing about his plan to steal the Jewish treasure. Possibly it would be Vespasian, his spies had reported, which concerned Florus differently. Now he could plan for all the riches of the Jews. Some of it would go to his father and uncle. But he would hide for himself a sizable portion with his *argentarii* in Alexandria.

Florus's relatives in Sycaminum had swapped out with bags of sand the treasure in the two wagons they'd captured from the Jews. Then they'd resealed the wagons with the original copper sheathing. The Thracians who had formerly guarded his warehouse, hiding the captured treasure, still believed it to be there. And he had made a point of continuing to sow that belief with Krateros, the mercenary leader. But—as was known only to him and Drusus—the contents of one wagon had gone with him on a small vessel to Clazomenae. The treasure from the other wagon went to Alexandria, hidden deep within a shipment of sand.

Drusus, who had accompanied the treasure, had seen it delivered to the *argentarii*. Then the diminutive Heracles had cut away a last loose thread in Alexandria. He had strangled the Jew glassmaker, Meshulam, who owned the sand ship, and then killed his family for good measure. The man's son, Ehud, who had spied for him in Jerusalem, was dead.

It did not matter if he could steal the Jews' treasure only a little at a time; that might be best. His men had captured a Levite from Jerusalem who, before he died in agony, had told them how the Jews had worked to hide their treasure outside of Jerusalem. Each temple team verbally received location details—they had to memorize them—to take them to a safe hiding spot. The Levite had given them the names of two Temple Guard officers in Jerusalem who had read those details—Matthew ben Mathias and Eleasar ben Ananias. He must capture one of them or the guide they read from. If the Jews had changed plans to hide the treasure within or closer to the city, those two men would know about that, too.

But something or someone had drawn too much scrutiny upon Florus, and he was sure Vespasian had spies watching him. With the last assassination attempt he had orchestrated, he had hoped to shift the general's focus to worry about Marcus Otho. But Otho was now dead and no threat to anyone. So Vespasian's attention might swing back to him, which was one of the primary reasons he'd spent the last three months away from Caesarea. Florus had traveled from Alexandria to Antioch to Clazomenae. In between, he had stopped at Tyrus after Governor Mucianus's visit. He had planted seeds there, suggesting that only Vitellius would continue to treat that city favorably. And those working for him there to tend to the crop of misinformation could not be traced to him. All he had done made him appear to be a loyal subject of the new emperor, Vitellius.

Florus had returned, pleased until he saw that cursed centurion friend of Cleo's. He pulled a sheet of vellum to him and picked up his pen, dipping the nib in the inkpot. He held it poised to write as thoughts spilled through his mind. Was the centurion's return tied to Cleo? Standing that close to him, he had seen the venom in the man's eyes. Though Nicanor had given him the barest nod of acknowledgment without speaking, he knew the centurion detested him.

It was time to make Galerius Senna earn his keep beyond what he had done in the past, undermining Cestius Gallus, the former governor, and then-commander of the 12th Legion. Gallus was out of the way now, Jerusalem was doomed, and Florus knew more of the Jews' treasure was within reach. Senna—or his pandering First Centurion, Tyrannius Priseus—must find him a spy within the legion headquarters. Someone must watch Nicanor and kill the centurion if he proves an obstacle.

Florus folded the message into quarters and closed it where the corners met with a blob of wax. He blew on the wax, pressed his seal, and called for Irad, who came quickly. "Find Drusus and send him to me," he commanded. "When you see him leave, bring your brother."

He sat back, his stinging, blurry eyes forgotten. In his mind, everything was clear. He knew what he must do. Drusus would carry his orders to Galerius Senna, who would find him a man to deal with Nicanor. And Boaz would bring into Jerusalem a man more reliable than the Alexandrian Hananiah had proved to be. Florus reached down to rub his legs, remembering the burning pain caused by Cleo and the Syrian Sayid. They both would pay. But now, more important than vengeance was to capture this Matthew ben Mathias or Eleasar ben Ananias and learn what they knew about the location of the rest of the vast Jewish treasure. *Mathew ben Mathias,* Florus considered, *was not Vespasian's Jewish prisoner Yosef—Cleo's friend—also named ben Mathias?*

XL

Augustus 69 CE

Caesarea

The horse trader Todros, Celsus had told Nicanor, was located just outside the city's Herodian walls at the nexus of the *decumanus maximus*, the main west-east road through the town that ended at a major north-south trade route. Nicanor turned the mount south—it was one of the *paraveredi*, the legion's extra horses he had drawn from the stablemaster. *Ahead on the right must be it,* he thought, through the gate of the fenced area surrounding the cluster of three new-looking buildings. The central and largest was the stable, a mudbrick structure.

The sound of riders behind him brought his head around. A dozen passed through the gate of the large walled villa across the road and just north of the junction. They thundered, churning dust and dirt until they reached the paved portion that began the road east toward the city. His eyes went back to the villa. Its walls had recently been raised, maybe thickened. And what looked like newly constructed platforms—not entirely watchtowers—topped the wall at intervals, a man at each. He thought, *A cautious man owns it and seems too worried*. Caesarea now had the largest concentration of legionaries Nicanor had seen since leaving Rome. No rebel attack was likely, even if some rich man's villa lay outside the city walls.

As Nicanor dismounted, a man came from the smaller structure beside the stable. "I'm told you're an honest trader," Nicanor said in greeting, "And I wish to buy a horse." The man, a Greek to judge by his dress, bowed, his long dark beard brushing his chest, and laughed.

"Of course—aren't all merchants honest?" The man's lips curled into a cunning grin.

"Celsus Evander, the legion quartermaster commander, tells me you are."

The slyness ended as fast as it had appeared. "Then, with you, centurion... I shall be honest. I wish to sell you a horse, but"—he crooked a finger for Nicanor to follow him.

Inside the stable, Nicanor walked upon stone floors more level than the paved road, covered by a litter of fresh straw. Storage bins of what smelled like barley were aligned along one wall, and there were several stalls, each with its own water trough. *No doubt this is all reserved for his finest horses,* Nicanor thought. This trader was doing well. Nicanor followed the Greek past empty stalls to the rear, where broad doors swung open onto a large corralled field with a single white-and-pale-gray horse.

"Yesterday, I sold all I had," the Greek trader continued. Spreading his hands palms up in mock remorse, he did not have a selection for the tribunus to choose from.

"Except for that one," Nicanor pointed at the big horse stolidly chewing and staring at them.

"Yes." The Greek, hands on his hips, studied the animal and blew through his lips. "They deemed him the least spirited. But I will have more soon."

"When?"

"Two weeks... maybe a few days more."

Nicanor looked through the length of the stable back to where his mount waited. The legion's extra horses always seemed under-sized or ill-suited to him. "I don't want to wait that long. Is there another trader you know with decent stock? Or tell me who just bought what you had, and maybe I can convince him to sell me one." Nicanor watched the man quiver. It was a sign he had seen in many merchants over the years—they were terrified at the thought of losing a sale.

"The others are truly men you cannot trust," the Greek said as he puffed up. "And the man whose major domus bought all my horses yesterday seems to need them." They had walked back through the stable, and shading his eyes with one hand, the trader looked toward the fortified villa. "There," he jutted his black-bearded chin in its direction. "I'm told he is an imperial tax collector." The Greek cast a sideways look at Nicanor and shrugged. "But it is curious... to need so many men that come and go."

"Do you know his name?"

"The major domus's name is Irad; I believe Lord Florus is his master's name."

Nicanor ground his teeth. Since seeing Cleo's husband at the taberna, he had struggled with a need to smash the man's face for what he had done to her. At sea with Marinus, Nicanor had explained more of what he had done to help Cleo and why he and Graius had sought Marcus Otho's help to protect her. When he heard Gessius Florus's name, Marinus had told him he knew of the man and his family in Clazomenae. And he had a warning: "They're evil men, Nicanor. Cutthroat traders and predatory moneylenders."

Nicanor studied Florus's villa through a haze of dust still hanging in the sun's glare. Clamping down his anger, he repeated what he had told himself since leaving Puteoli. *I must be wise in how I go after Florus.* He had to find out why the tax collector had hired so many men and what he was up to. Acting too quickly out of anger would be stupid. It would get him killed, and who then could help Cleo? He gave his legion mount another measuring look, nodded to the trader, and gestured over his shoulder. "Let's go look at that white horse again."

* * *

THE ROMAN ENCAMPMENT

"This is the horse, Todros sold you?" asked Celsus Evander as he stepped from his office to meet Nicanor, who stood beside the horse, his hand gripping its bridle. Man and animal had the same expression—a steady, serious stare.

"His name's Albus."

"You named a white horse 'White'?" Celsus said with a smirk. "Really?" His smile dimmed when Nicanor did not return it.

"My last three horses had names with meaning... and I cared a lot for them. Abigieus died at Antipatris, forty miles from here, from wounds received at Beth Horon. I left Tempestas behind after the Siege at Yotapta when I had to go to Rome. Then I left Carmenta back in Rome when I returned here. I'll keep things simple with this one—no attachment." Nicanor glanced at the horse, who flicked a side-eye at him and stared straight ahead as they walked through the camp. Minutes later, they reached the praetorium.

"General Vespasian's ship is in?" Nicanor asked the senior quartermaster, who nodded.

"A runner alerted the camp when its captain signaled from outside the jetties," the man said. "They've docked by now. And a courier arrived just before you. Sayid should be here tomorrow."

"Good..."

Celsus studied his friend, surprised he did not sound pleased. Over their first beer at the taberna, Nicanor had seemed to look forward to seeing his friend Sayid and General Vespasian. That had altered with the spilled beer and the moment he had witnessed Nicanor's exchange with the nobleman. Nicanor had not talked about it afterward but had clearly known him.

Nicanor and Celsus stopped outside the main entrance to the praetorium, where Nicanor tethered Albus to one of the hitching posts. From that corner, they saw two mounted, scarlet-caped officers in resplendent uniforms. They reined in before the building, and a cart containing two soldiers and another man rumbled to a stop next to them. The two generals dismounted as the two soldiers helped the man, bound in chains, from the wagon.

Nicanor strode toward them on the broad flag-stoned walkway. "Generals… it's good to see you both. I'm glad to report for duty with you." Vespasian and Titus both had slight smiles as they returned his greeting. Behind them, Nicanor saw the chained man stand up after arranging the shackles attached to his ankles. He was smooth-shaven and—it seemed odd to Nicanor—wore Roman clothing of good quality. Then, all at once, Nicanor's jaw dropped.

"Is that you, Yosef?" he murmured.

XLI

September 69 CE

Jerusalem

City of David

Miriam felt the rising sun's glow that also cast its aura around the crest of the Mount of Olives as she passed through the Huldah Gates and down the steps into the City of David. She had gone to bed angry with Matthew, and her agitation had not lessened during her fitful sleep. Miriam hoisted the bread, cheese, and fruit bag higher on her shoulder. She carefully looked through the area as she approached the hidden entrance to the tunnel leading to King David's Tomb. Even at the early hour, there were people already about, and more than usual were foreign. They moved in clusters, their dress, and manner unlike those of Jerusalem's citizens. She waited for several of them to disperse or move away from her.

Miriam leaned her staff—once Zechariah's—against the old wall and again shifted the bag she'd filled with food for Rachel and Leah. If only she had not been gone when they had arrived frightened and out of breath the evening before, seeking shelter from Yonatan. Miriam had heard he had begun beating Leah again, and more than once, she had thought she should stop his cruelty. Maybe it was time for 'The Hand' to reappear.

Miriam shook off her anger as she quickly slipped between the rough-cut and forlorn standing stones that seemed of no importance but hid the tunnel's narrow entrance. Matthew had brought Rachel and Leah to this, the only secure hiding spot he thought safe for them. But Miriam had hoped to continue to use it as her own. Now, too many people were aware of it. Had Nahum talked about it? Essenes still traveled to and from the city. And what about Yohanan ben Zaccai? The old rabbi was talkative—she'd warned Matthew long ago about his rattling on about how King David's Tomb should be resealed. What if someone overheard him and came to explore? Deep inside, they'd find the tomb's treasure chamber! Even the thinnest rumor would bring looting men from Yohanan ben Levi or Simon bar Giora. And many other greedy men were not allied with the two faction leaders.

Maybe the treasure should be moved. Matthew had already asked for her help to find a safe location below ground for some of the Temple treasures they could no longer smuggle out of the city. *I must talk with him about that*, she thought as she stepped into a cleft in the stone and the shadows that quickly enfolded her in complete darkness.

* * *

KING DAVID'S TOMB

Miriam followed the now-familiar passage without a torch, knowing she was near the entrance to the antechamber even before she saw the dim glow of a lantern inside. "It's Miriam!" she called out to not alarm the two women. As she entered the chamber, she almost smiled when she saw Rachel.

"You can put that down," Miriam said. "It's a little heavy."

Rachel lowered and then set down the iron-bound cudgel Miriam had long ago brought there from the depths of the tomb in case it was needed. "It *is* heavy," Rachel said with a wan smile.

Miriam saw the tear tracks on her friend's dusty, weary face. Behind her, still trembling at the alarm of Miriam's entrance, Leah also betrayed her grief and exhaustion... and more. She was utterly dejected. One eye was swollen shut, and that side of her face was livid with a bruise from her brow to her jaw.

"Thank you for helping us, Miriam," Leah said, coming forward into the lantern light, and Miriam gasped a bit to see her friend's split lips.

"I fear Yonatan will kill me as soon as he finds me," Leah murmured.

"He'll have to murder me, too," said Rachel, bending to grasp the handle of the cudgel again.

"What happened this time?" Miriam asked. It had been a while since the last real beating, but Leah had suffered her husband's abuse for years.

"This time," Leah's hand went to her face without touching it, "was one too many. I told him I was divorcing him... he screamed that he'd see me dead before that."

"He'd been drinking," Rachel added. "I shoved him away from Leah before he could hurt her farther, and he hit his head as he fell. While he was dazed, we ran to your house, and Matthew was there. After we caught our breath, we decided that being there put your family at risk and told Matthew we would go. 'Where?' he asked. But we could not think of anywhere. So, he brought us here, showed us the cistern, and said someone would bring food for us."

Rachel waved her hand around the chamber. "What is this place?"

"It's safe," Miriam said, though she did not know for how long. "That's what matters."

* * *

THE LOWER CITY, POOL OF SILOAM

Miriam sat in one of the stepped corners above the *Breikhat HaShiloah*. The vast—nearly 4000-square-foot—rock-cut pool that she, Yosef, Matthew, and Ehud swam in as children and as they matured, sometimes with Leah and Rachel. There she saw Yosef kiss Leah for the first time. Pleased and embarrassed, Leah looked away, her face turning a dark red in the summer sun. *And that face is battered and beaten now*, Miriam muttered. She and Rachel had finally convinced Leah to sleep, that she was safe. Then Rachel and Miriam had gone to another alcove to talk. There, Rachel told Miriam what she already knew but that Rachel had never said aloud.

And now Miriam had to sit with all that grief and guilt stirred up.

"When Yosef left to live with the Essenes," Rachel had begun, "Leah realized they would never be together. Our father was already arranging her marriage to Yonatan, and she thought she could learn to love him as much as she did Yosef. But she couldn't, and that stirred from anger to cruelty inside Yonatan—he had hidden it until they were wed. And... and..."

Miriam could see the revelation of years-buried truth was difficult but freeing for Rachel. "And I thought... with Leah married..." Rachel looked at her friend to gauge how she would take these words. She took a deep breath and said more quickly, "Somehow, I thought that when Yosef returned, he might fall in love with *me*. So, I was pleased my sister had married another man... even once I realized how horrible he was. Now, I hate myself..."

Miriam had let her talk and empty herself of the cold, sour laments that needed to come out. Finally, Rachel said, "I'm sorry. I cry about 'what was and is' for Leah and for my own grief, but I forget yours. I hope Ya'akov can—"

Miriam rose to cut Rachel off. Rachel's words had twisted like a knife in her chest and stirred the regrets and guilt she held within. Miriam needed no more pity for Ehud's death. Nor did she need someone's fantasy that Ya'akov could heal that wound she had inflicted on herself.

As Miriam had turned to leave without speaking, Rachel stopped her. "Wait!" she said, going to another alcove and bringing out two objects: a woman's woolen shawl and a wooden top. "I found these here, Miriam. Was someone hiding here before us? Are we safe?"

Miriam had forestalled the question with a raised palm, telling Rachel, "I'll bring more food tomorrow." Then she had fled.

Now, setting aside thoughts of Rachel, Miriam swirled her feet in the water, enjoying its coolness. She longed for the coming fall, though she knew each day drew them closer to the inevitable confrontation with the Romans. She thought instead of Ya'el and their last meeting. Ya'el had been adamant that they must use Hananiah to discover what Gessius Florus was up to. And then they should try to get that information to Vespasian. If Miriam could get a message to him showing that a Roman nobleman responsible for starting the war continued to act secretly in Judea for some selfish purpose against the interests of the empire. Maybe Vespasian would be willing to parlay before resorting to further battle.

By all accounts, Cleo had said Yosef was still alive, and why *was* that if Vespasian was not considering that course of action? For that, Yosef could be the bridge.

Miriam had disagreed with Ya'el's optimism, but she would let Hananiah live for now. She would continue to foster a friendship with him to see if it led to something helpful for her people. Whether yes or no, at some point, Hananiah *would* die.

Miriam swung her feet out of the water, dried them with the hem of her cloak, and slipped her sandals back on. She went up four *ashlar* stone steps to the esplanade and crossed the street. The 26-foot-wide pilgrimage road was paved with enormous stone slabs, forming a street that climbed 400 feet in its half-mile run to the Temple Enclosure. Minutes later, where the road made its more northerly bend, Miriam heard sobbing ahead and looked for the source.

The crying woman was at the base of a pyramidal stone podium set off the road. It was crafted of *meleke*, the finer stone used in many public buildings, including the Temple. Yosef had told her about this platform. Many stopped to rest at it when they entered the city for the most important religious observances: *Pesach, Shavuot, and Sukkot*. The *Even Hato'eem*, the Stone of Losses, was where people came to stand and proclaim what they had lost, hoping someone could find and return to them. And whenever someone found something that would be missed, they came here to describe it and return it to its owner. But the racking sobs of the prostrate woman declared a loss with no hope of restoration, her wails coming from a deep well of sorrow within her.

Miriam knelt as others continued their way up and down the street. She silently rested her forehead against the woman's brow, feeling her shuddering breaths that, after a moment, steadied. As the women quieted, Miriam stood and, not needing to know what the woman mourned, turned up the street, carrying the weight of her own unspoken sorrows. She must get home so that she could follow, unseen, when Matthew went to his meeting with the man Alvon, Yohanan ben Levi's jailer. After Matthew paid him, 'The Hand' would see that Alvon never threatened her father again and would never take another bribe.

Behind her, the cries welled up again.

XLII

SEPTEMBER 69 CE

JERUSALEM

THE UPPER CITY

Miriam hurried across the viaduct connecting the Temple Enclosure to the Upper City. She felt the sun hot against her cheek and knew she had lingered too long in the Lower City. She had strayed from her direct route to the Temple to take a longing look at Zechariah's place. A moment to remember the old blind Sicarii and settle her mind. He, too, had lost much to the Romans... his wife and daughter. But as she approached the shop, she saw strangers and stopped. If a family had moved in, that would have felt right, a continuation of the old goodness. Zechariah would have been happy that his empty shop and home now offered a dwelling to those in need and would have welcomed them.

But he never would have welcomed the group of swarthy, angry men, most with swords at their hips, within his old shop. She shook her head again. She had watched, wondering, *Have I removed all my things from there?* She believed she had taken everything to King David's Tomb and then to her home once her family knew her secrets.

But she had also thought she'd removed all of Ya'el and Elian from the tomb, too. And she hadn't. Now Rachel was suspicious—Miriam had seen the questioning look in her eye. She could not know that Ya'el and Elian had remained in Jerusalem. Miriam could not risk these rough men finding anything of hers or Zechariah's she might have left behind. But she'd waited a while and found no opportunity to enter the place and check.

So, now she hurried, hoping Matthew had not yet gone to make the payment to Alvon. Crossing the agora, she avoided armed men in twos and threes on every street—they were always drawn to the unaccompanied to accost and harass them. Her mother had asked her to stop going alone, for the fighting factions made everything dangerous. But that was impossible. For the hundredth time, she wished Ya'el was not forced to hide. She felt very alone.

Miriam had nearly reached the front street gate to her home when she realized her preoccupation had been a mistake. Zechariah had constantly warned her: "Always be aware of anyone who seems to follow or come close to you," he'd said. And now she recalled the heavy tread of trailing steps had been behind her since the agora. A large hand painfully gripped her shoulder and spun her around before she could turn herself.

"Where is Leah?" Yonatan growled, his voice low and menacing. His eyes darted side to side to see if they were alone.

Because they were alone, he squeezed harder, digging his fingers into her flesh, and she gasped. Miriam had been carrying Zechariah's staff in one hand, angled down, its mid-shaft aligned with her forearm. She snapped it up, cracking into Yonatan's wrist and breaking his grip as she took two steps back from him. She needed room.

"I would not tell you if I knew," Miriam spat at him. "I'm glad she's left you... glad she's divorcing you. And we'll help her... see that her certificate is filed granting a divorce no matter how you protest or what you do."

Yonatan took a step forward and paused as the sharpened metal ferrule of the staff came up to point at his chest, and they both heard a noise from the house behind him.

"Matthew, come quickly!" Rebecca called back through the open door.

Yonatan darted a glance at Miriam's mother, then back. Miriam could see in his eyes the prospect of facing Matthew, and his sword was far different from assaulting a woman. Even one with a staff she could use in ways he could not.

"Your father is already in our hands... it's a dangerous time for families like yours, Miriam. And being a woman won't protect you." He glared at her, waiting to see the effect of his intimidation.

"I don't fear you or your master. You obey Yohanan ben Levi like the dog you are." She angled the staff's tip toward the side of Yonatan's head. "Don't threaten me, my family, Leah, or Rachel... or you'll lose more than an ear." Though she would be the one to take it. She did not need Hananiah stepping in as he had done once before, thinking that protecting her would make her more willing to come to him.

Yonatan turned away with a dismissive chop of his hand in the air. Miriam waited until he was down the street and out of sight before joining her mother.

"Where's Matthew?" she asked, looking behind her mother into the house.

"I lied," Rebecca said and stepped inside, drawing Miriam after her. "Eleasar ben Ananias has returned, and he went to speak to him before he meets Yohanan ben Levi's jailer at sundown."

Miriam looked over her shoulder at the sun dipping low in the west. "Where's he meeting the cur?" she asked.

"You should not go, Miriam... let Matthew deal with him."

Miriam moved toward the stairs, her mother following. "That's just it, Mother," Miriam said irritably over her shoulder. "Matthew can't deal with him. He cannot do what must be done to end the man's greed. If he did, Yohanan ben Levi would target Father... *and* Matthew. I will not lose another brother."

Miriam reached the landing, entered her room, and began undressing. She felt her mother stare at the forearm sheaths as her undertunic came off. It was the first time she had seen her armed. She adjusted one of the daggers and saw a bar of sunlight through the shutter gleam against the metal.

Rebecca's expression revealed she finally understood that Miriam had actually done what she had confessed to her family.

"Your father never told you the old stories of Deborah and Ya'el... but he told your brothers," Rebecca said, musing. "Yes, the name Yossi chose for the child he lost, the name he gave Cleo. It is a good name." She sighed and said, "I thought only to show you examples of strong women, and I thought you should learn their stories, but your father did not."

Rebecca held out her hand to indicate the dagger sheaths. "It seems you needed no examples, but I will tell you now." Miriam moved aside as her mother sat on her bed and prepared to speak, so Miriam took the stool.

"Deborah was the only female judge of our people over a thousand years ago, during our war with the Kings of Canaan. In that war, she often ordered the killing of men, including the Canaanite general, Sisera. Hearing that call, the woman Ya'el lured the enemy into her tent, then, when he dozed after a meal, stabbed him through the head with a tent peg, killing him." Rebecca pointed at her daughter's knives. "Those look much deadlier—as if they would not take as much strength as Ya'el's rage gave her with the tent peg."

Miriam rose then, with a grim smile, her mother's eyes on her. She thought of those long-ago heroines as she finished dressing in her disguise: dark tunic, darker light-weight cloak, and a cowl, her hair tightly pulled back under a brown headscarf. She picked up Zechariah's staff and asked, "Where is Matthew meeting this man... Alvon?"

*　*　*

The sun was half-sunk behind the three towers along the western outer wall of the city. Hippicus, Phasael, and Mariamne—each over a hundred feet high—rose into the purpling twilight sky and cast long-fingered shadows on the street. Miriam moved across the narrow and broad swaths of shadows. She followed Alvon, who had just walked away from Matthew, where they'd met outside the building where her father and others were held.

Miriam was not surprised to see the man's destination—the palace. Yohanan ben Levi had displaced the affluent family that had lived in the former home of Antipas, King Herod's youngest son. The jailer did not hurry—he moved with the confidence of a bully who was never confronted. The pouch draped over his shoulder on a cord and hung heavily against his hip with the weight of the gold bars—two mina—Matthew had given him. The man patted the bag as he walked.

Miriam strode through a thinning crowd, intent, as the dark fell and people left the streets for the safety of their homes. She made no more sound than a soft breeze as she got ahead of the man, increased her pace, and slipped around the corner he would soon reach. He would turn there toward the guarded entry to the palace. Miriam drew a blade from its sheath. Her flesh prickled with anticipation and fear of what she was about to do. She had never overcome that fear.

As the jailer made the turn, she yanked him close, and the large man stopped his instinctive struggle when the Sicarii dagger slightly pierced the soft skin beneath his chin.

"Here!" the man blurted loudly and shrugged off the bag. The two gold bars spilled out at his feet, making a dull gleam on the street. "Take what I have."

Miriam pushed the knife tip in farther. "Some don't need gold to do what's right. Some don't need to be paid to stop those who do wrong." The blade plunged in and across, a smooth arc through the man's fleshy throat. His blood sprayed her as he sank to the ground, blood cascading down his tunic. Miriam stooped to return the gold bars to the pouch and laid them on his chest.

The ebbing of life, not the weight of the gold, slowed his breathing until it stopped. Alvon's eyes glassily stared at her as she grabbed a handful of the soaked tunic. She dragged the body closer to the wall and pressed a bloody hand upon it. From the sash at her waist, she took out a stick of charcoal and wrote above the handprint:

Free those you hold unjustly, Yohanan ben Levi, or I will come for you next.

Final Siege

She wiped her hands on the sash and let out the breath she had been holding. A clatter, likely a guard, came from the direction of the Gischalan's palace. Miriam ran into the night, thinking of her mother's story.

XLIII

SEPTEMBER 69 CE

CAESAREA

THE ROMAN ENCAMPMENT

Nicanor muttered to the horse, "Steady...." But Albus had no twitch to him, no impatience for the treat of an apple, carrot, or handful of salted barley that always came at day's end. Though his earlier mounts had needed such instruction, Albus would likely not grow spoiled. He was impassive and let things come to him.

Since buying Albus, Nicanor had put him through his paces and worked on his gait each day. The animal was a fine runner, though he did not show Carmenta's speed. He did not lose his wind or founder when pushed hard over distance. Though Nicanor doubted the animal had the endurance and strength of Abigieus. Thankfully, he had not shown the sharp temper of Tempestas, who had been a challenge. Albus was what he seemed—a stolid horse without quirks. But his eyes showed that he silently observed everything around him. Oddly, he seemed wise.

Setting down the brush, Nicanor pulled on coarse-palmed leather gloves and ran his hands over Albus's back and neck to smooth his coat, still damp from washing up after a day of riding. *And gauging each other*, Nicanor thought as he looked around the three-horse stall that fronted his new quarters. It was the standard barracks configuration, with animals in front on the *castra's* main road and living quarters in the back. He was with the row of officers closest to Vespasian's headquarters.

Albus had the entire space to himself, and Nicanor enjoyed his own living area, the extra room a benefit Vespasian gave his most senior officers. *And I like it*, Nicanor had to admit to himself, though he immediately regretted the thought. Not 600 feet away at the praetorium, Yosef lived in a cell, still chained. At least he was not secured to a post as he had been in Ptolemais. And it seemed from his recent meetings with Vespasian and Titus that Yosef's status was changing.

Still, that did not absolve Nicanor of the guilt he felt that he rarely thought about his friend, hardly through his whole imprisonment.

But, he rationalized, *so much has happened since last we met*. He wondered if they could be friends again. He had asked that Yosef be allowed to visit him or that he go to see Yosef without guards. General Vespasian had said he would consider it.

"Well... we live...."

Nicanor looked across Albus's back to see Yosef standing in chains at the entrance, with Celsus Evander at his side.

"That's what you said," Yosef continued with a smile as Sayid entered behind him, "after the wreck of the *Salacia* and again after the fire in Rome."

"And again, to me, after Beth Horon," Sayid added.

Nicanor smiled at his two friends. "In Rome, I remember you two saved Lady Cleo's bird from the fire... what was its name?"

"Cicero," Sayid said with a shake of his head. "That parrot did not like me. Yosef saved it when I couldn't... then you saved me and the old man—Lady Cleo's major domus, the old man."

"His name was Graius," Nicanor said softly, "and when I returned to Rome, he was a great help and died saving me." Seeing their puzzled expressions, he added, "I'll tell you that story another time," and shook off that memory. "The last few years, I've seen many good men die." He held out a hand to Sayid as if to offer the remembrance: "At Beth Horon... Yotapta...." He saw Celsus nod at that, his eyes darting toward Yosef. The Jew had been the rebel commander of that city, and Celsus had been badly wounded in the siege.

Yosef met Celsus's look, then locked eyes with Nicanor. "Many have died on both sides and more will, unless...." Yosef looked away, and Nicanor pondered Vespasian's plan for his Jewish prisoner again. Nicanor had not wanted to judge his friend. And Yosef had not—to his knowledge—contributed any information to Vespasian that would harm the Judeans or even help Rome. So, it must be as Titus had mentioned—the prophecy Yosef had voiced when he was brought before Vespasian after his capture at Yotapta had resonated with the general. Now it seemed to be coming true. So, Vespasian kept Yosef close to him. From what Nicanor had observed, he used him as a scribe. *But for how long, and to what end?*

The silence grew awkward, and then Sayid broke it. "It is good to see you, Nicanor." He came forward to stroke Albus's neck. "He's as big as Abigieus—is he as fine a mount?"

Nicanor saw how the Syrian favored one arm, slowly raising it to run his hand along Albus's back. *Or maybe it's his shoulder*, he thought. "Albus is not like him, and I don't plan to try him in battle." Nicanor closed his eyes and saw again with a pang the mound of dirt covering Abigieus's body. Wounded and staggering, Nicanor had made it from the valley of dead at Beth Horon to where the legion had retreated to Antipatris. There, he found Sayid had buried his horse to keep it from being butchered for food by the legion, as most carcasses were after a battle. Abigieus had been dying already as he carried Sayid to safety. Nicanor had remained behind, commanding a decoy cohort to fool the rebels so the legion could escape.

Nicanor looked at Yosef, knowing he believed the war should never have started. "Most of my command—over 400 men—died at Beth Horon," he admitted. He draped a rough blanket from a peg on the back wall over Albus. The horse turned his head to look at him and gave a slight bob as Nicanor left his side.

"Celsus," he said as he walked over to the legion command quartermaster, who had been silent, "thank you." He gripped the man's shoulder.

"For what?"

"You must have agreed to be Yosef's escort, so General Vespasian would let him come."

"Yes," Celsus admitted, "and he arranged for me to temporarily resume my former duties and remain here for a while." Nicanor noticed Sayid's unaccustomed stern look, and Celsus repeated, "Temporarily. Then I return to my unit."

"Yosef gave his word he would not try to escape... as if he could." Celsus motioned toward the shackles on Yosef's wrists and ankles.

Nicanor turned to his old friends and said, "It is good to see you both again—and together."

"We live...." Yosef said again as he settled on the camp stool Sayid unfolded for him. He reached down to rub the scars on his ankles. "But what about Cleo?" He looked up at Nicanor, and they both slid their eyes to Celsus, who noticed.

"I cannot leave him alone," he pointed at Yosef, "even with you, Nicanor. But I will report nothing about what I hear."

After a moment, Nicanor nodded to Sayid and Yosef. "I trust him."

"But," Celsus glanced out the door and shook his head, "you don't have long. General Vespasian wants you in his office at sundown."

"Why?" asked Nicanor.

"While I was with him, a courier delivered several letters from Rome. He leafed through them as we spoke and then said to tell you that one is for you."

XLIV

September 69 CE

Caesarea

The Roman Encampment, Vespasian's Praetorium

When Nicanor arrived, one sentry was lighting the large lanterns hung on either side of the praetorium's entrance while another entered to tell the general's aide of Nicanor's arrival. The aide announced him at General Vespasian's private office entrance three minutes later.

"Reporting as ordered, general," Nicanor said as he entered to find the general and his son bowed over the vellum sheets in their hands. Vespasian looked up. "Sit, Nicanor." He motioned toward the chair next to Titus in front of his desk. Moving the sheets around, Vespasian pulled out a square folded sheet, sealed. He handed it to Nicanor. "This is for you."

Nicanor was surprised. He had no one to write him; it had been a decade or more since he'd received such a thing. He slid the tip of his dagger in and snapped the wax, cupping the crumbled pieces in his hand as he unfolded the letter and skimmed it quickly.

"Would you like to see it, general?" he asked. "It's from a friend in Rome, Marcus Attilius."

"No, I trust you to tell me if there's anything in it I should know. Antonia tells me," he shook the sheet in his hand, "that your friend, Marcus Attilius, is working for her now." Vespasian scratched a heavy eyebrow. "Is he trustworthy?"

"Yes, general. I trust him with my life… He saved me twice in Rome."

"Good." Vespasian held a hand out toward his son, who gave him the pages he'd been reading. "Antonia also passed on a report from General Marcus Antonius Primus. You met him in Rome?"

Nicanor was sure the general already knew that but answered, "Yes, general… he seems a capable commander."

"He reports that Vitellius has ordered several legions to Italia's borders to prevent the entry of the eastern legions who've declared loyalty to me. One of his generals, Caecina, commands them—he was instrumental in Marcus Otho's defeat at Bedriacum." He set those pages down and picked up another. "Antonia says there are rumors Caecina is unhappy with Vitellius's administration. She has someone working to convince him to join us."

"But there's no certainty he'll turn," Titus said. "It's reported that Vitellius has dealt quickly with any lack of loyalty and with those who could threaten him by holding loved ones hostage—for leverage."

Nicanor saw concern furrow Vespasian's brow and commented, "Marcus Attilius is the best bodyguard Lady Antonia could ask for, general."

"Is he a good fighter?"

"The best I've ever seen. Marcus will protect her."

Vespasian nodded, and his frown eased. "Antonia says some men who fought at Bedriacum tell a story of two eagles they watched fight above the field before the battle. A third came from the rising sun and drove off the victor when one was beaten. Some now claim the eagle from the east is a sign."

"You are the eagle from the east, Father...."

Vespasian gave a slight nod to his son and turned to Nicanor. "Did you see this in Bedriacum?"

"No, sir. I was with Marcus Otho at Brixellum, miles away."

"A commander," Vespasian said, "even an emperor, if he takes the field, must be close to the action. Especially in Marcus Otho's situation when he tries to secure his rule."

Nicanor was not surprised at this response.

"I've read that he and the officers he chose to lead the battle lost the faith of many of their men," Vespasian said. "That was part of his undoing. I would never make that mistake. You believe I'm the eagle from the east, Titus. Maybe I am. But two attempts on my life have come close to ending it." Vespasian's face became grim as he leaned back and studied Nicanor. "You know about those incidents, right?"

"Yes, sir. General Titus briefed me."

Vespasian thumbed out another sheet on his desk. "At least once, someone in Caesarea has brought a dozen Thracian mercenaries here from Alexandria. For what purpose, I don't know yet."

Vespasian's hand moved, and Nicanor glimpsed a symbol at the top of what looked like a ship manifest. Marinus had shown him the same sign; it identified the vessel as one of his. *It's Florus*, Nicanor thought. *It must be*. Two hours earlier, Sayid had told how he set fire to Florus's house in Ptolemais to save Cleo. A jolt of pride had run through Nicanor when Sayid told of how he had kicked Florus back into a burning room. That had caused the scars Nicanor had seen on

Florus's legs in the taberna. He wished the bastard had died. But he had not—and it seemed he had moved to Caesarea. *Why?*

Nicanor had seen a dozen heavily armed riders at Florus's *domus* outside the city. Why so many? He had pondered how to get Vespasian to act against Florus. Marinus's canny reporting had raised suspicion and gotten Vespasian's attention. Now Nicanor could work to connect that suspicious activity to Florus. And he would work to come up with anything else that might indict him.

"Soon," Vespasian continued, "I'll leave for Alexandria. Before I go, I need to know if I should expect a risk there or another attack here. I want Titus—who will take command of all legions here—to be alert and ready for any threat against *him*. I want you, Nicanor, to find out who's hiring these mercenaries and why. In the morning, you'll have my orders assigning you that mission, and you'll have my support and that of General Titus."

"I'll begin immediately, general. May I request an aide to help me?"

"Bring on anyone you need. Who do you have in mind?"

"Sayid, the Syrian auxiliary. He's served me before, and I trust him."

Vespasian shrewdly studied Nicanor for a moment and nodded. "Get started."

* * *

NICANOR'S QUARTERS

"I know you were badly wounded there," said Yosef, "but I won't apologize for Yotapta, Celsus. You're a friend of my friends, so I'm glad you survived."

Sayid knew Yosef regretted that so many Judeans were killed and many more would likely die when the legions marched on Jerusalem. Yosef had said his people bore responsibility for the war, too. The tension between the two friends had increased after Nicanor left. They sat in silence for a while until Sayid told Yosef about Hebron.

Yosef replied with sadness, "The old name was Kiryat Arba... it was King David's capital before Jerusalem. So the one-time capital of my people is now destroyed, and the current one, my family's home, faces imminent destruction."

Sayid had wondered, *What if my mother and aunt were in Jerusalem awaiting an invading army, and I could not help them?* And Cleo must still be there, too. He felt sadness for Yosef even though he intended to fight against his people when the time came.

Then Celsus had said something about the rebels getting what they deserved at Yotapta. Yosef had diplomatically acknowledged it, knowing Sayid and Celsus felt the same. Celsus was more at ease then.

They had left the stall half-doors and window shutters open, hoping for a breeze in the still-warm night, so they heard steps coming from the street through the stall. Then Nicanor entered the room and announced without a greeting, "Sorry, Celsus—Sayid now works for me."

"What?" asked the quartermaster commander and Sayid simultaneously.

With his hands on his hips, Nicanor looked at Yosef and Sayid. "We're going after Gessius Florus."

XLV

October 69 CE

Verona

Central Northern Italia

The building Marcus entered sat across from the much more impressive and vast three-tiered amphitheater made of cement-and-rubble bricks, *opus coementicum*. Stone blocks set in square pillars created a facade of 72 arches, whose top row must reach nearly 100 feet high. The city was much larger than he had expected, and the arena was astounding now in daylight.

Entering the room he had been in briefly the night before, Marcus remained in the back while the chamber filled with senior officers. General Marcus Antonius Primus stood before a large map created from a dozen smaller ones pinned to a wall. Together they showed all of Italia and the provinces to the north and east. Blue markers showed the locations of legions supporting General Vespasian's bid for power and red those who would fight for Emperor Vitellius. He had seen only one other map before, at the *porticus vipsania* in Rome, the *orbis terrarium*. A map of the world. Last night the general had greeted them as his aides placed the maps on the wall, and he had explained the markers and their purpose. Nicanor had mentioned that he liked maps and that it was essential for soldiers to understand and use them, so Marcus was determined to study this one.

"Pomponius Mela...."

"Who?" Marcus asked Pugnio Nuntius, next to him. Antonia Caenis had bidden Marcus to accompany the man to deliver a sealed message to Marcus Antonius Primus. They were to receive a report they would return to her.

"Mela is a mapmaker in Rome, a good one. I looked closely last night"—Pugnio gestured at the maps. "They're his work."

When Marcus had taken Carmenta to Antonia Caenis as Nicanor had asked, he had been surprised at her offer to hire him. He had fulfilled his obligation to Gnaeus Batiatus and had no desire to keep fighting in the arena. So he had been happy to accept, thinking she required a personal bodyguard. Every noble in Rome hired experienced fighters, usually former gladiators and legionaries. Vitellius had brought an unruly rabble into the city, and many people with much to lose felt vulnerable. Or maybe she had plans for him to protect Domitian, who had joined a faction of powerful men planning to overthrow Vitellius.

Lady Antonia had offered the *scriba* Pugnio, a seasoned correspondent, to help Marcus with a letter to Nicanor, sharing the news of his hiring. Marcus was a better reader than a writer and was glad to accept the services of the scribe. Then Lady Antonia had asked Marcus to escort the man to Verona. She had not answered when he blurted out, without thinking, "Why Verona?" It was Marcus's place just to do her bidding, not to ask questions.

But the previous evening, when they had arrived carrying the letter from Lady Antonia, General Primus had accepted the message from Pugnio. He explained, "No need to write all this, but I will tell you, for her ears. I'm here with my men because Verona is a central strategic position. It sits on the Adige River, which has two stone bridges, the *Pons Marmoreus* and the *Pons Postumius,* that connect both banks. There's good transportation on the river and road; the *Via Postumia* and the surrounding plains allow superior cavalry movement."

He paused momentarily, commenting, "Our cavalry is much better than the Vitellians. Lady Antonia needs to know this and what I say to my staff in the morning. I know all this will be sent on to General Vespasian." He had waved the letter from Lady Antonia and said, "She doesn't say it here, but she's likely concerned and wants to know why I did not hold at Aquileia. As in his last letter, General Vespasian wished me to wait for Gaius Mucianus to arrive with his eastern legions. So, listen closely tomorrow morning."

Now it was morning. Marcus studied Pugnio as he arranged several wax tablets on a broad pedestal. The man had brought a bag full of the tablets and kept them carefully wrapped and out of the sun. Marcus noted that the scribe had large hands, oddly scarred, suggesting he had not always wielded only a stylus or pen.

"Quiet!" General Primus silenced the buzz of chatter among his officers. "Many in this room, some in Rome and elsewhere, have questioned my decision to move swiftly to establish this base in Verona." He turned to the map and pointed his rod at a spot on the coast of northeastern Italia on the Adriatica. "Aquileia is too far east to block any other legions drawn from Germania to aid Vitellius. Its lagoons, river, and proximity to the sea would limit our use of cavalry." The tip of the rod traveled southwesterly and stopped.

Final Siege

"At Bedriacum, six months ago," the general turned to face them, "two Pannonian and Moesian cavalry regiments cut their way through Caecina's and Valens's lines. The Vitellian forces did not defeat them, though their great strength was not brought to bear, and leadership was weak in other areas." Primus's voice rang out the warning beneath his words. "Our cavalry and infantry—by the din they create and the very clouds of dust they raise, will overwhelm and bury the Vitellians. Whether we fight here or on the plains of the Po Valley.... With their lines severed, their men separated... our infantry will crush those who Vitellius sends against us. Then we will move south to Rome." General Primus slapped the tip against Rome on the map.

"For those who think we should wait for Governor Mucianus and his legions," the general continued, "I must report that a conflict with Thracian dissidents has delayed him. He will deal with the Thracians and resume marching to join us."

He paused, and his eyes swept the room. "The Vitellian forces continue their celebrations," he said, "while billeted in affluent citizens' homes, not barracks. They are glutting themselves on Rome's riches in idleness." He spat on the floor in disgust. "Once sated, though, they'll recover their urge to fight."

Marcus Antonius Primus glared at his officers. "Give them time, and they will remember they are soldiers—something the men in our legions have not forgotten. We will force Vitellius's men to fight while they are fat and slack. We have left behind the skirmishes of our entry into Italia. Now we will ready our men for the *real* battle. Soon you shall hear that the gates of *Italia* have been unlocked and Vitellius's fortunes shattered. You will be glad you followed and that you tread in the footsteps of the victor."

* * *

The next morning...

Marcus Attilius reined Carmenta to get close to the general, who sat on his horse upon a hillock. Spread out on the plain before them were over 5,000 men, and Marcus knew two other formations shielded Verona to the north and west. Carmenta softly nickered and canted her head to one side to stare intently down at the field of men. A bugle call pierced the air, and the legion formed in ranks and faced east. The amber-gold of sunrise tinted their upturned faces under gleaming *galea*. The burnished metal of thousands of helmets flashed as every man saluted the rising sun.

"Is that done every morning, general?"

"It's a custom the 3rd Legion, *Gallica,* adopted in Syria," Marcus Primus said as he turned his horse. "Did your scribe get written all that was covered throughout yesterday's meetings?"

"Yes, sir." Marcus Attilius rubbed his eyes. "He was all the night through writing from his notes and asking me all I remembered. He also made a copy for you and is now taking it to your aide. Then we leave."

"He added the news the courier brought me last evening?"

"Yes, sir. I repeated for him exactly what you told me: Vitellius's General Caecina has met secretly with Sextus Bassus, commander of the fleet at Ravenna, loyal to Vespasian. The Vitellian general plans to turn from Vitellius and will support Vespasian."

"Good... when you deliver your report, tell Antonia Caenis that the clash is coming, the moment to determine General Vespasian's rule." The general looked at the sky, now dotted with the wheeling shapes of large birds, dark despite the streaming sunlight. Their shrill cries carried across the plain. "It's upon us soon."

//
ACT II

XLVI

October 69 CE

Jerusalem

Bezetha, the New City

Ya'el welcomed the rains, though Shammai fretted over them because his burning pits could no longer exude steady plumes of smoke. His longstanding routine of loading deep holes in the ground with wood, then covering, burning, uncovering, shoveling, and lifting and storing the charred wood had been interrupted. The first day of rain reduced the field to mere smoldering, and now another day had extinguished every pit. When the rains stopped, they would begin the cycle of charcoal-making again, but for now, she and Elian could rest from their weary duties. Still, there were meals to prepare and clothes to sew and mend for herself, Elian, and Shammai, too.

In the evenings, Shammai read scripture to them from a precious scroll, and their Aramaic and knowledge of the Jewish faith improved daily. Still, as Shammai read, Ya'el often slipped into a daydream of Rome. Of the time when she had had servants. Of the happy times before she'd married Gessius Florus and before she sailed to tour the eastern and southern provinces. Back then, she and Poppaea went to plays and parties long ago and far away. Now her life was here and as different as it was possible to have become.

As it is, she thought, studying her scarred and calloused hands—some of it was likely permanent, from handling fire and embers. Her face had weathered too, and she felt the still-livid burn on her neck from when she'd tumbled three days earlier into a freshly opened pit, and a smoldering log fell against her. The wound still stung. *But it stings more,* she thought, *that I was once a noble lady.*

"Can we go now?" Elian asked, interrupting her thoughts.

Ya'el knew he was as ready as she was to be away from the work and the smell of burned wood. Lifting a long tress of her hair, she sniffed at it. She and her clothing always carried that stench... as did the boy. They could not leave it behind, and she wondered if she ever would.

"Yes," she said, closing the window shutters against the drizzly morning that would surely turn into a downpour by evening. But then she stopped; Shammai was approaching with two men. She recognized one as Yohanan ben Zaccai and the other she had never seen before. The three entered Shammai's modest home.

"But first, Elian, we must see if Shammai needs anything."

* * *

Ya'el placed a few *matzot* on a platter between the bowl of olive oil and another containing salted water, with three linen cloths for the men to clean their fingers before breaking bread. "Here, carry this to them," she told Elian in the kitchen. "But be careful—don't spill it." She watched to make sure Elian was attentive to the task—he'd dropped things more than once—then turned away to fill a pitcher with wine, noting the almost-bare pantry.

The evening before, she and Elian had seen farmers with their carts trundle into Bezetha, headed to the city markets with bushels of dates, grapes, figs, and olives. She hoped to see Miriam today but must first replenish Shammai's larder. And that had become a challenge. Yohanan ben Levi's men and Simon bar Giora's men were at war but alike. When the farmers came in, the men descended on them—like the locusts she had heard Bezetha work women chatter about. They bought or confiscated large amounts of the food brought into the city. She had learned that each faction protected its food stores while the Sanhedrin labored to fill communal storehouses and those within the Temple. The ordinary people of Jerusalem saw some foods become scarce as the number of people entering the city each day grew.

Ya'el set the wine on the table next to the platter. Shammai, Yohanan ben Zaccai, and the third man doffed their cloaks and hung them on pegs on the wall, where they could dry over the charcoal brazier that warmed the room. As the men went to sit, Yohanan studiously ignored her. The stranger looked at her and smiled with a nod. He was nearly as old as Yohanan, to judge by the lines on his face and the streaks of white through his beard and short hair. But the lean man had sat easily without creaking down like the old priest. The man loosened the strap that had kept his head covering snugly against his brow. Ya'el noticed a decorative oval of pliant hide centered in the length of plaited leather. The man's hands unconsciously but expertly wound the leather around his muscular wrist and calloused fingers and then unwound it. It was as if his hands refused to be idle.

"You and the boy can do as you planned," Shammai said in pleasant dismissal, and Ya'el and Elian returned to the kitchen.

"Can we go now?" Elian asked as soon as they entered.

"Not yet," Ya'el said, quietly moving a stool next to the door to listen. Perhaps she could learn something here to pass on to Miriam later.

"Arins here," she heard Yohanan say, "works with my friend Boaz and will now take over his trade into the city."

Arins replied in a deep voice unusual for such a slender man: "Boaz is concerned about his family in Caesarea. The Romans are readying themselves for something, and continuing to secretly trade with Jerusalem is becoming even more dangerous."

"Are you not afraid, too?" Shammai asked.

"I have no one close to me alive to be concerned about."

Ya'el heard the scrape of a chair and thought Yohanan was likely stretching his stiff legs under the table, as he did at Miriam's home. His scratchy voice added, "Boaz was also concerned about the fighting within the city. It seems that now Eleazar ben Simon has split from the Gischalan to form a third faction." The old priest sighed. "They will cause even more killing. Many city elders and the Sanhedrin pray the Romans will come soon. They would rather face war from outside Jerusalem's walls than within."

"So, everyone wishes to govern the city?" Arins asked, but he did not wait for an answer. "I also heard that a Sicarii assassin had killed one of this Yohan ben Levi's lieutenants—to warn him against imprisoning citizens. Maybe this 'Hand' will eliminate the faction leaders, and I wish him success. Still, Jerusalem needs traders... so I will endeavor to supply the city. I might need a place to keep and repair my wagons near the northern gates. Yohanan thought you might let me use a small area."

"Of course," said Shammai, "I'll help you in any way to continue to bring goods into the city. Too soon, that will end once the Romans arrive."

"In Caesarea," Arins continued, "I heard rumors of the civil war in Rome. Powerful men there seek to keep or overthrow the throne, which occupies them for now. I did hear some questions about why Jerusalem has not been taken yet. Maybe they change their mind about attacking the city...."

The men grew silent. The scuffling of Elian's feet back and forth, brushing the floor as he sat impatiently waiting, prompted Ya'el to stand. She beckoned to him and quietly opened and held the door for him to go outside.

"And it is still believed a Roman noblewoman hides here," Arins said.

Ya'el stopped in her tracks, her ears attentive to the following words.

"The reward has been increased... some Roman wants her badly."

Ya'el looked at her hands again. *How long can I stay safe here?*

XLVII

October 69 CE

Caesarea

The Balinae

Yosef's hands had been freed, and he used a long-handled scoop for water to pour over his head. Then he used a swath of clean, rough linen to scrub his neck, chest, shoulders, and arms. The runoff soaked his loincloth, and he worked his fingers between the metal shackles and the skin of his ankles to cleanse and massage the calloused flesh where the cuffs held him.

"Thank you, Nicanor. This is my first bath since.... well, for a long time. I usually have all my chains on and guards hurrying me." Such little freedoms meant much, and this day held others. The trip to Har haKarmel and Berytus had been his first time outside the encampment in nearly two years. Even during those earlier trips, he still felt like a prisoner. This day—with his two friends—he felt almost free.

Yosef raised his head and breathed in deeply the sea breeze, its tang and freshness. This clean wind had not passed over and through the odors and effluence of a military camp of thousands. These baths used by Vespasian's officers were only 300 feet from the surf. A few had stared, affronted at the presence of Yosef and Sayid, but they turned away once Nicanor glared at them. They had come to the baths on a sunny day after recent clouds and rain, within sight of an undulating tide of blue water under an equally cerulean sky. It had raised his spirits, as had Nicanor's news.

He studied his friend, who had just immersed himself, and emerged from the water to sit on the steps next to Yosef. Nicanor had lost weight and become grayer. The old scar that bisected his right eyebrow was now a pale seam that created a chevron of the two halves when Nicanor raised his brows in question or amusement. How close that arrow gash had come to the eye! It was more shallow where the line ended below the curve of his cheekbone. Another ragged scar scored the length of his neck, and Yosef wondered what recent injury had left it. Nicanor's forearm looked like a layer of skin had been peeled off and stuck back on. There was a deep pucker of a puncture wound in his upper arm. And, in his side, a slash ran across his ribs.

Yosef wanted to ask his friend about it all but didn't. He still wasn't sure how Nicanor felt about him now.

Sayid has changed, too, he thought as he looked across the rectangle of the semi-private pool Nicanor had arranged for them. Out of the water and drying off, he could see the Syrian was still lean, though he had added weight—solidity. Faint lines had appeared on his face, too—he was no longer the boy Yosef had first known years before. The perforation scars in the thigh were likely from arrows, and a jagged stab wound in his chest had healed poorly. The fire he had told them about must have left the still-healing marks on his arm and shoulder.

Yosef had few physical wounds compared to how the past few years of combat had marked his friends. He knew Nicanor and Sayid also had unseen injuries, but Yosef carried far more unhealing wounds. He slept little at night, plagued by them. But he did have things to be grateful for. Like the bath, which he would not have enjoyed if Celsus still watched him. The legion quartermaster commander, Yosef believed, still held against him the battle of Yotapta. He was grateful that Vespasian had listened to Nicanor and let him assume responsibility for Yosef when he was out of his cell. Nicanor had greeted him with that good news earlier in the day. But then Nicanor had asked a question Yosef had not answered. Now he would.

"I don't know where this will end for me, Nicanor. I know how it will end for my family... for my city."

Nicanor stood and dried himself with a linen towel. "General Vespasian becoming emperor will not stop the war, Yosef. I think he respects you and even your counsel in some matters. But that will not keep the legions from marching on Jerusalem."

"Still, when they do," Yosef said, "I hope to speak to my people to convince them to surrender and to talk peace." Yosef stood, positioned his feet to ease their discomfort in their shackles, then reached for the rough cloth Sayid held out to him. "That's all I ask of General Vespasian."

"I cannot stop any attack, but I will speak to him about you getting that chance," said Nicanor. "But, consider this... and you probably have. Sayid has heard the talk... I've heard the talk, too, since returning. Your people think you are a traitor." Nicanor's words cut deeply. "I'm sorry, Yosef," he said, that broken eyebrow quirking, "but will they even listen to you?"

Sayid followed as they walked silently to the *apodyterium* to put their clothes back on. "The people of Caesarea know General Vespasian favors you," he said. "It's taken time, but you're safe with him, Yosef. Anywhere else in your country, you'd be at risk." Then Sayid turned to Nicanor, "I'll go to the stables of Todros—I'll watch Florus's house from there tonight."

Yosef had heard the two discussing that earlier. The trader who had sold Albus to Nicanor had been happy to earn some extra coin by letting Sayid bed down in the stable, with an arrangement that the Syrian would also watch over the place while Todros was away on one of his procurement trips. From that vantage point, Sayid had been compiling a count and descriptions of the men working for Florus.

"Be careful, Sayid," Nicanor warned. "Yosef and I go to meet General Vespasian now. When I'm done, I'll come and watch with you."

Yosef sighed. He did not look forward to returning to his cell and another night of fitful sleep.

* * *

VESPASIAN'S PRAETORIUM

Once Yosef had his hands manacled again, he and Nicanor were announced into General Vespasian's private office. The general did not stand at such an entrance, and Yosef was surprised when the man with him did. He had grizzled hair, a beard, and a weathered face, his once-fine cloak rimed with what seemed dried saltwater. He eagerly gripped Nicanor by the shoulders and grinned at him.

"Marinus, here," Vespasian said, "has a lead for you on who is hiring the Thracian mercenaries."

The man's eyes went from Nicanor to Yosef and his chains and then back to Nicanor. "I'm here to take you to him," Marinus said.

"Good," said Nicanor. "Let's go now if the general needs nothing else. Otherwise, first thing in the morning."

"I'm afraid not, Nicanor," the man said as his smile broadened.

Nicanor frowned.

"Marinus sails in the morning for Alexandria," Vespasian said as he slid a sheaf of reports and letters into a pack like Yosef had seen ordinary legionaries carry. "We go with him."

"We, sir?" Nicanor asked.

The man nodded, and Yosef thought, judging from his weathering and the reference to sailing, *A ship captain, evidently.*

"You and General Titus will accompany me... as will Yosef," Vespasian said as he came from behind his desk.

Yosef was surprised at the prospect, hardly hearing what Vespasian said next.

"Nicanor, the man you need to speak to about the Thracians, is there in Alexandria. And that is where I will put another form of pressure on Vitellius."

XLVIII

October 69 CE

Alexandria, Aegyptus

Portus Magnus

The Roman navy *quinquereme* ahead of the *Egeria* was abreast of Pharos when the ruddy light from the mirror at the apex of the lighthouse flared with the blaze of a massive fire within a giant bronze bowl. The flame would burn until daybreak, its glow reaching down from a 300-foot height to add its illumination to that of the waning sun. It brightened the white limestone and pale sandstone of the three descending sections of the tower: round at the top just below the beacon, then octagonal, and at the bottom a rectangle.

The lighthouse stood within a walled square on a small island linked by a manmade causeway to the larger island, Pharos. Which was thence connected to the city by the *Heptastadion*, another manmade land bridge forming the westerly arm that embraced the harbor. The other arm was the Lochias peninsula and its stone breakwater. The magnificent torch that reached into the sky was the sentry that proclaimed that a ship had reached Alexandria, the second largest city, in size and in wealth, in the empire.

The *Egeria* closed the gap between it and the naval ship as the *quinquereme* turned right to enter the Small Harbor. The setting sun glowed against the sweep of the big ship's three banks of stacked oars. The same type of vessel had saved Yosef, Cleo, Nicanor, and Sayid after the wreck of the *Salacia*. Yosef knew there were over 400 men on the one ship: 300 rowers, 20 to 30 sailors, and up to 120 auxiliary legionaries.

"We'll bear to the left and take the *Egeria* into the eastern part of the Great Harbor, past Antirhodos," Marinus told them. "Our mooring is within the Royal Haven, near the palaces." He turned from watching the two *triremes* behind them following the larger naval vessel. The three naval ships sent from the fleet at Ravenna by Marcus Antonius Primus had waited just outside the jetties at Caesarea to escort them on the 6-day voyage to Alexandria.

Yosef leaned toward Nicanor and pointed at the small island ahead. "Marcus Antonius's uncompleted palace, *Timonium*, is there on Antirhodos, as is a colossal stone head thought to be the image of Cleopatra's son Caesarion. I saw them both from the deck of the ship I sailed on from Rome four years ago." Twilight was upon them now; he could not make out the forms onshore.

As the *Egeria* skirted the island, a glowing line grew on the quay as they neared it. Beneath the lights, gold, silver, bronze, and other metals gleamed on the chariots and the dozen or more senior officers, resplendent in their finest ceremonial armor, who awaited Vespasian and Titus.

Amidships, where sailors would set the gangplank, General Vespasian and his son stood in full regalia. Nicanor, too, was attired as Yosef had not seen him before, even in Rome six years before. Now he wore the insignia of a *tribunus militum*, a rank below a legate, the general in command of a legion, but above other centurions. Under one arm, he held his *galea*, the helmet's transverse horsehair crest a dark red in the dusk. He wore a new gleaming cuirass—chest and back—of *lorica musculata* and *lorica segmentate,* metal shoulder plates, with *lorica manica* of overlapping bronze strips protecting his right arm from beneath the shoulder plates to the wrist.

Nicanor had explained all these armor parts to Yosef, who noted that one covered the scarred arm he had seen.

"Quite a welcome," Nicanor commented and crossed his arms, and let go a deep sigh. Nicanor was never comfortable with pomp and ceremony, and much of that was ahead for them.

Yosef raised his hands to wave away a cluster of midges as the wind dropped with their entry into the harbor. A cloud of the pests quickly descended on the *Egeria*. They'd shipped oars to maneuver to the pier, and he heard the oarsmen below swearing as the flying insects tormented them, too. His chains clanked, and he almost matched Nicanor's sigh. "The last time I was here, I was a free man headed home."

* * *

The Prefect's Palace

They had passed through an interior arch to a gallery, a meeting hall with a central platform bordered by short columns. The marble walls of the chamber were frescoed in myriad colors that climbed to a white limestone ceiling. Yosef leaned over and whispered to Nicanor, "It feels like we're back in Rome—when I joined you at the party for Cleo at Empress Poppaea's invitation. And *you* wore a toga!"

"Don't remind me," Nicanor grunted. "I felt naked in it."

The chamber held the prefect and his retinue, the senior legion officers—commanders and their seconds-in-command. A handful of citizens were also in attendance, notables of a rank that merited mingling with the general who planned to become the next emperor. Vespasian sat upon a simple *sella curulis*, but the dignity of his straight-backed posture gave the plain chair the aura of a throne.

As Yosef and Nicanor climbed the steps, Tiberius Alexander, the Prefect of Aegyptus, was speaking. "Yes, my countrymen... the *euggelion*... the good news spreads of the new emperor come from the east." He half-bowed to Vespasian.

"You frown, Yosef," Nicanor said quietly. "But the prefect is on General Vespasian's side."

Yosef realized he must not show his thoughts, a habit he had lost in Caesarea.

The prefect continued, walking around as he spoke: "When I received your decision, General Vespasian, I thought about it, considering its impact on Rome." The saffron-dyed fine woolen toga draped elegantly over his left shoulder and arm, swaying as he moved. The scarlet silk threads of the wide embroidered hem shimmered in the lamplight. "Rome has suffered from poor leaders in its highest office. We cannot endure yet another. So, I considered what General Vespasian's leadership could mean for Rome."

He picked up a goblet from a tray, turned to the man he spoke of, and raised the cup to him. "A good man. A strong man of principle. Rome needs both. That is why the legions of the east...." The prefect turned, and his eyes swept the gathering of men. "That is why the legions of Pannonia, of Moesia... that is why I, the legions and people of Aegyptus, swear an oath of allegiance." He walked toward Vespasian and stopped in front of him. "To this good, strong man, who will become our emperor."

Although hindered by his chains, Yosef raised his hands to join the clapping, and the sharp clank of metal drew stares from the men nearest him. Like the rest, Yosef thought Vespasian was a good man, perhaps destined to be great. But the man was also a supreme pragmatist. Yosef hoped to appeal to both traits to prevent his family's death in the assault on Jerusalem.

As he watched Vespasian accept the accolades and endorsements, he prayed that the quality of mercy was greatest in the great. Vespasian's uniform was not as ornate as those Yosef had seen on other Roman generals, even some within the room. The great man raised his large hand that gripped his vinewood rod and waited for the room to quiet. Vespasian's eyes locked on Yosef again, and the rod twitched to beckon him forward.

"My good fortune seems everywhere of late. But it is a rightful destiny foretold in different ways. While Nero still reined, one man prophesied what's happening now. The prophet was a valiant man. A general in his own right who fought bravely for his people. He suffered much—before and after the siege and his capture at Yotapta. Though he was an enemy of Rome and his people are still enemies of Rome, it is shameful that this man, who foretold the moment that has now come upon me, should still be held a prisoner."

Vespasian leaned toward the prefect and spoke quietly, then the prefect nodded and motioned an aide to come to him. "Bring a metalsmith," he ordered.

The aide returned with a workman bearing tools, a hardwood block, and a puzzled expression. Following the prefect's directions, the metalsmith set the block on the floor and took up his hammer and chisel. The prefect turned his eyes to Yosef, who stepped forward.

When the last bolt was sheared, cuffs and chains released, Titus spoke: "General Vespasian—Father—it is more than iron chains that should be removed from Yosef. This frees him from his bonds, but we must cut them to pieces, and he will be like a man that has never been bound."

At Vespasian's command, the metalsmith took the length of the chains and cut them into pieces. Then he stooped to gather the shackle cuffs, the severed bolts, and the links. Two connected links dropped as the man left the room, and Nicanor bent to pick them up. He turned to Yosef. "Hold out your hand," Nicanor said, placing the broken links in the Judean's palm. "You are free, Yosef."

Yosef closed his hand around the broken links and studied his fist for a moment, and when he looked up, all eyes were on him—and not with friendship. In the eyes of Vespasian and Titus was an acceptance that the right thing had been done. But the eyes of the prefect, the other legion officers, and the city notables differed. They seemed to hold questions or doubts about Vespasian's words regarding Yosef. Even with the chains off, many still saw him as an enemy. Yosef squeezed the metal links in his hand, felt the weight of those eyes, and nodded to Nicanor, wondering, *Am I truly free?*

XLIX

OCTOBER 69 CE

ALEXANDRIA

THE PREFECT'S PALACE

Nicanor saw the servant at the entrance leave Yosef in the antechamber. He approached Vespasian, who stood at the head of a long table strewn with maps and scrolls, his vinewood rod holding open one scroll filled with numbers.

An entire wing of the prefect's palace had been provided for General Vespasian. It included rooms for Titus, Nicanor, and Yosef. When Nicanor had left Yosef late last evening, his friend had seemed almost lost in the extravagantly furnished large room. A drastic change from his setting during more than two years of imprisonment. Nicanor had then gone to his own room of unaccustomed luxury and soon found he preferred his simple quarters in Caesarea with Albus in the connected stable. Still, he had slept well and risen early for this meeting with the generals and Tiberius Alexander.

Vespasian beckoned Yosef to enter as Titus, with Nicanor's help, began gathering the maps and reports. The old general said to Tiberius Alexander, "I've decided, then. There will be no further grain shipment to Rome without my release. I know it will bring hardship to Rome's people, but it will also pressure Vitellius—and pressure either hardens a man or cracks him. He will crack from all I've heard and know of the man."

Yosef looks like he didn't sleep at all, Nicanor thought as his friend reached the table. Vespasian asked the newly freed man: "How does it feel, Yosef?"

Yosef was clean-shaven, with threads of early graying hair at his temples. He was garbed as an affluent Roman in a tunic of white linen and a cloak of equally fine material. But, to Nicanor, it seemed Yosef was not at ease wearing them, and the scars at his wrists and ankles were not hidden by the new high-strapped sandals.

"Thank you again, general.... for my freedom," Yosef replied. Nicanor saw him brace for Vespasian to ask again and relax when the general did not.

"I'm told you are a writer and studier of history," Tiberius Alexander said. "You are in a city that values both. And here, there are centuries of learning to be drawn upon." The prefect's eyes narrowed. "But as a man who could enjoy that, you may one day," his eyes slid to Vespasian and back to Yosef, "become a citizen. And perhaps you should take a new name to better fit in."

Nicanor saw Yosef stiffen, and Vespasian's expression turned thoughtful. Then the old general said, "Yosef, you have the freedom of the city, but join me at sundown for *vesperna*." Vespasian held his hand up, interrupting the prefect, who had started to speak. "No, Tiberius... a light dinner tonight, no entertaining anyone, no entertainment. You can have your lavish *cena* tomorrow." He turned to Nicanor and said, "Tribunus, see to your mission, but you join me, too, for dinner."

Nicanor and Yosef watched as Vespasian, Titus, and the prefect left the room. "Where do they go?" Yosef asked.

"Somewhere called the *Serapeum*—a temple, I think. The general mentioned meeting someone there."

"That's the Temple of Serapis, a Greek-Aegyptian god."

"God of what?"

"He's like the Greek Zeus combined with an Aegyptian sun god." Yosef shrugged. "Is the mission Vespasian mentioned connected with your plan for Gessius Florus?"

Nicanor held a finger to his lips and beckoned Yosef to follow. They left the palace and walked down terraced steps toward the waterfront. He stopped at the gated entry to the promenade bordering the water along the Royal Haven. "It concerns Gessius Florus," he finally said, "but we must be cautious speaking of it and of the man. Florus could have spies anywhere... everywhere." They continued through the gate. The harbor was shrouded in fog, and a thin veil covered the island Antirhodos that served as a wave break for the palace waterfront.

"The fog is lessening," Yosef said. "It was much heavier earlier."

Nicanor glanced at his friend. "You've been outside the palace this morning?"

"I slept little. At first light, I wanted to see how it felt to walk alone again, in the open... in a new place." He rubbed the scars on his wrists, turned, and pointed east. "The Jewish Quarter of the city is that way. But I walked there instead," he turned around in the opposite direction, "to the Temple of Poseidon." Mist blanketed the lower part of the massive structure, covering its columns to a third of their height. "I stood there and thought about the sharks that circled us after the *Salacia's* wreck and the one that bit into Sayid's leg. You called them 'Neptune's demons.'"

Nicanor smiled. "They are. The damned cruel creatures. But the sea god's dolphins saved us that day."

"There," Yosef said as he gestured toward the area south of the temple, "is Alexandria's Great Theater. Your Julius Caesar turned it into a fortress where he withstood a siege after his legions conquered Aegypt." Yosef turned his head to indicate an arc around them. "A conquered country.... its capital taken. But today, it still stands and is still a great city. I hope that is my city's fate. Do you think it will be?"

Nicanor shook his head. "I don't know, Yosef." His stomach knotted because he knew. Vespasian had discussed that morning the grain embargo and how it would worsen conditions in Rome. The general had been adamant, telling Titus, who would command the siege, and Tiberius Alexander, who would be his second-in-command. "The vast treasure the Jews hold in Jerusalem must be taken," Vespasian had said. "It's needed to stabilize our economy and my rule, or it could be short."

To Nicanor, that meant Jerusalem's fate was sealed. But he could not tell his friend. He could not strip him of hope, not so soon. He changed the subject. "You should be careful, Yosef."

"Careful?" Yosef looked away from the water that was being slowly revealed as the fog receded.

"I saw your expression when you were near Tiberius Alexander... when you looked at him. I saw it just a while ago when he mentioned you becoming a citizen."

"I know of him, know what he's done. He comes from a wealthy Jewish family but abandoned his faith to rise in Roman rank. He was the Procurator of Judea 21 years ago when I was young. And he brutally put down a Jewish protest here in Alexandria three years ago. I heard a report of it from a witness. Prefect Alexander used two Roman legions and 2,000 soldiers from Libya. He ordered them to kill the rioters, plunder their property, and burn their homes. The soldiers pushed the protestors back into the Delta, what they called the area where the Jews gathered." Yosef paused.

"The Jews of Alexandria stood shoulder to shoulder with their most heavily armed men in front," Yosef continued. "They held their ground... for a while. Then the line gave, and they were slaughtered. Death came on them in every form. Some were overtaken in the open. Others were driven into their houses, which the Romans looted and burned down. The soldiers felt no pity for infants and children and no respect for the aged. They cut down old and young alike." Yosef turned and faced the Jewish Quarter. "Fifty thousand died there. Some were killed in the fighting, and others captured and burned alive." He stiffened and whirled around to face Nicanor. "I believe Tiberius Alexander thinks I'm like *him*," he said through gritted teeth. "He thinks I've abandoned my people in exchange for my life and freedom."

Nicanor could not speak. He knew his friend would do what he could to help his family and people. He thought again of Vespasian's command to Titus: "Soon you will march on Jerusalem. Take it... take the treasure." Nicanor knew the Jews would not give up their temple treasure. Not even to save their city. Jerusalem was doomed.

L

November 69 CE

Jerusalem

The Lower City

Miriam drew her cloak closer around her. The thin undertunic and light mantle over it were not the warmest. But being able to move more freely in lighter garb had saved her several times since she'd killed Alvon. She'd been able to slip away when there were too many to fight and was quicker when she faced only one or two. Her attackers from before dawn that morning were cold; their bodies left where they fell. *Let them be found*, she thought.

She took her practiced quick visual inspection of the street and the alley between Zechariah's old shop and Kefa's leatherworks. Which, oddly, had not opened all day with the other shops lining the craftsmen's street. She had been in the Lower City most of the day, moving from time to time, changing her headcloth, and turning her cloak inside out to change her appearance while staying near her current spot. She quickly checked on Leah and Rachel to find that Matthew had already brought them oil, charcoal, and food. They were both anxious to leave the confines of King David's Tomb, but that depended on Yohanan ben Zaccai's success today.

So many people were packed into the Lower City that anyone with shelter was glad of it. Many worked cheerfully at the tedious task of re-mudding the beams and branches of their roofs. Repairing the damage from the October rains. Newcomers to the city made do fashioning crude lean-tos of scrap wood and coarse, grease-stiffened wool blankets for roofs. That morning Miriam had heard an infant's cry and a woman's sobbing from one haphazard dwelling. She glanced inside. A young mother rubbed her squawling newborn with salt and wrapped it in a blanket. She held the baby to her chest as she lay down to gather her strength.

Miriam had dared not—disguised as a man—see to the needs of the young mother. She had seen the child was tiny but had a strong cry and wondered it she could return later to help them. She wondered if the young mother's tears were of joy or sadness at bringing life into such a tragic time and place.

That sight triggered thoughts she carried throughout the day. Miriam knew she would never be a mother, but she had wondered what it would be like. She recalled seeing how fatherly Ehud had been with the boy Elian. That had made her dream that maybe if there had been no war, no fear of what was to come—if things had been different—perhaps she and Ehud would be together now and have children. But those were tears of joy never to be shed. Her longing for that had died when she killed Ehud with her own hands. Now Ya'akov—she did not want to think of him but could not help it—had just the previous night explained his return and why they could still marry.

"Miriam," hissed a voice she recognized, cutting through her daydream and the murmur of people on the street. *Well, those thoughts were best interrupted,* she thought.

In the moment it took to raise her head, she lifted her mind from the downward spiral it was often drawn to since she had begun killing again. When she had last briefly met with Ya'el, she could see that the Roman woman, too, had become withdrawn, as single-minded as Miriam. That offered them a dark form of companionship. They must discuss it soon.

Miriam's eyes caught the movement of a shadow in Kefa's now-open door, where the voice had come from. She saw a flame flare inside the dim interior as a figure moved to the side and revealed himself in the glow of a small hand lamp. The Sicarii stood well back, so he could not be seen from the street and waved for her to cross to him.

"You watch for me?" Kefa asked as he backed three steps into the shop. All his windows were shuttered, and the inside lighted only by the small lamp behind him. "It is good you do, for Elazar ben Yair sent me back here to give you a last message."

Miriam felt uncomfortable inside the doorway with her back to the street. But Kefa would not retreat farther into the room. "Where's the message?" she asked as she held out her hand.

Kefa shook his head. "Elazar told me to tell you... this is your last chance to come—with me—to Masada and fight the Romans from there. He says we have already lost Jerusalem to men like Yohanan ben Levi and Simon bar Giora. When the Romans arrive, they will take what's left and destroy anything they don't want. Come to Masada, where we will stand together."

"I can't. Not as long as my family is here...."

"Bring them with you. We have *our* families at Masada."

"Yohanan ben Levi holds my father... If I could free him and if I could then convince him... maybe." But she knew that would never happen. Her father and brother would never abandon Jerusalem.

"But I have been looking for you to ask something of Elazar. Simon bar Giora wants me—as 'The Hand'—to ally with him. As the leader of the Sicarii, ask Elazar to announce this: 'The Hand' will never join with men who serve themselves and not Jerusalem.' I want ben Levi and bar Giora to know that, and they'll hear his voice."

"Then Simon bar Giora will want you dead, just as we've heard that is what Yohanan ben Levi desires. And the Gischalan even offers a reward for your killing. If you won't leave Jerusalem, you should stop being 'The Hand,' and they will never discover who you are."

"It's too late to stop, and what happens to me doesn't matter. Ask Elazar to please tell them what I ask. And tell them that 'The Hand' is not the last Sicarii in Jerusalem."

"But when I leave today... you will be." Kefa turned to lift the lamp from the table, his lips pursed to blow out its wick.

"No, I won't," Miriam said into the darkness.

* * *

THE UPPER CITY

Sundown in Jerusalem now signaled everyone in the city to go inside, where there was some hope for safety. From the southernmost end of the Lower City to the northernmost of the Upper City... the streets were terrifying. When there was no fierce fighting in sections of the city and around the buildings held by the factions, patrols and predatory men still roamed the streets. Miriam had moved fast that morning and was still forced to kill two men. She did not want to end the day with more killing. Despite what she had said to Kefa about not stopping, each death weighed on her, no matter how much it was deserved.

Now, men in the alleys and side streets of the Upper City's residential area had left Miriam access to her home only at the front entrance. Inside, she quietly doffed her cloak and heard Matthew's voice coming from the family room.

"Yohanan ben Levi's men and the Zealots have secured the area from Bezetha, north of Antonia Fortress, to the Water Gate in the south, where the City of David ends at the outer walls. Simon bar Giora and his men hold the rest of the New City to the third wall, all the Upper City and most of the Lower City."

Miriam entered and stopped at the sight that greeted her. Her mother was wiping blood from a ragged gash in her brother's upper arm. While the man Yohanan ben Zaccai had introduced as Arins deftly stitched the wound with Yohanan looking on. As Matthew turned his head toward her, she saw the bloody knot on Matthew's left brow just over his swollen-shut eye. "What happened to you?"

"Yohanan ben Levi's men. I came upon Yonatan handling Leah roughly while his men looked on and laughed... and I tried to stop him." Matthew grimaced as Arins tugged a stitch tight.

"It's my fault," Yohanan said. He looked tired and dejected.

"It's not your fault, Yohanan," Rebecca said as she rinsed the bloody cloth in a water bowl and wrung it out to wipe Matthew's brow.

"Leah asked Rebecca if I could help her... Because of the fighting, almost everything administrative has slowed down or stopped. So I pushed through her divorce decree and got the certificate issued and accepted. Leah's free from him, but..." The old rabbi shook his head.

Matthew finished for him. "It seems that, in retaliation, Yonatan wanted to punish Leah before Simon bar Giora's men either kill him or he runs back to the Gischalan. And he's threatened Yohanan, too."

Miriam's eyes went to Arins, who caught her questioning look but finished the last stitch before speaking. "I came to see Yohanan about a problem," he said.

"But he ended up helping me." Matthew flexed his arm carefully and nodded his thanks to the merchant.

"I came upon your brother while on my way here," Arins said to Miriam, then half-turned to Matthew. "Those men were leaving you—I just helped you home."

"He did a better job stitching the wound than I was doing," Rebecca said, "and I was glad to have him." She picked up the bowl and bloody cloth to take to the kitchen.

"I'm good with my hands," Arins said as he sat back, "and I have learned many things. Besides, like Yohanan said earlier, doctors and healers will no longer come out at night. You must go to them, and that's a risk."

"Still, thank you," Rebecca said as she brought out of the kitchen an earthenware pitcher of wine and cups to set on the low table.

The merchant filled a cup and took a sip. "So, can anything be done? My wagons are stopped at every gate. Most of their contents go to Yohanan ben Levi's or Simon bar Giora's storehouses. They claim they will distribute the goods to the people, but I doubt it."

"It's just another means of exerting control... of making people decide who to follow so they have food to eat," Matthew said. "We'd need hundreds—maybe a thousand men—to side with us to rout them from the gates and stop them from intercepting supplies coming into the city. We don't have that many men, and we have *no* hopes of raising more." Matthew replied.

"Yohanan, is there any way to enter the city without using the city gates?" Arins leaned toward the old rabbi, whose eyes went to Miriam. Arins followed the gaze, and he began to look puzzled as he studied her.

LI

November 69 CE

Jerusalem

North of Antonia Fortress, East of its Moat, Remnants of the Hasmonean Baris

Near Struthion Pool ran the moat that skirted the Antonia Fortress's northern and western sides. Miriam recalled walking there with her mother and brothers. As children, they were more interested in the pool, not the site their mother told them of, the citadel built by their ancestors. Herod's new fortress, named for his patron Marcus Antonius, now sat where once had been a Hasmonean stronghold, the *Baris*.

Men were working to repair damaged sections of the fortress walls, battlements, ramparts, and the cloisters that connected and overlooked the Temple Enclosure. Matthew prodded her to walk faster, and she hurried a bit, playing out the role of a young workman accompanying a Temple Guard officer. That guise should not draw attention, they thought. Despite the feuds within the city, the warring leaders agreed that they must continue to bolster its defenses against the Romans by strengthening walls and reinforcing the city's exterior gates. The supervision of that work had been left to Eleasar ben Ananias and the Temple Guard, who usually left the workmen alone. But Matthew insisted on escorting her.

She could no longer safely use Zechariah's shop and King David's Tomb. The Lower City, especially, had become dangerous. Miriam needed to find a place with enough room to spread out Zechariah's maps and the rough additions she had made. And she needed a place to meet with Ya'el unseen, close enough to reach quickly. Zechariah had told her about the tunnels dug by the Hasmoneans. And that the Romans had even used some of them, though they did not know them all. But many Sicarii did, for many came from families that had built much of Jerusalem over the centuries.

Zechariah had warned her to stay away from Fortress Antonia without an escort. The auxiliaries garrisoned there were not disciplined enough to leave the young women of Jerusalem alone.

Like they could hurt me more, she had thought, but she had heeded his warning.

When she had gone through all of Zechariah's maps and notes, she remembered the tunnels and made out his markings and notes with a close study. Adjacent to Antonia Fortress and the Struthion Pool was an open area that contained the stock of stone, both rough and cut, used for the repairs to the walls of the *Struthius*. Among the piles and stacks was a small building that housed common tools. If she had read Zechariah's note correctly, within, she would find a hidden entrance to the underground chambers and tunnels of what was left of the basement level of the Hasmonean Baris.

They reached the stockpile of stone and found the building. Matthew had to put his shoulder against the door and push hard to open it. Within were tools showing the dust of months of disuse, and Miriam hoped the building remained unused for a while longer. She took out the lamp she carried and lit it. Handing it to Matthew, she shoved the door closed with a grunt. "There"—Miriam pointed at the stone bench that ran the length of the back wall. "Beneath it should be the entrance." Setting the lamp on the floor nearby, she grabbed one end of the bench and Matthew the other. His lifting and her sliding revealed a bare dirt floor. With her hand brushing the back wall, she walked the span of dirt, testing it with her feet, and felt something give midway.

Matthew knelt and prodded the packed earth there, searching for the edge of the trapdoor. "Here it is!" He got his fingers under and lifted, and a thick layer of dirt clods fell away. The hole was just big enough for a person to slip into. He reached an arm in and felt around. "It's lined with stone—and wait... Here's something." He groped farther and announced, "Handholds carved into the side." Still on his knees, Matthew motioned, and Miriam helped him realign the bench. Leaving enough room behind it that they could slip into the opening. They would need to develop a better means of hiding the entrance when they kept this tunnel in use, or someone would have to remain outside to conceal it behind them.

Miriam hoped Yohanan ben Zaccai's instructions had been clear. And that he had told Ya'el to knock on the outer door when she reached the building but not to loiter if the door did not open immediately. That made her think of the old priest. "Matthew..." she asked as she bent to closely examine the hole. "Did you speak to Yohanan about Arins?"

"He says Boaz trusts him."

Miriam watched Matthew get up and begin pacing as he kept his eyes on the entrance, listening for Ya'el. He worried about their safety. But most of the fighting was around the Temple Enclosure, Yohanan ben Levi's palace, and Phaesel Tower, which Simon bar Giora used for his headquarters and residence. Still, thousands had died in all parts of the city, not just faction members. They were men, women, children... young and old, innocent people in the wrong place at the wrong time. That morning, fighting had begun within the Temple Enclosure as Giora's men fought to oust Eleazar ben Simon, one of Yohanan ben Levi's lieutenants who held the Inner Court. Rebecca had wondered if Simon bar Giora, who controlled the Upper City, would take the Temple. Miriam prayed for it to happen if that meant her father would be freed from Yohann ben Levi. She also wished the two faction leaders would kill each other and that their deaths would stop the fighting inside the city.

"But," Matthew continued, "you were wise to tell him Yohanan recalled how we explored the city as children... but that was long ago. He asked no more questions, so...."

"Arins is right, though." Miriam removed her cloak and adjusted her tunic, loosening it over her chest. She patted the pack full of maps, pens, and ink. Miriam had planned to learn all of Zechariah's tunnels so she, too, could reach many parts of the city without walking the streets. But with Ehud's arrival, she had lost motivation. *I won't let myself be distracted again, no matter how Ya'akov pleads.* Now she must learn everything Zechariah had documented with his maps and notes. And she would teach Ya'el, too.

"The tunnels to the hidden valley near Motza and the old Canaanite Tunnel we used for Nahum's escape give us those two means of leaving and entering the city," she said. "But there must be more. We should find them and see how they can be used."

"There she is, I think," Matthew said, and at the knock, he walked toward the door, his hand on his sword.

* * *

This chamber Miriam and Ya'el left was small but had tables and benches. Miriam set her pack of maps on the largest table. She followed Ya'el into a hall; their lamps cast small arcs of light so they could see its dimensions.

"There's enough room," Ya'el said, "plenty of distance to set up targets, but we would have to bring many lamps to light it completely." Ya'el studied the long empty gallery, its farthest end deep in shadow.

"I'll bring your bow next time, and you can begin. Do you have arrows?"

"Yes. Shafts... I keep Elian busy shaping them and forming sharpened points. But I need feathers for the fletching."

"We still have Cicero's you collected, and Mother has added more to the supply. I can bring them."

"Bring them, but I want to save the green feathers... can you get me some to use just for training?"

"I'll ask Matthew... or have him somehow get arrows from the armory at Antonia Fortress." Miriam wondered if any of the tunnels in the old Baris were still connected to the fortress above. If someone realized weapons and equipment were missing from the armory, that would lead to trouble for them. *But still,* she thought as she shook her head, *there's much we could take.*

They needed to start going over the maps. Miriam shook the lamp, gauging how much time had passed by the oil remaining, a trick Yossi had taught her long ago. Matthew would be returning for them before sundown.

* * *

"So, the tunnels here," Matthew pointed at the map Miriam had spread on the table in the chamber they would use for their workroom, "also connect to Zedekiah's Cave... within the quarry." He moved his pointing finger to another section of the map. "And to the Temple Enclosure, here and here and in the City of David near the Pool of Siloam. That is where the tower fell that once guarded the southern wall."

"And I think other places, too," Miriam said. "I feel sure of these from my own exploring, though I haven't been through them all. The one at the Siloam Tower likely also connects to King David's Tomb." She glanced at Ya'el, who had not smiled since arriving, then said, "We'll check them out and the others."

Ya'el nodded as they readied to leave. "Shammai has other helpers now, and I'll have time to help. Elian will keep working with him. I'll have to tell him something, so he doesn't think he'll be exploring tunnels, too." She paused. "I'd like to get Cicero from your mother... it would help entertain the boy if he has to care for him."

LII

November 69 CE

Mevania, Italia

81 miles north of Rome, The Roman Legions' Encampment

Marcus Atillius admired how the gradually darkening sunset painted golden the bridge's stones and the browning fields beyond it. The city of Mevania sat upon a small hill along the Via Flaminia at the western edge of *valle umbra* at the confluence of the rivers Tinia, Clitumnus, and Anio. The valley's locus of water transport and the crossroads junction created what he had heard was called a *trivio* on the Roman roads. Near the Ponte Lapidium, the bridge over the Tinia spread the lower part of the plain where General Marcus Primus had brought his legions.

Marcus Attilitus sighed and turned to enter his tent. Now he knew what Nicanor had meant about getting tired of being sent where others needed him, no matter how much you wished to be elsewhere. Repaying his debt to Gnaeus Batiatus had freed him from a financial burden. Yet, his friendship with Nicanor had led him to a different entanglement. Indeed, he felt a sense of duty to General Vespasian and his lady, Antonia Caenis. But it seemed things were coming to a head, and he hoped for another kind of freedom very soon.

He studied Pugnio, who was working at a small table, steadily transferring notes inscribed on stacks of wax tablets to a single report on a parchment. So many tablets they filled the extra cots in their four-man tent. They represented a dozen meetings the burly correspondent now labored over. The man was amazingly deft despite his big, scarred hands.

"Do you think Vitellius intends to renounce the throne in exchange for his life?" Marcus asked, daring to interrupt. The other man looked up and shook out his hand to ease it. *Maybe he's glad for the rest*, Marcus thought and continued. "I know he sent the message asking General Primus to meet him here to confirm the terms. But that could be a stalling tactic."

The scribe nodded, waiting to hear more.

Marcus explained his thinking. "The second battle at Bedriacum was over a week ago. The Vitellians were crushed, and now the road is open to Rome. Why give them time to regroup?"

Pugnio picked up a tablet and read from it. "The count is 30,200 of Vitellius's men dead to 4,500 of General Primus's. But that imbalance is large because Vitellius's General Caecina was in chains the night before the battle. He was not able to command the Vitellians in the battle." He picked up another tablet. "I was with General Primus and took notes when Caecina was brought to him—less a prisoner of our cohort than rescued from his own men. They planned to deliver him to Vitellius as a traitor. Caecina reported he had told his men this: 'With Vitellius, there is only the name of power. With Vespasian lies *real* power. It is better to gain favor with real power. We will be overwhelmed if we fight.'"

Pugnio closed the tablet and said, "Caecina was right... and his men were badly wrong. There were not many left to regroup."

"And though General Primus won, we wait here," Marcus said, pacing the tent. "So, I ask again... do you believe Vitellius's message from four days ago that he will quit the throne... leaving Vespasian to become emperor, unopposed?"

"Two days after the battle," Pugnio said, "they cut down General Fabius Valens and his escort, who were trying to raise more Gauls to fight for Vitellius. All the emperor has left are the legions in and around Rome. Vitellius is not a soldier, and I think he would rather live as a failed past emperor than die as a current waning one. General Vespasian's last letter to General Primus said he would let Vitellius live if he surrendered."

A draft had just fluttered the tent's flap, signaling the coming of a chill evening, when a camp runner entered. "General Primus requires both of you at his command tent."

* * *

"Release him to return to Rome," General Marcus Primus told the two legionaries on either side of the road-stained messenger. He looked again at the parchment scroll, then Marcus Attilius and Pugnio. The writer already had the two halves of a wax tablet spread open on his knees, taking notes as the general continued.

"Titus Flavius Sabinus reports that Vitellius was on his way to the Temple of Concord three days ago. There he planned to leave the insignia of the empire given to him by the Senate... before meeting here in Mevania. But he was stopped by senior officers of the Praetorian Guard, who forced him to return to the palace."

The general, his beaked nose made more prominent by taut, deep furrows on either side, re-rolled the scroll and tossed it on the campaign desk behind him. "So, they will fight. My army will begin our march to Rome tomorrow, and we will wrest the city from them." He picked up a folded square of vellum and handed it to Marcus. "This is for you, from Antonia Caenis. I've read it." He waited as the freedman unfolded it.

Marcus read the message and met the general's unapologetic gaze.

"You must leave now," the general said with a nod, "and get to Rome quickly... ahead of my legions. Should the battle go against them, they might kill the boy."

"Yes, general." Marcus turned and was a dozen feet outside when he realized the shorter, stouter Pugnio had caught up with him.

"What did Lady Antonia's message say?"

"Vitellius's men have taken Domitian. She wants me to lead a group of men to save him."

LIII

NOVEMBER 69 CE

ALEXANDRIA

"This is the Rhakotis area of the city, closest to the mouth of the Nilus," said Yosef as they turned toward the waterfront. "It is the oldest part still referred to by its original name." Since early that morning, they had walked the Via Canopica and many of its side streets. Gates at each end of the main avenue marked the city's boundaries. They had started at the east, the Gate of the Sun—Helios, and worked their way west toward the Gate of the Moon—Selene. They had just left the street of the Soma and Alexander's mausoleum.

"You know a lot for having been here only once before," Nicanor said. "Have you now seen all you missed then?"

"I've read much about the city's history and have always wished to visit here," Yosef said. "But last time here was my first time. After you returned to Antioch to serve under Cestius Gallus, Cleo and Sayid went to Caesarea with Gessius Florus... I came here from Rome. I went quickly from the ship and onto a donkey cart—I had a family I hurried home to in Jerusalem...." Even as the words came out, Yosef regretted speaking of his family.

Nicanor had spoken in jest about his knowledge, but now his expression showed *he* regretted causing his friend more pain. Still, Yosef did not need to correct himself and say he still had a family and a city he called home. He did not believe he would see either again, though he hoped. "Yes, my friend," he said. "I've seen all I wish to...." There had been the briefest moments here in Alexandria when he considered where he stood and what he looked upon. Before, when he'd stood before Alexander's resting place—if such a conqueror's soul could ever rest—he had pondered the city's history. And his worries were temporarily set aside.

What he had heard at the dinner with Vespasian and again at the *cena*, the extravagant dinner hosted by Tiberius Alexander on their third night in Alexandria, brought back Yosef's concerns. The grain embargo Vespasian had ordered would lead to great suffering in Rome. He had overheard Tiberius Alexander commenting to the general that grain traders and farmers were complaining about being unable to ship their harvested crops. Who would pay them and when?

If General Vespasian will make his people suffer and risk the anger of merchants who provided the primary food source for Rome. How can I expect him to treat my people, my city Jerusalem, with mercy? He had even mentioned his thoughts to Nicanor, who seemed not to want to discuss it. That, too, had bothered him.

"We'll go to meet Marinus shortly," Nicanor said as he squinted at the sun's slant against the Heptastadion, the causeway connecting the city to Pharos Island. Its bridge was high enough for ships to pass beneath. Where the two men sat in the Small Harbor wharf taberna on an outdoor terrace had a view of the Eunostos, the Harbor of Fortunate Return, and its southern mooring, Kibotos Haven. "I'm... well, *we* will meet him at the Moon Gate just before sundown."

Yosef had understood Nicanor's hesitation to include him in the meeting with Marinus. But they'd discussed it and decided. Whether for ill or good, they were being watched. Both had seen men's faces that became familiar, and they realized they were trailing them wherever they went—likely hired by Florus. Yosef shifted the Roman pugio Nicanor had given him—with Titus's approval—to a more comfortable position. He had not carried a weapon since Yotapta but would fight if the men watching them planned harm. Still, it was better to remain close to Nicanor should something happen. He noticed the *tribunus* studying him.

"I see you ease your blade, and your eyes sweep around us. Those men are not currently in sight... but they are nearby. I got a glimpse of one when we stopped here." Nicanor raised the mug of beer the serving girl had just delivered, tasted it, and smacked his lips. "That astrologer, Claudius Babilius, the man General Vespasian introduced you to at the prefect's dinner.... Do you think he is having you—or us—followed? I don't believe he liked it much when the general told him that you, too, have visions that foretell the future. He seemed intent on currying favor with the next emperor. When I was with the Praetorian Guard in Rome, I heard of him as the emperor's astrologer in Nero's court. That was before he came to Alexandria as Nero's prefect."

Yosef had felt the man's eyes on him throughout the dinner. "He's now the director of the Great Library," he said, "though it is not as great since Julius Caesar burned part of it. But something about Babilius raises my dislike. I've never cared for men whose words are measured to fit what powerful men's ears wish to hear." As he said it, he saw Nicanor's eyebrows twitch, and he questioned his decision to convey his visions to Vespasian. But he had had the dreams... could he not be forgiven for trying to gain a position with a powerful Roman to help his people? He shook that thought away, knowing it would return at night to keep him from sleeping.

"Do you worry, Nicanor, that they might be connected to those men Marinus told you of our first day here? Men of the *Ala Veterana Gallorum et Thracum*." Marinus had warned them about them, former legion auxiliaries who followed the cult of Sobek, men who bore tattoos of crocodiles on their hands. They had yet to see any, but the men they suspected of watching them never got close enough to show tattoos. Marinus believed the cult men were connected to Gessius Florus, and he was still trying to get something to prove that connection.

"They could be," Nicanor said. "Marinus told me he has something important to show me.... to show us."

* * *

KIBOTOS HAVEN

This bay was much smaller than the two principal harbors, Nicanor noted. Marinus stopped at the ship nearest the junction of the quay and the street leading to the Moon Gate, and Nicanor saw the carved symbol on the stern of the shallow-drafted vessel. "One of yours?" he asked, though he did not need to.

Marinus nodded. "For trade... this ship, the *Khonsu*, travels to and from Shedet, the capital of the Phiom region. Come on board."

Nicanor and Yosef followed the ship owner up a narrow gangplank across the weathered deck and down steps into a small central storage hold. An enormous man stood at a doorway at the end, his head grazing the underside of the deck above. He was shaved and gleaming in the light of a swaying lantern, with massive arms, thick as a man's thighs, holding two swords crossed before his chest.

"Amon," Marinus said in greeting, nodding, and the giant stepped aside. Within this inner space, the three men could barely fit themselves. A swathed object lay on a tiny table beneath another lantern, and Marinus unwrapped it. As the folds of cloth were laid back, the glint of gold was bright even in the low light.

"A man in Shedet asked if I could convert this to Roman coin... he had received it in payment for finding men—fighters—for a rich man who needed them. He arranged former Thracian auxiliaries for him."

Yosef lifted the object. "This is a tithing vessel from the Inner Temple!" He turned it over. "It has the identifying mark stamped in its base...."

"Who paid the man with this?" Nicanor asked, praying this was the proof Vespasian needed to conclude Gessius Florus was involved with the Thracians.

"A squat man, half the height of my Amon outside, but just as broad... and he had massive hands."

LIV

November 69 CE

Alexandria

The Prefect's Palaces, Vespasian's Praetorium

Nicanor crossed the central courtyard of the palace wing that had become General Vespasian's praetorium and quarters. Auxiliaries from eastern Syria were posted at every corner. They patrolled the grounds, and their like manned the fortified towns along the Euphrates, a natural border and buffer against Parthia. Tiberius Alexander had taken these fierce fighters under his command to provide security for Vespasian, and Nicanor respected them. Two thousand had arrived from Antioch in two giant ships. "They're *octeres*," Marinus had told him, "with 1,600 rowers—two banks of 800 each side—and they can transport 1200 soldiers. One is over 300 feet long and 33 feet wide, best used for coastal sailing. Out in the deep ocean current, wind, and waves... they'd twist and ultimately break in half at some point." Even to Nicanor's untrained eye, they had looked like unwieldy ships.

He passed through the atrium to the broad hall leading to the central chamber Vespasian had taken for his office and briefing room. Four armored guards stood outside its entrance. Nicanor knew another four were at the entry to a smaller courtyard and a connecting gallery to the rest of the palace. No one entered until approved by the general through his aide, Junius. The senior guard leaned into the entry and announced him. Junius appeared, peering around the guard's broad back. He nodded, and the guard captain stepped aside for Nicanor to enter.

The only remnant of the formal dining room was a long, broad table raised on decorative stone blocks to the height of a campaign desk. A *sella curule* at the head of the table and several folding camp stools along its sides comfortably replaced the low divans used by diners. Pitchers of water and amphoras of wine stood at both ends of the table, though only two men sat at the farthest end. Vespasian stood there looking down at an open *loculus*, its contents—a set of maps and sheaves of vellum and parchment scrolls—spread on the table. The old general lifted the legionary's satchel and set it beside his chair. Nodding at Nicanor, he pointed at the map. "Do you recognize where this is?"

Nicanor leaned over to study the map. "Yes, sir. That's the Po River, the *Via Postumia*. And the area between Cremona and Bedriacum. It marks the disposition of the Legions 3rd *Gallica*, 8th *Augusta,* 7th *Claudia,* 7th *Galbiana,* 13th *Gemina*... and their auxiliary cohorts and cavalry. Is this General Primus's army?" He looked up at Vespasian and his son. Titus nodded with a smile, so Nicanor went on. "And here are Legions 11th, *Rapax*, 5th, *Alaudae*, 1st, *Italica,* 12th, *Primigenia,* and 4th, *Macedonica* with their auxiliaries and cavalry... Vitellius's army." His eyes shifted to the sheets of parchment next to the map. Nicanor picked it up. "A battlefield report... from General Primus?"

"On his tremendous victory. He has broken Vitellius's army." Titus's smile broadened as he took the report from Nicanor and read. "Whoever wrote this writes well. He even tells how the Syrian legion, the 3rd *Gallica,* saluted the sun on the morning of the battle, and that disheartened the Vitellians. The captured legionaries thought it meant General Primus's legions were watching for reinforcements from the east. Of course, if that were true, it would have meant the Vitellian legions were badly outnumbered."

"How many of General Primus's men were lost?"

Titus checked the report. "Nearly 5,000 of our men went down, sadly. But over 30,000 of the Vitellians were killed."

"So, General Primus's army is mostly intact," Nicanor said, checking the battle date on the first sheet. "He must be in Rome by now."

Titus shook his head. "Afterward, Vitellius stalled General Primus's march on Rome by trying to negotiate his abdication. He was to meet General Primus in Mevania to confirm and sign terms, but events changed his mind, or he had it changed for him."

"Events, sir... what events?" Nicanor asked.

"The Praetorians stopped him."

"Why? They must know General Primus has a large enough force to enter Rome and take it."

"*Quis custodiet ipsos custodes?*" Vespasian said, his face grim. "Who will guard the guards? The Praetorian Guard will make him fight in and around Rome using his legions, for they want an emperor they can control. Their power has been decades solidifying and has become the expected path to the throne—for some, the *only* path. To become a ruler or remain one requires their support."

Nicanor thought of Ophonius Tigellinus and Gaus Sabinus, Nero's Praetorian Co-Prefects, and their intrigues. He nodded and saw from a glance at Vespasian that he was angry, an emotion he had seen only a few times. "But you don't require their support, sir?"

"No, I don't need them, but I will make them pay." Vespasian shook his head, his face drawn tight and deeply creased. He picked up a flattened scroll of parchment, and the remnants of sealing wax crackled and fell from the leather ribbon as he reopened the scroll. "My Lady Antonia tells me that Domitian has been captured and held hostage. And the Praetorians not only took my son but attempted to take my daughter and granddaughter, and separately my son-in-law Quintus Cerealis was captured or killed... Antonia does not know which yet. Domitilla and Flavia escaped, and now Antonia and the men she hired from Gnaeus Batiatus are protecting them in Tibur." He set the letter down and picked up another, still folded but without a seal. "For you," Vespasian said, handing it to Nicanor. "It also tells of Antonia's plan to save Domitian."

* * *

YOSEF'S QUARTERS

"How was the meeting?" Yosef asked eagerly when Nicanor entered the sitting room. "Did you tell General Vespasian about the payment for the Thracians?"

"No, we discussed other important matters." The tribunus nodded to Yosef, Marinus, and Anyte, who sat beside Yosef with a thick tablet, a metal stylus in her hand. Nicanor sat and reopened the letter he had skimmed as Vespasian—holding his anger in— continued their meeting. The resulting orders from the general were what Nicanor had expected but not looked forward to. "I will speak with the general later or in the morning," he said. His eyes went to Marcus Attilius's message. It was just a few rough-lettered lines, not as finely written as his previous message. The lines were enough to make him worry about his friend.

"Nicanor, my hand is not as good as Pugnio's, but he is busy finishing the report for General Primus. I write to tell you I go to Rome now to find where Vitellius's Praetorians hold Domitian, then free him. I leave Carmenta with Antonia Caenis. She is too fine a horse to risk in the chaos that Rome has become. She will be there for you when you return. *Vivamus moriendum est,* Marcus.

"Let us live since we must die," Nicanor muttered aloud as he read Marcus's closing.

"What is that?" Yosef asked.

Nicanor looked up at Yosef, and Marinus watched them as Anyte used the flattened end of her stylus to smooth away lines of writing on her tablet. "Something a friend, Marcus, in Rome told me once," Nicanor replied. "Life is short... enjoy it while you can. He now risks his own life to save Vespasian's youngest son."

"I pray he succeeds without harm."

Nicanor looked at Yosef and knew he meant those words.

"I think I am being followed, too," Marinus said, looking at Anyte, "and I fear more for her than for myself. We must tell the general about that and what we've learned about the Thracians."

"I'll speak to General Vespasian and Titus in the morning... there's another meeting with them and Tiberius Alexander." Nicanor turned to Yosef. "I'm sIy, my friend, *alea jacta est*... the die is cast. Tomorrow, we plan the march to Caesarea, and from there... the assault on Jerusalem."

LV

December 69 CE

Rome

Saepta Julia

Marcus Attilius reeled out of the southern side of the Saepta Julia. He staggered through its travertine marble porticus, dripping blood from the crude tourniquet Pugnio had applied to his half-severed arm. The limb felt dead beneath the pressure of the leather strap Pugnio had found to cinch around near his armpit. The writer had then cut long strips from a cloak to strap the numb limb to Marcus's chest to keep it from flopping. Or falling off. From what Marcus could see through all the blood, though, the bone was deeply nicked but not cut through.

He looked around for more soldiers but saw only the empty uncolonnaded, broad corridor leading to the nearby *diribitorium*, a public voting hall. He had been inside the impressive place before. The roof, supported by beams of Larchwood one hundred feet long and one and a half feet thick, had the widest span of any building in Rome. Small groups in the distance were moving north, leaving the city, and from one of the nearby streets, he heard the tromp of hundreds marching in what seemed the same direction.

Bending the arm at the elbow to support himself as he looked around a corner brought back the screaming pain. Marcus had bit his lip to bloody shreds as Pugnio treated him and still had not held in the groans. But no one was around then to hear him other than Pugnio, who now signaled his presence with the huff of heavy breathing. The writer was carrying Domitian over his shoulder and had only just managed to catch up with him. Vespasian's youngest son had a bloody gash on his brow that wasn't deep, but the blow had knocked him unconscious.

It had taken days and the work of Antonia Caenis's spies to find where Vitellius's Praetorian Guard held Domitian. He, Pugnio, and three gladiators from Gnaeus Batiatus's *ludis* had cut their way through the twelve Praetorians guarding the boy, and only the three had survived.

Final Siege

So far, he thought. He would probably at least lose his right arm, quite possibly his life. Marcus gripped his sword left-handed and laughed.

"You laugh?" Pugnio grunted. "Strange time for that. We can't escape the city; the horns blare across Rome. General Primus's army has reached the outskirts. Someone will soon check on Domitian, or his guard watch will change... and then we'll have more Praetorians upon us. Where do we go now?"

"I laugh... thinking, what good am I as a one-armed fighter?" Marcus gasped when he backed into a hidden area for cover and struck the wounded arm against the wall as he beckoned Pugnio to follow. They must take stock.

Built by Julius Caesar as part of the complex for citizens to vote, this building had been converted, under Nero, into a venue for gymnastic exhibitions he had once come to see. Marcus looked southwest toward the Pantheon. It did not seem that long ago he had met Nicanor there with Vespasian's brother, Flavius Sabinus and Domitian, as they strategized moving General Vespasian's youngest son to safety. The Pantheon's Plaza was too open and exposed, especially with streets as empty as they had become this close to nightfall, the people hiding from the fighting to come. Now any movement caught the attention of the city guard in its patrols. It would not do.

His eyes moved from the Pantheon to the Temple of Isis, almost directly south of where they stood, not a thousand feet away. The temple's exterior was decorated with Aegyptian objects. A pair of obelisks in red granite at the entrance were shading pink in the fading sun. But inside, the temple was dark, and surely no followers of Isis would venture out to worship with the city on the verge of battle.

Marcus eyed the writer who had surprised him when he prepared to leave Mevania. Pugnio had insisted on joining him in his mission, saying, "I was not always a writer. I can fight, and I owe Antonia Caenis my life." And indeed, Pugnio had fought. He did not wield a sword well. But inside Saepta Julia's halls and the chamber where Domitian had been held, he had closed on the Praetorian Guards, parried one thrust, dropped the sword, and grappled with the soldier who had expected a sword fight. Surprise was still on the Praetorian's face as the writer broke his back. The dried-wood snap had echoed through the hall, then Pugnio had cut the man's throat. The scribe had killed three more the same way, only two fewer than Marcus. Even the gladiators with them had not killed as many.

"Can you run with him," Marcus gestured at Domitian's slack form, "draped over your shoulder?"

Pugnio nodded, "Can you run and not leave your arm behind?" The writer seemed more concerned than sarcastic.

"Let's see... follow me." Marcus raced toward the temple, each stride a jolting bolt of pain. They had just reached the steps when they heard shouts behind them. Two armored Praetorians ran after them, moving quickly despite their armor. Marcus moved halfway up the steps and wheeled, lifting his sword to face them.

"No, Marcus!" gasped Pugnio as he set Domitian on the top step at the foot of a column. "I have this... you cannot fight."

The freedman knew Pugnio was right. "Here..." Marcus flipped the sword to hand it to the writer hilt first.

"Keep it... I'm not good with one," Pugnio waved away the blade. He took a pair of gloves from his broad belt, thick leather with metal studs over the knuckles and metal plates on their backs. The gloves protected the fighter's hands and punished whoever received one of their punches. "The others wore no armor, and we surprised them." He nodded toward the approaching Praetorians. "I'll need these now." Pugnio slipped the gloves on and said, "It has been a while since I wore these."

Marcus recognized their type. "Pankration." The practice of that deadly martial art explained Pugnio's scarred hands... and the prowess he had demonstrated in fighting the Praetorians.

"Do you need help?" a voice behind them called.

Pugnio continued to face the two Praetorians who had slowed at the bottom of the temple steps. Marcus half-turned to see a robed attendant step from the shadows inside the temple. "Yes... please help us." Marcus dropped his sword and, with one hand, grabbed the back of Domitian's tunic to drag him inside. The attendant gave the approaching Romans one look and helped pull Domitian by one arm.

Walking backward, Marcus watched as Pugnio spun and swept the legs out from under the first Praetorian in a graceful move he thought impossible for the burly scribe. The man went down with a clatter as Pugnio leaped past him, pivoted his body, and punched his metal-sheathed fist into the face of the second Praetorian. Despite his heavy breathing, Marcus heard the crack of the man's jaw as it broke, slewing to one side, and saw the lower part of the soldier's face masked with blood, his nose pulped. His mouth dropped broken teeth as he fell. Marcus's last sight was of the other Praetorian sprawled prone on the steps, Pugnio astride him, twisting his head back. The man's neck broke even as he reached over his shoulder and plunged his dagger into Pugnio's throat.

Swallowed by the shadows inside the temple, Marcus knew he could not save Pugnio. As a torch flared, casting a glow on him and the wide-eyed attendant, he looked down at Domitian and wondered if the general's son was worth the writer's death.

LVI

December 69 CE

Sycaminum

Florus's Port Warehouse

Sayid wrapped his cloak around him, thankful there was no wind. Despite the damp chill that had settled into his bones, he smiled. The memory that just came to him was a good one; Nicanor complaining about how he felt the winter and dampness in his bones and old wounds. Sayid shrugged his shoulder, loosening it and feeling the pull of the scar left from the sword thrust by Gessius Florus's military aide Caputo into his upper chest. Florus's enforcer had nearly killed him that night long ago. Perhaps he was getting old enough to have an inkling of what Nicanor meant, the ache in the bones. Or, more likely, he had accumulated enough wounds to feel now the impact of weather and its change.

Here at the water's edge, he also recalled killing Caputo even as the man's sword cut into him. In that forgotten building on the beach, half-buried in sand dunes and scrub brush near the residence of Gessius Florus and Cleo in Ptolemais. He had been hiding there to do what Lady Octavia had asked of him, what he would have done anyway for the sake of Lady Cleo.

But Sayid had also owed something to Octavia's husband, Cestius Gallus, the former commander of the 12th Legion. The man had granted him leave to see his mother, and Sayid had helped nurse her back to health. If he had not, she might have died without their seeing one another again. So Sayid had gladly gone to Ptolemais to help Cleo get free from Gessius Florus.

The area south of Sycaminum's port was much like the stretch of the seafront where Cleo had lived with Florus, windswept dunes that had piled and grown over the years. This part of the port was also the site of this warehouse set off from others, Florus's destination.

Since Nicanor and Yosef had left for Alexandria, Sayid had kept watch over Florus's fortified villa outside the walls of Caesarea. He had caught glimpses of Cleo's husband going to and from the city for a while. Always with an escort of armed men. Then, for the past two months, no sight of him. Then Sayid had overheard an idle conversation between two men who worked for the man. He had seen them come and go from the villa as they picked up feed from Todros, the horse trader who also stocked grain for sale. One had mentioned, "He returns soon... then maybe there'll be some action." Two days later, he had seen Gessius Florus, mounted with a group of men, come out of the villa's gates and head north. He had hastily saddled Albus and grabbed the pack he kept ready.

Sayid had trailed Florus and his escort, sure he was headed to Ptolemais, a little over a day's ride from Caesarea, so he was not worried he would lose him. But then he had been lucky to notice the fresh horse droppings where Florus and his men had turned off the Roman road leading through Sycaminum and onto Ptolemais. The horse's spoor was where the road passed two shrub-topped sandy mounds, and following the sign, Sayid had found a secret, well-packed gravel path wide enough to accommodate a wagon.

The road had led to a warehouse that he watched now at the southern edge of the port. Behind a rise big enough to hide him, Sayid had dismounted and looped Albus's reins over a length of driftwood buried in the weed-clotted hip of a sand dune. Staying low, he found a position where he could see the warehouse. A squat, powerful-looking man came out to meet Florus, and all went inside. From watching for things in Caesarea, Sayid knew the stocky man's name was Drusus. Sayid was also sure Drusus had been the man who had tried to kill him in Ptolemais, but Celsus Evander had saved him.

Sayid knew, then, that Florus wanted him dead because he suspected or knew Sayid had helped Cleo escape him. And Florus was behind the rumor and reward for the noblewoman hiding in Jerusalem. But what was he doing at a warehouse in Sycaminum?

Two hours had passed since the men had entered when Sayid heard the crunch of wheels and hooves. As he watched, a wagon approached the warehouse—the wagon heavily laden, judging by the pull of the mules and the wheel rims cutting ruts in the gravel. A wagon at a warehouse was a regular sight. But having six heavily armed riders as escorts, with two equally armed drivers? That was not.

The wide doors at the southern end of the warehouse opened, and Sayid could see they had been reinforced. He could see twelve or more men inside. With them were the taller figure of Florus and the short, broad Drusus. As the wagon pulled in, they all stepped aside, and four men closed the doors.

* * *

Well away from where the gravel road reached the warehouse, Sayid had pitched his cold camp among the dunes and scrub brush. A scattering of slow-moving clouds shrouded a nearly full moon, offering only the palest of light. Still, it was enough for Sayid's sharp eyes to see around him. But he would trust his ears more for warning. He was thankful Albus had kept his routine silent disposition as he followed Sayid's command to lower himself onto the ground. And he welcomed Albus's warmth. Sayid, wrapped in a blanket, leaned against the horse's broad rump while Sayid draped another blanket over the beast, whose even breathing proved he dozed.

Sayid was tired, but many thoughts kept him awake. He thought not of Florus, as curious as he was about what was happening with the warehouse. Instead, he thought about his father, whom he had not seen in six months—for that, he was thankful. He did not need his father's questions about why he was again occupied with something that was not a soldier's work. In Hebron, there had been a moment when he saw something in his father's expression change when he had looked at him. Not approval... but maybe the man showed consideration and not disdain. That scorn would probably come back if he saw his son now.

Sayid shook his head and adjusted the blanket over Albus to better cover his belly and broad back. The horse lifted his head to look at him, then lowered it again. Sayid's thoughts drifted like the clouds above. If not before, he'd see his father during the assault on Jerusalem. There he would, at last, show him he was a soldier.

* * *

"Hmmph... what?" Sayid woke as Albus's whiskered muzzle scratched the side of his face again. He straightened, the blanket falling away as the horse shifted. He heard the sound of hooves on gravel in the morning's stillness. The sound was as crisp and sharp as the chill settled in Sayid's rump. He stiffly got to his knees and crawled to see. Florus and his escort flashed past, kicking up a spray of gravel. Sayid spun back toward Albus, finding the horse on its knees, poised to stand but waiting for him. *Clever animal*, Sayid thought as he checked and secured the saddle. He hated leaving it on Albus, but the animal had not seemed discomfited by it. Now he was glad. He mounted and eased out onto the gravel road.

Florus and his men were out of sight and past the bend where the path arced toward the main Roman road. A minute later, as Sayid approached that junction, he held back. He expected Florus to turn south toward Caesarea. *Good*—Sayid could easily trail behind. Several minutes later, his mind wandered again as he thought about the warehouse and wagon. And suddenly, Sayid realized there was no sign ahead of Florus and his escort, just what seemed to be a merchant in a mule cart.

The roads to and from Caesarea had long since settled down. Rebels had stopped all attacks and harassment of travelers and merchants months before. Legion patrols routinely swept along the road to ensure there was no trouble. He heeled Albus into a trot to draw alongside the mule cart. "Did six or seven men pass you recently?"

The man blinked and replied, "Mounted men together? No." He shook his head. Some legion cavalry passed me as I left Ptolemais... told me they'd be up and down this stretch of road."

Sayid did not thank the man. He wheeled Albus in the opposite direction.

* * *

Near Ptolemais

Even in the spans between villages, towns, and cities, Roman roads often had waypoints near water sources where the road was widened. Travelers would find posts set to hitch animals and benches to sit on and rest. Sayid knew this part of the road, and he had reached where the road veered east before turning to run through Ptolemais to the Roman encampment on the other side of the city. This section of the road followed the level areas between a rolling series of hills that climbed toward the slopes of Carmel, the mountain the locals called Har haKarmel. The road was busy with carts and men on horseback.

Sayid saw ahead some mounted legionaries at the waypoint perimeter. With them were men he recognized as some of Florus's riders. Sayid angled Albus off into a long copse of trees that bordered the road. Albus's broad chest broke through an undergrowth of tall weeds, clumps of brush that grew thick on the slope above the waypoint. Sayid dismounted to push through a tangled thicket too dense to risk injuring Albus. Careful to avoid thorns from the scrub and dried branches on the ground, he crept closer to just above the back edge of the waypoint clearing. He stopped when he heard the muffled voices of the three men on the benches set there. Sayid stood partially from his crouch and craned his neck to see over the scrub brush he hid behind. He saw Gessius Florus and two senior officers of the 12th Legion: Galerius Senna, its commander, and Tyrannius Priseus, its First Centurion! Why did they meet here with Gessius Florus?

"You... what are you doing?"

Sayid jerked to his left to see two large men closing on him. He knew immediately that they were Thracians, to judge by the distinctive curved sword, the *sica*, they carried. The men's hands bore near-identical crocodile tattoos. Sayid straightened and hurled himself through the brush toward where he'd left Albus, the two cursing men lurching after him.

LVII

December 69 CE

Caesarea

Gessius Florus's Villa

Gessius Florus studied the Thracian mercenary captain who stood on the other side of his desk. The man had a seamed, scarred face, and he looked unconcerned. "So, it's been two days," Florus said in a challenge, "and your men, whose '*skill*' I pay you well for, have not caught the man?"

"No, Lord Florus...."

"Did they get a description so we know to watch for him?"

"Not a clear one, lord.... just of a young man with dark hair, in simple clothing, on a big, pale horse."

Florus was then similarly unconcerned—many young locals on the road matched that vague description. The one in the bushes near the Ptolemais waypoint was likely just curious, the glitter of Galerius Senna's uniform probably having caught his eye. The 12th Legion commander was a preening peacock, but Florus still needed him. Besides, the man at the waypoint could have overheard nothing from where he'd been seen lurking.

Florus frowned and feigned anger at the Thracian captain. "Continue to watch for anyone who seems to be interested in me. What of the Syrian auxiliary, Sayid? You reported he had returned... has he been found and dealt with?"

"He was back in Caesarea for a few days but is now gone again. We don't know where sir. But we have discovered that his father serves in Hebron. We have seen them meeting in the past, so maybe we could—"

"I *pay you* to solve things like this and to see that the solutions do not have consequences for me. Do what I want, or I'll hire others who can." Florus caught the flicker of worry in Krateros's eyes, which pleased him. He sat at his desk, flicking a stylus back and forth as he listened to the mercenary's tromping clatter recede down the hallway toward the atrium. Krateros' lack of results was disappointing, but what Galerius Senna had told him at their meeting near Ptolemais was even more dissatisfying. The 12th Legion's commander and his

First Centurion had failed to find a suitable spy to insert close enough to Vespasian to watch the centurion. *No*, Florus thought with a frown, *the tribunus now*. Upon his return, the messages he'd read indicated that the tribunus, Nicanor, would join Titus there. *And there I can have him killed without questions, just another fatality in the fighting*. He smiled as he reread the message. Finally, things moved in his favor: Vespasian had been swayed to remain in Alexandria. Titus would soon return to Caesarea to lead the legions against Jerusalem.

He lowered the sheet and stared thoughtfully at the ledger at one side of his desk. While Vespasian was looking ahead to becoming emperor, he would no longer be near enough to closely watch anything in Judea other than the attack on Jerusalem. As long as Titus succeeded, there was no need for the would-be emperor to loom over his son's shoulder. And he knew the young man would be victorious. Titus would attack, lay siege, and destroy Jerusalem. As he read another line, he thought, *the young man seeks to shine in his father's eyes... and to establish himself for succession when Vespasian dies.* Florus mused. *Titus won't pay attention to anything I do, and Nicanor will be with him. So, their eyes are off me.* But Florus had someone as his eyes and ears near Titus, reporting the decisions of Vespasian and the young general. *He will whisper in Titus's ear whatever I tell him to say.*

He set that message aside and picked up the one that confirmed the accuracy of the information tortured from the Levite guard. Indeed, Matthew ben Mathias was the key to finding the hidden Jewish Temple treasure. Drusus and his men had been fortunate to uncover one more wagonload, but all other searches had been fruitless. He read the last line of the following message, which explained that they believed more of the treasure was being hidden in the city or nearby. Certainly, this Temple Guard officer, Matthew, had knowledge of the locations. That pleased him almost as much as that this Matthew was the brother of Vespasian's pet prisoner, Yosef. Though he was not done trying yet, if Florus could not kill Yosef, he would kill someone close to him. Florus pushed the messages aside and took his pen and ink to a new sheet of parchment:

You must befriend Yosef ben Mathias's family. Find out what I need and be ready.

LVIII

December 69 CE

Caesarea

The Roman Encampment

Sayid led Albus into Nicanor's stable-quarters, thankful the orders he always carried with him now had not been questioned by the sentries at the main gate. Nicanor's tribunus rank as his direct commanding officer, endorsed by General Vespasian, meant there was no need to explain his arrival *post median noctem*. Though after midnight was an odd time to enter a Roman camp and not raise suspicion. He knew this was especially so for him, on an exhausted horse, both streaked with the long-dried blood of several scratches. And Sayid had been wrapped in a fetid blanket, one he still smelled after two nights and day of wearing it. The scene had raised eyebrows and swords. Sayid had silently handed the guard captain the orders, and he'd read them and told the guards to lower their weapons. Sayid did not think any Thracians had followed him but had not wanted to risk going to the horse traders. The legion camp was safer.

Sayid closed the stable doors behind them and stripped the saddle, blanket, and bridle from Albus. He tended to the cuts on the horse's chest, neck, and shoulders. Then, the horse watered and fed; he cleaned his scratches, glad the ones on his legs and arms were shallow. The deeper cut on his cheek, where a slender branch had whipped and scored him, had dried, broken open, and crusted again. He wiped it carefully, trying not to start the bleeding again.

The dense, thorny thicket had saved him at the waypoint outside Ptolemais. He had shed his cloak and moved fast, running for his life, not caring that the thorns tore him. The burly Thracians had tangled their own cloaks, which snagged on the thorns and slowed them as they had to cut their way through. That gave him enough time to reach and mount Albus, then heel him to surge and breast through another heavy thicket and into the trees. The horse had not hesitated even as the low tree limbs and more bunches of tangled scrub thorns made the going painful.

Sayid had not turned toward the road as his pursuers would have expected. There the Thracians and legionaries would spread north and south in their search. He didn't know how far, so he had kept to the countryside parallel to the road south until he was past Sycaminum. There he had turned onto the semi-hidden gravel road to the warehouse, still feeling the itch of his questions. They lingered still, and he must scratch.

Sayid had been chilled to the bone and still was. Sundown had increased the cold, and he and Albus had to find somewhere to rest for the night and add more time for the searchers to lose interest. The area around the warehouse had seemed worth trying, especially in a place they would not have expected he would dare to go. His thought had been to learn more about it if he could. And he *had*.

Sayid now mulled what he'd heard in the warehouse. He drank deeply from a skin of water hung from a peg on the wall and rolled himself into a heavy blanket to lie on his cot in Nicanor's quarters. Near that warehouse he had left hours before, almost in the same spot he'd hidden, he had settled Albus in the lee of a dune and covered him with his blanket. In their escape, he had lost his pack, a meager portion of food, and a small grain bag for Albus. Then he discovered the stopper had pulled from his waterskin. It hung upside down from the saddle, empty. A grumbling belly could be tolerated, but thirst would be harder to ignore. He knew he had to find water for them both.

He had crept to the warehouse and crawled its perimeter, seeking a well. But he found none. That meant a cistern would be on the property, or the men would store their waterskins inside. The last glow of the sunset's red-orange had faded from the western sky. Still seeing no movement, he had slipped from the thick fringe of scrub brush and crawled toward the eastern side of the building. He searched for an entry he would slip through without alarming the men inside. It had been quiet—not a sound... not a movement. Perhaps they had gone. He had followed the wall on that darker side of the warehouse, and his hands had crossed a recess. His probing fingers found an inset door in the warehouse's curiously thick walls. He had waited and placed an ear to the door, but still, he could detect no sound. He had tried the door, and though it was stiff with apparent disuse, it took just the push of his shoulder to open it with a low scraping sound that made him cringe.

There had been no light immediately inside, though some distance away near the southern end of the building had been a glow and the muffled sound of laughter. His eyes had adjusted and made out shades of gray among the deep-shadowed interior. With his hand touching the wall, he had moved toward the northern end, away from the light and sounds. He had come upon a room built into the wall and slipped inside. His exploring fingers had found wall-mounted chains and manacles crusted with something that smelled of rotted meat. He had been glad he could not see it.

He'd had a fleeting memory of when he had been wounded, and the Jewish rebel, Yohanan of Gischala, had captured and chained him in a cell. Sayid convinced the man that he carried important letters for Cestius Gallus, which could stop the 12th Legion's attack on Jerusalem. Finally, the rebel leader let him go. He had then reached Cestius Gallus just as he began his attack. The contents of the letters had indeed made Cestius Gallus pull back from Jerusalem.

If only things had ended then and returned to how they were before, Sayid thought.

Moments later, as he came out of the cell-like room, he stumbled to his knees into a depression in the floor, where the smell of ashes and old burned parchment had filled his nostrils and nearly made him cough. He had caught himself with his hand to the ground and brought up a fistful of what felt like charred sheets, some half-burned. Without thinking, he had tucked them into his tunic.

As he had circuited the building, it seemed much larger than it appeared outside. At what his sense of direction told him was the western wall, he had encountered more rooms. These were deeper than the one he'd found before and had been sealed by chains and locked doors. The feel of the huge links and locks had told him it would likely take less time to cut through the doors than through the chains. What was inside? The questioning itch had grown stronger.

Next, he heard animals in the warehouse. As he passed the corner of the last room, the glow of a lantern on a post in a corner showed him a row of horses tethered to a waist-high bar mounted to the wall. Four horses dozed, standing, and eight others lay on the ground on a thick bed of straw. His eyes had caught a glint of water in a trough below the hitching bar. And he had felt for his empty waterskin. But there had been no way to get to the water without disturbing the horses. He had stepped into the darkness where the corner lantern did not reach and turned again in the direction he thought would get him past the animals. But that direction was toward the glow of lanterns and the muted talk of several men.

As he got closer, he could make them out as they sat or lay on the ground in shadows at the edge of the arc of light from the lamps. He had angled toward the wall again, glad when he felt it, and inched close enough to hear the men.

They had spoken some Greek dialect he could barely understand. So he crept even closer, crouch-walking to where he could see and hear them clearly enough. They were drinking from water skins or wineskins, which had worsened his thirst, especially when the odor of sour wine and sweat wafted to him.

From what he could see, none of the men had a crocodile tattoo on his hand, and they had not looked Thracian. The largest stood and stretched, and one reclining man called, "Will Gessius succeed?" The questioner waved his hand at the dark western part of the building beyond the horses and asked, "Will he cover his family's debt?"

The big man had replied: "If the amount of treasure is what he claims, he'll have more than enough."

The lolling man sat up. "Pray to the gods that is so. My family has served his for a century and profited... we'd not wish for them to return to being mere olive and grain merchants again."

The standing man said, "Gessius himself put the family's fortunes at risk... he'll do what he must. As much for that as to enrich himself... he's always been a capable bastard... and a greedy one. Besides, he's got our best man in Jerusalem, come out of retirement to help; he owes the family that much."

Behind Sayid, there had been a shrill whinny and the thud of a stamp and kick with more animal cries. The big man called, "Antreas, go see about that noise—find out what's happening. You others look alive."

All at once, Sayid had found there was no time to retrace his route. One of the reclining men had already risen, grabbed a torch to light it, and turned in his direction. Sayid had turned toward the central darkness and prayed he'd not gotten turned around. He blindly walked toward what he believed was the eastern wall. As he reached it, he sprawled over a crusted wad of a blanket he had snatched up when his hands came upon it as he'd desperately felt for the door he had come through. At last, he found it and scurried from the warehouse, hurriedly pushing the door closed.

No longer trying to hide, he had sprinted to Albus, who rose without complaint. He did not know if his presence had alarmed the horses inside the building. But the men were getting up to check them and their surroundings. He had not risked finding out whether the horses and men were aware of him, and he wanted to get away as fast as possible. They had galloped up the gravel path and onto the road south, stopping only for small breaks, and had raced through the night until dawn.

They'd hidden to sleep a few hours during the day, and by late afternoon, they had continued to make their way to Caesarea.

Sayid was exhausted and declared that he was done reliving the answers that created more questions. He willed his mind to stop so he could sleep. His last thought was, *I wish Nicanor was here to talk about that warehouse.*

* * *

Next morning...

Sayid laid out the half-burned sheets of parchment he'd retrieved from his soiled, castoff tunic on the small table. Much of the writing was hard to read... lines translated from Hebrew and Aramaic to Greek.

"Sayid!" called a voice accompanied by a rapping sound on the side door, not from the street-front stable doors. He opened the door to find Celsus Evander standing there.

"It's good to see you, sir... what can I—"

Then he stopped, feeling his blood run cold at the expression on his former officer's face.

At first, Sayid thought it was because of how he looked after his adventures. But then, an equally tall man stepped around Celsus from behind the legion quartermasters' commander.

"So, you decided Hebron was enough war for you," his father said. "You've become a clerk again." Marcus Sabinus's tone had that sharp edge of disdain Sayid had heard before.

LIX

December 69 CE

Jerusalem

The Upper City

"So, they have bred a faction within a faction," Mathias said, returning to the room with one hand on Matthew's shoulder. After his arrival home, though wobbly on his feet, he had insisted on sitting in the courtyard, his favorite place, and hearing of any news. "Like beasts lacking food, they prey on their own flesh." Mathias shook his head in sadness and lowered himself with a groan onto a chair.

Miriam was at his elbow right away with a cup of water into which she'd squeezed an orange. He must replenish his body from Yohanan ben Levi's imprisonment.

Eleasar ben Ananias, still standing, commented: "Eleazar ben Simon has long believed his father disrespects him. He served well as one of Simon's lieutenants when they harried the retreating 12th Legion. Then he led well during the fighting at Beth Horon. But Simon never took note, and that resentment festered enough to bring Eleazar into the arms of Yohanan ben Levi... only to find little esteem under the Gischalan, either." He motioned toward the three Levite Temple guardsmen to indicate his readiness to leave. "And so," he said, "Yohanan ben Levi wants to use him as a stick to poke in the eye of Simon bar Giora."

Mathias chuckled grimly and replied, "That was indeed a sharp stick—Simon's son choosing to follow his rival."

Eleasar moved toward the door, the Levites with him. "I must go now. Matthew, we'll talk later, yes?"

Miriam noted Matthew's nod.

"Mathias," his father's old friend said, with a hand on her father's shoulder, "I'm glad we could finally get you home. Now you must rest." He and the two guardsmen left.

"You should, Father," said Miriam, "with Mother, who has slept little." She helped him up and over to the cushioned divan. That peaceful corner was shielded from drafts and closer to a brazier full of glowing embers. He sat beside Rebecca, spent with the emotion of her husband's long-awaited homecoming. Her mother had been weeping since the men had come through the door. After she helped him sit, he took Rebecca's hand in his own. Miriam took her place on his other side and, as she had as a little girl, rested her head on his shoulder.

Miriam was shocked at how thin he had become, how frail. For many minutes, she had had eyes only for her father. But now she took in the others who rejoiced, too, at the return of Mathias. Yohanan ben Zaccai, seated at the table, was smiling. Rachel and Leah were also undoubtedly glad they no longer had to hide in King David's Tomb. But their smiles were tinged with sadness and more than a little fear. Matthew still stood, and Miriam could see that his initial joy at bringing their father home had faded with the conversation.

"I can help you upstairs... to rest," Rebecca said quietly but firmly.

Her husband shook his head. "Later, I will. I have spent too long not knowing what is happening. I must know. Matthew and Eleasar told me some on the way here... but they moved so fast, I could barely keep up, much less ask questions."

"The lull in the fighting," Matthew carefully gestured as if afraid of stirring up the chaos, "we had no idea how long it would last. I could have carried you...."

"So, Giora's son holds the Inner Court and the Temple?" Mathias asked as he reclined against a cushion and let Rebecca smooth his tangled beard over his chest.

Mother would rather see him in his bed and not talk about what's happened and happening. But having him back was what mattered most, Miriam thought, with a rush of gratitude for the familiar comforts of housekeeping and family life. But no time for this—she must get the details of the fighting.

"He has 2400 men, all barricaded within," said Matthew. "They've sealed the courtyard gates, and Yohanan ben Levi is trying to breach their defenses and take the Temple for himself. Earlier this morning, he turned his catapults, now atop the cloisters and ramparts of Antonia Fortress, on the closest entrance into the courtyard, the Spark Gate."

Yohanan ben Zaccai picked up the explanations from there. "And once they've broken through, his men will pour through the Spark Gate. We remember from the writings that King Yechoniah was exiled through that gate when Nebuchadnezzar deposed him nearly 500 years ago." The elderly rabbi shook his head. "Now, a tyrant of our own making would control the Second Temple, the one built to replace what Nebuchadnezzar destroyed."

"What of Shimon ben Gamliel and the Sanhedrin?"

"The Sanhedrin no longer meets," he said wearily. "Shimon is seldom seen. He is a frightened old man."

"And he wishes to grow older instead of doing what is right," Mathias said, looking up at Matthew. "Will the Gischalan break down the gate and the wall and take the Temple?"

"So far," Matthew answered, "all his men have done is create more rubble to block the gates. This morning's attack brought down the two pillars that supported the loft over the gate. They had no care for the sacred fire tended there—in fact, they catapulted stones against the Levites working there. Sacrilege! And as for the tactics, all that did was add more obstacles for Yohanan ben Levi's men to clear."

"And Simon bar Giora just watches as the Gischalan attacks his son?"

"It seems so, Father. He has 15,000 men to Yohanan ben Levi's 6,000. Eleazar ben Simon and his men will kill some of them, and then Simon will face fewer opponents. We owe your release to the Gischalan's slipping grasp."

Yohanan ben Zacchai wiped his eyes with the back of his right hand. "The siege weapons of Rome, manned by our own people... used against our own people. We kill each other before the Romans reach our walls."

"Jerusalem has sinned grievously...." Mathias said in his own denouncement. Miriam sat up, remembering that tone her father had always used when reading scripture and how it always stirred her.

"She has become a mockery," Mathias went on. "Those who honored Jerusalem now demean her." He paused and tugged his beard. Miriam had dreaded that gesture of sternness as a child but welcomed it now with his return home. "Look, O Lord, at the anguish I suffer!"

Miriam remembered it was from the first portion of the Book of Lamentations.

"My stomach churns, and my heart recoils within me. How bitter I am!" Mathias pulled his beard again. "Outside the sword... inside there is death."

The dirge moved her with its fitness for their time. Death was inside Jerusalem's walls... and it came from their own hands.

* * *

That evening...

Miriam listened to the mutterings of Cicero in his cage as she took the dagger Hananiah had given her and struck its blade against the

Final Siege

ferrule of Zechariah's staff. That hardened metal tip rolled back the blade's edge; another sharp blow left a small nick.

She would use the damage as her occasion for calling upon Hananiah with the knife. She had promised Ya'el she would stop putting it off. *Tomorrow.* It was certain Gessius Florus had offered the reward for news of the Roman noblewoman hiding in Jerusalem. Ya'el—the Roman Cleo—must remain hidden, for the city still talked about the reward. Especially since the bounty had recently increased. Only the fighting had slowed down the bounty hunters scouring the city.

If and when the in-fighting stopped, everyone would remember the search. When the Romans finally descended upon them, the true value of the bounty would surge. That information could provide wealth and leverage or influence with the Romans—perhaps yielding safe passage from Jerusalem.

Through Hananiah, Miriam and Ya'el hoped to learn about Gessius Florus's efforts in the city and maybe find some way to protect Ya'el. Miriam squirmed at the memory of her seeming to accept Hananiah's flirtation after he overheard her rebuffing poor Ya'akov.

That tense confrontation in the Upper City market had seemed to cool Hananiah's interest in her former betrothed, and Ya'akov had stayed away from her. But she knew her mother still talked with him and was likely even now sharing the news of Ya'akov's current intentions with her father.

But perhaps Leah and Rachel were the topics of their conversation still. When Matthew went to his meeting with Eleasar ben Ananias, she had overheard the two women and her parents with Yohanan ben Zaccai. The old priest explained how he had used current circumstances and Yonatan's known brutality to push through the recording of a Bill of Divorce for Leah. Yohanan explained that there were precedents for such an action—the initiation of a divorce by a woman—though it was rare. Rebecca explained that she planned to take Leah and Rachel into their home and got Mathias's agreement. That move would offer them some security, but she knew Leah and Rachel would not feel safe for long.

Miriam thumbed the nicked blade and slid it into her forearm sheath. As she shrouded the parrot's cage so he would sleep, she whispered to him, "Soon you will see her." Taking a heavy cloak from a peg on the wall, she pulled it on, opened her door, and slipped quietly up the stairs. Miriam heard distant cries the wind carried to the rooftop terrace, which chilled her more than the December cold.

She thought of her father's words from Lamentations as tears ran down her cheeks. Night fell, and she listened to Jerusalem cry.

LX

December 69 CE

Jerusalem

The Lower City

Hananiah moved efficiently in the early morning darkness under the dim light from a single lamp. He settled the last blade and tang in the remaining open crate, completing his first task for Simon bar Giora's order for swords. Next, the hilts would be affixed, and the man crafting the weapons would return them, so Hananiah could put a cutting edge on the metal. Until then, they'd make good bludgeons but not swords. In the lamp's glow, he admired the ripple of light along the length of the blade. These were as good as Roman-made, with the last of his metal stock from Alexandria. From now on, he'd have only scrap metal melted down, reforged, and reworked.

The past months had been the busiest for the metalwork he had learned as a boy. War kept men in that trade busy. His teacher in metalworking had taught him his other—primary—profession, too, all the while abusing him. From these experiences, Hananiah learned deadly capabilities and cruel ruthlessness. But he had not practiced his primary skills of late, for he had not heard from the Roman, Gessius Florus. With a target assigned, he was relentless until he made the kill. He had last reported to Florus his capture of the woman Ya'el and the boy and experience with 'The Hand.' He was glad to have had the Roman's silence since then. It would likely not go well with him since he'd lost the woman and boy to 'The Hand' after sending that message. According to Miriam, Ya'el and her boy had fled to Masada with the Sicarii killer. But The Hand was back and putting his killer's mark on Yohanan ben Levi's men.

He had several possibilities and several necessities. The bounty Florus offered was significant. He had not made nearly so much for handling Ehud and searching for the locations where the Jews hid their Temple treasure. His report to Gessius Florus confirmed some had been moved from Jerusalem to disperse and hide from the Romans. And he had offered something even more valuable—a lead about where to find a list of directions to the treasure locations. Perhaps now he could just conduct that search for the treasure on his own—without Gessius Florus—but he would need to figure out how to get it safely out of Judea. And that could prove impossible.

He went to his small room and was drawn to his trophy bag of ears. He had not added to his collection since that Zealot, Yonatan, had threatened Miriam. His fingers caressed the bag. He wanted to sort through them and recall each moment of every kill the ears represented—but for Yonatan's—that Jew had escaped. But he had no time. Hananiah took down from its peg the small, decorative mat that covered a crevice he'd created in the mudbrick wall as a hiding place. He took out a scrap of parchment. Then replaced the mat, the only bit of color in the sparsely furnished room. All must always be in place, lest he be surprised.

He studied the latest message he had found on his counter when he returned from his stall in the Upper City agora the evening before. He suspected Boaz was no longer Gessius Florus's lone man in Jerusalem, for he had not seen him in months. When he first read the message... he sensed the anger in the Roman who wrote it. Then he remembered Florus had replied to his message about 'The Hand,' woman and boy with the parrot. So there was some justification for his anger. But he had lost that reply when 'The Hand' rescued Ya'el and the boy. The blow on his head from Ya'el had knocked him out and muddled his thinking for days after. He had forgotten about that unread—lost—reply until finding this latest message last evening. He unfolded the square of parchment as he walked back to the shop's front. As he reread it, his resentment at the first reading returned and soured further, turning into anger. Did Gessius Florus mean to cut him from any reward beyond what he had already been paid? That money was not enough for his plans.

"Hello," came with the creak of the front door opening. The hooded figure at the entrance to the shop was barely discernible with the first light of dawn. They wore a heavy cloak and carried a staff in one hand. The familiar voice did not match the image. Though surprised at the hour and the attire, he did not show it.

"Hello, Miriam," he said, beckoning her forward and sliding the lamp on the counter closer to him. "Are you out early for safety's sake? Most everyone on the streets now carries weapons and dresses for fleeing or fighting, and every day many must decide which. And always there are more, wanting to hide from the Romans." He patted his most prized weapon, the sheathed Iberian dagger, on his hip. It was cold-hammered to form the finest double-edged blade, the *parazonium* type preferred by higher-rank Roman soldiers. The blade was leaf-shaped and about 19 inches long, with a hilt, grip, and pommel of bone. It was a lethal work of art he could handle expertly. "This serves me well... but," he waved his arm at Miriam, summing up her attire, "a man's cloak and an old man's staff are little defense—and cumbersome."

"I would have come to your stall in the Upper City market," said Miriam, "but that is too public. And much of the fighting lately is around the Temple. I thought it best to bring this here." She drew an object wrapped in supple leather from her cloak and laid it on the work counter. She slipped the hood back to fall on her shoulders, and her face was pale and her eyes large in the lamplight.

Beautiful, Hananiah thought. He set down the parchment message he still held and unfolded the wrapping to reveal the Damascus-blade dagger he had given her. The raindrop pattern ran in rivulets along the length of the blade in the lamp's glow. It was one of his most beautiful pieces of using the *dimasq* process. He looked more closely at the damage and almost winced in pain. *How could she?*

"You've not handled this as you should," he said, the accusation giving his tone a sharp edge.

Miriam remained silent as she watched him go to his sharpening wheel and set it spinning. Deftly he smoothed out the nick and the folds in the edge. Hananiah returned it to the work counter, picked up a fine-grained file, and finished the smoothing, returning a razor-keen glint to the blade's edge. He stropped it on a wide strip of leather attached to a ring hung above his workbench. Checking the edge with his thumb, he next placed a drop of oil on the metal and polished it with a scrap of fine linen. His cloth-covered fingers rubbed away tiny scratches from the sharpening and grinding as he stroked the blade to a shimmering gleam.

As Hananiah worked, he kept looking up to study her. He had seen her discourage the man Ya'akov—her former betrothed, he had learned—from talking to her in the market. And had decided not to press his interest in her until he was sure he would not have to kill the man. That would not bother *him*, but it might disturb Miriam. He'd seen how she'd shrunk back at Ehud's death, though that killing had not been by his hand. He would not risk anything now when she seemed to be getting over that loss. Here she was now. That was promising...

He caught her eyes studying him just as he had watched her, and they exchanged looks of equal understanding. The repair of the dagger was a pretext. Women, even independent women like Miriam seemed to be, needed a man to protect them—especially in times like these. He wrapped the dagger in its soft leather again, tied it with the cord, and handed it back to her.

"I'll walk you home," he said. "I'm better protection than that...." He pointed at the staff. When she did not protest his offer, he reached over the counter and put his hand over hers, where she gripped the edge. He felt her stiffen, then relax. Yes, going slow and letting her come to him was working. Though he was a *castratus*, he still felt the slow build of anticipation within him, the likes of which he had only ever felt when stalking a man to kill. And then the culmination would sweep through him when the act was consummated. *Ahhh....* he savored the memory of the feeling. He took her hand, and he saw something flare in her eyes.

LXI

December 69 CE

Jerusalem

The Upper City

Miriam had never seen Hananiah so angry, and she was startled because he never showed emotion. She had glimpsed inside the folded message he'd set on the counter when she came in. It looked like the same hand as was in the message Ya'el had taken when Miriam had—as 'The Hand'—knocked Hananiah to the floor when she had rescued them.

Was Hananiah now angered at something in Florus's new message? A falling out between two evil men could help draw out Hananiah. She could use that vulnerability to find out what he knew of Florus's reward to anyone who found his wife. And Florus hid other matters from Vespasian and, before him, the 12th Legion commander, Cestius Gallus. Those things also could be reported to Vespasian with the hope that the information would somehow mitigate his attack on Jerusalem.

Ya'el—Cleo—had told her she believed her husband planned to loot the Temple treasure… but for himself, not for Rome. She had heard Matthew and Eleasar ben Ananias talk of the raids where some of the treasure was hidden or would be. Some of it had already been stolen. Those two had entrusted her with finding some unknown or forgotten place beneath Jerusalem or nearby where they could hide what they could not get out of the city. She and Ya'el would soon explore more of the tunnels and chambers.

On their morning walk to the Upper City, Miriam responded to his interest in her by asking him questions about himself. "What will you do when the Romans arrive?" Depending on the extent of his relationship with Gessius Florus, he might even know in advance what the Romans' timing would be.

Hananiah had replied not with an answer but with a question for her: "Do you wish to be truly free?"

They had walked silently as she considered what to say next and wondered at the streets' quiet. As they walked, she found what the brutes who ruled the streets were doing—preparing for a different kind of killing. Cartloads of stone and bundles of arrows were being wheeled toward the Temple Enclosure. There, men loaded sling nets. Rocks were hoisted for the catapults, and hundreds of arrows passed to the watchtowers on the walls. It would have seemed they were making common cause to fight the Romans, except that the weapons and bowmen were turned inward to Jerusalem instead of outward.

She had felt his eyes on her in silence as he waited for an answer. She turned to him and simply replied, honestly, "Yes. I want to be free." But he need not know that the freedom she sought was not from the walls of Jerusalem but from her memories. She wanted to be free of the pain she had suffered in herself and at the deaths of others, some of which she had caused—Miriam carried a great weight of responsibility.

Hananiah nodded, his eyes drilling into hers with the possessive gleam she'd seen when he handled his knives and said, "Good."

Miriam hoped her intent was accomplished... that rejecting Ya'akov publicly and pushing him away piqued Hananiah's interest and protected Ya'akov.

They arrived at her home as the sun cleared the Mount of Olives and fell on the Temple, turning it into a bright white beacon capped by a blaze of gold. The sight always took her breath away, but Hananiah had been impatient and unmoved as he waited on her to finish gazing at it. When she turned back, a man was just reaching the front gate of her home. "Who is that?"

Miriam wished she'd been able to enter unseen through the rear courtyard, but that was impossible with Hananiah accompanying her.

"*Sh'lam lak,*" Arins had said in morning greeting, and his gaze had swept her from toe to head with a long squint at Zechariah's staff in her hand. Then he gave a longer, sterner glare at Hananiah, whom she had awkwardly introduced, then thanked him for walking her home. She promised to soon come by his stall in the agora, and Hananiah took the hint and left them with a nod to her and a lingering glance at Arins.

"I know it's early, but I came by to check on Matthew," Arins said, raising the cloth bag he carried in explanation. "I will be out of the city for a few days and wanted to see how his arm is healing before I go. This is a medicine I just got from one of my suppliers. Its ingredients have become harder to find. So I bought all he had. It will help prevent wounds from becoming inflamed or reduce the fever if they already are."

She had him wait as she went inside to get Matthew, change her clothes and cloak, and leave her staff in her room. When she had come down, Arins was in the family room, unwinding Matthew's bandage with her mother looking on. She had seen the gray-haired man shake his head as he commented. "Some stitches have pulled loose, and the wound is swollen. It cannot be re-stitched until the swelling and redness are gone."

Matthew had not complained, but Miriam knew that must have happened when he had lifted most of the weight of the stone bench over the tunnel access they'd found to the remains of the Baris at the edge of and beneath Fortress Antonia.

"This," Arins said of the sealed earthenware jar he took from the bag, "is a compound of honey and *Ezov*, a cleansings herb, mixed with grease and boiled plant fiber. Use it to cover his wound... it will help." The old trader had handed the jar to Rebecca.

"Thank you for helping my son," she had said as she opened the jar, and Arins showed her how much of the ointment to slather over the wound.

"My own youngest son and daughtIhad they lived—would have been about your age," Arins said, gesturing toward Miriam and Matthew. "So, if I can help... I will."

Miriam had heard steps on the stairs and then her father greeting someone at the door and bringing them toward the family room.

"Matthew," Mathias said, with a bit of a surprised look at Arins, "Yohanan must speak with us and Eleasar ben Ananias, who should be here soon." Then he introduced himself and Yohanan ben Zaccai to Arins, thanking him for treating Matthew's injury.

Arins said, "You are welcome. I am grateful to learn that you have recently been released from the 'care' of Yohanan ben Levi." Then he turned to Yohanan ben Zaccai for what he said next, his deep, vibrant voice: "It becomes ever harder for me to bring stores into the city. Please help me bypass the gates... to bring food and medicine to others. I know these men— Simon bar Giora and Yohanan ben Levi— only from their actions. I don't think they have the good of Jerusalem in mind. Can you help me enter the city without their men interfering and redirecting supplies?"

Miriam held her breath, silently praying that the old priest would not betray what he knew of the tunnels nor betray with a glance that she had knowledge of them. She let out her breath silently after he turned to her father and Matthew and said, "We will discuss it, see if there is some way. There might be...."

239

Arins nodded thanks and used the cloth her mother had brought him to wipe his hands. "I will return in a few days and see you then."

As Miriam walked the trader to the door, she heard Yohanan ben Zaccai say: "I have a message from Nahum. His craftsmen in Qumran have created a copper scroll of the locations."

Arins had paused, cocked his head, and searched her face.

Did he hear that? she wondered, but then he said only, "Be careful walking the city. Never go out alone... have someone like that young man—Hananiah, is it?—have someone like that with you."

Shortly after she closed the door after Arins, there was a knock, and she opened it to Eleasar ben Ananias. She had helped Rebecca prepare breakfast and strained her ears to hear the men's conversation before returning to her room. "The Essenes list on the metal scroll some sites they have not used," said Yohanan. "I told Nahum to leave them as decoys should anyone try to follow the directions without the key."

Matthew offered, "We can find a place within or beneath Jerusalem for the balance of what we hide."

The conversation must have ended with the meal, for Matthew soon called for her through the door. She opened it, and he slipped inside.

"Eleasar told us Elazar ben Yair, the Sicarii leader in Masada, has sent a message to Simon bar Giora that 'The Hand' does not ally with any faction leader in Jerusalem. But 'The Hand' is not the only one who stands against those who harm the innocent in Jerusalem. What does that mean, Miriam? What are you doing?"

LXII

December 69 CE

Near Bousbastis, Aegyptus

Six Days Southeast of Alexandria

Nicanor had worked on the route map for General Titus with the legion's *mensores*. They were all experienced centurions, charged with surveying legion routes and identifying locations for marching-camps. Once in the field, they would proceed ahead of the marching order—the ranks of infantry on foot—to confirm the site's suitability or select another location for camp at day's end. A good camp would have the best ground available, with sources of water, forageable crops, game, and good grazing for horses and pack animals. The mensores drew from centuries of experience to set up camps that could be easily defended. Despite the work these camps involved at the end of a day's march, it was necessary to do everything according to that tradition. Nicanor had never heard of a marching-camp being taken.

    At the average daily pace of a legion, the journey from Alexandria to Caesarea would take 21 and a half days, so they planned many overnight stops. Winter was moderate along the coast of the *mare nostrum,* the sea at the heart of the Roman Empire. The nights were cool, and the days warm but humid. Even with these favorable conditions, three weeks would be tiring. Nine of the overnight stops would be in towns: Hierakonpolis, Naukratis, Bousbastis, then Pelusium, where they left the humid Nilus Delta. Then came the most brutal, arid stretch to Raphia, after which the land became more fertile again at Gaza. Then Ascalon, Azotus Paralios, and Lydda... the last overnight camp before Caesarea.

    The evening before they left Alexandria, at a private dinner with the old general, Titus, and Nicanor... Vespasian had told Yosef: "I want you to see Roman might, but not on a training field or while facing it as an enemy. One day I might ask you to write about what you have witnessed. You will not have to march but ride alongside the men from here to Caesarea, then up to Jerusalem." He had turned to Titus and said, "Nicanor will be an adviser to you, but he will stay with Yosef at all times. Let Yosef speak to his people in Jerusalem if there comes a fitting time for it. We must see if they will surrender to save their city."

Nicanor had seen the flash of joy on Yosef's face, which had saddened him. Once they were at Jerusalem, the truth would cloud his countenance. Surrender meant the citizens of Jerusalem would live... but as enslaved people. That had already been decided, and he still had not found the courage to tell his friend. Besides, that knowledge woI not help Yosef now nor change anything. Jerusalem's temple treasure would be taken, and the city would be stripped of everything of value... including many of its people.

It had surprised Nicanor at that dinner with Vespasian that Tiberius Alexander would be Titus's second-in-command. Vespasian intended to remain in Alexandria, not returning to Caesarea long enough for a final staff meeting with his officers there. As Nicanor had originally, many had come with Vespasian from Rome to Antioch and on to fight in Judea.

The morning their march began, Tiberius Alexander, at Titus's side, had explained that it was strategically safer for the next emperor of Rome to remain in Alexandria. Nicanor agreed with some of his explanation... but not strongly. The last reports from Governor Mucianus said Vitellius had no men nor means to project force beyond the city of Rome. A defense force had been scratched together from legions, including the Praetorian Guard and Urban Cohorts.

Nicanor was pleased that General Vespasian had ordered Tiberius Alexander to take the Euphrates guard to Caesarea and include them in the assault on Jerusalem. These men were utterly loyal to Alexander, not Vespasian. The general had replaced them in Alexandria with the 3rd Legion, *Augusta,* and its *auxilia* from Cyrenaica in eastern Libya. But Nicanor still felt General Vespasian would be safer in Caesarea with more than one legion protecting him.

Shaking off the thoughts that occupied many of the hours of dull plodding, Nicanor wiped his damp face and looked down at Yosef, who rode beside him. He wondered if the mule assigned as his friend's mount had been intended to slight the Jew. Or was it merely a precaution lest the former prisoner attempt to join his people? A mule could not outrun a horse. *But,* Nicanor thought, *a mule could better manage some of the rough ground we've covered.* The road was irregular, with uneven stones and loose gravel. It dipped and climbed, following contours of the land the engineers and their workers could not level.

"The town is ahead...." Yosef pointed.

Nicanor clenched his knees to grip his horse's sides and rise in the saddle. The low sun was full on their backs, casting long shadows on the road ahead. In the distance, the road passed through a massive carved stone gate. "So, these people prayed to cats?" Nicanor asked with a grunt. An Alexandrian who had been to Bousbastis before had ridden with them for hours that morning. Chattering to Yosef, who had asked him about the town's history as the center for the worship of... "What was their god called?"

"Goddess," Yosef said. "Baast... the Greeks called her Ailuros. Originally a fierce lioness warrior goddess."

"Hmmph... a lion's better than a cat." Nicanor watched as the mass of marching and mounted men slowed. The centurions and *cohort optios*, ranking just below legion officers, herded their men to set up a marching-camp that would spread on both sides of the road up to the gates. Legion senior officers, including himself, with Yosef, would find quarters or pitch tents inside the gates. Nicanor's eyes swept the ranks of legionaries and auxiliaries as they broke off into their assigned working groups. He had not served with these men but knew their type well from his nearly 25 years of service, most of which he was proud of. Some men were older than he and must be in their 30th year or more of service. Many of them were scarred by old wounds... their bodies had reckoned with the cutting edge of weapons of war and the crushing grind of army life. *All for two and a half sesterces a day.* He wondered if Yosef looked upon them now as Vespasian had expected he would and saw Rome's might. Truly, the legions were the greatest fighting force in the world—a world that was now predominantly Roman. Yet he saw now centurions prodding men who had marched all day, barking at them to work harder, faster. They wielded *vitis*, the wooden rods they carried as their rank badge. They were also handy flails for the backs of any recalcitrant soldiers.

"You wear a grim smile that does not reach your eyes, Nicanor. What is it?" Yosef asked.

"In I was young... in the legion for less than a handful of years, we called my centurion, behind his back, '*Da Mihi Alteram*.'"

"Give me another..." Yosef translated and looked puzzled at the phrase. "What do you mean?"

"He would break his rod beating my fellow rankers who moved too slow and then shout at his optio, 'Bring me another!' We hated him." Nicanor squinted again at the hectoring centurions and muttered, "*Semper idem*... it's still the same." He shook his head. "Let's find a decent spot...." He heeled his mount ahead to part the men milling around the gate. Nicanor glanced over his shoulder to check that Yosef was close behind him. As he often had since leaving Alexandria, he wondered whether Vespasian meant what he had said the last evening in Alexandria.

LXIII

December 69 CE

Bousbastis

The Roman Camp

Yosef had slept little, as tired as he was. General Vespasian clearly meant for Yosef to know what the would-be emperor had told his son Titus during their last evening in Alexandria. That had kept him awake, considering the opportunity to help his people. After tossing and turning, he hung a blanket from the rod that formed the peak of the tent he shared with Nicanor, shrouding the light from his small oil lamp.

He had taken out the satchel containing several splendid multi-leaved wax tablets Anyte had given him. "Made by my new manufactory in Forcella," she'd said, "just east of Rome." Her father, Marinus, had boasted of his growing ventures, adding, "Pan, the god of bees, has blessed the production." Whether that was so or not. The tablets were superior to what Yosef had used in Rome and less susceptible to the heat. He could easily bring one or two to write in when he carried no ink and parchment. His rear end sore from many hours on a mule, Yosef wished he and Nicanor were sailing on the *Egeria* to Caesarea with the father and daughter. But Vespasian had ordered the shipowner to begin regular sailing—his fastest, 32 days, and at risk in winter weather—from Alexandria to Ostia and back, bringing updates.

The first light of dawn peeked through the sliver of an opening in the tent flap, and Yosef heard Nicanor awakening on the other side of the makeshift partition. The tribunus muttered curses at the small brazier, which failed to warm the tent, then at his stiff knees and aching back. His big hand swept aside the blanket.

"What have you been up to all night?" Nicanor asked, wrapping a heavy blanket around himself and peering down at Yosef sitting cross-legged on his pallet.

"Writing...."

"You should have slept... from here, it's four long days to Pelusium, then a hard stretch from there to Raphia." Nicanor held out his hand for the tablet. "Writing what?"

Yosef gave it to him and watched Nicanor lean down to angle it under the light. "I can't read this." He handed the tablet back.

"It's *notae tironianae*, a quicker way to write that Anyte was teaching me. It uses signs and symbols instead of words and sentences. Your scholar and orator, Cicero, had it developed by his personal secretary, Tiro, to record his speeches and take dictation. It's handy... well, I've been practicing to make it more useful."

Nicanor yawned, palmed his eyes, and gestured at the tablet again. "What have you written?"

"What I plan to tell my people when we get to Jerusalem." Yosef waited, thinking Nicanor might ask him what he planned to say. But his friend stood there silently studying him. Yosef continued. "Also, I'm writing notes about what has happened to my people and me. When we get to Caesarea, I'll transcribe this all in ink on parchment and add to my store of writings."

"Why write about such pain and suffering, Yosef? Does it not hurt you again as you do?"

Yosef stood easily with the strength of a young man, and his eyes were then level with Nicanor's, but his slight frame took up less space in the tent. He moved to open the flap to let in more light, then blew out the lamp. He turned to Nicanor and said, "My lieutenant and friend Levi ben Altheus, who died at Yotapta saving two women and me, told me I must do it. 'Get the story written,' he urged me, 'or no one will know what happened, and no one will remember how we lived... how we died.' Also, being aware of how one's ancestors suffered to give you a better life helps you appreciate what you have."

* * *

They ate bread, dates, and cheese in silence. Yosef had expressed some anguish when he spoke of his promise to Levi. Writing hurt, as did even thinking of all that must be noted about the past and the things to come. But he had not meant to offend Nicanor or make him regret speaking openly. Yosef had missed having someone to talk to in that way, so he broke the silence. "It sounds like Vespasian wishes to reward you when you retire. He said that as emperor, he would double your *praemia*... I don't understand what that meant.

"It's a discharge bonus for retiring legionaries... the equivalent of 13 years' pay. It gives the most experienced legionaries an incentive to stay on until mandatory retirement."

"So, General—I mean, Emperor Vespasian would reward you with 26 years' worth of pay when you retire? That seems a lot of money."

"Enough to buy some land, somewhere quiet."

"Have you picked a place?" Yosef liked the thought of his friend being at peace. He had no idea where—or in what circumstances—he might be when that happened for Nicanor, but envisioning him safe somewhere on his land made Yosef smile.

"Marinus and Anyte have given me some ideas," Nicanor said. Then he wiped his mouth, gauged the angle of the sun and the sounds stirring around them, and stood. "We're breaking camp, and I want us to be closer to the front of the formation today. You pack our things and take down the tent while I get our mounts."

An hour later, the formation moved through the eastern section of the town. Nicanor and Yosef passed buildings and temples so old they seemed part of the land, but they still showed signs of use. The air was thick and dank, laden with the smell of rank water from the town's canals and the estuaries webbed around it, a nexus of the Nilus. A few tremendous scaly beasts had dragged their bodies onto the sun-warmed banks and watched them with cold-glittering eyes. Crocodiles. It made Yosef think of how the Book of Job, in the Hebrew Scriptures, had described the creatures—they feared no one.

"What do we do next about Gessius Florus and the Thracians?" Yosef asked.

"General Vespasian needs proof of Florus's direct involvement in something he hides from Roman authority. We'll have to find that proof."

Titus was at the vanguard of the formation with his personal guard and the *aquilifer*, the senior standard-bearer. Behind them rode Tiberius Alexander and a man he had introduced the morning they left Alexandria as Lucius Serenus, who was joining Titus's staff. Yosef gestured toward him. "What does that man with Tiberius Alexander do?"

"He's a *summus curator*, responsible for purchasing and caring for the legion and auxiliary horses and work stock... mules and donkeys. In Caesarea, he'll work with the legion quartermasters."

They were close enough to see the man laugh at something Tiberius Alexander said. The newcomer acted with familiarity with the Aegyptus Prefect, which seemed strange to Yosef. He glanced to see whether Nicanor had noticed, but his friend seemed lost in other thoughts. Maybe Yosef's distrust of Tiberius Alexander affected his perception of the man. When Yosef and Nicanor met with Vespasian and Titus to show them the gold tithing vessel from the Temple in Jerusalem, Tiberius Alexander had entered the room just as they finished. Yosef had covered the tithing vessel used as payment for the Thracians, but he was sure there had been a flash of recognition in the prefect's eyes as he did. But again, his dislike for Alexander made it hard to shake his suspicions about the man.

Yosef blinked in the sun's glare, and ahead, Serenus laughed again. To Yosef, the man seemed before to laugh little. He studied the canal on the right that had paralleled the road for a distance. When it started to bend away, he and Nicanor drew closer to the two men. Yosef saw that Lucius Severus's right hand was missing three fingers, and he wore a leather glove that covered the three stubs and reached his wrist. Yosef turned toward where he pointed at a man in a flat-bottomed boat that moved with them, matching their pace.

"Nicanor," Yosef said, "when you went to get your horse and my mule... I saw him, Serenus, talking with that man in the boat on the canal. I wonder what about...."

LXIV

Januarius 70 CE

Caesarea

The Roman Encampment, Nicanor's Quarters

Sayid had set up the camp stove beneath the window, its shutters open enough to draw the tendrils of smoke away. He had cooked his meal, a stew he had not tasted in over two years. Not since he cared for his mother in Laodicea ad Mare and his Aunt Yara made *yakhanit batata* for him. But this time, he had lamb for the stew and not the braised goat—the best she'd been able to get. He closed his eyes and could smell the aroma wafting from Aunt Yara's cooking again. Even the memory of it had lifted his spirits. The seasoning she made for the stew, the *bharat,* perfumed the surrounding air with its blend of black pepper, cinnamon, ginger, nutmeg, and cardamom. An aroma that always made him think of his mother and aunt. He took a bite and cursed that he had not written the recipe down. He had missed something... or perhaps he was just a lousy cook. Still, it was warm... and it did have a taste, just not a very good one.

He would not have tried to make the stew, but after his last conversation with his father, he needed something that meant family to him since his father did not. His father had lectured him as if he did not already know that auxiliaries were second-class to Roman citizens. And citizenship was impossible for *peregrini* until they served 25 years and received a military diploma, a notarized copy of the original *constitutio*—the decree issued by the emperor and recorded in Rome. He had once asked Nicanor to tell him about the process. Despite being familiar with Roman thoroughness, Sayid had been amazed.

The diploma was made of two bronze tablets hinged with inscriptions engraved on both plates documenting that the man's service commitment had been fulfilled. The full text of the diploma was on the outer side of the first *tabula*, while the outer side of the second *tabula* displayed the names of the required seven witnesses, their seals covered and protected by metal strips. The holder would take the sealed diploma to the main *civitas*—city—in the province where he intended to live in retirement and present it to the Keeper of Archives. The archivist would break the seals and check that the details on the inner inscription matched those of the outer. If all was in order, he would enter the diploma holder's name onto the register of resident Roman citizens. To become a Roman citizen was precious, and Rome protected itself from forgeries so that only the deserving could be recognized as citizens. That bronze tablet awarded citizenship to the veteran and his entire family.

His father had gone on with his harangue, telling Sayid to stop worrying about proving himself to Romans like Nicanor and Celsus Evander. He should instead earn the respect of his fellow auxiliaries. He should eat with them, roll dice with them, and become one of them. "Be a soldier all the time and stop shuffling paper for legion officers," his father had said. If he could not be a soldier, maybe Sayid should return to Laodicea ad Mare and care for his mother until he could return to marry her. His father still could not understand that he wanted to prove himself to just one man—his father. But he would not try again to explain what he had done to help Nicanor and to help Lady Cleo.

Sayid thought cooking the meal that always made him feel close to his family—his mother and aunt—would make him feel better. But the taste...

"Sayid!" called a voice outside the window.

He looked up and said, "Come in, sir." Celsus Evander stepped through the door.

"Would you like some of this?" Sayid asked, standing and offering to fill a bowl from the pot simmering on the camp stove.

The tall quartermaster commander leaned down, squinted into the pot, crinkled his nose, and shook his head. "No, but thanks. I came by to tell you orders from General Vespasian have arrived on the coastal courier. General Titus and Nicanor, with more men, are coming overland from Alexandria to Caesarea. We are to begin preparations for the legions to move out when Titus arrives to command the attack on Jerusalem. We have the marching order, unit order, and timing for each. Their field supplies and hundreds of pieces of siege equipment need to be re-checked and readied. I have all the quartermasters starting on it, but I could use your help especially. Can you work with some auxiliary commanders... at the warehouses to check, prepare, and stage their equipment?"

Sayid had not told Celsu' Evander anything of what he had seen or heard in Sycaminum and at the waypoint outside Ptolemais. Nicanor should hear about it first. So he had kept himself safe, mostly within Nicanor's quarters, since returning. He had not even checked

Gessius Florus's villa. He doubted anyone was looking for him, but he must be cautious until he could report to Nicanor. But the warehouses Celsus directed him to were within the encampment. The work should be safe from any prying eyes.

"Of course, sir. I can help until Nicanor arrives. Then I will ask him to release me to a combat unit." He saw an expression flit across the officer's face and asked, "What is it, sir? I'm grateful for having worked for you. I've learned much from it, and I'm glad to be of help. But I must go to a combat unit when we march on Jerusalem. I hope you understand."

"I know and do. But Marcus Sabinus is the first auxiliary officer you will work with tomorrow morning. Will you still help?"

LXV

Januarius 70 CE

Caesarea

Gessius Florus's Villa

Gessius Florus studied the ledger he had kept *editio rationum* for years. He was trained in this recordkeeping by his father, who had learned from his, and so on for five generations. His family in Clazomenae had used financial instruments and manipulation to control markets, having grown beyond their origins as olive and grain merchants and traders. The maxim passed down from father to the oldest son had been to always keep a correctly dated and detailed account management.

    He dipped his pen in the ink jar, underlined a large number on the page before him, and compared it to numbers from a different sheet. The assessed or liquidated value of the wagonloads of treasure he had captured so far was insufficient to pay his Clazomenae family's debt to the lender in Thessalonica. A debt from Florus's past poor gambles. He had to show them there was no risk of *foro fugre*, of his fleeing the forum as bankrupt senators once did. But he needed more. He had the means to securely move large parts of the Jewish treasure, but he must get his hands on it and then transport it quickly. That meant by sea. He might have to use Meshulam's sand vessel to get it all at once to Clazomenae. Or take the portion needed to Thessalonica, and let them deal with converting it to Roman coin—or they could hold it as they wished. The remaining treasure would still make him one of the wealthiest men in the empire.

    Florus had read how Cato the Younger had moved his massive wealth, seven thousand silver talents, by sea instead of overland a century before. A ship presented fewer opportunities for brigands to converge on it, but there were risks. He turned to another sheet with notes and a crude drawing of large, sturdy chests with 100-foot cords affixed to them and corks tied to the other end. Cato had used this method to mark his treasure's location if it had to be cast overboard in shallow waters to avoid a raid. He would do the same.

    "Lord Florus," Drusus said from the doorway, standing with a dispatch satchel, "I have messages for you."

"Set it down—I'll read them later. Come in. There's something I need you to do in Sycaminum."

* * *

Florus pushed the satchel aside. His most recent message to Hananiah had resulted as he had expected. With the merchant Boaz no longer the conduit, Hananiah was using the old message drop outside Jerusalem. Sending another man even more seasoned than the Alexandrian, Hananiah had been wise. It served two purposes, one allowing him to reengage with Hananiah.

As he kept a ledger of his and his family's finances, so did he keep a personal record of another kind. A list of those who attempted to interfere with him and those who angered him. Sometimes the person was guilty of both crimes. This private record needed to be balanced and accounts paid, just as in the financial ledger. He would collect from the likes of his wife, the Jew Yosef ben Mathias, that legion tribunus Nicanor, and the Syrian auxiliary Sayid. Their shipwreck had seemed to cement their friendship and loyalty to each other, which grated on him. They aligned with Cleo at points and contributed to his greatest embarrassment—her leaving him—and physical injury. He rubbed his legs; the pain from the burns had long gone, but the rough flesh and stiffness reminded him.

If Yosef stayed near Vespasian and Titus, there would be little chance of killing him. But others close to Yosef in Jerusalem—his family, maybe his brother Matthew, who Hananiah had identified as a source of information about the Jews' hidden treasure or sister—could be taken and used as leverage to reach Yosef. Or he could just kill them and cause Cleo's Jew pain. And the sister would pose no challenge to his men in Jerusalem. She was just a weak woman like Cleo—who could have never left him without help from those men.

LXVI

Januarius 70 CE

Jerusalem

The Upper City

"Mother, it's like I told Matthew," Miriam said. "If Simon bar Giora and Yohanan ben Levi thought 'The Hand' was alone, they would not worry that anyone could hold them accountable for what they do to innocent people. Father, you've said this yourself... no one in the Sanhedrin is stopping them, and anyone who speaks against them becomes a target. One thing they do fear, though, is the Sicarii. The Gischalan especially."

Miriam had gone over this before, but Matthew's question had only stirred her parents' fear. "I cannot let them believe I'm the only Sicarii in Jerusalem, alone. But I am." Miriam could not remove the raw emotion in her voice, and she saw the pain in her family members' eyes.

"Elazar ben Yair and his Sicarii have abandoned Jerusalem," she said sorrowfully. "He thinks our leaders have brought a lion and a jackal into the city, but he did as I asked when he told them 'The Hand' was not alone. But I fear it's all gone too far, and they think they're beyond reprisal."

"You're *not* alone, Miriam." Matthew stood and gripped her shoulders. "I'm sorry I ever let you feel that way."

"You didn't know that I kept it from you—none of you did. Now I'm glad you forced me to tell. But bearing that pain and fear made me learn to defend myself, and now I am fit for battle, ready to fight— as we all must be."

"Still, we want you to try to stay safe, Miriam," said Rebecca.

"There is no 'safe' in Jerusalem, Mother. How can there be? Matthew told us that Yohanan ben Levi used *sacred timber* meant for the Temple to build towers to attack Elazar ben Simon within the Temple courts. What blasphemy. When the men who claim they should lead Jerusalem instead murder our people on the steps of the Temple, how can anyone, anywhere in the city, be safe?" Miriam shook her head. "Mother, you told us stories of our Hasmonean blood and of women who fought when they must, for their people. Father, you've condemned those who do wrong to benefit themselves all my life. And show how doing the right thing can be hard but must be done. You should both understand what I've done and what I do now. I won't argue about it anymore."

* * *

"Matthew, here I am!" Miriam called to her brother, who stood in the rear courtyard, his heavy cloak open despite the chill, the swirling wind sweeping against his legs. He took in her usual disguise—men's garb, his old mantle, and the staff gripped in her hand.

"The fighting is becoming much worse, Miriam. Mother and Father must not go out on the streets unless absolutely necessary. You and I must take care of them."

I know, and we will. And we must Protect Leah and Rachel as well," Miriam said, her glance going to the bedroom shutter—once Yosef's—where their cousins now slept. "Ya'el and Elian, too... though that's more difficult."

Matthew nodded. "I go when I can, you know. I let Elian see me so he knows we're watching over him at Shammai's. Yesterday I saw Ya'el at the underground chambers."

"We've lost our brother, but our family has grown...." The wind gusted and gripped Miriam's cowl, and she pulled it back down.

Matthew shook his head. "We haven't lost him. The last we heard, he was alive."

"But that's been a while...." Miriam knew rumors still spread that Yosef could only be alive if he were helping the Romans. "It's just you and me protecting our family," she lied. Matthew did not need to know that Ya'el would fight, too. He would find that out when the time came. "I need a bow, strings, and arrows... as many as you can get for me. As soon as you can. Ya'el will teach me how to use it against anyone threatening us."

Matthew held out his hands as if beholding the sight of his sister's outfit and said, "Are your daggers and that staff not enough?"

"I need something with enough reach to strike from a distance."

"You're not going to be on the walls when the Romans come, Miriam."

"You don't know that... I will be where I need to be. But a bow might save one of us when the Romans are in our streets. No matter how strong our walls are, that will only stop them for a while. No one—not you, Mother, or Father—will care if a woman and not a man fired the arrow that saves them."

Matthew sighed and shrugged. "I'll get what you need... and can teach you here in the courtyard."

"Good, but I know enough to begin, and I'll practice and get better. But not here. It could draw too much attention."

"Practice where then?"

"In that long gallery room in the Baris." Miriam looked forward to an opportunity to test her marksmanship on the two primary faction leaders, the Gischalan first. Her father remained weak from imprisonment. She had heard her mother tell Yohanan ben Zaccai that she feared he would never recover. Yohanan ben Levi must pay for that.

LXVII

Januarius 70 CE

Jerusalem

The New City / Bezetha, The Baris, Underground Remnants

After Miriam visited Elian at Shammai's, six men from Antonia Fortress accosted her, demanding she stop. So she'd changed direction, and the chase had doubled back into the Upper City, through the agora, where another group of men in the market confronted the six from Antonia Fortress. As she ducked away among other scattering people, she heard the clang of metal, sword on sword, and men cursing behind her. At least one crying out in pain.

Inside the tool shed, gasping from the run, Miriam put her back to the door and pushed back to shut it. If Elian began staying here with Ya'el and had to come and go on his own, they'd need to find an easier way in and out. Maybe Matthew could adjust the door. Yossi was the family scholar, and Matthew worked well with his hands. *And what am I good for?* she wondered.

She pulled out the bench and saw the lines from the pulley arrangement Matthew had rigged. Two were attached high on the rear legs of the bench and a third to the underside center of the seat. The lines ran through a small opening in the wall and through pulleys. The four legs of the bench rested on small skids, and Matthew had even smoothed the stone beneath the bench to aid in sliding it back and forth, so a single person could manage it.

Lying across the bench, she reached her right arm down into the narrow space between the three lines. She lifted and slid the lipped access cover aside but kept it close enough to be easily replaced. She got on the ground then, backward-belly-crawled until her feet dipped into the opening, finding a rung as her legs entered farther. Her arms, then her hands, held her weight until she could descend and planted her feet on the rungs. Once clear of the opening, she reached up and pulled the cover back in place. Then she hooked an arm in the rungs and carefully, with an even pull, drew the lines down, pulling the bench back to the wall over the tunnel access. When she left, she'd climb up, open the trapdoor, push the bench away, climb out, and push the bench back. Then she would check that the lines were straight and no slack showed underneath.

When she reached the bottom of the shaft, in the dim light, Miriam heard the rasp before she saw Ya'el several feet from the ladder, her bow pulled with an arrow nocked. Ya'el eased her pull and lowered the bow.

"Did you check on Elian?" she asked.

"Yes. He's unhappy but well. He misses you."

"Matthew told me he still stays in the building Shammai let us use... but now it holds two other families. They barely speak to him, and he does their hardest work. When can he come and stay here with me?"

"Soon," said Miriam with an encouraging smile. "Shammai asked Yohanan ben Zaccai if Elian could work through the next month. He's the best at clambering down into the pits and back up. Shammai's new workers are old men, and they're slow. His woodcutters are bringing in less timber, as well. Two were killed at the Damascus gate for cursing at the men who stopped wagons to search them. Now the other woodcutters worry about the violence threatening them next."

Miriam followed Ya'el into the inner chambers. "The air is fresher now," she noted.

"Matthew brought a hole borer from Shammai to clear the above ventilation holes. There were several." Ya'el stopped at the table that held their charts of the tunnels beneath the city. She gestured at two earthenware pitchers. "There's water, and Matthew brought wine with the provisions. There's not much to eat, but enough. I'll need more once Elian is here."

"I saw Hananiah again. He hints he's working again on something that will reward him enough to leave Jerusalem, and he wants me to go with him."

"It must have to do with my husband, then. Have you figured out why Hananiah seemed angry at the message you got a glimpse of?"

"Yes, but how he is spurred on by some plan."

"We must find out what it is... what Gessius is doing," Ya'el said.

"He could run out of time before he has what he wants. A friend of Yohan ben Zaccai's told us the legions in Caesarea are preparing, which means they'll soon march here."

"Did you ask Matthew about bows and arrows?"

Miriam nodded. "And replacement strings. He and Eleasar ben Ananias are going to take them from Antonia Fortress. They must be careful, but he hopes to have them soon."

"Good. Until then, you can learn some of the craft with mine." Ya'el took her bow and released the string from one end with a push and pull. "You never leave it strung too long. And here's how to string it." She rested one nocked end of the bow against the inside of her foot. Then pulled the center of the bow toward her while pushing the other end down within reach of the end of the string hooking it in place. "It takes some practice and strength, depending on the draw weight of the bow being strung, but you should have no problem." Ya'el straightened up and held out the bow. "Now, you try...."

They did it several times—string on, off, on again—until Miriam could do it smoothly.

"Now we'll shoot...." Miriam followed Ya'el into the long gallery off the central chamber. "The lighting would be better with more lamps," said Ya'el, "but I have only a few you and Matthew have brought. They're not the best, the coarse wicks sometimes smolder, but the air holes are helping."

Miriam saw the target set twenty paces away. The lamps along the wall cast an uneven light. On the wall on either side of the target, a sputtering torch gave off a flickering illumination of the mark. Ya'el picked out an arrow from several in a reed basket. Its shaft was mainly straight, its tip merely sharpened wood, with ragged feathers for fletching. "These are not the best... but the straightest Elian could find in Shammai's woodpiles." She nocked the arrow and drew the bow. Miriam heard her softly let go of her breath. The shaft flew and caught the edge of the target, tumbling beyond to one side.

"I can do better with real arrows. You will, too." Ya'el took a leather guard from the basket that matched the one on her arm. "Remove your dagger sheath, and let's put this on; then you can try."

* * *

THE UPPER CITY

As she hurried, Miriam rubbed the inside of her forearm again where the hidden sheath chafed the skin rubbed raw from her practice with Ya'el. Though the guard had mainly protected her, the skin was still sore. She had promised to be home before sundown to help with dinner and to relieve the ailing Mathias, who worried about her. She no longer cared about her clothing being noticed, for people on her street no longer paid attention to their neighbors. She entered her home through the front door.

"Mother!" she cried out surprisedly when she found Rebecca inside the entrance. She heard voices from the family room.

"Miriam, don't ask or look to see who's here. Please go upstairs, change, then come down looking like my daughter." Rebecca gave a sharp nod that indicated she would not be crossed and was not moving until Miriam was on the stairs.

Minutes later, Miriam was back down and recognized the voice before she entered the sitting area. Her father stood as she came in.

"Before you say anything, Miriam, I'll speak, and then Ya'akov will say why he's here."

Miriam was surprised when he turned to her mother. "Rebecca, this is something you also do not know. When Ya'akov's and Miriam's *erusin* was broken... Ya'akov refused to take back the bride price, the *mohar* that tradition required. Since I could not force him to take it back, I've held it." He looked at Miriam then. "When your mother told me Ya'akov had returned to Jerusalem," Mathias said, "I tried again. But...." He motioned toward the young man behind him to come forward.

"Our engagement was broken," Ya'akov said as he stood and approached her. "But not my love for you, Miriam. That's why I have not married. I still want to—"

The loud knocking on the door interrupted him.

Stunned, Miriam watched her mother dart an angry glance at her father as she went to answer the door. She returned with Yohanan ben Zaccai, who looked upset. "Yohanan has something he must tell us," she said.

The old priest swallowed, his narrowed eyes going first to her father. "News has come about Yosef. General Vespasian, who it seems will become yet another new emperor of Rome, has freed Yosef. He is no longer a prisoner."

Miriam's surge of joy matched the flare of happiness on her mother's face.

But the worried look stayed on the old priest's face, and he said, "But Yosef remains with the Romans!"

LXVIII

Januarius 70 CE

Caesarea

The Roman Encampment, Legion Equipment Warehouses

Sayid knew well the vast warehouses, the *horrea* General Vespasian had constructed to store the over 700 siege engines to be used against Jerusalem. Each kind of equipment had its own section in a warehouse. Weapons like the *scorpios, ballistae,* and catapults were stored with their stock of missiles—stones chiseled and smoothed and large bundles of heavy bolts and javelins. The compounds and materials for the incendiary munitions—fire arrows and the heavy hollow balls filled with flammable oils—were stored separately in a warehouse a safe distance from the others.

In another warehouse were *testudos*, shelters on wheels that protected the men with rams as they worked to break a gate or wall. There were also components that, when assembled, would become siege towers constructed to protect assailants and their ladders as they approached the defensive walls of a fortification. An archer atop a tower could extend their effective reach while reducing the range an enemy requires at ground level. This strategy also helped against a wall with ramparts. The towers were rectangular, with four wheels, their height set roughly equal to that of the wall, or sometimes higher, to allow archers to shoot down into the fortification. The tower frames were wooden and flammable. Some were covered in iron or fresh animal skins for the towers used on the ground too soft for a heavier structure.

Yet another warehouse held breaching equipment—rams for breaking walls and gates... and ladders for assaulting walls. The rams reminded him that Nicanor had talked with the senior *armamentarii*, weapons engineers in Rome, about an improved design after he saw how defenders at Yotapta dropped rocks heavy enough to destroy a testudo and break a ram's shaft just behind its metal head. That new design—with the thicker, longer iron sheathing of the neck—is what they would take to Jerusalem.

Sayid and his father had worked through each piece of equipment the auxiliary units would help assemble and position at Jerusalem's walls for the breach. Their first day together had been silent but for exchanging brief questions and answers and noting things completed or yet to be done before they completed their work. Sayid saw his father lose some of his severe stiffness over the following days, though neither had spoken of opinions nor feelings. It seemed best to keep personal thoughts and personalities out of it. Sayid began their last morning with some regret. All his life, he had dreamed of serving with his father one day. And he had... without his father's past acrimony creating friction... for a few days.

"The *libratores* will inspect everything when set up in the field." The statement was not a question, but Sayid confirmed it and gestured toward one of the *immunes* working a row over from them. The man was one of the non-combatant specialists who checked, repaired, and leveled all the legions' siege equipment. Missile throwers—*tormenta*—especially required constant maintenance. Rain and dampness affected their torsion components. The leather, sinew, and hemp skeins loosened and lost their ability to hold tension.

"They'll evaluate every piece of equipment here and change anything that needs replacing," Sayid said. "They'll do that again in the field."

Sayid and his father entered the area filled with undermining equipment. Shovels and pickaxes for digging and bracing and brackets for the frame that would collapse a section of an undermined wall according to a predetermined schedule. Sayid watched his father bypass that equipment and head straight for the mass of ladders. At Hebron, Sayid had seen firsthand how effective an *escalade*, a ladder assault, could be. Breaking through walls and gates was often the method that ultimately worked in a siege. But a faster means of gaining control involved getting ladders in place and men up them. A ladder assault could also result in many dead, so two factors mattered greatly. The number of ladders you could get onto the wall with men securely anchoring them and how fast the operation could be completed to keep a stream of men moving up and over.

"We'll adjust the height when we see Jerusalem's walls," Marcus Sabinus said as he kept moving among the rows of stacked ladders.

His father had just alluded to a third important factor, and Sayid confirmed it. "Right, sir. I know the walls to be 40 feet high and 8 feet wide. There are 90 towers on the first outer wall, 14 on the second, and 60 on the third. That newest third wall—the outermost northern one—is twice as wide. But the engineers will measure the wall height, so we're accurate." Sayid saw his father's eyes narrow, but not in irritation, and the slight nod of his head, as if approving his words.

Accuracy was important. Sayid had seen one too-tall ladder quickly pushed away by the defenders at Hebron. Spilling the men to sprawl on the ground and quickly becoming the focus of volleys of arrows from archers on the walls. Most of those men had died. Another ladder that was too short left the lip of the wall, its rampart, out of reach. The men's attempt to stretch and grasp it slowed them, so they became targets for archers shooting from where the wall jutted out enough for their angled line of fire. The siege forces also had to account for the distance the base was set from the wall—too close, and the ladder could more easily be pushed over.

"Let's walk the stacks and look for any with dry rot," Marcus Sabinus announced. "Afterward, if you're willing, I want to go to the port and see that shipment just in—the new-style helmets. If possible, I'd like my men to be allotted those, too."

Sayid nodded. "Then let's go see about it."

* * *

THE PORT

Marcus Sabinus lifted one helmet from the crate, packing straw falling from it. The Imperial Gallic type had hinged cheek guards covering the largest part of the face without restricting the soldier's breathing, sight, or shouting range. A horizontal ridge across the front of the bowl acted as a guard for both the nose and the rest of the face and reinforcement against downward cuts and blows from above. Ear guards protruded from the side of the helmet but would not obstruct hearing. The shallow neck guard was angled toward the bowl to prevent chafing against a metal cuirass.

"This is much better than what my men have," Marcus said. "Can you have them let me take this one to show them?"

Sayid waved over a clerk he recognized, who was checking in the shipment. "I'll sign for a crate opened and one helmet removed," he said when the man had hurried over. "I will report it to Celsus Evander." He turned to his father with a smile and said, "It's yours...."

With a nod, Marcus Sabinus tucked it under his arm as they left the busy dock at the junction of the quay and the city's central avenue, where a babble of conversation came from a group of men waiting outside the largest taberna in the area.

"Do you want to join us?" Marcus said.

Sayid turned to his father, who said, "Some men asked me to meet them here. You're welcome to join me... to join us."

As his heart rose, Sayid heard a man behind him, "General Titus and the Alexandrians have arrived. The word is he'll soon set his sights on Jerusalem."

Then Nicanor was back! *I must tell him about Sycaminum and the waypoint outside Ptolemais.* "Sorry, Father... I wish I could, but I must do other work now." Sayid stood watching as his father turned away, but not before he saw the flash in the other man's eyes. His expression had hardened as he took the steps to the taberna without another word.

* * *

NICANOR'S QUARTERS

Sayid watched as Nicanor finished feeding Albus a second handful of salted barley. Then they went into the living quarters. While Nicanor looked understandably tired, Yosef seemed exhausted, with dark half-circles under his eyes and shoulders slumping as he set aside one of the half-burned sheets of parchment.

Sayid had told them what he had seen and heard when he'd followed Gessius Florus, and Yosef had immediately sat at the table to look at the scraps of parchment.

"These rough translations mention items that can only be from the Temple in Jerusalem and locations where they are now... or will be," Yosef said. "A name mentioned on one page, Nahum, is someone I know in Qumran." He looked at Sayid and said, "You found these in Gessius Florus's warehouse?"

"They were outside what looked like a prison cell inside the warehouse in Sycaminum. It was close to the large chained and locked room I mentioned."

"Nicanor," Yosef said as he carefully stacked the scraps, "we must learn what Florus has inside that room."

LXIX

Februarius 70 CE

Jerusalem

Outside Antonia Fortress

Eleasar ben Ananias said to Matthew as they stood at the base of the imposing tower at dawn: "I agree that we should stockpile our own weapons. Yohanan ben Levi's men have taken the extra ones held by the Temple Guards. But we can't walk into' Antonia Fortress and take them from under the noses of the Gischalan's men," said Eleasar ben Ananias. The fortress rose over them, its corner towers just now showing the pale tinting from the dawn growing over the Mount of Olive's shoulder.

"We'll go in the same way we did four years ago. When the Roman garrison held Antonia Fortress, and we needed weapons to fight Gessius Florus's men. I wanted to see if the outer guard positions had changed." Matthew turned south toward the Upper City and the agora and took a last glance at the fortress. "I wish it were held by a man who helped defend the city, not tear it apart."

Herod's Fortress Antonia walls had at their base an imposing glacis—blocks cut at a steep angle to deflect battering rams and tightly and smoothly joined so no attacking soldier could get a foothold. A dry moat accompanied the glacis inside the Temple courtyard. *This place,* Matthew thought, *should become the last redoubt for Jerusalem's defenders against the Romans.* But under Yohanan ben Levi's control, he doubted it would.

The generously-sized stronghold had once housed most of the Roman garrison in Jerusalem, a cohort of about 500 men. There was ample room for even more within the structure and its open courtyard. Sentries patrolled the walkways Herod had provided atop the four walls of the Temple Enclosure, allowing the Romans to guard against insurrection by any Jews still angry at Roman rule. A would-be Jewish ruler of Jerusalem now used it against his own people.

"Do you think the Gischalan's men know of that secret passage?" Eleasar asked quietly as he and Matthew passed into the agora and headed toward a hidden entrance to the tunnels connecting the Temple area, the fortress, and the Northern City.

"He might," Matthew replied, "and if so, he either guards it or has it sealed against any attack by Simon's men. But maybe they don't know since so many are Galileans and others are from outside Jerusalem. We have to try."

* * *

THE UPPER CITY, AGORA

Matthew led them through the empty market where, as soon as the day fully began, the bravest—or neediest—would venture out to shop. The agora, surrounded by porticos, was the city's forum, where prosperous citizens conducted their business, shopping and being waited upon by the commoners who mostly lived in the Lower City. Parts of the agora had grown up over the years by chance, unplanned, so there were many unexpected paths and alleys. Most people knew only the familiar ones they took for their usual business. But the children of the Upper City, especially those full of curiosity like he, Yosef, and their friends had been, knew all the turns and where the alleys started, led, and ended.

Matthew turned into the alley he had first entered with Yosef two decades before, passing the bend straight to the alley's surprising blind dead-end. In a corner grew a shoulder-height dense shrub thick with thorns planted long ago in that overlooked corner. It served as the protector of a fitted trapdoor in the ground. Careful of the thorns—some dagger-sharp and inches long—he slipped behind the bush, swept away a thick layer of dirt from the hatch, and felt for the edges of the door's metal frame. Sliding closer, he hooked his fingers under the notches and lifted. The door opened with a dry rasp and spill of dirt so fine some of it hung in a current of air.

Matthew leaned forward to be sure it was as he remembered. Just inside, he saw the top handholds of a long ladder secured to the wall of the rough shaft that sank into the darkness below. "I'll go first and light the lamp," he said. Jerusalem's soft limestone bedrock could be easily chiseled through, allowing many underground passages. Two decades ago, Yosef had cached lamps and oil for them at different areas of the tunnels, including near the foot of every access and exit point. Miriam had told Matthew they were still there—she had replaced lamp wicks and stored new skins of oil—and he could find them by feel.

* * *

Final Siege

Antonia Fortress, Northern Wall

Matthew and Eleasar fled the armory, cursing at their burdens, pausing to catch their breath and wipe their sweaty brows, anxiously checking behind them. Both still held the strung bows they'd had to use against the six men guarding the sally port, Matthew feeling a pang at striking them from behind. They had not even reached to sound an alarm.

Matthew and Eleasar hurried through the passageway leading to the opening at the base of the northern wall of the fortress. This opening passed through the slanted flagstones at the bottom of the wall. It was familiar, but they had never used it. The passage was narrow, meant to be defensible, forcing them to enter and exit single-file. Each man carried a double-sized Roman *loculus,* legion infantry haversack, stuffed with arrows. The large bags swung over their shoulders, swayed, and kept catching on the rough sides of the passage, slowing them until they reached the way out.

The fortress behind them was in an uproar. They had heard the shouting and echoes of running men and tramping feet as they stole from the armory. Their way in would not be the way out. Burdened with bows, strings, and as many arrows as they could stuff in the Roman packs, they'd run to the only exit they knew in the opposite direction. Beyond it, the slender cut-through of the slanted flagstones of the fortress foundation did not widen until it reached the stone path encircling the fort. They filed through at a stumbling run.

Outside, they could hear more shouting from their left and behind them, accompanied by screams and the clang and clamor of battle. "I'll go look," Matthew said, shrugging the pack strap off his shoulder and following the path to the northwest corner of the fortress. He soon came running back, snatching his pack from Eleasar.

"There must be a thousand of Simon's men up there!" Matthew cried. "They're attacking the Gischalan's men on the western wall, atop the cloister and porticos. They are lined up all the way to the Temple. I couldn't tell how many... it is too far away... but it seemed dozens... maybe hundreds of the Gishalan's men must be on the double colonnades. At this end, on the ramparts of the corner tower, archers and slingers are firing to the south to shower Simon's men with arrows and lead bullets. That's where their attention is right now." He looped the bow over his free shoulder and gripped his sword. "So, let's go."

"Where? We planned to leave these," Eleasar slapped his pack, "in the tunnel for later. Where can we take them?"

Matthew cursed again. He had no choice. "Where they're meant to go."

LXX

Februarius 70 CE

Jerusalem

The Upper City

Miriam waited until she heard Matthew leave, for she did not want him to think he must change his plans and go with her. Aggravated at being wakened, Cicero squawked and muttered as Miriam wrapped his cage in a blanket and picked it up. She knew the risk of carrying anything on the streets that might seem valuable, especially an object hidden by a blanket. It could, and likely would, rouse interest from the men who roamed Jerusalem's streets. What would she do if confronted? She'd fight if it were one or two men. But what if there were more? Would she drop Cicero and run? How would she explain that Ya'el... to Cleo? Their lives had changed for the worse through no fault, and Ya'el had few meaningful things left of her former life: Elian, her bow, and the bird. Ya'el already had her bow back, and soon—Miriam hoped—Cicero.

Mother will miss him, Miriam mused, for Rebecca liked the bird's company and was the best at keeping him quiet. Until the previous night, Rebecca had kept him in her bedroom, taking the poor creature out only when Leah and Rachel went to the market with Matthew and Mathias. But Ya'el, Elian, and Cicero would be pleased to be together again.

The streets were eerily empty, even for that early hour. Cicero sensed something in that strangeness and sounded a faint cluck, then a sharp squawk. But at least it wasn't one of his screeches that they had tried hard to keep quiet at home lest neighbors or passersby hear him. "Shhh... shhh, Cicero...." she crooned, and he became quiet. Her eyes watched for men who might pose a threat. With the blanketed cage tucked awkwardly under one arm and Zechariah's staff gripped in her other hand, she walked toward Bezetha. She would get Elian and bring him with her to join Ya'el.

*   * * **

Bezetha, the Shed Over the Underground Baris Remnants

Elian was excited as Miriam lighted the small lamp kept inside the door. "Careful, don't move around. I'll show you where...." Cicero squawked as she handed the boy the cage and lamp and went to close the door, but someone on the other side pushed back. A worried jolt shot through Miriam as she shoved to close it again. Harder.

"Miriam! It's Rachel... Miriam, please!"

"What are you doing?" Miriam called anxiously as she pulled her cousin inside and pushed the door shut with a grunt.

Rachel glared at her. "What are you doing... here... dressed like that?" she asked accusingly. "I followed you and heard the bird... then saw you with a boy... Elian!" she exclaimed, getting a better look at the boy, his eyes wide in the lamp's glow. "I thought you and Ya'el were in Masada!" Rachel stared wide-eyed again at Miriam and repeated, "What are you doing here... dressed like that? I couldn't sleep... I started to come to your room... to talk about Yosef. Then I heard you leave."

"So you followed me?" Miriam said. "Do you know how dangerous that is?"

"I don't care," Rachel said defiantly. "I wanted to know what was going on. But I hung back and eventually lost sight of you. I don't know Bezetha, other than the cistern where we used to play, the *Struthius*. I went there to sit and think about what to do next, then I heard men shouting and what sounded like fighting. I hid and was about to try and get home when I saw you again. This time hurrying along with a boy... you must've heard the fighting too."

"Rachel, there's no more time for all this," Miriam interrupted her cousin. "You must leave now. Go and—"

A wrenching and pounding on the door cut her off. Miriam nearly panicked until she thought of Zechariah's words welled up in her mind: *Always keep your head about you.* Suddenly she felt settled, and her mind cleared. Pressing her weight against the door, Miriam looked around for something to wedge under to give them more time. A suitable chunk of wood with a narrow end was just the thing, and she kept her foot braced while she shoved the wedge in place.

"Elian, pull that bench from the wall," Miriam ordered in a tone that required obedience and fast. She pointed it out for him. "It's heavy—help him, Rachel."

Elian had set the cage and hand lamp down to struggle with the bench, and with Rachel's help, he managed to slide it away from the wall, and he now stared at the lines affixed to the bench. "Don't worry about that," Miriam said. "Move it all aside. See the hatch underneath?"

Her foot slid backward an inch, and she knew that whoever was on the other side was strong, and if he had any friends, she was in trouble. She instinctively turned her shoulder into the door and leaned her weight against it, feeling the muscles in her arms and back knot with effort. "You must hurry, Elian," Miriam groaned. She could not hold out much longer. "And tie a line to Cicero's cage."

Elian was a flurry of movement as he tied a length or rope to the cage and revealed the trapdoor.

"Lift the cover, Elian, and lower Cicero. Then hurry down after him. Rachel, you follow." The door inched open more, and as she pushed it back and heard a man's curse outside, she saw the wedge was no longer helping. "Rachel," she grunted, "go now, follow him!"

As Rachel lowered herself into the shaft opening, the door crept open an inch with each push. Miriam shed the cloak with her forward foot planted and her hip against the door, and she pulled both daggers from her forearm sheaths. Her last glance at Rachel caught her cousin's wide-eyed stare.

"Tell Ya'el to be ready to run," Miriam ordered, offering no explanation. "I'll buy time for you all to use one of the tunnels. Hurry—smother the lamp and go!"

Rachel pinched the wick and, plunged into darkness, Miriam backed away from the door.

LXXI

Februarius 70 CE

Jerusalem

Bezetha, The Entrance to the Baris Underground Remnants

Matthew led Eleasar at a hard run until he took a sliding stop before the shed, looking around to see if they'd been seen. Armed men were everywhere, many armored and with Idumean and Roman equipment combinations. Some still carried lighted torches, though the sun now cast plenty of light onto Bezetha and the New City.

Gasping, he told Eleasar, "Go." He waved his hand to dismiss his friend. "Drop your bag. I'll do this and meet you at Yohanan ben Zaccai's in two hours."

Eleasar had melted away among the stone piles, and Matthew watched to be sure he had drawn no attention. Matthew lay the two large packs at his feet and could not open the shed door. He pushed again.

"What are you doing?"

Eleasar, hands on his knees, had gasped out the question, and Matthew answered with another: "Why did you come back?"

"I don't know whose men they are, Simon's or Yohanan's, but they are everywhere, like hornets spewing out of the nest—Antonia Fortress. At least a hundred are marching this way—short swords, spears, and shields." He waved his arm wider as he took another big breath. "I saw others in the distance, moving toward the Upper City."

The wind shifted and brought the stench of smoke from an oil-stoked fire nearby. Matthew straightened and turned into the path of the smoke, then looked up. Low in the sky, a pall covered the areas he knew from all the preparations they'd made for the expected siege by the Romans. The garners were burning where the grain was stored.

"I heard a rumor... but didn't think they would do it," Eleasar said, gazing in the same direction. "Simon bar Giora and Yohanan ben Levi are burning each other's food stores. Yahweh save us—what are they thinking?"

The shouting grew louder around the rock storage field.

"Help me with this," Matthew said as he returned to the door. Finally, it gave, and they dragged the packs inside. As they dragged them through the entry, strident cries and the clash of swords on shields echoed from among the piles of stone outside. In the slanting sunbeams into the shed, he saw what Eleasar was staring at.

Miriam. The sunlight through the doorway glinted on the blades in her hands. There was nothing for it but to enlist the help of their friend. "Eleasar, help me shut the door," he said, and they both shoved it closed.

In the darkness, Eleasar said, "Matthew, why is your sister here, dressed as a man... and holding daggers like she knows how to use them?"

* * *

Ya'el lowered her bow, and Elian piped out, "Matthew!" The boy ran to him and grasped his short robe, looking up and smiling.

With an unconscious hand, Matthew caressed the head of the boy while looking around in awe. *The chamber is well-lighted, and the lamp flickers—good air flows here.* He had not been back since clearing the holes for Ya'el, and he blinked away his ridiculous desire to comment on it with pride. Elian had returned to Ya'el, who now had one arm around him as the boy spoke in low tones to the bird. Cicero preened, and Eleasar and Rachel stared at Miriam, who stared back at them.

No one looked at Matthew, but he must answer the questions. He must explain in such a way as to ensure that both Eleasar and Rachel kept secret what they'd learned—about this place, about Ya'el and Miriam.

"There are things you've seen today," Matthew said to them, "and you must give your word to never speak of the with anyone who is not now in this room. The reasons... will be explained later." He was confident in Eleasar's nod but must watch his young cousin. Miriam knew that, too, and was watching Rachel intently as she nodded, still stunned.

Matthew continued. "Right now, three men have turned our city into a battlefield: Simon bar Giora, his estranged son Eleazar ben Simon, and Yohanan ben Levi. And then there are the Romans, who we've heard are marshaling and preparing in Caesarea. That means only one thing. Sooner rather than later, they will be outside our walls. And no matter if it takes months to get here, they will be within our walls at some point. But the three Jews—our countrymen—are now a bigger threat to us. The fighting used to be confined to the Temple and its surroundings, but now it has spread. All three are responsible for the deaths of the worshippers who still come to the Temple from nearby countries. Their blood has pooled in the courts of Yahweh."

"How many do they lead?" Ya'el asked.

Matthew was surprised, and he studied her for a moment. When he had come down the ladder with Miriam and Eleasar at the bottom, one glance had told him Ya'el's arrow was ready to take the life of any man she did not know and trust.

Now he knew—and Eleasar must realize, too—that Ya'el's expert handling of the bow revealed that she had killed the Idumeans who had threatened his family. Their bodies in the courtyard had testified to a capable archer's work. *Perhaps Roman women have this skill?* He speculated. Perhaps that was part of why Rome's power reached as far as it did. *Yosef would know these things.*

He shook himself out of his wonder and answered Ya'el's question: "Simon bar Giora commands 10,000 Judeans led by 50 officers and 5,000 Idumeans led by ten officers. He's often seen with them on the streets of Jerusalem, close to the fighting. Yohanan ben Levi commands 6,000 led by 20 officers and rarely leaves the mansion he rebuilt and fortified for his use. As we came here, the Gischalan's men attacked Eleazar ben Simon, who holds the Temple's inner courts with 2400 men. They also hold Fortress Antonia and its adjacent walled open spaces from the fortress ramparts and the double-colonnade to the Temple. They stood off an attack from below by Simon bar Giora and his men."

"When the legions come," Ya'el said, "there will be 60,000 soldiers or more—will these men join one another to turn and fight as one people?"

"I don't know," said Matthew with sorrow. "I don't think anyone does."

Eleasar stirred and spoke. "Above us are some followers of those men—hundreds from all the groups are moving throughout the city. I hope they did not see us enter the shed; else, we may have a fight on our hands down here."

Matthew saw no need to comment that none of them would survive it. He added, "Or we can flee through the tunnels. The question," he said as he looked at Miriam, "is whether, if we do, we can come up within the city in a place that would be safe?"

As he asked that, he saw Elian's nose crinkle. The boy was used to the smell of wood burning. But this was the odor of the source of the plumes of smoke over the city. Grain was stored in massive jars of clay and wickerwork, and it would all have to be soaked in oil to burn effectively. And this odd smell confirmed that it had been done. *Likely a year's worth*, he thought. Surely some underground stores might remain, but that would not be nearly enough to feed all confined within the city. They must talk with Yohana ben Zaccai about trusting the merchant and trader Arins with a secret way into and out of Jerusalem. If they could not get more food supplies into the city before the Romans arrived, they had no hope of standing against the siege for long.

"There must be some safe place within the Temple to get to from here!" Rachel spoke for the first time in a quavering voice.

The ruffling stir and answering squawk were loud in the chamber. "Temple gold!" Cicero croaked.

LXXII

Februarius 70 CE

Caesarea

The Roman Encampment, Nicanor's Quarters

Nicanor had heard Yosef toss and turn through the night. *Perhaps it was the storm*, he thought, remembering the rumbles from the late evening into the early morning hours. A particular flash of lightning and crash of thunder had woken all of them. He had checked Albus, who looked sleepily at him, unconcerned. The horse slept better than any of them. As he returned to his cot, Nicanor had seen Yosef, his eyes open, staring into the orange-red glow of the charcoal brazier warming the room. Above him, in the corner, was a small hand lamp he must have lit and set on the shelf. It cast a small circle of illumination, and Nicanor could see Yosef had one of his wax tablets on his lap and held a stylus. When Nicanor had awakened at dawn, Yosef was in the same position but writing, and he continued while Nicanor made breakfast.

"What's wrong, Yosef?" Sayid asked, setting his empty bowl aside. "You've not said a word this morning and little last evening."

Nicanor finished his gruel, too, and added, "What troubled your sleep? It cannot have been just the storm."

Yosef rubbed his eyes with the heel of his palms. Behind him, sunlight shafted into the room through the slats of the shuttered window now that Sayid had pulled away the rectangle of waxed canvas that had held out the blowing rain during the storm. Yosef lowered his hands, and the slightest hesitation and twitch suggested he might turn his head away and keep his silence. But then Yosef spoke.

"A dream. A woman stood under an old almond tree 30 feet or taller, lush, with light pink blossoms surrounded by smaller, white-blossomed trees. She spoke to me, but I couldn't hear her. She remained under the large center tree, and its laden branches drooped and formed a veil over her face. Her hand raised to beckon me closer."

Yosef stopped and looked at his friends, saying, "The Hebrew word for almond tree is *shaqed*... it also means 'to watch,' and it can mean 'a promise of judgment.'" He swung his legs off the cot. "So, to my people, the almond symbolizes Yahweh's watchfulness... and reminds us that he measures us. Trees with light pink blossoms bear bitter nuts, and the white bear the sweet. The sweet are for those who follow Yahweh. The bitter seeds are for those who have forsaken him...." Yosef's voice thickened in a dry throat rasp.

Sayid poured water into a cup and took it to him. "What does your dream mean, Yosef?"

Yosef sipped and nodded his thanks. "I walked toward the woman... so I could hear her. She raised her hand to sweep the blossoms from her face."

Sayid turned to Nicanor and shrugged.

"Who was the woman? Nicanor asked.

"The same woman I first dreamed of the night before I left for Caesarea to sail for Rome on the *Salacia*... Lady Cleo."

He still cares for her, Nicanor thought with a jab of regret for his friend, tinged with his feelings for Cleo. All four of them had survived the shipwreck of the *Salacia*. And it was there, and in Rome later, before her marriage, that he had come to quietly admire her. The stories Graius had told of her during the peaceful stretches of their journey to gain Marcus Otho's help had endeared Cleo to Nicanor even more. He still intended to hold Gessius Florus accountable for what he had done to her and eliminate the threat he still posed. "What did she tell you?"

"That Florus wants the Temple treasure. The golden tithing vessel Marinus discovered in Aegyptus is connected to the Thracians here in Caesarea and came from the Temple. We have waited too long and must soon go to Sycaminum to see if he holds more in the warehouse."

"First, I have to talk to General Titus," Nicanor said. "I can't just leave." He stood and reached for his cloak. Titus had not wasted time having the men from Alexandria added to the legions' organization and plan for the coming assault on Jerusalem. Though he was a *tribunus*, Nicanor had not been given specific legion responsibilities or duties. General Vespasian had explained he would be an independent adviser to Titus. He had charged him to continue looking into the Thracian matter to determine whether it threatened them.

Even without official orders, Nicanor had helped with the final battle preparation for Jerusalem, working with the legion commanders and their staff who weren't part of the planning in Alexandria. With that completed now, they waited on the orders from

General Titus to assemble and march on Jerusalem. He must find out about that timing before leaving Caesarea.

* * *

THE PRAETORIUM

Nicanor still felt odd entering the command general's office and finding Titus—not Vespasian— sitting behind the large campaign desk. The only other difference was the bare spot where Vespasian's *clepsydra* once sat on the narrow table behind the desk. General Vespasian's water clock now performed its duty for him in Alexandria... maybe already in Rome.

Titus looked up from the contents of the dispatch pouch on his desk, sweeping away a few fragments of the red wax. "The courier vessel is in from Alexandria," he said, gesturing for Nicanor to sit. "Rome is settling down. The released grain shipments relieve their concerns about famine, lessening the people's anger."

"The legion talk is that thousands died in Rome," Nicanor said, "our men and those of Vitellius... and many citizens." Nicanor had been surprised at the scarcity of official updates other than that Vitellius was dead, and Rome had acknowledged General Vespasian as the new emperor. As with everywhere he had served, absent official news, men filled their conversations with rumor.

Titus nodded. "My uncle, Flavius Sabinus—I believe you met him—was killed on the last day of fighting."

"I'm sorry to hear that, sir. I met him when he was protecting Domitian. He seemed a good man."

"He did what he could. The dead have been cleared from the city, and soon more work will begin to rebuild what was destroyed in the fighting. The Temple of Jupiter Optimus Maximus will be first."

"Is General—I mean Emperor Vespasian now in Rome?"

"No. Not yet." Titus's face tightened into a frown. "He will remain in Alexandria until the winter storms end and Rome is stable." Titus took a wrapped square of vellum and handed it to Nicanor. "It seems my father and I are destined to be your messenger," he smiled slightly, a rare sight. "This is from Marinus, for you."

If Rome was settled, Nicanor wondered why Vespasian did not go there yet. Overland would take a long time, 80 days by horseback, stopping only for camps each night. And it would likely be longer since now an imperial movement. But Marinus's ships and the grain vessels must be sailing. He wanted to ask Titus if he or his father had discussed it with Marinus. Still, the general had not explained, and it wasn't Nicanor's place to ask.

"I need another minute of your time, sir," said Nicanor. "I must go to check something in Sycaminum that might be connected to the Thracian mercenaries General Vespasian has asked me to investigate. I'll be gone two or three days, and I need to know when you will give orders to march on Jerusalem."

"Sir," the aide called from the entryway, "your guest is here."

Nicanor saw a flash of excitement in Titus's eyes, and his expression lost some of its severity. Then he looked at Nicanor and said, "Not for at least two weeks or more...."

***

Nicanor's Quarters

"So, do we go now to Sycaminum?" Yosef asked as Nicanor entered the room.

"Sayid and I will leave in the morning, but you must stay here."

"Why!?" Yosef asked. "Am I free or not?"

Nicanor saw the flush on Yosef's face and understood his friend's need to help. Titus had ended the meeting by flatly ordering that someone trusted must keep an eye on Yosef while Nicanor was gone. Which forestalled his telling Titus he planned to take Yosef with him. "It could be dangerous for you, Yosef. General Titus ordered you must remain here." Nicanor didn't add that Titus had made him feel like a mortal male version of Cunina, the goddess who watched over children.

"Did General Titus say when we go to Jerusalem?" Sayid asked with a sideways glance at Yosef.

"No. But expect orders in two weeks or more." Nicanor didn't understand the delay, or perhaps he did. He had seen General Titus's beautiful guest as they passed in the antechamber to the general's private office. And then he'd heard her name as she was announced: *Queen Berenice...* he said to himself. *Who is that?* He sat down on his cot and took out the packet he'd tucked into his *cintus*, the broad leather belt that would soon bear his over-the-shoulder baldric when he wore armor.

"What should I do as I wait here for your return?" Yosef asked with a grimace.

Nicanor studied Yosef. The tension in his shoulders, smudges beneath his eyes, and the taut lines of his jaw betrayed his poor sleep.

"You should rest... get some sleep." *Likely little enough of that soon enough—in Jerusalem,* Nicanor frowned.

Yosef didn't reply, but the scowl deepened. He reached for his journals, set them on the table, and got his ink jar and pen.

Sayid stood. "I'll see Celsus Evander and tell him we'll be gone for a few days."

"Tell him I will come to see him later," Nicanor said with a quick look at Yosef. Celsus still had ill feelings toward the Jew but would watch out for him again if Nicanor asked. He slipped the ribbon of leather from the letters Titus had given him. He read the short one first. "Marinus and Anyte send their greetings to you, Yosef," he said after reading the first lines. Nicanor had sensed an affinity between Yosef and Anyte, the two writers, on board the *Egeria* and in Alexandria.

Bent over his own sheet with pen in hand, Yosef looked up and nodded. "If you reply, give them mine."

"Marinus says Anyte is now in Crete and will remain there until Vespasian goes to Rome," Nicanor said before setting aside that letter. When he began reading the one from Marcus Attilius, he stood suddenly at the news before he knew he did so.

"What's wrong?" Yosef said, looking up at him.

Nicanor lowered the sheet clenched in his fist. "My friend Marcus lost an arm saving Vespasian's son. A surgeon could not save it."

"I'm sorry, Nicanor."

"He lives... that's what matters. As does Domitian, and that was his charge. Antonia Caenis has taken Marcus into her home." Nicanor read on. "He says he'll be glad when the war ends and the fighting is done. Then when I come to Rome, maybe he won't have to save me," Nicanor put down the letter and grinned at Yosef, "says it would be harder with just one arm." Then his heart sank as he read on. "Yosef, you've often spoken about how men, leaders of your country, your city... have put their desires above your people's. And you wondered how that could be." He rattled the parchment.

"Marcus tells me many places you and I saw together in Rome that survived the great fire were destroyed in the fighting between General Primus and Vitellius' forces. Temples... places of study... of law... burned or torn down for no military reason. Soldiers ravaged the streets of Rome. Men defending Rome set fires that created more terror among the besieged than among the besiegers. They used mobs within the city for the defense of Vitellius. Hundreds and thousands fought and died, and Rome's citizens watched and cheered as if in the arena. Then the mobs turned on the citizens, too, killing and looting."

He went on reading. "But Rome is secure now. Gaius Licinius Mucianus has command of the city, and the Senate has appointed young Domitian as Emperor Vespasian's regent in Rome. Yet outside the city, there is still unrest. The legions in Germania refuse to accept General Vespasian as emperor. An uprising by the Batavi has become a rebellion led by Gaius Civilis. Our new emperor's son-in-law Quintus Cerialis is one commander of the legions against them."

Nicanor thought that could be the real reason for Vespasian choosing to wait. During the unrest in provinces just north of Rome, being in Rome would make him vulnerable. In Alexandria, he was more secure and still had his hand controlling the grain shipments to Rome. He looked up to see Yosef taking notes on the details he had just shared. "I'll go on, Yosef, since I know these things are of interest to you for your accounts." He smiled. "I'll give you this letter in a moment—no need to write so furiously."

Yosef looked up, nodded, and shook out a cramped hand.

"Marcus says the city became a nightmare version of itself. The spilling of blood and the litter of bodies in shops, restaurants, the baths.... everywhere. Citizens, nobles, merchants... freedmen, prostitutes, slaves... no matter their station or status. A mingling of bodies throughout the streets of Rome." He stopped to stare at Yosef. "You've told me how your people fight against their own countrymen. These past years in Rome prove it is not something only *your* people do."

He folded the letter and set it down next to Yosef. Marcus's dispirited words left him feeling as he had seen Yosef look when speaking of the Judean factions he blamed for the war. The news—the recounting—from Marcus was not the dry, sterile official report Titus had summarized for him. He wondered again at Titus's postponement of the assault on Jerusalem. Yosef once told him that Jerusalem existed beneath a Sword of Damocles, an imminent peril. And that writer and philosopher Cicero—who he had never heard of—had even written of the old parable. As hard as the attack on his city would be on Yosef, the waiting must be more torturous.

He thought about Titus's visitor, speculating whether she was the reason for the delay. "Yosef, a Queen Berenice has come to see Titus... who is she?"

That stopped the scratching of Yosef's pen that had resumed after the short break. He stared at Nicanor. "She's the sister of Agrippa, Rome's client-king for regions surrounding Judea and their last authority over Jerusalem. You've heard me speak of my dealings with him. He tried to convince Judean leaders to not rebel, which would start a war they could not win. I agreed with him."

"Still, you fought for your people. But he did not?"

"No. Agrippa is completely loyal to the empire. Some used to call his sister Berenice the Princess of Judea. Tiberius Alexander is her former brother-in-law."

"Why would she be here to see Titus?"

"I don't know, but she enjoys powerful men, and Titus is now the son of an emperor."

* * *

Next morning...

"Did you not sleep again?" Sayid asked Yosef as he came in from hitching up his horse outside, ready for the mission. From the stall came the sounds of Nicanor saddling Albus.

Yosef shook his head, "Very little...."

Sayid sensed his friend still did not want to talk. He wished there was some way to help Yosef, but how? He could not stop the inevitable. A jolt of guilt shot through him, not for the first time since Yosef and Nicanor had returned from Alexandria. He was torn between his need to prove himself as part of the attack on Jerusalem and regret over the fear Yosef felt for his people and his family. Nicanor had shared with Sayid what Vespasian had told Titus, though he pledged Sayid to keep it to himself. Jerusalem was to be stripped of everything and anything of value. But Yosef must already realize that, did he not?

"I'm ready—let's go," Nicanor said, poking his head in from the stall side of their quarters. His eyes shifted from Sayid to Yosef, who muttered something.

"What's that, Yosef?"

"'What do you see, Yirmiyahu?' The Lord asked. 'I see a branch of an almond tree,' he replied."

Nicanor glanced at Sayid, who shook his head, puzzled. "What does that mean?" Nicanor asked.

"Consequences... destiny...." Yosef said no more, and Sayid and Nicanor shrugged and left the man to his musings.

LXXIII

Februarius 70 CE

Caesarea

The Roman Encampment, Nicanor's Quarters

Yosef had never argued with Nicanor about what physical action to take, not in the aftermath of the *Salacia's* shipwreck or Rome during the great fire. In matters of struggle and risk, he had deferred to the Roman's greater experience. But the night before Nicanor and Sayid left for Sycaminum, he reasoned with Nicanor that he must go with them. On the march from Alexandria to Caesarea, he had been too tired to dream or chase around in his head all the regrets of the past seven years. With little in the camp routine to tire his body, his dreams and tormenting thoughts had returned. Traveling with Nicanor and Sayid would have taken them from his mind for a little while.

Nicanor understood but would not go against Titus's orders and let Yosef join them. Explaining they must enter the warehouse without notice or getting caught. It would be too dangerous for Yosef to go with them without an adequate escort, and even a few extra men would defeat their purpose of stealth. So, Yosef must stay in Caesarea.

Yosef had said bitterly that Titus did not want to risk harm to his father's prized prisoner. And he would hear nothing from Nicanor about that he was no longer a prisoner. Though freed of chains, Yosef knew he was not entirely free and probably never would be. But perhaps it was best, for he could not risk something happening to him before Jerusalem.

He had not told Nicanor and Sayid that he felt he knew what the dream of Cleo and the almond tree meant. For her to speak to him from within the blossoms of bitterness was a sign his people—that Jerusalem—had forsaken Yahweh. And a judgment was due. The dreams had also revived his belief that it was his destiny to live so he could at least *try* to stop something that seemed preordained. Yahweh had stopped other preordained judgments several times, as with Jonah and Nineveh. The only way to facilitate such a change of destiny would be to sway the Roman emperor, Vespasian, and his son Titus to consider letting the people of Jerusalem surrender.

After Nicanor and Sayid left, he reread the scraps Sayid had found. The Essenes had clearly drafted them. Florus had somehow gotten his hands on their list of locations where some of the Temple treasure had been hidden. And Florus—or someone working on his behalf—had used a precious object from the Temple to pay for the recruitment of mercenaries. For what purpose? It could only be to steal even more from the Temple, which meant he had a plan and the means. And Florus would do anything so his plan did not become known to the Romans charged with settling this war.

After reading, with the remnants of the scrolls fresh in his mind, Yosef had fallen asleep and dreamed of Qumran. The images were vivid, just as when he had last seen Qumran years ago. The settlement sat on a dry highland above a gorge only a mile northwest of the shore of Lake Asphaltitis. The settlement's inhabitants slept by the dozen in nearby cave residences in the sheer cliffs overlooking the gorge and the wadi. They had constructed most of the buildings from large, undressed stones. The most prominent structure was their assembly hall, which had a watchtower in one corner and housed the hall where the community ate. Many scholars and researchers did their work on the long tables between meals.

A large circular cistern and two smaller rectangular ones sat above ground, next to the cluster of buildings, and were fed by an aqueduct rain-collection system connected by channels. There were flour mills, a stable, laundry, and various workshops near the cisterns. As with all Essene communities, Qumran was as self-sufficient as possible.

Yosef knew the Romans had attacked Qumran and that much he recalled had likely been destroyed. In the dream, he stood on a cliff overlooking the gorge, holding a scroll he recognized as written in Greek, not Hebrew. A long slash on his right forearm dripped blood, but Yosef paid it no heed in the dream. He got an overpowering sense that the scroll was connected to Jerusalem's fate.

When he woke, as daylight grew, the last vestiges of the dreams had faded to be replaced by a conscious decision. Yosef's conversations with Titus during the journey from Alexandria revealed that the emperor's son had already contemplated what was next for him. Titus had hopes for portents such as his father had received, but he did not say so outright. So Yosef would tell him of his latest dream of the scroll in Qumran. He was sure Titus would send him there to find it, and then he could read what the Greek scroll held—hope or despair—for his people.

***

THE PRAETORIUM

Though he resented being watched, Yosef was grateful Celsus had stopped to check on him. He knew Nicanor must have requested it because the legion's commander of quartermasters still treated him stiffly, as the friend of a friend... but not his own friend. In fact, to Celsus Evander, Yosef was a former enemy and had no reason to believe he was no longer one.

Still, the soldier had accompanied Yosef to see Titus, which meant the general's aide must treat the meeting request seriously and Yosef respectfully. Yosef was aware as he sat there with Celsus that they were similar—tall, clean-shaven men. One was in the uniform of a senior officer, and the other in the clothing of a well-to-do Roman freedman, perhaps a scholar with the ubiquitous wax tablet tucked into the sash at his waist.

As he and Celsus awaited Titus, Yosef realized his people might see his appearance as becoming less or perhaps no longer Jewish. But he could not refuse the clothing nor the quasi-freedom the Romans had given him—how would that position him to help his people? He prayed his family would understand if he could see them or hear him if he could speak to the city leaders.

In his solitude on the march from Alexandria, when Nicanor was occupied with other duties, Yosef had another perspective on his decision, while a Roman prisoner, to help his country. Many supporters of General Vespasian were especially interested in his two young sons. The lack of a bloodline had been a weakness in past imperial regimes, leading to rampant sycophancy that undermined the empire's stability. Yosef was sure that such avarice in men, whether Roman or Jew, had ignited this war between Rome and Judea. If his words—conveying his visions—could help bring to power men with better intentions than their predecessors, that could help Rome and those Rome ruled. Helping Titus could thus still change the course of events for Yosef's people.

"Ah, Josephus."

Yosef looked up at the sound of the familiar patronizing tone. Tiberius Alexander beamed as he came from Titus's private office with Lucius Serenus, who slightly sneered at Yosef and gave a curt nod to Celsus Evander. He rubbed his chin as he passed, and Yosef could see his mutilated hand up close. An arc of faded green discoloration in his skin peeked from beneath the glove. Once they passed, Yosef heard Celsus mutter under his breath.

Yosef leaned toward Celsus and said, "There's something about that man...."

"I don't like him," Celsus murmured and started to say more, but the aide interrupted.

"General Titus will see you now."

LXXIV

Februarius 70 CE

Sycaminum

Florus's Port Warehouse

"Albus remembers this place from when we were here before," Sayid commented. The big white horse had already angled toward the two shrub-covered sandy mounds that marked the broad gravel path hidden from the road. "This path runs directly to the warehouse at the southern end of the port. I think he heard us planning this and knew where we were going."

Nicanor grunted and drew his heavy cloak tighter around him. Since they had started for Sycaminum more than once, he had uttered curses at the chill. His hip, leg, and shoulder ached afresh after they'd calmed while he'd rested from the long ride from Alexandria. "What are you smiling at?" He glared at Sayid. "Wait until you're old... you'll know how it feels."

"I smile because the last time I was here, it was cold and damp, and I, too, felt it in my bones for the first time. I thought of your grumbling... just like you grumble now."

"Hmmph..." Nicanor shifted in his saddle.

A few minutes later, without command, Albus stopped next to a piece of driftwood sticking out from a dune made of tangled weeds as much as sand. "Don't tell me," Nicanor said. "This is where you stopped before."

"Albus knows... he's a wise one."

The horse turned his head to look back at Nicanor and offered a blank stare to Sayid.

Nicanor dismounted, and once he was clear, Albus knelt beside the dune. Nicanor shook his head and eyed the horse, who stared back. "We'll wait until well past sundown, then check inside this warehouse," he said, unpacking the large bundle tied behind his saddle. "Here," he said as he tossed a blanket roll to Sayid.

Sayid unrolled it to find clothing inside—Judean, not Roman, and not very clean. He wrinkled his nose but changed into the garments, wrapping the greasy, stained cloak around him.

Nicanor did the same with items from his own blanket roll. Then both repacked their Roman clothing and resecured the bundles behind their saddles. Soon they sat huddled near their horses in the windbreak between dunes. As darkness grew, a scattering of evening stars sprinkled the indigo sky.

"In Jerusalem," Sayid asked, gazing up into the night, "do you think Titus will still let Yosef talk to the city leaders about surrendering? That's what Yosef hopes for... the chance to talk to his people."

"Yes," said Nicanor, "but I don't think Yosef realizes the conditions of surrender Titus will demand. The conditions will not include a punishment of fines or more taxes or anything like that. It will not be a return to how things were before."

"When I was in Jerusalem with Cleo, I heard the talk... among the differing sides within the city. I do not think the Jewish leaders will accept surrender unless they change their feelings about Rome."

"That might be best...."

"What do you mean?" asked Sayid. "Would it not be better that the people live?"

"Would they wish to live as slaves? That is what they will become. Their city will still be destroyed... they'll have no need for it. They will be sent to slave markets, and who knows where they will be enslaved within the empire? Families and loved ones will be separated—the Romans know that as the best way to keep them weak." Nicanor sighed. "And Yosef will blame himself for helping to convince them to surrender. If they don't surrender, they will die, and Titus will still loot and destroy the city, then pick from the remains whatever is of value. No matter the outcome, Sayid, it will be tragic."

After a pause, Nicanor added, "And either way, our friend's heart will be crushed. But if they refuse to surrender, perhaps Yosef will not blame himself... but small comfort in that."

"If Cleo is in the city, will she die, too?" Sayid almost whispered as if he were afraid to ask it aloud.

Nicanor struggled with his answer—all he had was a prayer to whatever gods or god who would listen and might grant it. "I hope not. I hope we can find some way to get her out of Jerusalem, to save her."

* * *

They had waited and watched for two hours and seen no activity beyond lights and movement at the nearest dock on the single giant vessel moored there. Far enough away that they did not fear anyone seeing them. But they had seen no activity around the warehouse in the dim glow from the waning gibbous moon hanging in the cloudless sky. With night-adjusted eyes, Nicanor and Sayid made their way to the eastern side of the warehouse. They found the door Sayid had used before.

"Stay close," Sayid whispered to Nicanor as he eased open the door. They skirted the outer wall inside, working east to north to the west as Sayid had before. They stopped at the room that jutted out.

Nicanor elbowed Sayid and whispered, "There's a dim light over there." He pointed south.

"That's where the men were before," Sayid replied. "Where the big doors opened to let the wagon in."

"Let's see how many are there." Nicanor crept toward the light.

"More last time—twice as many," Sayid whispered as they studied four men stretched on pallets on the floor. None moved, and snores came from at least two of the men. A single lantern cast a small circle of light down upon them.

"We'll risk it, then." Nicanor turned to retrace the way they'd come and stopped at the chained door, its surface in shades of gray that offered little detail without more light to see.

Sayid strained his eyes, looking at it, and ran his hands over the chain. "It seems only the one chain and a single lock."

Nicanor pulled the pry bar he carried at his hip, where he usually wore a gladius. "A dozen times since we came in here," he said, waving the pry bar, "I've reached for this, wishing it was my sword.... Give me your pipe."

"Here." Sayid handed him an arm's-length metal pipe he had carried at his hip. He heard Nicanor slip it over one end of the bar, a simple way to lengthen his lever.

"Light the lamp but shield it with your body."

Sayid took out a small hand lamp, knelt, and struck sparking stones to its wick. The flame flared, and he stood, bringing its light closer to the chains and lock. He watched as Nicanor wrapped the lower half of the lengthened pry bar in a thin blanket and inserted the narrow end into the hoop of the lock.

"Pray to the gods those men are asleep... or better... that they're drunk-sleeping." Nicanor pulled down on the lever with all his might. The blanket helped lessen the sound of metal on metal, but the lock snapping still made a sharp sound in the silent warehouse.

Sayid smothered the lamp, and Nicanor did not move. They listened. After a moment of utter silence, Sayid's heart pounding in his ears... the sound of snores came again.

"Good..." Nicanor said with the release of his held breath. Sayid moved swiftly but carefully to prevent any noise as they pulled the broken lock away and removed the chains. They pulled one of the doors open far enough to slip inside.

There before them was the wagon, a shadow within a lighter shadow. Sayid relit the lamp.

Nicanor pulled back the canvas tarpaulin to reveal the ruddy glow of a sheet of copper sealing the wagon box. He jammed one end of the pry bar under an edge, gouging the wood to make room for the beveled end to slide under and give him purchase beneath the copper sheet. Nicanor heaved, and the metal groaned as it came free and peeled up. He gripped the freed end and pulled it farther to see what lay beneath. "Bring the lamp closer."

Sayid raised it over the end of the wagon.

"Bags?" Nicanor said as he pulled his pugio and cut a six-inch slit in one bag. He plunged his hand in and withdrew a handful of...

"Sand?" Sayid wondered, taking his own handful. It trickled through his fingers as Nicanor cursed in a whisper: "Futuo! What game does Gessius Florus play?"

Sayid was at the door momentarily, holding the lamp to one side as he peeked out and gasped to himself. He turned and whispered furiously, "I think those men are awake!"

Nicanor ordered, "Throw your coins on the ground, here"—he pointed at his feet, then cut a ragged swath from the dirty cloth pouch at his waist and hooked it on the sharp edge of the curled-back copper sheet.

Sayid pulled out his handful of Judean rebellion coins, bronze *prutah* minted in Jerusalem. Each had an amphora symbol, the date, and the inscription *Herut Zion*—Freedom of Zion—which Yosef had translated for them. Nicanor had gotten them from a merchant in Caesarea when he bought the castoff clothing. Celsus Evander knew the merchant who supplied the coins.

"Let's go quickly and pray they blame rebel looters," Nicanor said. They ran through the darkness to the lesser dark outside and then to their horses. Two men shouted at them from the walkway near the dock, but Nicanor and Sayid ran faster.

LXXV

MARTIUS 70 CE

JERUSALEM

THE UPPER CITY

Early spring winds cleared the smoke from the sky, but the smell of ashes and charred grain lingered. In the storehouses around the city, men and boys still worked at sifting through the remnants to recover the least-damaged grain. So far, that had not amounted to much, but Matthew knew that even that would be needed.

"How are Ya'el and Elian?"

Matthew turned from his view of the city to see Miriam at the rooftop terrace steps. She pulled her cloak close as she walked toward him. "They're worried and feel trapped, but I tried encouraging them when I took enough food to last a few days. Will you be going to see them tomorrow?"

Miriam nodded. "In the morning. Did you have problems at Antonia?"

"No, but that twenty-foot stretch of tunnel between the Temple and Baris seems a long way when crawling through it. It's good that those old storerooms don't seem to have been visited for a long time." Matthew rubbed at the fresh scrape on his chin and showed it to her. "I got this when I discovered Ya'el's trap with ankle-high lines. I stumbled over one, and she was ready with her bow when I came out of the tunnel. She showed me how the trip lines rattle some gravel she's put in bronze urns. That's clever."

"Zechariah told me about something I mentioned to her."

"It's a good idea. King Herod's escape tunnel from the Temple into Antonia Fortress lets us reach yours—it's safer than entering and leaving through the shed. There are still too many men watching the area. We were fortunate none checked inside the shed that night and discovered the entrance."

"We could've made it away through that tunnel."

"Yes, but with men coming after us, Miriam, we could have come up within the Temple among the warriors of Eleazar ben Simon or Yohanan ben Levi. Eleasar and I could talk us through them—make a good story for you, him, and me. But Ya'el and Elian... if they were found not to be Jews...." Matthew shook his head.

Miriam recited: "You all know no foreigner may enter, no gentiles. Whoever is caught... death will ensue."

Matthew nodded. "Exactly. The *Soreq*—the warning on the wall in the Court of Gentiles—has been enforced for a long time. Ya'el and Elian would be executed, probably right then and there—and the men of any of those factions would be happy to do it. They'd agree on that, at least. That's why we were lucky no one entered that shed, and all we had to do was wait out the night and sneak home."

"There has to be a way that doesn't pose a risk to them. I'll check the other tunnels marked on Zechariah's map. I think one within the Baris underground leads to Zedekiah's Cave, into one of the galleries of Solomon's Quarry. But that's to the north."

"The oldest part of the quarry is a labyrinth," said Matthew. "It's too risky for—"

The expression that flashed on Miriam's face stopped him. "You know that already, don't you?"

"The one tunnel I know there... is dangerous," she said, "but it does run south, through the drops and rockfalls, and it led me to King David's Tomb in the City of David. One, maybe two, or three others seem to lead out of the city to the north and east. But we need something more accessible in the Upper or Lower City. Not under the Temple or the enclosure. Here, look at this." Miriam bent to the low table between them and unrolled a roll of parchment she had carried tucked under one arm. She sat and motioned to him to do so, too. She pinned down the corners of the map with the empty earthenware pitcher and three cups on the table.

"That night, as we waited in the Baris underground chamber while you were all talking, Eleasar looked at the charts I had spread out there. He asked me about them, and on one," she tapped the map with a finger, "he saw something I'd missed." She traced a faint line that began at the location mark for the Baris subterranean chambers and ran along the wall of the Temple Enclosure. "Eleasar told me it looked like the tunnel—if that's what the line is for—ended beneath the Hall of Hewn Stone. I know the hall has doors into the Sanctuary. But doesn't it also have doors to and from the outside? Eleasar said the Music Room is below the chamber—where they store the Temple's instruments, right? Maybe a hidden entrance leads to a tunnel under the Hall of Hewn Stone."

Matthew studied the map. "Do you know where it begins under the Baris?"

"No, but down at the lowest level, two walls have sealed entrances. I don't know whether passageways were closed intentionally or blocked by an earthquake and then had to be sealed for safety. That's not in Zechariah's notes. We'd have to open them up and see."

"That'll be a lot of labor."

"It's worth exploring," Miriam said and smiled. "I know Ya'el and Elian want something to work toward."

"I know the entrances to the Music Room," said Matthew. "They're on either side of the Nicanor Gate, but I've never been there. I'll ask Eleasar if he knows more about it." Matthew's finger trailed along the line to the Hall of Hewn Stone. "I think Yosef knew of this tunnel and a chamber beneath it, but we never explored it when we were kids because he was chased from there by a Levite guardsman. That might be the Music Room, and we never went back there. Maybe Eleasar knows more about any rooms that might be beneath the Hall of Hewn Stone. It's a good time to check because it's not being used now."

"Eleasar asked me why Ya'el and Elian were hiding. And about Ya'el's bow and my daggers...."

"What did you tell him?"

"I promised Mother and Father would invite him to dinner... and I would tell him everything then."

LXXVI

Martius 70 CE

Jerusalem

The Upper City

Though it was just past dawn when Miriam returned home, she saw her parents at the courtyard table through the row of fruit trees. As she slipped through the rear gate, her mother said, "I heard the three trumpet blasts earlier... why do that? Doesn't Eleazar ben Simon still block the gates and bar entry to the Temple? No one can enter to worship since his men took it over."

"Yohanan ben Zaccai told me last night that Eleazar ben Simon has decided to open the gates and allow worshippers into the Temple today." Mathias saw her among the trees and beckoned her lovingly: "Miriam."

She saw their looks of concern and knew he wanted to ask where she had been, so she went right to the answer. "I've been to see Ya'el and Elian." *No need to say what we did there.* She had helped them sort out tools from the shed above, then showed them where the branch tunnel entrances seemed to be and commissioned them to begin clearing them. She wished she could have stayed with them, but she had promised to help her mother prepare for the dinner, and Rebecca would start early. Eleasar ben Ananais would be there for the explanation she owed him, so Rachel and Leah would hear it, too. She did not look forward to that moment. But Matthew and their parents thought it best to share the truth. Otherwise, Eleasar's and Rachel's suspicions would create questions and lead to talk at an inopportune time. That could be even riskier.

Still, she would not tell them one part of the truth... that she had been raped. Instead, she would explain things about the Roman who had attacked them in their house nearly four years before, during the massacre ordered by Gessius Florus. Rachel had been in the house then, though she had remained with her mother in hiding while Miriam went upstairs and knifed the legionary, her first kill. Her family had also decided she should tell a partial truth about Ya'el and Elian. Ya'el had known Yosef in Galilee; her father had been a warrior without a son, so he had taught her how to use a bow. Just before the siege of Yotapta, Yosef had sent her away to seek refuge in Jerusalem.

Miriam needed to make sure Rachel accepted this explanation, too. She had been there when Ya'el and Elian arrived in Jerusalem escorted by Sayid, who she would explain was a Syrian Yosef had hired to accompany them. Then, one of Yohanan ben Levi's men recognized Ya'el and sought to take her to the Gischalan. So Ya'el had to hide. She would explain that Yohanan ben Levi still hated Yosef because he thought her brother had usurped his power in Galilee. Miriam hoped all this was believable, for it carried much of the truth. With all the extra turmoil of recent days, outlandish things seemed possible.

"I wish they could join us... and it would be like before," Rebecca murmured.

Miriam knew her mother thought of Ya'el as the wife of the new Roman Procurator, Lady Cleo, who had enjoyed Passover with them four years before. But Gessius Florus had ruined that memory a month later, turning loose his soldiers on the citizens of Jerusalem. And it was all because he felt slighted and made fun of over his tax collection efforts.

A sound of distress came from the rear of the courtyard, and Miriam heard the gate open and close. She hurried to it, her right hand inside her tunic's left sleeve to grasp the sheathed dagger's hilt. Then she took a breath when she saw the intruder. "Yohanan!"

The old priest had a lamb squirming under one arm. "To keep until needed for dinner," he said. "Arins brought it. Here," he gave the unwieldy, unhappy lamb to her, "take it." Then he went over to her parents, taking a deep breath and wiping his hands on his robe.

"Shalom, Mathias, Rebecca." Yohanan turned back, gestured at the lamb, and said, "Rebecca, do you mind if I ask Arins, the merchant, to join us tonight? He has no family to be with."

* * *

That evening...

Miriam studied Eleasar ben Ananias. Matthew had told her the Temple Guard commander's wife and young son had gone with her family to Masada. But Eleasar felt his duty was to Jerusalem, so he stayed. *Still*, she thought, *Masada is probably safer than Jerusalem.* She looked at Arins, who thanked her father and mother again for inviting him. The half-smile on his lips had not eased the lines of his face or the glint of his gaze. As they were now, she had caught his eyes on her throughout dinner. And there was Ya'akov, too, Rebecca's not-so-surprising surprise guest. He, too, had his eyes on her throughout the evening. She did not like being watched.

"Excuse me—what was that?" she said, shaking herself out of her thoughts. Arins had said something she had missed.

"I was apologizing if it seemed I stared at you, Miriam. But you do remind me of my daughter. She would have been about your age."

"Would have been?" she asked.

"She died."

"I'm sorry, was she sick?" Miriam asked, feeling uncomfortable with the conversation.

"No, the Romans killed her...." Arins's tone hardened, and she regretted her question. The man's face tightened, and his eyes narrowed for a moment. Then a sideways shifting of his eyes at Ya'akov widened them again. "It seems you have more than one young man who wishes your attention."

Miriam felt the heat rise in her face and knew it would be mistaken as a blush of embarrassment. But it was anger. She was angry at Ya'akov for still loving her and unknowingly putting himself in danger by staying near her. And at Hananiah—the threat—she would rather kill him than see him again, as she soon must. That afternoon the knifemaker had waved her over to his stall. He asked her to come to see him in his shop. He had something important to privately tell her.

Arins was speaking to her again. "I did not mean to intrude. I'm happy you have suitors... I just wish it were in better circumstances." The rangy man rose from the divan and said, "I must speak with your father and Yohanan now."

Miriam watched as her mother, Rachel, and Leah cleared the dishes, taking them into the kitchen. Suddenly, she was alone with Ya'akov. He stood and took a step toward her. She quickly stopped him with a palm-out gesture.

"Not now, Ya'akov. I will talk to you soon," she lied, stalling him. "But not tonight." Leaving him to watch her go, she climbed the stairs to her room and cracked open the shutter. Sitting in the moonlight, she listened as Matthew, Eleasar, her father, and Yohanan told Arins about the tunnel to and from the Motza Valley. The men had agreed it must be used to bring food into the city, bypassing the city gates, and that Arins must be told. With much of the food supply burned, the city was now much more vulnerable to siege. They did not tell

Arins that the tunnel had served to get some Temple treasure out of Jerusalem, only that it would work for trade.

She heard her mother's voice call out: "Mathias, Matthew... Ya'akov is leaving." Her father and brother went into the house to see him out, and she inched open the shutter and peeked down at her father's oldest friend and Arins, still at the table. "Yohanan," Arins asked, "did you think of someone who can be trusted to take in that young woman I know? She seeks refuge in Jerusalem but does not know anyone, and I don't want her to be alone and afraid."

Yohanan coughed, clearing his throat. "My friend, Shammai, who makes charcoal, has done that before. I will take you to see him."

LXXVII

Martius 70 CE

Jerusalem

Bezetha, The Baris Remnants

"So you told them Yosef and I were lovers," Ya'el said, her expression unreadable, "and Elian is my child from another man?"

Miriam could not read Ya'el's expression. And she could not understand why telling Ya'el the story she had told Eleasar ben Ananias, Rachel, and Leah that morning seemed awkward to share. But Ya'el and Elian needed to know it to support the story if asked. Eleasar had believed it. Though when she explained how she had learned to protect herself after killing the Roman legionary, his eyes shifted to Matthew and her parents. Knowing she had killed a Roman in a bedroom above him disconcerted Eleasar more than her explanation of who Ya'el was. And how she had skill enough with a bow and crude arrows to kill the Idumeans who had come to loot their home and slaughter them as others had been.

Leah had looked crestfallen upon hearing of Ya'el's 'relationship' with Yosef, and she seemed to listen to little after that. But Rachel was another matter. She had been there when Ya'el arrived at Jerusalem's gate seeking safety with Yosef's family. But Miriam could not recall whether Rachel had read Yosef's letter telling them who Ya'el really was and his asking that they take her in. Or had she only heard Miriam's response when they went to the gate to vouch for Ya'el, Elian, and Sayid so they could enter the city. So Miriam wagered Rachel had not read the actual letter and did not know the truth. After she had spun the story to them all, Rachel remained silent. But something in her cousin's eyes told Miriam she would have to watch Rachel closely; a casual comment from her about Ya'el could draw dangerous attention.

"No, I didn't say you were lovers," Miriam answered, "But I told them that he felt responsible for you after Yotapta." She turned to Elian and said, "You must both understand this and say nothing different. Right?" She studied the dirty Elian she'd interrupted from his eager tunnel work when she came down the shaft to them. When Ya'el smoothed the rooster tail of Elian's hair and smiled down at him, Miriam stopped to consider he was just a boy. In her zeal to protect them, she'd been severe with him. And Elian was not such a boy as he had been, either—he was growing.

"That's our story, Elian, but it is just a story," Ya'el said more gently. We do not expect any man to take care of us. We've learned we must defend ourselves and not count on others."

Miriam recognized that sentiment and sighed. Ya'el was right to feel that way, but now Miriam had many more people than herself to be concerned about.

"Now, I must go see Hananiah," she said. "He has something he wishes to tell me."

* * *

THE UPPER CITY

Miriam entered the agora wondering why she'd seen none of Yohana ben Levi's nor Simon bar Giora's men in Bezetha. And as she reached the path toward the shed, she saw Yohanan ben Zaccai and Arins heading to Shammai's. Miriam wished the old priest had kept silent about secret ways into—and out of—the city. Since she had not been to talk freely in front of Ya'akov and Arins the night before, she had to wait to tell Matthew what she'd overheard.

"I agree with your caution, Miriam," he had said, "but Yohanan thinks we can trust Arins. Besides, Shammai does not know where Ya'el and Elian are now, so he cannot let it slip."

But much Miriam wanted to keep hidden was becoming known, which troubled her.

More people were in the market than in the last few weeks. The order by the Roman general, Titus to let all travel freely who wished to come to Jerusalem for Passover created a massive influx. Many had taken that hopeful sign the new emperor, Vespasian, had decided to relent in his harrying of Jerusalem. Maybe that meant a change—maybe there would be no attack, and Rome would merely seek fines and extra taxes.

No matter what they were thinking, the people were swarming the city, going about business that had long been put off. But without a threat of Romans at the gate, would the rebels within the city continue their battle for supremacy?

Mathias had told Matthew that he thought Yosef being freed had something to do with the forbearance in Titus's decision. Matthew disagreed—he did not believe the Romans were that gracious or willing to accept anything less than a military resolution to the rebellion. From her hiding place where she had listened to them, she had whispered to herself, "I am of your mind, brother." Miriam's treatment at Roman hands made her scorn her father's optimism.

But then Ya'el was really a Roman noblewoman, and Sayid had been a Roman auxiliary. She trusted them and cared very much for Ya'el and Elian, the serving boy who escaped with her from Gessius Florus. Yosef cared for all three: Cleo, Sayid, and the big centurion, Nicanor. She had seen him only once and could not help fearing his similarity to the men who had attacked her. Yet Yosef considered him a friend. Miriam would reserve her own judgment on the meaning of Yosef's freedom until it was clear whose side he was now on.

Behind her, Miriam heard a hornet's nest of buzzing chatter grow from the eastern end of the market, close to the Temple. She was only a few strides from Hananiah's stall, his eyes on her, when a hand grabbed her arm and spun her around.

"Hurry, come with us now!" Matthew wheezed. His face and light cloak were dusted with the tunnel dirt, as were Eleasar's, behind him. They must have just come out of the blind alley. "Hurry!" he said again, tugging her away from Hananiah's stall toward the street leading toward home in the Upper City. With a glance over her shoulder, Miriam saw Hananiah's eyes flash angrily.

"What's wrong?" She asked Matthew as she took nearly-skipping steps to stay with him.

"Dozens of Yohanan ben Levi's men entered the Temple, disguised as worshippers. Once inside, they shed their disguises to reveal weapons and armor. Now, they're cutting down Eleazar ben Simon's unarmed men after killing him. Now the fighting will begin again. Though Simon and his son were estranged, that cursed Gischalan killing Eleazar will enrage Simon. The Temple floor is not the only place in the city that will run red with blood."

LXXVIII

Martius 70 CE

Caesarea

The Roman Encampment, Nicanor's Quarters

Nicanor paused outside the street-side entry of the stall and quarters he had enjoyed having to himself at first. Soon, Sayid and Yosef joined him with their respective horse and mule. They still had extra room without the fourth man or animal the place was built for. But they would be there not much longer, according to what General Titus had told him not an hour before.

He entered through the stall, pulling a *develah* from the pouch at his belt. The block of dried figs, given to him by Titus's horse master as they waited for the general and his guest to return from their ride, had proven to interest Albus, to Nicanor's surprise. He had once tethered the stoic horse beside a fruit seller's stand. Albus quickly snatched and ate a dozen dried figs before the fruit seller's shout got Nicanor's attention. Albus had seemed pleased with himself as he stared at the angry man. That fruit seller had been one of the local merchants who refused to sell to Yosef, cursing him as a traitor to his people. Nicanor had paid the man and had not regretted Albus's plunder.

Taking out his pugio, Nicanor cut the block in half. Then split one of the halves evenly, giving one piece to Sayid's mount and the other to Yosef's mule. He moved to the back stall with the other half of the fig cake in his hand. Albus was waiting with his head up and his ears tilted forward. The usually stolid horse curled his lips back when he saw the block of figs, and Nicanor returned his smile.

"Here you go...." he said, patting Albus's neck, and the horse canted his head to press against Nicanor's hand for a moment.

"What did General Titus say?" Yosef said from the entry into their living quarters.

"Exactly what you said he would," Nicanor replied. "Tomorrow, I will escort you to Qumran, where you are to find the scroll you saw in your dreams and bring it back to General Titus. A cohort of cavalry—480 horsemen—will accompany us."

Yosef nodded and turned to go inside, asking over his shoulder, "Did you tell General Titus what you and Sayid found at Sycaminum?"

Nicanor followed him. "About the bags of sand in the warehouse?" He shook his head. "No. I told him there was nothing there."

"But *something* was. We should tell Titus we think something was there that came from the Temple."

Nicanor thought about Vespasian's instructions about the importance to the imperial treasury of anything of value taken from Jerusalem. Someone was stealing what Titus had been instructed to obtain for his father. That should and would raise his concern. If we tell him that without proof, we will look foolish in his eyes. We—I—will lose his trust, and nothing will be done to Gessius Florus. That will only alert the man to cover his actions further or even send him into hiding. That cannot happen. I've made a vow to see him punished." Nicanor did not elaborate that the vow was equally for Graius and Cleo. "Where's Sayid?"

"He went to meet Celsus at the port taberna."

"I'll see him and ask if he wants to go with us to Qumran," said Nicanor.

"I hope he will... and I wish he would change his mind about returning to his auxiliary unit. My hope is to bring about peace. I pray they will listen to me. Still, I do not wish to see Sayid in danger should there be fighting."

Nicanor nodded sadly. He had asked Titus about his decision to let pilgrims travel to the city, and the general had replied: "They won't leave alive."

* * *

AT THE PORT

Nicanor spotted Sayid and Celsus as they left the taberna and stopped to talk to a tall auxiliary officer about to enter. Another large, rough-hewn man in a plain tunic and light cloak stepped from inside and skirted behind them. Nicanor was now close enough to see sunlight sharpening the furrows of old scars on his face, and the man swiveled toward the three as he slowed and stopped near them. His cloak billowed to show a weapon sheathed at the man's hip, and Nicanor recognized the curved blade of a *sica* used by Thracians. It was a sword common in the ports of the empire.

Celsus's voice carried in the lull of the cool wind's gusts: "I must leave you so that I may see the master of the *Vesta* before he sails." The legion quartermaster turned toward the quay without noticing Nicanor. The man with the *sica* still stood at the corner of the taberna, facing the street. His eyes seemed to cast sideways at Sayid and the officer, who seemed to be in a heated conversation.

"Sayid!" Nicanor called. And as he had hoped, the man with the sica looked toward him, his eyes sweeping over the breastplate and other trappings of a tribunus that Nicanor still wore after meeting Titus. The man's eyes lit upon the gladius that Nicanor instinctively gripped. With almost a sneer, the man wheeled and strode away.

Nicanor's eyes trailed him, and then he walked up to Sayid. "I wanted to see if you would go with me tomorrow to Qumran... or whether you wish to stay here."

Sayid looked up at the officer beside him and said, "This is the tribunus I told you I've served with." Then he held a hand toward his friend and said, "Nicanor, this is *Centurio Princeps* Marcus Sabinus, my father."

"A pleasure to meet you," Nicanor greeted the man, who studied him coolly and then responded with a salute.

"So, tribunus, you know Sayid." There was only the slightest note of deference in his tone. "We are of a similar age and experience, it seems, though my experience of our army has never before been with my... with Sayid. He has spoken much about you. But I do not understand why you have not told him—nor made things clear."

Nicanor blinked at the tenor of the man's voice. His eyes cut sideways to Sayid, whose face had stiffened as if expecting what his father was about to say. "Told him what... made what clear?" Nicanor asked.

"You have not told him that the legion and the auxiliary are not equivalent and never will be. Sayid will never be accepted as an equal."

"No, I have not told him that."

"You should."

Nicanor now knew the man had misunderstood his son's intent. Sayid—out of pride, he understood—had likely not told his father what he truly wanted: to earn respect from the father he had never known. But that was not for him to explain. He would instead tell this auxiliary officer a part of the truth.

"No, *Centurio Princeps* Sabinus. I should not tell him that; I never will because he already knows it. That status is not what he seeks. But," Nicanor looked at Sayid, "I will tell him he should not need to prove himself to anyone. Your son is a good soldier and a fine man. I trust, respect, and accept him as one."

Nicanor waited a moment, and then his voice hardened. "Why can't you?"

LXXIX

MARTIUS 70 CE

CAESAREA

GESSIUS FLORUS'S VILLA

A late quarter moon hung high above Gessius Florus and Galerius Senna as they sat in the central courtyard. A lantern on a low table, amid the two goblets and amphora of wine, cast a flickering light on each man's chest. Florus was glad to see that the 12th Legion commander had, as directed, not worn any metal or finery. Even the vain noble had agreed it was better to dress simply for a meeting that must not be known to any but his closest men. Senna must not draw any attention. "So," said Florus, summing up the conversation thus far, "Vespasian already plans his reforms but does not announce them because of the continued unrest outside of Rome."

"I'm told he is concerned about the financial state of the empire," replied Senna. "His advisers warn him that he will need three times the previous tax revenue if the empire is to become solvent. He plans to increase provincial taxes, in some cases doubling them. He will also revoke the tax immunities previously granted to some provinces and favored cities."

Hearing that, Florus wanted to explore immediately how he could use the information as a rumor of what would come under Vespasian. That would continue to stir unrest; he believed the ensuing retaliation would create opportunities. He clamped down on the anger he felt beginning to swell up in him. Such an opportunity as stealing the Jews' treasure had been so simple to arrange with Nero. All it had required was for Cestius Gallus, then-commander of the 12th Legion, to continue the assault on Jerusalem that had begun three and a half years ago. Carrying it out only long enough to give Florus's men within the 12th Legion access to the temple. But the fool had halted the attack and retreated, only to be embarrassingly defeated by the rebels.

Florus wished Gallus was alive so he could have him killed again. After that, he had endured Vespasian's delay and now his son's. Once Titus had command, Florus had thought he would immediately march on Jerusalem. Then the Jews' treasure would have been in his hands long ago.

Before, the debt owed by his family came due because of his own mistake. Still unpaid, the interest charge had begun to eat away what Florus had planned to be his portion of the treasure. A share easily large enough to make him one of the wealthiest men in the empire.

Galerius Senna's nervous shifting drew him back to the moment. Florus studied the man, trying to read his face in the shadows. "Have you learned where the 12th Legion will be positioned when Titus finally decides to attack Jerusalem?"

"The initial planning has it on the city's western side with 5th, *Macedonia,* and 15th, *Apollinaris.* 10th *Fretensis* will be to the east on what the Jews call their Mount of Olives."

"That must change. You must have at least half your legion to the north... here." Florus handed the legion commander a copy he had made of the map he had received that morning. He tapped the area with a finger. "There...."

Senna leaned forward to study the map. "That's a large area. Do you have the location for your camp?" He looked up with a puzzled expression.

"Just make sure your men are assigned where they can cover the area north of the city." Florus bent to bring his face into the light and squinted at the legion commander. "Note that the patrols are to pay no attention to any men in that area."

"What if they're rebels?"

"They won't be... and if any are around, they'll flee for their lives. They will pose little danger to the legions."

"But when the siege begins," Senna said, "I'll need to know where to send the wagons and mules you requested."

"When you need to know, I will tell you." Florus leaned back, feeling the shadow envelop his face. "What else do you have for me from your meetings?" Florus caught sight of a squat man walking toward them behind Senna through the courtyard portico. He held up his palm to him and waited for whatever additional information the commander had for him.

"Tomorrow," Senna said, "General Titus sends the tribunus Nicanor to Qumran with a cavalry cohort."

"To Qumran? Why?"

"They escort the Jew, Yosef ben Mathias. I don't know why they go there... only *that* they go."

"Hmm." Florus lifted his cup from the table and took a generous swallow. "Is the Jew 'princess' doing well with Titus?"

"'I'm told he's enamored and spends much time with her."

"Good... good." Florus waved Drusus into the light and asked him, "Are the men ready to see the legion commander back to his room at the inn for tonight?" Drusus nodded, and Florus caught the expression of distaste that Galerius Senna flashed at him. "The Thracians will follow you closely to ensure some rebel or brigand does not harm you. But they will be out of sight unless needed."

He waited until the legion commander rose and went alone out of the courtyard. Then Florus turned to Drusus and said, "Take ten men and get to Qumran as fast as you can. It usually takes three days... do it in less. Set an ambush to kill the tribunus Nicanor and the Jew Yosef, who are leaving Caesarea tomorrow, escorted by a cavalry cohort. Make it look like rebels killed them."

"There are only five of your men from Clazomenae here. The rest are in Sycaminum, on the vessel."

"Are enough there to protect it if someone tries another raid at the warehouse or on the ship itself?"

"I think the warehouse was done by locals, sir, and they were likely disappointed at what they found—or did *not* find. They won't come back. And yes, lord... the men on the ship won't be surprised like the Thracians in the warehouse were."

"They're poor guards when bored but good fighters; take five of the Thracians from here with you."

Drusus betrayed the distaste Galerius Senna had just exhibited.

"What you think of them does not matter!" Florus barked. "*Use* them. Before you leave for Qumran, find Krateros or send word to him to see me in the morning."

Florus watched Drusus go, then took out the original of the map he had copied for the 12th Legion commander. Setting his new reading crystal on it, he smiled and peered at the mark indicating the valley. He had been told the place was almost impossible to find without directions. It hid the entrance to a tunnel leading into the city's heart, straight to the Jews' temple, its treasure still waiting. Or so his new man in Jerusalem believed, and he had proved reliable. And now, even Hananiah promised results. So, getting information about where the treasure had been hidden—inside and outside the city was still possible. Then, with Yosef and Nicanor dead, Florus could balance the entries in his ledger. The Syrian Sayid would be taken care of by Krateros. Or he could die in battle at Jerusalem—that was not hard to arrange.

The wind dropped with its last sough, and Florus heard the women crying. Only two were left, and once he was done with them, there would be no more until the Jews' treasure was in his hands. Then—in the ruins of Jerusalem—there would be many for the taking as his reward. Cleo, and maybe even Yosef's sister, would also serve for his entertainment. Florus regretted that Yosef would be past hearing of the pain his sister would receive at his hands. Still, perhaps in the Jewish god's Heaven or Hades, he would somehow learn of it and suffer more. Florus smiled up at the moon. The thought pleased him.

LXXX

Martius 70 CE

Qumran

The Essene Community

The column slowed, and the main body of it stopped as the road climbed toward Qumran. Brasus, the *decurion,* had sent a patrol ahead, though Yosef had asked Nicanor if they could not do that. He had noted the signs of rebuilding from the previous destruction the Romans had brought them. He said it would alarm the people, who would think it was another Roman attack. Their hearts would sink at the sound of Roman armored cavalry approaching their community.

"You say they call themselves the Sons of the Lightness?" Nicanor asked as he reined Albus in and slipped the waterskin from the pommel of his saddle. "Why?" He took a drink and handed the vessel to Yosef, who drank and passed it to Sayid.

"They believe they know of the coming darkness for my people, and the darkness is their enemy. Their way of fighting it is to live as brightly and rightly as they can despite what they believe is to come." Yosef had been surprised at Nicanor's curiosity and even more by Sayid's silence since they had left Caesarea.

On the ride, Nicanor had asked Yosef about his years with the Essenes. Yosef explained how his mentor, Bantus, had taught him the Essene principle of community, which they called *Yahad,* which meant "together." Nicanor had nodded and said something odd, almost as if speaking his thoughts aloud: "To be together with someone...." His words had seemed a mix of hope and regret. It was the type of comment Yosef would expect from Sayid. But the young Syrian had been mostly silent the whole way, speaking only when spoken to and not much then.

Sayid had returned with Nicanor the night before they left, and he still wore the somber expression he had that night. At their overnight in Scythopolis, as Sayid tended to their mounts, Nicanor had told Yosef about meeting Sayid's father. How could finally having something he had wanted so badly, Yosef wondered, Sayid finding and meeting his father, have changed the Syrian so much? When Yosef first met him, Sayid often talked of his plan to find his father.

To show him he had grown to be a man who served the legions as his father did, an auxiliary and a soldier. Sayid felt that would be the bond that could bring them together. After all, his mother believed that when his father retired and could marry, he would do as promised and return to her.

But since the three old shipwreck friends reunited, Sayid said little about his father. What Yosef and Nicanor had learned had come from Celsus Evander. It seemed that Sayid's decisions to help others had created not a bond but a wedge between him and his father. And now, the young Syrian had become more withdrawn.

Nicanor heeled Albus and pulled ahead toward Brasus. The decurion had maintained his stern expression of worry since leaving Caesarea, and Nicanor had explained it to Yosef, adding his concern. Instead of an entire *cohort equitata*, capable enough but not quite legion cavalry, their escort would be only a half *centurae* of 40 men and not with the 240 men he had expected. There had been no explanation why, and Titus was elsewhere with Berenice, presumably. Nicanor had said, "I don't understand why it changed. Fewer men mean less protection, and we must keep the wing patrols and rearguard closer." When Brasus had ordered the advance patrol, he had agreed with the decurion: "It's necessary to warn of any trouble ahead." Yosef had understood the military needs but hated that it meant alarming the people of Qumran.

Yosef saw the dust plumes ahead, the billows growing as they descended toward them. As the leading riders of the returning patrol reached Nicanor and Brasus, he kicked his mule forward to where they conferred with the patrol leader. Nicanor shifted in his saddle toward Yosef. "The town seems deserted... but only recently... as if within the last few hours."

"They have men watching the road, hiding now but still watching. Let me enter the town alone. I hope there are some still there who will recognize me." Yosef saw the concern spread across Nicanor's face. "What is it, friend?" he asked. The expression changed to discomfort, and Nicanor locked eyes with him.

"Yosef, you know many of your people no longer trust you. I dislike saying that so plainly... but you cannot deny it. If you enter alone, so soon after a patrol has scouted the town, someone angry with you could try to kill you."

The knot in Yosef's stomach tightened, a tension that never seemed to ease, but he knew Nicanor was right. "Then you and Sayid escort me in. At the first sign of any attack, we'll turn and retreat to where Brasus holds here with his men."

Final Siege

* * *

The clopping sound of twelve hooves echoed as they entered and stopped in the central square formed by the community's main buildings. Yosef turned his head this way and that, searching for the sign of a friendly face or gesture. Nicanor and Sayid did the same on either side of him, but he knew they watched for threats instead. Nicanor had not been pleased, but the only way to do as Titus wished was for Yosef to be able to speak to someone who could direct him to what he sought. His friends were each equipped with two shields: legionary *scutae* larger than those typically carried by cavalrymen—Nicanor had insisted. One scuta was slipped across their backs, and the other carried on an arm, ready to raise and cover Yosef, who was unarmed and unshielded.

Yosef recalled the sounds of the community he had enjoyed on his visits before—lively and friendly, giving visitors a genuine sense of a people who got along well and lived happily. Now there was only silence. He faced the *Beit Knesset*, the synagogue, where a curious Essene leader would be if he knew the Roman patrol had not immediately resulted in an attack. On the plot of land at the rear of the building was a broad array of date palms. The community's primary crop, watered by the aqueduct fed by the Nahal, the flood torrent of rainwater that drained from the Jerusalem area less than a day's ride away. The trees looked well-tended.

Clenching his knees to grip the mule's sides, Yosef raised himself and called out. "I am Yosef ben Mathias... and these Romans mean you no harm." He waited and then repeated. After another moment's pause, his second call brought a man from the synagogue.

"Despite all we've heard, you are still welcome here, Yosef," Nahum replied loud enough to carry to others hiding nearby. "But I am surprised to see you. Why do you come with Romans?"

LXXXI

MARTIUS 70 CE

QUMRAN

THE ESSENE COMMUNITY

"It's safe for all of your people to return," Yosef assured the community leader when only a handful had come at Nahum's call. These few had silently prepared an evening meal for their leader and the three guests and left them to themselves. But Yosef knew they were watching to be sure nothing happened to Nahum.

Though Nahum said I am still welcome here, Yosef thought, *certainly not all of them feel that way.* As the Essenes had cleared the table, replacing the clay pitches of water with wine, he had caught their stares—none friendly, but at least none hostile. Nicanor and Sayid had gotten those looks. Those two had been allowed to stay, though Brasus and the rest of his men would camp outside the city, despite Nicanor's caution. But the tribunus had done what he could to allay Nahum's fears.

"Before we left," Nicanor said, "I read the reports on the last action here." He seemed relaxed though he and Sayid sat slightly away from the table, leaving their arms and hands free, their swords accessible.

"The action in which your men attacked and largely destroyed a peaceful community," Nahum had said.

That tone of accusation had come out during dinner conversation as well. Yosef saw Nicanor's jaw clench, a sign his friend was losing patience. Yosef started to answer for the tribunus but held his tongue. He could not be seen as a mouthpiece for the Romans.

Nicanor repeated what he had read. "The men from the 12th Legion, led by Tyrannius Priseus, responded to a report that your town was a haven for rebels who gathered to attack the legion cohorts at Scythopolis."

"We posed no threat then and are no menace to you now," said Nahum, glancing at Yosef.

Nicanor nodded. "I'm inclined to agree with you."

"You are?" Nahum said, surprised.

"Hmmph... I know the officer, Priseus, who led the attack," Nicanor said with a scowl. "And I trust him and his commander, Galerius Senna, no farther than I can throw my horse."

"Then why did they come here and attack us?"

"I do not know," Nicanor lied, not even glancing at Yosef or Sayid. But Yosef realized the tribunus was right not to tell Nahum the truth, even if it gave Nicanor a guilty twinge. The Essenes cherished their role as archivists, scribes, documenters, and even protectors of the Jewish people's history and scriptures. The Romans had sought that information—not the breaking of a rebel stronghold—and had taken Qumran forcibly, violently. As Yosef now believed, it did not matter that the Roman soldiers had come at Gessius Florus's instigation. Yosef, now accompanied by Romans, had come seeking information, too—that common purpose would cause the Essenes alarm.

"The men from the 12th Legion acted wantonly, which should not have been allowed," Nicanor stated firmly.

"I have known the tribunus for years, Nahum," Yosef said. "Before the war, even, and I consider him my friend. I trust his word."

"I, too, consider Yosef and this man"—Nicanor nodded and cocked a thumb at Sayid—"my friends." Nicanor leaned toward the Essene leader and said, "I command the men with us, and as long as we are not threatened or harmed... you and your people will not be hurt."

Nahum bowed his head momentarily, then turned to Yosef with a sigh. "So, you are only here to see the scroll you described from your dream."

"I know that is an odd request... I never saw the Essenes create Greek writings in my years with you. Banus, my mentor, told me the Essenes write only in Aramaic and Hebrew." Yosef was encouraged to see Nahum relax.

"We do, but I recall a collection of writings from a Greek man named Loukas. Levi ben Alphaeus, a former tax collector turned disciple of Yeshua ish Natzrat, left a copy of his writings. Levi had been comparing his own accounts with those Loukas wrote."

"Who is this Loukas?" Yosef asked.

"A Greek physician from Antioch who traveled across Judea recording accounts of the teaching of Yeshua ish Natzrat. Loukas was a companion of the now Jewish-Christian convert, Paul, who was preaching about this Yeshua everywhere. Loukas had time for research—interviewing eyewitnesses—and writing while Paul was imprisoned in Caesarea, awaiting the appeal of his case to Caesar. You know he was a Roman citizen...." At Yosef's nod, he added,

"When Paul was taken to Rome, Loukas left with him. But one of Netzarim—a former Essene—brought copies here for safekeeping."

"I knew this Paul... in Rome."

Nicanor's words turned Yosef's and Nahum's attention to him. Yosef saw the Essene leader's eyes were wide and questioning as Nicanor added, "He told me of your messiah."

"There have been many," Nahum said with a nod and a sigh.

"Paul called him in Greek the anointed one...." Nicanor said. "Yesous Christos... and spoke of his words to me, told me what the man taught his followers. Paul was a man of great learning, was he not? *He* believed him to be the messiah foretold of in Hebrew Scriptures."

"He tried to sway you to his beliefs?" Nahum asked.

"He talked... I listened. I thought him a good man." As Nicanor continued, Yosef saw a flicker of regret on his friend's face. "In Rome, I have visited where many Christians believe Paul is buried." Yosef again heard more than a hint of remorse in his friend's voice and a questioning... a longing he'd noted before when Nicanor spoke of his time in Rome when he met Paul.

Yosef looked from Nicanor to Nahum, considering how Nicanor had changed since he'd first met him on board the *Salacia* seven years before. The Essene must know that Nicanor was unlike the men who attacked Qumran.

The Essene smiled at the Roman. "How did you meet Paul?" Nahum asked.

"I was his jailer...."

LXXXII

MARTIUS 70 CE

QUMRAN

THE ESSENE COMMUNITY

Nicanor and Sayid looked troubled as they reluctantly followed Nahum. Both soldiers constantly swept looks around them, holding their lamps aloft for a better view along the dark path. Yosef had thought he would find the scroll in the town and that they would bed down there and leave early the following day. But when, after dinner, Yosef asked for details about the Greek scroll, Nahum said he would take them to it and that they could camp there. They were behind Nahum, descending a winding path from the town into a wadi, away from where Brasus and his men now camped.

Yosef knew Nicanor was cursing that Nahum had persuaded them to leave the shields behind, as they'd be cumbersome in the caves. The tribunus had darted a tense look at Yosef, who shrugged as they took the first descending step. "I must send Sayid to tell Brasus where we go," Nicanor whispered to Yosef. Who was glad he had kept his voice low to not alarm Nahum several paces ahead of them and striding confidently with only the light of a crescent moon and a small hand lamp. *He could probably traverse this way in pitch black, with his eyes closed*, Yosef thought.

"Nahum takes us to what we came for, Nicanor. Besides, Brasus and his men... do you really trust them?" Yosef did not expect an answer but let Nicanor go ahead of him on the path and spoke to Sayid, who trailed behind. "Do you know any of those men?" He held a hand out in the direction in which Brasus had taken the soldiers to camp.

"No, Yosef," came the hushed reply.

Yosef had visited many of the Qumran caves before. Where some of the Essenes of the community slept and where some worked their crafts to support their people. But he had never been so far from the settlement as they were going now with Nahum. After minutes of walking that he knew seemed longer in the darkness, he murmured over the sound of their shuffling steps on loose stones and grit, "Are we near?" He touched Nahum's shoulder to get his attention.

"Yes," said the Essene leader, pointing ahead and up the rock wall. In the murkiness, on the light gray-brown of the wind and water-sculpted stone, he could just make out a dark opening with a protruding ledge over the smooth face of the rock. "The way up and in is behind that ledge. We will be there soon. Tell your friends there is a climb to come, and all of you watch closely and follow where I put my feet."

When Yosef turned to tell Nicanor and Sayid, the Syrian whispered, "We heard noises behind us." Yosef saw the dimmest glimmer that indicated Nicanor no longer carried a lamp, his gladius now in one hand, his pugio in the other. The men stopped and listened. The scuffling of rocks and rasping of sand on stone continued for a moment, stilled in response to their having stilled, and then came a snuffling sound and the scratching of claws or cloven hooves—but not men.

Nahum seemed unworried. "Jackals... or the Ya'el.... they are busy at night."

"Did he say, 'Ya'el'?" Sayid asked Yosef as he and Nicanor exchanged a glance.

Yosef nodded. "Ya'el... means 'ibex' in Hebrew... it's a type of wild goat."

"And the name of another of your friends I've met, Yosef," said Nahum. The Essene leader gathered his robes behind him, up between his legs and through the sash at his waist. Nodding to indicate they should do the same. "She is an interesting woman—and I met her in King David's Tomb in Jerusalem. Does she know that the name you bestowed on her is that of one of our people's heroes?" He turned toward Nicanor and Sayid and said, "The original Ya'el delivered our country from King Jabin of Canaan by killing his general, Sisera."

Yosef let Nahum's challenging allusion hang in the air. His thoughts kept shifting to what the man had told him at dinner about the fighting within Jerusalem and his father's imprisonment by Yohanan ben Levi. It pained him to hear of his mother's careworn appearance and that Matthew was doing his best to protect his parents and sister. And Cleo because of the reward offered for the Roman noblewoman who hid in Jerusalem.

He mused over Miriam's boldness in taking Cleo to the tomb, her boldness in having explored underground to find what had been sealed for centuries. Everyone had assumed it was protected, not to be disturbed. But his sister—dressed as a man!—had taken Nahum through a tunnel to escape the city when the Zealots led by Yohanan ben Levi tried to kill the Essene leader.

At least now they all knew that, recently, Cleo was alive. As Nahum told the story, he saw Nicanor and Sayid's relief.

"As amusing as that story is, Nahum," Nicanor said with a centurion' resolve, "we must get moving and be done with this."

Nahum turned and began the climb.

* * *

THE CAVE OF THE COPPER SCROLL

As they entered the cave, Yosef and Nicanor had to bend at the knees and lower their heads. Even Sayid slightly bent his head to pass through. The shorter Nahum had no problem.

"That way in is a little precarious," Nicanor said to Nahum as he straightened. "The flat stones jumbled above the brow of the entry worried me as I passed under them." He stood awkwardly with his head almost touching the ceiling of the low chamber. "And the footing is treacherous. If you had not shown us where to step...." The tribunus looked from side to side, inspecting the cave as Yosef held up his lamp, then Nicanor stretched, pressing his hands into the small of his back.

"You were wise to follow my steps. Else you would have likely fallen or tumbled back into the wadi," Nahum said as he lit a splinter of reed from his hand lamp and used it to light a large lantern hung from a peg on the wall.

They could see the cave's central room in the arc of greater light. Lined up along the floor at the base of the walls were large jars, most sealed, but some not. Shelves cut into the stone walls held even more jars, these smaller than the urns on the floor.

"There are so many in just this cave..." Yosef said in wonder, brushing his hand along them as he circled the room. Here were the writings of his people—he wished he had time to study them all.

"Forty or more in here," said Nahum. "It is the work of men who have recorded our history... our beliefs... our...." He paused with his eyes on Yosef.

"Our people's fate," Yosef said.

"Yes," Nahum said, holding out his hand and waving it along the length of the storage area. "That's written of too... in what you see here."

"Do you know which one holds the Greek scroll I saw in my dream?"

"I know what each holds, for I put all the scrolls within these containers. And this is where I sleep. The writings are my companions, and I guard them." The Essene went to one of the large urns on the floor and detached its seal. Reaching inside, he retrieved a thick sheaf of parchment rolled and tied together with a leather cord. "This is some of Loukas's writing. This part might contain what you seek—some of the prophecies of Yeshua ish Natzrit. But Yosef, does your reading the portents of what lies ahead for Jerusalem somehow give you the power to change it? I do not believe fate can be altered."

* * *

Later...

"Yosef," Nicanor whispered as he knelt close to his friend, "it's not long until dawn, and we must get back into the town. After sunrise, Brasus will come to check on us. If we are not there, he will assume someone has taken or killed us—I won't be able to stop any action he takes in reprisal." Nicanor rose and asked, "Have you found what you wanted?"

Yosef looked up and around, dazed. Loukas's words—his recounting of what Yeshua ish Natzrat foretold—still stirred his thoughts. Sayid dozed in one corner, and Nahum nodded in another. He had been slightly aware that Nicanor had not closed his eyes through the hours of the night Yosef had been reading.

"Yes... I have it," Yosef said, picking up the scroll he had set on the floor beside him. He had found it an hour before but kept reading, hoping the other words were not as final or as determined. But all the words had been clear, and he now faced the problem that he had not figured out how to convince Nahum to let him take the scroll with him. He rose and stretched, letting out a yawn that roused Nahum.

"Is that what you wanted to see?" the Essene asked, yawning himself and pointing at the cylinder of parchment clenched in Yosef's hand.

"Yes... but I need to make a copy to take with me." Yosef saw Nahum's eyes narrow and a frown furrow his once-smooth brow. "Please, Nahum," Yosef added.

"You think you can use what is in there to help Jerusalem? To persuade this Roman General Titus to allow you to convince the city to surrender to save itself?"

"I'll use it and try..."

"Bring it here." Nahum went to an alcove next to the entrance.

Yosef followed him to find the alcove deeper than it seemed. A deep ledge that served as a desk was cut along the back wall. One side held a stack of thin sheets of parchment, and on a shelf above, ink jars, stylus, and pens beside a bowl of charcoal sticks used for marking the outsides of scrolls and storage jars. The right side of the ledge was taken up by a burnished sheet of copper incised with line after line of writing.

"What is this?" asked Yosef, who could hear Nicanor saying something urgent to Sayid, probably muttering an imprecation for the delay.

"This copper scroll is the fruit of your idea.... and that of your father and brother. It details where the Temple treasure has been hidden in Judea. Well, some of it. Not all the locations we surveyed and prepared have been used. Your brother and his captain of the Temple Guard had to stop moving the treasure when fighting broke out between Yohanan ben Levi and Simon bar Giora. Still, this copper sheet is now done and will withstand the elements. Your brother and Yohanan ben Zaccai in Jerusalem have a copy of its contents and the key to its use. I plan to roll this one into a scroll over a wooden dowel, then hide it."

Yosef recalled his conversation with his father and Matthew before he left to take military command of Galilee. They'd discussed protecting the Temple treasure by hiding it from the Romans. Now he knew how Gessius Florus must have gotten his hands on some of the treasure. The former Roman Procurator had learned enough from the scraps previously stolen from Qumran to get his men positioned so they might be lucky.

A noise brought Nahum and Yosef out of the alcove just as the wooden lattice used as a screen over the cave entrance was shoved aside. Sayid stepped inside the cave, striking his head on the stone lintel in haste. "We must go now... or be trapped here," he reported to Nicanor, who met him at the entry. Sayid's face was white in the lantern's glow. "You were right, Nicanor. Outside, I could hear men on the rocks above us. Many... and they rattle with the weapons of armed men, not Essene ascetics."

LXXXIII

Martius 70 CE

Qumran

The Essene Community, Below the Cave of the Copper Scroll

Nicanor was the first of the four men down the steep dry rill that snaked to the bottom of the wadi. Immediately pulling sword and dagger, he turned his back to the others—who descended several strides-length apart—and checked up and down the gorge and the heights above them. He could not see far in the pre-dawn dimness. Sayid joined him on the gorge floor in a few moments, his weapons out and his eyes scanning, too. The sliding, scraping sound behind them told Nicanor Yosef had reached the part without the carved footholds. That forced him to rely on the grip of the soles of his sandals and hold on with his hands to lower himself.

"Do you see wh—"

Yosef's question was cut off by the body of a man crashing down on him. Nahum cartwheeled atop Yosef and came to a crumpled stop at the feet of Nicanor and Sayid. The Essene leader's neck was transfixed by a long, curved blade, and a torrent of blood flowed down the body and splashed over Yosef, who had been toppled from the rill by the dying man. From above came a chorus of shouts and the sound of many men clambering on rocks and cursing.

Sayid searched the face of the escarpment and either side of the rill where he knew it ended just behind the entrance to the cave. "I see shapes and shadows but cannot tell how many men."

Nicanor had learned long ago to roughly gauge the number of armed men around him by the unique rattle of their equipment, breathing, and mutterings. There were at least nine or ten above them. They had weapons, and judging by the clink and clank of shifting metal plates, some wore armor. "I'll stand in the gap at the foot and take them individually," he said. The arrow arcing down the rill, nearly skewering him, made Nicanor curse his not having a shield.

His change of mind came quickly. "Or we run and find a better place to make a stand." If he recalled correctly, they had passed through a narrow bend in the gorge, a nearly blind turn, somewhere between the town and the cave. If they could reach it, he and Sayid could meet them one or two at a time as they came through the bend. "Up, Yosef!" he cried. His friend struggled to his feet, only to sink back down, gripping his ankle with a grimace.

"Go... leave me." Yosef stared at Nahum's body, the eyes open but lifeless, and he fumbled to pull his sword. "I'll stay—you and Sayid go." He tried to rise again and could not.

"*Futuo!*" Nicanor cursed and bent, grabbed Yosef by the tunic, and heaved him over his shoulder with a grunt that threatened to become a groan. His shoulder, hip, and thigh protested at the strain of Yosef's weight. "Sayid, cover us from behind." Nicanor gritted his teeth and lurched into a shambling run.

* * *

Nicanor was surprised to reach the narrows without Sayid left dead behind him and without a blade or arrow in his back—and Yosef's. The men who had killed Nahum and were now after them, moved slowly as if looking or waiting for someone to join them. He heard them calling a name but could not make it out. When they reached the bend, Nicanor, gasping with a stabbing pain shooting down his side, ordered Sayid, "Give me your sword and run for Brasus, I'll hold them here..."

He did not add what he was thinking: And pray they don't find a way to climb above to shoot Yosef and me full of arrows.

Sayid instantly saw sense in Nicanor's decision and turned up the wadi toward Qumran.

Nicanor grabbed his arm. "If you cannot return until it is too late, find the bastards that killed Yosef and me... and kill them back." He let go and watched the Syrian sprint away.

The wind from the east brought a dank, fetid smell of brine and rotted eggs. Above them were the first rays of daybreak cutting through low clouds in the slice of sky between ridges of stone. "How's your ankle?" Nicanor asked, but he could see it had already swollen, and the distended flesh purpled around the bone. Yosef shook his head, his face frozen in pain or anger.

There would be no running away unless he left Yosef to die alone, and that he would never do.

Nicanor knew Yosef was upset at leaving Nahum's body behind—he had filled his ear with it as they ran—but the Essene was not his friend. Yosef was. So Nicanor carried him to where he could turn and fight the men who were after them. *Maybe*, he prayed to the gods...

Sayid can reach Brasus in time. He heard the tramp of feet drawing near and moved closer to the bend, leaning close to the rock's shoulder without exposing himself, a sword in each hand. It seemed that he and Yosef had no time left.

The muttered conversation of the approaching men reached them. "For all his strutting, the little Heracles proved a coward and disappeared on us," a gruff voice snarled. "Krateros'll laugh at that; he couldn't stand the short shit. He'll have something more to report when he collects our pay from the—"

The blast of a legion clarion shook the wadi, the bugling call to attack ringing off the rock walls. From the ridge above them rolled the thud and clatter of hooves from riders on both sides of the narrowed part of the gorge. Behind Nicanor and Yosef, the sound of running men thundered down the wadi from the direction of the town. The heavy tromp of many soldiers' thick-soled hobnailed military sandal-boots grew louder.

A dozen men, led by Sayid, with Brasus at his side, reached them simultaneously with the cries of the men who had killed Nahum and were only moments from killing Nicanor and Yosef. Horsemen on the ridge fired heavy crossbow bolts, and the deep twangs filled the air. Then there was silence except for the labored breathing from Brasus and his winded troop as they gathered in the open span before the narrows.

"I met Brasus as he and his men searched the town," Sayid gasped.

"When you get your breath," Nicanor said, "help me with Yosef..." He greeted the Syrian auxiliary with a hard clasp of his shoulder.

Sayid reached for Yosef's other arm, and they got him up, hopping on one leg between them. Nicanor led them around the bend, following Brasus and his men. Ten dead men, each with three or more arrows in vital parts of his body, were strewn on the ground. As the wind stilled, the coppery tang of blood spreading on the stone floor of the wadi replaced what they had smelled earlier, wafting of salt from the sea not far away.

"Jackals," Nicanor said, pointing at the crocodile tattoos on five men's hands. "Nahum was right... they're busy at night." He felt Yosef shift and steadied him as Yosef reached into his tunic smeared with Nahum's blood.

"I still have it!" Yosef said as he brought out the Greek scroll.

"Good... because I'm done with caves and climbing," Nicanor declared, and Sayid nodded in agreement.

LXXXIV

Aprilus 70 CE

Caesarea

The Roman Encampment, Nicanor's Quarters

In Qumran, Nicanor had overheard Nahum telling Yosef—because Yosef insisted—what he knew of Yosef's family in Jerusalem. Sayid had been listening, too, and later said the only good news had been that Ya'el, Lady Cleo, was alive. But she was in danger, for Gessius Florus had offered a reward for her capture. But the news of Yosef's family's predicament and then Nahum's death had added to the gloom. On the return from Qumran, Yosef had barely spoken to them.

"Before we meet with General Titus at *meridiem*"—he gestured toward the sun almost at its apex—"will you tell me what that says?" Nicanor touched the scroll Yosef had flattened on the table. One edge still showed the faint scarlet smears of Nahum's blood, though Yosef had tried to wipe them away. "Or must I wait until you tell Titus?"

Yosef lifted his wounded leg with a grimace and propped it on a footstool. "It prophesies that Jerusalem will be surrounded by armies and fall within the lifetime of those who have heard these words." Yosef tapped the scroll. "The words were written by Loukas but spoken by Yeshua ish Natzrat. Not only that but the Temple itself will be wholly destroyed. Levi's writings in the cave at Qumran had the same prophecy."

"Is this Yeshua the Christ that Paul spoke of... the messiah, the Christians, worship?"

Yosef frowned down at the scroll, then squinted up at Nicanor. "I have two thoughts about that. The messiah is believed to come and sit on King David's throne. But that won't happen unless the messiah regains independence for us. And Yeshua did not do that. Also, we Jews do not believe that god inhabits humans, though the Spirit of Yahweh can at times, as with our prophets of old. Whether it is a Greek hero, a Roman emperor... or a poor Jew, we are all still human, no more and no less. The teachings of Yeshua ish Natzrat are admirable, but now his followers claim he was partly, if not entirely, divine. That goes against what Jews have always believed."

Yosef tapped a stylus on his upper lip in thought, then said, "So, no. I don't believe Yeshua is the messiah, though his followers do. Loukas makes this clear as he refers to him frequently as the 'Son of Man.' That is a clear reference to a future semi-divine persona envisioned by Daniel. This Daniel, who lived in Babylon six hundred years ago, also foretold Jerusalem's destruction. As I recall, he prophesied that centuries from that time, the messiah would be cut off, leaving no heirs. Not long after, a prince would come with his army and destroy the city and the Temple. The Essenes knew this prophecy well and thought the time was near for a great battle between the Sons of Light and the Sons of Darkness. In that battle, the current Temple would be destroyed. But no one knew for sure the timing. Yeshua now seems to have narrowed this speculation considerably by predicting his generation would not die out before witnessing the destruction of the city and Temple."

"And men still live today who have heard this Yeshua teach and give this prophecy?"

Yosef nodded. "My father and mother... and others close to me... they knew him but did not subscribe to his teachings nor believe what he foretold. They were not among his followers then nor now."

"But you believe the prophecy? And what of this prince the prophecy mentions? No prince is threatening your city."

The frown eased on Yosef's face as he straightened up and looked into Nicanor's eyes. "Is Emperor Vespasian not the ruler of Rome's empire... does he not have a favored son, who will become his heir?"

"Titus...." said Sayid, who had just returned from tending the horses.

"Yes, Titus. Is he not a prince?"

"He'll be happy to hear what you tell him from that scroll," said Nicanor. "He wants an official portend of his glorious future. That seemed to work for his father."

They all knew what that meant if the prophecy were to come true. Everything that occurred over the last seven years was coming to an inevitable conclusion. The quarters grew quiet, making them aware of the shuffling of hooves from the horse stalls and the sounds of men moving through the camp.

"What about what we saw on our way here?" asked Sayid. "That upset you a great deal, Yosef."

Nicanor nodded. He, too, was curious and concerned by how unsettled Yosef had been afterward. Brasus had been right to insist on a different route to return to Caesarea. The decurion knew General Titus would hold him responsible for Nicanor and Yosef being ambushed and nearly killed. Though saving them had restored some confidence in his mission. Still, Brasus would not risk traveling the predictable road where other men might plan another attack.

The rougher secondary road to Caesarea had led them through a series of low hillocks. They had come upon a grove of trees in a clearing between them. Where Yosef had reined in his mule and stared. Nicanor had turned Albus back to join Yosef at the copse of blossoming trees that Yosef studied intently.

"What is it, Yosef?" Nicanor asked. "What do you look for?"

"Not what, who... to see if she's under the veil of that one." Yosef had pointed at the large central tree, its branches laden and drooping with pink blossoms that draped nearly to the ground.

"She? Who?" Nicanor asked as Sayid joined them. Then he remembered Yosef's dream.

"Cleo. This is where I saw her." Yosef had heeled his mule forward and away from the trees. He had spoken no more about it in the days since.

Yosef rose and limped to the window, then turned to them. "Almond trees are the first to bloom in spring. They are also the first to lose their leaves in the fall." Nicanor did not understand the import and saw Sayid blink with bewilderment.

"Why was the pink-blossomed tree so much larger than the ones with white?" asked Sayid. "It had many more buds than the others."

Yosef winced as he stepped away from the window, putting too much weight on his injured ankle. "To my people, the almond tree also tells the story of the resurrection and destruction of the Temple." Sayid nodded his understanding, and Nicanor remembered Yosef mentioning this idea.

"I wish we had not gone that way, Yosef." Sayid shook his head. "Then you would not have seen those trees that disturb you."

"No, Sayid, it was meant to be part of my destiny. Jehovah's hand has been upon me since I left my home to sail from Caesarea to Rome on the *Salacia*. It has not all been bad—I met you and Nicanor... and...." Yosef sighed and turned to Nicanor. "Let's go now to see General Titus."

LXXXV

Aprilus 70 CE

Caesarea

The Roman Encampment, General Titus's Praetorium

Yosef looked up as he finished reciting from the scroll and saw Titus was delighted. The general's eyes were bright and sharp, and his smiling gaze went from Yosef to Nicanor and back to him again.

"Does this not indicate that now a prophet of your people has foretold my victory?" Titus asked, studying Yosef for a reaction. "Your visions have seen this just as you saw my father would become emperor."

"But it does not mean the destruction of Jerusalem and its people, my lord," Yosef replied. "There have been other portents from my people's god that did not come to pass. Yahweh told the prophet Jonah at Nineveh during the great Assyrian Empire that that capital city was doomed because its people had become evil. Our god, Jehovah, vowed to smite and destroy it. So, it was as if the Sword of Damocles Cicero wrote of was hanging over the city. But the citizens repented when Jonah warned the people of Nineveh, confronting them with the threat of Yahweh's punishment. And Yahweh spared them. So, he may also spare Jerusalem… if you allow me to speak to my people's leaders and convince them to surrender."

Titus nodded. "I will do as my father told me. You will have an opportunity." The general reached across his desk, took the Greek scroll from Yosef's hands, and glanced at Nicanor. "Tribunus, your friend Marinus and his ship entered port this morning. I will send word of your visions and about this scroll back with him to my father in Alexandria."

Meanwhile, the decree of Nero still stands, that all Christian writings are seditious to Rome and to be burned." Titus placed the end of the scroll in the brazier next to him. Yosef watched in dismay as the flames consumed the precious words so many had worked, suffered, and died to protect.

"So shall it be with Rome's enemies." Titus sat back and steepled his fingers. "In two days, the legions will march on Jerusalem."

"About the men who attacked us in Qumran, general," Nicanor said, having been quiet since Titus, anxious to hear Yosef, had rushed him through his report. "We cannot prove they are connected with Gessius Florus, but I believe they are. I'll prepare a report of recent events for Emperor Vespasian."

"Bring it to me tomorrow, and I'll include it with mine. I will ask Emperor Vespasian if he wishes to retain Lord Florus as an imperial tax collector. And I will send for the man before we leave Caesarea and ask him his purpose here. We'll discuss Lord Florus again after I speak with him. You may go." Titus waved for his aide to enter as Nicanor and Yosef rose to leave.

Moments later, they passed through the antechamber into the broad hall that connected the praetorium's two main entries and exits. As they neared the rear door leading to the main avenue of the encampment, a high voice behind them called. "Yosef ben Mathias!"

Yosef, surprised at hearing that name, turned and Nicanor with him.

"I would like to speak to you, Yosef," Berenice said, beckoning him to follow her. "Alone."

* * *

AT TODROS, THE HORSE TRADERS

Sayid dismounted, noting the empty corral. That afternoon, Nicanor arrived at Celsus Evander's office, explained Yosef's absence, and asked Sayid to trade in Yosef's mule. They would ride with the legions in two days, and their friend needed a proper mount this time. Nicanor had already put in the requisition with the legion stable master.

But the stable master had refused to provide the Jewish rebel with a horse. So back to Nicanor, he had gone, and the tribunus had decided that was an argument and confrontation not worth having. Many in the legion looked disapprovingly at a tribunus who quartered with a Syrian auxiliary and a Jew, who had been an enemy—perhaps still was one. It was suspicious that Nicanor preferred their company. Sayid knew Nicanor did not care what others thought... but going into a battle, especially a complex and sustained siege, was dangerous. The threat did not always come from the enemy you faced but sometimes from within—if fellow soldiers were angry. Many a score had been settled between allies under cover of war.

Todros greeted Sayid as he entered the horse trader's small office beside the stable. "Hello, my friend... I'm sorry, but I have no work for you...."

"I need to buy a horse," Sayid said, jingling the pouch of coins Nicanor had given him.

"And I would love to sell you one. But right now, I have none... the man who bought many from me before has just returned to buy many more... all I had."

Sayid swore under his breath, turned, and left. He had spent the whole afternoon returning Yosef's mule. Then waiting on the stable master to get around to him, only to be told Nicanor's requisition would not be filled. Then back to Celsus Evander's office for Nicanor to send him to Todros, who had no horses. Exiting the horse trader's gate, he looked north and across the road. A group of riders from the west slowed as they approached Gessius Florus's villa, arranging themselves to file through the fortified entry. The last pair entered, but the gate did not close. A moment passed, and then a wagon came out and turned east.

Sayid checked the position of the sun low in the west. He would meet Nicanor, Celsus, and Yosef at the port taberna for dinner if that woman was done with Yosef in time. They were all to go at the invitation of Marinus, recently in port. He studied the wagon. Nothing rose above the sideboards that he could see, but the wagon moved as if it carried weight; there was no bounce as it rolled over the ruts in the road. Curious, Sayid waited for it to get farther away, then heeled his horse forward to follow it.

* * *

EAST OF CAESAREA

Sayid could not see what the two men dumped into the shallow ravine, not from his angle and the wagon's position. The back end of the wagon was in the shadow cast by the front end, which sat higher on the lip of the gulch. At the edge, the driver took a flat piece of wood and scraped dirt from the wind drift piles of dirt to toss down upon what he had just unloaded. The second man had already carried a similar board down into the gully. After a few minutes of scraping, scuffling sounds, he climbed out as the driver finished and threw his board into the wagon. Stepping up, the two men settled on the bench by the driver, who snapped the reins. The horses easily pulled the empty wagon up the slope toward the road.

Sayid waited until the wagon was out of sight before removing his hand from his horse's muzzle. Thankful, the animal had stayed quiet as he watched the two men. Sayid walked to the ravine's edge to stand where the wagon had been. The last rays of sun ended at that edge, and shadows were deepening within the gulch. Seeing the marks of where the bulky objects had tumbled from the wagon, he followed them down. His foot caught on a rock or root near the bottom, and he stumbled to land on his knees among oblong mounds covered by gritty dirt and loose clumps of brush. He reached out to one bundle and felt it move under his hand. The dusting of dirt spilled from the face of a young woman, pale gray in the twilight.

LXXXVI

Aprilus 70 CE

Caesarea

Gessius Florus's Villa

Gessius Florus studied the three thin sheets of parchment, carefully passing his crystal lens over the surface. They were considerably smudged with charcoal, but the characters had been deeply incised and formed distinct letters. Drusus had not rushed his work. The rubbing had yielded legible text.

"When the tribunus, the Syrian auxiliary, and the two Jews left the town," Drusus explained, "their movements and voices carried among the rocks of the gulley. My men and I followed them from atop the ridge. Good thing the townspeople had scurried to their caves when the Romans appeared. That warned us to let them pass and then get above and ahead of them, to see who entered and left the town. It was a dark night, but the Roman wore armor that caught enough of the lamplight to show us he was with them. Him and the Syrian. They all went inside a cave far past the others. I could hear enough talk between the tribunus and the Syrian to tell the two Jews were doing something important inside. Finally, just before daybreak, I gathered my men above the cave they had entered, and we made enough noise to draw them out. Instead of just killing them, I thought it best to see what was inside the cave they'd spent so long with. I slipped inside after they fled as my men readied to follow and kill them." Drusus rubbed his face with the palms of his large hands.

"The only thing that seemed of value inside the cave was a sheet of copper filled with lettering, like some kind of ledger."

Florus lifted the crystal and set it aside. "Why didn't you just take it with you?"

"It's hard to carry a stiff sheet of metal that size. And I thought it must be important to be carved into the metal. I didn't want them to know I had the information if it was about the treasure."

Florus looked up at the thickset, exhausted man, impressed with his forethought, though he would not say so.

Drusus continued. "So, I did the next best thing and brought you the rubbing."

"Did your men kill them... both Jews, the tribunus, and the Syrian?" Florus asked.

"I don't know, lord. The Romans had camped on the other side of the town, so they could not interfere if my men struck swiftly. There were only four of them against ten of our men. And the two Jews were not fighters. I heard a man scream—one of the Jews, I'm sure—and then the sound of a body falling through the crevice they had climbed to reach the cave. The rubbing took me some time, and I wanted to protect the sheets I rolled and carried. When I came out of the cave, my men were down on the gorge's floor... going after them. They called me, but I thought it best to bring this to you as soon as possible instead—not get caught up in the fighting. Except for brief breaks to water and rest my horse, I rode straight here."

"Lord..." called a man at the doorway.

"Yes, Irad," Florus said as he turned to his major domus.

"The men just returned from disposing of the last of... of them." Irad hesitated, then asked, "Do you need me to buy more at the market in Caesarea tomorrow?"

"Yes, as soon as it opens."

"How many, lord?"

"One."

"Only one, sir?"

"Just one. A man." Florus smirked at the expression on the man's features. "Find one that's been a scribe or with enough learning to translate Hebrew writing for me." He did not look at the sheets on his desk but saw the major domus's eyes go to them.

"I'll try to find one with that skill, lord."

"Do not try... carry out my order *exactly*," Florus said, turning back to Drusus. "Get some rest. After Irad brings me a translator, you will leave tomorrow with the new men. I'll leave orders for your men from Qumran to follow us once they return."

* * *

THE ROMAN ENCAMPMENT, NICANOR'S QUARTERS

Nicanor saw Yosef stir on his cot, so he set down the letter from Marcus Attilius that Marinus had handed him at the taberna. He knew his friend had been awake since Sayid had reported what Gessius Florus's men were doing. It preyed on his own mind, as well. Florus's cruelty to Cleo was known to them. It was unsurprising that

Florus continued his brutality with other women—women he could dispose of.

"What did she want with you?" Nicanor asked.

"You mean Lady Berenice?"

"You said nothing about her when you joined Marinus and me at the taberna."

"It was not something to bring into the conversation when I arrived. You seemed interested in hearing Marinus tell about Anyte writing your story—the brave Nicanor and the old gladiator Graius, on a quest to help Lady Cleo. You have not told me much about it, but hearing what I did from Marinus makes me believe it is an epic worth writing about." He gave his old friend a smile.

"Marinus loves to talk," Nicanor scoffed. But he *had* been pleased to hear of his daughter's writing. He had seen how intently Yosef wrote down everything he could recall, documenting everything that transpired, as if for the perusal of people in the future. He had developed a sense of appreciation for that effort. He was not a scribe... and he had no children to tell stories to, so his life—the things he had seen and done—would never be known. If Anyte could record what he had shared on their voyage from Puteoli to Caesarea, perhaps some of his experiences would live on. His experiences and the feats of men like Graius and Marcus Attilius. Even the crimes of those like Gessius Florus.

"But it was good to see him," Nicanor continued. "I doubt I will again until the fighting is over." He regretted saying that as tense silence settled between them, and he broke it with his question again: "So, what did Berenice want?"

"To tell me what Titus already had about letting me try to talk to the leaders in Jerusalem. She said she had not told him what she knew about Yohanan ben Levi and Simon bar Giora. That they are not rational and are unlikely to listen. She wants me to speak with them, but I should not get my hopes up."

"It sounds like she cares for your people."

"I always thought of her as having once been a *Nazarite* woman, someone willing to give her life to my people's god. Her last time in Jerusalem four years ago was to fulfill her vow. Instead, she attempted to stop Gessius Florus's violence... but to no avail. Now, I don't know if she cares or just what she wants. She does seek status with a powerful Roman close to the throne. She talked of following General Titus to Rome once this war ends."

That sting of remorse came again into the tenor of his voice, Nicanor thought.

"She acted as if that was my goal too," Yosef said, "as if we sought the same things." Nicanor could think of no way to ease his friend's pain, and he was glad when Yosef changed the atmosphere by pointing at the letter Nicanor held. "You've heard from your friend in Rome?"

Nicanor nodded. "Marinus brought it to me. Marcus says he is healing well. The grain ships from Alexandria arrived just in time to prevent even greater riots in Rome... the local granaries had less than 10 days' supply left. The legions there continue to put down the remaining unrest inside and outside the city. Emperor Vespasian's son-in-law Quintus Cerealis leads one legion against the revolt by the Batavi in Germania." He glanced down where his finger still marked where he'd stopped reading. "Hmmph... he says Vespasian's youngest son, Domitian, has become quite the manipulator. Listen to this: 'He often speaks publicly as his father's representative... and can blush on command to seem modest and sincere, while privately he is anything but... Antonia Caenis says Vespasian has discreetly admonished him for usurping power.'" Nicanor shook his head and read silently for a moment.

Here's something different, he thought. "Antonia Caenis wants to breed Carmenta with her best stallion, saying she will make a fine broodmare and bloodline. She will hold and care for all the foals on my behalf. They will be mine when I return... should I wish to start my own *equus admissae*. I suppose she wants to put me in the business of breeding horses to supply to the legions."

"I cannot see you as a horse trader... where did that idea come from?" A half-smile curled Yosef's lip.

"I mentioned to Marcus that maybe I'd do as Vespasian had done when he retired. I'd find a place and deal in horses... sourcing and selling them to the legions. It seems he must have said that to Antonia Caenis."

"So, you *have* thought about what comes after this...." the half-smile faded.

Nicanor heard his friend's loneliness in the unsaid words. His despair had grown since talking with Nahum about his family in Jerusalem. Sadly, Nicanor realized that no matter how strong Yosef's sense of destiny had become. No matter how urgent his need to write the story, to live only to document the war for his people, it would never compensate him for all he had lost. *And he will lose even more in the coming months.*

LXXXVII

Aprilus 70 CE

Jerusalem

Bezetha, The Baris Remnants

Miriam watched as Ya'el struggled to take a deep breath, her breasts tightly wrapped with the same kind of linen band Miriam wore under her disguise.

"I know," Miriam said. "It took me some time to get used to it. I breathed too shallowly at first, but Zechariah made me focus on breathing normally until it felt almost ordinary." She tugged down Matthew's old tunic and was glad it was a little long on Ya'el, helping to hide the shape of her legs. Ya'el had long since given up the Roman lady's practice of removing the leg hair, which also helped the disguise. "After a while, when the strapping loosens, I'll show you how to quickly tighten it again."

"Elian!" Ya'el called to the boy, "You can come here now and bring my bow and quiver."

Miriam picked up Matthew's worn leather girdle and handed it to Ya'el to put on. "Mother helped me attach the ring to the back of it." Ya'el snugged the broad girdle around her, fastened it, and felt for the ring. The squawk behind them announced Elian and Cicero from the passageway. The boy was still unhappy at learning he would not get to explore with Ya'el the tunnels he had helped clear the entrances of. The parrot, who had quickly grown tired of the chambers, had helped keep Elian occupied, but neither was pleased.

Ya'el took the quiver of arrows from Elian and slipped her arms through the straps affixed to either side. She felt for the cords trailing from the bottom of the quiver, and she groped to feed them through the ring. "Got it," she said, passing the cords through again to double them, tucking the loose ends into the loop and finally pulling to tighten it all snugly to her back. There was enough slack in the shoulder straps that she could shrug off the quiver if she needed to without untying it from the girdle first.

Ya'el turned to Elian and tousled the boy's already-mussed hair, and he relented from his displeasure and gave her the slightest grin. "Want to see me make that shot again?" she asked. Elian nodded, and Cicero, perched on the padded leather square strapped atop the boy's shoulder, bobbed his head. Ya'el took the bow and stepped to the line she had marked on the stone floor. With Cicero screeching, Elian ran the length of the gallery and snuffed out the wicks of half the lamps.

"I still don't know how you can see to hit anything," Miriam said as she peered at the target, nearly lost in the gloom of the far end of the long gallery.

Elian raced back to stand beside Ya'el as she strung her bow. Then as fast as Miriam could pull her daggers, Ya'el straightened, reached over her shoulder, plucked an arrow, nocked it, and released it. Repeating that again and a third time. The whistling flight of the three arrows almost merged as one sound, and Miriam heard their thumps hitting the target more than she witnessed them striking.

"Come, let's look!" Elian cried as he waved a hand at them and ran to the target.

Miriam was glad for the smile beaming from Ya'el, a sight Miriam had seen only in those rare moments when she spoke of her life before Gessius Florus. They followed Elian, who had relighted the lamps nearest the target.

The arrows were grouped within the span of a hand at the center. It was only because Ya'el had taught her how to use one of the bows Matthew and Eleasar had brought them that Miriam realized what a feat this was. With plenty of light at half the distance of Ya'el's shot, Miriam could reliably hit the target, but not often in the center. "I'll never be as good as you," Miriam said admiringly.

"Well," Ya'el said affectionately, "I've handled a bow since I was younger than Elian. And I'll never wield a dagger or staff like you do."

"That reminds me," Miriam said as she slipped the blade she had brought from her sash. "Here"—she slid it into the sheath attached to the leather girdle. "You still need one to carry... though I pray you never have to use it."

"Isn't this the one Hananiah gave you?"

"I don't use it since it's from him, but it is a fine blade. And if you do as you wish to, which is a risk, you might need it."

"I want to go outside with you," Elian announced, crossed his arms defiantly across his chest, and stared down at the two women dressed as men.

"We must see if it's safe first, Elian." Miriam leaned toward the boy, regretting she had mentioned Ya'el's intent. "The city is packed with people; we must blend with them. But because many more children are on the streets now, too, if it seems safe enough, you will go outside with Ya'el later. Your Aramaic has become good enough for you to seem a Judean boy, but it will only be for a little while each time, understand?"

The boy nodded. "When?"

"Maybe soon." Ya'el smoothed Elian's hair, but it sprang back up. "Now go put Cicero in his cage and cover it... it's time for you both to settle down for the evening."

They watched the boy and parrot move toward the side chamber that had become their sleeping quarters. Ya'el and Miriam returned to the central room. Miriam took a cord-bound parchment packet from her sash and put it on the table. "Here are Zechariah's letters you asked for—for your reading practice." Miriam almost wished she had not mentioned them. Miriam had so little left from Zechariah, and these were the most personal of his belongings. The letters Zechariah had continued to write to his long-dead wife, Bayla, and his daughter, Meira, had always moved her. The latter ones mentioned Miriam, as well. They had helped bring her out of the darkness that had returned to her with Zechariah's death. But Ya'el had asked for something to read, and the letters were all she had to give. They would help her Aramaic, too.

"Thank you."

"You have enough water and food here now?" Miriam asked. Food was increasingly becoming a problem, though Arins, as he had promised, had begun delivering perishable food to the valley near Motza to store it at the tunnel entrance. The supply had not amounted to much yet, and her father, Matthew, and Eleasar ben Ananias feared what would come to them all very soon. The fighting over food would be worse than the fighting between Yohanan ben Levi and Simon bar Giora. And the rumblings foretold that fighting would soon recommence.

"Yes... enough for several days. The time will allow me to get used to these clothes before we test this disguise."

LXXXVIII

Aprilus 70 CE

Jerusalem

The Upper City

This Feast of the Passover required Miriam's devoted attention to her family and the preparations. She thought it might be the last time for that feast and for *Hag Hamatzot*, the Feast of Unleavened Bread. She hated that Ya'el, Elian, and even Cicero were confined to the underground chambers of what was left of the Hasmonean Baris. But now, she must focus solely on her father, mother, Matthew, Leah, and Rachel.

The preparation of meals was permitted only on the first and last days of the feasts. But before that, every household underwent a tremendous amount of cleaning. When younger, Miriam had complained when her mother and father refused to hire servants to do such tasks. But she did not even consider shirking or commenting about the work this time. With the help of Leah and Rachel, everything in their home was scrubbed: walls, ceilings, floors, and furnishings. Cookware was boiled and cleansed, special utensils were set aside that had not been soiled with leaven, the yeast that made bread dough rise.

Once they had finished, Mathias carried through with the tradition of the Search for the Leaven. At sunset, with the house darkened, he took a lighted lamp and searched the house, looking for any hidden leaven. A home that was truly clean of it was free from the corruption of sin before a Holy God. If anyone ate anything with leaven during the feast days, that person would be cut off and cast out. All the Jewish people remembered then that Jehovah called them out of Egypt to become a separate people who followed only Him. The feasts commemorated their deliverance from Aegypt and all oppression and suffering.

At *Pesach* dinner, the family had completed the four rituals: the *paschal* offering, the lamb, eaten alone and then with *maror*, bitter herbs; the eating of the *matzah*, unleavened bread; and the reading by her father of the story of the *Yezi'at Mizrayim*, their people's exodus from Aegypt.

When Mathias ended the tale, Miriam felt Eleasar ben Ananias' eyes on her. Her parents had invited him but seemed unable to relax in their hospitality. He kept looking at Miriam, no doubt trying to understand her killing a Roman, even if it had been to save herself. Miriam felt a pang, knowing Eleasar's concern for his wife and child he had sent to Masada for their safety.

The knocking at the door startled everyone. Matthew went to answer it and returned with Yohanan ben Zaccai, who was nearly breathless. The old rabbi had been invited to dinner, but Matthew had announced that Yohanan sent his apologies. He unexpectedly had to meet someone just south of the city. She had wondered, but not asked, who or what could draw Yohanan from Jerusalem during the feast days.

"I met with an Essene from Qumran," Yohanan explained, looking around at all of them, "The Romans went there again, and Nahum is dead." Then, naming Mathias, Matthew, and Eleasar, he said, "I must speak with you later on that matter." Yohanan pulled at his beard, his eyes sad, as he took the seat Mathias offered and the cup Rebecca pressed into his hand. He looked at both of them and said, "The Essene told me that Yosef was with the Romans at Qumran, and now General Titus and his legions are approaching Jerusalem. They will be here soon."

* * *

Days later...

THE UPPER CITY

For the next several evenings, men gathered in small groups in front of Mathias's home and cursed Yosef's name in the shadows of night. The news Yohanan ben Zaccai had brought the family... of Yosef accompanying the Romans in Qumran... had spread quickly. This early morning, Miriam and Matthew sneaked from the courtyard at the rear of their home, Miriam expecting every moment to encounter the men angry at the family of a traitor. But the men on the streets, alone or in groups, seemed to have another purpose.

"They pay us no mind!" said Miriam, then lowered her voice to practice sounding more like the young man she was dressed to resemble.

Matthew strode with purpose as they turned onto the main street through the market, seeming to not want any men to have time to recognize and accost him. Or perhaps he was just angry at what they

Final Siege

had decided the evening before. She had to quicken her pace to match his, then she nearly ran into him as he stopped abruptly.

"Wait"—he held a hand out to wave her back to the side of the street under the just-unfurled awning of a merchant's shop. Six heavily armed and armored men had taken possession of the street ahead. A man in regal robes strode close behind them with another six equally equipped and menacing-looking men on his heels.

"Yohanan ben Levi goes to meet with Simon bar Giora," Matthew said. "After you went to bed last night, Eleasar stopped by to tell me they had called a truce to discuss the Romans—to study their approach and decide how to fight them. They have sent most of their men to the walls, and the others have begun moving the war machines and missile stockpiles from their positions, threatening each other to use against the Romans."

"So they'll aim them at the Romans instead of one another? Instead of us?" Miriam asked irritably, in her low tone. She ground her teeth together. "That man, more than anyone, hates Yosef and stirs others to hate him.... He stirs them to hate *us*, though we've done no wrong. I should find him when he has fewer men to protect him...."

"Leave him alone, Miriam," Matthew ordered with the maddening command of a brother. "Do not even threaten him. We have enough already to bring the Zealots' animosity upon us."

She heard the irritation in his voice and realized she was furious at Yohanan ben Levi and Yosef. How could her brother be with the Romans still if they freed him? *Surely he would have come home to his people... to help us!* Yet he seemed to be working with them. And Yohanan ben Zaccai was certain it was Yosef in Qumran. The Essene, who now waited in a cave in the Hinnom Valley to carry any reply to Qumran, had served Yosef and the Romans the meal they shared with Nahum. And the Romans later killed Nahum. *How could he be part of that?* she lamented to herself. The stories Yohanan ben Levi spread about Yosef's treason, further spewed by Yonatan Hilel, Leah's former husband—how could it be true?

The previous evening, she watched the light of hope fade from her father's and mother's eyes as Yohanan ben Zaccai spoke. That same light had first appeared when they heard Yosef had survived the destruction of Yotapta. Then the light had grown into warm blazing when they'd heard the Roman general, Vespasian, had freed him. But now the light was gone, replaced by pain. Yohanan had reported that the copper scroll was completed and safe, and the plans were to be hidden. He had pressed Matthew and Eleasar to do what must come next. They must hide the key, the code that completed the copper scroll and revealed the locations of the stores of the Temple treasure.

Yohanan and Mathias had determined it was best not to hide the key within the city. Jerusalem had become a kicked hornet's nest as the factions resolved their differences. And they must before they all faced the Romans. The soldiers of that empire had bided their time until many thought they would never come.

But where would they hide it, and who would see to it? Matthew offered to take the key out of the city and secure it in a safe place, but Eleasar had said Matthew could not be absent when the call to arms was sounded. Then the Temple Guard Captain surprised her when he said, "Miriam is the only one able to do it." Even more surprising was Rebecca's recommendation of the best place to hide it.

"Let's go"—Matthew touched her shoulder, startling her from her reverie. She hurried to follow him on the now-empty street.

* * *

BEZETHA, THE SHED OVER THE UNDERGROUND BARIS REMNANTS

"Matthew!" Miriam called to him. "We must go. Mother said it took over nine hours to get there when she was young. We can't risk it getting too dark to see the landmarks." She tucked the folded sheet of parchment with her mother's hand-drawn map and directions into the sash around her waist.

"Then nine hours back, too, if you don't rest. The Romans will be here by the time you return. I should be the one to go." Matthew shook his head, and his eyes narrowed. "You've never traveled alone outside of Jerusalem." He glanced at Ya'el, dressed similarly to Miriam, with a prominent dagger at her hip but her bow in her hand and a full quiver on her back. Like Miriam, she also had a waterskin and a small bag of pressed dates, their only provisions, slung over a shoulder.

"You know you can't go," Miriam replied. "Eleasar is probably already at his post in the watchtower on the western wall, at the Gennath Gate, right?"

He nodded.

"You'll be expected at the northern gate, else you will be considered a deserter, a traitor like...." Miriam did not finish. Matthew's grip on the outer door tightened as he looked over his shoulder to study her for a moment, then his eyes shifted to Ya'el beside her.

Ya'el replied though Matthew had asked no question: "I will not be a hindrance for Miriam—I can help her get there and back."

Miriam had seen the surprise on Matthew's face when they arrived in the subterranean chambers, and they first saw Ya'el with her hair shorn, though now she covered her head with a cloth. It had jolted Miriam, too. Driving home that the former Roman noblewoman was made of sterner stuff than she had assumed when she first saw her four years earlier. The Roman woman, Cleo, was no longer among them.

"We can't change this, Matthew," said Miriam. "Once the Romans are here, it will become even harder, if not impossible. And by now, Yohanan ben Zaccai is with the Essene messenger, telling him our hiding place. Then he can retrieve it and take it to Nahum's successor. We know where it must go."

"Where Judah the Hammer rests," said Matthew.

"Mother says it is safer to hide it where her ancestors are buried than in Jerusalem. And you know Father agreed. It is long since settled."

Matthew drew a deep breath, held it momentarily, and released it. "Then we will do this...."

"You'll check on Elian and Cicero later?" Ya'el asked.

Matthew nodded. "Yes... my post is close by." He pulled the door open and waved them through, seemingly two workmen about their foreman's bidding. Once outside, he stepped ahead of them onto the path that wound through the piles of stone and materials. "I'd rather you go through Herod's escape tunnel to leave the city through the valley near Motza. But Arins has one of his caravans due this morning—his last before the Romans should arrive. They must not see you. I'll leave you at the Schechem Gate." He squinted at Miriam. "You know where to turn from that northern road?"

Miriam patted their mother's directions. "Yes."

Matthew passed between two tall stacks of building stones, turned toward the path leading to the northern wall, and stopped as a harsh voice boomed: "Why is a Temple Guard officer not on the walls? Ahhhh, I know who you are! You're the brother of that traitor, Yosef ben Mathias. Yohanan ben Levi speaks much of your family. What are you doing here?"

Miriam and Ya'el crept closer until they saw Matthew standing just past the bend, his hands at his side. Hearing their faint steps, Matthew used the hand nearest them to signal for Miriam and Ya'el to back away. The man, out of sight to Miriam and Ya'el, noticed the gesture and asked, "Are others hiding with you?"

The tip of a sword, level with Matthew's chest, came into the women's view, but they could not see the man who wielded it. Matthew replied to the man, "No," and his hand flicked again to tell them to stay out of sight, to return to the shed.

But with a glance at Ya'el, and in three steps, the women joined Matthew at his side, and Miriam saw the flash of anger and concern on his face as they did.

The man backed away several steps, his sword up, and pointed it at Matthew's chest again. He glanced over his shoulder, keeping a side-eye watch on them. He seemed about to shout to someone when the bow Ya'el had carried down at one side came up and met the arrow the other hand had pulled from her quiver. The shaft flew and struck the sword hilt with enough force to make the man drop his weapon and back farther away. The man rubbed his hand, eyes on the second arrow Ya'el had nocked and ready. He stood aside to let them pass.

Once they got beyond him, Miriam heard Ya'el whisper to Matthew, "You see that I'll help her, not hinder her."

LXXXIX

Aprilus 70 CE

Gophna

14 miles north of Jerusalem

Nicanor had not been surprised that they had marched unopposed from Caesarea. Only an insane rebel leader would have tried to interfere with the Roman juggernaut that could not be slowed, much less stopped. This was not the flawed march from Antioch nearly four years ago, the 12th Legion alone and led by the ill-advised and militarily inexperienced Cestius Gallus. General Titus's three Legions—5th, *Macedonia*, 12th, *Fulminata*, and 15th, *Apollinaris*—had moved south and east to converge in their approach to Jerusalem. A fourth, 10th, *Fretensis*, came from Jericho in the east. A full-strength auxiliary force accompanied each legion, and Nicanor estimated nearly 70,000 fighting men would soon assault Jerusalem.

The vanguard, marching first, were the troops sent by the empire's allies and client-kings, accompanied by the auxiliaries. Behind them came the Roman surveyors, engineers, and cohorts of workmen, the *immunes* whose duties were to grade the roads and plan the encampments. With armed escort and support personnel, the legion baggage and supplies were safely centered within the formations. After these came General Titus and Tiberius Alexander, surrounded by their elite troops and heavy infantry, followed by the cavalry of the legions. Behind them came the war machinery of the Roman Army pulled by mules and loaded pack animals, accompanied by dozens of heavily laden wagons of missiles for the throwers and bowmen. Then, following the siege engines, came the senior tribunes of the legions, he and Yosef among them. Nicanor had maneuvered them to be closest to the rear rank of the auxiliaries supporting the siege engines, which included Sayid's unit. Behind them came the cohort leaders with their select units, then marchers with the Roman flag, and standard bearers with the golden eagle. The legions' *aquila* preceded the trumpeters. Then came the massive body of legionaries in their ranks six abreast. Finally, the wave was followed by the mercenaries in the rearguard and the legion servants.

As they entered Gophna, Yosef commented, "One hundred and ten years ago, your General Cassius sold Gophna's population into slavery for failure to pay taxes. Then Marcus Antonius freed them shortly after he came to power. But since their surrender two years ago, General Vespasian has held several rabbis and local leaders here." A handful of minutes later, as the leading edge of the column entered the gates of the Roman encampment, Yosef turned in his saddle. "You asked me about Yeshua ish Natzrat... if he is the messiah. There is a story of a local man who visited Jerusalem during Yeshua's last days. He claims to have seen him, Yeshua, return from the dead. At that, he immediately became a follower, a Christian. He came home to Gophna and told his wife what he saw, and she refused to believe him unless the rooster she had just killed returned to life. As she mocked him, the rooster arose and flew away toward that mountain." Yosef pointed south of the town. "Now it's called Mount of the Rooster."

Nicanor laughed. "Is the story of a mistaken woman all it takes to convince people to believe in this messiah, the Christ?"

"We both saw in Rome that Yeshua's followers believed strongly enough in him to die themselves to follow him and spread the word of his teaching. But I do not believe Yeshua ish Natzrat is the messiah my people watch for. Although the people's passion suggests there's more to his followers' belief in him than mere stories. You have told me in Rome you found Paul's stories interesting, and they made you think."

"Hmmph...." Nicanor grunted as he turned Albus off the main road toward the huge cleared area for the massive influx of troops. They would camp here.

*　*　*

THE ROMAN CAMP

The night was still crisp, but they needed only enough fire to warm their meal and offer light for the three men sitting around it.

"So, your father is your commanding officer?" Nicanor asked as he set his empty mug between his feet, reached for the waterskin beside his campstool, refilled the mug, and pulled his cloak up farther on his shoulders. He looked again at Sayid. "Was that ordered intentionally... on purpose?"

"Not mine... but his, I think." Sayid shifted uncomfortably on the folding camp stool.

"Maybe he realizes now that you are a good soldier, worth having under his command." Nicanor almost made the mistake of saying, 'Worth watching over.' Sayid had seemed hesitant to accept Nicanor's invitation to join him for the evening meal once the camp had settled. He looked across the flickering flames at the young Syrian, acknowledging again to himself that Sayid had become a man and a comrade worth respecting.

"Where's Yosef?" Sayid asked.

"He dines with General Titus, who wanted to talk to him about what he plans to say to his people when we reach Jerusalem." Nicanor paused. "I haven't spoken of it... but I apologize if you think I was rude to your father when you introduced me to him."

"My *father* was rude," Sayid said with a shake of his head, and Nicanor let it go as the younger man shifted the subject back. "So, Yosef will try to get them to surrender the city?"

"Yes." Nicanor couldn't help the conflicting thoughts he knew must cross and clash in his expression, which must be apparent to Sayid.

"What's wrong with that?" the Syrian asked.

Nicanor looked at Sayid for a moment before answering. "Yosef does not realize—or chooses to ignore—that the conditions of Jerusalem's surrender do not mean returning to the way things were before."

"When I was in Jerusalem with Lady Cleo," Sayid said, "from what I learned of the factions within the city, it seemed they'd never accept Roman rule again. I cannot see any good outcome for them."

"Or for Yosef," Nicanor said. "If they surrender, they will live as enslaved people, and Yosef will blame himself for helping to convince them to surrender. If they fight, Titus will kill all he must... to get what he wants from the city, and any survivors will become enslaved. Then he will take whatever value remains and destroy the city. If the leaders in Jerusalem don't listen to Yosef, the people will be slaughtered, imprisoned, and sold. The city will be destroyed. Yosef might believe it was not his fault and that he had done what he could to help them. But I doubt that will be much comfort. And few of his countrymen will see it that way."

Nicanor sighed and looked up at the moon rising in the night sky and then at Sayid, who sat with his head down, staring at his clasped hands before him. "Soon, our friend will have much to deal with," the tribunus said, and I wonder how he will cope." Even as he said it, his thoughts went to Cleo. *Does she still live?* How could he find out... how could he find her... in the chaos Jerusalem would become once the siege began?

ACT III

XC

Aprilus 70 CE

Near Jerusalem, Gibeon

Nicanor returned from Titus's staff meeting to find Yosef sitting outside their tent, staring south down the length of the descending valley. "What do you look at?" he asked as he settled on a stool beside him.

"This is called the Valley of Thorns," Yosef said, sweeping his hand in an arc. "We're only four miles from Jerusalem."

"I've been here before, though I did not know the name of this valley when I was with the 12th Legion on our retreat from Jerusalem." Nicanor had no wish to tell Yosef how close they were to Beth Horon. The site of the 12th Legion's ignominious defeat and where the men he commanded had been killed—they were decoys to enable the legion's escape in the night. Sayid had been wounded in that battle and barely survived—but not his poor warhorse, Abigieus. His fingers traced the scars on his face and neck, pushing away the memories that had become nightmares for months. "Titus plans to take a force of 600 to observe Jerusalem before the siege begins."

"When?" asked Yosef.

"Tiberius Alexander is forming them up now."

"What can General Titus see today that he could not see tomorrow when he brings all the legions before Jerusalem's walls?"

"I don't know, but he wants to see today what his legions will begin to take tomorrow."

"When I dined with him," Yosef said, "he told me that once the siege starts, when my people see what they face, perhaps they will surrender. If the people of Jerusalem can overcome the power of the Zealots and the seditious and if they truly want peace."

"Do you believe they will?" Nicanor asked as he entered the tent, came out with his chest and back plate armor, and began to put them on.

"I pray they do," Yosef replied, looking questioningly at him. "Are you going with General Titus?"

"Yes, and you are, too. Bring your shield."

* * *

Near Jerusalem's Walls

Yosef knew Nicanor had seen Jerusalem twice before. The tribunus said he did not relish thinking about what it would take to breach the walls, even with Titus's greater force and resources. This time the Jews had had over three years to prepare instead of three months. Every Zealot in the country was behind those walls. Three walls fortified Jerusalem in the areas of the city not protected by two steep ravines, where they had only one wall. The city sat on two hills opposite one another, with a third valley dividing them within the walls. The hill containing the Upper City was much higher and had a straighter ridge line than the lower part of Jerusalem. The Temple complex with Antonia Fortress sat atop the lower hill, and the rows of houses on each hill seemed to begin and end at the edge of those walls.

Nicanor shifted in his saddle to look at him. "How long has it been since you left?"

"Three years." Yosef did not turn from the city. They were not close enough to see it, but he knew the ramparts would be lined with men, all gaping at the mass of Romans on the road leading to the gates of the western outer wall. He considered that he should have avoided the destiny—the duty—he now believed was his. Something in him wished he had drawn a different lot in Yotapta. If he had, his remains would have long ago become part of the ground beneath the rubble of its walls and buildings, among the bones of all who had died fighting beside and for him.

Yosef finally broke his gaze to turn to Nicanor. He had never sat alongside someone tasked with attacking Jerusalem, who saw his city only as an objective to be accomplished. An obstacle to remove... a people to be beaten into submission. He looked at his city and tried to see it through Roman eyes, dispassionately and gauging.

The four towers on the west side appeared much more elevated because of the high ground from which they rose. Even though Yosef had grown up with them, the gigantic stones seemed marvelous to him after not seeing them for three years. They were not common stones, as were the walls of Yotapta, nor even stones that a man or two men might be able to carry. These were stones of fine limestone cut out of King Solomon's quarry. Some were 30 feet long by 15 feet wide by seven and a half feet deep. They were so perfectly fitted together that each tower seemed formed of one massive stone carved and polished by the skilled hands of Jerusalem's stone cutters. The rocks were so tightly joined that their joints were almost

FINAL SIEGE

imperceptible. And each had a glacis and dry moat at its base, an angled set of blocks that would deflect any siege ram. All had been designed by Herod with the best Roman engineering.

A ripple of movement broke Yosef's concentration. He saw Nicanor rise higher in his saddle to look ahead to the leading element of the six hundred, General Titus, at its center.

"The general is moving us closer."

Yosef heard the concern in Nicanor's voice and watched him grow tense as Titus led a group of his men up the road that ran straight to the city gates. The formation pulled up, and cavalry wings flanked out to face the walls. They could now clearly see men upon the walls, some scurrying along the parapets and descending into the city while others raced up to reinforce those remaining. But nobody came forward to call out to the Romans nor came from the gates.

Titus rode forward with some of his men toward the nearest tower. "That's Psephinus," Yosef told Nicanor as they watched. "It is 115 feet tall. The Gate of the Women's Towers is near its base."

Psephinus was octagonal and situated near the northwest corner of the city walls. To Yosef, those towers were larger, more beautiful, and stronger than others in the known world. Herod had been a great benefactor to the city. Though he built these impressive structures to satisfy and gratify his affectation. He dedicated them to the memory of those most dear to him: his brother, friend, and wife. Hippicus, named for Herod's friend, was a square tower that rose 45 feet above the wall and was also built of enormous stones bonded together to seem like one piece. It held a reservoir 30 feet deep, over which a two-story house rose another 40 feet. Over this were battlements three feet high and turrets of almost five feet, so the tower's entire height was about 120 feet. Herod's second tower, named for his brother, Phasael, was 30 feet square. Its solid stone base rows were 30 feet in height, over which a 15-foot-high cloister was shielded from enemy missiles by breastworks within the walls. Over the cloister was another tower adorned with more battlements and turrets than were the others. Its entire height also reached almost 120 feet. Now that he had been to Alexandria, Yosef could see how it resembled the Tower of Pharos, which held a fiery beacon to warn sailors as they approached that splendid harbor. But Phasael was much larger in diameter than Pharos.

Pride swelled within Yosef as he thought of how his people's buildings matched many magnificent structures he had seen. Miriamne, the third tower and named for Herod's queen, was solid rock 30 feet wide and deep. Though it was shorter at only 75 feet, its upper structure was more magnificent and varied than the designs of the other towers.

Shouts and a claxon blast from a Roman bugler broke Yosef's reverie.

"That's a recall!" Nicanor shouted and rose again to watch as hundreds of rebel fighters charged out of the gate at the tower's base to intercept Titus and his men as they approached the tower. The rebel force cut off Titus's smaller group of horsemen from the main cavalry on the road. "He can't move forward to curl around to outflank the rebels, for those trenches protecting the base of the wall are in front of him."

Yosef looked where Nicanor pointed at the channels cut into the hard-packed earth around the walls. Those were new to him, an additional defense someone had wisely constructed. Titus couldn't return to the main body of his men, with the Jews between them outnumbering his men, and there was no way to outmaneuver them. As he and Nicanor watched, Titus, his standard-bearer at his side, wheeled his horse around and cried out to those with him to follow. Then Titus galloped violently into the midst of the Jews to cut his way through to his own forces. It suddenly registered with Yosef that Titus had neither his helmet nor his breast armor on; he had not expected an attack. Still, Titus ran over anyone in his path with a sword in hand, his horse's hooves pounding them into the ground.

The Jews cried out at Titus's boldness and shouted to one another to kill the Roman general. Yosef had to quell his desire to cheer the rebel fighters as they renewed their efforts to reach the emperor's son. The men surrounding the general quickly took arrows through their chests and backs, reeling in their saddles. Many fell as the archers on the city walls rained arrows upon them. But the ones left formed a screen shielding Titus so he and his escort could cut through the Jewish attackers. The blast of another bugle call sounded as Titus escaped with a few of his men and safely returned to the Roman lines.

A thousand voices from the walls jeered the Romans' retreat.

"It seems your people would rather curse at us than talk peace," commented Nicanor. "And nearly killing Titus won't help their position... it will only increase the legions' wrath."

XCI

Aprilus 70 CE

Jerusalem

The Roman Encampment Outside the Western Wall

All the legions still trembled with the shock of almost losing their commanding general, the emperor's oldest son, within an hour of sighting the walls of Jerusalem. Nicanor knew General Titus needed better preparation to avoid being surprised again. Titus had ordered him to take the next steps methodically. So Nicanor had gone to requisition Sayid's help that morning. Marcus Sabinus had not been happy, and Sayid even less so, if possible.

With a large escort, the commanding general had gone to meet with the commander of the 10th, *Fretensis*, Marcus Ulpius Trajanus. That legion was working to resurrect the 12th Legion's encampment on Mt. Scopus from four years before and fortify it. A mile north of Jerusalem, Mount Scopus loomed 200 feet over the almost 3000-foot-high plateau Jerusalem sat upon. Titus had taken Yosef with him to view the city from that vantage point and answer questions about it.

Nicanor had elected to remain at the base camp erected for the legions 5th, *Macedonia*, 12th, *Fulminata*, and 15th, *Apollinaris*. He had requested a copy of the map prepared for the Jerusalem siege by cartographers back in Caesarea. The map was spread on a table outside his tent, and he regretted it was too large to fit inside. "What do you recall from when you were with Lady Cleo in the city?" he asked Sayid.

"We were careful to stay out of sight as much as possible and, at first, did not walk about. But later, I noticed the gates had been strengthened compared to what I saw before. There were reinforced beams on the doors and stonework added on either side, where the gate doors were mounted."

"I saw the trench network outside the gate area of the west outer wall," said Nicanor. "How far do they run, and are there any running parallel inside the walls?"

"The trenches weren't there when I was last here... so, I do not know. The outer wall will be hard to breach—you have seen its height.

The ramparts are 15 feet wide, so there is plenty of room for *ballistae* and two-man *scorpios* to throw stones or shafts from the wall. There are 90 watchtowers 400 feet apart. The second and first walls within the city are also nearly as thick and 45 feet high. They secure inner city sections, and each has dozens of watchtowers." Sayid lifted a charcoal stick and marked the map to show their locations.

Two men came to them from around the side of their tent. "So, you've both been to Jerusalem before and know the city?" asked Tiberius Alexander.

Nicanor worried how long the two had lurked there, listening. He nodded to the Aegyptus Prefect, General Titus's second-in-command. "I've been in Jerusalem twice, sir, the last time with Lord Cestius Gallus and the 12th Legion."

"Ahhh... a poor commander and a terrible defeat," Tiberius Alexander commented and swung his gaze to Sayid. He seemed nonplussed at finding a Syrian auxiliary sitting with a Roman tribunus as if they were friends, talking about a city's defenses. "You have been in Jerusalem also?"

Sayid glanced at Nicanor before answering: "Yes, lord. When I accompanied Lady Cleo and again when serving in the 12th Legion under Lord Gallus."

"Lady Cleo? She who abandoned Lord Gessius Florus?" The prefect shook his head and glanced at the man with him. "Who knows what crimes she runs from? Do you think the rumor is true... that she hides with the rebels inside Jerusalem?"

Nicanor felt his jaw clench and the muscles in the forearm nearest his pugio flex. He forced himself to relax.

"Perhaps you should add this auxiliary to your staff, lord," said Lucius Serrenus, the legion *summus curator,* leaning over the map to inspect Sayid's marks. He laughed and turned to Tiberius Alexander. "If we may go, sir, I must show you where the wagons, draft, and pack animals are staged, as you requested."

A camp courier raced up before the two men walked away. "General Alexander, I bring a message from General Titus." The man handed a scroll to the Aegyptus Prefect. Alexander unrolled it, and a stern expression formed and hardened on his face. "We'll look at that later, Lucius. Still, come with me." The men strode away.

Once they were out of hearing range, Nicanor turned to the courier, still catching his breath. "What did the message say?"

The auxiliary courier shook his head and said, "I must return to my post."

Nicanor gripped the young courier's arm. "It was unsealed—I know you likely read it."

"It said the rebels have sortied from the city," he said quickly, twisting out of Nicanor's grasp. "They killed many men from the 10th Legion who cleared the area between their encampment and the city's eastern wall. General Titus would lead a counterattack." The soldier hurried away.

"Yosef's people are brave," Sayid commented.

Nicanor turned to sit again before the map, his finger tracing the Kidron Valley east of the city up to the slope of Mount Scopus. "Yes. But that means more of them will die... their courage will not save them."

XCII

Aprilus 70 CE

Near the Modi'in Valley

Miriam followed the surprisingly sure-footed Ya'el through the narrow course that cut through the high shoulder of a craggy hillock. The fading light cast by a waning sun did little to help their footing on the rough trail of uneven, brown-gray dirt, loose rocks, and ridges of upthrust stone. The blanket roll containing her bow and quiver, now slung across Ya'el's shoulders, barely dipped side to side as her gait and balance adjusted as they climbed. Miriam shifted her steps and weight away from where the crumbling trail dropped off into the ravine below. She said, "Watch for a level open area to make camp, and we'll stop for the night."

At first, she had bristled at the thought that Ya'el was better suited to lead them from Jerusalem to the valley where her ancestor was buried. But Matthew was right. She had never traveled alone outside Jerusalem, and Ya'el had. And when she did travel with a group, it was never on rough paths through rugged terrain like this. Once they were outside the city, on the northern route to Shechem, she worried about the next westward turn when they reached the landmark. The trail followed the contours of the land, rising and falling to twine its way for miles through gulches and gorges, up and over terrain that seemed to repeat itself.

Miriam could easily navigate the maze of streets in the Upper and Lower City, the City of David, and even below ground in the tunnels. But the open sky, craggy rocks, escarpments, the rills and gullies, and the myriad sensations and sounds were so different from the city. It was disconcerting, which must have shown. Because an hour into the trek, Ya'el said: "When I told Matthew I could help you, he told me Sayid had described our trek with Elian from Ptolemais to Jerusalem through groups of Romans, rebels, and bandits. That's why I could help. I learned from Sayid how to make a concealed camp, start a fire, find water, and forage for food. I even learned how to use the night and morning stars as a guide. That made him feel better. Do not worry—I will help."

So Miriam had waved Ya'el forward to take the lead, wondering if Ya'el's experience and confidence had silenced his objections. But for

Miriam, nightfall was worrisome. She had long ago come to grips with the darkness in Jerusalem's tunnels, streets, and alleys. She had lived a nightmare beneath Jerusalem, in a blackness that consumed her recollections. The ordeal almost consumed her, but for Zechariah and all she learned from him. She learned that darkness could be dealt with and could become an advantage. So, she accepted that idea and now moved easily in its realms. But the darkness within tunnels and on narrow city streets was not like this.

Miriam scanned the area outside the tiny arc of light of the small fire Ya'el had built in a scooped-out hole and banked against the flat stones she gathered. Shielded by the rocks and a blanket strung up to screen the side away from the cliff face, the fire was almost indiscernible, a dim glow only for someone nearby. Beyond that firelight, things moved in the night, making unfamiliar noises through the soft sough of the wind.

Miriam turned back to Ya'el, both women purposefully not staring into the fire, so they preserved their vision to better watch their surroundings. Miriam had learned from Zechariah not to stare at any torch or lamp light in the tunnels: "You will never see what is in the darkness if you gaze at the light." It seemed Sayid had taught the same lesson to Ya'el.

With a sigh, Miriam answered the question Ya'el had asked moments before. "Zechariah told me he wrote to his wife and daughter so they would always live in his mind and heart. He said that by doing that, he never felt alone."

"I read and reread those letters you brought me," Ya'el said with a nod of understanding. "In the later ones to his wife, it was good to see that Zechariah cared enough for you to tell her about you. And he wrote of how his daughter, had she lived, would be your age."

More moments passed, and the cool night wind picked up. Miriam drew her cloak closer around her. "He saved me, but I lost him...."

"Still, you're not alone, Miriam. You have your family, and you have Elian and me." Ya'el paused. "You *could* have Ya'akov."

"For how long? There is no future, Ya'el. We'll return to see the Romans at our walls and the beginning of the end."

"Until that end, whether weeks or months, you could be with him. Do you care for Ya'akov... did you not love him?"

"At one time, I did... not as I loved Ehud, but enough. There's no time now, and I think Hananiah will kill him if I do not continue to turn him away. If Hananiah thinks I care for him...."

Rising above the wind, the call of a jackal echoed among the hills, and she turned her head one way and another to study the night. "Hananiah thinks his opportunity is coming and will act soon."

"Because the Romans are here?"

"I think so, and I must find out what he plans to do for Gessius Florus."

* * *

Daybreak...

THE MODI'IN VALLEY, THE TOMB OF THE MACCABEES

As Miriam trusted Ya'el with the directions from her mother, her thoughts shifted to stories Rebecca had told her and her brothers when they were children. How the land she and Ya'el now walked upon had been the place of battles fought long ago against the Canaanites and others who continually tried to subjugate her people and their faith. There were few settlements in the barren landscape they traversed. But revolutionaries and fugitives—her ancestors—found it a perfect place to hide and from which to mount their rebellions.

Rocks, whole and shards, had tumbled from the peak and littered their way down onto the valley floor. As they climbed the narrow path and drew nearer the crest, Miriam could see shapes like those her mother had described. The stone structures seemed dug into the hill, and columns rose from the ground to gabled roofs.

The two women reached the summit and made their way toward the central, largest building, and they found the wind had carried dirt and dried brush over the rugged land to collect at the entrance. The buildings clearly had not been visited in some time. *Perhaps because of the Romans*, Miriam thought. Even though it was important to her mother, she had not been here in decades.

As the stories went, a rabbi named Mattathias had rebelled against the Seleucid king Antiochus, who all but banned the practice of their faith. Antiochus had placed a statue of his people's god, Zeus, in the great Temple in Jerusalem. In response, Mattathias and his five sons raised an army and fought against that Hellenistic rule. When Mattathias died, his son Judah took over as leader, defeated the Greek Seleucids, and retook the Temple. That victory freed their country and launched the Hasmonean dynasty. When the Temple was re-dedicated and worship allowed again, the victorious Jews could find only one jar of the holy olive oil needed to burn constantly to cleanse the Temple. Yet that single container of oil burned for eight days. The sacred, cleansing flame was kept alight until they found more holy oil. They now celebrated that miraculous event each winter.

Within the shelter of the massive, deep stone lintel of the entrance, Miriam's cloak no longer whipped around her. She placed both hands on the broad door and pushed. It took effort, but with Ya'el's help, the door gave way and opened with a rasp of its wood on the gritty stone floor. Inside, she took out her hand lamp and struck sparks to ignite the wick. The small light revealed a prominent central chamber in the mausoleum. To the left was a single crypt, and a more sizable vault came into view on the right as she moved farther inside. Then Miriam stooped and entered the *kokh*, the low vault, for a single burial. She stepped down into a square pit cut into the floor. Before her, in the wall opposite the entry, was a long narrow recess and a stone chest. Miriam swept her hand over the ossuary's carving and held her lamp close to read its inscription.

"Who is it?" Ya'el asked

"Mattathias, the Hasmonean."

"I thought your ancestors were Maccabees. Is he the one you seek?"

"No, he's the father... I seek his oldest son, Judah, who became known as the Maccabee... the Hammer." Miriam backed out of the pit, waving Ya'el from the entrance where she crouched. She crossed the central chamber to the other opening, Ya'el following. Within the antechamber, Miriam bent to enter the far larger vault. Inside, along the facing wall, was an *arcosolia*. The ledge was carved into the stone, as was a recess within the arched ceiling of rock. On the shelf within were five limestone chests similar to the one she had just seen. Miriam went to each from right to left, smoothing away dust from the letters carved into each casket so that she could read them. "Here are the five brothers who took up arms when their father died—they revolted against the Seleucid Empire."

Miriam returned to the center ossuary and said, "This one is Judah's. Help me open it."

Ya'el moved to her side and gripped the stone lid of the ossuary, pausing when Miriam did not move to lift her end.

Miriam had had misgivings about disturbing her ancestor's bones until her mother had explained: "He is your family. You, through me, are of his bloodline. You are like his granddaughter... seeking to save your people, as he did. You will not trouble his peace, nor will what you place among his bones."

She took a deep breath, nodded to Ya'el, and lifted. Carefully setting the lid aside, Miriam took from her pack the small, sealed, earthenware jar Matthew had given her. Within it was the parchment, the key to the copper scroll. Yohanan ben Zaccai had told Matthew the parchment had been prepared with a preservative coating of a salt he had gotten from the Essenes. She carefully nestled it among the crumbling bones and prayed all would remain at peace until the Temple treasure could be restored.

* * *

THE HIDDEN VALLEY NEAR MOTZA

As they neared Jerusalem, the women realized a large group of men on horseback were not far behind them. At first, Miriam had worried that they must run to lose them... but where? They could not outdistance horses, and if they fled into the nearby range of hill caves, when would they be able to come out again and reach Jerusalem? Then Ya'el had observed that the horsemen moved at a walk—they drew no closer. So, they continued but at a faster pace, despite their fatigue. They had just entered the hidden valley to find it empty, with no sign of a camp. Arins and his men were gone.

They were halfway across the valley floor when the thud of pounding hooves shook Miriam from the plodding stupor of exhaustion. She gathered what little energy she had left, grabbed Ya'el's arm, and yelled, "Run!" The echoing clatter of armored cavalry grew louder behind them.

XCIII

Aprilus 70 CE

Jerusalem

The Roman Encampment Just west of Jerusalem

"Were you in the fighting?" asked Nicanor.

"No," replied Yosef. "Titus and I were up on a promontory at the Mount of Olives, overlooking the city, when reports came to him. The workers assigned to clear the lower area of Mount Scopus, leveling and flattening the land to make it more traversable from the base into the Kidron Valley, were under attack. A force of," Yosef paused, and Nicanor realized he had wanted to say 'my people,' "streamed out of the city. Titus summoned a cohort from the 10th Legion, and with heavy infantry and cavalry support, we went to the fighting. The commander there told us that the workers dropped their tools and ran when the rebels came from behind the walls. Even those with weapons turned their backs on the rebels and did not stand their ground. Many were killed before they could face the enemy. Then more rebels swept into the valley to join the attack. I could hear their shouts, celebrating that they'd made the Romans run."

As Roman soldiers arrived, the workers regrouped and forced the rebels back. They retreated toward the city as we watched. Once they were on the rise back up to the city, they turned, faced the Romans, and fought them fiercely hand-to-hand. Then more men poured from the city, and soon that part of the Kidron was full of fighting men. That's when Titus left me with an escort and descended into the valley to rally his men with a mix of heavy infantry and cavalry. I could hear him exhorting the men to stand their ground and fight. With 60 of his cavalrymen, Titus led the attack on the rebel's flank and turned them back toward the city. Then the men on the valley floor followed him, pressing the attack on the retreating rebels."

"Vespasian's son is brave," Nicanor mused and almost mentioned seeing Titus in the field at Yotapta but not directly in combat with Yosef's forces. He knew the young general wished to prove himself to his father. He studied his friend, whose downcast demeanor had deepened further since returning to their camp. "So, the real fighting begins... you knew it must, Yosef."

"Yes, but it still saddens me. What pains me most is that I looked down on my city from the Mount of Olives and could see its parts damaged from fighting—but not by Roman hands. Deserters from the city captured last night say the city is overfull. I saw that, too, in the spread of tents across Bezetha and other formerly open areas in Jerusalem. I have never seen the city so full of people.

"Titus had me interpret when he questioned the fugitives. They also said the hostilities between Yohanan ben Levi and Simon bar Giora had destroyed almost all the city's grain stores. I was not surprised at those two fighting but at their stupidity. Their need for power had led to destroying food, which shocked me. I accused the deserters of telling lies. One spat upon me, calling me a traitor even as he pleaded with Titus for his freedom. He again claimed he told the truth of how Jerusalem's leaders had turned upon each other. Then from our position, I could see where the granaries and storage had been burned to ashes. The truth was there before my eyes."

"Did Titus free the man?"

"No," said Yosef. "The general ordered him and the others captured to be taken to a camp to the north. It is a camp under construction for Gaius Aeterius Fronto and his men. I've not heard of that Roman. Who is he?"

"An eques, an imperial administrator from Alexandria, with Tiberius Alexander's staff. General Titus has assigned him responsibility for the rebels captured during the siege and afterward." Nicanor did not elaborate that Fronto would be in charge of selling Yosef's people into slavery.

The surrounding camp buzzed with organized activity. Yosef watched as cohorts of legionaries moved past them. "Is that the 12th Legion?"

Nicanor nodded. "Tiberius Alexander asked General Titus if the 12th could be positioned between the northern gates. So, they move there."

"Has Titus decided where he will attack first?"

"Siege towers and engines are positioned outside the gate leading to the Joppa Road. Sayid is there now, helping to assemble the towers." With a grunt, Nicanor stood. "Let's see how he fares."

**

OUTSIDE THE WESTERN WALL NEAR THE JOPPA GATE

There was no movement along the walls, and it was eerily silent save for the grunts and curses of men, the braying of mules, and the barks of commands from officers. They had already unloaded wagons of smoothed stones at points where the siege line formed. Catapults and ballistae were in varying setup stages, with only a few completed and in position. Behind them was the staging area for the significant components of the siege towers being hoisted into place, joined, and tested. "The engineers have smoothed the ground up to the trenches," Nicanor said as he pointed after reigning Albus to a stop behind the siege line. "When the siege commences, they'll either fill in the trenches to get the machines and towers closer, or the underminers will use the trenches for cover for their work." Nicanor studied the area. He saw Sayid, who raised a hand in greeting and then returned to his labor. His father, Marcus Sabinus, strode from machine to machine among the bustling men, speaking to some and shouting commands or curses at others who lagged in their work. The auxiliary officer saw him watching, gave a curt nod, and moved on.

"This one's not complete. Why do the men move it forward?" Yosef pointed at one of the siege towers rolled closer to the gate. It was only three-quarters assembled—up to the platform just before the top piece. Nicanor motioned to dismount, and they led their horses to the side, away from the still massive partial tower as it slowly moved past them. The staccato clop and stomp of several horses coming to a stop on packed earth behind them made them turn. Titus, accompanied by a sizable escort, beckoned to them in full armor and helmet. The sun was low on the horizon behind him, casting Titus's shadow over them as they stopped beside his mount.

"When it is in place," Titus said as he gestured toward the partially assembled siege tower, "when the heavy ballistae are ready, you will call to your people. Offer them an opportunity to discuss their surrender with me."

He turned to Nicanor. "Tribunus, you and a handful of men go on the tower with him."

Nicanor saluted and saw the emotion on Yosef's face as he thanked General Titus. He could not tell if it was hope or dread his friend felt.

* * *

The sun was much lower, and no one from the walls had replied to Yosef's calls to speak with Yohan ben Levi or Simon bar Giora... or both men. Yosef had stood there for an hour, periodically shouting his request. He was accompanied by Nicanor and five other legionaries in armor and carrying their scuta, the shields they would use to protect Yosef if his people fired at them.

"They must be waiting until we bring up more towers and machines and then try to destroy them where they are more exposed," Nicanor remarked.

"Yes... that was what we did at Yotapta," Yosef replied, his voice a dry rasp and his eyes never leaving the ramparts of the walls.

Nicanor glanced over his shoulder at the last sliver of the sun and then at the city. He heard Yosef mutter, "So ends the Feast of Unleavened Bread...."

"What's that about bread?" Nicanor asked, but the movement below made him look toward General Titus, hoping for a signal to come down from the tower. He did not care to remain a promising target for the rebels. The Jews could decide it was time to fire upon the few Romans stupid enough to be so exposed.

"It is a time when my people remember our exodus from slavery in Aegypt over 1500 years ago when they gained their freedom from that oppression. Do you remember from your Passover visit four years ago?"

Nicanor saw Titus's hand move, but it was a gesture to the commanding officer of the ballistae, who ordered three *ballistarii* to load their weapons. All set, the officer looked at General Titus, who nodded. The ballistae released, and three nearly-75-pound rocks flew in arcs that took the stones through the last slanting rays of sunlight. Each missile became a bright white rough sphere streaking toward the wall.

Now a response came from the rebels. There was a cry that sounded like "The son cometh..." The heavy stones struck the wall with a thunderous multiplied crash. Nicanor saw Titus's order to reload and fire again. A token gesture until all the weapons were brought to the siege line. But still, it was a response to the silence of the Jews when Yosef called out to them. That silence foretold what was to come.

"What do they mean about the son coming?" Nicanor was puzzled as he heard that warning cry repeated along the wall ramparts.

"I think the watchmen mock Ya'akov, the brother of Yeshua ish Natzrat, a leader of the Christians. He spoke of Yeshua—after his death—as the messiah our people had long waited for."

"What happened to him?"

"Eight years ago, the High Priest, Ananus, ordered him thrown from the Temple wall here in Jerusalem. Yet the fall did not kill him, so they stoned him. As he died, he told them, 'The Son of Man is about to come in the clouds of Heaven.'"

The meaning of the Jewish rebels still baffled Nicanor as he watched the second salvo of three stones, bright in the waning sunlight, as it struck a wall section. The rebels there prepared for the impact by tracking the stone's flight. Two thoughts came to him: they must darken the missiles to make them harder to see, and with the crash of the first stones against Jerusalem's walls, a statement was made. What was to come was a foregone conclusion. This time there would be no exodus for the Jews. He could not tell and would not ask, but he thought he caught the glint of tears on Yosef's face as they climbed down the tower.

XCIV

Maius 70 CE

Jerusalem

The Upper City

Miriam and Matthew were alone in the courtyard as day broke over the city. It was quiet now, a peace they had come to cherish in these hours together. But that would soon end. With the day came the sounds from outside the city walls. A din that grew with the work of the Romans. There would be a multitude of harsh sounds from thousands of men's labor and machines, where there were no sounds before, and all the clamor had been inside the city. That unfamiliar human and animal noise added to the buzzing within Jerusalem, and the constant hum heightened the sense of fear in every man, woman, and child. Soon would come the first stirrings in protest of the food rationing as many people woke each day with hunger. Refugees, pilgrims, and the people of the Lower City were the most affected. These poor souls had come to Jerusalem because they feared the Romans who were now upon them. They'd been drawn to the city—even in such disarray—by the divine command to worship at the Temple. For the poor, life always had a narrow margin.

"I'm glad you two had no trouble returning to the city," Matthew said, "but you came very close to being overtaken by those men outside the hidden valley."

"They sounded like armored men on horseback to us. Arins says they were not his men, so they could have been only the Romans, but we should sneak into the valley to make sure."

Miriam was tired of arguing with Matthew. Since their return, he had insisted they be more careful, staying close to home or concealed in the underground chambers. It was understandable—they were all shocked at what had happened the day after they returned from the Modi'in Valley to her parents' welcome of joy. On that next day, Matthew had actually seen Yosef! He had almost called to him and would have, had Eleasar ben Ananias not convinced him not to. The men they were with were already angry at the news of what Yosef did at Qumran. Seeing him with the Roman army outside the walls of Jerusalem, acting as the Romans' spokesman, had incensed the men on the wall. They were ready to fire upon him and those who were with him.

Yohanan ben Levi and Simon bar Giora had stopped the hotheaded men because their targets had been outside the range of their best slingers and archers. "Say nothing," they told their men, "and when they come closer, and the shot is certain, kill Yosef first and then any others you can strike."

But Yosef had not moved closer, and soon Roman missiles were striking the city. Matthew's words to them after returning from the western wall stunned her and devastated her mother and father. "It is Yosef," he said. "I could see him clearly. He is clean-shaven, wears Roman robes, and has soldiers *escorting* him, not guarding him as a prisoner. I watched him on that Roman platform for an hour while he was calling to speak with Yohanan ben Levi and Simon bar Giora. Now all the city wishes to see him dead."

Miriam still did not understand how Yosef could ally with the Romans. Still, it seemed he had. His words had been an offer to discuss surrendering the city he had been born and raised in. As if the Roman general's offer could be considered trustworthy. If Yosef had mentioned peace, there might be a reason to speak with him, to speak with the Romans. All the loudest voices in the city agreed there would be no discussion of surrendering.

But it was clear what the Romans thought—next came the rain of heavy stones on the western wall, immediately after Yosef's plea to those on the wall. Offering to talk was a ploy to make it easier for the Romans, not for the Jews of Jerusalem.

"We've concealed the tunnel," Matthew said. "Arins says the outer entrance looks like just part of a cave now, not a tunnel. All the food Arins's men brought has been moved into the gallery beneath the Temple and divided among public storehouses under the control of men who can be trusted."

"What of Yohanan ben Levi and Simon bar Giora?" Miriam asked. "Are they not still at one another's throats?"

"Their men are on the walls and at critical areas of the city. The Gischalan's men routed the Romans in the Kidron Valley. They showed the Romans we can fight—and *will* fight."

"But we will lose, Miriam said.

"Yes," Matthew admitted. "Yosef was right years ago. We cannot stop the Romans. Still, I need you and Ya'el to focus on two things: find somewhere in the tunnels to take Mother, Father, Leah, and Rachel when the Romans break through the walls. Someplace no one can find without knowing how to reach it."

"What about you, Matthew? You must stay with them... they will need you."

"I ask the same of you, Miriam. I plead with you to join them and take Ya'el and Elian there when the walls are breached. If a safe place can be found, who knows? Some of you may survive long enough to escape once the Romans take the city. You know the tunnels better than I do. That is another reason you should plan to go with them. Also, you must try to find other ways into and out of Jerusalem... a different means of escape than others know about."

"What of the Temple treasure you still have left to hide? Do you still have plans for it?"

Matthew shrugged. "Maybe. But the most important treasure is our family, Miriam. Though I fear we've lost our brother, we must try to save everyone else."

* * *

Hananiah quickly turned away from watching Miriam's home when he spotted her leaving—he had not expected that. He knew she preferred to go through the rear courtyard to the alley and side streets on her way to the market. Miriam's awareness, comfort with silence, and desire for independent action had appealed to him since he first met her. Until Miriam, no woman had ever drawn his attention. The thrill of seduction was weaker to him than the thrill of stalking and killing someone... a sport and vocation that engaged all the senses. In the hunt and the kill, he had ultimate control. The feel of metal thrilled him, the exquisite pain when its finely honed edge parted the flesh with a bare touch, drawing blood—it was a pleasure he could not describe.

There had been few opportunities for killing, none since 'The Hand' had fled Jerusalem, taking with him the boy and the woman Gessius Florus sought. Now there was no one to hunt, but his latest message from the Roman nobleman—bought by the still unknown courier—had directed him to watch for a chance to take Matthew. If he delivered him, he would be paid handsomely—it would be enough money to escape and take Miriam with him. Long ago, she had wished not to see or be with her family—that was her true feeling. He would take her to a new life with him, thinking her brother had died with the rest of her family in the destruction of Jerusalem.

Hananiah straightened as Matthew came out of the house. He would follow him and learn the pattern of his movements. He would be ready once he was sure of his reward, and then he would seize it.

XCV

Maius 70 CE

Jerusalem

The Wall Near the Women's Gate

The lanky man climbed the steps to the battlements with the agility of a much younger man, outpacing the younger men weighed down by armor. He stepped onto the rampart at a watchtower and gate into what the Jews called the New City, Bezetha. Only in the sun's light did his cropped iron-gray hair, white-streaked beard, and seamed face show his age. He smoothed his beard with powerful hands as he looked out at the Roman line, then touched the braided cord about his lean waist as he moved along the parapet, watching for the signal. He unwound the long cord, feeling for the pouch halfway down its length. He pulled the drawstring of a small bag secured at his waist and selected from its contents. The men who had followed him up the steps spread out, giving him room, filling the ramparts on either side of the tower and gripping the hilts of their curved blades.

* * *

The Roman Encampment, the 5th and 15th Legions

Yosef looked up from the writing-filled parchment sheets on the table before him, leaves he would bind into his journals. He rubbed his weary and smoke-stung eyes and asked Nicanor, who had just returned, "Anything new come from your staff meeting with General Titus?"

"Patrols continue to pick up deserters, mostly city dwellers not used to night outside a city—they don't know to hide and keep still." Nicanor sighed and tugged at his beard. "One of them told Titus of a recent incident at your temple, Yosef. You—I mean, the rebels—have a leader called Yohanan ben Levi?"

Yosef nodded. "What has he done?"

"Apparently, he and his men killed many followers of one of the other rebel leaders... inside the temple. I believe Titus recalled the man, this Yohanan ben Levi, from when he and his men prepared to attack his town—Gischala. The man abandoned his city the night before the siege, leaving his people to face Titus's legion alone."

Yosef closed his eyes, feeling the anger surge through him that his city was partially in the hands of such a man. He breathed deeply to settle his emotions and then blinked at Nicanor. "Sit," he said, gesturing to a stool.

Nicanor shook his head. "I'm here to take you to Titus. He has questions for you."

"What questions?"

"About this Yohanan ben Levi, I think...."

* * *

GENERAL TITUS'S COMMAND TENT

The commanding general and Tiberius Alexander were seated at a huge campaign desk as Marcus Trajanus, commander of the 10th Legion, finished his report, and Yosef and Nicanor were shown in.

"General, as you ordered," said Marcus Trajanus, "I've moved the 10th Legion into the Kidron Valley nearer to the city. Engineers are directing the filling of ditches and chasms. The *immunes* and auxiliary laborers, protected by cavalry units on the flanks and a line of heavy infantry between them and the city, have broken down walls the Jews used to mark off their gardens. Destroying the crops and cutting down groves of fruit trees. I have 400 men with iron hammers who now level the rocky outcroppings of the valley slopes and floor to ease the movement of cavalry, men, and war machines. We'll be done in a few days and will move our siege engines to within range of the rebel walls."

"Good. Tomorrow I will come to see how you progress." Titus dismissed the legion commander, who nodded at Nicanor, squinted at Yosef, and left.

"So, Yosef," said Titus, "Has Nicanor told you what one of your countrymen told us... of Yohanan ben Levi?"

Yosef shook off his gloomy thoughts and said, "Yes, lord. It dismays me."

"Does this Yohanan ben Levi truly represent your people?"

"I wish it were not so, lord, but it does seem so. He, along with Simon bar Giora."

"I know something of Yohanan ben Levi—"

"I told Yosef of your experience with him, general," Nicanor interrupted.

"Then you know, Yosef, that I think little of him as a leader of men. What about this Simon bar Giora?"

"He is a more capable leader, lord, though he, too, desires to lead my people only to serve his own purpose."

"So, they fight and kill each other… even within your place of worship."

Yosef replied though it was not a question, "Yes, lord. It sickens me."

"Well," Tiberius Alexander said with a slight smile, "They help us by killing each other. But it is time to focus on our assault, and there's another question we need to ask of Josephus, General Titus."

Yosef ignored the name Tiberius Alexander used for him but saw the general's eyes cut sideways at his second-in-command.

"Where is the greatest weakness in Jerusalem's defenses?" Titus asked.

Yosef struggled to face the moment he had feared most. If he answered, he would prove himself the traitor his people likely believed he was. How, then, would he ever convince them otherwise? He was no traitor but must say nothing for that to remain true. He looked at Tiberius Alexander, who likely knew the answer because of his familiarity with Jerusalem. The Aegyptus Prefect's lips curled as he stared at Yosef. Time seemed to stop, deepening the silence, then Nicanor shifted a step toward the desk and the two generals.

"General Titus," he said, "I know the weakest section from my experience with the 12th Legion. It's near here."

Titus turned his gaze from Yosef to Nicanor. "Take Yosef with you and see if it seems as you recall." His eyes went back to Yosef. "Determine whether your people have made any defensive improvements that change Nicanor's assessment."

"I will go with them, General Titus," Tiberius Alexander said as he stood, "and I will report back to you."

XCVI

Maius 70 CE

Jerusalem

The Wall Near the Women's Gate

Yosef had seen Nicanor glance at him several times after leaving General Titus. It made him uneasy, so he remained quiet as he strode north with the two Roman officers along the siege line. They were close enough to their camp that Tiberius Alexander had deemed an escort unnecessary, which seemed odd to Yosef. But he let it go and wrestled with his feeling of being trapped in the expectation that he would help Titus with military advice. Nicanor had saved him from the general's probing question, but Yosef had seen Titus's expression. If the general asked for military details about the rebels or his city's defenses, how could he evade answering them?

Nicanor broke in on his thoughts. "In all my service, I've known only one or two slingers—both mercenaries from the Balearic Islands off the coast of Hispania—who might reach this far."

"Many Jews train as slingers," Yosef commented. "A past great king of Israel had a great skill at slinging—which he practiced endlessly while guarding sheep as a boy. In one battle, he killed a giant that all the soldiers feared."

"Stay to my left, Yosef," ordered Nicanor. "You wear no armor."

Yosef glanced at his friend, noting that he had worn the unadorned armor of a centurion in the field: *lorica hamata*, chain mail, instead of the plate armor, *lorica segmentata*. He carried an infantryman's shield and wore greaves that protected his legs from knees to the *caligae* on his feet. The heavy-soled sandals were the same worn by the legionaries in the ranks. His cloak was simple and brown... just like the one Yosef wore. But when they left Titus's campaign tent, Nicanor had donned a centurion's *galea*, the helmet with its transverse crest of horsehair. In his usual practicality had foregone the *torques* and *phalerae* that would display on his torso the awards he had won in battle.

Yosef studied Tiberius Alexander on Nicanor's left. The Aegyptus Prefect was resplendent in pristine scale armor, bronze chest and back plate, and ornate helmet. All perfect and unmarred by the nicks, cuts, and dents of having been in combat. His scarlet cloak billowed around him like a martial cloud of command authority.

Yosef knew where Nicanor was taking them. North of the city was the only area suited to support an assault, despite its reinforced walls. He was sure Titus knew this, and battle maps showing the best approach and means of attack from the north had long been prepared. Except for a swath of land around the western wall, the deep ravines of the Hinnom Valley to the south and west and the Kidron Valley to the east made attack difficult from those three sides of the city. The 10th Legion could successfully attack the city walls from their new position. But they would have to fight uphill to enter the city through any breach. The northern area had the only sizable level plain from which the legions could both breach the walls and attack with enough men to clear the defenders from their path and penetrate deeply into Jerusalem. Knowing this, King Agrippa I had reinforced these walls years before.

As they neared the Women's Gate, over small, loose stones that littered the ground, Tiberius Alexander, who had moved next to Yosef as if to study the city walls, stumbled. He caught himself by grabbing Yosef's shoulder. The motion turned both men toward the crenelated battlements. Yosef felt the Aegyptus Prefect grip him harder, not letting go. Instinctively, Yosef shrugged him off, twisting away, but his still-weak ankle buckled, and he staggered. Nicanor stepped toward him to offer a steadying hand. Just then, Yosef felt more than heard something streaking past his head and cracking into Nicanor's shoulder, and his friend went down with a grunt of pain.

Yosef bent down to Nicanor and saw a lead bullet on the ground, now slightly deformed from the impact. He picked it up, tucked it into the sash at his waist, and knelt to help Nicanor stand.

The shouts behind them made both men look for the cause of the noise. A flood of rebels came through a small door inset in the Women's Gate. Yosef hurried to Nicanor, and the tribunus, his right hand pressed against his left shoulder, cursed as Yosef helped him onto his feet. "Where did Tiberius Alexander go?" he growled.

Yosef pivoted, searched, and pointed at the swirling red cloak as it passed behind the wall of shields at the siege line. "We need to fall back, too," Yosef said. He had no desire to be taken by his people. It might not be the reunion he had once wished for.

Nicanor grunted as he looked over his good shoulder at the Jews outside the wall. "What are they doing? They look unarmed and act like they've been chased from the city."

Several stones thrown from the walls landed near the rebels.

"What do they shout?" Nicanor asked, each step making him bite his lip. He stared at the men who seemed confused about whether to run toward the Roman line or back to their city.

Yosef stopped then, realizing what words he had heard. "They cry out that they desire peace with the Romans!"

"Now they push and strike each other," Nicanor said, his face twisting in pain. But he could not turn from watching as the rebels broke into two groups. "Some of them call back to your people on the ramparts. Do they know who they fight?"

"They are begging to be let back in."

Behind them on the Roman lines, they heard a bugle call that urged them back toward the siege line, where Titus had just arrived with his escort. Beside him was Marcus Tittius Frugi, the commander of the 15th Legion. Next to him was an *aquilifer* carrying its eagle standard.

A tumult of yells from the walls turned their attention to groups of men clustered at the two watchtowers on either side of the gate, fighting each other. The skirmish did not last long; soon, men from one group fell out of sight as the victors called out to the rebels outside the walls.

"What do they say now? Nicanor asked.

"They will open the gates and let them back into the city. They call out to the Romans to join them, too."

The knot of rebels outside the walls took up the cry, beckoning to the Roman line: "Follow us—we want peace! We will let you enter our city."

"We can't keep stopping and gawking," Nicanor said, gesturing for Yosef to follow him. Minutes later, they crossed the siege line and moved toward the band of men and horsemen around the commanding general. Tiberius Alexander, now on horseback, was in the group.

Titus leaned down from his mount as they stopped before him. "Can we trust that your people now want to talk, Yosef?"

Before Yosef could answer, legionaries at the closest point to the beckoning men bellowed a battle cry, lifted their shields and swords, and charged forward with many a gladius flashing. The men—his people—retreated to just outside the gate.

"Futuo!" Nicanor hissed in anger. "They're going to draw those fools within range of the towers—of the men on the walls."

The running rebels stopped and wheeled back on the Romans, crashing into their shields and pulling them away as they grappled with the legionaries. The air filled with arrows and stones from the

Final Siege

city that landed behind the Romans and fell upon them as the rebels adjusted aim. The ramparts were now filled with men, each with a bow or sling, and small *ballistae* quickly trundled into place with a team of two men who fired heavy stones from the parapets.

"If they drive the legionaries to the wall, the defenders will be ready with boiling oil," Yosef said, pointing at the parapet, where the wall jutted out on either side of the gate. The corbels below supported a large extruded section of stone blocks with vertical slits and openings at the base. "They'll pour it from there."

"They don't have enough men on the ground," Nicanor said with a grimace, still gripping his shoulder. "Not enough to drive the legionaries to the wall."

The rebels must have realized that, too. Dozens of armored men streamed from the port in the gate. They encircled the Romans before the legionaries could form a defense. It was a single legionary against two, three, or even four rebels. The Romans retreated, fighting for every step, leaving dozens of dead behind and helping the wounded fall back behind their shields.

A bugle call sounded behind Yosef and Nicanor for a cohort of the 15th's armored cavalry to sweep around the endangered legionaries and charge the Jews. Who ran for the gate and safety as more arrows and stones rained down on the charging horsemen.

"I'm getting you to a medicus...." Yosef said as he took Nicanor by the elbow and steered him away from the entourage around Titus. The general angrily ordered the 15th Legion's *buccinator* to blow an immediate recall. The man's cheeks bulged as the bugle call blasted from him so that his face became as red as that of the infuriated commanding general.

XCVII

Maius 70 CE

Jerusalem

The Upper City

The clamor in the streets had become a softer murmur with the day's end. Eleasar ben Ananias leaned back stiffly at the table in Mathias's courtyard. He crossed his arms and said, "They still celebrate as if two minor skirmishes mean they've won the war."

"Yohanan ben Levi takes the credit when Simon bar Giora is not near," replied Yohan ben Zaccai, then he slumped with fatigue. "But it was *Simon's* plan at the Women's Gate."

"You should go rest, Yohanan," Rebecca said, patting his arm. "You can stay here if you wish. The night air is pleasant, despite the Roman noise beyond the walls. From daybreak to dusk, that ring and clang of metal on stone echo from the Kidron. We can prepare a divan for you here, under the trees." She stood and walked over to the space she meant for him.

"Yes, stay with us, friend," said Mathias. "The streets are still full of Zealots flush with their false bravery—I hope that will sustain them... We all need something to sustain us in the coming days."

Matthew was glad to hear something from his father, who had spoken little since Yosef's arrival outside the city walls. He knew Mathias meant something more substantial than foolish courage or bravado. That afternoon Mathias and Yohanan ben Zaccai had attended a rare meeting of the Sanhedrin. There, Mathias had confided to Matthew as a shaky and weak-looking Shimon ben Gamliel announced the looming dire shortage of food.

The silence and darkness grew around them. Rebecca lit the lamps on the table and each of the four torches in the courtyard. Matthew wished Miriam were here, but she had stayed with Ya'el and Elian in the underground chamber to start their search in the tunnels. If she found a safe way out of the city, past the Romans, could he convince their parents to flee before it was too late? He wished Yosef were here, though his presence alone would raise thorny questions— and maybe answers Matthew did not want to hear. Yosef spoke well— if anyone could compel their parents to save themselves if the opportunity presented itself, Yosef could. Though his brother was near, he felt Yosef was far from them.

Earlier in the day, Matthew had found Rebecca on the roof terrace looking westward to where they could see the Roman line, though it was indistinct. She stared as if she could discover Yosef among the thousands. Matthew, too, found he unconsciously looked in that same direction several times in the day. That day, as his father and Yohanan ben Zaccai were in the Hall of Hewn Stone, Matthew was on the wall by the Women's Gate. He had scanned the ranks of Romans, conflicted about whether he wanted to see Yosef. But the Roman line was too far away to discern an individual man. He had seen the success of Simon bar Giora's ploy, though, even if the older men objected to it. Matthew had cheered to see the Romans fall before they reached the walls of Jerusalem.

"Has no one come forward who might have witnessed it, Yohanan?" Mathias asked. "You've been searching for weeks."

"No, Mathias. I've inquired everywhere. I even spoke with Arins again, for he had gone with me to see Shammai the day before we found him dead." Yohanan shook his head, where untidy wisps of gray hair stuck out like a spray of weeds. "Why would someone kill a charcoal maker?"

"I saw Arins on the wall today," Eleasar said. "He had his men with him—that was a surprise."

"I glimpsed him, too," Matthew said. "With the Romans outside our gates and in the valley near Motza, Arins must do something helpful for us all. We need every man now." His next thought was of Miriam and Ya'el dressed as men, crossing a dangerous countryside from Jerusalem to the Modi'in Valley, doing what must be done. They were so unlike Rachel and Leah, who helped his mother as necessary but kept to themselves—and they never offered more. They were above, now, in Yosef's old room. He doubted they would fight when the Romans broke through the walls and ravaged the city. But Miriam and Ya'el would fight at the foot of broken walls, in the streets... wherever they must. He prayed they would never have to, but it did not seem their God heard any of the prayers that rose from Jerusalem. Only cries streamed up to the heavens without a response.

Matthew turned his gaze toward the western sky, now blue-black, with the first freckling of stars. But he did not look at those points of light; his mind was on his brother. Yosef also stood below those stars. *What will happen to him?*

XCVIII

Maius 70 CE

Jerusalem

The Roman Encampment, Nicanor and Yosef's Tent

"Nothing breaks the skin—no bone protruding, and it seems intact...." The medicus lightly traced his fingers along the line of the bone from the base of Nicanor's neck to the end of the shoulder. "But you must take care." The medicus lifted a triangle of linen knotted at two ends to form a loop he put over Nicanor's head. "Slide your arm into this sling, and rest it there when you sit up or are on your feet."

"For how long?" Nicanor grunted with a grimace.

The medicus shrugged. "Two weeks, maybe more, tribunus. It depends on whether the swelling and your pain recede. I have an elixir for the pain—it's made from poppy leaves and seeds." He placed a small, sealed amphora on the low table between the cots. The medicus had never acknowledged Yosef standing to one side and still did not. He said to Nicanor, "I'll check on you tomorrow. Send for me if anything becomes worse."

* * *

Next morning...

Nicanor had barely slept, deciding to not use the elixir, but had drank the cups of wine Yosef had brought him. "I've seen men use the poppy to ease their pain when wounded. Then they kept using it after they were healthy... or maybe some only healed on the outside and still needed the poppy for what tormented them within. I drink because I like my beer and wine, but I'll not become a man who drinks or uses the poppy because he must." He smothered a groan as he stood, reaching for his cloak. "Help me with this, Yosef. I must go—it's time for the staff meeting."

* * *

Titus's Command Tent

The sides of the large tent had been rolled up and pinned in place. Inside, General Titus paced, his staff officers in a line behind him. Nicanor had been the last to arrive and stood at one end as Titus faced the men gathered in ranks just outside the tent. Some were wounded, unable to stand independently, and held up by the men beside them.

"These Jews are not ruled by their madness," Titus said. "Everything they do is done with careful planning. We have already experienced their clever strategies and ambushes. They've succeeded because the Jewish fighters are obedient, honoring their faithfulness to one another. We Romans, too, rule fortune by obeying orders and always move with proper discipline and complete submission to our officers. But you have not acted as Romans. Your inability to restrain yourselves from action caused needless deaths."

Titus spun on his heel and took three steps toward the men, now standing outside the tent and shouting at them. "You went off without orders from your commanders and did it in my presence!" He walked up and down the line of men.

"The rules of Roman warfare weigh heavily on all who serve Rome. My father, who will be angered when he hears of this debacle, never made an intentional mistake as grievous as yours in all his days in battle. Our rules of warfare call for those who break them to forfeit their lives. I have seen you disobey and how it led to disorder and death. Those of you who have acted insolently will be made quickly sensible. You will not be able to disobey orders again."

Nicanor had no doubt Titus intended to execute the men. A breach of discipline was severe, but condemning so many to death would not send a good signal to the legions. He looked down the line of staff officers to Tiberius Alexander. *This is where the man—who was presumably a leader—should ask to speak with Titus privately*, Nicanor thought. But the second-in-command did not speak up. Nicanor then looked at the soldiers outside the tent. The wounded had sunk to the ground, and the others, their faces drawn tight in despair, realized their fate, too.

"General," said Marcus Trajanus, commanding officer of the 15th Legion, as he left the staff line and went to Titus's side. When the general did not turn to him, he moved closer and spoke in even tones.

"These are men under my command, though they did not obey the officers under me. That has never happened before. I believe they wanted to close with our enemy. The rebels deceived them as they tried to deceive all of us. Some of those before you," Trajanus waved his hand at the men, "broke ranks only when their comrades were under attack. Then they went to their aid. I ask you to pardon their rashness. They must be punished, but I ask that it not be a final punishment. These men can make amends and prove to be better soldiers of Rome in the days ahead."

The silent moment grew into a minute before Titus replied. "I'll consider your question and tell you my decision this evening."

* * *

Hours later...

TITUS'S COMMAND TENT

The sides of the tent were rolled down this time, and only staff officers were in attendance. Titus sat behind the large campaign desk, his fingers steepled before him.

He looks like his father, Nicanor thought.

"I've decided not to execute the men who bolted to attack the Jews. Though it seems prudent to execute individuals for their misdeeds, punishment of the whole group of men should only be in the form of reproof. So their punishment will be to work with the *immunes* and laborers on the earthwork barrier built around Jerusalem. Go and tell your men." Titus dismissed the staff with a wave. "Tiberius, you and Nicanor remain."

When the others had left the tent, Titus said to the two remaining with him, "It's time to make the Jews pay for their cunning hoax."

* * *

JERUSALEM'S WESTERN WALL

"There, where the wall bends west and north," Nicanor said as he gestured beyond the wall, where rose the pointed roof of a large building higher than the wall. "The fortifications are weaker here. When I was here before the war, I learned," he did not say it was from Yosef, "that the builders in Jerusalem neglected to strengthen these walls. When this new area of their city was established, it was not very populated, and reinforcement did not seem necessary since a second wall protected the city's main areas. This section will be easier to break through. When we do, we will find room to the north to bring an entire legion inside the outer wall to position along the second inner wall and spread the rebels thin. Then we can punch through it, giving us entry into the Upper City and the Antonia Fortress. From Antonia, we can take the temple."

Nicanor winced as Tiberius Alexander turned to Yosef, who had accompanied them. "That tall building close to the wall," said Tiberius. "Is that not the monument to Yohanan Hyrcanos, High Priest, long ago? He was related to your ancestor, right, Josephus?"

Yosef nodded but did not speak.

Nicanor was beginning to find the Aegyptus Prefect's comments to his friend irritating, but it seemed to be his nature. Tiberius Alexander had forsaken his Jewish heritage to embrace Rome and seemed to goad Yosef for following in the same direction.

"We'll move the 5th and 15th Legions two *stadia* from their wall at this point," Titus said, interrupting that line of conversation. "It is well within our ballistae range at 1200 feet. We can hurl a one-talent stone and easily reach their walls, and a steady shower of 75-pound rocks will wear them down." He glanced at his second-in-command and said, "Tiberius, you say the rebels have only lighter ballistae from the Roman garrison armory in Antonia Fortress, right?"

"Yes, general," said the Aegyptus Prefect, his eyes shifting to Nicanor and then back to Titus. "They also have the ones taken from the *12th* Legion... during their defeat and retreat. But they have nothing that can reach this distance."

"Have the rocks painted black," said Nicanor, ignoring the glance and the reference to his defeated legion. He had earlier explained to Titus that the brilliant white of the incoming stones had given the defenders a chance to call out warnings. He was growing used to giving advice on how to do more damage to the city his friend called home, and it seemed Yosef was growing used to it, too. But the Jew stood away from them, his arms crossed as he stared at Jerusalem.

* * *

Upon the level area that would become General Titus's main assault point, the two legions marched into place in seven ranks. The infantry was in the first position in three rows, with the cavalry behind them also in three ranks. Titus had placed the legions' archers in the center of the seven ranks. Then the legions with their auxiliaries and the beasts of burden with supplies and pulling siege machines moved in without fear.

Sitting on their mounts among Titus's entourage, Nicanor and Yosef appreciated the general's intent. This was not just the display of power as a show for the rebels. With such a large body of Roman troops, the Jews would be foolish to attempt ground attacks against them, and perhaps less blood would be shed. Careful to keep his left arm in its sling held close to his chest, Nicanor turned in his saddle to study how far the earthworks wall progressed. On their arrival outside Jerusalem, Titus had ordered the leveling of all villages around Jerusalem, stripping them of anything of use to the legions.

The trees from around the city and surrounding area were immediately cut down, men began to gather timber to use in the siege, and the countryside now lay bare. A unit of engineers and two cohorts of laborers had worked daily from sunup to past sundown, erecting a barrier around the city. Each worked with his *dolabra*, the entrenching tool every legionary carried, and baskets to move the dirt and stones. Thus, the trenches and earthworks were developing quickly.

As the legions settled into re-establishing their encampment, Nicanor turned to Yosef and said, "Let's go see to our tent site."

* * *

NICANOR AND YOSEF'S TENT

Nicanor looked across Albus's back to see Sayid approaching and tossed the brush into the bucket at his feet so he could go greet his friend.

The young Syrian auxiliary looked exhausted, but he said with concern, "My father came and told me you'd been injured, Nicanor. How is your shoulder?"

"It hurts like Vulcan struck me—if the armorer of the gods were ever to wield his hammer on a man. But I'm mending...."

Sayid turned to Yosef, sitting quietly on a camp stool outside the tent, and said, "My father also said that the rebels... did not respond to your request to talk... I'm sorry, Yosef."

When Yosef did not reply, Nicanor asked, "How are you holding up, Sayid? Your father is driving his men hard."

"We work intensely with the laborers and engineers... for the pace at which Lord Tiberius Alexander drives us is twice normal. We will soon begin to move siege towers and rams—the ones with your design improvements, Nicanor—onto the ramps. They will be moved to follow our progress, so they can strike as soon as the ramps reach the walls."

Sayid studied Yosef in his silence and asked quietly, "Will you get another chance to speak to your people?"

The steady march of men loading baskets of dirt for mule carts, then trundling them to the growing ramps, had become a constant sound. Nicanor thought Yosef looked like their loads had been poured onto him. His shoulders seemed bowed with age and weariness as he looked up at Sayid and said, "I hope so... I have to try again...." Then he rose and left the tent site.

"Where's he going?" Sayid asked Nicanor.

"Each evening, he climbs one of the mounds of dirt when the sun goes down. He watches until Jerusalem's lights appear... he does not come back until late."

XCIX

Maius 70 CE

Jerusalem

The Upper City

The dense, scudding clouds obscured the vestiges of sunset as the light of torches and fires spread low beyond the third wall. In some places, the flames climbed high above the ground, illuminating the line of Roman infantry and siege weapons. One by one, the bronze bowls set atop the Roman watchtowers were filled with wood and set ablaze.

"The rain of rocks seems to never end," Rebecca commented, though all of them on the rooftop terrace watched, spectators to the never-ending Roman missiles crumbling their city. They all knew that, at some point, the rocks would reach them. In the distance, dark shapes arced over the wall and then came the thuds and muted crashing of the stones, followed by thin cries. "The Romans surround us on three sides, spreading outside our wall. It all feels like a fever dream." She passed her hand over her brow as if to wipe it away.

Matthew knew his mother would say more; lately, all her observations referenced what Yosef had done or said. *She tries to make those memories offset the present.* But Mathias barely mentioned their second son anymore.

"Yosef had many dreams that troubled him as a child and then as a young man," she said. "The last I sat through with him was the night before he left for Caesarea to sail to Rome. I feared for him and wanted him to stay." She turned to Mathias and added, "But you insisted he was the one who must go."

"And that proved to be the right decision, Rebecca," Mathias sighed. "Yosef did bring home the rabbis imprisoned in Rome."

"Then he left to fight in Galilee in a war he did not believe in," she lamented.

Matthew had never felt overshadowed by his younger brother. He'd never longed for the importance of what Yosef had done nor yearned to see things far beyond Jerusalem. He had been content to live and die in Jerusalem. *And that will not be long*, he thought wryly. But there was no escaping the fate brought on, in part, by Jerusalem's leaders. "Mother," he said, "Yosef believed we should not have contributed to that war at its start. But once it was underway, he fought the Romans."

"Yet now he is with them." Mathias jutted out his chin, pointing his beard west.

"Mathias," Yohanan ben Zaccai said as he leaned forward, "he is your son. It's right for you to praise him for what he accomplished in Rome, and I saw much of Yosef in Galilee, as I shared with you all. We were all proud of him. We do not know why the Romans freed him. Still, I suspect it's because he has taken a position to serve as an intermediary between us and the Romans. You once thought so, too."

Matthew watched as his father's eyes narrowed, but he did not respond to his oldest friend. Instead, he asked him, "Do we know yet who the man is?" The beard swung back toward the Romans, where a cross was silhouetted against the fires.

"Eleasar is still trying to find out who was crucified," Matthew answered. "Simon bar Giora's commanders do not have current rosters of their men since so many are new. They were poor refugees and pilgrims who came for Passover and remained. And now they are pressed into service. Most men attacking the siege weapons at the western wall were killed, and the survivors do not know who the Romans captured."

"Terrible it is that the man suffers, and we don't even know his name," Rebecca said, shaking her head.

"He suffers no more," Matthew said. "When I was at the western wall, near the where the Romans crucified him, I no longer heard his cries. He is not the only one now silent...."

"What do you mean?" Yohanan asked.

"Yeshua, the doom crier, has met his end." Matthew had been amazed at the man striding along the streets closest to the western wall, even once the Roman ballistae were positioned close enough to fire into the city. Stones rained all around him, yet his "Woe to Jerusalem!" rang out between the crashing of the rocks and the screams of people struck by the falling buildings and debris. His "Woe once more to the city, to the people and to the Temple!" had carried to the men on the wall. That morning, Matthew had seen the black-as-death stone thunder fully into his chest, driving him to the ground. Matthew had scrambled down the ladder from the ramparts and rushed to find him crushed beneath the rock. "And woe to me" were his last words.

"Can Simon bar Giora's men hold the wall?" asked Mathias.

"He has 10,000 Jewish fighters and 5,000 Idumeans," Matthew replied. "Simon positioned them at the approach to the Tomb of Hurqanos on the ramparts. And behind the wall at the Hippicus tower." *But that will not be enough to withstand the Romans,* he thought.

"Can they hold?" His father asked again, beard jutting.

Matthew looked at his mother, then at Rachel and Leah. The truth was inevitable, whether unspoken or not. "Giora's men still sortie from the wall," he said. "They kill some Romans and damage some of their machines, but most of our fighters die in the attacks. And the wall cannot withstand the beating. It's crumbling and will fall no matter how quickly we repair it. Soon." He saw alarm in the young women's eyes and resignation in his mother's.

"We'll have to pull back behind the second wall...."

"Yes, Father. Yohanan ben Levi and a little over 8,000 men defend Antonia Fortress, the north portico of the Temple, and the wall facing the Kidron Valley. They are a mix of Zealots and his Gischalan and Galilean militia. Simon bar Giora's s men will have to move inside the second wall to protect the Upper City."

"What of the Lower City?"

"Father, we cannot defend it...."

"How long can we hold out?"

"Not long before the Romans breach the third wall." Matthew shook his head. "At the second wall, we'll have our men spread less thinly and can mount a stronger defense, but I don't know."

"We don't have food to last," Yohanan noted. "Neither the Gischalan nor Simon bar Giora want anyone checking into the extent of their folly—and both are fully responsible."

With the words bitter on this tongue, Matthew said, "They expect the people to think more about their fear of the Romans now and less about how their own 'leaders' have cost them dearly."

Yohanan continued. "Yes, that fear now keeps anyone from asking hard questions. I could not get accurate information from them, so I found and met with the last remaining prominent food supplier to the city, Ben Kalba Sabbua. He reports the Zealots and Giora's men burned ten years' worth of supplies. Sabbua's quartermasters have inventoried what remains. It's almost all gone. But a young shepherd named Akiva, who works for Sabbua, knows of a cache of supplies they cannot figure out how to reach. Akiva took command of Sabbua's last supply caravan when the trainmaster fled upon hearing the news of the Romans being so near Jerusalem. Akiva diverted the caravan into the Hinnom Valley and hid it in a large cave."

"*Ge Hinnom!*" A sour expression now spread over Mathias's face. "This kiva hid it where Jerusalem casts its refuse, and the bodies of sacrificial animals from the Temple...."

"And the city's sewage," Yohanan ben Zaccai added.

"Cohorts of the 10th Legion patrol there from the Kidron," Matthew said. "But they move fast—the stench is too much even for them—so they don't check the caves. Still, with the patrols, we can't reach the hiding place through the valley."

"Maybe Miriam knows of a tunnel that runs near that cave in the valley," Yohanan said.

"Is she still with Ya'el?" Rachel asked, seeming to want to say more. But she glanced at Leah, who shook her head.

"They have explored the two most promising tunnels coming from the sub-chambers in Baris underground," Matthew replied.

"They must leave that place—Elian and Cicero, too. They must leave that place and come home." Rebecca stood and darted a look west, then faced north. "Before..."

"Before the Romans breach the third wall into Bezetha." Mathias nodded at Matthew. "Get them, son. We must be together to face what is to come."

"Eleasar's tour on the wall is done at dawn," Matthew said. "I'll be there when he's relieved from his post, and we'll go to our moles and bring them out into the light of day." He smiled a little, though humor was far from them all. "But first, we'll seal the tunnels at that end."

C

Maius 70 CE

Jerusalem

Beneath the City of David

Miriam unrolled her map on a handy boulder. She took a charcoal stick to note the location of the two tunnels. The only ones that led from the underground chambers of the now long-gone Hasmonean fortress and wandered far to the south and east. All the others they'd cleared and checked were just stunted stubs of passageways. The map marked the passage of the long tunnels from the deepest section of the Baris to the City of David. She rubbed the side of her nose and studied her marks—remembering the route they had found.

"This is the tomb of one of your queens?" Ya'el asked as she took a long drink from the waterskin draped over her shoulder.

Miriam looked up from her chart. "Not of my people. Queen Helena was of *Hadaiav*—you may know it as Adiabene. Yosef told me of her and of her country that borders the Parthians. Rome has had past conflicts with them."

"Why is she buried in Jerusalem?"

"Her family converted to our faith; she built the palace above us and chose to live her last years here."

"And now her former palace is her tomb?"

"Hers and that of one of her sons." Miriam returned to the study of her new map.

Ya'el spilled a little water from the skin bag onto a strip of linen and handed it to Miriam. "Here—you have charcoal on your nose and cheek."

Miriam smiled and wiped her face, studying Ya'el's weariness revealed in the slump of her shoulders and the furrowed lines of her face. "I have maps of the connecting tunnels into King David's Tomb from here," she said. "They reach farther to the Hezekiah Tunnel and its workers' passage, then out into the hidden exit into the Kidron Valley. So, let's fill our lamps and head back. We'll make better time returning."

Relief spread over Ya'el's features. Miriam knew she hated to leave Elian alone for such a long time. Still, it had been necessary." I hope we have better luck with the other tunnel," she said. As they moved into the side passage that would take them to the central tunnel north and east, Miriam prayed they would find a safe place for her household to hide.

Deep underground for several days, Miriam had heard little of the recent events and seen none of the increased fighting herself. From her last talk with Matthew and Eleasar ben Ananias, she knew the Romans' most potent attack would be from the north and northwest. Time was running out for those between the third and second walls. The war surrounded them on both sides. *And which side are you on, Yosef?* She wondered. What had made the brother she was closest to join the Romans? Was Yosef now her enemy, too?

* * *

BENEATH BEZETHA, THE BARIS UNDERGROUND REMNANTS

Cicero's raucous squawks echoed harshly, warning them something was wrong, so Miriam and Ya'el hurried to the mouth of the tunnel.

"Elian!" Ya'el called as they approached the steps to the higher level where they lived.

"Elian!" Miriam echoed. The boy had been upset when Ya'el told him he must stay behind, and they discovered that, except for the irate parrot in his cage, the chamber was empty. "He's either gone up—outside—or into the second tunnel," she said. She did not need to add that they would split up to find him.

Ya'el was already changing into her mercenary archer's garb, donning it quickly. Miriam refilled a skin bag of oil and inserted fresh wicks into her lamp, adding extras to the pouch at her waist. Ya'el strung her bow and swung a large quiver of arrows onto her back.

Miriam did not tell Ya'el to be careful as they moved toward the ladder leading to the shed above, but she gripped Ya'el's free hand. "We'll find him," Miriam assured her friend as Ya'el reached for the first rung. Then Miriam sped into the second tunnel.

* * *

BEZETHA

The sound of the fighting at the wall struck Ya'el as she left the shed. She instinctively faced the direction of the boom—a Roman heavy ram was battering a gate in a rolling martial rhythm as if from so many drums. Ya'el was drawn by the clamor and the sight of the flocks of small, dark shapes in the distance. But the stones must be terrifyingly large to those they flew toward.

Ya'el moved toward the sound, as she knew Elian had likely done. Ya'el had seen Roman might before but in peaceful camps. Or the hurried, frantic legion patrols Sayid helped her escape when Gessius Florus pursued her in Ptolemais. But she had never witnessed the fury of a legion assault. The noise was nearly deafening. The curses and screams of men tore at her heart. As did the fearful torsion-released twang of the ballistae she saw firing from two siege towers down into the mass of men defending the wall.

As she drew closer, her eyes swept the area for Elian, but he was nowhere in sight. Miriam had told her that the tomb of a long-dead ancestor was across from the nearby monument. Ya'el climbed onto a large wagon loaded with timber and stone slabs, material that was probably positioned to use shoring up the wall. She looked in every direction for signs of the boy as a tremor shook the ground as she straddled the load on the wagon. The discordant cry of one of Jerusalem's walls breaking made her soul recoil as sections of the western wall crumbled, spilling down and falling to the sides. An iron ram's head now protruded through the gate as Romans with flashing swords, the morning sun glinting on their armor, poured through the splintered opening and the broken wall. A tide of metal and men crashed into the dazed defenders and washed them away in its surge, leaving bloodied stone and riven bodies in its wake.

Transfixed, Ya'el just stood there as hundreds of Roman heavy infantry moved into Bezetha, followed by even more who had been waiting to enter. The rebels fell back or died before the legionaries who flooded through the breach.

Ya'el took her stance without thinking as the Romans came into her range. Bow in hand, she nocked and fired again and again. Most of her arrows found exposed flesh—throats, faces, arms, legs... whatever vulnerability her instincts could target. But her fusillade of shafts had drawn attention. Twenty legionaries now sprinted toward her, some with her arrows lodged in their armor. They moved far faster than she imagined possible for such heavily laden men. Finding her quiver empty, she turned and ran, praying to the gods all the while—not for herself, but for Elian, that he was safely hiding or that Miriam would find him. Bile rose in her throat; she spat it out to the side and ran faster.

* * *

In the Second Tunnel

Miriam had been slowed by stopping and checking side passages to see if they showed signs of Elian. It had not taken far into the second tunnel to sense that it ran more east-southeast than the one she and Ya'el had just explored. The step count Miriam kept unconsciously told her she was now past the Antonia Fortress. Zechariah had been pleased with her awareness of her position in any space. That sense told her she now veered toward the Temple Enclosure. She passed through a long stretch without side passages and then came upon one with a large opening. Stumbling on the loose rock, she caught herself with one hand at the rim of the rock wall to the left of the space. Her fingers explored the lines cut into the stone, and she held the lamp closer, wiping dust and grit from the incised characters, but she still could not read them.

She entered the passage she soon realized headed due east, and she saw the tunnel was littered with broken stone on the floor, most of it small, like gravel. Along its length, rock hunks and slabs were set to one side as if stacked up for a particular use.

A few minutes later, she passed two passage entrances, branching left and right. Each was utterly sealed by similar slabs of stone fitted together and mortared to fill the crevices between the rocks. She was curious about them but passed them by to continue on. This eastward tunnel soon ended with a similar barrier of sealed rock. They were finely fitted stones, mortared in place. But in one spot was a jagged fissure where something had dislodged a corner of a stone, and someone had enlarged the opening by pulling a larger section free.

Miriam set her lamp on the floor and Zechariah's staff beside it, and she studied the opening. Shifting the light closer, she reached in and brought forth a green feather. Elian's! It came from the simple necklace Ya'el had braided for the boy, twining in some of Cicero's feathers to add color.

Miriam tucked the feather into her pouch and lifted the lamp to see what lay beyond. Barely able to fit, she belly-crawled with the light held out before her. Once through the opening, she reached back to drag Zechariah's staff to her. Then she carefully stood in the chamber beyond, raising the lamp to cast its glow farther. Six feet from the now-partially-sealed opening, a dozen narrow steps descended and then arced into a spiral that continued lower and lower.

"Elian!" She hazarded a call, for no one else could be this far down. Her voice echoed into the depths. Down more steps, she repeated it. "Elian!" The echo came back sooner, more distinct. A minute later, she reached the bottom.

* * *

THE CISTERN WATER BUCKET CHAMBER

In the center of the modest chamber were scaffolding and a mechanism with a line that held buckets and traveled up through an opening in the ceiling and then presumably came down—emptied—on the other side. Though the pulleys or mechanism at each end was out of sight. The bottom opening seemed larger, and Miriam knelt to find that the stone lip on one side had fractured. She brought her lamp closer, and a moan came from below. Startled, she rocked back on her heels and then shifted forward again to bend down toward the opening.

"Elian?" she called. The groan was louder, and she lowered the lamp into the hole and bent farther in. The boy was a dozen feet below her, his tunic caught on an attachment connecting the bucket to its line. The lamplight barely reached him, but as he swung around, the side of his head came into the light. A gash glistened red, and a scarlet rivulet ran down Elian's cheek—his eyes fluttered open.

"Mir... Miriam, help me!"

CI

Maius 70 CE

Jerusalem

The Roman Encampment, Titus's Watchtower

Nicanor and Yosef climbed the steps of the 16-foot-high watchtower Titus had ordered erected near his command tent. Its square platform, 10 feet on each side, gave a good view of the nearby siege line, its ranks, and the queue of men and equipment. They could also see the progress of the earthwork wall of timber, stone, and dirt that Titus had ordered. Erected according to the standard siege doctrine, the barrier to seal the city already spanned in both directions, curving to the north where it reached the 10th Legion's location. Behind and before them stretched a train of wagons loaded with dirt, stone, and timber for the ramps that seemed to extend and grow even as they watched under the bright sun that made them shade their eyes. Workers with wicker hurdles met the heavily laden wagons at the far end of a ramp. They used their baskets to scoop out the dirt they delivered to the workers at the other end of the ramp.

"Backbreaking work," Nicanor grunted, rearranging his left arm in its sling. His shoulder still hurt, but the handsbreadth bruise of mottled yellow, dark blue, and purple on his upper chest had begun to fade. "Titus promises rewards to the men who finish first."

"And they're now within range of the defenders," said Yosef, "and of the ballistae on the walls." As he said it, another salvo of rocks and arrows landed on the movable wooden protective cover that shifted along with the workers as, foot by foot, they drew closer to the city.

"There goes the Sagitarii," Nicanor said, pointing at the auxiliary cavalry archers from Provincia Creta. "About half the regiment...." The 250 horsemen barely slowed as they swept in and fired volleys at the defenders on the walls, then arced away to come around for another pass. Most remained unscathed, but many peeled off with arrows embedded in their armor or sunk into the neck or hindquarters of their mounts. Blood splashed crimson on their sweat-sheened coats. A dozen horsemen were fully down, their horses terribly wounded or killed under them. The men scrambled for the cover of the workers' wooden shed as it crept toward them.

"By the end of the day, they'll reach the wall...."

Nicanor did not even need to look to know that his friend's eyes were on the scene they'd witnessed day after day, but Yosef would have the look of someone seeing something beyond. It was a haunted shadowing that showed first in his eyes and, more often, drew his face into tight lines of discomfort. That would not ease any time soon, if ever, for Yosef.

* * *

AT THE ROMAN RAMP

In the hours before dawn, the auxiliary units, Sayid's among them, had helped bring up the light ballistae. The *catapulta* and *scorpios* were now on either side of the ramp but not at its end, where it reached nearly flush with the city wall. They kept the weapons well back, at their maximum range, to strike the defenders' ramparts and towers without the engines being destroyed by the Jews. It had been slow, hard work under desultory fire from the rebels that increased with the morning sunlight. With their interlocked shields facing outward and above them, the testudo he and his unit formed deflected most of the rebel arrows. But almost every man bore a ragged gash on his arm, shoulder, or leg, where the streaking shafts found openings between the shields.

The wooden shed they'd left in place when the ramp was completed now bristled with arrows. The jagged rocks hurled from the walls above gouged its thick roof. But the sturdy wood and the iron plate sheathing had held so far. Next would come the ram, now that the weapons were in place to counter-fire on the rebels as the ram commenced its work.

Sayid wiped sweat and grit from his face with the back of his muddy hand and realized he had just smeared himself with blood. A ragged scarlet furrow ran across his forearm to his wrist. He was thankful the arrow had cut only a thin channel through the flesh, but it bled profusely. Then came the blast of a bugle, and Sayid and the others recognized the call to pull back to their designated rally point and meet the next piece of siege equipment.

* * *

TITUS'S WATCHTOWER

Final Siege

"They're moving your battering ram to the line," Yosef said, thrusting his chin toward a team of men and mules sweating as they pushed and pulled the ram. Its lengthy shaft—the trunk of a large tree—was strapped onto the wagon bed that moved toward the foot of the ramp at the siege line.

Nicanor moved closer to Yosef's position on the platform and looked down. The tip of the ram, the impact point, was fitted with a massive piece of iron in the shape of a ram's head. It would be mounted within a protective structure on four large wheels broad enough to traverse dirt or semi-packed sand with enough men or animals to pull it. Nicanor was proud of the largest ram he had ever seen, and its iron sheathing ran from the head nearly the entire distance of the long shaft.

At the siege of Yotapta, Nicanor and Vespasian had witnessed the Jewish giant Dov throw a rock that two strong men could not lift and shatter a ram's shaft just behind its iron head. He did not know if Jerusalem had any giants. Still, he had seen to the design of a battering ram almost impossible to break and supervised as the men of the 15th Legion assembled at the vast *castra stative* outside Rome. That was where he had met with the army's senior *armamentarii* on Vespasian's behalf to discuss these design improvements for siege rams.

As the men toiled moving the ram, he heard them chant a name. Throughout his years of service, it was customary for men to name their personal weapons and the machines they manned. He did not see sense in it. But he had thought he heard the *armicustos*, the weapons quartermasters, speak to the pieces as this superlative battering ram came together. The largest and heaviest needed naming. Now he heard what they called it: "Nico is coming... Nico is coming...." Only one person knew the nickname his mother had given him as a child but that he'd put behind him when he joined the legion. *So, Sayid, you must have told Celsus Evander*, and the legion's commanding quartermaster had passed it down.

The massive ram inched closer to the ramp where it would be mounted within its *tortoise*. A framework of solid timbers with planks and wicker hurdles on the sides covered with uncured hides. Inside, the ram would be suspended from a beam like a balance arm with cables around its middle. That, in turn, was supported at both ends by posts fixed into the ground. Once set in position, the ram would be drawn back by a team of brawny men who then pushed it forward in unison with all their might so that it struck a gate or a wall with its iron head. In a flash of pride, he wished he could see 'Nico' in action against the thick gates of Jerusalem.

A creaking sound grew louder, and Nicanor turned to see a large team of men and mules moving one of the 75-foot siege towers toward the packed-earth area beside the ramp. They would stage there and then move into place for the ram to come up from behind.

Yosef finally spoke. "Jerusalem's gates are stronger than Yotapta's, but they cannot withstand your ram, Nicanor."

* * *

AT THE WALL ON THE SIEGE RAMP

Sayid had seen battering rams before but never one like this... and never one for an enemy gate. The ram was secured beneath its tortoise, and the wheels of the contraptions were chocked to fix it in place. Two men released the blocks and wedges, and the ram swayed slightly. And all at once the ram was deployed. A team of eight men, muscles straining and feet digging in, pulled back on the tethers and released it. The gate shuddered and shook with each blow of the heavy iron head. Soon the 15th Legion's battering ram had displaced the corner of a tower but not done much damage to the gate itself.

The hissing and whooshing of arrows and stones filled the air from the siege towers and the return fire from the rebels. Sayid had never been more exhilarated, not even at Beth Horon, where he had fought at Nicanor's side, secure in the knowledge that the burly centurion would help him in the thickest, deadliest time of the battle. When sword and shield clash heavily, and breath comes in gasps, fear settles on a soldier that the next breath won't come. After Beth Horon, on his mission for Cestius Gallus, Sayid had braved many things and fought on his own a time or two. But combat like this stirred him much more—the primal feeling of shared readiness and duty in the face of the enemy. It radiated from the men surrounding him and filled him with pride.

The men on the ram kept the chant, "Nico.... Nico," and Sayid smiled despite his weariness. Gauging from the half-ball of molten orange sinking low behind them, he knew the recall for his unit would come soon. And he was ready.

The blast of a sounding horn came... but behind him, from the walls. Sayid shook himself and braced his shield and sword as he wheeled toward the scores of men that poured from a hidden door at the base of the gate.

Final Siege

The rebels ran boldly to the siege machines. They cast sealed jars of oil among the structures that broke on impact as rebels from the walls threw lighted torches upon them, setting the siege engines afire. The more courageous rebels leaped upon the machines' coverings and tore them to pieces, falling upon the Romans underneath. Each rebel carried bulging goatskin bags full of a sticky, flammable pitch they tried to spread on the siege tower and the ram's tortoise.

Roman soldiers reeled under the crash of rebel bodies and the stones from above as the testudo fell apart. Sayid blocked the thrust of a man wearing Roman armor. Only the man's long beard and expression of pure hatred marked him as a rebel wearing stolen armor, not an ally. Sayid spun as Nicanor had taught him, got inside the man's reach, and thrust his gladius into the flesh of the rebel's neck. He felt the blade strike bone, withdrew it as the man fell, and planted his feet to meet another armored rebel who slammed into him, trying to rip his shield away. Gripping it, he dropped, and his weight drove the bottom edge of the shield onto the man's sandaled foot. As the rebel's toes shattered, the man let go, and Sayid shot up to bring the top edge of the shield crashing under his jaw. That bone broke too, and the man's scream sprayed blood and bits of teeth. Stooping to retrieve his sword, Sayid stabbed into the man's stomach, and the rebel fell to the side.

Sayid gasped, wanting to retch after the shattering violence of the last few moments. Thankfully the defenders on the ramparts above them had ceased their barrage once the fighting on the ground began. Then he realized another bugle call had sounded as he fought. It was Roman this time, and he took heart at the supporting wedge of cavalry, Tiberius Alexander's select soldiers, drove into the remaining rebels. He saw Titus in full armor at the tip of the charge, his spatha at the top of its arc catching that last glint of daylight as his long sword cleaved rebels right and left, leaving a dozen dead behind him. Men on foot followed, rushing with baskets of dirt to throw on the fires that were chewing away at the siege towers and the ram's tortoise. All were scorched, but none had burned long enough to be badly damaged. More Romans arrived to defend the siege machines as the rebels died around them.

A Cretan auxiliary cavalryman reined beside Sayid, leaning down and offering his hand. "You look tired, brother. Let me carry you to camp...."

Sayid grasped his hand and swung up behind him. At rest, finally, he breathed in the smell of burned oil and wood, the coppery tang of blood... It was his own blood and that of the men killed, the bodies strewn on the ground while the wounded were being helped away as he was.

Sayid lived..., and though he no longer dreamed of proving himself, he wished his father had seen him fight.

CII

Maius 70 CE

Northwest of Jerusalem, The Hidden Valley

The long-limbed man moved through the tunnel slowing only to bend when the ceiling dropped. Never faltering even when the footing became uncertain where the loose rock had fallen from above or flaked from the walls. The torch in his hand would soon not be needed. After a slight bend in the tunnel, he saw a glimmer that told him the torch in his hand would soon not be needed. As the mouth of the exit brightened, the close-cropped iron-gray hair, white-threaded beard, and seamed face showed his years.

On either side of the tunnel exit, the men outside closed on him quickly. Then stopped at the familiar sight of the older graying man who moved so lithely, now shielding his eyes as they adjusted to the daylight. One guard waved his tattooed hand to indicate the way was clear outside, and very soon, he could see the world outside that he'd left an hour earlier. Before him was an open field within a small valley among four hills that mingled and stretched into ridges of varying height and slope. Winding among those hills was a road that had been for a long time overgrown with disuse. But now, the scrub was matted down with newly formed ruts from the wagons waiting in line nearby, where a few low buildings hugged the hills. Their weather-worn steps led to entries half-buried in drifts of sand and dirt. The structures appeared to be as long-disused as the road had once been, perhaps long forgotten. But now, the place was busy, and several tents had been set up in the clearing before the buildings.

The man moved past the wagons, taking stock of the equipment. Some were captured locally, but most were built for the Roman legions, with broader beds and higher sides, heavy enough to require drawing by two bullocks or oxen. Or by four of the mules in the nearby corral. As he approached, two massive, armored men outside the large, central tent offered the man a much better salute than had the Thracians at the tunnel. The two men from Clazomenae were deadly killers who recognized their equal. One swept the tent flap open with a long, massive arm for him to enter. Inside, his eyes adjusted again to the dim light in the tent, whose side had been half rolled up to let in some light and breeze but not the valley sand.

Gessius Florus looked up at him from where he sat at a sizable legion-commander-style campaign desk covered with parchment and flattened scrolls, and two maps. The short, powerfully built man standing beside Florus began to roll up the maps and asked, "Do you want me to stay, Lord Florus?"

The newcomer eyed him, his stare as harsh and merciless as the two men outside the tent.

"No, Drusus. Return to Sycaminum and send Krateros to me." Florus's attention shifted to the newcomer to gesture at the camp stool in front of the desk. "Sit...."

"I see you have your wagons and mules ready," the man said, passing his hand over his cropped gray hair, dislodging some of the dirt that had fallen on it during his trek through the tunnel.

"I hope soon to use them," Florus replied, "now that the outer wall has been breached." He leaned back to study the man. "Since we last spoke, you have acted on the signal I arranged...."

"Yes, lord. It was at a great range... I was close but missed the Jew, though I struck the centurion with him. I'll try again if we can bring the Jew close to the city's second wall."

"General Titus will soon ask him to speak to his people again if an opportunity should arise."

"I can arrange such an occasion, lord. More and more, the people in Jerusalem are going hungry. I know a man in the city, Castor, who commands a tower at the second wall. He looks ahead and fears what is to come. He wants food for his family. Let me know when to plan to use him for this, and I will have him plead to speak with the general, offering what Tiberius seeks."

"And Titus will probably send Yosef on his behalf," Florus replied, the rings on his hand glittering as he tapped his lips with two fingers.

"Yes, lord. I'll watch for one of your messengers...." The man stood to go but stopped at the sight of Florus's raised hand.

"The centurion you wounded was Nicanor, now a tribunus. So, though you failed to strike Yosef ben Mathias, you still struck a blow against another man I want killed. When the chance comes again... do not miss."

Arins stroked the long slinger's cord wrapped around his waist as if a part of his sash. "If he and Yosef come close enough, they will die."

"Good... good...." Florus's smile matched the flash of the gems on his hands.

CIII

Maius 70 CE

Jerusalem

The Roman Camp, Bezetha, Nicanor and Yosef's tent.

"Levi!"

The cry brought Nicanor up from his cot, and he reached for his pugio. The dagger was never far from his hand, even at night, within his tent. Blinking, pawing sleep from his eyes with one hand, he took his bearings. They were in a new campsite between the city's third and second walls. The camp had its usual nighttime thrum of activity, and the rebels were very close.

He looked down at Yosef sitting in the tangle of his thin, sweat-soaked blanket. His hands ran over his face and head as if searching for something he could not find, confusing him.

"What is it, Yosef?" Nicanor picked up the small lighted lamp and brought it nearer his friend.

"Is there blood?" Yosef held his hands out beneath the lamp's glow.

"No," Nicanor said and blinked again. "It's just one of your dreams, Yosef."

"I was in Yotapta during the last battle inside the walls. Levi screamed, 'The Romans are too close... save Ariella!' Then he shoved me back as a sword thrust through him from the back and came out of his chest."

In the dim light, Nicanor could see Yosef's eyes wide, his friend reliving the memory as he continued. "Levi cried to me to trigger the deadfall Dov had crafted in the cellar behind us. But it was too late to collapse the escape passage... the Romans were already upon us. Tripping the deadfall would bury Levi, who was nearest the Romans. I couldn't do it!"

Yosef violently rubbed his eyes as if to wipe the vestiges of his dream away. "Levi kicked me in the chest, driving me back, away from him and the Romans. Somehow, despite that sword piercing him, Levi leaped for the lever and pulled it. The mass of stone and dirt was released and buried him and the Romans." Yosef's eyes narrowed as he shook his head. "He died to save me. Ariella accused me of letting him die. I told her I did not, but still...."

"Men die in battle, Yosef... you can't assume responsibility for everyone under your command." Nicanor knew that was not true for him, though. He was still haunted by the ghosts of his men who died at Beth Horon. He and Yosef alike keenly felt the guilt.

"Women die too, Nicanor. Soon after Levi's death, Dalit died. She was Dov's wife and also a fighter. She and Ariella were caught taking water to where the siege survivors hid in the cave beneath Yotapta. Dalit fought against Roman armor and swords, though she was armed with only a goatherd's crook. Ariella lived, though, and later sought to make me suffer for Levi's death... as if I did not already suffer."

Yosef tipped back his head and gazed at the dark canvas of their tent. "Ariella had finally forgiven me and been set free from her rage. But she was killed, her body cast on the dirt outside the gate of the Roman encampment at Ptolemais. So, her death is on my hands, too."

Yosef's last word was followed by a tremendous crash that broke through the routine sounds of the camp that echoed within the confines of the walls.

Nicanor grabbed his sword and shield and rushed outside to the chaos of running, shouting men, and the blare of a bugle call to action. He headed for the source of the crash, the staging area for three 74-foot-high siege towers they'd brought through the shattered section of Jerusalem's outer wall to be used against the inner second wall. A cluster of torches held by a group of men showed the pile of rubble that had been one of the towers.

Yosef ran out behind him, pulling on clothing. "How did that happen? An attack—"

Nicanor cut Yosef off. "I heard no alarm. No rebel infiltrator could get this far into the camp. Titus has ordered sentries and patrols thick as fleas on a dog."

"Still, maybe they slipped through."

Nicanor shook his head. "I don't think it's possible. Even men garbed as legionaries or auxiliaries could not move about the camp at night without being challenged for the daily password. Titus sets it each morning in the staff meeting. Anyone who doesn't know it or has it wrong... is cut down on the spot."

A thudding of hooves came from behind them, where Titus's command tent and quarters had been set up. Yosef had called it the "Camp of the Assyrians," explaining that 800 years before, another army had staged an unsuccessful siege of Jerusalem—before they built the third wall.

"The general goes to investigate...." Nicanor explained. Though he did not see Titus, the flash of his standard-bearer among the horsemen galloping past assured him the general was among them. They would inspect the collapsed siege tower. "Let's return to sleep... if we can," he told Yosef. "I'll learn more in the morning, and we can see Sayid." Nicanor turned to follow Yosef inside the tent and stopped to look at the night sky.

"*Media nox*, midnight, and the *kalends* of Junius are upon us," he muttered, shaking his head at how time passed so swiftly. Since arriving at Jerusalem, he had pushed down thoughts of Cleo, letting them slip free only long enough that he could pray to the gods that she wasn't still in the city. Or if she was, somehow, that she would survive and that he could find her, even though she might choose Yosef.

The waning gibbous moon above the city cast its light upon attackers and defenders, the guilty and the innocent. It drew forth from Nicanor a memory of Graius's story of Cleo as a young girl, shooting arrows at the moon. The old gladiator's memories of her had warmed his heart on their long journey to seek help from her brother, Marcus Otho.

But now he was left with a longing he did not know would ever end. With a sigh, Nicanor turned and entered the tent.

CIV

Junius 70 CE

Jerusalem

Beneath the Temple, the Cistern Water Bucket Chamber

"I'll get you out, Elian!" Miriam called to the boy. "Stay still... try not to move." She studied the place where the lip of the stone had fractured. The opening to the space below had been cut through a thin layer of rock beneath her. She slid closer, gripping Zechariah's wooden staff in one hand, and reached her free hand up to the bucket-hoist's rope. *Will it hold me?* She tugged. It creaked but seemed secure. She unwound her sash and tied one end to the looped handle of the lamp and the other end to the line just within reach below the hole.

Miriam swung her legs into the hole, moving the staff with her so that it spanned the opening, its ends well past the rim on either side. The stone beneath her gave way with the sharp crack of rock splitting, and she dropped. Elian shouted from below as her hand clamped on the staff to bear her weight. Her dangling feet struck the hoist line, nearly striking the lamp and bringing another strident cry from Elian below her. As she brought her other hand up to grasp the staff, the rimstone broke farther, and her sweat-slick hand slipped. She was directly over Elian and would knock him loose if she fell. Both of them would plummet. How far, she did not know. Yosef had once told her of the caves believed to be beneath the Temple, but he and Matthew had never explored them.

Already exhausted, Miriam could not hold on much longer, but she would not bring harm to Elian. Carefully, she raised her legs and swung her lower body away from the hoist with small motions. As her momentum increased, she extended her legs to fall into the darkness clear of the hoist and Elian. Her arms trembled with the strain, and the ache of cramped abdominal muscles spread to her ribs. A tremor through the staff signaled there was no more time, and as the stone and the staff came loose, Miriam tumbled away from the hoist line and buckets. Zechariah's staff grazed her as it fell into the void below.

She barely had time for the wrenching pain of regret and grief as she lost her most important keepsake of the man who had saved her before she crashed against the edge of a coarse stone platform. Her head slammed hard, and the darkness enveloped her.

* * *

THE GREAT SEA CISTERN CAVERN

Miriam blinked her eyes open to nothingness as splitting pain shot through her head as she raised it from the rough rocks she lay upon. Carefully her hands searched to either side of her. One hand met a stone wall, and the other found an unevenly hewn edge over the nothingness. She blinked again, focusing on the blurred, dim glow above her. Where the lamp was miraculously still tied, revealing Elian dangling from the hoist many feet above her over the abyss.

"Elian... Elian...." she called plaintively, her head pounding so it was hard to focus. The bundled mass of her hair beneath her headdress had cushioned the blow, but she felt a tender knot at the back of her head, and her fingers came away sticky. She shook her head, increasing the pain, and she widened and narrowed her eyes, allowing them to see more clearly. "Elian!" she called louder this time.

"Miriam! I saw you fall, and I thought..." Elian's voice choked off. "I knew I would die, too."

"I landed a rock shelf down here that seems cut into the cave wall." *Likely from the workers who rigged up the mechanism*, she thought. Gingerly, she sat up, knelt on the narrow shelf, and explored the walls with her hands. She found a few spikes driven into the stone and supposed they had once secured lines used by the workers.

"Can you save me again, as you saved us from the knifemaker?" Elian's voice had a pleading sound. She struggled to think. *How long have I been out?* She and Ya'el had already been tired when they returned to the chamber to find the boy gone. The surge of strength that had coursed through her with the urgency of finding Elian had now burned away. She was faltering with that loss and the blow to her head.

"Miriam... I'm scared... I think your lamp will go out soon. The light flickers...."

Miriam gauged time by the full lamp reservoir she had topped off before descending the steps from the passageway above and the now sputtering wick. It had been hours. Without the lamp, Elian would be in pitch black as she was. That glow her eyes were drawn to had anchored her. When it was gone, they would both be trapped in nothingness. "I can't climb out to save us, and I can't reach you from here," Miriam said. She would not lie to the boy. But she could offer hope, the only one she had. "But Ya'el will come looking. She's a strong woman... she'll not stop until she finds us... until you're safe."

"You will be safe, too," Elian said. "She told me you're her sister, in her heart." His voice broke with a parched croak, and he coughed. "I'm thirsty, and my head hurts...."

Miriam swallowed, her throat dry. "Mine hurts, too... but don't despair, Elian." She could hear the boy cry in the silence and knew she must cheer him. "One day, when I was younger," she said, "my father found me crying in our courtyard beneath one of the trees."

The sniffles stopped. "Why were you crying?"

"I was sad because someone I loved had left Jerusalem, and I thought I would never see him again. My father sat with me and told a story. Our *Shlomo Hamelech*, King Solomon, was a mighty ruler with many responsibilities that often weighed heavily on him. So, at times, he was sad about how hard the burden was to carry. He brought his advisers together, and they were wise men all—he asked how to deal with that feeling when it came upon him."

"What did they tell him?"

"Well, they went away to think for a long time, then came to him and said, "O King, make yourself a ring and engrave up on it '*Gam Zeh Yaavor*.'" The king immediately understood their wisdom. He had the ring made and always wore it. Every time he was distressed, he looked at his ring, which improved his spirits."

"What does '*gam ze*...' what you said... What does it mean?"

"This, too, shall pass....' So, Elian, we'll wait and watch for Ya'el. This, too, shall pass." Miriam settled back as best she could on the narrow shelf, her back against the wall. Mathias had been right. With time and when Ya'akov entered her life, she had gotten over Ehud. But then, so much had gone wrong. The attack upon her, Ehud's return, and his death—his blood on her hands! And now Ya'akov. But she could never love him again. That would dishonor the feelings Ehud's return had brought back. So much had happened... and now the Romans were at Jerusalem's walls. Guilt and her regrets would never pass—she would bear those burdens until she died. And her revenge on the Romans and their collaborators had yet to make her feel better about anything.

Miriam wanted to sleep but wouldn't. She would stay awake for Elian. She leaned forward to stare into the darkness below until dizziness made her sit back. "It cannot hurt me, it cannot hurt me..." She murmured what Zechariah had made her repeat over and over.

Mostly she had come to believe that darkness could not hurt her. But what was *in* the dark could....

CV

Junius 70 CE

Jerusalem

Beneath Bezetha, the Baris Underground Remnants

Dawn was breaking as Ya'el reeled off the ladder from the shed above. The evening and night hours had been spent moving and hiding, then moving to hide again as the horde of Romans spread across Bezetha. At one point, she had taken a galea and scutum from a dead legionary. She used the helmet to mask her features and the shield to hide her garb that differed from the legionaries and auxiliaries establishing their positions facing the second wall. She had cast the Roman articles from her once her third circle of the area around the shed, and the stone stockpiles seemed clear of invaders. Even with her mind focused on staying alive and reaching the Baris underground, she had mused on that thought—Romans as invaders.

Jerusalem had become her home because she had grown close to Yosef's family. They had accepted and protected her and Elian. They had become family, and where "family" was... was home. Now the army of her countrymen was here to destroy that home, which made them invaders. She regretted having shot all her arrows as she avoided the soldiers more than once through the night.

"Elian... Miriam!" she called, praying Miriam had found the boy. Bezetha above had become a field of slaughter. The men of Jerusalem—fighters or those trying to run away—were butchered with no offer of surrender. She had witnessed a handful of cornered women who were so hungry that they asked even these soldiers for food. The men had laughed and dragged them off. Ya'el shuddered to think of their fate.

She entered the chambers used as their living space and found only darkness. "Miriam...." Only Cicero's squawks came in reply. She went to the bird's cage and removed its shroud. The parrot's glare, the disarray of his feathers, the raucous complaint... told her no one was there. She released Cicero, who took wing and flapped an angry circuit of the chamber to land again next to a water bowl he gulped from. He settled and began to preen, watching her.

So she is in one of the tunnels... and I hope so is he, Ya'el thought as she took a drink from a waterskin and slung it over her shoulder. Then she went to a shelf and took down the largest lantern she could carry one-handed. She filled it with oil and checked the blade Miriam had given her to ensure it was secure on her belt. She began to pick up her bow but left it—impractical for a tunnel. With a last glance at the bird and taking the lantern with her, she descended to the lower chamber where she would access the tunnels.

At the entrance to the second unsealed long tunnel, Ya'el paused and took a deep breath. It had never become easy for her, even with Miriam, to go into the tunnels. And now she was about to enter one she had not explored—and she was alone.

A clatter echoed from the short passage to Antonia Fortress, and she reached to unsling her bow—it was not there! She pulled the blade and turned to face the two men at the mouth of the tunnel.

"Matthew... Eleasar!"

* * *

AT THE END OF THE SECOND TUNNEL

"Miriam still marks her passages well," Matthew commented." He was in the lead, with Ya'el in the middle and Eleasar ben Ananias behind them.

"We have to be below the Temple by now!" Eleasar called from the rear. "Have you been down here before?"

"No," said Matthew, "though Yosef has. I had hoped to go with him before he left to study with the Essenes. But we never did. And soon after he returned, he sailed for Rome."

At the sound of his name, Ya'el had a feeling she had not experienced since she'd left Yosef's family, a feeling she missed. She always cared for Yosef, and every mention of him reminded her of that. She loved hearing stories of him from before they met on the ship to Rome. When Yosef had arrived with the Romans, it had jarred her. But not as much as it had his family. It was curious that Matthew's tone was level when he referred to his brother. He was unemotional. But Miriam always grew heated at any mention of his name. "Despite my mother's belief—or hope—about his intentions, I don't understand why my brother accompanies the Romans. He knows as well as does anyone that our leaders do not listen to reason."

Ya'el agreed with her about Jerusalem's leaders. They seemed as self-interested and power-hungry as many Roman nobles. After the shipwreck in Rome, Yosef spoke of his people and their relationship with Rome. Though he was no longer in chains, Yosef seemed still imprisoned by his duty to save his people. *Or to try.*

"I wonder where the sealed passages lead?" Eleasar commented as they passed one of them.

"We'll have to come back and see...." Matthew stopped. "This passage has been closed, too, but opened again," he said as he knelt. Ya'el could see the opening through the mortared stone that had once sealed it off. He lay flat, pushed his torch through, and crawled in until he was out of sight. "It continues to a set of steps going down," Matthew said, his voice echoing.

* * *

THE CISTERN WATER BUCKET CHAMBER

"I think we are east of the Temple Sanctuary," Matthew said, holding his torch high as he entered the chamber at the bottom of the steps. "Below this is the cistern that serves the Temple."

Ya'el pushed past Matthew and Eleasar, crying, "Look!" She ran to the bucket-hoist, stopping once she saw the jagged edges of broken stone. Lying flat, she crawled to the rim and lowered her torch into the opening; it bumped against an empty lamp tied to a rope.

"We have you!" Matthew called, and Ya'el felt her ankles gripped by strong hands.

Ya'el strained her eyes as they grew accustomed to the darkness below. There he was! "I can see Elian!" she cried, her voice more full of relief than she expected. Tears stung her eyes. The boy's eyes were closed, but she could see the rise and fall of his chest. "Elian!" she called softly, but he did not respond. "He's alive... but he's not answering me, and he's caught on something."

"Do you see Miriam?" Matthew asked.

Ya'el swung the torch to cast its light farther. "I can't see her... or anything more."

"We're pulling you up to rig a line. I'll go down and get Elian."

As she backed away from the edge and stood, Ya'el breathed heavily. "What's down there... beneath him?"

Eleasar and Matthew took loops of rope that lay near the wall and searched the walls for something to secure them. As he worked, Eleasar told her, "It's said the cistern is carved into a flattened spire of rock that juts from a massive cavern wall. But surrounding it is an abyss. The stories say the cavern below still holds waters from the great flood. Some believe it is where our souls go to await judgment. Some say it holds the chamber where Abram ben Terah prepared his son Yishaq as a sacrifice to Yahweh. Others believe the *Aron Ha-Brit*, the Ark of the Covenant, was hidden here when the Babylonians captured the city over six centuries ago. The sacred vessel containing the *Aseret ha'Dibrot*, the ten commandments given to Moshe upon Har Sinai, commandments that he brought down to our people. No matter what stories people like to tell, this massive cave holds a reservoir of water, fed from the aqueduct, that supplies water to the Temple above. Priests draw from it to fill the upper smaller cisterns and the containers used to wash away blood from the sacrifices during festivals."

"I don't care what's below. I just want to save Elian and find my sister," Matthew commented. He knotted one end of his rope around a bent spike protruding from the wall behind the hoist frame and moved toward the hole in the floor.

Ya'el agreed. *Then we must get through Antonia Fortress*, she thought. While hiding nearby in the night, she had watched it once the Romans were inside the third wall, and the ramparts were thick with men. She hoped the armory passages would be empty later. The Romans were close, but others who were threats remained... much closer within Jerusalem's intact walls.

CVI

Junius 70 CE

Jerusalem

Beneath the Temple Enclosure, The Cistern Water Bucket Chamber

Matthew touched the crusted gash on the side of Elian's head and called up to Eleasar, "He's struck his head and got quite a cut, but it's stopped bleeding!" He gripped his rope with one hand and searched behind the boy with the other, speaking comforting words, but the boy did not respond. Elian's tunic was rucked up and torn where the bucket's loose metal fastener had caught and pinched it, wedging the fabric tight. "Send down another line—with two loops in it—and I'll use my rope to secure Elian while I free him."

A minute later, Ya'el called down, "Here...." Matthew looked up and saw Ya'el prone, her arms through the hole, lowering a rope. He worried about the thin slab giving away, and she seemed to answer his unspoken question: "Eleasar has the rope secured... and me, too. When you are ready, he'll take up the slack."

The rope came down alongside him, and when the loops neared the level of his feet, he called out, "Stop and hold." He waited a moment, then put his foot in one loop and tested his weight. It held, but it threatened to spin him around. He carefully slipped his other foot into the loop, then pulled the slack end up to pass around Elian's torso and under his arms. He tied it tight. "Take up the slack on Elian's line," he ordered.

Grasping the boy's tunic at the shoulder, Matthew carefully pulled Elian toward him and, with his other hand, took the knife from his belt sheath. He shifted the blade close to the trapped cloth. It was hard to see in the dark and with the boy's shaggy head casting a shadow, so he had to feel where to cut the bunched, knotted cloth with one hand.

"What?" Elian cried as his eyes fluttered open close to Matthew's cheek, and he jerked away, setting them both swinging. "What?" he cried again.

"Steady, Elian... don't move, and I'll free you of this thing...."

"Matthew?" The boy's eyes were unfocused, and he blinked several times. "Can you see Miriam?"

Matthew's heart lifted with hope as the boy half-twisted, grimacing at the discomfort of the rope, and craned his neck downward. "She fell, and I think she's hurt."

Matthew followed his gaze into the depths of the cistern, but he could see nothing. *Must get him up first*, he thought.

"Elian," Ya'el said soothingly but firmly, and the boy turned his face up in the glow of the lamp she was lowering. When she had his attention, she said, "Be still, Elian. Matthew will free you, then Eleasar and I will pull you both up. Then we will see about helping Miriam."

* * *

THE GREAT SEA (CISTERN) CAVERN

Once freed and in Ya'el's arms, Elian had told them how Miriam had fallen and been silent for so long that he had thought her dead. Then she spoke for a while but sounded like she was in pain. Then she had been quiet, but he could not tell for how long.

Now Matthew was down into the shaft again, and Ya'el lowered the long torch tied mid-shaft to the line alongside him, so he pivoted in a short arc. A current of air fanned a tongue of flame to lick sporadically at the rope. He would have to check it closely before it bore any weight. He had an unlighted torch tucked into his sash so he could light it if needed once he reached the floor of the cistern cavern.

Ya'el called from above, "Eleasar says you should be close!" That warning came at the same instant the swaying torch revealed a glint of water near his feet. "Hold!" he cried out, and both lines stopped. He stepped from the loops and slowly tested the water depth beneath him. Eleasar knew more than he did about what many priests called the "Great Sea." It was the largest of the 30-odd cisterns and underground water chambers beneath the Temple Enclosure. It was an immense limestone cavern, its ceiling supported by pillars as grand as those of the above buildings. It held a vast measure of water. Enough to fill the entire Holy of Holies, someone had told him once. Water was diverted to it regularly from the aqueduct and withdrawn with the buckets on ropes draped over a water wheel mechanism above. He'd once seen that it could be turned by men or animals.

He and Eleasar had re-rigged the lines to drop farther from the bucket-hoist. He could see the lowest containers floating in the still water nearby. Water sloshing up to his knees, Matthew pulled the lighted torch from its line, stuck the end of the rope through a loop on the belt at his waist, and knotted it. Holding the end of his line and raising the torch, he turned to his left, looking in the direction Elian thought Miriam had fallen.

The water he moved through maintained an even depth until he reached a rocky shelf that formed what seemed to be a walkway that followed the base of the cavern walls. As he stepped up on it, a sound turned his head to the right, and he followed it. He quickly came to a rocky ledge over a head's height above him, projecting from the wall. A foot dangled from the shelf at arm's reach. He touched it.

"Miriam," he said softly, and a low groan came from the ledge. He jammed the butt end of the torch into a crevice where the shelf joined the wall and pulled himself onto the ledge. Miriam was slumped against the wall, her head lolling on her chest, which rose and fell steadily.

Matthew knelt beside her and touched her shoulder. Her eyes flew open, and she rasped out, "Matthew!"

"How did you end up here, sister?" he teased to reassure her. "Did you think you had fallen into the abyss Mother used to warn us about? She always hoped she'd frighten us enough to stop our exploring." He smiled and helped her sit up.

"Elian?" she asked after swallowing painfully.

"He's safe with Ya'el and Eleasar above. And now we'll get *you* out of here."

Miriam nodded and winced. Matthew leaned closer and gingerly cradled her head, hesitating when he felt the lump at the back of her skull. "I'll take you home," he assured her.

Dread gripped him then, wiping away his relief at finding the boy and his sister. He thought about the Romans above them, inside the third wall. Once the Romans breached the second wall, they had to fight them in the streets.

CVII

Junius 70 CE

Jerusalem

Bezetha, The Roman Encampment, Nicanor, and Yosef's Tent

"How is Yosef?" Sayid asked, settling on the camp stool and taking the cup of water Nicanor offered.

"He spends most of his day writing his journals and working on a manuscript recounting this war for Titus—well, I think *that* order came from Emperor Vespasian. A box of legion reports arrived today from Alexandria via Caesarea. General Titus is reviewing them with Yosef this evening—so he can use their information."

"How can Yosef write a history from those reports of men who have killed so many of his people? And no doubt they record their assurance that they will defeat the city he calls home." Sayid shook his head.

Nicanor studied his young friend's deeply tanned face, shining with sweat in the firelight. That afternoon he had visited Sayid at the siege works along the second wall of Jerusalem. He had waited for Sayid's shift to end, then asked him to join him for supper. Nicanor no longer needed to study him—Sayid was no longer the boy he had first met years ago. Still slender, not thickset like most soldiers, the young man had nevertheless proved he could work at least as hard as other men.

Nicanor had come upon Marcus Sabinus watching Sayid work and was irritated at being caught doing so. Marcus had nodded a curt greeting and walked away, but not before he gave a last approving glance at his son.

Nicanor answered Sayid's question. "I asked Yosef about that myself. He said all he could do was put as much perspective as possible in the writing to balance it. Ultimately, Vespasian and Titus will render judgment on what is written. But Yosef's personal journals, too, detail this war as *he* wishes, the portions that will not go into his work for Vespasian."

"Do his dreams still trouble him?" Sayid asked as he poured water from his cup into one palm, splashing it on his face with a sigh of pleasure.

Nicanor tossed him a cloth. "I am sure they trouble him still, though he has stopped mentioning them to me."

"I dream of the battle... the last man I killed...." said Sayid as a glistening drop of water fell from his chin. He wiped the back of his neck and looked up at Nicanor. "Do you have such dreams? Or am I weak that I have them?"

"I'm glad you weren't hurt... and I've heard from others that you fought well." Nicanor took a deep breath, held it for a heartbeat, then let it go with a sigh. "I dream, too. For a long time, I dreamed of Beth Horon... about my friend Graius and how he died saving me. I have dreams about the men I cared for who died. The men I've *killed* do not haunt me, but it's good that you dream as you do."

"How so?"

"Before meeting you and Lady Cleo, I saw wars, mostly battles fought for Rome, as maybe not righteous battles.... but right. We, the legions, brought order... or kept it. That's why the empire has lasted so long and become vast."

"But now...."

Nicanor's thoughts flitted to Paul the Christian sitting in his dark prison cell in Rome, talking of his own beliefs and opinions but equally interested in Nicanor's.

"The people I've met since we met on the *Salacia* years ago... you people—not events—have made me who I am. I now realize war can be rational for both sides and that war is not always the best means to resolve differences. But in combat, Sayid, when it's your life or death... reasons and differences do not matter. Have no guilt over the men you kill in combat. Learn from the experience, but let their ghosts fade."

"So, you've never dreamed about a man you killed?"

"Of course, when I was a young soldier. I have seen many a good soldier badly affected by memories of battle long afterward. But I learned to move past it, and that experience strengthened me. "

"That's why it's good I dream of him?"

"Yes, you know now that it's common—there's nothing amiss with you. You will defeat the dream as you defeated the man, making you even stronger." Seeing Sayid's thoughtful expression, Nicanor continued. "There is one man I fought that I've recently dreamed of— I suppose Yosef's dreams of Yotapta stirred my own. They attacked our siege weapon at that place—what you just experienced, but at night. A truly giant warrior led the rebels. I later learned he was named Dov, and he was mighty. I came against him and felt like a boy against a man. He beat me down and could have killed me. But he broke off his attack to save one of his compatriots. I got a glimpse of the face of the man he saved."

He paused then, and Sayid looked at him expectantly.

"It was Yosef," Nicanor said. "If I had killed Dov, our friend Yosef would have died. If Dov had stayed fighting me... as things were, *I* would have died. The rebel Hercules was remarkable, a juggernaut no one man could stop. He did not die that night, but later in the siege, he died for his people in an act of heroism I doubt I will ever see equaled."

Nicanor leaned toward Sayid, bracing his hands on the table. "Dov showed selfless courage. I gained true respect for Yosef's people that day—I now regret that we are fighting them. But I pray Jerusalem has no more giants like Dov on their second wall."

"They will bring Nico forward in the morning... readying it for duty," Sayid commented slyly. "Your namesake...."

Nicanor snorted. "Wipe that grin off your face. I should never have entrusted you with my nickname."

"It was Celsus who—"

"Yes, I'll speak with Celsus about that the next time I see him." Nicanor turned at the sound of creaking wheels. Newly constructed siege towers, large shadows in the night, were revealed in the torches and bronze fire bowls set on pedestals around the perimeter of Titus's command tent. "Yosef told me his people call this area, between the walls, the Camp of the Assyrians. Maybe centuries ago, your ancestors fought here."

"I still want to fight... and I *will* fight, but when I see Yosef... I wish.... Will he get another chance to speak to them, encourage them to surrender?"

CVIII

Junius 70 CE

Jerusalem

Bezetha, The Baris Underground Chamber

"Matthew and Eleasar are barricading the shed door and blocking the access to these chambers," Miriam said as she entered the underground room a little unsteadily. "We don't want to leave any entrances from Antonia Fortress. When they're done, we'll go." Rubbing her head, careful of its tenderness, she glanced at Elian, who slept on a pallet of blankets, his arm curled around Cicero's cage, the parrot dozing, too. The boy's hair was wet and smoothed back, a cloth around his head holding a bandage. Ya'el, with unexpected strength, had carried him all the way from the cistern while the men assisted Miriam and carried the torches and ropes.

"It's your turn," Ya'el said as she motioned to Miriam to sit next to a low table holding jars of water and a bundle of clean linen. Miriam gratefully took the cup of water and piece of bread Ya'el pushed toward before, cloth in one hand and a jar in the other. Ya'el poured water on the tangled, clotted mass of Miriam's hair, saying, "This may sting." Carefully she cleared the matted strands, freeing them from the skin. She set the pot down and raised a lamp for better light over the wound. "I think it needs sewing, but I cannot tell, for the surrounding flesh is swollen, and your hair is thick. You are lucky to be alive, I think."

"Cut the hair away, then... cut it all... as short as yours. I have no need to be seen as a woman."

Ya'el did not hesitate, and in minutes, it was done. "The wound is clean," she announced, "but we'll need to close it up when we get you home." She wrapped Miriam's head as she had Elian's. "I have fresh clothes for you over here," Ya'el said as she took up a basin of water and cloths and walked to an alcove out of sight of the main chamber.

Miriam followed her. With a grimace and grunt of pain, she lifted her tunic over her head, careful not to dislodge the bandage.

"Oh, Miriam," Ya'el said, raising the lamp so Miriam could see how badly her side was bruised from her hip to ribs. "Why did you not tell me about this? From your fall?"

"Complaining doesn't make it hurt less."

"Still..." Ya'el helped her remove the soiled tunic, then took the daggers Miriam unstrapped from her forearms. Ya'el then waited as Miriam unwound her linen bindings around her chest and sponged off her body. Then Ya'el handed Miriam the length of linen and waited as she wound it around her torso, flattening her breasts.

"Perhaps that will support your ribs," Ya'el said. "They must be sore." She helped Miriam get one of Matthew's tunics over her head and a broad sash around her waist. Finally, she watched Miriam strap the daggers back in place. As they left the alcove, Miriam instinctively adjusted the long sleeves of Matthew's old tunic to cover the sheathed daggers on her forearms.

Footsteps then announced Matthew and Eleasar, and the two sank down by the low table, took gulps from the cup there, and crammed bread in their mouths. "We're done," Matthew said wearily around the lump of bread in his mouth, and then his eyes widened as he took in Miriam's short hair beneath her head bandage. "Rouse Elian and get Cicero wrapped in a blanket," he said, "and let's go. Pray we don't get stopped in the Antonia. If we do, that's likely where we'll die."

* * *

THE UPPER CITY

The last Miriam had heard of the rhythmic sound of the Romans battering Jerusalem's wall, it had been distant and echoed. But the harsh clangor of the Roman assault on the second wall was close and sharp as they came out of the tunnel in the dead-end alley at the northeast corner of the agora. Matthew left the alley first to check the street, then returned.

"The market is full of people," he said. "They're fighting for scraps around the food stalls. Stay with me—don't run and don't draw attention, but move quickly."

Miriam had led them through the tunnel, each breath and step sending darts of pain through her side, but now she moved to stay behind Elian and Ya'el. After the silence in the caves below, the discordant noise was disturbing. It was not only the Romans' attack but also the shouts and screams of her own people fighting among themselves. She wished Eleasar had not left them so he could draw away the men in the passageway in Antonia Fortress's armory. But because he did, they could pass through from one tunnel to the next unchecked.

Miriam was concerned for Eleasar's own sake and the rest of them—they might need his sword. Matthew was well-armed, and Ya'el had her bow and a full quiver. Still, she could not effectively stand off an attacker without Zechariah's staff. She would have to get close to use her daggers.

As they neared their home, Miriam moved ahead as they entered the side street leading to the rear courtyard entry. Matthew was last to ensure no threat followed. Miriam opened the gate with relief, passed through the row of trees, and stopped short. A man sprawled face-down in the courtyard, his headcloth awry.

"Father!" she shouted and ran to him, falling to her knees in a pool of blood still spreading beneath the body. Ignoring the stabbing pain in her side, she turned the man over. *Ya'akov!* she cried, seeing her one-time love dead. But she also found herself relieved. *It's not Father!*

Someone had slashed their friend's stomach open, and his eyes stared but could no longer see. Her heart pounded in her ears and throbbed inside her head, drowning out the sound of the Romans beating on the second wall. Matthew had already rushed by her and headed into the house. She sensed Ya'el and Elian kneeling beside her, Ya'el's arm around her shoulders. Miriam suddenly surged to her feet and twisted out from under Ya'el's arm toward the house. "Father! Mother!"

Matthew was inside with a crying Rachel and a hysterical Leah. "Yonatan and his men have taken them," he said.

"Why?" Miriam asked, gripping his arm.

"When Mother, who was talking with Ya'akov, saw it was Yonatan, she sent Leah and Rachel to hide." Miriam knew what they always talked about—her. That sent a deep pang through her.

"Yonatan told them he came for the traitor's father," Matthew said, his jaw clenched. "Ya'akov tried to stop him, and Yonatan drew his sword and killed him."

Miriam asked Rachel and Leah, "How do you know this if you were hiding?"

Rachel wiped her face with the sleeve of her robe. "Yohanan ben Zaccai was here and tried to talk Yonatan out of taking your father but could not. After Yonatan and his men left with your parents, Yohanan ben Zaccai came to tell us it was safe to come out. We heard some of what was said, and he told us what else happened."

"Why did Yonatan take my mother?"

"When he struck Ya'akov down, and his men roughly grabbed your father, Rebecca took Yohanan's staff and hit Yonatan, nearly felling him. So, he took her, too."

"Where's Yohanan?" Matthew asked.

"He said he would see Simon bar Giora and Yohanan ben Levi—to protest and try to free your parents," Rachel replied.

"I must go, too," Matthew said, turning to Miriam. "I'll be back as soon as possible. When Eleasar gets here, ask him to stay with you."

Miriam nodded and murmured, mostly to herself, "I'll take care of Ya'akov." She walked slowly toward the courtyard.

Ya'el suddenly appeared at Miriam's side and said, "Should we take his body somewhere?"

Miriam shook her head. "We can't bury him as should be done." She closed her eyes and continued. "At one time, he would have been my husband and become family to us all. I will wash and prepare the body, then bury him here under the trees, where we used to sit together."

* * *

The light wind did not carry away the scent of the spices and oils Miriam had used, the ones she could find. The comforting, mournful aroma hung over her where she knelt, sweat-soaked, next to the dirt mound Ya'el insisted on helping her dig in the garden to make a grave. They had lowered Ya'akov's body into it, covering him with the beautiful blanket Miriam had chosen for his graveclothes. Miriam had asked to be alone, and Ya'el had gone inside with the others while Miriam filled in the grave.

Silent tears left trails in the dust on Miriam's face, and she looked up at the sound of Ya'el's approach. "I loved him when I was a whole... and unsullied woman," Miriam said. "The memories of Ehud, the one I loved first, would have been bitter for the rest of my life... but I could have been happy with Ya'akov."

"I'm sorry, Miriam," Ya'el said, reaching down to help Miriam, holding her hand, and gazing into her eyes.

Rachel joined them, then, and said, "Leah and I warmed what soup remained in the kettle from yesterday. We are out of food now, for Yonatan's men took the rest of the little we had left."

"I'll get Elian." Ya'el sighed. "He's always hungry." She walked to the house.

Miriam looked at Rachel, who was watching Ya'el enter the house. "How are you and Leah?" Miriam asked.

"Leah is still upset. Even hearing Yonatan's voice scares her... that and hearing the hatred of Yosef so many express." Rachel rubbed her own reddened eyes.

"And how are *you*?" Miriam asked again, and Rachel took a square of parchment from the sash of her robe and turned it absently between her fingers.

"Yosef is not a traitor," Rachel said. "I know it in my heart. Don't you?" Then she looked down. "You must think me stupid to love him. He was a man my sister loved. A man Ya'el has feelings for... or once did. A man who both married and divorced... while he was a Roman prisoner. A man not far from us now... yet so far away. Still, I love Yosef, Miriam. He is trying to save us in his own way."

Miriam nodded. "I know... and I understand how that hurts you." She pointed at the folded parchment. "What's that?"

"Just before Yonatan and his men arrived, a workman—to judge by his clothes—brought this. He said his name was Kefa. I told him you weren't home, and he told me to give it to you." Rachel handed it to her.

Milam looked at the sealed message. "Did you read it?"

Rachel could not look at her. "Yes."

"Did you show it to my parents or tell them about it?"

"No." With tears, Rachel finally looked at her again and then walked away.

Miriam unfolded the square and read:

"One more traitor to kill. If Yosef speaks again for the Romans, get within reach and kill him. If he asks to see his family, that will give you the chance. If you do not, others will die instead."

It was unsigned, but she recognized the Sicarii leader's writing. She knew Eleazar ben Yair's connection with Simon bar Giora, who could clearly get messages to and from Masada. The Sicarii knew far more about the tunnels into and out of Jerusalem than most. And she knew who Eleazar meant by "others"—her family. How could she carry out such an order? Kill her brother, or risk another family member's death?

CIX

Junius 70 CE

Jerusalem

Bezetha, The Roman Encampment, Nicanor, and Yosef's Tent

"The fighting begins at sunrise but doesn't really stop, even through the night," Yosef said from the opening of their tent.

Nicanor stretched, trying to loosen his tight muscles and stiff joints in what had become a morning ritual. His jaw cracked with his massive yawn. In a close-quarters siege like this, neither side got much sleep. And the nights were more challenging than the days—for both sides. *The rebels fear we'll overrun the wall in the darkness. And we stay on alert, for the Jews might come out from behind their defenses and attack at any time in one of their flashing raids.*

He joined Yosef just outside, where he had been up before dawn to watch the sunrise behind the Jewish temple and the Mount of Olives to the east. Nicanor, too, appreciated the beauty of the sun's rays haloed behind the structure, turning gold into a radiant gleam and brightening the brilliant white stone.

Nicanor looked about, thankful his tent was positioned farther from the siege line. Trying to sleep in his armor, as did the men closer to the wall, would have made it even worse. Likely, the Jewish fighters on the wall and behind it also slept in their armor, given their sudden attacks. Hours before, they both lay blinking into the dark, listening to the reaction force meet the rebels' attack. "Your people attack so recklessly," he said. "They kill some of our men and damage some equipment but cannot drive the legions back."

Yosef sighed and sat on a camp stool he'd brought out of the tent. "I know the men who command them. Jewish warriors are aggressive, desiring to satisfy their officers. The rebels are unconcerned with their welfare—they care only about what injury they can inflict on the Romans. It does not matter that they will probably die if they can kill an enemy. That's what their leaders now expect. Simon bar Giora is the field commander who drove back the 12th Legion when it assaulted Jerusalem years ago."

Nicanor did not need a reminder that Giora had led the rebels at Beth Horon. That rebel commander was responsible for the death of many of his men and his warhorse Abigieus. That memory sparked a thought about Carmenta, now in the care of Marcus Attilius at Antonia Caenis's estate. Then Tempestas, his warhorse after Abigieus. He had learned from Titus she was still at the legion camp in Ptolemais. Before moving their tent inside the outer wall, Nicanor had visited Albus to feed him two handfuls of salted barley. The treat he always brought for the animal. From there, he planned to order the exchange of mounts—request Tempestas from Ptolemais—and he would never again see Albus, who was not a true warhorse.

The animal had greeted him with his usual stolidity. But after he had eaten the treat, Albus had nudged Nicanor's head around with his muzzle to look him in the eye. Somehow, he had sensed something—maybe his thoughts—and took a step closer. He draped his head over Nicanor's shoulder and rested it there. Then Albus lifted his head and backed away with a nod. Nicanor had left him, then, instructing the commander of the auxiliaries responsible for the legion mounts to have someone continue to bring Albus his treat each morning. Though not a warhorse, he had decided to keep the animal.

Nicanor sat next to Yosef as the camp busied in the growing light of morning. "As disciplined as we train legionaries to be," Nicanor said, "I've seen men act rashly since this siege started. Romans are emboldened by what seems to be our perpetual training and warfare. They have helped the empire grow and hold what we have gained. Now they see General Titus with them at every moment, bravely fighting beside his men. The general sees who fights nobly and rewards him. Sometimes that recognition leads men to do foolish things."

Yosef nodded but did not say anything.

"Yesterday, I saw a man," Nicanor said. "I later learned his name was Longinus. He suddenly leaped from his line to charge rebels that had sallied from the wall. He broke through their ranks and killed two, spearing one in the mouth as he rushed at him, pulling out the spear and using it to kill the second. He then ran unhurt from the Jewish ranks and back to Roman lines."

"And Titus saw... and rewarded him...." Yosef said.

"Yes. Everyone could see that Longinus showed courage. But Titus did what any outstanding field commander should do—to prevent others from seeking to imitate the man. After they repulsed the rebel sortie, he ordered the men engaged in that combat to form into ranks. He told them that such a lack of discipline as Longinus had just displayed was madness. As their commanding general, he told them, he would see that they recognized the *true* bravery of fighting—and winning—with discipline and orderly conduct. He directed them to be vigilant and to prove their courage without taking unnecessary risks."

"It's a fine line between acknowledging and encouraging such courage... and enforcing discipline. At Yotapta, I had to do that as well." Yosef shook his head and continued. "Titus has had me interpret for him as he questions the men and women he's captured. From what I've heard, Yohanan ben Levi and Simon bar Giora have far less concern for their men than Titus does for his."

Nicanor rubbed his aching shoulder, smothering another yawn. "Titus told me the patrols capture hundreds each day who are deserting the city. Are there so many secret ways out of Jerusalem?"

"There are some... most are very old, but some men still know of them. But few can escape that way." Yosef stood and entered the tent. As he passed inside, Nicanor heard him say to himself, "Not enough by far...."

* * *

AT THE SECOND WALL

Nicanor joined Yosef, who watched the auxiliary units, including Sayid's with his father in charge, move several larger war engines to the middle tower. The armored rebels defending the wall seemed frozen in place as the wall shook with the heavy blows of the ram. As the siege weapons crept closer, a man rose from behind the ramparts beside the tower.

"My name is Castor, captain of this tower!" the man called out in clear Greek. "I would speak with your General Titus. We ask for his mercy. If the great Roman general should promise that, we will surrender to him."

"Is this a trick?" Nicanor asked Yosef. "Would one of the captains surrender this easily?"

Yosef shook his head. "I knew of a Castor in Galilee who was one of Yohanan ben Levi's lieutenants—those men can never be trusted. But it is for General Titus to decide."

The line commander had passed the message back, and an order soon came to cease the ram's battering and the assault on this wall section. Titus came forward, surrounded by his guard and accompanied by Tiberius Alexander, and joined Nicanor and Yosef. He shouted to the man on the rampart, "Speak your mind! Tell me what you wish."

"General, I'm Castor, and I lead these men." His arm swept to include those nearest him on the rampart. "We will leave this tower and come down from our position, leaving it undefended, if we have your right hand of security. I want the Roman to guarantee that I and any men I bring will not be harmed if we surrender."

Titus leaned toward Tiberius Alexander, saying, "Order the men to lower their bows. No weapon is to fire until I command it." When his second-in-command left to pass that order down the line, Titus turned back to call calmly to Castor, "I'm pleased to hear this. I would give the same guarantee to all of Jerusalem."

Several of the men with Castor began begging for Roman mercy, but as many others cried out, they would never submit to Roman slavery while it was in their power to die as free men. The quarrel between the men grew more heated, and those who resisted faced the Roman line and shouted with gestures and pointing.

Nicanor whispered to Yosef, "Those men are not speaking Greek. What are they saying?"

But Yosef did not answer—his eyes were locked on those men.

Nicanor turned to Titus and said, "General, I think this is just a stalling tactic to delay the attack."

"Perhaps, but let us see what this man does." Titus kept his attention on the rebel captain.

Castor called upon his five stubborn men to accept Titus's offer. But the men grew angrier and slammed the bare blades of their swords against their chests, and then the five who would surrender rushed the resisters.

"They fight among themselves," Titus said with a shake of his head as the hand-to-hand conflict took the ten rebels out of sight below the battlements. Titus looked at Yosef and said, "Surely these men are in earnest that they wish to surrender. Is that not what you wish?"

"General Titus, we cannot see what is happening beneath the ramparts," Yosef replied and then involuntarily ducked, as did they all, when from behind them flew a volley of arrows, striking near Castor. He stood while one of the next flight of shafts grazed his face. But the man did not duck below the bulwarks.

"Stop the firing, and do not fire again until I command!" Titus roared, and Nicanor knew some would later pay for the continuing lack of discipline.

Titus turned to Yosef and ordered, "Go forward and talk to him—offer my right hand. I guarantee they will live if they surrender."

Final Siege

"General, you cannot trust him," Yosef replied. "You cannot trust any of the men led by the rebel leaders. If they were civilians, true civilians, then... maybe." Yosef studied Castor again, saying, "I think this is just a lure to draw you closer. Or perhaps to draw me. They could want someone close enough to kill or wound. I should not talk with him, and you should not."

Titus frowned but nodded. He turned to an aide. "Bring up the man Eneas... the deserter we captured yesterday."

The aide returned in a few minutes and reported that the prisoner was willing to go forth if he would either be rewarded or freed if he could get Castor and his men to surrender the tower. Titus agreed, and soon Eneas climbed atop one of the siege engines to call out to Castor. With all eyes on the prisoner, all witnessed the large stone that flew from the wall and struck the Roman next to him.

And just then, the ten rebels who had fallen out of sight behind the rampart appeared, firing arrows toward the general and his entourage. All the arrows fell just short of them, as had been ensured by the placement of their observation point.

At the proof of yet another hoax, Titus stepped over to Tiberius Alexander, who had just returned to the gathering. "By showing mercy to rebel fighters," Titus said, "I show a weakness I can no longer afford to suggest to men such as these. Bring the rams forward and more siege weapons as well."

* * *

That evening....

The Pool of Towers

"Aren't we near the gate where I met you and your brother four years ago? I recognize that stone arch." Nicanor pointed across the vast water reservoir—over 240 feet long and 140 feet wide—now being used by the legions. Yosef had told him the reservoir was known by two names. The Tower's Pool, for the three structures at the juncture of the third and second walls, or Hezekiah's Pool, for a king of several centuries before. More than once in conversation, Yosef had explained that Rome and Jerusalem had documented great spans of history and warfare. Something they had in common, those experiences embedded in the *pneuma* of both peoples. *Gods, let not my future be determined by the bloodshed in my past*, Nicanor prayed.

"Yes. The Gennath Gate is near, but four years seems an eternity ago."

"I think I told you then that your visions had likely not foretold that meeting...."

Yosef nodded with a smile that quickly faded. "I was glad when Cestius Gallus stopped the assault to attempt a peaceable resolution; many of my people were happy too. Cestius Gallus trusted we were serious about peace. But those who wanted to fight broke his trust—and yours—with their attack even as he spoke. I can still see that heavy rock striking you."

Nicanor rubbed his shoulder. "It seems your people manage to strike the same part of my body each time!" He watched his friend study the second wall that began next to the Gennath Gate at the city's oldest—first—wall that extended north and around to the Antonia Fortress. The torches and brazier fires of the legionaries and auxiliaries manning the siege weapons clustered at the central section of the second wall cast the only light that revealed the wall. The defenders were wise not to reveal any lights that might help the Romans aim.

But the darkness shrouding the crenelations did not slow the rebels' own fire. Their arrows created their own night noise punctuated by the cries of men the shafts found.

"Yosef," Nicanor said, now that things were quiet enough to allow for the question, "the rebels were shouting today while that man, Castor, attempted his ruse. What did they say?"

Yosef's hand went up to his clean-shaven chin. He glanced down at his tunic and cloak. "They spoke in Aramaic and said I'm no longer a Jew... said that I have forsworn my people... and my faith. I've become a Roman. I'm sure Tiberius Alexander enjoyed hearing that."

Nicanor knew what he meant—Tiberius Alexander always seemed to be watching for Yosef to join him in renouncing his people. *As if doing that as a means to rise in power or place was not something to be ashamed of,* Nicanor thought.

"Afterward," Nicanor said, "they abandoned the tower, probably knowing as we do that the wall section there will fall by tomorrow. After what happened today, do you still want to speak to your people? Who can you find to trust if Titus asks you to speak to them again?"

"Yohanan ben Levi will have men try to kill me if I get close enough to strike. Perhaps Simon bar Giora would, too. But I hope to reach the other people who will surrender despite those two. I would speak with any of them if it might save some. But my family are likely the only ones who would not harm me."

CX

Junius 70 CE

Jerusalem

Bezetha, at the Second Wall. First Breach

"Ready!" Titus's command rang out over the field at the last strike of the ram's head and a klaxon blast from the legion's senior *buccinator*.

A thousand men of the heavy infantry surged through an opening Nicanor thought was too small for it, slowing the assault. *We should have widened it and better cleared it, too, so the men would not have to lower their shields to clamber over the rubble,* he thought. He had warned Titus of this when he and Yosef met with the general the hour before dawn. What he saw now proved his point.

Yosef had offered Titus his own caution: "The area behind the wall there is part of the Upper City's marketplace. It has slanting, narrow streets crowded with the shops of merchants who sell wool and cloth." He did not need to say more to suggest the innocence of those who might be first run over by the Romans.

"Good," Titus replied with a harsh tone. "There's less chance it will be well defended."

Nicanor added, "Narrow streets like Yosef describes will limit our movement and our ability to bring more force to bear on the rebels in those streets. And what if we have to pull back and regroup?"

Titus had been adamant: "I have twice shown the rebels my generosity, despite two hoaxes meant to deceive me. Still, I do not wish to strike them harder than necessary. With my demonstration of moderation, I believe they will not set traps and risk my anger. I've ordered those who are not armed and do not fight against us to be spared. I've ordered their property not to be burned. Those who relent in their obstinacy will live. That will lessen resistance."

That had ended their talk, and Yosef quietly returned to their tent to write in his journals while Nicanor accompanied Titus. Vespasian had ordered Titus to preserve as much of the city as possible. And—most important of all—not to destroy the temple and its treasure. So the general demonstrated his restraint to Yosef's people as an incentive to comply. While Titus had presented the measures as being "for the sake of Jerusalem's people," Nicanor was sure that was only partly true. The empire badly needed to loot Jerusalem to replenish the imperial coffers, Nicanor had gathered from what he'd overheard, though he had not thought it wise to tell Yosef.

But the rebels saw Titus's overtures as a sign of weakness. They probably thought the Romans were afraid they could not take the city. *Fools*, he said to himself, mouthing the word.

As the last men of the breaching force passed through the wall, Nicanor could hear the crash of metal in the streets and the screams of fighting and dying men. The leading edge of the assault units had already clashed with the rebels. *We should have razed this part of the wall completely*, he thought. Minutes later, the shouts and screams grew closer instead of moving further away. From the city to him came the noise of many men—hundreds—a rhythmic tromping, with the braying of animals and the clatter of wheels on stone. From the north, the upper gate of the second wall, came the swelling sound of men running and yelling as they hurtled toward the Roman line behind the wall.

As the sounds and fighting men converged, Nicanor instinctively wheeled and raised his shield in time to deflect a spear as another hissed by his head. Then he twisted away and felt a shock to his shin. A slinger's lead bullet had fallen short and skipped off the stone to strike him hard just above his *caligae*, where the open-faced heavy-soled hobnailed sandal-boots met his greaves. Titus's personal guard moved between this new threat and their general. A cohort of heavy infantry and another of auxiliaries peeled from the line to form a screening barrier. Bugles echoed as Titus ordered men to move up from the staging area of the encampment in Bezetha. He brought forward a half cohort of archers, held in reserve, to put the wall at their back and fire over his men at the onrushing rebels.

Nicanor spun back to the wall to see the first men scrambling through the breach, some staggering as they carried others and some spilling back through the opening. He spotted the commander of the archers and ordered, "Split your men and turn half into the breach to provide covering fire for our men falling back." The man stared at the opening, where wounded men were struggling through the gap, and he nodded and shouted at his men to reposition them.

Climbing atop a high pile of rubble, Nicanor stared through the gap riven in the wall. Stumbling backward, fighting as they went, dozens of Romans fell to the street dead or too injured to reach their feet. These were the remnants of the breaching force, far fewer than a thousand. The wagons he'd heard were loaded with stone, pushing the Romans out of the city. He could barely see the heaving shoulders of oxen that drove the wagons before them. A teeming mass of armored rebels followed the animals, and the side streets he could see from his angle of view were also full of armored men surging toward the break in the wall.

The tops of buildings now bristled with bowmen and slingers. Nicanor did not know whether it was an arrow or a slinger's lead that caromed off his helmet to knock the *galea* from his head and tumble it down among cracked blocks of stone from the wall. Cursing, he steadied himself and raked a forearm across his brow to wipe away the sweat stinging his eyes. He heard another shrill bugle call and the thud of horses closing on his position, probably mounted archers coming fast. He darted a quick look through the breach. There would be no stopping the rebels. They would reseal the wall and retake it. He climbed down from his surveillance point, and when he reached the ground, an arrow struck and stuck between his feet. He blinked to clear his eyes.

A white shaft.

What? He stooped to pull it free. The arrow had been fletched with green feathers. He strained his eyes, looking above the wall, trying to see the rooftops of the buildings he had just glimpsed. *Cleo!*

CXI

Junius 70 CE

Jerusalem

The Upper City

Matthew had gone two days without sleep, and Miriam hated to wake him, so she spoke softly. "Matthew, Yohanan ben Zaccai is here...."

"What?" His voice was thick, and he rubbed his puffy eyes and wiped his mouth. "Any news?" he asked as he swung his legs from the cot to the floor.

"Not of Mother and Father, other than that Simon bar Giora won't intercede. Yohanan ben Levi still holds them." Miriam gritted her teeth, wishing she had killed the Gischalan long ago and Yonatan, his attack dog, too. "Eleasar sends word from the second wall at the central tower. Yosef was seen there when the Romans set up to attack, and Eleasar thinks he will try to speak to the rebels again... maybe you can talk to him?"

"What should we speak of?" His weary cynicism struck painfully within her. How much of their old connection the siblings had lost in these years!

Miriam heard the hurt in Matthew's voice, too. He was torn between his father's dismay that Yosef had become a collaborator with the Romans and their mother's adamance that Yossi would never betray his people. Miriam herself felt a wave of anger against Yosef, and the message from Eleazar ben Yair weighed on her mind. What if Matthew should return with arrangements for them to speak with Yosef? What would she do? What *should* she do?

"Tell Yohanan I'm coming," Matthew said. "He and I will see what our brother has to say."

* * *

The Rooftop Terrace

Though it was still early, the summer day's heat was already upon them. Beyond the terrace, the sounds of battle at the second wall to the north had become alarmingly distinct. The shrill sound of Roman bugles was much more strident than the round bleats of the *shofar*, the ram's horn that called the Jewish people to action. The random harsh blasts of the Roman bugles made them all edgy. Cicero had several times tried to pull free from Elian. Miriam had started to tell the boy to put the bird in its cage but relented when he finally settled on the leather pad wrapped around the boy's forearm.

A final blast of a Roman horn was soon followed by a swelling thrum spreading from the marketplace area inside the second wall. It was not the sound of despair Miriam had expected after hearing the echoing crack and crash of stone that surely signaled a Roman breakthrough of the second wall. Instead, this growing noisy hum became a raucous surge of joy... the cheering of victory. Soon the streets were full of people chattering as they learned the Romans had broken through, yes, but then had been beaten back. Rachel and Leah had jumped up and danced joyfully, but Miriam sat still, nursing her side. Besides, she knew—anyone with common sense knew—whatever respite that victory might gain them... it would not last.

"I see Matthew and Ya'el!" Elian exclaimed, moving closer to the baluster around the rooftop terrace.

With a grunt, Miriam stood, pressing a hand against her ribs. Despite her aches and pains, she felt relieved. Matthew had been eating less, so there was more for the others, especially Elian and Yohanan ben Zaccai. Miriam had insisted she would accompany Matthew to the second wall. "Everyone in the Upper City is at risk, and we grow weaker daily. None of us should go anywhere alone." He had pointed out how gingerly she moved and asked what good she could do until she healed, so Ya'el had gone in her stead, dressed in her bowman's garb and gear. Miriam breathed too deeply and winced even as she welcomed the sight of them coming home.

As the crowd on the street thinned, she noticed a tall, rangy man following behind Matthew and Ya'el. He slowed when they slowed, stopped when they stopped, and kept to one side of the street as if ready to dart away. When they drew closer, she recognized it was Arins. Matthew had gone to talk to him the evening before, explaining what had happened to Ya'akov and their parents and that Yohanan had finally found a witness to Shammai's death. The charcoal seller had been killed by a man with a peculiar creature tattooed on his hand. Matthew and Eleasar had both commented that Arins's men had such tattoos. It seemed senseless these days to dig into the cause of Shammai's death, but the man had been Yohanan's friend, so Matthew wanted to ask Arins about it. Matthew had returned home late, so she had not learned what he had found out.

And now Arins followed Matthew but stayed back, seeming not to want to be noticed. *Why?*

Miriam had seen more of Arins's men throughout the city, and that disturbed her. "Those men have the eyes and the bearing of the man who tried to kill me," she'd told Matthew, "after I slew Yehudah ish Krioth." Matthew and Mathias had been startled to learn that Yehudah had been one of Gessius Florus's spies in Jerusalem and an informant within the Sanhedrin. Were it not for Zechariah, Miriam would have died that day, too. Zechariah had saved her after she stabbed Yehudah in the throat. As the traitor fell, a Roman mercenary, surely sent by Florus to keep Yehudah in line, attacked her. Zechariah had thrown himself over her body and taken the blades meant for her. She had then killed the mercenary with Zechariah's staff. So much had happened in those brief moments.

Miriam squinted at Arins on the street below, wishing she had Zechariah's staff to lean upon now.

"Cicero!" Elian cried as the parrot shot from his arm and sped directly for Ya'el, almost below them. Miriam could now see Arins's face as he stared at Ya'el and Cicero. A smile of recognition slowly stretched the creases on his face, making Miriam uneasy. The trader looked pleased as he stood there watching as Ya'el settled the bird on her shoulder before continuing toward the front entry of their home.

Miriam had stopped wondering about Arins after the man helped tend Matthew's wound not long ago, but perhaps she should keep watching. But the trader had brought some food into the city, which had helped many. Arins had also been vouched for by Boaz, who had been a friend of Yohanan's for many years. But no one had seen Boaz for some time, even before the siege. Yohanan believed he had retired to be with his family in Caesarea. Under Roman control now, even more so than when Gessius Florus had lived there as Roman Procurator.

In the past, she mused, Florus had proved to have more than one agent in Jerusalem. Could there be someone other than Hananiah still in the city? Could it be someone like Yehudah ish Krioth, someone they believed they could trust? He thought then of Esau ben Beor, the Idumean whose secret hatred of Jerusalem had enabled Florus to leverage him as his new spy within the Sanhedrin. Despite what each of those men had seemed to be, she had learned the truth and killed them.

Miriam decided. "Elian," she said, "stay with Leah until Ya'el comes for you—she will be here in a few moments. Rachel, I need your help. Please come with me."

Miriam quickly and awkwardly stripped off her clothes in her room, grunting with pain. She directed Rachel to wrap her ribs with enough additional binding to flatten her chest. "Say nothing about this—but tell Matthew and Ya'el I left to follow someone." She would give Arins the benefit of the doubt by not naming him, but she would follow him to see what she could learn of the man. With Matthew's old tunic in place, the sleeves hiding her daggers, she returned Rachel's wide-eyed nod and donned a dark cloak with a hood.

With a last warning glance at Rachel, she slipped down the stairs and through the courtyard just as Matthew and Ya'el entered the front door.

* * *

The Tunnel

Once he passed through the hub of tunnels and connecting passages near the Temple Enclosure, Miriam realized where Arins must be going. But his men had sealed it after she and Ya'el had returned from the Modi'in Valley, where they'd hidden the key to the copper scroll. She took a shuddering breath before passing through herself, as much to calm her nerves as to be sure he did not detect her behind him. Her skin crawled every time, and worse when she was alone where she had seen Gessius Florus meet with Yehudah ish Krioth. She had accidentally jostled the loose rocks that had alerted the Roman that someone was there listening to them. Here, Florus ordered the two legionaries to find and deal with the noise source. She shuddered at the memory of their groping hands and thrusting bodies that had not stopped until Zechariah killed them. Her tremors did not end until her sense of direction and distance overrode them. She must follow Arins through to the last part of the passage, where it exited into the valley.

Ahead of her, a challenge in Greek stopped Arins, and she crept closer to see what would transpire. During their passage through the tunnel, the fringes of light cast by Arins's large torch had been enough for her to see well enough to silently follow him. She used her extraordinary vision well even in the dimmest illumination and not had to risk lighting the small hand lamp tied to her waist.

Arins's reply was more distinct. "If I cannot join Lord Florus because of his visitor, ask him to come to see me. What I have to say will not take long."

Minutes passed before there were voices again before her. "Lord Florus," Arins said, "you'll be pleased to hear I've just seen your wife in Jerusalem...."

CXII

Junius 70 CE

Jerusalem

Bezetha, The Roman Camp, Nicanor, and Yosef's Tent

Nicanor could not believe what he had heard all through the night—joyous celebrations from the rebels at their great victory. "How can they rejoice?" he murmured before turning over again, rearranging his limbs and thin blanket.

Still, that was not what had kept him awake. He had not told Yosef of the green-feathered arrow that meant Cleo was still alive—she had recognized him and sent him that signal. He cherished the arrow, now hidden under the pallet on his cot, as he cherished the hope that he could somehow save her. And lamented that he had not told Yosef—could not tell him... yet. He wanted to treasure the knowledge of Cleo by himself. But if he did save her, she would perhaps be drawn to Yosef again. Nicanor could not hold that against his friend, but he held from Yosef the precious knowledge. And that reality was bitter in his throat—it galled him that he withheld from the other man who loved her most in the world that she was nearby!

He rubbed his burning eyes as he tried to heed what Yosef was saying. His friend, too, had been restless in the night—Nicanor had heard him leave the tent for several hours.

"My people begin to think the Romans will not attempt another attack. They believe they forced the Romans back behind the second wall and are thus impossible to defeat." Yosef hung his head as he clasped his hands between his knees, where he sat dejected at the table in their tent. "They cannot imagine a larger Roman force than they have just pushed back. And in their jubilance, they do not feel the hunger creeping up upon them."

He looked up then at Nicanor and said, "I've been to where the captured are held. I spoke with some who fled the city only to end up in the slave pens of the Romans. Yohanan ben Levi and Simon bar Giora feed themselves at the people's expense, creating great misery for those they purport to serve. I have seen the sites of the food stores they've destroyed, setting fire to the grain so that their enemies among their own people cannot have it. What treason against my people!"

"A famine cannot be avoided," he added. "Some are just now feeling it, as shortages of what they prefer become shortages of what they must have to live. That will worsen. The soldiers already tell of Jews asking them for food in exchange for their enslavement. The soldiers jest that they're making it very easy!"

Nicanor shuddered, a response he never had, no matter the reason. But now, something deep within him had been touched, and he was affected by it all. Roman sieges often forced cities to exhaust their resources, weakening their will—or ability—to fight. These tactics had served the empire well—as at Yotapta, against Yosef and the people he commanded. Yotapta had plenty of food stores—its leader had not foolishly destroyed them—but lacked a water supply within the city. Jerusalem was the opposite—they had plenty of water, so their sustained deprivation would affect them slowly. They would begin to behave differently, become ruthless in what they were willing to do... and dull in their response to the outrage. That shook him. He did not want to see Yosef's people suffer so. "Will the threat of starvation be enough to convince your people to surrender?" he asked.

"I know how men like Yohanan ben Levi and Simon bar Giora choose to think. They are so crazed with their cause that they see the people's destruction working to their benefit. Their pride makes them believe they will survive this war with Rome, so the Gischalan and Giora oppose any who want to surrender. They call them weak even though they have done the weakening! Their every decision hurts my people." Yosef stood and paced the small space of the tent in his agitation. "They are willing to let many die for them. I don't need a dream to see Jerusalem's *leaders* have blinded themselves to their guilt, their sins against the people. Last night you told me they made a wall out of their comrade's bodies to fill the breach in the second wall. What little sleep I might have had was lost thinking of that."

Yosef sank onto the stool again and added, "I often went with my mother when she shopped along those streets as a child. Some of the dead are surely people I know... people I knew." Yosef lowered his head again as if his thoughts were too great a burden. With his elbows on his thighs, he gripped his head, pressing his fingers against his skull.

Nicanor became aware of the glow growing at the openings of the tent flaps. He rubbed his eyes again, felt his stomach roil, and decided

Final Siege

to tell Yosef no matter what. *But later.* Now he must prepare to join Titus and the command staff for the attack to retake the second wall.

"I can only imagine your thoughts, Yosef. I would not add to your pain, but your accounts," he waved his hand at the writing materials on the table, "your accounts should tell of it. Some who retreated from the city yesterday told me the rebels were cutting the throats of shopkeepers about to surrender to us. So do not weep or lose sleep, my friend, for the rebel fighters killed." Nicanor clasped Yosef's shoulder. "Titus will not make the mistake of too small a breach, too light an effort, nor too little discipline among the force breaching the wall today. He will send in his hardest legionaries, and they are merciless. While the rebels have retaken their second wall, it will not be for long."

* * *

Later...

Nicanor and Yosef's Tent

Nicanor stripped off his armor with relief outside the tent, reporting the day's work to Yosef, writing at the table he'd set up outside. That morning the sun had risen to reveal the 2,000 heavy infantrymen in place with 500 engineers protected by two cohorts of auxiliary armored infantry. Titus had not hesitated to show his might, and there had been no restraint on this day. "In the night, the rebels dragged off the dead oxen, more concerned about the food than the risk of retrieving it."

"More important than gathering the bodies of our dead, too, I expect," Yosef said grimly.

"I think they intended the dead to become a gruesome part of the obstacle for the legionaries." Nicanor focused on undoing a strap.

"I saw Sayid," Nicanor said, "and he said he'd worked all night under torchlight to position three rams against the wall. The assault began with four hundred archers and a dozen ballistae sweeping the defenders from the battlements. As the wall came down with the massive force of Titus's will, the rebels were forced to flee from the most powerful onslaught I've ever seen. Far greater even than at Yotapta."

At that, Yosef raised his head. "I did not watch today," he said dully. "They've fallen back to the first wall?"

Nicanor nodded. "The rebels now hold only the areas behind the first wall—Antonia Fortress, the Upper City, and your temple and the hill upon which it rests."

"The Temple Mount, we call it," said Yosef. "Why hasn't Titus attacked the Lower City?"

"It is not an area of significant resistance, not during this stage of the siege, at least. Instead, as the populace becomes hungrier, the resistance is strongest where the rebel leaders are, and the rich always manage to have food. That is where Titus focuses his effort, that he might weaken those who still have strength."

"Including my family...."

"Yes, Yosef. One thing, though, should cheer you. Titus has decided to pause the siege to allow the rebels time to reconsider their position. After seeing the second wall destroyed so quickly and thoroughly, they may find their minds may change. Still, Titus believes they need more proof that what they face is a mightier army than they imagine. He ordered his commanders to form the army tomorrow morning to receive their pay. All the legions and auxiliaries will line up for it in full battle gear, so the people of Jerusalem can see them. He expects you and me to join him tomorrow morning to begin that display."

* * *

INSIDE THE PERIMETER OF THE SECOND WALL

The entire area before the first wall was full of dazzling sunbursts reflected by the armor of the Roman army confronting Jerusalem. As was the custom, each man drew his sword and marched with the weapon in their hand. Ahead of the foot soldiers rode rank upon rank of cavalry on finely equipped horses.

Yosef stood with Nicanor upon a platform erected overnight where the second wall had stood. He gazed upon the part of the city he had best known all his life. The Upper City and the agora were encircled by the entire first wall. Within that wall were packed the people of Jerusalem. Some in the Upper City stood on the roofs of their houses to see the army so close. Yosef craned his neck to glimpse his home, but he was too far away. From what he could see, every part of the city was filled with crowds unable to ignore the spectacle before them, and the crowds moved in waves that made them seem one body. All wanted the best view of the Romans—the empire's might—that controlled their fate.

"You'd think this would dismay even the most courageous rebels," commented Titus to Tiberius Alexander beside him. The words rang out clearly to all nearby. "They witness the polished weapons and armor of Romans who display such order and discipline. One would think that the rebels would change their minds."

Yosef noted the looks occasionally cast his way by Titus and the sharper darts, seemingly sly, from Tiberius Alexander. Yosef ignored them and kept silent. The crimes of Jerusalem's leaders against his people were horrendous. Men like Yohanan ben Levi and Simon bar Giora would never change their minds, for they knew the Romans would never forgive them. They understood theirs would not be a simple death before a Roman tribunal's judgment of punishment. It would, instead, be torment, so it was better to die in battle. So they would declare, though Yosef doubted the Gischalan had faced much danger in this siege. Still, their fate was settled—and the innocent would die with the guilty.

It took four days for all the Roman soldiers to receive their pay, and he and Nicanor were there each morning for a portion of the spectacle.

* * *

THE ROMAN CAMP, NICANOR, AND YOSEF'S TENT

On the morning of the fifth day after the destruction of the second wall, Yosef roused from a semi-sleep to find Nicanor entering their tent. "I've just come from Titus's command tent. The rebels still do not seek peace, so the general has divided his legions and raised embankments for specific assaults. The 5th and 12th Legions will attack Antonia Fortress, which they'll use to stage the assault upon the temple. The 10th and 15th will be at the monument to your ancestor—Hurqanos—and from there, Titus will take the Upper City."

Nicanor stood silent, hands on hips, watching Yosef, then, with a decisive grunt, went to his cot and reached under its thin pad, bringing out a white arrow with green feathers. Yosef could not believe what he saw and looked at Nicanor with confusion.

"I should have shown this to you days ago," Nicanor said. "I will explain why I didn't—I owe you that. But what is most important... Cleo is alive."

CXIII

Junius 70 CE

Jerusalem

The Tunnel Near the Hidden Valley

As Miriam backed away from the guards at the tunnel's exit, she realized it was Gessius Florus's men, not legion soldiers, who had entered the valley behind her and Ya'el on their return from Modi'in. She must get home to tell Matthew, so he and Eleasar could seal this tunnel, too. But not before she ended Arins's life.

She dared not make an attempt so close to Florus's mercenaries, so she returned to the nexus area, where the central gallery would give her enough room to maneuver. Just past the last bend of the passage, well out of sight, she took the handlamp tied to her sash and lighted it to see her way through.

As her mind roiled with what she had just heard, she was surprised when it seemed only minutes later that she reached the nexus. She settled into a wall cleft just wide enough for her, extinguished the lamp, and tried to ease her breathing. Deep breaths hurt, her head throbbed, and her side ached. It was difficult to wait, but she must deal with Arins. Was he connected to Hananiah, too? Did Arins tell him of the tunnel, and was that how Hananiah planned to escape the city with Florus's help? She could see how Hananiah might take her to deliver whatever information Florus would pay for.

With the Romans pressing their attacks, she had remained in the Upper City or out of sight in the *Baris* underground chambers with Ya'el. She had not seen the knifemaker in some time, but he could still be watching her, waiting for a chance to speak. Ya'el had said she was certain Gessius Florus wanted only two things: the Temple treasure and Ya'el—Cleo—herself. Hananiah could provide him access to both through Miriam. Of course, Miriam had told him she wanted to be free of her family—that had been true during her darkest times. Hananiah could take that to mean she would abandon them and flee the city.

For Gessius Florus, it all meant he needed to capture someone with knowledge of the Temple treasure, wherever it lay, before the city fell into Roman army hands. He would come after her father,

Yohanan ben Zaccai, Eleasar ben Ananias, or Matthew to get that knowledge.

Ya'el had told her of Florus's hatred of Yosef, so he must want Hananiah to take Matthew. He was the youngest and likely the most actively involved—other than Eleasar—in hiding the Temple treasure. And there would be less opportunity for vengeance with the Temple Guard Captain. It must be Matthew.

If Arins had realized Ya'el was really Cleo... did Hananiah know that too? Miriam had convinced him that Ya'el and Elian had fled to Masada. But with the chaos within the city, Ya'el had stated she was done with hiding, so it would be easy enough to find her. Miriam would kill Hananiah—if she could—before he ever harmed anyone in her family, including Ya'el. But first, she must take care of Arins.

A scuffling of rocks on the stone floor echoed ahead of the torch glow. Arins was coming. The torchlight grew as she shrank back into the alcove and pulled her hood around her face. Just as he passed, she exploded from the cleft with a last wish that she had Zechariah's staff. She hooked an arm around the lanky trader, trying to pull him to her as her blade arced toward his throat. Arins surprised her with his strength and broke her grip almost immediately.

"Whoever you are," he said, "you breathe too loudly... but that won't be a problem for you too much longer."

In the light of the dropped torch, she saw Arins back away and, with practiced ease, pull a pouch from his belt and twine its long pull cord around his hand and ball it all into a fist, the pouch dangling. She, too, had retreated to reset her feet for another attack, but suddenly Arins closed on her before she expected it. He snapped out his arm, and the bag struck her shoulder heavily, and the impact sent jolts of pain through her arm. Still, she raised her blade in her fist to slash at the man's face. And missed.

Arins ducked and spun on a heel, slamming the heavy bag into her injured side beneath her overextended arm. As she gasped and stumbled, Arins's free hand, now a clenched fist, punched the side of her face. She staggered away, outside the reach of the light from the torch burning on the ground. The bag flailed again, striking her right arm above the elbow, and the whole limb went numb, and her blade fell from her hand. Despite her sudden weakness on that side, she instinctively thrust her hand forward to claw at his face while she brought her left hand up with its dagger.

One of Arins's long legs shot out and swept her off her feet so that she struck her head in the same place as in the cistern. The stitches burst with a tearing stab of pain, and she tumbled onto the hard-packed floor littered with chunks of stone. Dazed, she tried to roll as another kick connected with her ribs. The movement took her closer to the sputtering torch.

Arians landed astride her as she bucked and twisted. Her fogged mind locked onto the sensations long burned into her memory. The weight of a man upon her. His heaving breath—foul—and the stench of his sweat. She melted into weakness with the salty taste of her tears as she cried out in vain.

Her old nightmare was happening again, in the same place as before.

Her arms pinned beneath her, she twisted onto her side while Arins's hand gripped her throat with fingers hard as the stone beneath her. His fingers dug in deeper, crushing her throat and closing off her breath.

In a single moment, the glow from the torch revealed his snarl of fury, which kindled her rage. Gasping, she bucked harder, working to free her left arm, despite the man's strength. She felt the sinews of her neck strain to their utmost and the throb of a vein near her eye as she raised her head to challenge him.

"I—will—not—die—here!" she screamed.

She wrenched her left arm free and punched into the side of his head with her fist closed around the dagger, feeling the blade pierce the soft indention beside the eye. For a half heartbeat, she held it there, then grunted as she heaved up and shoved it in deep. She watched the light in his eyes flicker and go out as the torch died, and she was in darkness.

CXIV

Junius 70 CE

Jerusalem

The Upper City

Though the Romans never stopped their attack, the market grew busier at night when the barrage lessened. People moved quickly from stall to stall, merchant to merchant, not to haggle over the prices but to scuffle with others over the dwindling foodstuffs that became more costly daily. *What will Jerusalem become when no food is left?* Miriam wondered as she made her faltering way among the people. The buzzing in her ears was not the hum of the market but the blows to her head. She put her hand on the burst wound at the back of her head and took away a smear of blood she wiped on her tunic.

The market had no sellers of cloth, bronze-work bowls, earthenware containers, or the myriad practical items and luxury goods that no one needed anymore. Frantic, grasping people focused on two things—food and wine. The first was to survive and the second to cope, and there was plenty, in comparison, for coping. The trade for wine was like in former days, though the angry, fearful voices rose shrilly at the food stalls as people snatched at what they needed. Her stomach growled, accompanied by twinges and spasms gripping her injured side with each step.

This day no one would notice her limping, head down, cradling the injured arm she pressed close to her stomach as she trudged toward the Upper City. She was just one of many fighters seeking their homes and loved ones to tend the wounds they'd incurred defending the first wall, for the medical stations nearest the fighting could help no more. Some walked on their own, and others were carried by their friends. In any case, no one took heed of another poor soul seeking refuge and healing.

It seemed to take hours in the dark, but she finally reached the street to her home. She was barely through the rear gate when Ya'el came from the darkest shadows within the row of trees. "Thank the gods... Rachel said you had left, and we've worried ever since." At the sight of her faltering steps, Ya'el rushed to Miriam to help her, extending an arm Miriam gratefully leaned upon. "Who did you follow and why?" Ya'el asked anxiously.

"Arins is not the man we thought him," Miriam said with a breathlessness that evidenced her exhaustion and pain. "He works for your husband, who has a camp in the hidden valley. I followed him there, where he spoke with Gessius Florus... telling him you are alive in Jerusalem—"

Ya'el stiffened with a quick intake of breath, and Miriam finished, "And he knows where. But don't worry," Miriam patted Ya'el's supporting arm, "don't worry—I killed Arins in the tunnel."

"Oh, Miriam," Ya'el replied in sympathy and relief. "I'm not afraid," she added, "but now I have the means to draw Florus near." Ya'el flashed Miriam a look that seemed almost bitter joy, "I'm the bait to trap him...."

Miriam understood vengeance but warned her friend, "That could prove deadly to you, too."

"I don't fear him... nor what might happen to me, as long as he pays for what he has done. Besides, if I die and he lives, it might not be long anyway. I saw Nicanor during the second wall attack. I fired an arrow he would know by Cicero's green feathers with a message that we're alive. I know he'll watch for other messages if I can get them to him. He detests my husband... if he learns of Florus's plan... and I don't survive this siege, I think Nicanor will kill him anyway."

"Was Yosef with him?"

Ya'el shook her head as they entered the house. "No, Miriam...."

* * *

The next morning...

Matthew rubbed the scar on his chest absently, and Miriam could guess his thoughts. Arins, who had stitched up that wound, was a Roman spy—it did not matter that he was Gessius Florus's agent and not one of the Roman army—and that enraged him. She had convinced him to send a dozen Levite guardsmen to defend the tunnel, where it narrowed to a choke point before the nexus gallery. That was another thing she had learned from Zechariah, though Matthew knew the stratagem, too. He wanted to collapse the tunnel and seal it, but she persuaded him it could still be useful. Their family might escape if they could get their parents released. Mathias and Rebecca would never want to leave, but they would if things became too dire... and that seemed to be what they were heading toward. For now, though, she was not telling him Ya'el had contacted Nicanor.

Despite her misgivings about that, she was willing to see if it offered some hope of help. But she would not say anything to Matthew, and raise his alarm, until something became certain.

"You mentioned what Yohanan ben Zaccai told you," Miriam said. She brought out one of Zechariah's maps showing the Lower City and the areas west and south of it. "He said that Akiva ben Yosef hid the last supply train of the merchant Sabbuas," she pointed to the Hinnom Valley south of the city, "in a cave here. Do you know which cave? There are dozens, maybe hundreds, of them."

Matthew shook his head. "No... I haven't spoken with him."

"We must find out." She traced a line on the map, wincing at one of her many pains. "Here's the branch passage used by the workers in Hezekiah's Tunnel," she said, drawing her finger from the city to the west. "It reaches the Kidron Valley. That's how we got Nahum out of the city." She paused. They had sneaked the Essene leader from the city to escape Yohanan ben Levi and his Zealots. He had made it to his home in Qumran, only to be killed there by the Romans. She squeezed her eyes shut at the idea that Yosef had been a witness to his murder. *But we must be on with what is before us,* she thought. "At about its midpoint," she said, "another tunnel split off to the south toward the Hinnom Valley. That entrance was also choked with dirt and stone, but I didn't investigate to see if it was entirely blocked."

Matthew leaned back from the table. "We need that food for us and to help whoever we can... maybe even to bribe the men guarding Mother and Father..."

Leah came to the steps of the house into the courtyard. "Matthew, someone is at the door. You said we shouldn't open it...."

Matthew rose and returned a minute later, with Yohanan ben Zaccai following him. Miriam greeted him abruptly: "Yohanan, I must meet with this Akiva you told Matthew about."

"Yes... yes... I'll bring him to you later, Miriam." The old rabbi looked upset.

"It's important—"

"Yohanan came to tell us, Miriam," Matthew interrupted, "that Yosef is at the earthworks before the Antonia Fortress, where the Romans are preparing their attack. He's asked to speak to Simon bar Giora."

CXV

Junius 70 CE

Jerusalem

At the Antonia Fortress

Miriam had convinced Ya'el to stay at the house with Elian, Rachel, and Leah while she went with Matthew—who also required convincing since he wanted her to rest— to listen to Yosef. Now she stood, in the garb of a man, with her brother, Eleasar, and Yohanan ben Zaccai on the parapet of the northwest corner of the fortress battlements overlooking the Roman earthworks and siege line. Along the western wall of the fort stood Simon bar Giora, flanked by his personal guard. Eleasar muttered to Matthew, "Yohanan ben Levi doesn't care to come, it seems, or he fears confronting Simon."

Miriam looked out to the platform built upon the Roman earthworks. A large man stood upon it with a sword and glittering full combat armor. Next to him, an unarmed man dressed in the robes of a Roman civilian of some good standing, judging by the apparent fineness of his clothing as it swayed in the light breeze. "A tribunus," Matthew had said of the man with the unsheathed sword in his right hand and a large infantrymen's shield in his left. And Miriam recognized her brother's bare, clean-shaven face even from a distance. She was glad their parents could not see Yosef standing there with the Romans. It would crush their hearts. She felt anger boiling up in hers.

A hush grew over the crowd of men on the ramparts of Antonia Fortress. It spread to quiet the multitude of men and women in the courtyards within the walls. The Roman soldiers surrounding the platform stood quiet as Yosef began to speak.

"Spare yourselves," he called out in a voice that carried across the space between them. "Spare your city and our Temple, do not be more obstinate than are the Romans. They respect sacred Jewish rites and our Temple, even though you have become enemies. The Jews, who alone had the benefit of these things our people value and hold holy, now have leaders who seem in a hurry to destroy them. The Romans and I have heard the stories of the fighting within the city I still call home. Your leaders have already seen Jerusalem's strongest walls demolished. We all know that the remaining wall is weaker than those already breached. The leaders of our people must now believe Roman power is invincible and acknowledge that we Jews have long been ruled by Rome. Why do they now believe it is just and our right to fight for freedom? Why didn't our people fight in the first place?

"Having fallen under Roman power and submitting ourselves to Rome for so many years, the Jews now pretend they must shake off that yoke. But that is not to love liberty—it is to love death. Man may rightly resent the dishonor of having despised masters rule over them, but not if those masters possess the entire inhabited Earth. For what part of our world has escaped Roman control? It's evident that the Romans have fortune in their hands and that Jehovah, who has all the world under his dominion, now accepts them as rulers.

"Men must bow to those too strong for them and allow those mighty in battle to rule. Consider your forefathers, who were far superior in soul to the Romans and had many more advantages. Yet they submitted to the Romans because they knew God was with Rome. And now that the Romans have taken much of Jerusalem, what will you depend upon to help you oppose them? Although the last wall still stands between you and the Romans, all of you within Jerusalem suffer more now than if the city fell. The Romans are aware you do not have enough food to eat. The signs of famine now show, and hunger will join the Romans as an ally against you, even if the Romans stop the siege and do not attack the city.

"As it is right now, the war inside the city is insurmountable and grows worse every hour. You will die unless you somehow control or set aside the enmity between the factions within Jerusalem and your hostility against Rome.

"If you are aware of what consequences may come, it is proper to change your behavior before a catastrophe falls upon you. Listen to the advice that might save you while the opportunity still exists. The Romans will not hold against you your previous actions against them—unless you persevere in fighting. There is no profit for Rome to leave Jerusalem devastated and its inhabitants slaughtered, nor to turn Judea into a depopulated desert. For these reasons, Titus offers you his right hand of surety, guaranteeing that you will live and the city will not be destroyed. But no one will be spared if he has to take the city by force if you reject his peace proposals."

Miriam felt Matthew stir as a roar of laughter came from the men aligned with Simon bar Giora. Some raised bows and fired a handful of arrows, while others threw rocks. The immense Roman tribunus stepped in front of Yosef to protect him, and three arrows struck his shield.

Yohanan ben Zaccai whispered to Matthew, "Don't do anything...." Miriam gripped his arm to keep him at her side as he shifted to turn toward the men who had fired at their brother. She heard Simon bar Giora bark a command to his men, and they lowered their bows.

"You mock and insult me," Yosef continued. "But remember your history—our history. Any man is a good man who flees from a house full of sin. You've convinced yourself that Jehovah, who sees all hidden secrets and hears all private conversations, will now overlook your sins. But I ask you, what crime has been kept secret or concealed among you? What is it you do that even your enemies don't know? The current leaders of Jerusalem pompously boast of their transgressions as they contend with one another. They have made, perhaps still make, a public demonstration of their injustices as if they were virtues. They have turned Jerusalem into a 'house full of sin.' Despite the actions of these men, there remains a chance to preserve your life if you're willing to grasp it. And Yahweh is quickly reconciled to those who confess their sins and repent. Do not be like the hardhearted wretches who say they 'lead' you. Throw down your arms and take pity on your country that is already in ruins. Have regard for the city you are betraying. Save that most excellent Temple with the many holy offerings within it. Who could bear to be the first to set it on fire? Who is willing that its sacred contents should no longer exist? What in all the world deserves preservation more than our Temple, and what is within it? If you cannot all see this with judicious eyes, at least have pity for your families. Look at your children, your wives, your parents, who are gradually consumed by deprivation and this warfare. I know that danger extends to my mother, father, brother, and sister among you. The risk is to all my family still within the walls of Jerusalem, and they have not been dishonorable. Perhaps you're imagining I give you this advice only on their account. If that is how you judge the matter, then kill me. Shed my blood if it may preserve your lives, for I'm ready to die if you will only surrender to Rome after I'm dead."

Miriam watched as Yosef moved ahead of the tribunus, holding his arm out to keep the armored man behind him.

CXVI

Julius 70 CE

Jerusalem

Bezetha, The Roman Camp, Nicanor and Yosef's Tent

"The rebel leader who spoke to you after you addressed him... was that Simon bar Giora?" Nicanor asked Yosef, who sat in his accustomed place of an evening on a camp stool facing the city.

"Yes," Yosef said curtly.

Nicanor knelt beside his friend, settling the sealed wineskin on his knee. "When you moved before me," he said softly, "refusing my shield arm, I understand why you did. But why did he order his men not to 'waste' an arrow on you?"

"If I'm alive, Simon can continue to mock me and point to me as a living traitor... not a Jew who sacrificed himself on principle, as he purports to do. He does not believe that I stand with the Romans and speak on their behalf only that I might save my people... save the city."

Nicanor stood to unfold his stool and place it on the other side of the small campfire that warmed their uneaten dinner of wheat grain and lamb stew. The sun, a molten crimson orb half below the horizon, had not yet relieved the day of its heat. He felt the trickles of sweat form on his brow and trickle down his neck and into the collar of his fresh tunic. He wiped the droplets with his inner forearm, dried the damp with the tunic's hem, then studied his friend. "Had I a bow in my hands," he said, "I would have made this Simon bar Giora a *dead* hero of your people—for he led the men who killed mine at Beth Horon."

Nicanor took a drink from the cool wineskin he had kept in a bucket of water, shaded within the tent throughout the day, then held it out toward Yosef.

Yosef shifted on his seat to glance at him without reaching for the wine. "I wonder if you had met Simon at Beth Horon and killed him there," he said, "if my people might have been better led." Yosef sighed and shook his head at the offer of the wine Nicanor held out again. "If only I had dealt with Yohanan ben Levi in Galilee and ended his selfish desires. That would have stopped him from coming here."

Yosef looked upon the city before them and said sadly, "Then maybe my people would listen to me. And I could stop all of this...." He swung his arm back to encompass the legion surrounding them, spread across Bezetha. The mass of the army arced north to the siege works at Antonia Fortress and stopped at the works along the first wall, the agora of the Upper City just beyond it.

"I told Titus what to expect behind the second wall at the point of the attack, hoping he would protect the civilians there," Yosef continued. "I believe he tried. But the Zealot leaders of my people sacrificed them—as you told me, their men cut down those who would have surrendered. Then they suffered more when Titus, in retaliation, sent his harshest legionaries to retake the second wall and decimate all in that area of my city." Yosef shook his head. "Simon bar Giora mocked me even more by denying his men a chance to kill me... and then saying what he did...."

"About your god's temple?" Nicanor asked.

"That the world was a better temple for Jehovah to reside in than was our Temple here in Jerusalem." Yosef's face hardened, and lines furrowed his brow. "I cannot contemplate how he, or any of my people, would say such a thing... much less believe it. Simon talked as if the Temple meant nothing to him. Maybe it doesn't... but it does to the true ones of our people. Only with the Temple can we make sacrifices for our sins and seek atonement with our Lord."

"The rebel fighters do not cease... they fight for your city, for your temple, too. Is that not true?" Nicanor wanted to make clear that he respected Rome's enemy. "At Antonia Fortress, the four new siege towers are repeatedly attacked, no matter that the rebels suffer massive casualties each time."

"The Zealots will not stop until all the fighters are dead, even though their leaders never came from behind the first wall while their men and mere shopkeepers were slaughtered. Hundreds of my people die daily, escaping the city to flee or find food. Some 500 a day, Titus told me this morning. He has them crucified in front of the city walls. The legionaries amuse themselves while planting this cruel crop by nailing them up in different postures. Desecrating the dead...."

Nicanor could see it was not perspiration coursing down Yosef's cheeks. He reached to touch his friend in sympathy, saying, "I spoke with Titus earlier and asked him to order it to stop. They are less likely to surrender if they fear such a fate."

The two sat as the silence and twilight deepened, and their dinner bubbled, neglected, over the fire. Sensing Yosef's desire to talk had ended, Nicanor rose from the stool and said, "I'll turn in now."

Yosef looked up at him and asked, "You still plan to be at the siege line of the first wall in the morning?"

"Yes. Each day from sunup to sundown, if I can, until this is done. Cleo might watch for me to send another message. She—"

Nicanor stopped and turned from Yosef to face north. A blossom of fire grew and climbed, and with it came shouts of hundreds of men now surging through the camp toward whatever was burning. A strident bugle call pierced the night... then another.

CXVII

Julius 70 CE

Jerusalem

Bezetha, the Roman Camp, Nicanor and Yosef's Tent

Two siege towers had been destroyed, the remaining two at Antonia Fortress had been heavily damaged, and the rebels undermined the siege works along the first wall. After that, the soldiers cast many sullen glances at Yosef, so he was careful to remain out of sight when Nicanor was not with him.

On this morning, he sat just within the tent's opening, relishing the breeze that had picked up after dawn, offering welcome relief from the stifling air within the tent and refreshment before the day's blazing sun. A large square of wood on his lap served as a writing desk, as he didn't want to block the entrance with the table. He could hear an officer speaking to his men, and from the snatches of the words carried by the breeze, he could tell the man was passing on what Titus's augurs had discerned. But to Yosef, the assessments seemed much what men could conclude. And what their leaders would say to build up the soldiers under their watch. The Roman gods' favor can ebb and flow... the tides of circumstance and fate can and will turn, especially in battle and war. Roman soldiers are physically trained for those reversals in combat but must be just as strong mentally.

Yosef felt proud to hear the centurion commend the Jews—that they now fought better than before. They had learned to handle weapons taken from Antonia Fortress, which had once been the Roman garrison within Jerusalem, and their tactics had improved.

But the encouragement just as quickly dissipated with the truth the centurion then shared. No matter how well its men now fought, the city of Jerusalem had become like a cornered wounded animal... fighting its fiercest as death closed in.

"I see you listen to the talk of the camp."

Yosef started at Nicanor's sudden appearance. He smiled wryly as he moved aside to let his friend into the tent, "It seems even Roman legionaries need to be inspired at times."

"Titus is concerned about the men's spirits," Nicanor said. "Recent advances have not come easily—each has come one step forward, with a half-step back."

"But each half-step you gain means more of my people die...." Yosef could not help his bitter tone.

"You and I did not start this war, Yosef," replied Nicanor sharply. "We have each shed blood and lost people we care for...." The tribunus took a deep breath, held it for a heartbeat, and let it go. "At the staff meeting after briefing General Titus, Marcus Sabinus told me Sayid was hurt in the attack on the siege towers at Antonia Fortress. I go now to see him... if you want to join me."

* * *

SAYID'S AUXILIARY UNIT CAMP

The two auxiliary soldiers sitting with Sayid outside his tent stared at Nicanor and scrambled to vacate their stools. "These are my friends," Sayid said to them, flashing a wan smile.

Yosef was unsure whether Sayid referred to the two auxiliaries now cowed by Nicanor's glare or himself and Nicanor. It didn't matter, though, for the two soldiers scurried away with a last puzzled look at Nicanor and then Sayid.

"So...." Nicanor settled on one of the vacated stools. "Let's see the damage...."

Yosef thought the burn on the Syrian's cheek and neck looked painful but superficial. Nicanor gestured at the linen bandages wrapping Sayid's upper leg.

As Sayid unwound the bandages, the swollen flesh revealed a much deeper burn that went well into the meat of his thigh, from above the knee to the groin.

"That does not look good, Sayid," Yosef said, glancing at Nicanor, who had far more experience with these things.

"It shows signs it may be beginning to fester," Nicanor said with a frown at Sayid. "I'll send one of Titus's doctors to treat it before it worsens." The tribunus leaned back and said, "Now, Sayid, how in Hades did you get that?" He pointed at the wound.

"My father ordered my unit to save as much timber as possible from the burning siege towers and the undermining framework. Part of it collapsed and pinned me for a few minutes until others freed me." Sayid shrugged and winced at the burn's sting on his neck.

"Why would your father order such a risk?" Yosef asked. "Why not let it burn?"

"Because there isn't any wood of any length left within 10 miles of Jerusalem," Nicanor answered. "Every tree has been cut down... almost all of the legions' stock of lumber has been used."

Sayid nodded, and the weak grin returned. "And your namesake, Nico the ram, needs a new shaft."

"Hmmph," Nicanor grunted. "One will be found. Titus has had enough of a two-pronged assault. This morning he ordered all focus on taking the Antonia Fortress, the temple, and the Upper City."

"Good," Sayid said, then grimaced as he repositioned his leg, then cast a worried glance at Yosef.

Why must they always apologize? Yosef thought, then he said, "Nicanor already pointed out this morning that he and I did not start this war, and neither did you, Sayid. But we are all caught up in it, my friend."

"I know, and I'm sorry for your family here...."

"Cleo, too... she's still alive," Nicanor said. At Sayid's shocked expression, he explained the message of the green-feathered arrow.

As Nicanor spoke, Yosef noticed Sayid rubbing the puckered scar on his chest. Back in Caesarea, Sayid had told them of the events when he had saved Cleo from Gessius Florus. The scar came from when Florus's military aide stabbed him. Still, Sayid had managed to kill the man.

"We must get Cleo out of the city before it falls," Sayid said.

"I don't see how to reach her... but I'll search for a way," Nicanor replied. "It will be even harder now, though, for Titus also ordered the reworking and tightening of the earthen wall the legions built around the city."

"Why rework it?" Yosef asked.

"It was first set as a *circumvallation* barrier, more effective outwardly. To prevent aid and supplies from getting into the city. Engineers and two labor cohorts will now dig ditches nine to ten feet deep in front of that barrier on this side of it. That will convert the barrier to a *contravallation*... a construction that will encircle the entire city and be better able to keep people within its boundary. That will stop people from escaping the city or searching for food. He has also increased patrols in the valleys surrounding the city to ensure any who try are captured."

A series of bugle blasts cut through the air. Sayid raised himself on one leg to look to the west and north, where a billow of dust grew and expanded.

Yosef stood to look, too. "What's this?"

Nicanor did not stand, did not look. Instead, he commented on what he knew: "Titus empties the encampments outside the city... the 5th *Macedonia*, the 12th *Fulminata*, and the 15th *Apollinaris* will entirely move within Jerusalem's outermost wall... here. They will become the Roman spear point to thrust at Antonia Fortress and the rest of the city."

CXVIII

Julius 70 CE

Jerusalem

The Upper City

"You need more rest...." said Ya'el, but Miriam moved past her and started downstairs.

"I need to talk to Matthew before he leaves," she replied, but she stopped when Ya'el put a hand on her shoulder, and she felt the kindness and concern in that touch. "I'm fine, Ya'el," she said more gently.

Behind them, Cicero squawked angrily, and Elian soothed the bird, though he, no doubt, was hungry, too... but he did not complain. Ya'el glanced over her shoulder into the room, then turned back to Miriam.

Miriam answered the question in Ya'el's expression—the concern of a "mother" for a child when everyone now went to sleep at night with an empty belly. "That's what I need to see Matthew about—going after that hidden food supply."

"After you speak to him, do you want to talk about Yosef? I know you were upset...."

"I don't need to talk about Yosef. Finding food is more important." She heard Matthew downstairs, about to leave, and called, "Wait!" She hurried down to him.

"I have to meet Eleasar and Yohanan ben Zaccai," Matthew explained. "Yohanan ben Levi's success defending Antonia Fortress and Simon bar Giora's success at the first wall has given us a few days' respite. But the Romans used it to their benefit—they've put thousands of men to work and took only three days to dig a deep trench at the inner foot of their wall encircling the city. Everyone within Jerusalem is even more of a prisoner now. The Roman fist clenches harder. We're going to talk to Yohanan ben Levi about releasing Mother and Father.... now is the time to free everyone he holds."

Miriam asked what she had planned not to ask him. "Why didn't Simon bar Giora order his archers to kill Yosef?"

"Killing him would signal that what Yosef says is true... that he is trying to help us. But not to win this war; we cannot defeat the Romans." Matthew rubbed his face with the palms of his hands and paced. "Bodies pile up all over the city, with more added daily—we cannot bury them all. Our people grow hungrier each day. The old grow weaker each day." He stopped to face Miriam. "Like Father, I was upset over the news of Yosef's freedom that seemed to indicate he had fallen in with the Romans." He put his hands on her shoulders. "You have said little, but I see your expression when we talk of him. I saw your face at Antonia Fortress as Yosef spoke. You, too, think he has abandoned us."

Matthew shook his head as Miriam shrugged away his hands. "But after seeing him, hearing his offer to give his life if it would change the minds of Jerusalem's people. Like Mother, I believe Yosef is trying to help our people survive. And I have heard from many who believe that, too. They want to surrender but won't—or can't." Matthew moved toward the door, and Miriam followed him.

Then he turned around and said, "Simon bar Giora and Yohanan ben Levi would rather Yosef remain alive and hated. Then our brother is the one they can point at and rail against to take attention away from what they've done to bring ruin to us. Frightened and weak people will believe the loudest voice, even when it tells them something untrue, when the lies are spewed often enough. All while, under orders from Simon and the Gischalan, the Zealots imprison the remaining prominent men of Jerusalem. Not because they speak against them, but because they have food and supplies they need for themselves."

"Do you think Mother and Father know of Yosef's attempts?" asked Miriam.

"I'm sure Yohanan ben Levi has told them and that he also twists what Yosef says for those who have not heard our brother's words directly. Distortion and lies suit his purpose, and I'm sure he enjoys how his lies hurt Mother and Father."

"Do you think you and Yohanan ben Zaccai can get them freed?"

"He has tried several times, and we will try again today. But there is no power or authority except that of the Zealot leaders. I worry Yohanan has pressed so much he has become a target, too. Were it not for all the young men he has taught and still tries to teach, including the children of many Zealots, Yohanan would likely be confined as well. And Yonatan hates him for getting Leah's divorce decree enforced. He hasn't yet threatened Yohanan... but he *is* a threat."

"Then we must get the food the shepherd boy hid," Miriam said. "Maybe we can bribe the guards with it."

"The Gischalan feeds them from what his men steal, but the city is so poor now that perhaps we can try. When I see Yohanan, I'll have him arrange a meeting with Akiva."

* * *

Miriam heard Elian's voice haltingly speak words that took a moment for her to recognize. She reached the doorway and stepped inside to see Ya'el lift the sheets of parchment and read another line for Elian to repeat. As he recited, the boy turned over and over in his hands the silver hamsa with a deep scratch on its surface. *The hamsa given to her by Ehud.* Miriam shook that memory away. The scored metal also reminded her she still must deal with Hananiah. His thrust had damaged it during their encounter when as 'The Hand,' she had protected Matthew from his attempt to take him.

"You don't mind him playing with it, do you?" Ya'el asked, seeing Miriam's look as Elian angled the hamsa to catch a slanting ray of sunshine and cast its dancing light upon the wall.

"No... not at all. But be sure he doesn't lose it... Ehud gave it to me—a gift to keep secret—long ago, just before he left for Alexandria with his family." Miriam pointed at the letters in Ya'el's hand. "Your Aramaic has become very good... those are Zechariah's letters?"

"Yes. Thanks for sharing them... reading them has been helpful." Ya'el refolded the letters. "In the later ones, he talks about you to his wife, Bayla... how you're the age his daughter, Meira, would have been... that you *are* what she could have grown up to be—beautiful and strong."

"The Romans killed them," Miriam said quietly.

"I know... and Zechariah held never-ending love for them. It squeezes my heart that he continued to write to them after they were gone."

Miriam saw the tears welling in Ya'el's eyes and felt the same in her own. "Now we will all lose everything to the Romans."

"There are still ways some can escape—through the tunnels leading from the city," Ya'el said as she glanced at Elian.

"Matthew and I'd never leave our parents, but if you want—"

"No, I would leave none of you behind... you are my family now." Ya'el looked again at Elian, who was now at the windowsill. Cicero preened at his side, studying the courtyard below. "But maybe we could get Elian out of the city, save him." She leaned toward Miriam and whispered, "But let's play pretend... if we all could escape someplace safe, where would you want to go?"

The whisper reminded Miriam of this room... sitting on this bed late at night when bad dreams awoke her, and she came here to Yossi, not to her mother or father. Yossi would whisper stories to her, keeping his voice low until she fell asleep to wake the following day in her bed as if she had been there all night. Yosef would greet her with a smile and wink at their secret. *No matter his reasons, how could Yosef stand to remain with the Romans and speak for them?* Miriam felt her anger stir again.

"Miriam?" Ya'el sat on the bed and looked up.

Miriam pushed thoughts of Yosef aside and turned the question back on Ya'el. "Where would you go?"

Ya'el did not hesitate. "Someplace—a real home—overlooking the sea with a path down to the beach. To walk at sunrise and sunset with seabirds in the sky and my face turned into the sea breeze!" Ya'el's eyes searched Miriam's face as the glow that had momentarily illumined her own dimmed with the impossibility of that dream. "Miriam," she murmured, "where would you go?"

Miriam could not answer. She had not traveled like Ya'el—like Cleo—had. She knew little of other places and could not see beyond the present. She did not realize she had closed her eyes until Rachel's voice at the door made her open them.

"Miriam, Ya'el... I want to talk about Yosef."

CXIX

Julius 70 CE

Jerusalem

The Upper City

"Elian, please take Cicero to the courtyard," Ya'el told the boy, then went to the corner table and picked up a large jar. She had the boy cup his hands and tipped the pot nearly bottom up to pour a handful of seed. Elian smiled up at her, and she set the almost empty jar down and smoothed his unruly, sleep-tossed hair. "Stay close to him and see if you can help him find bugs to eat beneath the trees." Ya'el considered stopping the boy and using a silk cord tied to one of the bird's legs and the other end to Elian's wrist to keep the parrot from flying off. But as long as there was food, Cicero would be content. Matthew had brought her a bag of seeds, enough to fill the jar again—but only once—saying, "This is the last I could find." After that, it would be only what she could share from her meager rations and what Cicero could forage for in the courtyard. When there was nothing for him to eat... she would have to free him to find food for himself. And she would pray no one took him to feed themselves.

When boy and bird left, Miriam asked Rachel, "What about Yosef?"

Rachel looked at Ya'el. "Do you love him?"

Ya'el blinked and darted a look at Miriam, who gave her a slight nod.

"You know who I really am?" Ya'el asked Rachel.

"I know who you were... and that you meant enough to Yosef for him to give you Leah's *kinyan*," Rachel gestured at the sash around Ya'el's waist. "You keep it tucked away but always carry it."

Rachel reached in and pulled out the small coin on its cord. "Yosef gave it to me so—"

"So his family would know you came from him seeking help... and that you were important to him... somehow." Rachel kneaded her hands nervously. "Do you love him... and does he love you?"

"I haven't seen Yosef in a long time, and I cannot speak for him now."

"But you did love him, and did he love you?"

"I think we were falling in love, but...." Ya'el sorted through her thoughts to find something she had pushed aside.

"Leah still loves him, and I—" Rachel stopped and shook her head. "Yosef has the favor of the Roman general." Rachel darted a look at Miriam and then back to Ya'el. "And I know you were—are—a highborn Roman lady. Your brother was even briefly emperor."

A pang of regret shot through Ya'el at how little she had thought about Marcus. Hardly believing he had been emperor for three months before his death a little over a year ago. She was numb to so much in her past.

"Yes, he was," Ya'el answered. "What are you asking?"

Rachel turned to Miriam instead, saying, "If she gave herself up to the Romans, proved who she really is... maybe the Roman general would listen to her."

"Listen to what?" Ya'el asked. "to a plea to save Jerusalem? Titus has offered opportunities to surrender through Yosef, and your leaders reject those pleas and mock Yosef."

"Then maybe the general would let Yosef see us... let him speak with us...."

"Rachel, Ya'el cannot give herself to the Romans. There's a reason she came here, seeking safety."

"Where no one is safe." Rachel's eyes flared, glistening with tears. "We all will die here. Leah would like to speak to Yosef, even if it's the last time. I would like to also... if only to tell him...." Her eyes closed, squeezing out the tears that trickled down her cheek.

Miriam went to Rachel and clasped her shoulders, "Ya'el can't do that... Please accept that Yosef is lost to us. I have." Miriam took her by the arm. "I'll come to talk to Leah and make her understand. And I hope you will, too."

Ya'el remained in the room and went to sit by the open window. She could get another message to Nicanor. He now knew she was alive and would be watching for other messages. She could count on him to help her. Could she somehow sneak into the Roman camp with his help? Perhaps even see Titus? She would have to ask him for protection from Gessius Florus. And Nicanor would shield her. Yosef would defend her, too... but did he still love her? She had heard of his marriage while imprisoned. What of Yosef's wife?

In her darkest moments, filled with memories and regrets, Ya'el had often thought of the last time she had spoken with Yosef. Newly imprisoned and chained to a post at the Roman encampment in Ptolemais. Then she thought of all that had happened since. Her friendship and affection for Yosef had survived it all. As she thought it through, she realized her gratitude for him had grown, but not her love. She squeezed the small coin on its cord. It symbolized what Yosef and Leah had called her "kinyan" for him. Since arriving in Jerusalem, she had learned its significance. A kinyan was a symbol of love, signifying two people transforming to become one. There was a time when she thought she and Yosef were on the verge of such a singular love. But it had no chance to grow; now, it would never be. Now her bond with Miriam, Matthew, and Yosef's parents—her love for them—was stronger than what she felt for Yosef. She could turn from revenge, forego killing Gessius Florus, and even risk her own death if she could save Yosef's family, Elian… and Cicero.

The parrot's raucous squawk echoed up from the courtyard, followed by the ring of Elian's laughter. The pure innocence of the sound drew her to look at them below. Laughter was now rare—had been for some time—in Jerusalem, where there were only cries.

CXX

Julius 70 CE

Northwest of Jerusalem

Gessius Florus's Hidden Camp

Gessius Florus looked up from the floor of the sunbaked valley and longed for a cooling breeze. The sun beat down, and the surrounding hills shouldered away all but the most gusting winds, refusing to release the heat. *Perhaps that's why they abandoned this place*, he mused, contemplating the neglected buildings behind him. Who would wish to live here during the summer months? He had not planned well—before having Drusus eliminate Irad, he should have had the *major domus* send an extra two slaves to fan his tent and cool him. Perhaps Tiberius Alexander could provide a few healthy deserters from the city, rebels easily disposed of when he was ready to leave this fiery place.

He detested the valley and nearby Jerusalem... and all of Judea. For that matter, he disliked all the empire's southern and eastern provinces. With the treasure he was keeping for himself, he could one day live in luxury in far better climes.

He wiped the sweat from his blurred eyes and wiped with a cloth the crystal lens he had been squinting through. He positioned the lens again over the copy of the text Drusus had made by rubbing charcoal over the Jews' copper scroll. Then he looked up at the squat man standing before his desk. "You found just one more site?" he asked.

"Yes, lord." It was clear from the man's begrimed appearance that Drusus had not had the benefit of a proper bath in weeks. Using the information from the rubbing, he and a dozen men had traveled as far as northern Galilee. Then down to the east of the vast dead sea, the Romans called Lake Asphaltitis... and on to Gaza in the southwest and back. They tried to make sense of the list of locations found in the Essene cave in Qumran and investigated promising sites. But the directions on the list needed another piece, a key to decipher the vague references and make the locations precise. "We were lucky to find that one," Drusus answered. "And it was a heavy haul, like the others."

"I do not see it—did you bring it here, into the valley?" Florus set the lens down.

"No, lord," Drusus lowered his voice. "I still do not trust these Thracians. I re-hid the treasure north of here and left your Clazomenae men to guard it."

"Good." Florus settled back in his chair, disgusted at the feel of the clinging damp tunic on his back. He could trust those men from his birthplace—some were family.

"I thought that we could figure it out by getting close to what seemed to be the locations." Drusus gestured toward the list. "We tried."

Florus rested his chin on his fist, feeling his many rings, the stones digging into his flesh. Then he tapped his lips with two fingers, a mannerism he borrowed from Emperor Nero. He thought with a smile of when he'd first proposed to steal the treasure from the Jewish temple, and Nero had eagerly encouraged him.

So what was next? Arins had not yet returned to confirm that Hananiah, the Alexandrian assassin, had captured the Jew. This Matthew, the brother of Yosef ben Mathias, could give him the key to the treasure locations. And where was Cleo? Arins had promised he would deliver his wife to him, too. Florus squirmed a little in his chair in anticipation of what he would do to her—and that thought stirred him perhaps even more than did the prospect of getting his hands on the Jews' treasure.

He studied Drusus for a moment. The powerful killer had proved trustworthy because of self-interest. "Return to your men and take the wagonload of treasure to the ship in Sycaminum," Florus ordered, "and store it onboard with the rest. Remain there with the ship, and have the men ready the vessel to sail on short notice once I join you."

"Yes, lord."

"And Drusus, before you go, find Krateros and send him to me." Florus saw the flash in the man's eyes—his intense dislike of the Thracian captain showed. *And perhaps something can be made of that,* he thought.

"Yes, lord."

* * *

"I did as you asked, lord," Krateros reported. "I took the tunnel, following the way the man Arins had led my other men into the city."

Gessius Florus studied Krateros, the mercenary captain, without the equanimity he had previously felt about Drusus. This man

Final Siege

deserved no trust. "You're back far too soon to have gotten through the chaos of a besieged city," he said. "Surely you could not have found Arins nor Hananiah yet."

"I never reached the city but found one of the men you wanted." After a brief pause, he announced proudly, "That old Balearic Islander, Arins."

"Where is he, then?"

"Dead, lord. His body is half-jammed into a crack in the wall where all those tunnels join. Someone dug a nice hole into the side of his head. He'd been dead for days, judging by the smell. One odd thing, though...."

"Odd? What? Another wound?"

"No, a mark. Whoever killed him cut his tunic open and left a bloody handprint on his chest."

Florus did not let his fury reach his voice, but he watched the Thracian stiffen as he glared at him. *Good—you should be afraid of me.* "Call in all your men and send for more from Caesarea," he ordered the Thracian. "I don't want to enter Jerusalem too soon, but we will be ready, so we are not too late."

CXXI

Julius 70 CE

Jerusalem

The City of David

The ancient, narrow tunnel closed in on Miriam, reminding her of the confined feeling of her first days exploring tunnels beneath the city with Zechariah. This rough-hewn tunnel ran between the Kidron Valley and the Gihon Spring, a water supply at the city's eastern wall at the edge of the Kidron Valley. But another branch bent south toward the Pool of Siloam and, she thought, went beyond, under the city wall, and into the lowermost Hinnom Valley. The wiry shepherd, Akiva, had helped her clear the fallen rock just within its entrance and again at two of the narrowest sections. Thankfully, the flow of air was not blocked, and their torch flames continued to sway even when they stopped to drink and wipe their sweaty faces that quickly coursed again with sweat.

"Do you think Yohanan ben Zaccai and your brother will get Yohanan ben Levi to release your parents?" Akiva asked as he slid the pack from his shoulders. He turned sideways to slip through a place where rocks bellied out and formed the most naturally constricted point they had encountered in the passage. The stone above seemed to have settled. The weight had buckled the slabs and blocks of the side walls at mid-height of the tunnel.

"I don't know, but I pray they do." Miriam let out a held breath, a prayer that the tunnel would not further buckle while they were in it. Her chest binding constricted her breathing but allowed her to pass through the confined space.

"You have known Yohanan ben Zaccai a long time?" Akiva asked.

"All my life. He is one of my father's best friends."

"Yohanan told me he is also a good friend to your other brother and was with him in Galilee. I've heard that the Romans captured Yosef at Yotapta, but he now speaks for them?"

Miriam heard the question in Akiva's statement or his curiosity, but she would not satisfy it.

The shepherd said, "I have long heard of Yohanan and admire how he teaches. One day I hope to be a learned man, too, and maybe I can become a teacher like him."

"You'd give up the freedom of being a shepherd?" Miriam was glad he had moved on from the subject of Yosef. "You would teach the young?"

"There is freedom as a shepherd, but also hard work and responsibility for my flock. In that, Yohanan ben Zaccai and I are alike."

"Alike... how?"

"Yohanan's students and those he mentors are his flock... but they can grow up and become teachers or good keepers of our faith. My flock is only for shearing, butchering for meat, or Temple sacrifices. I would rather have a human congregation such as Yohanan's... though he fears they now face the same mortality as my sheep. He prays that though the Temple might fall as it did 600 years ago, the teaching of our faith will survive." Akiva stopped and drank deeply from the water skin draped over his shoulder. "How much farther do you think we have?"

Miriam checked her mental count of steps since they had entered the tunnel and matched it against her assessment of the distance to reach the Hinnom Valley. "Another third of the way... maybe less... another quarter." She rubbed grit from her eyes, squeezing the bridge of her nose between thumb and forefinger, and considered the harder work to come. They would have to hand-carry what they could not drag in tow through this narrow tunnel. She shrugged and rolled her head to loosen the tightness in her neck and shoulders. The food would save her family, Yohanan ben Zaccai, too... it did not matter how many trips it might take. She continued leading the way, Akiva following her.

* * *

THE HINNOM VALLEY

The Hinnom Valley always had a stench that wafted from the east from the city's workmen's quarter and was added to where refuse and animal carcasses brought from the city were burned or left to rot. In the past, the odor had been masked slightly by the perfumery in the southernmost part of the Lower City. She and Akiva had likely passed under it by now. She had always associated her mother with the scent of the *spikenard*. The perfume was made from myrrh, nard, cinnamon, iris, and sunbul oil. Her mother always had a small pear-shaped, clay-stoppered bottle of it. But with the coming of the siege, the perfumery had long ceased production. The only odor from the city now was of death from the thousands of bodies piled in alleys and side streets.

"We're not far from it," Akiva said as he pointed. "See the big stone, about 30 paces from here, that looks like a fist with a thumb? A broken half of a wagon wheel leans against it, marking the rough path up to the cave."

Miriam gauged the distance and thought Akiva had it right. But they also had to descend from the cave where the branch from the tunnel ended. Then reach the level plain of the valley, that thumb-rock, and its marker. Anyone watching would easily see them in the daylight. "We have no choice now—we must keep going—but we'll have to move the supplies at night." Miriam turned to Akiva and said, "Let's go—"

"Wait!" the shepherd whispered fiercely, pulling Miriam behind a large boulder.

The thunder of hooves explained why. Leaning out from behind the rock, Miriam squinted with one eye. She saw a Roman patrol, the sun glinting on the small round shields and armor of twelve or more horsemen coming their way. The thud of their gallop slowed to a rhythmic clop of hooves on the hard-packed sections of the pathway. It seemed the Romans only patrolled this valley, not leaving permanent sentries to endure the smell.

"When they are on us, stay low behind this rock," he said, "and I will lead them away. Run for the wheel when I do." He pulled his two remaining torches from his pack and gave them to her. "Then turn toward the city, and look for the signs of the rough trail leading to the cave where I stored the supplies."

"What about you?"

"I'm a fast runner—I chased down goats on rocky ground as a boy. I'll lose them and come back to join you." Akiva peered around the boulder. "Get ready...."

Miriam pulled her man's tunic higher between her legs, girding herself to run. Though she was ready for it, the speed of Akiva's surge and sprint from behind the boulder startled her as much as it did the Romans. Their shout did not slow Akiva, and after a heartbeat's pause, the horsemen charged after the young shepherd in a thunder.

Miriam kept her tunic tucked and ran faster than she ever had in the direction he had ordered. Skidding to a stop at the broken wagon wheel, she glanced back toward where Akiva led the Romans. A cloud of dust now hid horses and men, assuring her that they had not caught the shepherd yet. As she watched, the dust cloud broadened to show the Romans must have spread out, maybe trying to encircle Akiva. She shook her head, spotted the track she would have missed if she were not looking, and headed up the slope toward an escarpment speckled with the shadows of recesses or caves in the stone. The path broadened at its base, where several openings seemed like the mouths of caves. She cast about for another sign. There were no traces of wagons, carts, mules, or even human footprints, but then Akiva said he had thoroughly cleared them to not leave anything to lead toward the caves. Only then did he return to the valley floor to take a path toward the Gate of the Essenes.

At the far left, beside the next-to-last opening, Miriam found another piece of a broken wagon wheel. She pulled one of the torches stuck in her sash and stepped inside. Waiting until deep within the shadowed mouth, Miriam struck a streamer of sparks to ignite the torch. In the large cavern, she found the tracks of wheels, many feet, and a lot of blood that had dried into a crust on the cave's dirt floor. Far in the back, she found the remnants of handcarts and wagons, all the large pieces of their wood missing. *Taken for firewood?* Miriam thought as she searched the rest of the cave. The wood was not the only thing taken. The food was gone. Someone—nearby villagers or deserters from the city—had found and fought over it. When they left, they, too, had enough presence of mind to clear away any signs of traffic to the cave.

Miriam sank to her knees, emotionally spent and her mind numb. *What will we do now?* The thought tumbled over and over in her mind. Finally, she realized Akiva still had not appeared. She returned to the cave entrance and cautiously looked for any sight of him. The Romans had not only returned but were joined by another patrol from the direction of the Kidron Valley. Now, the two groups of Roman horsemen were pitching camp where Akiva had begun his run. There was no way, even in the dark, she could slip by them. She turned and studied the arrangement of caves closest to her along the lower face of the bluff. She was trapped here unless she found another way out.

CXXII

Julius 70 CE

Jerusalem

The Cave in the Hinnom Valley

Miriam welcomed the dawn from where she sat just within the cave's mouth. She had not slept and wished for the sun to rise faster. The previous evening, she had kept her torch lighted only long enough to fully explore the cave. She found a large bag of grain and several pounds of pressed dates hidden within a niche she had discovered in the back wall. It was not much, but something. Her stomach growled, but she ignored its complaint. She would not touch the food until she had it home to share.

Sitting in the darkness close to the opening to hear the night sounds and listen for any approaching Romans, her mind had drifted back to the uncomfortable conversation with Rachel and Leah before Yohanan ben Zaccai returned to the house with Akiva. Rachel seemed to have a spiteful expectation. That Ya'el—as the Roman Lady Cleo—should do something to convince the Roman General Titus to let Yosef return to his family. Miriam did not know what purpose that would serve except fulfilling whatever desire Rachel felt for her brother. Leah, too, wished to see Yosef again... though she seemed more and more detached from the reality of current circumstances. Neither of her cousins would listen to her advice that they should forget Yosef. It seemed a rivalry over her brother might sever their sisterly bond.

Her own feelings about Yosef were hardening. She now believed he had struck a deal with the Romans to remain alive. *I wager you never go hungry, Yosef, as do most in the city you once called home,* she thought. Yosef did not suffer as his family did. He might still fear death—for surely not all the Romans, his former enemies, had accepted him—but his would not be the demise all in Jerusalem now faced. At least the end Akiva must have met had been swift. She had not known the young shepherd long, but he was brave. It seemed he was more courageous than Yosef.

Miriam got to her feet with a final worry that made her restless. *Will Rachel do or say something to disclose who Ya'el really is?*

Yohanan ben Levi and Simon bar Giora would happily use her... if only to make a spectacle of executing her in front of the Romans. That would not be rational. But all the two Zealot leaders had done since gaining power defied rationality, at least insofar as best serving the people of Jerusalem was concerned.

She inched outside and moved to a point where she could see to the east and west. Clusters of Romans were in both directions, and a patrol traveled east toward the Kidron Valley. Another group of horsemen in the distance seemed to be working their way west into the Hinnom. There was no way for her to reach the cave containing the branch passage to the Canaanite Tunnel, at least not yet. She returned to the cave that once held Akiva's hidden supplies.

Inside, Miriam took a cylinder of stiffened leather from her pack and pulled a rolled map and two thin charcoal sticks from within it. Flattening the map on a stone, she marked with a tiny drawing of a wagon wheel the cave where she and Akiva had entered the Hinnom Valley and the cave she was in now. Next to that, she shaded in the locations of what appeared to be other caves at the base of the bluff. She could not reach where she and Akiva had entered the valley; that was the only hidden way out of the Hinnom and into the southern part of the city. But maybe she could find one yet unknown. She rigged a sling to carry the bag of grain and pressed dates; she wouldn't risk hiding them somewhere while she explored.

***

IN AN UNKNOWN TUNNEL

Miriam lighted her last torch and prayed she would find a way out before it burned out. By now, she knew she was well under the city. She did not want to consider returning to the Hinnom Valley and did not want to die there with its stink her last breath. The first three caves she checked had held no tunnels she could find. She had been lucky in the fourth. Her steps into its deepest recess had kicked up enough dust to show the slightest swirl of a current coming from a man-sized opening that seemed to have been hidden behind rocks piled up to screen it from the central area of the cave. The space was rough-fashioned as if whoever had created it had started with a natural fissure in the rock and expanded from there. Miriam stepped far enough inside to see the passage continued toward the north—into the city, she prayed. Parts of it seemed to have been hewn by following the natural cleavage in the stone. She left the tunnel to return to the cavern's central chamber and updated her map.

Then she went just outside the cavern and gazed over the area. The Romans were still there. Searching the ground, she found a fist-sized rock with a somewhat flat side. Regretting that the operation dulled her dagger's point, she used it to scratch the shape of a *hamsa* on the flat surface. Cautiously, without stirring up plumes of dirt from the trail, she crept to the thumb-stone and set her rock on the ground beside the broken wagon wheel. Someone might take the broken wheel—for what reason she could not imagine—but they would pay no attention to a rock.

She continued northward in the tunnel, realizing she was probably in a storm drain beneath the Tyropoeon Valley. She pressed farther into it until a strong current of air fanned her torch flame, and Miriam felt a coolness that relieved her hot cheeks and broke her reverie. She breathed deep, tasting the moisture-laden air as the tunnel opened into a vast grotto. Miriam walked straight ahead for several steps until her torch showed the lip of a tremendous underground sea stretching into darkness. She was where Elian had been trapped, where she had fallen, and where Matthew, Eleasar, and Ya'el had saved them both. Nearby was a flat stone platform that jutted several feet into the water. At its end, she knelt to cup a handful of the cool water and bring it to her mouth, soothing her dry throat. In the torchlight, the rim of the stone glistened with a different color and texture; a yellowish plaster coated the stone wall beneath the water. She returned to where the platform joined the lip of the massive reservoir. Kneeling again, holding her torch low, she could make out the hand prints in the plaster left by the workers who had created this enormous cistern generations ago. Matthew had told her about them.

Miriam followed the stone perimeter until, with the torch held high, she saw what must be a line hanging down from above. One of the ropes Matthew had used to save her was still there as if it might be needed again. She hoisted the heavy pack of dates and grain to ride higher on her back. She studied the area. It had two ways in and out that could be defended by a few against many. And it would be difficult to find without precise directions... this could be a safe place to bring her family. If only Matthew could get their parents freed with Yohanan ben Zaccai's help. And if they could find more food somehow, somewhere. Then maybe they could survive the siege, take this way out, back through the storm drain to evade the Romans in the Hinnom Valley, and escape.

Despite the 'ifs' and 'maybes,' Miriam stepped into the water with her worry about finding a safe place for her family resolved. She felt something hard bump her leg where the water rose to near her knees. Careful to not let the food pack slip into the water, she bent at the knees to feel for what had struck her leg. The faintest shiver passed over her at the flashing memory of her mother's cautionary tales of a creature from the depths. Her mother had hoped to frighten her and Matthew and Yosef to keep them safe, and that brought a bittersweet smile to her lips.

The object was a wood rod, slick from its place in the water for who knew how long. She lifted it from the water and became aware of the familiarity of its heft just as its metal ferrule gleamed in the torchlight. Zechariah's staff! She thought it had been lost forever. The bittersweet smile became pure joy, and she even laughed aloud.

Shuffling through the water, she reached the dangling rope and knew that just beyond it was the bucket-hoist that ran high above her into the opening she could not see but was there. She secured the staff on her back and gripped the line. Miriam began climbing, forgetting the soreness in her ribs and feeling stronger than she had in some time.

CXXIII

Julius 70 CE

Jerusalem

The Upper City, Agora

Miriam climbed from the tunnel and snagged her arm on the thornbush concealing the trap door. Suddenly memories came flooding back to her of Yosef holding the trap door so she could slip in after him while exploring as children. Also, of the day she snagged herself on a thorn shortly before the two Romans had raped her in the darkness below. She seemed to recall a story that Roman soldiers had made a crown from these thorns to mock Yeshua ish Natzrat. Miriam looked at the blood seeping from the current scratch, stanching it with a scrap of cloth, wishing she could as easily wipe away the memory of her tragic day four years earlier. She rested to catch her breath. The booming and crashing sounds she had begun to hear below were very loud here, rolling over the Upper City market, seeming to funnel into her blind alley. Still, the noise was not as worrying as it had been when she passed through Antonia Fortress not an hour earlier.

The Romans were bringing their full force against the fortress, and the rain of rocks from their siege weapons was far more frightening from within the fort. The walls shuddered from what seemed an unending fusillade of large stones. She had exited one tunnel to cross the lower-level armory and reach the entrance to the tunnel that the off-shoot passage to take her to this entrance within the agora. Even at the depth of the armory, she had heard the screams and shouts of the men above fighting... and dying.

Thankful to be away from there, Miriam had approached the meeting of the tunnels expecting to be confronted by the Levite guards Eleasar ben Ananias had posted to secure the tunnel from encroachment by men from Gessius Florus's camp in the hidden valley. Arins's men might still be in the city, but Matthew and Eleasar had not seen them; maybe they had returned to Florus. But none of Eleasar's Temple Guard were there. Perhaps they had moved down the tunnel toward the valley to interdict Florus's men closer to the Roman nobleman's camp.

Still... someone had moved Arins's body... but not removed it. The stinking corpse, no longer an unusual odor within the city, had been laid out next to the fissure in the stone where she had tried to hide the body. Anxious to get home, she glanced at it only as she passed.

With a groan, Miriam stood and pulled Zechariah's staff from its strap on her back. She still relished holding it in her hands again. She straightened her clothing and adjusted the cowl of the light cloak from her pack that she had donned to disguise herself in the city. With a tired sigh, she moved down the alley toward the agora. She would have to return at dark with Matthew or Ya'el to retrieve the bulky package of grain and dates. She could not risk someone realizing the pack contained food and trying to steal it from her.

Miriam paused where the alley began at the marketplace. It was nearly empty. Only a few merchant stalls with scant wares to offer, manned by glum, anxious-looking shopkeepers with arms crossed and furtive eyes watching all around them. She stepped out and immediately felt their glare, but she ignored them and moved with a firm stride and purpose. Zechariah repeatedly told her, "Whether you are acting as yourself or as a Sicarii... move confidently as if defying anyone to challenge you. Weaker men step aside from those who move with purpose." She had seen that for herself in the year following Zechariah's death.

"Miriam...." The voice was low but had an edge that cut through the stillness.

She turned toward the sound to see Hananiah step from the shadows between two stalls. His unblinking eyes studied her as he waved her over to him.

"I recognized the staff and your walk." Those eyes passed over her clothing. "Dressing like that is better protection than a woman's garb... if you have to be on the streets." The knifemaker paused, and his eyes stared into hers. "Why must you be on the street?"

"Searching for food to buy."

"There is little or none here." Hananiah's head pivoted to look around the market and returned to her.

"Still, I must try."

"I have food... enough to share with you...." Hananiah stepped closer and put his hand on her forearm. Thankfully, Miriam thought, it was above her dagger sheath. "The Romans attack the Upper City and Antonia Fortress... not the Lower City. Come stay there with me."

"I can't leave my family."

"Once you said you wished to leave them, you even did for a while. Now your brother Yosef is called a traitor, and people hate him. The

Gischalan, Yohanan ben Levi, has imprisoned your parents." Hananiah stroked her upper arm, "Your brother Matthew can care for himself. Come with me." He paused, rubbing together the fingertips of the hand he had used to caress her arm. "This is blood... are you hurt?"

"Just a scratch... I must get home to tend to it."

Hananiah took a step back as if releasing her. "Come see me in the morning, and I will share my food with you." He turned from her and stopped, then said, "You are friends with the old priest, Yohanan ben Zaccai?"

"Yes, he's a family friend."

"You should tell him to leave the city tonight or to hide where he can't be found. That man Yonatan bar Hilel, who threatened you and now has only one ear. Earlier in this market, I overheard him tell some men he will kill Yohanan tomorrow."

Miriam watched him walk away, still massaging his fingertips as if he enjoyed the sensation.

CXXIV

Julius 70 CE

Jerusalem

Sayid's Auxiliary Unit Camp

"Well, they've done it without your help," Nicanor said, gesturing toward Sayid's bandaged leg. "New siege works and assault towers at Antonia Fortress. I'm glad you are finally letting that wound heal."

"I had to try working... my father came to see me."

Yosef handed Sayid a cup of the wine Nicanor had brought. "That is well," Yosef commented. "I'm glad you are talk—"

"He told me if I could not perform my duties," Sayid said with a frown, "I should stand down."

Nicanor grunted. "Your father is right—let your leg heal. Now drink that wine and enjoy it. It's from Titus... for his staff."

"He did not say it outright, but he wants me to admit I cannot do my duties." Sayid shook his head and gulped the wine. "I know he thinks I should return to being a clerk or an attendant...."

"To some other Roman noblewoman... like Cleo." Yosef leaned forward, his elbows on his knees. "Sometimes I dream of being back in Rome, after the shipwreck but before the great fire. Back when I came to know you all, but also looked forward to coming home."

Sayid's frown eased into an expression of concern as the young auxiliary nodded at Yosef. "I wish that too, sometimes. You wanted to return here to help your people. I wanted to return to Judea to serve the legion, hoping to find my father. I've done both... but it has not made me as happy as I once thought."

"And I've failed to help my people...."

"Hmmmph." Nicanor set the half-full amphora of wine and his cup between his feet and rubbed his shoulder, flexing it to loosen its stiffness. "Yosef, I've heard them refuse to listen to you. And I have listened to your stories of the faction fighting. Theirs is the failure, not yours." He put his hands on his thighs and looked over the area of the auxiliary camp within sight. "Gessius Florus, Nero... other Romans, along with your Judean leaders. They all failed. They all played a large role in this war. Old men... younger men... all greedy...

They are the power seekers or wielders who start the wars that other men—often the young—fight and die in."

"And women, too."

Nicanor knew Yosef meant the woman Ariella, who was briefly his wife. Then there was the wife of the Jewish giant Dov and other women in Galilee and at Yotapta.

"Have you heard any more from Lady Cleo?" Sayid asked.

"I'm at the siege line of the last wall every morning and stay as long as possible," Nicanor replied, "but nothing yet."

"I hope she is—"

Just then, two Syrian auxiliaries, cursing and kicking, came tumbling into the open space between the rows of tents. Nicanor stood to glare at them until they stopped, but in the struggle, a small glinting object flew from one man's hand and landed near Sayid's camp stool. Nicanor bent to pick it up. A small gold coin. *But auxiliaries are not paid in gold!* He thought.

"Where did you get this?" Nicanor demanded. The two men untangled themselves and stood truculently before him.

"It's mine," said the one man, "and," he pointed at the other as if he were a child complaining of another, "he thinks I should share with him. I told him to get his own. But now he'll have to chase it down...."

"I asked you, where did you get this?" Nicanor took three steps to loom over the two men.

"At the camp north of the city, tribunus," the man answered, flinching away from Nicanor. "I saw one of the Jewish prisoners, done with his squat, and what he did then made me go see what he was up to." The man looked up at Nicanor's stern expression and continued. "He picked through his filth and came up with that coin. He tried to hide it when I approached him."

"He swallowed it so it would not be taken from him," said Yosef, who took the coin from Nicanor to study it.

"Another guard saw it, too, but he did not try to steal it from me." The Syrian auxiliary glared at the other man. "But he grabbed another prisoner taken with the one hiding the gold. He cut him open and found three more gold coins in the Jew's stomach. Now he and the others run down the Jews inside the camp to see if they, too, carry gold."

Yosef gripped Nicanor's arm and said, "We must go to General Titus to stop this!"

* * *

Final Siege

Next morning...

THE ROMAN PRISON CAMP AT THE BASE OF MT. SCOPUS

Nicanor surveyed the carnage of the clearing within the camp, saying to Yosef, "Titus is furious with Aeterius Fronto, the *eques* who commands this camp and is warden for all the prisoners. He will administer their eventual sale. But it seems the auxiliaries—maybe at his command—thought a quicker profit could be made by gutting the prisoners to find what valuables they might have swallowed in their entrails."

"Two thousand men and women killed in one night." Yosef was pale as he stared at the field strewn with ripped-open bodies.

"Titus swears it will not happen again... he has warned Fronto and his officers that those responsible will face a death penalty."

"That's too late for them," Yosef said with a wave of his hand.

Nicanor gave Yosef a moment's silence, then said, "Titus wants to see you about a man he saved from all this."

* * *

THE ROMAN ENCAMPMENT, TITUS'S COMMAND TENT

General Titus sat behind his campaign desk, Tiberius Alexander off to one side with two legionaries, the escorts for the man standing before the general. The bedraggled man in a stained tunic had shackles on his feet and hands. Yosef shivered with the memory of himself in similar conditions before Titus's father, Vespasian, at the Roman encampment at Yotapta.

"Yosef," Titus said, "I know Nicanor has told you I regret what has happened at Lord Fronto's camp." Titus pointed at the prisoner before him. "This man," he flicked his hand and asked, "what is your name again?"

The man lifted his head, revealing large bruises almost encircling his neck. "Mannaneus ben Lazarus, general," he croaked.

"This man was saved from the killing of the people he led some from the city because conditions have become so terrible." Titus gestured at the man. "Tell him," he pointed at Yosef, "what you told me."

Mannaneus ben Lazarus turned to face Nicanor and Yosef. He ignored the tribunus and said, "You're Yosef ben Mathias... I do not know you... but know *of* you." The man's voice quavered with strain or anger—Yosef could not tell which. "There are so many dead that the streets are lined with the bodies. Some abandoned buildings and houses are full of corpses. Whether under the sky or sheltered by a roof... they rot. We listened to you about surrendering, so I tried to bring some people out, hoping to save them from that fate. All I achieved was a different place of death for them." The man hung his head, his tangled mass of hair falling over his face to shroud it.

"Yosef," Titus said, "I have decided to offer again to your people my grace and consideration. Go to them and tell them that, starting tomorrow at sunrise, I will let them bring out their dead. Choose a gate away from here that does not interfere with my men, and they will be free to remove the bodies from their city."

He glanced at the prisoner. "This man, Mannaneus ben Lazarus, in exchange for his life, will count the dead and report to you. And you will report to me."

* * *

THE NEW ROMAN BREASTWORKS AT ANTONIA FORTRESS

"Careful, Yosef... We're closer to the rebels this time. You must stand in line with us." Nicanor nodded to indicate the two legionaries on Yosef's left and the one on his right. Each was armored—as was he— and carried an infantryman's *scuta*, the tall rectangular shield that provided more protection. "Do not step out in front."

Yosef nodded. "Make the signal, Nicanor."

Nicanor leaned from the platform's edge and nodded to the *buccinator* on the level below. "Sound a cease-fire," he ordered.

The bugler's clarion call rang out, and the Roman *ballistae* slowed their fire and then stopped. The last rock crashing against the fort's rampart was surprisingly loud in the new quiet. It took a moment for the parapets to fill with rebels, curious about the cessation of attack.

Despite Nicanor's warning, Yosef took a half-step forward and spoke forcefully: "General Titus is aware of the hardships people in the city now endure. He will let you carry the dead from the city... but only briefly. You cannot hope to offer any funeral or burial rights or observances, as is our tradition. Still, you may relieve Jerusalem of the burden and risk the dead present to the living. Tomorrow at dawn at the Gate of the Essenes, cartloads will be allowed to go to the Hinnom Valley to dispose of the bodies."

The hiss of the stone cut through the air at the same time the missile scored a bloody groove along Yosef's brow. He went to his knees as Nicanor and three legionaries rushed to cover him. Stunned,

Yosef lay still as cheers erupted from the fort. The rebel celebration quieted as Yosef staggered and shrugged off the hands, pulling him to safety. He turned back toward the fortress. "Fools!" he cried. "I try to help you. Titus is gracious, and you spurn him. Since you do not trust me, listen to a man you may know—recently captured—Mannaneus ben Lazarus. He has told Titus of the city's plight caused by the number of dead. He will be at the Gate of the Essenes tomorrow at sunrise with General Titus's guarantee you may bring out the dead. Mannaneus will count the dead for General Titus. Use the time the general gives you to help those still alive in Jerusalem."

CXXV

Julius 70 CE

Jerusalem

Below the Gate of the Essenes in the Hinnom Valley

In the dawn's light, Yosef saw the first cart trundling down a path from the plateau skirting the Gate of the Essenes. Mannaneus ben Lazarus, now bathed and dressed in a rough but clean tunic, stood beside him, his hair swept back and beard combed. Mannaneus's hands were now free, but his legs remained hobbled by the chains attached to manacles at his ankles that were already chafed bloody from the bonds.

Mannaneus lifted his face to the low sunshine, and Yosef saw more clearly the mottled skin of his throat. He noticed Yosef's look and said, "Two soldiers held me down while a third had me by the neck. That one was ready to plunge his knife into me when the general and his escort entered the camp."

"You were fortunate," Yosef replied.

"Was I? Am I? Unlike you," he said with disdain, "I do not know if I will live or die at the Romans' hands."

Yosef was angry at the tone, but now was not the time or the place to defend himself. "Mannaneus, I chose to live to try to help our people," he said simply. Then stepped back to the line of Romans selected by Nicanor: twenty armored, heavy infantry and ten mounted cavalry archers that formed their escort. As his friend had told him, there were "enough men to protect you until one of the circling patrols can react, but not so many as to be an overt threat to the rebels."

The first cart reached the valley floor, escorted by two armed rebels. Mannaneus turned toward Yosef and said, "They've sent a man who knows me. I'm going to speak to him."

Yosef heard Nicanor tell the decurion commanding the escort to order his men to be still but ready. He watched as the two men on the cart glared at him, and then the driver bent to greet Mannaneus. The driver looked up again at the Romans, scowled at Yosef, and nodded to the man at his side. The rebel took a swath of white linen and affixed it to a long pole he pulled from among the corpses in the cart's bed. He raised the flag high to signal men atop the bluff, and the strip of cloth caught a sunbeam. Soon the clops of many mules and the creaking of wheels and wood broke the dawn stillness. Looking up toward the gate, Yosef saw a line of wagons and men on foot coming down the path with their burdens.

"Where will they take the bodies?" Nicanor asked, wrinkling his nose as the breeze carried to him the odor from the first cart. "This valley will reek even more."

"Caves and crevices," Yosef replied and noted Mannaneus finishing the first wagon's count and writing in the wax tablet he had provided him. He would collect the tablets each day and tally the totals for Titus. "But they must move fast to get as many bodies out as possible in what time the general allows." Yosef saw Nicanor search the face of the escarpment for the honeycombed shadowy openings.

"There are many places for them," Nicanor said as he gauged the sunrise. He waved flies from his face as he turned toward Yosef. "Now, I must go to the siege line. You don't need to be here for this? Let that man," Nicanor gestured at Mannaneus, "do as he's been tasked. Come away with me."

"No... I'll stay. I feel I must witness this." Yosef replied.

"Well, I trust this decurion leading these men. Are you at ease that I may leave?"

Yosef nodded, and Nicanor mounted Albus and rode away. He turned back to the spectacle as the first cart moved by him toward the slope to the caves. Bitter bile rose in his throat, and he forced it down with a grimace. He did not want to look, but he could not turn away. He was compelled to search the faces in the cart... even as he prayed he would not recognize any of them.

CXXVI

Julius 70 CE

Jerusalem

The Upper City

Miriam entered the rear courtyard to find Elian sitting with Cicero, digging his fingers into the dirt beneath the trees. He brought up a grub to the keenly watching bird perched on the leather pad on his shoulder, and Cicero accepted the result of the boy's labor. Miriam ruffled the boy's tousled hair as she passed them, not pausing to allow him to ask questions. But she looked forward to offering him and the bird the grain and dates waiting to be brought home.

Miriam looked toward the house, alarmed to see that at the courtyard table, Ya'el was bent over Yohanan ben Zaccai. She inspected a swollen-shut eye and dabbed it with water on a linen hand towel that Rachel and Leah had brought her. Both Ya'el and Yohanan turned toward Miriam as Leah lighted a lantern. Miriam saw that the old rabbi's brow and cheek had been badly bruised. "What happened?" she asked.

"Matthew and I finally found Yohanan ben Levi," Yohanan said, flinching as Ya'el softly pressed the wet cloth to his eye. "We convinced his guards to let us see him, and he..." The old priest winced again, reached to take the cloth from Ya'el, and held it to his eye himself. He shook his head to free the words too hard to speak.

Miriam looked at Ya'el, who responded, "He just got here, and I think the blow to his head has muddled him. We don't know what happened."

"Has Yohanan ben Levi harmed my father and mother?" Miriam asked, her voice rising in alarm. Cicero squawked at her change in tone.

"I don't know," Yohanan said. "We found him overseeing the melting down of the Temple's vessels. It is a desecration I never imagined him capable of... though I've long known of his greed. But I thought his longing was only for power. But his men were drinking from casks of sacred Temple wine and then drunkenly tossing the golden vessels into iron smelting kettles over blazing fires. Matthew confronted him, accusing him of making the gold easier to steal. That was a clear sign that he planned to abandon Jerusalem to the Romans as he had abandoned Gischala in his own town in Galilee. Two of the Gischalan's men grabbed Matthew, and I tried to help him, but another man struck me in the face and knocked me to the ground. I lay there looking up at Yohanan ben Levi and asked him, 'Why?' He stared down at me and said: 'Because I can employ these divine things on behalf of the Divinity....'"

The old rabbi's head dropped to his chest, and Miriam saw tears trickle from his open eye. In all her life, she had never seen her father's best friend lose his composure. A chill shot through her. "What about my parents?"

"The Gischalan's men dragged us from the chamber and threw us onto the street. I do not know if Mathias and Rebecca have been harmed or if they suffer, but they are still imprisoned."

"Where is Matthew?" Miriam gritted her teeth.

"He went to find Eleasar ben Ananias... to tell him about Yohanan ben Levi's latest transgression against our people... and against our faith. Then they will go to Simon bar Giora to convince him to stop the Gischalan, to punish him."

"So, even now," Miriam said with disgust, "with the Romans assaulting our last wall... we fight each other."

"I know, Miriam, but ben Levi cannot do such things. He has become an enemy within reach with this sin, and we must hold him accountable."

"No... I think Yohanan ben Levi must be punished fully. He must die for what he's done." Miriam took in a deep breath and released it. She was exhausted and feeling the weight of so much to do before she could rest... if she ever could again. "But first, we must hide you until I get you out of the city."

"Yohanan ben Levi won't come after me."

"He might not, but Yonatan, his attack dog, will. I was told on the way home that in the agora, Yonatan boasted to his men that he would kill you tomorrow." Miriam heard Leah's quavering gasp. From the corner of her eye, she saw Rachel put her arm around her sister.

Yohanan stood and teetered, his hands pressed to the tabletop as if that alone kept him from falling. "Then I must go... Yonatan must not come here."

"Wait here and gather yourself. Then I will take you out of the city through the Canaanite branch tunnel into the Hinnom Valley. You can rest in the cave there, and then we'll see if you can get away."

"You and Akiva found the hidden supply wagons? Good! But where is he?"

"The Romans were there in the valley where the tunnel comes out in one of the caves. Akiva led them away so I could get to the cavern he used to hide the supplies. He's gone... just as the supplies were when I got to where Akiva had hidden them. Someone found the food and took all but a small part. It was hidden away in the back of the cave."

"Did the Romans catch him?" The old rabbi's voice changed from anger to remorse.

"I don't know...." Miriam shook her head but thought they *must* have caught the shepherd. She prayed the Romans had moved from the area so Yohanan would have a chance to escape. If he could escape the valley, nearby villages would take him in... if the Romans had not destroyed them, too. *What then?*

She blinked away the worries of the future to focus on the present. "I brought back that little store of food and hid it in the tunnel near the agora alley. Now that the sun is setting, with Ya'el's help, I can go get it and bring it home in the darkness. Then tonight, I'll take you through the tunnels to that cave in the Hinnom Valley. We'll see if the Romans are gone at daybreak, and you can escape." Miriam gestured to Ya'el to follow her as Yohanan sank back into his chair. "We'll be back soon with some food."

* * *

"Is Matthew not back yet?" Miriam asked as she shrugged off the pack, and Ya'el reached to open it. Elian, with Cicero, gathered with Rachel and Leah around the courtyard table. With a look that asked permission and after Ya'el's nod, the boy broke off a piece from a cake of pressed dates and shared it with the bird.

"He was here, then left quickly...." Rachel said as she took the bag of grain from Ya'el. They had all discussed that Matthew, Miriam, and Ya'el would forage for food and that what they found would be strictly rationed. Rachel had that responsibility.

"Where's Yohanan? Is he inside, resting?"

"He's gone," Leah answered, and Miriam heard what seemed like relief in her voice.

"What?"

"Two of his students arrived out of breath, beating at the door to warn him. They had been running to get here ahead of Yonatan, for they'd heard he would not wait until tomorrow. He and some of his drunk men boasted they would find Yohanan tonight." Fear had crept back into Leah's tone but eased again as she continued. "Yohanan's students plan to smuggle him out of the city in the morning."

"How?" Miriam feared Yohanan's well-intentioned followers would get him killed.

"Word has spread that the Roman general, Titus," Rachel glanced at Ya'el, "is letting us take our dead from the city through the Gate of the Essenes. At dawn tomorrow, some of Yohanan's students plan to hide him in a casket and get him out of the city."

Miriam rubbed her eyes with her hands and shook her head wearily. "You said Matthew was here and then left again."

"He got here right after Yohanan left with the two students. We told him what had happened, and he went to find Yonatan, to stop him from coming here. Or delay him to give the students time to get Yohanan from the Upper City."

"Ya'el...." Miriam turned to see her feeding the parrot a tiny pile of grain cupped in her hand. "You and I will be at the Gate of the Essenes before sunrise to see that Yohanan gets safely out of the city."

CXXVII

Julius 70 CE

Jerusalem

The Lower City

"Do you think something has happened to Matthew?" Ya'el asked, speaking for the first time since they'd left the Upper City.

"I hope not," said Miriam. "But my worries have stolen my sleep—and I much needed it!" She had awakened in her dark room just past midnight, finding her exhaustion had left her sleeping in the same position as when she'd stretched out on her bed. With a groan, she sat up and checked, finding that Matthew still had not returned. Consumed with worry, she could not return to sleep. "After this, we'll go home, and if he's not there... I'll search for him."

"I'll come with you."

Miriam nodded. Ya'el had proven she would not shirk her friends... her family. That thought turned Miriam's thoughts to Yosef. Men were already moving about in the pre-dawn as she and Ya'el went from the Upper City to the Lower City. She overheard bits of discussion about General Titus's decision to let them remove the dead from Jerusalem. Upon hearing Yosef's name, she slowed her steps to hear more, waving Ya'el on for a moment, and learned that Yosef himself had announced that order.

"And when that sling-stone landed square on his head, I was glad to be done with that traitor," the man said, and Miriam's hand went to her heart. But in the following words, the man cursed that he had not died. "Only stunned, the dog!" the man complained. But Miriam's hammering heart began to still at that assurance.

By then, Ya'el had retraced her steps to join Miriam, and she listened, too. Miriam knew the distress on Ya'el's face was mirrored in her own. *But we must be about our business*, she thought.

Miriam moved along the parapet to the steps down to the Gate of the Essenes. Dawn was breaking, and far below, a group of Romans watching extinguished their torches. A yawn gaped her mouth, loosening the cloth across her face. She quickly secured it, glad she and Ya'el fit in with the men. They were even better disguised now that everyone tried to filter out the stench that had settled over the Lower City.

As Miriam and Ya'el reached the gate level, they saw cartloads of bodies being brought into a long queue. Near the front of the line, six men—really boys with patchy beards—now stood three to a side next to a wooden casket, their eyes cast down. The mutterings of men and the soft noise of mules in harnesses broke the morning stillness. As she and Ya'el waited, watching the boys who were surely Yohanan's students, Miriam heard men say once they hauled away the dead, the animals would be butchered for meat. She wondered how to steal some of it.

"What's this?" called out a booming—bullying—voice in Aramaic, silencing the whispered conversations around them. Yonatan bar Hilel, flanked by a dozen men, approached the nervous boys by the casket. "Is the body within too good for the wagons?" he asked, gesturing toward the carts piled with bodies, some with a limb dangling over their sideboards. "Let us see."

Yonatan motioned to his men. Two of them took the long iron pry bars from one of the wagons used to shift the dead. They walked to the casket and plunged the long rods into the wood. The iron easily passed through, and the tallest of the boys threw himself at one man, yelling, "Stop!" With a sweep of his iron bar, the man knocked the boy down as the others scattered.

That shout echoed from within the casket as Yohanan ben Zaccai shoved the splintered lid up and away and stiffly climbed out, ripping a length of his tunic pinned by a rod into the bottom of the casket. The other iron rods had narrowly missed him, too, though he did have some blood along his neck.

A miracle! Miriam thought and suddenly realized Ya'el was not beside her any longer.

The old rabbi glared at Yonatan with his one open eye. "Stop! Do not hurt these boys. They have done nothing to you.... Nor have I."

"But they took my wife from me because of you!" Yonatan shouted and moved toward the old rabbi.

The hiss of an arrow cut through the silence that had fallen over the crowd around the gate. It struck one of the men in the chest, and the iron rod he held fell feebly to the ground. His hands went to the shaft and gripped it as he sank to his knees. Miriam sensed Ya'el nock, pull, and release again. Another arrow skewered the neck of the second man closest to Yohanan.

Ya'el's action was unplanned, but Miriam moved as if it had been. "Meet us at the tomb!" she called over her shoulder to Ya'el. Miriam raced to Yohanan ben Zaccai as more of Ya'el's arrows flew, striking several of Yonatan's men and driving the Zealot to find cover. Miriam reached Yohanan ben Zaccai, grabbed his arm, and pulled him away from the casket where he had stood in shock.

"Please, Yohanan," Miriam cried, "you must run like you're young again… or we will both die here."

CXXVIII

Julius 70 CE

Jerusalem

The Hinnom Valley

Nicanor watched as Titus waved the perfumed swath of silk around his face, dispersing the plague of flies and attempting to mask the stench that grew stronger as they drew closer. The odor of putrefaction and vast clouds of insects now hung over all the Hinnom Valley. Nicanor had braided a whisk from Albus's tail hair, affixed it to a handle, and wielded that to keep his mouth and nose momentarily free of the pests. He wished he'd drenched it in some scent to counter the smell. He leaned forward along Albus's neck every few minutes and whisked the flies away from the horse's muzzle. Albus did his part by angrily blowing through his nose and lips, dislodging the flying pests. Nicanor took a little comfort in seeing the first sign of the animal's imperturbable nature.

Titus turned to him, holding the silk to his cheek. "I see the numbers Yosef has brought me each night, the count of the dead, but...." The general shook his head at the spectacle of the valley that butted up against the craggy bluff of the city.

Nicanor nodded with understanding. In his most recent years of service in the legions, he had read many reports of the results of major battles, small actions, and minor raids. Each had a count of the dead and wounded. For some *eques* on Titus's staff, men who had received their position through connections or wealth, not service, the impact of the reports did not resonate as they did with Nicanor. Only those who had observed—or survived—combat firsthand, seen the aftermath of strewn bodies, and suffered their own torn flesh carried scars within and without for the rest of their lives. Titus had witnessed war, seen combat, been endangered, fought and killed men, and seen many men killed. But neither had seen death on this scale—it was staggering.

The caves that lay closest to the path were filled, as were the ravines and gulches along the valley nearby. The cartloads now must travel farther along the escarpment that formed the valley. With the general's escort leading, Nicanor and Titus followed the line of wagons so the general could see for himself.

"Yosef says the flow of wagons does not stop," Nicanor commented. "At night, they continue under torchlight, stopping only when he needs a few hours of sleep." Nicanor directed the cavalry officer leading Titus's guard to shift the formation to one side and to move faster around the line of wagons. He kneed Albus to pick up the pace.

They reached the line's end, where a team of men from the city unloaded the carts. He saw Yosef off to one side, on the edge of the gulch, with the Jewish deserter, Mannaneus ben Lazarus. As he approached, Yosef looked up from the tablet in his hands. It probably marked the latest wagon load's count. Mannaneus ben Lazarus stood next to Yosef, who gave him back the wax tablet. How his face has thinned, Nicanor thought as he studied his friend, who now had severely drawn lines alongside his nose, and his brow more deeply furrowed. He seemed oblivious to the flies that flitted about and landed upon him. Yosef did not greet him but watched Titus move away and upwind with his escort.

Before Titus could motion a command to come to him, Yosef stepped away from Mannaneus, turned to Nicanor, and gestured at the gully. "Tell me what you see," he said.

"I don't need to look, Yosef... I know what lies there." Nicanor dismounted, holding Albus's reins in one hand while he continued to wield the horsehair whisk. "And *you* do not need to be here to see them. Titus does not expect that. I've told you I can have Mannaneus's tablets brought to you. You do not need to be here," he repeated.

"Look, Nicanor." Yosef's tone was demanding, stiff but with a hint of cracking.

Nicanor stepped to the rim. The narrow gulch was filled with bodies upon bodies, too many to count. He could see they had laid some out in somewhat orderly rows. Others, more haphazardly, were tumbled down by men weary of the hours of hauling, carrying, and handling the weight of the dead. Though his friend had touched none of the bodies, Nicanor saw their weight in Yosef's dull eyes and slumped shoulders.

"Do you see?" Yosef asked.

Nicanor did not answer him. Yosef did not seek an answer.

"When this started, there were many younger men, fighters who had died from their wounds. But soon, just as many were old men and women, frail and ill. Then the younger bodies became not just fighters. The dead seem younger each day, sometimes with—each—wagon—load." Yosef's voice broke. He paused and swallowed to bring it back together. "And this morning..." Yosef beckoned him to follow.

"Yosef," Nicanor said, lengthening his stride to catch up to his friend while Albus trudged behind. "This will end soon... Titus told me after the staff meeting this morning that they are on the verge of breaking through the walls of Antonia Fortress. He will soon order the end of bringing out your dead. Titus is re-sealing the city." Nicanor stopped next to Yosef. "Did you hear me? When Antonia falls, he will attack the temple, and there will be no more defensible positions for your people."

"Look," said Yosef stubbornly, not listening to him, pointing at the wagon they had reached. Three small bodies were atop the pile—two girls and a boy. Nicanor was a poor judge of children's ages, but they were probably three or four years old... not older than five. Yosef moved to the next wagon. "Look." The young woman must have been in her teens and seemed asleep, with the tiny newborn baby clutched to her breasts.

Nicanor closed his eyes. When he opened them, he saw Yosef's had filled with tears. The first spilled down his friend's cheeks but did not disturb the flies.

CXXIX

Julius 70 CE

Jerusalem

The City of David, King David's Tomb

Miriam studied Yohanan ben Zaccai as he took another gulp of the stale water from one of the water skins she had left stored in this antechamber, now what seemed so long ago. Miriam was no longer thirsty, but she took another gulp herself, giving her stomach a sensation of fullness. She had given Yohanan some of the food she found left behind by Ya'el and Elian. *Even Nahum found shelter here,* she mused. She hoped that the days he had left after his brief time of hiding in Jerusalem had allowed more of the Temple treasure to be secured by the Essenes.

It was nothing but hard cheese and a handful of nuts, but once his breathing had settled and color finally returned to his face, the old priest had gnawed them with appetite. She handed him a small bundle. "Here's some dried fruit. It's not much, but I hope you reach safety and someplace where you'll find more."

"Thank you, Miriam." The rabbi nodded and leaned back against the wall with his legs stretched out, hands folded over the food packet on his lap. He had been mostly silent since Miriam had led him on a stumbling run from the Gate of the Essenes to King David's Tomb. It had taken all his breath to run, even though she had slowed her pace for the old man. Then, once safely inside the tomb, he began to experience the aftershock of being so close to a violent death. Miriam knew moments like that made a person draw inward, so she let him have the silence.

"Do you think Ya'el is in trouble?" Yohanan finally asked. "She should be here by now."

That worry had nagged at Miriam for the last half hour, her anxiety growing as the time flowed by. Had Yonatan's men or some other Zealot at the Gate of the Essenes taken Ya'el? Or had she forgotten how to find the entrance to the tomb. *No, not that.* Ya'el might have been born a Roman noblewoman, but she kept her wits. But even if she were safe, Ya'el might not come to them. "There have probably been too many of Yonatan's men on the streets. There's time... and we must wait until dark before I get you into the other tunnel to Hinnom Valley."

"I should stay in Jerusalem," Yohanan said quietly but firmly.

Miriam leaned down from her seat on a bench to look at the old priest. "There's nothing you can do," she said. "Your students are right. You must get out of the city and continue your teaching. That's a reason to live."

"Now Yonatan will kill Leah...."

"You could not stop him from trying—both of you could end up dead at his hands."

"But—"

"But nothing...." Miriam slipped from the bench to crouch on the ground beside the old priest. "There's nothing you can do to help her."

Yohanan sighed. "She's never gotten over Yosef, and unless he's changed with all that's happened since I talked to him last in Yotapta, he still loves her."

But he has changed. Miriam had turned that bitter thought over and over in her mind. It could not be denied that Yosef had joined their enemy, which settled it for her.

"Rachel," Yohanan continued, "loves Yosef, too. Even my tired old eyes can see the light in hers when there's talk of him, even if it's talk against him."

"Leah and Rachel should let go of what will never be. Yosef has turned his back on us."

"No, Miriam," Yohanan said as he leaned toward Miriam and took her hand, "I'm certain he has not turned his back. I know Yosef still tries to help our people, mostly his family. He loves you all—"

"He helps himself and doesn't suffer as we do," she said, interrupting him. "You've seen all the bodies taken through the Gate of the Essenes. Soon, even more, as we sit here, and more to come. Soon there will be no one to carry them. Those who remain in Jerusalem will fall or lay themselves down and become another body and another among the thousands and thousands. Only then will the legions and Romans go away... Yosef with them."

Miriam looked into Yohanan's tired, wrinkled face framed by thinning hair and a long, coarse beard now more white than gray. She squeezed his hand, and her stomach growled, loud in the antechamber's quiet.

"If gold were food," Yohanan gestured at the passage she knew led to the tomb's treasures, "we would not have to worry about eating." He smiled, and Miriam had to offer him a smile in return, though it hurt. She watched his smile fade and his expression harden. "I should stay."

Miriam shook her head and reached for his hand again. "No. I'll see you to the Hinnom Valley when it's dark and wait until you're away. Then I'll return. I'll protect Leah and my family."

"Even as a little girl, you always cared for others more than yourself," Yohanan said as his features softened, and he reached up to brush his gnarled knuckles along her cheek. "If teaching is the reason I should live, what is yours, Miriam? To take care of your family?"

Miriam closed her eyes and whispered. "It's all I have...."

"There is strength in you, Miriam." The old priest gripped her shoulder. "After I go, give my love to them all."

"I will. Now rest a while." Miriam watched as the Yohanan settled back and closed his eyes. She mouthed silent prayers for her father and mother... and for Ya'el. Where was she? Where was Matthew?

CXXX

Julius 70 CE

Jerusalem

The Lower City, the Pool of Siloam

The men she had heard near the ruins all day had finally gone, so Ya'el carefully crawled from beneath the rubble of cracked stone and fractured rock that seemed to have been picked through for decades. What was left of the Tower of Siloam that Miriam had told her about falling many years before had been useless to anyone. But it provided a hiding place for Ya'el. Lying beneath the stone and dirt, faint from the heat, with no food, no water, Ya'el felt her mind wander. Trailing through her memories of recent events and what loomed over them still to come from the Romans. She thought of all the dead. Miriam and Akiva had undertaken to find some last food supply for them. But Miriam had returned alone, reporting most of it was gone. The grain and dates Miriam had salvaged would last them only a few days.

She moved slowly, drenched in sweat, exhausted, stiff, and aching from being immobile all day. The waning moon above cast little light, and everything around her was in shades of gray and black. That morning after her attack defending Yohanan ben Zaccai, she had pinned down Yonatan and his men for a few minutes while Miriam and Yohanan ran north toward the City of David. With her last arrow spent, Ya'el had sprinted east toward the Pool of Siloam and outrun the men. Miriam had told her of a short tunnel she thought was under the tower's foundation and connected it to King David's Tomb. But Ya'el could not find the tunnel entrance—only a hollowed-out space large enough to hide her.

During that long day full of nothing but her thoughts to occupy her, Ya'el had recalled that Yohanan ben Zaccai told her a story when she mentioned seeing the Pool of Siloam for the first time. In the time of the supposed messiah, Yeshua ish Natzrat, Pontius Pilate, the Roman Prefect, had ordered several Galileans killed for causing a public disturbance as they worshipped. Also, around that time, the Tower of Siloam collapsed, killing 18 people. Yeshua had often debated Jerusalem's religious leaders, and they questioned him about why misfortunes befall people who have done no wrong.

Yeshua had replied that good and evil men and women, those who sin and those who do not, all have something to repent. Those who would not repent would perish. She had not understood all Yohanan had talked about once he discovered her interest. But one thing was evident—terrible things can and do happen to people through no fault of their own. It was how they responded to them that mattered most.

Ya'el approached the vast rock-cut pool, sensing as much as smelling its moisture. She stepped into the pool to slake her thirst and sluice water over her face. Dripping, she climbed four precisely cut and uniformly shaped *ashlar* stone steps to the walkway surrounding the pool. Which led to a broad avenue paved with massive stone slabs, where few people walked the stepped street that climbed toward the Temple. Soon she passed a pyramidal dais set to the side. Miriam had told her it was formed from *meleke*, the finer stone used in many public buildings, including the Temple, unlike the limestone paving of the street. She stopped at a stage where many rested when they entered the city for Pesach, Shavuot, and Sukkot. The *Even Hato'eem*, the Stone of Losses, was where people stood and declared their loss, hoping someone could find their belonging and return it to them. She thought of what she could declare lost. But her personal loss could not compare to what this city and people had lost, nor could her sufferings match the anguish of Yosef's family.

The self-measuring cleared her thoughts. Miriam did not need her help to get Yohanan from the city. Ya'el was out of arrows, and though she had the dagger Miriam had given her, she would be useless in a fight. Instead, she would ready herself to go to her countrymen and plead with General Titus. Rachel was right—she should try, even if that meant Titus sent her back to Gessius Florus. Then, if he did not kill her first, she would kill at her first opportunity. Her death did not matter if she could convince Titus to save Yosef's family.

* * *

Next morning...

THE UPPER CITY, THE AGORA, THE FIRST WALL

Compared to the noise of battle around the Antonia Fortress, this first wall area was almost peaceful. The Romans kept their siege line manned, but they had moved nearly all the ballistae and other missile throwers, as well as the siege tower, to assault the fortress, their main point of attack.

Ya'el cautiously stepped along the parapet to the nearest tower across from the center of the Romans' siege line. It was quiet, other than the small sounds of sporadic volleys of arrows or slingers' bullets. Watchmen were spread thinly along the wall, and most hungry and exhausted rebel fighters still slept though dawn was breaking. She took the steps to the tower's peak, then looked out on the Roman line and worried about Matthew. He had still not returned, and when she got home from the Lower City, she had found Rachel and Leah in a panic. She was thankful Eleasar ben Ananias had been there to bring her a scant supply of arrows. He had agreed to stay with them through the day until she, Matthew, or Miriam returned.

Looking down, Ya'el gazed over the Roman line, searching for Nicanor. After several minutes, a large Roman carrying a shield, his metal breastplate catching the sunbeams now slanting down, passed through the line to stand several feet before it. Red cloak swirling, he raised his muscular arms to lift the helmet from his head and tuck it under one arm. *Something about him,* she thought. A man behind him, another officer on the line, called something to him she could not hear. The giant soldier half-turned to face the other officer and shook his head. Then he turned back toward the wall, scanning the rebel bulwarks.

Ya'el prayed it was Nicanor as she stepped up on a stone from a ballista that had landed perfectly within the tower's crenelations. It raised her by a foot or more to the height of a very tall man. She lifted her bow, then nocked the white-shafted, green-feathered arrow and held, ready.

The Roman looked in her direction, and she loosed the string, arcing the arrow perfectly to strike the ground in front of the man. He stooped to pick up the arrow and straightened up with his broad back still to the line. Setting his shield on the ground, propped against his leg, he loosened the message wrapped to the shaft. He glanced at it and snapped the arrow into halves, casting the point to the ground on his left and gripping the feathered end in his right hand. He stared up at her.

CXXXI

Augustus 70 CE

Jerusalem

The Roman Encampment, Nicanor, and Yosef's Tent

"So begins the *kalends* of Augustus," Nicanor announced. He stepped into the arc of light cast by the lantern hanging outside the tent where Sayid had spent his impatient hours healing in company with Yosef.

Sayid looked at him and said, "So that rumbling was the wall...."

"Yes, Antonia Fortress is coming down," Nicanor said, "though the legion engineers had hoped to breach it today." He put his head back and gazed into the clear night sky and the waxing crescent moon. "They were close." Nicanor settled onto the stool across from Sayid and an empty seat where Yosef must have sat recently. *At the privy?* He wondered. Sayid seemed saddened by the news, perhaps in sympathy with Yosef, who had told Nicanor earlier that the final count would be over 111,000 dead. It was a staggering number.

"Your infantry will pour through and take the fortress at dawn, then," Yosef said as he returned to the arc of light and took his seat, handing a cup of water to his friend.

"No," Nicanor replied, and both his friends looked up, surprised.

"What?" Sayid exclaimed, wincing as his shifting on the seat pulled at his wound.

"The rebels have built *another* wall behind this one. The engineers could not assess it in the dark, but the rebels were ready to defend the new wall even more fiercely than the old. When the engineers and their support came close with torches, the rebels showered them with arrows and dozens of stones. Many legionaries, including three engineers, were killed before they could pull back out of range. Titus has ordered a counter barrage to commence at dawn once we see what we're shooting at. Then the engineers will re-assess the wall and how to breach it."

"Then there's still a chance—" Sayid cut himself off and looked away into the night.

Nicanor studied his friend and continued with his news. "Titus plans to speak tomorrow afternoon to the men of the 5th Legion, who will attack once the new wall is evaluated."

FINAL SIEGE

"I will be there."

"To listen only, please, Sayid. I know I'm not your commanding officer, but...."

"Sayid, you still limp badly," Yosef said, clasping the Syrian's shoulder and glancing at Nicanor. "Like Nicanor told me... the end is near. You've proved your bravery over and over. You need do no more."

Tightlipped, still looking away, Sayid did not reply. After a moment, instead, he faced them and said, "Nicanor, before you left us to meet with General Titus, you said you had something to show us."

Nicanor emptied his lungs with resolve, reached behind his *balteus*, the broad belt supporting his sheathed *pugio*, and pulled out a message. The contents had troubled him all day so that the crash of the fortress wall had been a welcome distraction. "This was attached to another arrow from Cleo...." He handed it to Sayid next to him, and Sayid, in turn, unfolded it and leaned closer to Yosef so he could see it, too, under the lantern light. Sayid read aloud in a hushed voice:

'All dying. I must plead with Titus to save Yosef's family. Help me. When Antonia falls, ask Y about the branch tunnel. Herod's Tunnel, the passage to the agora. Meet me there. Break arrow if agreed. Show fletched end here at second dawn. I will send time to meet after Antonia taken. If no, drop whole arrow—and pray for us.'

"She can't do that!" Sayid exclaimed. "Florus will kill her!"

"Cleo says 'all dying'... she means my family." Yosef stood, clenching the message in his fist. "I have to do something. Nicanor, do as she says... but *I'll* meet her in the tunnel."

"No." Nicanor shook his head. "You'd never get through Antonia Fortress alone. Where's the tunnel entrance?"

"Down at the armory level...."

"Then it's certain you'll never reach it. Tell me how to find this tunnel, and I'll go."

"You can't, Nicanor," Sayid said as he stood with a lurch and a grimace. "If you get caught, how would you explain?"

Nicanor pinched the bridge of his nose and rubbed his eyes with the spread of his fingers. "It does not matter. I won't get caught, and I'll protect Cleo from Gessius Florus." He looked up at Yosef. "I will do my best to help her save your family."

"And I will go with you," said Yosef. "You don't know those tunnels."

"*Futuo!*" Nicanor swept his hand through his hair, smoothing it back. "Then *you* will come with me, Yosef."

"Now I pray Antonia Fortress falls soon," Yosef said, looking north across the camp toward the looming shadow of Antonia Fortress.

CXXXII

Augustus 70 CE

Jerusalem

Near Antonia Fortress

There was no wind, not the faintest air stirring, even upon the raised platform. *Helios takes little pity on the emperor's son,* Nicanor thought, squinted at the scorching sun, *and much less on others.* Sweat stung his eyes, and he wished for a cloud or breeze to lessen the sweltering heat. He looked down upon the ranks of soldiers, where the stifling air seemed to shimmer beneath the *meridiem* sun around all those armored bodies. Titus's staff, with Yosef, faced the rubble of an outer wall of Antonia Fortress. Nicanor heard Yosef sniffing the air as if searching—hoping—for a scent. "What are you doing?" he whispered.

"This is the season when figs, peaches, apples, and pears ripen. As a boy, I loved the aroma of the groves, even in this hottest month of summer, for it promised fresh fruit. My mother told us, as children, that it was a cycle that lasted forever. But she was wrong." Yosef dipped his chin to his chest and then raised it to stare over the rows of men. "Now, there's only an odor of death in Jerusalem."

All the trees around Jerusalem were gone for some distance. The hungry inside the city would have long since devoured even the green fruits on what spindly trees were left as the legions had taken the rest. *The trees will take many years to grow and bear fruit again,* Nicano thought. *Will they grow wild, or will any people still be here to tend them and eat the fruit?* Yosef might be brooding over that prospect or perhaps remembering the harvests of years gone by.

Titus strode from the awning set up to shade him and Tiberius Alexander from the blazing sun, and he took the platform. Before him spread almost the entire 5th Legion. Ranks of men arranged in cohorts of legionaries and auxiliaries filled the ground below him, ending before the piles of rubble. The new wall the legion engineers had evaluated that morning was a short distance behind the debris.

Nicanor's eyes swept the crude battlements of the new wall and could still see no rebels. But they must be there, watching and waiting.

"Have you spotted Sayid?" Yosef whispered, leaning toward him.

Nicanor shook his head and lowered his gaze to the cohorts. "I see what I think is his unit—Marcus Sabinus in front," he thrust his chin at the middle mass of men, "but I can't find Sayid."

Yosef's eyes followed Nicanor's line of sight. "Maybe he's not here," he said. "Maybe he decided to rest his leg after all."

Nicanor shook his head, certain their friend meant what he had said. "He's stubborn, Sayid is... I'm sure he's there."

Titus motioned with his hand, and the legion *buccinator* raised his horn and let go a sharp blast. The ranks of men became entirely still. Nicanor wiped the sweat from his brow with one hand and sensed Yosef shifting a half-step closer to Titus and concentrating. He would later be able to recall and record almost exactly what Titus said so he could record it on one of his tablets for the general to review.

Titus cleared his throat.

"My fellow soldiers, to drive men to achieve that which offers no danger is a dishonorable waste of time for those hearing such a speech. It is the same for the speaker, even a sign of timidity. I believe that such reassurance should only be made in dangerous situations. Men can hearten themselves in other circumstances—they need no speeches. And so, I will tell you what you know: attacking this new inner wall will be dangerous.

"But it is right that those who want to be remembered for their valor undertake perilous missions. It is a brave thing to die with glory. The courage that emboldens those who go first will not go unrewarded. My first reason to inspire you to attack seems like an argument that might be used to the contrary... to persuade you not to go. I mean the determination and persistence of the Jews, even under their difficult reverses and losses. But you are all Romans."

Titus paused, and his eyes swept the cohorts of both legionaries and auxiliaries. "You are my troops. You have been trained in peacetime to fight, that you might win at war. It would be a shame to you to now suffer defeat by the Jews, who are inferior, both in skill and in valor. This is especially true when victory is at hand. We have suffered setbacks, mainly because of Jewish madness in the face of looming defeat. But your boldness and their god Jehovah helping us have caused their woes.

"The Jews have rebelled against one another even before this war. They are now suffering famine. They must now endure our siege engines and the destruction of their walls. What can this be but a demonstration of their god's anger at them and his help for us? It is not right to show yourselves as less than those who are your inferiors. Embrace their god's divine providence, which is your ally.

"Even more dishonorable would be not conquering those Jews who expect defeat. They rebel against being slaves and run from slavery, preferring to die. So, they continually sneak from behind their walls—of which only one remains—and present themselves before our forces, not expecting victory but only to show their fearlessness. We, Romans, have taken possession of all the Earth's land and the seas. What a disgrace it would be if we could not conquer such as these because we were afraid to go where the danger lies but would rather wile away the hours in our armor while our enemies died of starvation. All this when we have them in our power with only one wall standing between us and victory."

Titus pointed at the collapsed wall and the newly built one behind it. "I know many of you are tired... many have been in this land for far longer than expected. The city will be ours if we take and hold the Antonia Fortress. Once it is under our control, I think the fighting in the city will end. We will have the high ground, closest to the most valued part of their city. We will strike our enemies before they know what has happened. I say that these advantages will enable a quick and certain victory."

"But I won't speak further about that certainty. And I will not now speak of praising those who die in warfare. Nor will I talk about the immortality of those slain fighting bravely. I cannot cease to speak against those who want to die in peacetime by some disease or another. Those whose bodies and souls are forever condemned to the grave. For what worthy man among you does not know that those souls severed from their flesh by an enemy sword are received into the ether. The purest elements join with those brave men whose home is amidst the stars. Who among you does not know that they become heroes, showing themselves as such to all who come after them?

"But upon those souls that succumb to disease and old age comes subterranean darkness into which they dissolve into nothingness, never to be remembered even though they are innocent of the world's defilement. In this death, not only do the soul and body die, but also any memory of them. Since an end will come upon every man, a sword is a better instrument than any disease. Why shouldn't we yield to dying for the greater good rather than leave death to fate?"

Titus stepped closer to the edge of the platform and spread his arms. "I have made my speech assuming that those who make the first assault on the second wall will be killed in the attempt. You are soldiers and know this risk, though men of real courage have a chance to escape even the most ominous actions. I speak of taking this new wall behind the old one we just brought down." Titus pointed at Antonia Fortress. "The demolished portion of the first wall can be quickly ascended, and the new wall will be destroyed, but it will take brave men to scale it. Will you all gather your courage, inspire and help one another to set about this work? Your bravery will soon break the enemy's heart, and, just possibly, your glorious mission may be accomplished without bloodshed. Rightly presume the Jews will try to stop you. But if only a few of you get over the wall, the Jews cannot keep the rest out. The man who gets over the wall first, I will bestow upon him so many honors that he will be the envy of all the army. Disgrace will be upon me if I do not. If that man survives, he shall command those who follow him who become his equal. Upon that man, I'll bestow an honor reserved for the bravest who serve Rome in battle, the *corona muralis*. So ... who will volunteer for this chance at glory?"

Titus lowered his arms, took a half-step back, and studied his men expectantly.

Nicanor knew Titus must exhort the men and that his speech was intended to motivate volunteers to come forward. Acts of bravery on the battlefield often broke stalemates, impasses, and even the lassitude of men. How could they not become disheartened at discovering yet another wall to breach? The heat, the stench, and yet another obstacle to overcome weighed heavily on the legions.

The men remained still in moments of silence following Titus's words.

Nicanor caught the impatient twitch of Titus's shoulders and the slight shift in his stance, a mannerism he had noticed, too, in his father. He glanced at the other staff and saw a hint of nervousness on the faces of all but Tiberius Alexander. Then a movement drew Nicanor's gaze back toward the legions.

A man had stepped from one auxiliary cohort and turned toward the platform. Titus had ordered the soldiers not to wear helmets in this heat to hear him speak. But this man wore his as he strode toward the platform. As he neared, Nicanor noticed his build, the hitch in his stride, and that he favored one leg. But many auxiliaries were slighter built than legionaries. Many had suffered wounds that made them limp though they could still serve.

"Nicanor...." Yosef clasped his arm.

No, gods, let it not be him, Nicanor prayed.

CXXXIII

Augustus 70 CE

Jerusalem

Near the Breach into Antonia Fortress

Nicanor and Yosef moved nearer to Titus to see the ground before the platform. The soldier came closer, his face mostly hidden by the hinged cheek guards and the ridge across the front of his helmet. The shallow leather neck guard was not as protective as the metal ones others wore, but it covered his hair at the nape of his neck. But with a glimpse of the thick bandage wrapped around the man's thigh, Nicanor felt his heart sink.

"General, I will be the first to climb the wall," said the man as he approached within a few feet of the platform, pulled off the helmet, and tucked it under his arm. Sayid looked up at Titus, his thick hair tangled and matted, his face sweat-sheened, and his eyes burning.

"What is your name, soldier?" the general asked.

"Sayid Sabinus, General Titus. And I pray for good fortune, though, if ill luck denies it, I know that my death will not be worthless." Sayid's eyes flicked to Nicanor and Yosef, softened momentarily, and then sharpened again as he looked at Titus. "I choose to volunteer... though I might die." Sayid put his helmet on, lifted his shield over his head with his left hand, and drew his sword with his right. As he turned to march toward the wall, eleven other men from his auxiliary cohort broke ranks to follow him.

"The fool!" Yosef said too loudly. "Why is General Titus allowing this?" The complaint had drawn the attention of Titus's personal guard, and several scowled and moved toward them.

Nicanor appeased them with a palm-out gesture. He then firmly gripped Yosef's arm, tugging him away from Titus. "Be quiet and stay put, or you'll get yourself killed. We can't stop Sayid, but maybe his father can." Nicanor pointed at Marcus Sabinus, who had moved before the stacked cohorts and was shouting orders. But by then, Sayid, sensing others had joined him, charged forward, nearly at a sprint. Surprisingly quickly, given the pain it must have caused him, he covered the distance and scrambled over the rubble to reach the roughly-built new wall.

Even from a distance, Nicanor could see that the jutting blocks and stones offered footholds and handholds. Then he caught the motion atop the wall. Rebels lined up above where Sayid climbed, with the other auxiliaries now close behind him. The Jews shot arrows, but Sayid, hooking one arm over an outthrust rock, deflected them with his shield. Luckily, the big rocks the rebels now cast kicked out and over Sayid but landed on three men below him, crushing them.

At the midpoint of the new wall, Sayid had to resort to the strength of his arms. Nicanor could see his wounded leg threatening to buckle with each push higher. Twice it gave way, leaving the Syrian hanging by a single handhold as he deflected more arrows and stones that nearly knocked him from the wall. *Go Sayid, keep going*, Nicanor prayed as grudging respect grew to replace the anger at his friend's relentless climb. "The men behind Sayid have fallen...."

"But there are fewer men above him now," Yosef said.

Nicanor eyed the top of the wall to confirm Yosef was right. "The rebels must think it a full assault and have pulled back to regroup or to gather more arrows and stones." Nicanor shook his head. "Sayid might pull this off." But he saw on Yosef's face what he felt must be on his own. They were surely watching their friend die. He and Yosef had talked about the fortunes of war and combat after Yotapta. Yosef had spoken about the death of his lieutenant and friend, Levi, and the sacrifice of the giant Jewish warrior, Dov. At times like those, one could understand the whims of gods and goddesses, how Fortune is jealous of Valor and interferes in glorious achievements. As they watched, Sayid reached his goal: the wall's top. His injured leg gave way as he clambered over the rough battlement, and he stumbled and fell, gripping the leg.

"No!" Yosef cried. "The rebels now see it's just him!" Indeed, the Jewish archers and slingers came forward and fired their missiles at the one prostrate Roman soldier.

"Look!" Nicanor said, pointing for Yosef. Marcus Sabinus now had a team of auxiliaries with ladders at the foot of the wall. *Why couldn't you have waited, Sayid?* Getting ladders in place and sending men up was slower than attempting to climb—but it was a better means to gain control of a defensive wall. But even a ladder assault resulted in many dead men. Success depended on how many ladders you could get onto the wall, how many men anchored it, how well, and how fast you could get a line of men moving up.

Marcus was on the first rung before they anchored the first ladder, and he climbed with a lurch up each rung. At the top of the wall, Sayid was trying to cover himself with his shield as the stones and arrows hailed down on him. Nicanor looked at Yosef beside him, frozen, staring wide-eyed. Though he had told Yosef to stay put, he could not. "You!" Nicanor called out to one of Titus's guards. "Give me your shield." Titus turned and asked, "What is this?"

"General, your volunteer is my friend. I'm going to him... now." Nicanor matched the general's stare and glanced at Yosef, who had moved beside him.

"And I'm going with Nicanor."

"You cannot go, Yosef," Nicanor said, and his friend's stubborn frown forced him to turn back to Titus. "General, we will wait for men ahead of us to clear the way. I will protect Yosef. He'll come to no harm."

Titus's own frown eased, and he nodded. "Give them your shields," he ordered two legionaries, turning to Tiberius Alexander. "Bring up more men and the archers to go ahead of them."

CXXXIV

Augustus 70 CE

Jerusalem

Atop the New Wall at Antonia Fortress

Sayid had risen on one knee, still protecting himself with the shield. Drawing his sword, he met the rebels who rushed at him one by one. He cut the first one down easily, for the man, too anxious, overreached his thrust and left himself open to a quick stab through the neck. His body cartwheeled off the wall to fall on the rebel side. The next came in low, and Sayid managed to one-leg hop backward, catch the blow, deflect it down, and cut deep into the man's side with his counter-strike. As the rebel gasped and tilted to one side, Sayid crashed his shield into him, driving the man backward and onto the rebel behind him. Sayid surged forward then, biting his lip hard at the pain in his leg. He hit the man again with his shield and lowered it to thrust his sword over it and into the man's chest. The rebel fell, and the fighter behind him leaped forward, the tip of his sword slicing a furrow along Sayid's neck. He beat down the man's blade, angled his shield, and arced it edge-on into the man's face. Jaw bone askew, the rebel staggered, dropped his guard, and Sayid stabbed him through his gaping mouth. The rebel crumpled at his feet.

With a shuddering breath, and a moment's reprieve, Sayid faced more men coming at him. But there was no room to maneuver, and—favoring his wounded leg—he could not set his feet securely enough to block the burst of attacks. A flashing sword beat past his guard and cut into Sayid's shield arm. The heavy *scutum* spun from his hand to tumble down the face of the new wall. Another sword thrust went through Sayid's chest as a short spear from one of the crowding rebels deeply pierced his upper ribs and caught there.

As he fell, a shower of arrows swept the wall of the rebels.

* * *

Sayid struggled to sit up and tried to pull the spear from his side with one arm. But it had gone too deep. The pain from this was worse than being stabbed through the chest. Again. As the pain narrowed his vision, he focused on the puckered scars of the old arrow wounds on his thigh—so long ago, a lifetime, it seemed. When he had sought to reach Cestius Gallus with letters from his wife and Lady Cleo. The evidence that he should stop the 12th Legion's first assault on Jerusalem and get answers about Gessius Florus's involvement in starting this war. He had succeeded and won the reward of getting leave to see his mother and help nurse her back to health. The memory of the time with her took him far away for a moment.

Then the whistling and wheezing of his shallow breaths brought him back, gasping. The hiss and swish of another volley of arrows keeping the rebels back was less than the sound of his struggle to breathe. He needed a minute of rest, perhaps to revisit those memories... then he'd pull out the spear from his ribs and continue as he promised General Titus. He would not quit.

The rattle of shifting loose rock made him blink open his eyes—he had not realized he had closed them. Half-slumped, his right arm supporting him, he had trouble focusing. He tried to raise his left hand to clear his eyes. As his vision steadied, it did not shock him to see his useless left arm had been cleaved to the bone, and there was a ragged tear where the muscle had been torn free at its upper end. *Why do I feel no pain?* The arm lay half across his lap; try as he might, he could not lift it. He felt his eyes slide closed, a slow curtain coming down.

"Sayid!"

A voice called to him, cutting through the hornet nest buzzing in his ears. His right arm and hand worked. He massaged his eyes open and saw clearly.

"Father?" he said, feeling a wave of relief. Their last words had been in anger. As he had stepped out to answer General Titus's call, his first thought had been of those words... not what he was about to do—what he had just done.

"Steady, Sayid. I'm going to lift you, and it will hurt."

"Why, Father?"

"I'll get you up over my shoulder and carry you... bring you down from here to a *medicus*. They will take care of you...."

Sayid did not realize it was he who screamed, but he tasted the blood that frothed his lips. "No, Father... let me stay here. Let me rest."

Marcus Sabinus lowered his son, careful of the part of the shaft from the still-protruding spear. He checked for any rebels, but the archers kept the air full of arrows, driving them back with each rebel attempt to charge. "Then, when my men are here, I will go for help and return for you."

"No, Father. Sit with me... don't leave me." Fuzzy shapes and shadows moved by. *More men coming up the ladders*, Sayid thought. *They'll beat the rebels and take the fortress.* The blood was sticky, and his lips felt gummed together as he tried to speak.

With a groan, his father sat beside him. "What did you say?" He leaned closer.

Sayid worked up enough spittle to thin the blood. "I was first, Father... I was first...."

"Yes, my son... you were...."

"It will be fine... everything is fine now," Sayid said, then coughed a spray of crimson. He felt someone take his hand, and he stared at it. "It's good, Father." He tried to squeeze it, but his hand was so slippery with blood could not tell if he had. Time passed, and the sounds around them lessened as he and his father sat quietly. No anger came between them; all that had happened and been said before was gone, leaving them at peace.

The sunlight dimmed as two shadows stooped over him. He blinked his eyes clear again and looked up at Nicanor and Yosef. Sayid smiled at them. "I was first, Nicanor... no one will doubt me now."

"No one will, Sayid. No one. Titus promised a *corona muralis*. Any Roman soldier brave and strong enough to be first to scale an enemy wall gets that reward. It is yours now, and none has deserved it more than you."

"Father...."

"Yes, son."

"Give it to my mother and take care of her." Sayid coughed again, licked his lips, and tilted his head to look up at Yosef. "Will you write about me?"

"I have, and I will... about all that you've told me." Yosef gestured at Nicanor and added, "And everything we know of you."

"Good..." Sayid smiled. "You must do two more things for me. You both must live, and you must save Cleo." His head lolled, his eyes too heavy to keep open, and the wheezing slowed. "Father, tell Mother I love her. Tell her I got what I wished for—I'm a soldier like you."

"And I'm proud of you, my son. I love—"

The wheezing had stopped.

"He's gone, Marcus." Nicanor swallowed to clear his throat. "He heard you, but now Sayid's gone...."

CXXXV

Augustus 70 CE

Jerusalem

The Upper City

"We were all worried about you," Ya'el said as she took the dust-covered pack from Miriam. It wasn't heavy, but Miriam was exhausted and unsteady when she entered the courtyard gate. Ya'el had been watching for her in the stifling heat unrelieved by even a whisper of a breeze.

"I waited with Yohanan ben Zaccai for the Roman patrols to become less frequent. I think it's the heat we can thank for them letting up. That's the only thing we can thank it for...." Miriam followed Ya'el across the courtyard into the house.

Inside the kitchen, Ya'el opened the pack. "Where did you get this?" she asked as she pulled out a bundle tied within a square of linen. One corner came loose, and some dried fruit spilled out.

"It's Yohanan's... what he was to take with him. But he left it behind, I'm sure, on purpose... for us. I discovered it after waiting a couple of hours where I could view the valley to make sure the Romans had not seen him. When I started back, I found the pack just inside the tunnel entrance within the cave." Miriam shook her head. When she had found the bag, she sat and cried. It was a meager amount, just enough for two or three days if each ate only a handful daily. But that's what the purpose had become for them all. To find a way to live, a day at a time. There was no "tomorrow." By giving up what food he had, Yohanan had done as he had said to her while they waited, putting trust in their God. But she did not think He cared anymore, or perhaps the sins of Jerusalem's leaders had condemned them all in His eyes.

"Do you think he got away?" Ya'el asked.

"I don't know." Miriam shook her head and regretted it when it made her feel faint again. She steadied herself with Zechariah's stiff still gripped in her hand where she sat. She had been so tired in the Hinnom Valley cave she had not noticed Yohanan had left without his pack. He took with him just a water skin slung over his shoulder and cast a last smile back at her as he strode from the cave. She was even more spent now—all she wanted was to rest for a little while. "In the Lower City, I heard talk some people have gotten through the Roman trench and over or around their wall. But I don't know if that's true or only hope."

"I pray he does get away," Ya'el said, dumping the dried fruit into a bowl of water and beginning to wash the dust off it.

Maybe it was because she was so tired that it seemed Ya'el avoided looking at her now. Miriam rubbed her eyes with the heels of her hands. "Where is everyone?"

"Back asleep now... or what passes for sleeping now." Ya'el continued to focus on the fruit. "Yonatan showed up at dawn threatening to strip and beat Leah, then drag her through the streets. Eleasar confronted him while Rachel and I tried to calm her. I thought it would come to blows, but one of Yohanan ben Levi's men showed up to get Yonatan and take him to Antonia Fortress. Something was happening there."

"Eleasar? Matthew's still not back?" That suddenly returned worry straightened Miriam's back, forcing her wooziness to recede. *Has something happened to Matthew? Is that why Ya'el will not meet my eyes?*

Ya'el's kept her head down but said, "No one has seen Matthew, and we've heard no word. After confronting Yonatan, Eleasar left to search again." Ya'el finally looked up. "I'm glad you are here. We thought something had happened to you, too. Yonatan not only cursed Leah. He said the family," Ya'el hesitated, then finished quickly, "the family of traitors like Yosef should be executed... and that it was not just Zealots who felt that way. Others wished to see the house of Mathias punished if Yosef himself was not to face justice."

Miriam felt a chill despite the cloying heat and the sweated-through men's garb she had worn for days. The 'others' could only mean the Sicarii. They wanted Yosef killed, and since they could not reach him—since she had not reached him—they might have taken or killed Matthew as punishment!

CXXXVI

Augustus 70 CE

Jerusalem

The Lower City

During his life, Hananiah had endured violence and deprivation. And had seen much of it inflicted on others. He had been an instrument of pain and suffering on those he was paid to hurt or kill. But even he had been struck by the cruel and selfish depths reached by many in Jerusalem. The Zealots, especially leaders like Yohanan ben Levi and Simon bar Giora, still had food while most people starved and died. They did not enjoy the same amount and quality of food from months ago. Still, they remained relatively safe even as the Romans methodically destroyed the city. They had killed thousands in their attacks and many more—slowly—by sealing the city and forcing a famine upon its people.

But Hananiah was a survivor. He had killed one of Yohanan ben Levi's chief hoarders, taking the food for himself and offering to share it with Miriam. She had not come to ask for it as he thought she would. But that might have worked out for the best.

The morning after speaking with Miriam in the Upper City agora, a man appeared in Hananiah's shop doorway. Big and scarred, with a tattooed fist, he had the bearing of a capable brute-for-hire. Hananiah had seen many mercenaries like that in Alexandria and killed a few. They were often hired to protect the men he had been paid to kill. The memory made him wish to sort through his bag of trophies—he'd recently added to it with the ear of the Gischalan's hoarder. He always found pleasure in telling over the evidence of his exploits.

The man had stood there, his bulk filling the door frame, and asked: "Are you Hananiah, the knifemaker?"

He had not answered the man but raised the sharpened blade he was working on in reply. Rotating it to let lantern light play on the pattern in the metal and along the dagger's keen edge. The man had stomped toward him and, without preamble, asked, "What or who have you found that can help Lord Florus? It is time to deliver."

The weak thumping sound—another reason it was best Hananiah went to Miriam instead of her coming here—had drawn the big mercenary's eyes toward the rear of his shop. But they quickly snapped back to him. Hananiah had become concerned something had gone wrong with Florus—he had received no messages for a long time. But he knew Lord Florus's greed would not let the Roman give up. And Hananiah would act when the time was right—that time must be close. He had told the brute, "I have someone who can direct him to what he seeks."

"Then I'll take him from the city to Lord Florus." The man had looked expectantly at him as if he should produce the "someone" at that moment.

Hananiah had thumbed the knife's edge and eyed the mercenary. "First, I must get a guarantee from Lord Florus. The amount we agreed upon, authorized under his seal and payable to me by his *argentarii* in Alexandria, and the lesser sum in Roman gold coin, also agreed on. Bring the bank draft to me with instructions on where to deliver what I have for Lord Florus. Along with the draft, bring the gold coin owed me."

After a long moment of staring at each other, the man turned and left. The soft thumping had sounded again. He ignored it and waited, watching the door in case the mercenary returned, thinking to force the situation or renegotiate. His fingers stroked the blade, and a slight grin curled his lips—there would be none of that.

Hananiah got off his stool and went into the back of the shop. All was quiet as he shifted the crude bars of metal stacked against the storeroom door, freeing it. Inside was a bedraggled, soiled man tied to iron rings fresh-set into the rear wall. He still mused how poorly the man had fought, but then he had given him no chance to draw his sword.

He took off the prisoner's rough cloth gag only long enough to provide one of the infrequent swallows of water he allowed. He saw the man had struggled against the gag enough to rub raw the corners of his mouth, splitting the flesh. The leather bindings wound around wrists, and bare ankles had chafed the skin until it bled. The man was quiet from weakness, but his eyes still showed his confusion and flashes of anger.

"Soon... soon...." He looked down at Matthew ben Mathias and let his anticipation rise. He would go to Miriam now.

CXXXVII

Augustus 70 CE

Jerusalem

The Upper City

Ya'el crept from the room, trying not to disturb Elian and Cicero—an angry parrot could wake the house. And Miriam, most of all, needed to sleep. Ya'el went down the stairs, entered the still-dark kitchen, and felt for the small lamp on its shelf, lit it, and set it on the table. Ya'el took her day's handful of the dried fruit from the large bowl and then returned half. With a growling stomach, she tightened the sash at her waist to draw the light robe snugly over the men's tunic beneath. She felt her body had shrunk. Once upon a time, in her life in Rome, she would have checked her figure in one of her many elegant mirrors. A Roman noblewoman's affectation acquired through her friend Poppaea.

The smile on Ya'el's face slacked and died as it was born when the flash of that pleasant memory quickly vanished. Poppaea, once the wife of her brother Marcus... who had been forced to divorce her so she could marry Emperor Nero. So, she had become an empress. But Poppaea was always her friend, and Cleo had had very few friends when she had gone by that name.

Then Nero had killed Poppaea, and Ya'el's only remaining friends who had known her as a woman of status in Rome were Sayid, Yosef, and Nicanor. And they were all now so close yet far across those battlefields. But that must change.

Nicanor had done as she asked in her arrow message. At dawn, two days after that message, she had seen him again, helmetless, with a bright crimson cloak. He was no longer a mere centurion—he now wore the trappings of his senior rank, tribunus. She wondered what he had gone through since she and Sayid left him in that port taberna in Ptolemais long ago.

Nicanor, like Sayid, was a steadfast friend. She had watched his enormous hands grip half the green-feathered shaft as his eyes swept and searched for her. She had fired another arrow with its optimistically pre-written message:

'*Gratias tibi*, thank you. Come here at dawn each day with the feathered half. If the fortress is secure, drop the half-arrow. I will try to meet you at the tunnel nexus at each next dawn.'

Ya'el had told no one of her plans, and keeping it from Miriam shamed her. Yosef's sister had become a friend like no other, not even Poppaea. But that was why she must do what she could to save Miriam and her family.

The graying of the pre-dawn just beginning; carrying a cup of water and a piece of dried fruit, Ya'el went into the courtyard, enjoying the faintest whisper of a breeze. She closed her eyes and hoped for more, then opened them to see Miriam quench the lamp's wick on the courtyard table. Before her was a sheaf of parchment bound by a cord run through holes along one side. "Miriam, you should still be sleeping," Ya'el said.

"I've slept enough. Now that day breaks, I'm going to search for Matthew."

"I'll go with you," Ya'el said without thinking but then strategized her double mission... I'll ask her to split up to cover more of the city. I can go check for any signal from Nicanor.

"No," ordered Miriam. "Someone must stay here to protect Elian, Rachel, and Leah."

Ya'el felt Miriam studying her and realized her expression had revealed her conflict. She must watch for Nicanor's signal, but there was no news that Antonia Fortress had fallen. Even in the depths of night, that would have become quickly known throughout the Upper City.

"What is it, Ya'el?" Miriam asked.

"Nothing. I'll watch over everyone." Ya'el needed to redirect Miriam's inquisitiveness, which still showed in her look. "What is that?" she pointed at the bundle of parchment in front of Miriam.

"My father's notes... this is his study of the Book of Lamentations." Ya'el saw the fatigue return to Miriam's features and recognized she had aged beyond her years—the lines were drawn in a face grown more haggard each day. *Probably like my own!* She thought with irony. *Perhaps I should be glad there are no mirrors.* "While I waited for sunrise, I read the notes. They fit the times."

"Read something to me...."

"It's not heartening... but I will if you want. Then I must go." Miriam picked up the notes and read aloud: 'How solitary sits the city, once filled with people. She, who was great among the nations, is now like a widow. Once a princess among the provinces, now a toiling slave. She weeps incessantly in the night, her cheeks damp with tears. She has no one to comfort her from all her lovers. Her friends have all betrayed her and become her enemies.'"

As Miriam read the last line, Ya'el saw the furrows in her brow deepen and tears form in the corners of her eyes. Something beyond current circumstances tormented her friend. But how could she find out what... without Miriam asking *her* again what she kept from her?

CXXXVIII

Augustus 70 CE

Jerusalem

Northwest of Jerusalem, Gessius Florus's Encampment

"Lord Florus," said Krateros, crossing his thick arms over his chest, "the knifemaker Hananiah says he has someone who can lead to the hidden treasure."

"So, he must have finally laid hands on the brother of that Jew traitor." Gessius Florus still fumed over the delay he'd endured since the death of Arins. He tapped two fingers on his lips and leaned back from his desk. "Did he say anything about a woman?"

"No. He only said that before he delivers this person to you, he wants his payment as agreed."

Florus was not concerned about that. The treasure found so far, stored onboard the vessel at Sycaminum, would clear the remainder of his debts with a good deal left over. He had just returned from meeting with Drusus there to better gauge the value and check the ship's security. There was plenty left to pay Hananiah. Besides, perhaps the Alexandrian assassin would not live to collect on the draft though that could prove perilous if he failed to have the man killed. He studied the Thracian mercenary captain and considered that though the man was fierce, experienced, and skilled, Krateros alone could not kill Hananiah.

"I'll prepare the bank draft, and then Hananiah must deliver. I agreed to get him safely away from Jerusalem, and then he can collect the rest."

"When you have the draft ready, I'll take it to him," Krateros nodded.

Florus studied a map of Jerusalem spread on his desk. "So, the Jewish rebels no longer guard that tunnel?"

"No. But if you send many men through, the rebels might catch on and seal the tunnel so we do not have a way into the city."

"Antonia Fortress will soon fall." Florus's forefinger tapped it on the map. "Once it's secure, we'll have another way. As the Judean Procurator, I learned that the Jews' King Herod had created a tunnel from the fortress into their sacred temple area and the Upper City.

We can use that." He saw the wariness in the mercenary captain's eyes. "What?"

"Lord Florus, that's a great risk, too, when Antonia is full of legionaries and auxiliaries."

"That's why I'll have Tiberius Alexander issue orders you can carry to answer questions and eliminate risks. Even when I force this Matthew ben Mathias to decipher the instructions on the copper scroll, I will not take only the treasure hidden outside Jerusalem. I want more of what the temple still holds."

"Good," said the Thracian with a nod. "The additional men I brought from Caesarea are bored and need to earn their pay without fighting a legion."

"Have your men ready...."

"Yes, lord." The burly mercenary turned and left.

Florus stood and paced, thinking. *It's coming...* he felt a flush of excitement and expectation. All the years of planning and manipulation would end with a nation's riches in his hands... the wealth of an emperor. He stooped to rub the scars on his legs that pained him only within his memories now. But that was enough—Cleo would pay for the burns. He had heard of the death of the Syrian auxiliary, Sayid Sabinus, which greatly pleased him. He hoped she grieved her accomplice. But he wanted his hands on Cleo's throat as much as he wanted them on the Jews' treasure.

He stepped to the tent entrance and called to the courier always stationed nearby. "Go to General Titus's camp," he said, "and find Tiberius Alexander. Tell him I need to meet with him." He watched the man hurry away and worried little whether Titus discovered Tiberius Alexander's digression from duty. *Exitus acta pro bat*, the result justifies the deed... *that* was something he believed in. And soon, he would have his result.

CXXXIX

Augustus 70 CE

Jerusalem

At the Northern Wall of Antonia Fortress

Nicanor and Yosef found Marcus Sabinus just inside the northern wall of Antonia Fortress. A cohort of *immunes* laborers and one auxiliary unit had cleared the breach of rubble and debris. Now shielded mules and men brought siege equipment, materials, and weapons through the opening, under heavy fire from the rebels.

Nicanor did not know how to greet Sayid's father, so he made an observation as they neared him. "Antonia's armory must hold more arrows than I imagined… still, the rebels must be close to running out." Nicanor's voice, pitched loud enough to carry, caught the auxiliary officer's attention. He turned and reluctantly nodded as Nicanor beckoned him to join them outside the rebel archers' range as volley after volley of arrows rained upon the soldiers.

"They attack in waves," Marcus Sabinus replied, "but we'll have this area secured by nightfall. Then the final assault on the temple can begin." The auxiliary cohort commander nodded to Nicanor and cast a questioning glance at Yosef. "Why are you here?"

"We did not get to tell you on the wall or afterward," Yosef replied, though the man had asked Nicanor.

"Tell me what?" Sayid's father narrowed his eyes at Yosef.

"That we are sorry for your loss…."

"But my son died in an attack against *your* city." Marcus Sabinus shook his head, puzzled.

"He was our friend." Yosef gestured at Nicanor. "Our good friend and a fine man."

Nicanor saw anger in Marcus's eyes and almost stopped Yosef from explaining what they had discussed about Sayid's death. Yosef would never condemn Sayid, just as he did not hate Nicanor for Yotapta.

"Too many good people have died in this war trying to do what's right from their perspective," Yosef said. "Many do their duty for their country. To serve some obligation put upon them by others or by themselves. Sayid was our friend, and his death saddens me. I will always remember how he lived with loyalty and honor. Not how or why he died."

Marcus Sabinus was silent, staring at them long enough for the moment to grow uncomfortable.

Nicanor broke the silence. "I spoke with General Titus. Once his staff completes the formal confirmation required for such a high military honor, you will receive Sayid's *corona murialis*." Nicanor nodded at Yosef and then continued. "I know how Yosef feels about why a friend could fight against his people. And I appreciate his understanding because I am doing that, too. I will also honor and remember Sayid's bravery and how well he fought. I'm proud to claim him as much a comrade-in-arms as a friend."

Nicanor saw some depth of emotion in the auxiliary officer's eyes for the first time. The stern demeanor did not soften but eased enough to show what seemed remorse. "I am proud of my son and regret not showing him that sooner."

"At the end was enough. Sayid knew you held his hand, and he heard your words as his *pneuma* rose to Elysium." Nicanor said it softly, clasping the man's shoulder. "He rests there now with that knowledge."

"On the day General Titus brings me Sayid's reward, I will retire from the legion and return to his mother in Laodecia ad Mare. Tahir will know of her son's...." Marcus Sabinus paused. His gaze went to the soldiers maneuvering equipment into position, then returned to Nicanor and Yosef. "Tahir will know of *our* son's courage." He then looked beyond Nicanor's shoulder. Nicanor half-turned as a junior officer he knew stopped, out of breath, sweat streaming down his face.

"Tribunus, General Titus commands your presence and that of the Jew, Yosef ben Mathias. Now...." The junior aide's eyes cut sideways at Yosef.

"What for, Petran?" Nicanor asked.

"More deserters trying to escape the city were caught early this morning. One of them asked to see the Jewish trai—"

The man stopped and collected himself. "The man claimed to have important information for the general alone and was given leave to speak with him. Then the general sent me to find you both."

CXL

Augustus 70 CE

Jerusalem

The Roman Encampment, General Titus's Command Tent

It surprised Nicanor when he and Yosef entered to find General Titus alone at his campaign desk. The general looked up at them and stated what they already knew: "Yosef, someone from the city has asked for you."

Nicanor had had to lengthen his stride to keep pace with his friend's hurry to reach Titus. As they moved against the tide of men and material moving toward Antonia Fortress, Yosef had not said a word, his expression tight with concern. But Nicanor's thoughts had jumped to the notion that the deserter who had seen Titus could be someone from Yosef's family. And if it was, maybe Nicanor would not have to do what he had promised. Cleo's idea to plead directly with Titus was too risky for her, for Gessius Florus would have her killed at the earliest opportunity. Nicanor would do all he could to protect Cleo. But for Nicanor to propose that he and Yosef enter the rebel-held part of the city to get her out, without orders, through some secret tunnel... that was madness Nicanor wished not to undertake.

Nicanor had heard enough of other deserters' talk to know most of Jerusalem now hated Yosef. Though it would be a serious problem if any Romans found them in the tunnel, it would be even worse—fatal—if the rebels found them there. Nicanor blinked. What if this request from a deserter was just to get someone close enough to kill Yosef somehow? Someone might sacrifice himself to do so—Nicanor had seen hate consume men. He started to speak, but Titus spoke first.

"See if they have cleaned the man up and bring him to me," Titus ordered Silvius, the aide, who hurried away.

"General, you know there's enmity toward Yosef among the Jews," Nicanor warned.

"Yes," Titus nodded, "but this man claims to be a friend. And he says that, like his friend Yosef, he has had a vision. It was of my future, and what he told me was reassuring." Titus smiled then. "He seems harmless, so I've agreed he can see you, Yosef."

Yosef seemed puzzled—*perhaps he doesn't know who else sees visions?* Nicanor thought. Then Titus's chin tilted as the aide and a legionary returned, grasping their prisoner's upper arms. Water dripped from the old man's matted white beard, and the empty flesh of his haggard face sagged in folds as he brought his head up. He looked impossibly frail, Nicanor thought. Titus waved for the aide and guard to release the man, who looked at Yosef, a slight smile bending the seams of his face.

"Yohanan!" Yosef cried out and stepped toward the man with his hands out, then stopped, unsure if it was permitted. He looked back at Titus.

"So, you know him," Titus asked.

"Yes, Lord Titus... he's Yohanan ben Zaccai. I have known him all my life."

"Do you wish to have some time to speak with him?"

"I would very much appreciate that," said Yosef, who took a more decisive step toward Yohanan and stopped when the legionary put his hand on the hilt of his sword. "Could he come with me to our tent to eat and rest?" Yosef asked Titus.

"I'll allow that. I want you to hear him retell and record what he told me." Titus looked at Nicanor and said, "Tribunus, you will be responsible for him, then." Titus stood and walked to Yohanan ben Zaccai. "You understand that if you try to escape, you will die," Titus said. "It does not matter about your auguries and what you've foretold for me." He turned to Nicanor, "Tomorrow morning, Nicanor, you will report to me all he says."

* * *

NICANOR AND YOSEF'S TENT

Beyond his thanks, Yohanan had said nothing as they moved through the camp. Still, Nicanor saw the old man's eyes nervously jump at the clamor and clatter and the stares of many Roman soldiers. When they reached their tent, Yosef got out a bowl of fruit and sliced it, and they watched the old priest slowly and steadily eat it all. His hunger was evident. But the man was careful with each bite, not too much or too fast for a stomach that had gone without for some time.

"What of my family?" Yosef asked.

"I was thinking of them when I spoke to the general, hoping it would help him listen. You must get him to help your family, offer his protection, or provide some means for them to leave the city, or they will not survive. It is horrible, Yosef. Even the strongest now stagger with hunger. Like maddened dogs, men, women, and children no longer worry about the Romans." Yohanan's eyes went to Nicanor, then back to Yosef, and he continued. "They seek anything to eat... anything."

Nicanor knew a little about this old priest, who had been Yosef's confidant during his Galilee campaign. "What did you tell General Titus?"

"What all men with power want to hear," he said with a little smile. "They all want to hear that they will keep their power and watch it grow."

"What happened to the others with you?" Yosef asked.

"Miriam got me out of the city through a tunnel into the Hinnom Valley." He held up a finger to stay Yosef's question while he finished his account. "After leaving her, I came upon others hiding, avoiding patrols. We made it through the trench together and tried to climb over the Roman wall. That's where the horsemen came upon us. The others ran, but I could not, which saved me. They were run down and killed. I told the horsemen the only thing I could think of that might save me... and your family."

Yosef leaned toward Yohanan and said, "Tell me of Miriam—she got you out of the city?"

"Yes, after she and Ya'el saved me from Yonatan bar Hilel and his group of Zealots."

Yosef shook his head. "How?"

"Ya'el killed several of them and held off Yonatan and his men while Miriam led me to safety," Yohanan explained.

"Who is Ya'el?" Nicanor asked, not understanding.

"Ya'el is Cleo...." Yosef replied.

"What?" Nicanor said with a gasp.

CXLI

Augustus 70 CE

Jerusalem

The Upper City

Miriam had searched most of the Upper City for Matthew from Herod's Palace, avoiding Simon bar Giora's fortified buildings since she could never get past his guards. She traversed streets from the north, running west to east and back until she ended at the southern wall. Then followed the aqueduct north to where it bent east to the bridge that joined the western wall of the Temple Enclosure. She had yet to search the area below the viaduct because it contained Yohanan ben Levi's quarters and that of his chief lieutenants and followers. It was the last place and most dangerous, but she must do it. Next, she would have to search the Lower City.

Miriam approached the palace of the old Hasmonean dynasty, her ancestors. Her mother and father had taken the family into it long ago to see where the leaders of her mother's people once lived.

"Dressing as a man won't hide who you are!" called a loud voice. "Sister of a traitor."

Miriam stopped and turned to see Yonatan bar Hilel striding from the shadows of the entrance to a smaller, less ornate building next to the palace. There had been a few people on the street, but now there were none. She was alone.

Yonatan was a large man, and his torso had once been like the trunk of a mature tree. His legs were as thick as its lowest limbs. But hard times had consumed the fat that had once padded his form. His face was thinner, and his midsection had shrunk so much that the lean breadth of his shoulders was exaggerated. He had not yet pulled the weapon at his hip, a Roman longsword Matthew said was called a *spatha*.

Miriam pointed at it and said, "I doubt you took that weapon in combat." She loosened the daggers within her light robe sleeves and shifted Zechariah's staff to rest in the crook of her left arm. "You're brave only with women. And I doubt you dare to face Roman soldiers without a wall between you." She did not trust the crazed look that came into Yonatan's eyes and set her feet to be ready if he charged at her. The brute pulled his sword and took a step toward her.

"You have one left," said a calm, familiar voice behind her. But she did not turn from Yonatan.

Hananiah was beside her now, with a long, broad-bladed dagger in his hand that she saw when she risked a sideways glance. *Has he been following me... out of sight?* She wondered. Yonatan's eyes widened as his hand touched where an ear had once been.

"You have one left," Hananiah said again, pointing the blade's tip at Yonatan's remaining ear. "Only the one, so decide wisely." His free hand thumbed the edge of the blade.

"What have you done with my brother?" Miriam asked as she glared at the Zealot lieutenant, hating him for all his abuse of Leah over the years of their marriage. If he confessed to hurting Matthew, she would kill him right here. *Now. Even if Hananiah witnesses it.*

"Nothing... yet. But for *all* in your family, retribution is coming." Yonatan backed away three steps, then turned and walked away.

Miriam stood silently until the Zealot was out of sight. Her first impulse was to tell Hananiah she had not needed his protection. But instead, she turned and told him, "Thank you."

"Do you worry about your brother... Matthew, I mean?" Hananiah's voice held no emotion when he spoke of others, even when he spoke with her. But his eyes, when he had touched her, had not been cold. They were deep-set and dark but simmered with a black heat.

"He's missing," she said.

"Many disappear in this city every day," Hananiah replied, slipping the dagger into the sheath at his hip.

Miriam stepped to the side, saying, "I must get home now."

He moved closer to her, his gaze fixed on her face. "You did not come to see me... for food."

"I was busy. I did as you suggested... I helped Yohanan ben Zaccai."

"So, the old rabbi has escaped the city?"

"Yes." Miriam wanted to move away from him but stood still. She still longed to kill this man for murdering Ehud. But Ya'el wished to use Hananiah to entice Gessius Florus into a trap? *She wants revenge against her husband—for his abuse.* That was the only reason Miriam had not yet confronted Hananiah over Ehud.

"Any who can leave should," Hananiah said, pausing to lock his eyes on hers. "I will have a way soon. For you, too...." Then he turned and walked away toward the Lower City as the shadows lengthened.

Final Siege

Miriam checked the street. *Still empty.* The sun was a deep orange half-orb, the color spreading through a thin bank of low clouds. Yonatan would have boasted if he had killed or harmed Matthew or if he had heard the Sicarii had done so. With a sigh, she turned toward home. At night, men, women, and even abandoned children crept out into the streets to find what they could eat—she shivered at the stories she'd heard. For the first time, she thought perhaps it better for her parents to be imprisoned so they did not see what now occurred in Jerusalem.

Tomorrow she would search the Lower City. She would also seek out Kefa, one of Eleazar ben Yair's chief Sicarii in the city, to ask him about Matthew. But it had been a long while since she had last seen Kefa. He must have fled to Masada before the Romans truly sealed the city. Still, she would check. Miriam hurried through the dark streets, noticing that no one left the shelter of homes to light the lanterns. Jerusalem had become a city of darkness.

* * *

Miriam shot up from her bed. The thin, sweat-dampened blanket fell to her lap. Despite her fatigue and the weary prospect of another long day looking for Matthew, Miriam's hunger pangs kept her sleep light. But the blast of so many shofars would have roused her from the deepest slumber. The sound of Roman buglers had become more common than the dwindling instances of calls from the shofars of the Temple.

What prompts the shofar calls tonight? A second round from the rams' horns echoed, and she recalled Mathias telling them as children the story of Yeruba'al defeating the Midianites. One night he ordered his 300 men to carry shofars and torches in baked earthenware jars. They had blown their ram's horns on his command. Then broke the pots from around the lighted torches among the sleeping Midianites, convincing them Yeruba'al commanded a much larger army. The plan had worked, and the Midianites fled. She did not know why so many rams' horns had just trumpeted in the night.

Miriam rose from the bed, wrapped a light robe around her, and stepped to the open window. The soft breeze was too warm to cool her much. She glanced down into the courtyard below, remembering her father's storytelling more clearly. After the recitation, Matthew and Yosef acted out the battle. Matthew, as the oldest, was Yeruba'al, the Jewish hero, and Yosef, the enemy Midianites. That seemed ironic after the heralding of so many trumpets in the night... since

Yosef was now an actual enemy. She wondered if he could hear the horns.

A pounding at the front door brought her back to the moment, and she reached it with Ya'el close behind, her bow in one hand and a lighted lamp in the other.

Miriam cracked the door enough to shed some light outside. Eleasar ben Ananias, his face bloody, gasped out, "The Romans have taken Antonia Fortress!"

* * *

Ya'el emptied the bowl of bloody water and washed out the cloth rag Miriam had used to clean the deep slash across Eleasar's brow. Miriam had placed a thick pad of linen over the wound and wrapped it tightly. She planned to try to stitch it closed in the light of morning.

As Miriam worked on him, Eleasar had explained the night attack on the fortress. "I think the watchmen had fallen asleep. My men and I had finished our watch and had turned in. I had just dozed off when one of the inner courtyard sentries came rushing in, shouting that the Romans had breached the defensive perimeter. Then I heard a Roman bugler signal. The Zealots took that as proof that the Romans were making a full-scale assault. I couldn't confirm it because one of Yohanan ben Levi's lieutenants ordered all the Zealots to fall back to the Temple. I tried to get him to countermand the order—hold our positions—until we could verify the Romans were in force and not just testing our defense. But I failed, and they ran, leaving us behind." Eleasar pointed at his brow. "He's the one who gave me this wound. I ordered my men out of there and to the Temple and came here to warn you."

Within minutes of finishing his report, the former Temple Guard Captain had fallen asleep on the divan near the courtyard. Ya'el had told Miriam she would sit with him and that Miriam should go upstairs and try to sleep some more before dawn. Reluctantly, Miriam had gone.

Ya'el settled onto a chair close to Eleasar. Just before sunrise, she would leave to see if Nicanor was at the wall to signal her. When she returned, she would do all she could to convince Miriam to take Elian, Rachel, and Leah into the Great Sea cistern cavern and remain there until she came for them. But to do that meant she must tell Miriam her plan, and she did not know how that would go.

But no matter. I must meet Nicanor and have him get me to Titus. Miriam had told her of the encounter with Yonatan, and she had heard stories of starving men who hunted the streets at night. And how some even entered homes and carried off the sleeping. Would any of her new family survive to even face the Romans when they entered the Upper City?

General Titus was the only means of saving them.

CXLII

Augustus 70 CE

Jerusalem

The Upper City

The moment had come that Ya'el dreaded but had asked for. At the first wall, Nicanor had dropped the feathered half of her message arrow and nodded. Now she must meet him tomorrow at dawn in the tunnel nexus. Half her thoughts were on that meeting. And that she now must tell Miriam about it. The other half were on the people on the streets. She had learned to watch their eyes and posture, especially the men's. All showed their hunger. She had learned that once that hunger became unrelenting, a person's emotions and decisions were affected as much as the body. But this morning, she saw no aggression, just a little fear—no panic but ultimate resignation. All knew the end was near. Whether delivered by the Romans or by the people succumbing one by one to weakness or illness or at the hands of the ravenous skulkers in the night... the end was near. She plodded home, feet heavy and heart dragging at what she must do next.

Inside the house, all was still quiet. Eleasar ben Ananias sat on the divan near the rear courtyard entry but stood at the first sound she made, his sword ready in his hands. The former Temple Guard Captain's face beneath his bandaged brow was pallid in the wan sunlight spilling through the window above him. He relaxed and sat again. She returned his nod but did not reply to his questioning look. Glad not to speak, Ya'el silently moved toward the stairs and up. In her room, she carefully lifted Cicero's cloth-covered cage. Gingerly to avoid waking Elian, she turned and left the room. She shut the door and went toward the steps to the rooftop terrace.

"Where have you been?" Miriam asked, coming from her room dressed in men's garb. "I was preparing for today's search for Matthew in the Lower City and heard you come through the courtyard."

"Shh" Ya'el held a finger to her lips, cautioning Miriam, then turned and continued to the rooftop.

Miriam followed her, not lowering her voice. "Where did you go?"

"Please, don't wake Elian."

"What are you doing?" Miriam asked as they stepped onto the rooftop terrace.

Ya'el set the cage—Cicero stirring within it—on a low table. She removed its cloth cover, shed her cloak, then slipped off and set down the bow she had looped over her shoulder.

The sunrise had lost its haze, and the sullen orange was now a sharp, brightening yellow against a clear blue sky. Ya'el turned her face toward it for its blessing. She felt she must look as stark and haggard as Miriam did as she removed her headdress. "I'm freeing him," she said.

Ya'el reached into the cage and brought Cicero out, perching him on the leather guard she had put on her left forearm in the bedroom. She stroked his head, which he bent and cooed for, and she smoothed his feathers, calming him. A warm breeze picked up, swirling over the terrace, and she felt it stirring her now-boyishly short hair, and she swept the short locks from her eyes with the back of her free hand. Tears pooled in her eyes and then broke free to run down her cheeks. *After all I have been through, why does this cause me such pain?* She wondered. She felt a grip on her shoulder, turning her.

"What is happening?" Miriam asked, her fingers digging in.

Ya'el saw the mix of fright and anger on Miriam's face. "I'm freeing him... saving him in case I fail."

"Fail at what? I don't understand." Miriam's look hardened, and her hand moved down Ya'el's arm, pinning it down so she could not lift Cicero to the heavens.

"Wait," Miriam said again. "Tell me why you're doing this."

Ya'el steadied her thoughts and then began. "Days ago, I sent another message to Nicanor. I told him I must meet General Titus... to plead with him to save you. I do not ask for the city... it is lost. But I want him to save you, Elian, Rachel, and Leah... Matthew, too if he reappears or if you can find him." Ya'el could not tell Miriam she thought her oldest brother was dead. "Maybe Titus can send men to reach your parents in time to save them, too." Ya'el let out the breath she felt she'd held since that first contact with Nicanor. "I must meet Nicanor tomorrow at dawn. He'll take me to Titus."

"Meet you how... where?" Miriam stared at her without speaking for several moments.

Ya'el broke the silence. "He will have Yosef tell him how to use your King Herod's secret tunnel connecting the Temple and Antonia now that the Romans hold the fortress. I will meet him at the nexus, and he will take me back to Titus from there."

Ya'el winced at the tightening of Miriam's clutch of her arm, but she did not shake free. She knew Miriam was shocked—even angered—that she had told Nicanor about the tunnels. And beyond that, she was asking for Yosef's help to use them.

"You don't know that Titus will help," Miriam said, her eyes drilled into Ya'el's. "When you appear among the Romans, Gessius Florus will have you killed if he doesn't do it with his own hands as soon as you're within reach."

"There's no other hope, Miriam... we face certain death anyway. It walks every street in Jerusalem. It comes for us."

"I'll go to Hananiah and get food," Miriam said. "He has offered it."

Ya'el shook her head. "What if he wants something from you in return?"

"I won't go with him... but I'll give him what he wants." Miriam's eyes burned, but her face had gone pale.

"That will save us for only a while. And it won't stop the Romans." Ya'el sighed and shook her head again. Cicero squawked, and she clucked softly to him and let him nibble on her thumbnail. "The end is upon us... I want you and your family to live."

Ya'el fixed her gaze on Miriam, who finally released her pressure on the arm holding Cicero. Ya'el raised her arm level with her face so that the bird sat calmly, his head tipped as he watched his mistress. He leaned in toward her, and she whispered to him. Then she quickly raised her arm to launch the bird and stood staring after him as he became a speck in the sky to the east.

"What did you say to him?"

Ya'el choked past her tears. "I told him it was time to fly... never to return. It is a twisting of the poet Virgil's words in his *Ecologae*." She had not considered those words as she said them, but she must with tomorrow's dawn. *They may prove true for me, too,* she thought. Whether she succeeded or failed to get Titus's help, Gessius Florus would come for her. And she would never return to see whether Miriam, Elian, and the others survived.

CXLIII

Augustus 70 CE

Jerusalem

The Upper City

Hananiah had watched the slender man in a cloak that partially disguised a bow and a quiver full of arrows. The archer had hesitated at the front entrance to Miriam's house, then gone down the side street, where the home's courtyard had a gate. Hananiah settled back into the shadows of the columned entry of the vacant dwelling—its owner fled or dead and kept watching for Miriam. With the fall of Antonia Fortress, he expected to hear from Gessius Florus's mercenary messenger soon, and he must tell Miriam he needed her decision. Her only chance of surviving would be to go with him. With her parents imprisoned, probably dead, one brother a traitor, and the other missing... who or what did she have to remain in Jerusalem for?

There was something in Miriam he related to. She held the kind of deep pain he knew only came from an unjust injury... something tragic had created it. Hananiah did not need to know what, only that the connection existed. He gauged the sun breaking over the city and decided to wait longer, then cross the street and seek her out. Surely she would join him now.

The street was empty after the bowman passed, and the house remained silent as the shadows lightened around him. Then the sound of voices above drew his eyes to the rooftop. There on the terrace, two people seemed to be in conversation. He recognized Miriam immediately and then realized the other person was the bowman. He must have entered through the rear courtyard. Puzzled, he stepped from the shadowed gate and moved closer to Miriam's house for a better view.

The bowman's cloak came off, as did the bow. And then he removed the headdress and bent down, straightening up with a bird perched on his arm—its colors caught the dawn light.

Hananiah crept as close as he could while still seeing Miriam and the bowman. He could hear them arguing... not their distinct words but tones, both high voices. Suddenly he knew... Miriam had lied to him! Cleo had not fled to Masada—this was her with her bird! The anger coursing through him only sharpened the biting coldness hardening inside, arming him against his slight regret at taking Miriam's brother to serve his purpose. With Miriam, he had ignored his principle to never become close to anyone. People were targets to capture or kill for reward... or—he stared up at Cleo as she raised her arm with the bird—leverage to ensure he was paid what was owed him. *And even more*, he thought.

The bird soared into the sky as he glared at Miriam and Cleo. A flash of color drifted down on a current of air to settle on the street. He went to the spot and picked up a green feather, tucking it into the sash at his waist. *This will be proof*, Hananiah thought, proof to Gessius Florus that his wife—the woman he so badly wanted to get his hands on—was still in Jerusalem.

The sound of shouting turned him to look down the street, where a cluster of armed men was approaching. Hananiah took his dagger out to show them he had a weapon, but they took little notice of him. He slowed one man who reeked of sour wine and asked, "What is happening... where do you go?"

"To the Temple to watch Yonatan bar Hilel. He has challenged the Romans to single combat."

CXLIV

Augustus 70 CE

Jerusalem

Antonia Fortress

The new summons from Titus surprised Nicanor. Yosef had already delivered to the general his report of what Yohanan ben Zaccai had told him and Yosef. There were shocking details of what existence had become for most Jews within the city. Yosef had gone pale and silent as the old rabbi struggled to speak the words he probably thought he would never have a chance to say outside the city. In his over two decades in the army, Nicanor had seen horrific things and heard of even more terrible and tragic war-related incidents and events. But what Yohanan shared had left him as speechless as Yosef was. Titus's messenger with Titus's summons had been a welcome interruption to break the appalling silence that filled his tent.

"Why do we come here?" Yohanan asked as they entered Antonia Fortress, and the messenger led them to the tallest of the fortress's four towers. On the southeast corner, it rose 120 feet into the air, nearly 40 feet taller than the other three, commanding the best view of the Jewish temple and its surroundings.

"Titus commands it. Something to do with a challenge from the rebels." Nicanor glanced at Yosef, who remained silent and ashen-faced. He thought *I'd feel the same if I had family in Jerusalem and heard Yohanan recount what's happening there.* But he realized he did have dear ones in the city. He, too, worried about Yosef's family, and Cleo faced the same peril. Today he would have to tell Yosef of the meeting planned for the next morning—with Cleo in the tunnel.

They stepped onto the top level, the peak of the southeast tower. Beyond its crenelated battlements spread the Jews' Temple Enclosure. In the distance, bright sunlight dazzled from the temple's white stone and gold adornment. Nicanor studied the cloisters in double rows with pillars almost 40 feet high supporting them, each column carved from a piece of white marble. The roofing, made of simply and beautifully cut cedar, had neither paint nor elaborate engraving. Nicanor appreciated the natural finish and fine joinery of the Jews' handiwork. The outermost porticos were 45 feet wide and stretched over 1000 yards. The central courtyard was open and paved with every imaginable stone.

Traversing that open span, facing a heavy missile defense, will be tough, Nicanor thought. *I hope the rebels spent most of their stones and arrows defending Antonia Fortress.*

"Josephus!" called Tiberius Alexander, who was standing beside Titus. At their attention, he beckoned them and gestured for the escorts to make an opening for them to pass through.

Nicanor saw Yosef's jaw clench as he stared at the Aegyptus Prefect and former Alexandrian Jew.

"Who is Josephus?" Yohanan ben Zaccai asked with a puzzled expression.

When Yosef did not answer, Nicanor did. "It's what Tiberius Alexander calls Yosef. Lord Alexander, who gestured at us, is General Titus's second-in-command." Nicanor touched his friend's shoulder to get him moving. "We must join them."

"He's here, General," Alexander announced.

Titus turned to them and nodded. "Tiberius thought you might know this man." The general walked to the battlement's edge and pointed down, waving for Yosef and Nicanor to join him. They left Yohanan ben Zaccai with a guard and joined the general.

A solitary man strode on the floor of the vast courtyard between the fort and the temple, 30 or 40 feet from the porticos that ran along the fort's southern wall. Several men who must have accompanied him were 20 or 30 feet from him. A much larger group was farther from Antonia Fortress, near the vast courtyard's center. Beyond them was a structure closer to the temple and a cluster of more people. *They are all watching... or waiting... but for what?* Nicanor wondered.

Yosef studied the rebel fighter, who carried a Roman longsword in one hand and gripped a dagger in the other. Nicanor noticed the man was too lean, and every distended cord and sinew on his arms stood out in detail. His frame and clothing seemed to belong to a larger man, but his broad-shouldered, barrel-thick torso had shrunk if it were his own clothing. Still, he seemed strong. "I don't know him, Lord Titus.... what has he done?"

"Sentries reported he marched from your temple alone... trailed by a few other rebels. My men were so surprised they let him approach unopposed. Then the rebel did something only a madman would do."

Yosef continued to study mutely while the lone figure glared up at them.

Nicanor caught the eye of Titus's guard captain and nodded toward the general. The officer understood, swept his eyes over Yohanan ben Zaccai, saw no threat, and nodded, allowing the old man to join them to look down into the courtyard. Nicanor asked, then, "What did he do, general?"

Suddenly, with a cracking voice, the rebel bellowed: "*Ego te provoco*, I challenge you!"

Nicanor blinked, shook his head, and looked at Titus. "He demands single combat?"

"So it would seem," the general replied with a smirk. "He's been insulting my men since he arrived. He stopped his taunts to stare sullenly and then shouted his challenge."

"I know who he is," Yohanan said as he leaned over the parapet. The man came closer so they could hear his cry clearly.

"*Ego te provoco*, I challenge you!"

The old priest turned to Yosef. "He is not as you remember him. It's Yonatan bar Hilel." Yohanan moved closer to Yosef and whispered, "I did not think to tell you... he and Leah are now divorced."

"He does not seem a worthy warrior," Titus said, shaking his head. "Still...." He turned to the guard captain. "Send Pudens and Priscus from my escort down to face him. Let's see if he can fight."

Nicanor leaned toward Yosef. "You know him?"

Yosef nodded... his eyes on Yonatan below.

"Is he a friend?"

Nicanor saw a flash of anger cross Yosef's features as he shook his head.

Yohanan ben Zaccai added, "He's a Zealot and hates Yosef and his family."

"Well, that will all end soon for him." Nicanor watched the rebel below, but the Zealot did not turn away when the two legionaries reached the ground and neared him.

Pudens, his *spatha* out, had not carried his shield. *Foolish*, Nicanor thought as the legionary circled the rebel who turned with him. He had a momentary flash of memory of the crude arena in Marianum, where Graius, the old gladiator, depended on him to win. The only way they would have enough money to continue their journey. That was another effort to save Cleo by finding her brother, Marcus Otho, to lend his help. Now Otho was dead... Graius was dead... Sayid was dead. All who had hoped to help Cleo survive this war were gone. All but him and Yosef.

"Ho!" Titus's exclamation brought Nicanor's full attention back. Pudens had slipped on the courtyard stone—the hobnailed soles of the legionary's *caligae* could be treacherous on smooth surfaces. The legionary rolled to get to his feet, but the rebel was on him, riding his back. Twisting around, dropping the longsword, the gaunt Zealot tore off Pudens's helmet and yanked his head back with a strength Nicanor was surprised to see in the man. The rebel slashed Puden's throat with his dagger and held onto the legionary as he bled out. Viscous crimson streamed down the Roman's gleaming bronze breastplate. Priscus moved forward. The rebel, in response, roared, his voice breaking, "*Ego te provoco!*" He let Pudens slump to the ground, spurned the body with a heel, and charged at Priscus. The remaining legionary calmly set his feet and cast his *pilum*. Throwing the seven-foot spear with such force that it impaled the rebel. Its three-foot iron tip passed through him to protrude from his back.

Yosef stared at the fallen body, and Nicanor said, "General, do you need Yosef or me for anything else?"

"No." Titus's eyes fixed on Yosef and lingered, but Yosef did not look away from the dead Zealot. "Now, I go to meet with the assault commanders," said the general, turning toward the Jews' temple.

* * *

THE ROMAN ENCAMPMENT, NICANOR AND YOSEF'S TENT

Nicanor pointed his empty wine cup at Yohanan ben Zaccai, who snored lightly on Yosef's cot. "Do you believe all he told us, especially about the Jewess who killed her child and—"

"Enough!" cried Yosef, causing Yohanan to stir but resume his slumber. "You and I can only imagine what their hunger could make them do...." Yosef cradled his head in his hands. "But Yohanan never lies."

"Then we must do what we can to save your family," said Nicanor. "I've had another message from Cleo. We will meet her in the tunnel tomorrow at dawn to bring her to Titus."

Yosef lifted his head, and Nicanor saw fear and hope wrestle in his eyes. "The Leah Yohanan mentioned... is that the woman you loved but could not marry?" Nicanor asked, filling his friend's cup and handing it to him.

Yosef nodded.

"Then we must try to save her, too." A qualm stirred in Nicanor... he hoped he had said that for Yosef's sake and not for his own.

CXLV

Augustus 70 CE

Jerusalem

Antonia Fortress

Nicanor and Yosef passed between a narrow gap through three cohorts of heavy infantry filing rank by rank into Antonia Fortress.

"Last evening's staff meeting was grim," Nicanor said. "Titus read from what Yohanan ben Zaccai recounted to you. Most were as repulsed as you and I were at the sufferings. Some officers spoke up about shocking things their men had witnessed and heard from the captives. The general told all the commanders they must act even more aggressively to end this siege."

Nicanor did not add that he had left that meeting, certain Titus would not listen to any plea from Cleo. Now he wrestled with whether to lie to her just to get her away from the city. The clank and rattle of over 1,000 heavily armored men echoing around them in the gray light before dawn was just the tip of the Roman spear about to thrust into the heart of Jerusalem. He gestured at the soldiers. "There's already a cohort of archers in position on this end of the cloisters—to support the infantry." Past the legionaries, Nicanor cut through an inner courtyard to one entrance to the lower levels of the fort. "The good thing is that no one is likely to be below, in the armory. They will all be up here watching the assault." He cocked a thumb at the battlements around and above them, every space lined with men.

Nicanor pushed open a thick wooden door reinforced with iron bands. Inside he stopped and turned to Yosef and asked again. "You're sure your friend won't try to escape?"

"I told you when we left, he gave me his word. Besides, Yohanan's still frail. He doesn't have the strength to go far."

"Well, if he wanders... some auxiliary or legionary may cut him down and check his guts for gold or silver."

"Yohahan won't leave the tent. There's food and water for him... he'll eat, drink, and probably sleep more."

Nicanor took a torch from a bracket mounted on the wall. "Get the other"—he pointed to an alcove beside the entry. "Put yours out, and we'll use them one at a time." He led the way down the passage and turned into another, ending at descending steps. "Careful now..." He'd discovered the stones had been worn down. Many had chipped edges and crumbling lips from years of legionaries' hobnailed sandals going to and from the armory. Though it was well-lighted, Nicanor kept his torch burning when they reached the equipment and ordnance level. He glanced at Yosef. "You'll need to lead the way from here."

Yosef moved ahead of Nicanor down the corridor. He walked past two smaller storerooms and the vast central storage area. Yosef stopped at an opening into what Nicanor thought must be a small, seldom-used room, judging by its stiff single door. Entering, Nicanor saw it was full of dusty and broken bits of equipment.

"Here... hold your torch closer," Yosef directed him to the rear wall.

Nicanor saw nothing but a blank stone wall with two waist-high benches strewn with a tangle of what had been rope and animal sinew twined together to create the torsion part of two or three missile throwers, small *scorpios,* or *ballistae.* Between the benches was a space the width of his shoulders. Nothing but gray stone.

Yosef reached over the tangle and pressed and pulled something behind the left bench. Nicanor saw a thin vertical line appear on the right of the open space in the wall. He watched as Yosef gripped, tugged, and slid a panel aside to reveal an opening. He touched the panel and found it thick wood cleverly painted to seem stone. "So, your temple grounds and Upper City could've been entered this way all along," Nicanor mused.

"I'm sure some Romans—the previous prefects—knew of this... but probably not Titus. It's not practical for a sizable attack. It's easy to defend the other end or to seal it off. King Herod, who built all this, had this tunnel dug as a getaway passage for him—just in case." Yosef gestured for the torch, but Nicanor kept it and stepped into the darkness as he pulled his *pugio,* its blade gleaming in the torchlight.

CXLVI

AUGUSTUS 70 CE

JERUSALEM

HEROD'S TUNNEL

Once the tunnel widened, Yosef walked beside Nicanor to guide him. He had been surprised when Nicanor admitted that close spaces bothered him. Yosef had thought nothing frightened his burly soldier friend, but he could sense his tension as they went farther underground. The muscles bunched and knotted along the Roman's forearm as if holding the torch required effort. Nicanor's other arm, bent at the elbow, was cocked and ready to thrust the dagger gripped in his hand. "Stop," Yosef whispered and tapped Nicanor's shoulder.
    "Why?" Nicanor asked but stood still.
    "To listen... if someone ahead of us moves, we'll hear them if we're quiet. Bends in these tunnels shield torch or lantern light... and some receive little or no light from along the passage. But sounds carry."
    "Then they might hear us before they see our torch?"
    "Yes, just as we can hear them. That's why we stay close to one side of the tunnel wall, so we have only ahead and the opposite side to watch."
    "And we can hear any coming up behind us"—Nicanor nodded and gestured at the darkness ahead. "How far to this nexus Cleo mentioned?"
    Yosef had not been in this tunnel since finding Miriam's *hamsa* there years ago... before he took command in Galilee. And then he had not been in it since before he went to Rome to free the Jewish priests and to try to stop a brewing war between the home country he loved and the empire he admired. He searched his memory to gauge the distance. "I believe it's close," he said.

***

THE NEXUS

"Put away your blade." The voice from the darkness where the torchlight did not reach was low yet sharp.

Yosef had convinced Nicanor to forego his armor and trappings of rank, to carry no shield, and to keep his gladius securely sheathed unless needed. Yosef wanted nothing to catch the light if they needed to retreat into darkness, but mostly nothing that could make a noise that might warn of their approach. But the 11-inch *pugio* remained in Nicanor's fist—its telltale glint had revealed the bared weapon. Even just the whisper resounding in the underground gallery, Yosef knew well. "Miriam!" he said with deep emotion.

Nicanor raised the torch. "Where's Cleo?"

"I'm here, Nicanor." A tall figure came into the reach of the torch's light. Dressed as a man and equipped as an archer, bow in hand, a full quiver peeking over her shoulder, and with a leather forearm guard on the arm, Cleo raised to beckon to her companion. Beside her, Miriam entered the fringe of the torch's glow, her eyes locked on Yosef.

Yosef was shocked at how thin Miriam had become. Her eyes were oversized in a face that had lost all vestiges of the plumpness he had teased his sister about when they were younger. "Miriam...." He stepped toward her, his arms out, but stopped at his sister's cold glare.

Cleo tried to get her attention. "I asked her not to come with me," she explained and added, "Miriam, do not do this with your brother. I'll go with them now, and you know I vow to do all I can to convince Titus."

Yosef watched his sister nod but not shift her gaze from him, even when Cleo grasped her shoulder.

"I did not expect you, Yosef," Cleo said as she turned to him. "Despite all that has passed," she glanced at Miriam, "I am glad to see you free." Cleo turned to Nicanor then and said, "We must go. There's no time to delay."

Yosef stood rooted, stunned by Miriam's expression. He had seen men in combat during the siege of Yotapta whose eyes had looked like hers did right now... and that was just before throwing themselves at the enemy. From the corner of his eye, he saw Nicanor shift his keen watch from Miriam to Cleo, and the taut lines on his face softened. But that momentary ease faded quickly. The deep-scored furrows returned as his friend took a deep breath as if he were reaching a decision and preparing to say something he would rather not.

"There is no time, Cleo," Nicanor said simply. "Any hope Titus would listen to you... to anyone... is gone. Nothing can happen other than what is happening now over our heads. It would be foolish to try. Let me—let us—take you from here, but do not expect to sway Titus. Do not fear Gessius Florus—I'll protect you from him."

Cleo came closer. "How will you do that, Nicanor? Hide me from him? I'm done hiding.... and I do not fear Gessius Florus."

In the flickering torchlight, Yosef saw that once a soft alabaster oval, Cleo's face had sharpened into a duskier, angular form, with prominent cheeks and a defined jawline. A hardness within, the same he saw in Miriam, had changed her. He and Nicanor exchanged looks, and he knew Nicanor was shaken, too.

Cleo continued. "You do not know how bad things have become... the things some have done to survive."

"We know. Yohanan has told us," Yosef replied.

"Yohanan ben Zaccai?" Now Miriam came as close as Cleo was.

Yosef saw where the sleeves of the men's tunic she wore had pulled up to reveal the hafts of daggers in sheaths on her forearms. His eyes went then to Miriam's face. The fondness, the love once there for him, was gone. They were replaced by a glare of accusation. Yosef had not thought his heart could be more broken. But it could. Sadly, he turned away from his sister. "Cleo, go with Nicanor."

"No," said Cleo. "If you say there's no chance with General Titus... then I'll stay... with the only family I have left." Cleo moved closer to Miriam and linked arms with her.

Nicanor sheathed the *pugio*, his face stern. "Then find a safe place to hide... Find a place that Yosef knows, where I—where we—can find you once the city falls."

Cleo surged forward and clenched Nicanor's arm, bringing Miriam with her. "We're starving... can't you see?" She tugged at the slack in her tunic and Miriam's. "We won't last...."

I'm stupid, Yosef thought. *Why did I not think to bring some food for them?* But then, he had expected Cleo to be alone and that she would come away with them. Earlier, Nicanor had surprised him with his certainty that Titus would not listen to Cleo, but he realized Nicanor was right. Yet there must be *something* he could do to help his family.

"There is a place where I think we'll be safe... where you can bring us food," Miriam said, glaring at Yosef.

"Bring food?" Nicanor blurted.

Yosef heard the alarm in Nicanor's voice and ignored it. "Where?"

"I can reach a cave in the Hinnom Valley from a tunnel in the Lower City. You can bring the food there, and I will take it to where we hide."

Yosef nodded. "I know of the caves and the stories of tunnels from some of them. How do I find the one you speak of?" He focused as

Miriam described the cave's position and how it was marked; her voice lost none of its bitterness. She merely spoke the words of necessity. He nodded to her. "We'll have food there at sundown tomorrow."

"Wait..." Nicanor shook his head, "Yosef...."

"We have to, Nicanor. You said you would do all you could to help my family." Yosef studied his friend, then his gaze went to Miriam, who returned it, grimly unblinking, and on to Cleo, who smiled. At that moment, she was the Cleo of years ago, before she'd married Gessius Florus... before the war. His eyes returned to Miriam. The women's voices had sharpened and risen, too much so. *So much they have suffered,* he thought. He whispered, "Yohanan told me about Mother and Father—how is Matthew?" If anyone were to have escorted Cleo here, Yosef had thought it would be his brother.

"He has disappeared... I fear he's dead."

Yosef felt another piece of his heart fall away. "The Romans have not captured him... not that I know of...." He could imagine nothing but death would keep Matthew from taking care of his family. "What of Leah?"

"Leah is divorced from Yonatan... but he still threatens her," Miriam replied.

Yosef nodded. "Yohanan told me he had recorded and certified the divorce decree."

"I'm glad Yohanan's alive," Miriam said, with the only break in her bitterness he'd heard.

"I am, too," Yosef replied.

The silence grew, and Nicanor used the nearly spent torch to light the other. "Cleo, please come with us," he pleaded. "We must go... we've taken too long."

"I will not go." Cleo shook her head.

Nicanor shifted and rolled his head and neck as if loosening tight muscles before combat. He drew a deep breath, released it, nodded to Cleo, and caught Miriam's eye to include her. "Then we will bring food for you all, as Yosef said."

"Miriam, tell Leah to fear Yonatan no more," Yosef said. "He is dead... I witnessed it." He sensed Nicanor's urgency and knew he was right, but still, he hesitated. "Tell her I hope to see her soon... when this ends."

Nicanor pulled Yosef's arm. "Now, we must go...."

CXLVII

Augustus 70 CE

Jerusalem

Antonia Fortress

Nicanor had been silenced by many thoughts as he and Yosef—also silent—had made their way through the tunnels to the fortress, leaving Cleo and Miriam far behind in the trap the city had become. Miriam's cold delivery of the news that their brother was believed dead must have dismayed Yosef. What else could he expect but coldness and rage from those who saw him with the Romans and thought him a traitor? Nicanor clenched his fists in exasperation at Cleo, though he could not begrudge her bravery or loyalty to Yosef's family. Now he wrestled with the problem of how to steal enough supplies to save Yosef's family. Getting caught stealing would be a problem, even for a *tribunus*. As the light of the inner courtyard beckoned from ahead, he heard the now-familiar clamor of battle.

Nicanor looked up at the southeast tower as they emerged and remarked over his shoulder to Yosef, "Titus's standard flies there—he'll have his staff with him. I should make an appearance."

"I'll go with you, then check on Yohanan." Yosef followed him to the steps leading to the higher levels of the fort.

The upper bulwarks of the fortress were thick with men at each level that they had to push through. Then one scarred old *tesserarius*, who recognized Nicanor, cried, "Make way for the *tribunus*!" Nicanor nodded his thanks to the veteran watch commander as they passed him. Soon, they were atop the southeast tower, where Titus and his men were ranked along the ramparts, all gazing south.

As Nicanor and Yosef joined them, they could see the central section of the portico ablaze below them. The outer courtyard was strewn with the dead, mostly rebel bodies full of arrows.

The rebels don't lack bravery... they died in the burning of it, he thought, and more closely studied the strangest battlefield he had ever observed. "Look there," Nicanor said as he pointed at the central part of the western portico. The rebels were trying to cut it away even as heavy infantry rushed to drive them away. Securing the cloisters was vital, for their height provided a tactical advantage and a means to surge men toward the temple and attack from above. With that advantage, they would not have to rely solely on a frontal ground assault that would cost the lives of more men and take much longer.

More Roman soldiers poured onto the veranda atop the cloisters, and finally, the rebels retreated at a run. A roar of Roman cheers poured from the parapets. The legion would surely secure that advantage for the coming full-scale assault already in preparation around Antonia Fortress.

Yosef nodded toward the southwest, squinting into the afternoon sun. "See those men," he said, and Nicanor followed his gaze. A group of rebels on the ground were sprinting toward the western colonnade. Above them, the Romans were unprepared and could hurl down only insults.

"They should have archers with them," Nicanor muttered. On his left, a shorter cropped-gray-haired officer, a former centurion raised to junior officer rank, gave him a sideways look and nodded agreement.

"Fire arrows!" someone cried out, and Nicanor watched as the rebels, now with bows strung, lighted, nocked, and let fly their burning missiles. The flaming arrows struck the north end of the portico and the wooden supports beneath. Immediately, flames sped along the decking, preventing the Romans from returning to the fort to escape. The rebel archers nocked and fired again, and a lengthy section south of the Romans ignited, cutting them off.

"They were ready for us," Nicanor commented at the odor that blew in their direction. "They've soaked the wooden joists and under the decking with oil and pitch." He shook his head again—who was in charge of all this? A scout unit should have been sent to check; even if not, the men advancing should have smelled the danger before committing to going so far. Now they were trapped, and the two burning sections were converging, bringing on the first screams of the burning legionaries. Some jumped to their deaths or to injury, rendering them helpless against the rebels who rushed in to cut them down.

"They destroy the other porticos, too," said the seasoned legionary beside Nicanor, pointing east at the large group of rebels chopping away the decking while others sawed into the supports. A large section of the joists cleaved away and fell to the ground with a crash.

Yosef said something Nicanor could not hear over the din. "What was that, Yosef?" Nicanor asked, turning to his friend. Yosef looked forlorn, his shoulders sagging as he stared south. To Nicanor, the view of the destroyed porticos meant they must make a head-on attack with no maneuvering, no probing from the wings for weakness in the defender's lines. But Yosef was not thinking of this. "What is it?" Nicanor asked.

"Now the Temple stands alone." King Agrippa's warning echoed from four years earlier.

CXLVIII

Augustus 70 CE

Jerusalem

The Roman Encampment, Nicanor, and Yosef's Tent

As he expected, Yosef found Yohanan ben Zaccai sleeping deeply after eating his fill. Yosef had not awakened the old man but sat thinking in the relatively cool shadows just inside the tent. He sat in a Roman army camp surrounded by thousands of soldiers attacking his birthplace. The singular moment unnerved him as he judged himself and others from the past while listening to the martial noise of the present. These men had devastated so much and killed so many in Judea. And in the not-too-distant future, they would destroy his glorious city and the people he loved.

He was grateful for the interruption by the sounds of Yohanan stirring behind him. He could not dwell on so many whirling worries mixed with too little hope. But he still clung to that fragment of hope as an anchor.

"Yosef," said the old priest behind him with a tone that carried both satisfaction and regret. Yosef turned to see the old priest stiffly rising from the cot and asked, "Did you sleep well?"

"I seem to have slept the day away," Yohanan ben Zaccai replied. "How long have you been here?"

"A while," Yosef said, wondering how long his thoughts had wandered. He turned to face the old priest and said, hoping to pin down at least one of his whirling thoughts, "So, Leah is divorced under our law? She is not a widow?" He stood to give the older man his camp stool.

Yohanan said, "You kept silent after we all saw Yonatan die. I wondered when you would ask. Do you still dream of her?"

"Yes," Yosef said but had no more to add.

"I pray Leah lives so you can have her—she is legally free." Yohanan rubbed his eyes and smoothed his beard, flattening it against his chest. "Has Nicanor taken Lady Cleo to General Titus?"

"No, Cleo did not come with us. Titus moves faster now, and Nicanor believes he will not divert his attention to any requests from her. As much as I wish to get my family safe by those means, I agree with Nicanor. In the past few days, I've seen Titus's determination. He has a fixity in his eyes and bearing. We explained that to Cleo and tried to get her to still come with us, but she would not." He paused before adding, "Miriam was with her."

Yosef grew silent, and Yohanan let him have the somber moment, likely understanding all that went through his heart. "When we left Miriam and Cleo," Yosef continued, "we came out to witness an attack on the Temple grounds. I watched as the cloisters were destroyed... severing the Temple from Antonia Fortress."

Yohanan closed his eyes and shook his head. "So that prophecy will come true."

"I fear it will." Another silent moment stretched into many. "Why does Miriam hate me?" Yosef asked quietly and watched his father's oldest friend take a deep breath and let it go before answering him.

"She has seen two of her loves die: Ehud and Ya'akov... but you cannot have known that. But even before their deaths, something happened to her after her betrothal to Ya'akov. It was after Gessius Florus became Judean Procurator while you were still in Rome."

"When I returned, I could tell she had changed. What happened?"

"That is for Miriam to tell, not I. Know that she has also seen your parents imprisoned and thought you dead. Then she learned of your imprisonment and later of your freedom—why, she must have asked herself, would the same hands that bound you free you? And now your other brother is missing and likely dead. That and the horrors of our city—created by this war with the Romans—have turned her. She believes, as much of Jerusalem, that you've allied with the enemy and turned against your people."

"I haven't."

"I know, Yosef... but she cannot see that for herself."

"When I survived Yotapta," Yosef said, "I thought I had been given a purpose to stop this war. When I was captured, I told Vespasian my dreams—that he was the ruler I saw in my vision. I sensed he was a good man—Nicanor believes him so—who could gain enough power to end the conflict. I thought he could bring peace. Events have confirmed my dreams and convinced him to believe in his destiny."

"We heard a prophecy had emboldened Vespasian, and that support from others added to his ascent to power. When we learned you lived, Yosef, I told your father that the prophecy must have come from you since you had been so long with the Essenes."

"But it did no good, Yohanan... Vespasian did not stop this war."

"I, too, used a prophecy to save my own life," Yosef, "because I believe I've been given a purpose. The Laws given to Moshe cannot die with Jerusalem nor become forbidden because of what happens here. You did what you must to survive and end this madness. Vespasian did not stop this war, but Titus offered *many* chances for the Zealots to surrender the city and halt the bloodshed. What has happened is not your fault. Just as the Romans have men who manipulated them for their own purposes... so do we. The leaders of Jerusalem and men like Yohanan ben Levi, Simon bar Giora, and the Zealots—all the irrational and greedy bear responsibility."

"I must convince Miriam," said Yosef, "but can I make her understand?"

"How will you see her again if Ya'el—if Lady Cleo does not plead to Titus?"

"Miriam will hide the household in a place Miriam says is safe," Yosef said. "Nicanor is securing food now, and tomorrow at sundown, we will take it to her... to a cave in the Hinnom Valley. They plan to hide until the Romans finish their grim work and it is safe to move again. With Nicanor's help, I will do all I can to save them. Will Miriam *then* believe me?"

"All you can do is just that, Yosef. Show her you have not turned on your people, your family... and her."

CXLIX

Augustus 70 CE

Jerusalem

The Roman Encampment

Nicanor had separated from Yosef and turned toward the stockade area, thankful that the legion officers' horses had been moved inside the outermost wall as the rebels were driven into the residential and temple area of the city. The northern half of Jerusalem was entirely in Roman hands. He had turned to watch Yosef heading toward their tent, noting that he moved quickly but heavily, with his head bowed. His friend had far more to bear than Nicanor's own concern about smuggling food into a city besieged by his own legions. It would have been even more difficult to hide Cleo from her husband, for a Roman noble could wield influence with powerful men. Still, he must do as he promised... and try to save more than Cleo alone.

By Yosef's count, Nicanor needed to get enough food for eight people. Two were Yosef's imprisoned parents, and one was Yosef's missing brother. But how long must he feed them? He knew more than most about Titus's plans—a month, maybe less, and the city would fall. They might have to remain hidden even longer. But there was no way he could get a month's worth of supplies into the Hinnom Valley unnoticed without facing questions or challenges. He would have to cache the food where he could easily reach it, and then he and Yosef must move it in small quantities in several trips. But that increased the risk.

Though his memory of the stench in the Hinnom Valley sickened him, it had a decisive advantage. As the citizens of Jerusalem weakened, fewer had the strength to flee the city. At the request of the 5th Legion commander, Titus had reduced the number of patrols in that valley.

When Yosef was out of sight, Nicanor roused himself from his ponderings, which yielded a curious feeling as he hurried. He smiled to himself at the thought that he looked forward to seeing Albus. He had spent little time with his mount since witnessing the massive Jewish burials in the valley they would soon revisit. He looked forward to the brief ride northeast to the legions' main supply camp.

He wished it were a much longer ride, for he yearned for this war to end so he could put Jerusalem and Judea behind him.

The ending could lead to a new beginning for him and for Yosef and his family if the gods helped him to save them. And most of all, he realized, it would be a new beginning for Cleo.

* * *

NORTHEAST OF JERUSALEM, THE LEGIONS SUPPLY CAMP

Nicanor reined in Albus outside the southern gate of the walled supply camp, noting that it appeared to be manned by the 12th Legion to judge by the standard at the guarded entrance. Was the 12th still being punished for its retreat from Jerusalem and defeat at Beth Horon nearly four years earlier? To the east sprawled an even larger prisoner camp that seemed to swallow the endless line of women and children herded by cavalrymen and heavy infantry. The line seemed to trail most of the way back to the city. These were thousands of new slaves-to-be. *Gaius Fronto will be pleased*, Nicanor thought.

He turned back toward the supply camp and saw to the west a billowing cloud, too large to be a patrol. He kneed Albus forward and neared the gate where one sentry, likely the senior man, came forward. Nicanor did not dismount, and he scanned the man to determine his insignia of rank—*optio custodiarum*. This was the commander of all the camp's guard posts, not just the *tesserarius*, sergeant of the guard, he had expected. He pointed at the cloud. "Do you know who that is?"

"The resupply caravan from Caesarea, tribunus."

Nicanor nodded, understanding why the guard commander was there. After a moment's pause, the man joined the other sentries at the gate. Nicanor watched the cloud move closer, and soon the lead escort of cavalry was in sight, with heavily laden wagons trundling behind them. The organized bustle of a significant replenishment could work to his advantage.

* * *

Nicanor drank deeply from the fist-sized mug of beer drawn from a fresh cask. Behind him, just over his shoulder, Albus munched enthusiastically from a bag full of barley seasoned with a handful of salt. The ordinarily impassive horse seemed as contented with his grain as Nicanor was with his beer. He rested the mug on a knee and

FINAL SIEGE

wiped his lips with his free hand. "It's good to see you, friend," Nicanor said. "I was surprised...."

Celsus Evander raised his own large beaker of beer. "I hoped I'd have enough time to seek you out." The tall quartermaster commander stretched his long legs and added, "And Sayid."

The fresh beer no longer tasted as good, and Nicanor would not delay telling him. "Sayid was killed in battle. He was the first man to scale the last wall at Antonia Fortress." Nicanor set the unfinished beer at his feet.

"I'm sorry to hear that," Celsus said, looking down as if studying the contents of his cup. "He was a good soldier."

"He was a good man... a great friend." Nicanor hoped his curt tone ended the talk of Sayid. Over the years, he had lost so many he served with... but Sayid's death had cut deep, and the wound would take much longer to heal.

Celsus nodded, and Nicanor knew he understood. The quartermaster commander looked up and said, "As we approached, guess who we came across?"

Since seeing his friend, Nicanor had been thinking about how best to ask Celsus for help to secure—then hide—enough food to save Yosef's family. Though Celsus accepted that Nicanor and Yosef were friends, the senior quartermaster was not friendly to Yosef. Who had commanded the rebels at Yotapta, where Celsus had been badly wounded. Nicanor blinked, realizing Celsus was waiting for his response. "Who?" he said, then took a sip.

"Tiberius Alexander, Lucius Serrenus... and Gessius Florus."

"Florus! Why is he here?"

Celsus shook his head and shrugged. "What an odd trio... and with a mix of hired men and legionaries from the 12th escorting them."

"Hired men?"

"They were clustered around Florus near some hills at the road's edge. As we filed past... I saw several with that crocodile tattoo on their hands.

"Thracian mercenaries!"

"Yes, and I bet from Alexandria."

"What does Florus do here, and why with Tiberius Alexander and Serrenus?"

"I don't know," said Celsus. "But Serrenus reported several wagons and draft animals stolen by rebels. I included their replacements in my caravan."

Nicanor shifted his eyes from the lanky senior officer to where the low sun had become veiled with a haze of dust that would bring on twilight sooner than usual. He set aside the question of those three men. Later, he would consider the meaning of their meeting and whether he should warn Titus of the suspicious behavior of his second-in-command. But now, he said, "Celsus, I have an important favor to ask. It comes with some risk."

CL

Augustus 70 CE

Jerusalem

The Upper City

Miriam stepped into the courtyard and eyed the muddled sky. The setting of the sun, its light reduced by the dingy overcast of dust, made her feel more uncertain. If not for Ya'el, she would not trust this plan. But Ya'el—Cleo—trusted both Yosef and Nicanor without reservation. But with every new discovery, it seemed to Miriam that Yosef had wholly allied with the Romans, and if so... he should die as traitors die. But despite her misgivings and anger, she knew this plan was their only hope of survival. *Though what do I have to live for?* She wondered. Life would never be as it was; her long-ago dreams would never come true.

She returned to the house and looked at Rachel and Leah, pale with the fear of leaving the relative security of their new home and what lay ahead. The sisters sat, each with a small bundle of belongings in her lap—all Miriam had allowed them. But Elian, beside Rachel, held an expression that was not fear. He was holding onto his sadness that Cicero was gone. No matter how Ya'el had explained why she had released the bird, he gripped his sorrow with anger against her.

Miriam studied the boy sitting next to his pack. Ya'el held her bag in one hand; her eyes seemed shadowed by thoughts. But she had her bow over one shoulder and two full quivers of arrows on her back—only one shaft boasting distinctive green feathers. An errant gust had overturned Elian's last bowl of feathers left on the rooftop terrace, and the wind had carried them away. With Cicero gone, there would be no more green-feathered arrows.

Miriam had a small pack, judging it best to keep her hands free and move quickly if necessary. Besides, she had only a few things from her old life that she wished to take with her. And there was scant food left. The last days' worth, little more than a mouthful each, occupied little room.

When Miriam and Ya'el had told them of the plan, Rachel and Leah had been relieved... even hopeful. Then she told them they would leave in that brief period at dusk between when people emptied the streets at sundown and before the predators hunted. That rekindled their fear. But it must be so. Too early, and they would draw attention. The light of day brought its own risks—thieves and brutes would stop them and take what little they had. After sundown, the hunters would take that and more. The thought made her shudder as the blurred smear of rusty light edged into a darkening band. It was time.

"It is time," she said. She would lead them to their redoubt in the Great Sea cistern cavern, and in the morning, she would leave Ya'el to guard them while she searched again for Matthew. Next, she would meet Yosef and his Roman friend at the cave in Hinnom Valley.

* * *

Hananiah had watched Miriam and Cleo return to the house and hoped to catch Cleo alone at some point. His eventual accounting with Miriam must be between just the two of them. He was curious about where Miriam was leading the household—the three women and the boy—so he followed, focusing on movement within the deepening shadows on the street.

CLI

Augustus 70 CE

Jerusalem

West, Outside the First Wall

Albus snorted and shook his head a little, enough to let Nicanor know he disliked going south toward the worst of the smells, though he'd taken delight in their brief ride north the day before. Nicanor patted the horse's neck, muttering in his ear, "I agree with you." He realized Yosef had heard and said with a rueful smile, "But we must."

A sober Yosef shook his head and said, "Celsus was not pleased when you brought him to our tent last night."

Nicanor did not reply. There was tension between his two friends over Celsus's wounding at Yotapta when Yosef was in command of the Jewish forces. But Celsus was right to be concerned, for he took risks helping them. "We needed a reasonably safe place for his men to hide the supplies so we could easily reach them this morning," he explained. "So, I had to bring him to you."

Nicanor studied the wall they passed on their left. The defenders grew fewer toward the south. They had passed what Yosef told him was Herod's Palace inside the walls. Marked by the 150-foot-tall Phaesel tower at the northwest corner of the palace grounds, from which hopeful or desperate archers fired arrows that fell far short of reaching them. Soon the surviving rebels would be swept from their positions, as had been their fellows. According to Titus's battle map and signaled by the massing of the legion cohorts, they would take the temple. Then Titus would swing the legions through the Upper City first and then into the Lower City to kill or subdue any remaining fighters.

"What is this place you chose?" Nicanor asked, looking ahead.

"It is a reservoir built to trap runoff from the Hinnom Valley. It fills when the rains come."

"Do they come soon? I hope so... to break this perishing heat." Nicanor lifted his helmet, wiped his face, and smoothed the sweaty hair on his brow. Judging the distance from the wall again, easily over a thousand feet, he deemed them safe from archers. He settled the helmet on one saddle pommel, letting the light wind cool him.

"The heat will lessen, and the rains come with the end of September," Yosef said, clamping his knees and raising himself in his saddle. "There it is," he pointed ahead. "The Serpent's Pool."

Will we still be here in a month to greet the cool rains? Nicanor wondered. Titus was bringing all forces to bear... the broken city must soon fall. He followed Yosef's gesture and saw the twinkle of water in the late afternoon sun. The slanting light glanced off the water's surface a foot or two below a stone rim that contained the pool. As they neared, he saw stone slabs covering the channel cut into the ground from the pool toward the city, now 2000 feet away. The stone sheets Yosef had told Celsus about were stacked on the eastern edge of the pool.

"The slabs covering the watercourse get broken, so having a supply of them here makes replacement easier," said Yosef as he dismounted and checked between the stacks. "I told Celsus about them."

Nicanor remained on Albus to watch for any movement in the distance, and he saw that the deep shadows of the stone slabs did indeed make good hiding places. When he had brought Celsus into the tent last night, the quartermaster commander had seen Yosef and Yohanan ben Zaccai—to the Roman, yet another enemy. Nicanor saw Celsus's expression of distaste and worried he would change his mind about helping Cleo and abandon the task. He had stayed for the conference with Yosef. But it was still possible that he'd decided against it later and that Yosef would find nothing here.

After Celsus had left with his marked map the evening before, Nicanor told Yosef about the quartermaster commander seeing Gessius Florus on the road. "He's here to steal more of the treasure once the Temple falls!" Yosef had cried. "We must stop him!"

Before Nicanor could answer, the old priest had said no one could stop what was destined for the temple and its treasure. The focus must be to save Yosef's family and Cleo. And the old man was right. Celsus had mentioned Marinus was in Caesarea, refitting the *Egeria*. So, Nicanor had sent a message back to Marinus, asking to have one of his trusted ship captains watch Florus's vessel in Sycaminum. The vessel surely held some of the treasure Florus had already stolen. It was kept there until ready to carry Florus from Judea with his spoils. Nicanor would go there to stop Florus and prove the man's crimes to Titus if he could.

"Found them!" Yosef called from a dark recess in the jumble of stones, and Nicanor walked Albus and led Yosef's mount to him. Yosef said, "Celsus was clever to have his men bring small bundles."

Then he looked up, sweat streaming down his face, and asked, "Can he trust them?"

"Celsus is a good man, a fine officer, and uses his head, so I hope he chooses men he knows are loyal to him." Nicanor dismounted and took from Yosef a fat satchel of what felt and smelled like bricks of pressed dates, securing it behind his saddle. Beside him, Yosef tied a sack of grain—barley or wheat—to his own saddle. The next bag Nicanor lifted gave off the distinct odor of aged, hard, salt-brined cheese. He gripped the sack and mounted Albus—whose nose crinkled at the scent of the food—and settled it across his saddle's front pommels. Yosef climbed onto his horse to balance before him another package of foodstuffs he had handed to Nicanor to hold until he was mounted.

A *tribunus* and a Roman-looking civilian could not carry more without looking even odder so far from the Roman encampment. Nicanor prayed the schedule he had seen for the patrols that morning was correct. He would be hard-pressed to explain these precious burdens if they were stopped. He gazed west and saw the first shades of purple-tinged black above the horizon, night readying for its fall. "Let's hurry," he said.

* * *

THE HINNOM VALLEY, ROW OF CAVES

Nicanor's worry had increased. He constantly turned his gaze east and west, watching for the telltale plume of dust that meant a cavalry patrol as Yosef scrambled to find the markings Miriam had made at the cave. *Find it, man!* He fumed to himself.

"Here!" Yosef finally called out. "But these are not the caves I knew of before, with a tunnel connecting to the city." Yosef turned in his hands a rock with what looked like a handprint carved into its flat side.

"You're sure this is it?" Nicanor asked.

"It must be...."

They followed the little-used path to the cave entrance, and Nicanor secured both horses to the thickest branch of a gnarled bush growing from the fissure of a splintered rock. He patted Albus on the shoulder and pulled out a torch and his leather pouch of sparking stone and rod. "Yosef, wait!" he called, but his friend had already stepped inside the shadowed entry. As he entered, a gray shape shot from the inner darkness into the dull light of the opening, and

Nicanor saw the faint gleam of a dagger come up and hold just before Yosef's throat. Nicanor dropped the torch and grabbed for his pugio.

"Put your knife away, Roman," ordered the voice flatly. "Pick up your torch and light it."

Nicanor could not reach Yosef in time to prevent the knife's work, so he did as he was told. A streamer of sparks flew and caught on the oiled head of the torch. It flared, casting its light.

"Miriam!" Yosef cried out in relief.

CLII

Augustus 70 CE

Jerusalem

The Hinnom Valley Cave Tunnel

Miriam's back bowed with fatigue as she carried the sack of grain and cheese for which she was grateful, despite it coming from the Romans. Everyone she knew was growing weaker by the day. Her family craved meat, but they would all be grateful for this food, too. She would return the next day for the rest of the small amount Yosef and his Roman friend had delivered, promising to bring more as soon as possible.

That moment in the cave with Yosef had unsettled her; weary, her thoughts drifted despite her determination to remain alert. That morning she had searched the city again for Matthew and tried to find medicine for Leah, who was now feverish, her belly tender to the touch. Miriam had found no medicine at her home, already bare of anything useful since the looters had been there. She had not cried at finding crushed on the floor the hand lamp Zechariah had made for her, but she picked up the piece of the base carved with the *hamsa*. Zechariah had told her, "It's not the lamp that's important. It represents the truth that you can find the light within yourself and from others who love you... to lead you from any darkness." Miriam had found that light. It had come from Ehud, Ya'akov, her mother and father, Matthew... and Ya'el and the boy. It did not matter that some despoiler had trod upon that precious lamp, for she had its message in her heart. But in her mother's room... seeing her finery missing, soiled, or broken... that was when she cried. Then a call from below interrupted her tears.

She had gone downstairs to find Eleasar ben Ananias, the former Temple Guard Captain, glad to see her. He reported he could not find Matthew and that the Romans were massing to break through into the Temple Enclosure. Thousands would then pour through.

She told him she had taken all the household to the redoubt and asked him to join them, but he said, "The Temple will fall, and there's nothing left to fight for in Jerusalem. I'll try to get out of the city to my family at Masada. If I cannot, I'll join you."

Eleasar had given up, but she would not. Still, grief filled her mind as she waited in the cave for Yosef to bring the food. The glimmer of the Roman officer's trappings had startled her, and she had reacted instinctively. The pain, anger, and hate had boiled over, so she had pulled her daggers and leaped. Part of her had known it must be Yosef and his Roman friend, Nicanor, but another part had not cared. It was hard to control the urge to kill the brother she felt had betrayed them all. But she had held her hand.

Pushing that memory away, Miriam focused on the present. Ahead, beyond the reach of her lantern, the inky black of the tunnel had lightened to dark gray. As she got closer, the shifting of dull shades showed she neared the opening into the great cavern. She would have to move the fire farther from the tunnel entrance and into a side gallery to better shield it from sight.

The Redoubt within the Great Sea Cistern

Miriam stepped from the passage, and Ya'el greeted her with a drawn bow and nocked arrow. But then her strained features relaxed. She slung her bow over her shoulder and walked toward Miriam, relieving her of the heavier burden, the grain.

"Did you find any medicine?" she asked.

Miriam had expected Ya'el to ask about Matthew. *But no—she believes him dead*, Miriam thought. And she had not asked about Yosef, either. "No," she said. "All is gone or ruined at our house, and none to be found elsewhere. Is Leah any better?"

Ya'el silently shook her head and turned toward the lambent fire.

"I'll try again in the morning," Miriam said, following to where they had settled their meager belongings around the fire. She greeted Rachel, holding out the bag of hard cheese to her. Ya'el had set the grain bag next to a bronze water kettle already bubbling on the fire, then cut the bag open and cupped handfuls of barley to pour into the water. Rachel took a block of cheese from her sack, trimmed the thick rind off, and dropped it in the pot. "For savor," she said. Then she cut slices of the pungent cheese, and Miriam found her mouthwatering despite the fatigue and grief.

Two strides beyond the fire, in an alcove inset in the cavern wall, Miriam saw the huddled shape of Leah on the pallet of blankets and small cushions made of wool-wrapped straw. Elian sat at her feet, facing the fire that ruddied his forlorn expression. He gripped a braided leather cord twined with green feathers that looped around

FINAL SIEGE

his neck. She handed him a slice of cheese. "Eat slowly...," she cautioned him, and he tore into it.

Near the boy was a pile of short lengths of splintered wood and blocks used for shoring, left behind by the men who dug the tunnels long ago. The dried wood burned quickly.

With Leah growing weaker, Rachel had not wanted to hide in the dank cavern, but she knew no homes were safe any longer. If anyone found they had food, it would draw scavengers and worse.

Miriam moved to sit at Leah's head and used a wet cloth from the bowl next to her to wipe her face. Leah's eyes fluttered open. "Did you see Yosef?" she asked.

Miriam answered, averting her eyes from Leah's yearning look, keeping the emotion out of her voice: "Yes, I did." Rachel, hearing her sister, had taken a step toward them.

"Good," Leah said. "He will save us." Her eyes closed, and she slipped back into a fitful sleep.

Miriam swallowed the bitter words she had almost said about Yosef. She watched the emotions in the play of light and shadows on Rachel's face. Sadness for her sister, yes, but also—Miriam knew—a desire for Yosef.

She shook her head at Rachel's delusion and gazed upon the feverish Leah. Remembering when Leah was young and achingly in love with Yosef before her forced marriage to Yonatan. He had battered her body and crushed her soul. Miriam leaned back against the rough stone wall with a sigh. All that had been her life before the war spilled through her thoughts. Ehud, Ya'akov, and her mentor Zechariah... all dead. Mother, Father, and Matthew were likely dead, too. All gone, their 'light within' extinguished... leaving her with barely a flicker against the dark. Leaving her with only Yosef for family... though he was not family anymore.

The nagging thought returned that she had forced down as she trudged from the cave in the Hinnom Valley. She should have made that thrust, do as the Sicarii were trained to do... kill all traitors. No exceptions.

* * *

Next morning...

THE LOWER CITY

The fighting around the Temple Enclosure and Antonia Fortress had grown fierce. After seeing what remained of her home the day before,

Miriam had steered clear of the Upper City. She wondered if Eleasar had escaped or even attempted it. Miriam realized she stood before Zechariah's old shop on the craftsmen's street of the Lower City, and she stopped. At some point that morning, she had stopped looking for Matthew and wandered, her mind adrift, and her feet had taken her where they willed. She stared at the shop. Zechariah was long dead, but he had taught her to fight and not be afraid in that shop. Miriam shook off the memories—she must get to the cave and retrieve the rest of the food. Maybe Yosef had brought more.

"Miriam!" The voice was not loud but as sharp as an accusation. "I know what you are!"

She turned to see Hananiah behind her.

CLIII

Augustus 70 CE

Jerusalem

Near The Roman Encampment

The silence of their return from the cave was not just to keep them hidden from any patrols. Nicanor had seen Yosef's sister move with instinct; her leap from the dark was a killing act. And even after Miriam recognized her brother, Nicanor could see she struggled to lower her blade. Yosef must know that, too, though he'd scoffed at his soldier's concern.

But it was clear by Yosef's sister's businesslike acceptance of the food and curt words, "When will you bring more?" that she was caught between need and deep anger and bitterness. He had seen battle-weary men pushed so hard they became savage without regard for themselves. And she had suffered—and still endured—the desolation and danger of the people of Jerusalem. It was not over yet, but it would be soon. She was not a soldier trained for that life from childhood. Miriam was a young, highborn Jewess. That was what shocked him.

So he and Yosef rode silently but for the clop of hooves on stone and the crunch of gravel. But then, as they veered more toward the city and neared the camp, the sounds of nighttime warfare filled all the silence. Soon they passed the challenge of the gate sentries, Nicanor's rank stopping questions.

He had kept their mounts close by at their tent—*I will have to explain it*, he thought, as few cavalry commanders did that. But having their horses near was more important than worrying about questions.

* * *

Nicanor and Yosef's Tent

When Nicanor finished tending to the horses and ducked into the tent, Yosef handed him a square of parchment. In the lamplight, Nicanor could see his face was furrowed by a frown.

Yohanan ben Zaccai explained: "A runner from Titus came looking for you, and I told him I did not know where you both were. He left and later returned, out of breath and unpleasant, carrying that message."

Nicanor noted the broken wax seal of Titus. He glanced at Yosef, who nodded at him. "I read it." Nicanor let pass his flash of irritation at his friend and unfolded the note. He read it aloud: "You have been absent from duties. See me at dawn. Bring Josephus with you."

* * *

Next morning...

Titus's Command Tent

It had been a sleepless night for Nicanor and Yosef. But the old priest had slept well, to judge by his snores. During the night, Nicanor had brushed and cleaned every inch of his uniform and polished its metalwork. Then he bathed from a water bucket and trimmed his beard. With less to do, Yosef brooded, but he, too, had taken heed of his appearance, shaved, and donned clean clothing. Both men sensed the underlying danger in Titus's brief note. And the use of 'Josephus' emphasized Yosef's Romanization and suggested he had a debt for his freedom. Titus had not mentioned it until—it seemed—now.

The sentries at the entrance acknowledged Nicanor was expected. They let him and Yosef enter to find Titus at his campaign desk. The young general's features had thickened and grown heavier with his cares, the abundance of food, and the lack of active combat. Nicanor saw much of Vespasian in Titus's face. To one side, slightly behind him, stood Tiberius Alexander, smirking, as usual, in contrast with the severe countenance of the young heir to the throne.

"You wanted to see us, general," Nicanor said as he stopped in front of Titus, adding just enough change of tone to show the half-question.

The general's eyes flicked from Nicanor to Yosef. "I needed you... only to find you were not available." Behind him, the sneer on Tiberius Alexander's face broadened.

"I—we—are at your service, General Titus," Nicanor replied, gesturing at Yosef. Experience had taught him that with a fair commanding officer, as Titus had proved to be, it was best to not explain or defend. Instead, he offered that any offense or problem would not be repeated. Then he must make sure it was not. Nicanor became even more aware of the Aegyptus Prefect from Alexandria, surely the source of the news of their absence.

Titus nodded, and his stern look eased. "Very well, then. In the days to come, you will both remain immediately available. Report every morning to the staff meeting and stay within reach of my call throughout the day. I will require you both."

"Yes, General." Nicanor and Yosef left the tent. Once out of earshot of the sentries, Nicanor muttered, "This comes from Tiberius Alexander. What is he doing with Gessius Florus?"

Yosef stopped, and Nicanor was forced to halt and look at him.

"How will we get more food to my family?" Yosef asked.

CLIV

Augustus 70 CE

Jerusalem

The Lower City

Hananiah heard them enter—from the sounds of their footsteps, likely three or more men. Word must have spread that any who thought to steal from the knifemaker would be found dead in the street, so he had not been disturbed in some time but was still wary and had hardly slept. A large lantern always burned on his counter, and he stayed back in the dawn shadows beyond its glow, hidden and with his blades ready. He saw four move toward the front bench, and the lantern revealed a smudge across the fist of the largest—a tattoo, and thus Lord Florus's man. The man stepped into the rim of light, and Hananiah greeted him. "It's been some time...."

"Lord Florus has arranged all you asked." The big man tossed a drawstring pouch, heavy by its sound, to land on the counter. "There's your coin." The man took from his tunic a rectangle of parchment sealed with a blob of wax. "And here's what else you demanded." He set the folded sheets next to the bag.

Hananiah stepped to the counter, picked up the rectangle, broke the seal, and read. The first sheet was a confirmation from an Alexandrian *argentarii*. The money had been deposited in his name. He could transfer it—once back in Alexandria—to another banker of his choosing. The second page was Florus's letter that he now possessed. Duly authorized documents signed by General Titus's second-in-command to protect Hananiah and provide him an escort from the city and Judea. Hananiah would receive it once he delivered what he owed. "Excellent...."

"Lord Florus expects you here." The brutish mercenary unfolded another sheet of parchment on the counter, flattening it with two scarred, massive hands. The faded green depiction of a Nilus crocodile on one, now clearly seen under the light. A thick finger tapped a mark on the roughly drawn map. "Tomorrow, at *prima noctis hora*, the 1st hour of the night... be there with your prisoner." He stopped, and his eyes flicked toward the back of the shop, but there was no sound to heighten their interest. Hananiah readied for any movement from the three men accompanying the man before him. They remained still as their leader continued. "Can you get your prisoner there? The crazed walk the streets, and the city reeks of death even more than last time."

Hananiah stepped closer to study the crude map. "This is the Upper City agora. And that," he touched the marked location with the point of his knife, "is the end of an alley I believe leads nowhere." He looked up questioningly at the brute.

"At its end, you'll find a trapdoor entrance to a tunnel. Follow it, and you'll find where we meet."

That makes sense, Hananiah thought; no place on the streets is safe. *And if the Romans could get into the city through it, he could use it to get out more easily.* "I will be there with what I have for Lord Florus, but can't meet that soon."

"Why?" The massive brute bristled and seemed to grow larger. The men with him stiffened and shifted their feet, and hands went to grip hilts at their belts.

Hananiah took out the green feather from the sash at his waist. "Give this to Lord Florus... and he will not mind the delay. Tell him I ask that he double the amount held by the Alexandrian *argentarii* for me. If he does, I will deliver his wife back to him." He could see the man consider this recent development, his eyes narrowed, squinting at him. He took the feather.

"I'll give him your message. When can you meet? There is not much time...."

"An extra half-day," Hananiah tapped the location on the map, "the day after tomorrow at noon. And Lord Florus must be there." He saw the man's jaw clench and thick muscles bunch along the ridge of his shoulders.

"I will see you there..." The man loomed over the counter and turned away.

Hananiah waited a moment after they left, then went outside. The few people on the street moved from the four mercenaries' way. At a discreet distance, he followed them into the Upper City, to the marketplace, now one in name only. He watched them turn into the alley marked on the map still held in his hand. His eyes turned north and east toward the Temple Enclosure. He stared at the Temple rising over the wall. *The brute's right; there's not much time. Now to take Cleo from Miriam.* He turned toward the Upper City residential area to Miriam's home. He doubted she and Cleo were there; they had seemed to be headed toward the Lower City. A trio of scavengers he had been forced to kill had interfered with his following them the other evening as they abandoned their home. Even he dared not search at night. He had lost Miriam, her two cousins, Cleo and the boy, but he would find them.

* * *

Hananiah entered the Lower City, his thoughts fixed on where Miriam and Cleo could be. He considered where he had seen Miriam most often. As he neared the craftsmen's row, he saw her. Miriam stood with her back to him, staring at a closed shop. An unfamiliar jolt of rage shot through him. He had thought of Miriam as he did the metal he forged into beautiful, malleable weapons that could be made to serve his bidding. His only love before meeting her was the heft of a well-made knife, its keen edge, and the use of its killing point. That changed because he felt they shared some marring, a past terrible event that altered everything. He thought her something he too could shape but as a companion. Then she had proved a liar, a deceit. Before considering his words, he called out to her. She turned at them, and he saw a flash... of contempt... of hate. He was unsure; it passed quickly but turned his anger into a bitter cold.

"What am I, Hananiah?"

Her expression had become composed, and she faced him. Hananiah swallowed his bitterness. His declaration: 'I know what you are,' had come out too harshly. He needed Miriam alive, but only long enough to find Cleo. Then he would kill her. He softened his words, but only a little. "You are a sister grieving the loss of another brother."

"How do you know Matthew is still missing?"

"Because I have him. Bring the Roman lady, Cleo, to me."

"You want to claim the reward once rumored for her."

She drops all pretense now. "It's real. Bring her to me, and I'll let Matthew go." Hananiah watched her hands on the wooden staff, her knuckles whitening as her grip tightened and thought, *lies to a liar.*

CLV

Augustus 70 CE

Jerusalem

The Outer Courtyard of the Temple, atop the Memorial over King Alexander's Tomb

Yosef wished he was dealing with Simon bar Giora instead of Yohanan ben Levi, but he would do as Titus commanded. But it might not have been any better with Simon bar Giora, who had been lured to "take Jerusalem" by Matthias ben Boethus, one of the Temple high priests. When that had not gone well, Giora, suspecting the man supported the Romans, had ordered the High Priest and his sons executed atop the wall in the view of the Romans. *Giora likely harbors similar plans for me*, Yosef thought.

"General Titus asks me to tell you," Yosef called across the ruined land, "that if you want to continue to battle his legions, you should bring your men out of the city to fight, as many of them as you want. Doing so will save Jerusalem from further destruction and end the threat to the Temple. Yohanan," he pleaded, hoping the other man could hear reason, "General Titus does not want to see you defile the Temple and offend Jehovah—*Adonai Eloheinu*—the Lord our God. He asks that you spare the city and prevent what will otherwise happen. Spare the Temple and the people of Jerusalem by taking the fight outside the city."

"You speak as if I am the traitor to our people, Yosef ben Mathias," Yohanan ben Levi sneered. "Do you have a Roman name yet? I have never feared the Romans taking Jerusalem. It belongs to Jehovah alone. He shall help us against the Romans."

Yosef cried out in a loud voice, "Until you have taken it for yourself, the city is pure and the Temple untainted. You sin against Him to whom you pray for help. You're a vile wretch to hope our God will support you. You have taken away His daily sacrifices and risked the loss of His eternal worship. And now you blame the Romans for your own sins. You, a Jew educated in our traditions, have become a greater enemy than the Romans, who have taken great care to allow us to observe our holy laws."

Yosef bowed his head a moment to gather his composure and try again. "Again," he said, "General Titus asks that you recommence the sacrifices. That will calm the hearts of devout people within the city. I plead with you. It is not dishonorable, even at this late hour, to repent and seek to make right what has been wrongfully done. Remember the actions of our King Jeconiah. When the king of Babylon assaulted Jerusalem, Jeconiah, by his own volition, left the city before it was overrun. He and his family voluntarily went into captivity, so the Sanctuary might not wind up in enemy hands and that he might not witness Jehovah's house set afire. His actions are still celebrated by all Jews, and his memory will be immortalized through the ages. His example is appropriate in these dangerous times. I swear that Titus promises he will absolve you if you end the fight now." He paused to highlight the choice. "But if you must persist, take the battle outside the city."

Perceiving Yosef's choking voice and the tears in his eyes, Yohanan ben Levi and his men poured more insults and jeers upon Yosef. But some among the rebels and many surrounding them seemed to listen as Yosef continued: "Why do you trample over the dead bodies on the Temple floor? Why do you pollute the Holy Sanctuary with the blood of Jews and Gentiles? General Titus asks me to tell you he appeals to the gods of his own country and all gods who have held this place in high esteem. He will testify to the Jews and rebels who still confront him that he and his army are not forcing you to defile our Holy Sanctuary. If you choose another battlefield, no Roman will come near our Temple nor commit any offense against it. General Titus will try to preserve our holy house, whether or not you will."

"Josephus," came a firm voice behind him, and, hearing the name, Yosef clenched his eyes shut, opened them, drew in a breath, and released it. He turned from Yohanan ben Levi's insolent and derisive tirade to Titus, who stood a few feet away surveying the rebels hurling insults. Next to him stood Nicanor, who—he knew—watched for any sign the rebel invectives would be followed by arrows and stones.

"Yes, Lord Titus."

"It seems the rebels are neither moved to have pity upon themselves nor concerned over their temple. So be it... what comes next is upon them." Titus motioned to the captain of his escort and said, "I return to the Antonia Tower." He turned then to the aide who always accompanied him. "Notify my staff to meet me there."

Final Siege

Titus looked at Yosef and said, "You go to your quarters." Then the general gestured at Nicanor and said, "You come with me, *tribunus*. Our major assault begins tonight."

CLVI

Augustus 70 CE

Jerusalem

The Roman Encampment, Nicanor and Yosef's Tent

Yosef returned to the tent, as Titus had ordered, but hesitated when he saw the two legionaries standing there. "What is this about?" he asked, but the men ignored him, so he went inside and found Yohanan ben Zaccai putting a rolled blanket into the haversack on the cot.

"I hope Nicanor does not mind me taking two blankets," the old man said, "and thank him for the clothing."

"Why are you packing?" Yosef asked, and the priest straightened his back to look at his dear friend's son. "General Titus has freed me," he said. "So he has written." He handed Yosef the sheet of vellum still bearing the crumbling bits of wax pressed with the general's personal seal.

"This gives you safe passage to Yavneh, a city now under Titus's protection," Yosef said, feeling decades of memories flowing through his mind, memories of the old priest who had been with him through so much in Galilee. "Why?"

"When General Titus heard my prophecy for him, he said, 'If I free you, what would you do... where would you go?' I told him I wished to go to Yavneh and join the sages there." The old priest pointed at the decree in Yosef's hands. "The general has agreed that no elders in Yavneh will be harmed, and I can establish a school there."

"Must you go?" Yosef asked.

"Please don't be sad, Yosef. I must. Jerusalem can no longer be the center of our faith. Our people need a new, safe place for study." Yohanan put his hand on Yosef's arm. "Perhaps after this war ends, we can see each other again. I'll pray for you and your family." The old priest's hand moved to grip Yosef's shoulder, and he continued: "Your purpose is to write about what has happened before and during the war. Record it all so it is not lost. My purpose is to teach the young so our faith is not forgotten while we are in exile."

Final Siege

* * *

"You sit in the dark," Nicanor said, entering the tent with a small hand lamp and almost stumbling over Yosef on a stool. He set the flickering lamp on the small table beside his cot.

"So has my life become," Yosef replied. "Yohana ben Zaccai is gone... now it's even darker."

"Titus told me."

"You knew he was being sent away and did not tell me?"

"I found out not an hour ago as Titus dismissed his staff for the night. I understand he decreed Yohanan's freedom and promised that the place he goes to settle will be protected."

"Yes... he will be safe." Yosef rose from his stool and stepped outside.

Nicanor followed Yosef to stand by the horses tethered at the back of the tent. A night wind swirled, kicking up ashes from the extinguished campfire and the dust along the paths worn between the tent rows. Yosef stood facing Antonia Fortress and the Temple to the south.

"When will it begin?" he asked.

"*Vigilia quarta*, the ninth hour of the night. Titus will not delay, for he is still angry at the rebels' insults. Before dismissing the staff, he donned his armor, planning to lead the attack personally. But we convinced him it was best to remain in Antonia Fortress and command from there. The soldiers would fight as bravely if they knew he was watching."

Nicanor studied his silent friend, imagining his thoughts. His sister would likely have returned to the Hinnom Valley cave by now and found they had brought no more food. And she would probably think Yosef had betrayed her yet again. He touched Yosef's shoulder. "We should rest. Titus expects us to join him at dawn."

CLVII

Augustus 70 CE

Jerusalem

Beneath the Temple Enclosure, The Great Sea Cistern Cavern, The Redoubt

Miriam's relief that Matthew was alive soon sank under the weight of her frightening exchange with Hananiah. *What to do next?* she thought as she returned to those in hiding. How could she save Matthew yet not risk Ya'el—Cleo? And how could she do that and still kill Hananiah? And even if she did all that... then what? Death by starvation or at the hands of a Roman soldier? Or by her own hand? For she would never let another Roman touch her. She would fight until she could not... then end her struggle—stop her pain.

But what of the others? She saw Elian and Rachel now, looking up expectantly as she approached. Leah was asleep or too weak to raise her head. She knew Ya'el would soon reveal herself from within the dark, where she watched the passage into the cavern.

"There was no more food at the Hinnom Valley cave," Miriam said dully, and their countenances fell. They all knew they had food for only a few days. Her anger rose, but not at the ones who depended on her. Her hatred of Yosef supplanted her worry about how to deal with Hananiah without risking Matthew's death. 'Yosi,' her once-dearest brother, had either lied about bringing more food or proved too cowardly to risk the effort.

"Maybe Nicanor and Yosef were delayed," Ya'el said as she came from the shadows. "Maybe they will bring it later... or tomorrow." Once again, Miriam saw the effects of worry on her friend's face and knew she bore the same. "Did you hear any word of Matthew?" Ya'el asked tenderly.

"Word of him, yes." Miriam was aware of Rachel's keen attention and of Leah shifting with a groan to turn toward her, both hands pressed to her lower belly at her right hip.

"What word?" Rachel asked with a glance at her sister.

"The knifemaker Hananiah has him," Miriam said plainly, then turned to Ya'el. "He will exchange Matthew... for you."

Final Siege

Ya'el turned her face fully into the light, her chin thrust up. "Then he'll deliver me to my husband and receive the reward."

Miriam nodded. "That is what he hopes. But he will not collect. I plan to get Matthew from him, but I will keep you safe."

* * *

Ya'el heard Elian's breathing change and felt him stir. She waited to see if he would rise to sit by the fire as he had done before or if he would try to explore the dark areas of the gallery and cavern despite her warnings. He lay still for a moment, then got to his knees and carefully crawled to where Miriam slept, several feet away, farther from the fire. Ya'el had learned to judge Miriam's sleep by sound and knew her friend did not sleep. She was undoubtedly going over and over in her mind the plan she had outlined. She had told Hananiah she needed time to convince Ya'el to return to the city, suggesting their hiding place was beyond the innermost walls. Rumors had circulated that some people had escaped the horrors of the city and found safe places nearby and out of sight of the Romans. *Likely hopes or lies*, Ya'el thought.

Surprisingly, Hananiah had not pressed Miriam to deliver Florus's wife sooner. Miriam promised Hananiah she would say she had found Matthew alive but wounded and in hiding and that she needed Ya'el's help to move him.

Hananiah acknowledged that a plausible explanation and Miriam insisted on not meeting at his shop. It must be another location... out of sight as much as possible. Miriam had not been surprised he had told her to use the Upper City agora alley entrance to the tunnels beneath the Temple Enclosure, for she knew that beyond the nexus gallery was the only passage from the city to the hidden valley where Gessius Florus secretly camped with his mercenaries. This arrangement also served Miriam's plan. From there, they could get Matthew into the tunnel leading to the bucket-hoist room, then they could descend to the Great Sea cistern and reach their redoubt within its cavern.

They would do that only if they could kill Hananiah and only if the Romans had not yet found and now controlled the tunnels. Both possibilities were doubtful.

Elian softly called Miriam, and Ya'el wondered if she would feign sleep. With Elian's second whisper of her name, she answered him just as quietly.

"You should be asleep, Elian. You need your rest."

"Ya'el gives me half her portion of food. She makes me eat it. I wish I didn't, but I do, and then I feel selfish. I cannot sleep."

Ya'el shuddered, hearing the lament in Elian's voice.

"I know she does that," Miriam replied, "but don't trouble yourself. It is her choice... a gift to you."

Ya'el's food sacrifice was little compared to what others had given to help her. Miriam's parents had taken her in despite the risk and all the pain, suffering, and danger that had come ultimately because of her father's greed in arranging her marriage to Gessius Florus. She suddenly realized her concern had been for Miriam's parents, not considering they were Yosef's parents, too. She prayed that Leah, on the pallet next to Rachel's, would live and that Leah and Yosef could be together at last.

"I heard you talking about saving Matthew," Elian said in a low voice, and Ya'el held her breath to hear what came next. "Please don't let Ya'el die or get taken away—don't let my... my mother—die."

"I'll do all I can to protect her, Elian," Miriam answered softly.

"Why do the gods let so many bad things happen? I pray all the time! Don't the gods listen?"

Ya'el understood Miriam's silence. Whether they worshipped many gods or one... it was a question everyone asked. *But what can even a god say about this?* she wondered.

"Why are there so many evil men?" Elian asked with the heat of anger. Ya'el could almost see his little fists balled up in the struggle of it.

"There just are...." Miriam replied. "But I swear to you that soon there will be at least one less of them."

After a quiet moment, the boy crawled back to his pallet and pulled his blanket over him. Soon the evenness of his breathing told her he was sleeping. But she could not. Matthew must be saved no matter what happens at the exchange with Hananiah. Even if she had to deliver herself to the knifemaker. Gessius Florus would never be rash enough to enter the city to seize the treasure he sought. He had hirelings to do that, and the only way she would ever get close to the man she hated more than any would be to put herself in the charge of Hananiah. When she was led before her husband, she would be demure, appear frightened... as she had been when they were newly wed. Gessius Florus had liked her like that—fearful and compliant. He liked all his women like that—including the slave girls he abused. She would let him think her just as broken as they, show him her fear one last time. She would get him to drop his guard, and then she would try to kill him—barehanded if necessary.

Final Siege

You're right, Miriam, she told herself. Soon there will be one less evil man.

CLVIII

Augustus 70 CE

Jerusalem

The Outer Courtyard of the Temple

Yosef studied the men and siege equipment surrounding King Alexander's tomb. The Romans had massed there in the early morning sun, facing the northern wall separating them from the Temple Sanctuary's inner courts.

The two assault platforms and the new battering rams had failed despite a week-long effort against the precisely joined massive stones that formed a structure stronger than even the outer walls of Jerusalem. The siege engineers had tried undermining the foundations at the northern gate. They had little to show for the effort, as only one or two outer stones had been loosened. The inner foundation beneath the gates remained stout and immovable. If they could not go under to bring the wall down, Titus was determined to go over, and he had ordered scaling ladders brought forward.

Yosef had watched with Nicanor and wondered if his friend had shared his memories of Sayid just then. But the rebels made no attempt to stop the placement of the ladders, and the counterattack began only when the legionaries began climbing. The rebels used poles to push away several ladders full of armed men, pitching them headlong onto the stone floor of the outer courtyard. The defenders cut others down as they reached the parapets before they could raise their shields to protect themselves. Hundreds of rebels died or fell fatally wounded themselves as they ferociously defended the Sanctuary wall, but they drove the Romans back.

In the next assault, Titus had ordered legion *aquila* bearers to lead the men up the ladders, believing there was no way that legionaries would fail to protect their eagle standards. He challenged their honor and stirred their pride, only to be shocked that the rebels killed every soldier scaling the wall and captured the eagles in a triumph shameful to the Romans. Though every Roman soldier had taken an enemy with him as he died, the rebels forced the legionaries to withdraw.

Final Siege

In one lull, more men deserted the rebels, and among them were two men Yosef had heard of but did not know personally. Ananus of Emmaus had been a brutal member of Simon bar Giora's personal guard and Archelaus ben Maggadatus, one of the rebel general's lieutenants. They asked to see Titus and begged for his pardon and their freedom.

Titus had wanted to put them to death, having read what Yohanan ben Zaccai reported about the cruelty of Simon bar Giora and Yohanan ben Levi against their own people. When the two defectors met with Titus, he declared, "Men who hurry to leave their city when it is in flames through their own fault and that of the leaders they supported, those men do not deserve mercy." But he had already given his word that any who surrendered would live. Though they would not be as well treated as others, who had proved to have played no role in prolonging the war.

The evening before, Yosef had left the meetings at sunset—dismissed by Titus. Later that night, Nicanor had told him what was to come. After the siege engineers failed in their attacks on the Temple's boundary walls, Titus ordered all wood and timber available to be brought to the wall. "The wood piled against the Sanctuary's northern gate has been soaked with oil and pitch and will be set afire," Nicanor said. "Titus plans to melt the ornamental silver to get at the wooden frame beneath. Destroy the gates... pour men through, widen the breach, and bring more men directly against the temple."

So Nicanor had said, and now Yosef witnessed the final preparation for that action in the slanting sunbeams passing through broken clouds.

* * *

TITUS'S COMMAND POST NEAR THE TEMPLE

The gates were now destroyed, and two Legions—5th *Macedonia* and 15th *Apollinaris*—had encircled the massive temple in the innermost court. Its front side spanned 150 feet with 12 steps to the opening, and it reached back 150 feet as well, but the building tapered to a back width of just 90 feet. The fine stone was overlayed by sheets of gold, and the inner walls bore gold. Yosef had always been in awe of them whenever he visited the Temple. All the walls not covered in gold were of an equally-dazzling pure-white *melekeh*, the finest royal limestone, used only for buildings most important to the Jewish people. And none was more important than the Temple.

Nicanor had attended General Titus's staff meeting with Tiberius Alexander, the commanders of the 5th and 15th Legions, and the Procurator of Judea. He told Yosef that some had recommended destroying the Temple, claiming it had now become more a fortress than a place of worship. Titus had said he did not wish to see it destroyed—it was too grand and beautiful. But Nicanor and Yosef were witnessing just that destruction now.

The most sacred building in Jerusalem and Judea now showed the abuses of man, the marks of violence, and the damage of war. Stone missiles and fire now marred and scorched the once-unblemished exterior that had before radiated such a flash of brilliance with the rays of the sun that people averted their eyes. But no longer. The conflagration grew and began to consume the structure itself. The white-hot flames had softened the precious metals, incinerated finely crafted wooden decorations, and heat-fractured the exquisite *melekeh* fitted by Judea's most skilled stone masons.

The day before, the rebels had sortied from the temple through the remnants of an eastern gate to attack a legion cohort at the boundary of the Inner Court and the Outer Court. A three-hour battle had forced the rebels back within the Inner Court, and only a few hours later, they clashed again. This time, a unit of the 5th Legion paid the rebels back for the earlier dousing of hot oil and fire arrows that set dozens of their number ablaze, burned alive. In the frenzy of fighting, the legionaries forced the rebels back into the Temple Sanctuary. A soldier had thrown a burning length of timber through a doorway into one of the northern side chambers. The fire spread as a messenger had roused Titus with the news. Orders had gone out to extinguish the fire, but those orders had been ignored or could not be acted upon. The battle had spread deep into the Sanctuary, up to the Altar in the Priest's Court. The flames had raced through the Temple with all its holy oils and fine, flammable fabrics. Yosef ached inside as he imagined the conflagration of the massive veil-tapestry that separated the Holy of Holies from the Inner Sanctuary.

"It's like everything—even stone—has become one immense flame," Yosef observed, feeling detached by shock and disbelief. He pointed out the 12 steps that now coursed with streams of crimson and at the bloody flagstones surrounding the Temple. "The desecration of blood from the fighting is as tragic as the fire." He was silent momentarily, then added, "And today is Tisha B'Av—the eighth day of this Jewish month."

Nicanor turned to him. "What's that?"

"Exactly 656 years ago, on this very day, the Babylonian King, Nebuchadnezzar, captured Jerusalem and burned King Solomon's Temple... our first Temple. Now the destruction happens again." Weary, for he had not slept in a day, Yosef felt his thoughts return to his failure to get more food to his family. He had not told Nicanor that he could wait no longer. *Tonight, I will go alone to take more food to the cave.* He was sure Miriam had checked it and hoped she would continue to do so. But no doubt she hated him even more for not keeping his promise. He prayed she had found Matthew alive and unharmed.

Nicanor's heavy-handed slap against his shoulder shook him from his thoughts. "What is it?" he asked, blinking away the wanderings of his mind.

"I've seen that man before," Nicanor said, thrusting his chin toward a massive man escorted through the guards around Titus and his staff. The large man, his scarred features drawn tight in a scowl, moved toward Tiberius Alexander. The Aegyptus Prefect stood next to Titus and the commanders of the 5th, 10th, and 15th Legions—Sextus Cerealis, Lucius Lepidus, and Titus Frigius, Yosef remembered from his written accounts of the war. On the other side of General Titus was the new Procurator of Judea, Marcus Antonius Julianus, newly arrived from Caesarea.

Yosef could see that the scarred man in mercenary garb carried two daggers at his belt and a long sword sheathed at his hip. Those weapons required rare permission for anyone who would get near Titus. The man raised his hand in a brief salute to Tiberius Alexander.

"There!" Nicanor's voice was sharp. "See his hand... the crocodile tattoo. What does that Thracian mercenary want with Tiberius Alexander?"

They watched as General Titus's second-in-command stepped away several feet... the mercenary following him. The two men, heads bowed close, spoke briefly, then the large man turned to leave, and Tiberius Alexander followed him!

"We should see what he will do next," Yosef whispered to Nicanor.

Nicanor and Yosef were at one end of the ranks of Titus's staff and entourage. The *tribunus* frowned, and his eyes turned to study General Titus, who seemed deep in conversation with the new procurator. Yosef watched his friend's eyes shift, and the lines on his face deepened. Yosef was newly reminded of his friend's age and weariness.

"Very well," Nicanor replied. With a last glance at Titus, he slowly followed Tiberius Alexander and the mercenary, and Yosef followed him.

* * *

ANTONIA FORTRESS, THE ARMORY LEVEL

Yosef did not need to ask if Nicanor, too, wondered why Tiberius Alexander had followed a Thracian mercenary to Antonia Fortress and descended to the armory. For what purpose?

The voices came from a small room off the worn steps to the right, just before the double-wide entrance to the main storeroom. The door was open, and Yosef could see the bulk of the mercenary filling the entry. All the man had to do was glance over his shoulder, and he would see them. With a tug at his sleeve, Nicanor pointed at a broad recess in the opposite wall, filled with barrels stacked three high. There was just enough room to slip behind them, which was a tight fit for Nicanor.

An irritated voice carried sharply from the room. "Your message insisted we meet here as soon as possible. Why?"

The voice and tone teased Yosef. As he tried to place who it belonged to, another answered, and he recognized that voice! He held his breath as he listened for every word, holding a hand palm out for Nicanor to stay quiet.

"Things are moving quickly," Tiberius Alexander said. "General Titus is readying for the destruction of this fortress, which could collapse the tunnels beneath. It could affect the passage to your camp. You must move fast."

"How long do we have?"

Now Yosef was sure, and he looked with wide eyes at Nicanor, who stared in the direction of the room and did not acknowledge him.

"A day or less... the new procurator Julianus brings news that Emperor Vespasian has already left Alexandria for Rome... the city and region are now stable. Titus will push hard to end this so he can join his father in Rome. Send word when I should meet you back in your camp."

The shifting movement of the man in the doorway was their only warning that the meeting was over. The big man stepped aside to let Tiberius Alexander leave the room and go up the steps, then he pulled the door almost closed, shutting himself in with the other man.

"*Futuo!*" Nicanor muttered, and Yosef saw him wiping his hands on the hem of his cloak. "Oil seeps from these barrels. They're probably for soaking the support timbers down here so they can burn them away." He looked up at Yosef and said, "You heard that voice?"

Just then, a clatter of hobnailed sandals came down the steps. Several auxiliaries descended and entered the main storeroom, shutting its wide doors.

Yosef watched the small room door open fully, and the tattooed mercenary peered from within, then came out. Another man in fine clothing followed him. Behind him came two more big men, mercenaries, to judge by their weapons. The Roman nobleman squinted down the corridor. "Now, let's go get them," said Gessius Florus.

Though Yosef had recognized the voice, he was still stunned to see the Roman who had caused so much strife for his people and, even worse, brutalized Cleo. He had not seen him since the early days of his imprisonment as Vespasian's prisoner.

Gessius Florus and his escort moved down the corridor to a room Yosef knew had access to the tunnel leading into the city.

Nicanor spoke first. " 'Get them,' but who?" He stepped sideways and pressed against another barrel, smearing oil on his leather chest piece. Wiping it with one hand, spreading it farther, he joined Yosef to follow Florus and his men.

CLIX

Augustus 70 CE

Jerusalem

The Upper City, The Tunnel

Where my darkness began may be where I end, Miriam recited the refrain that had begun amid her sleepless night. And then, when she and Ya'el entered the trapdoor to descend into the tunnel, it echoed again in her head: *Where my darkness began may be where I end.* She would gladly die in this tunnel if it meant saving Matthew.

"Miriam?" Ya'el asked with a grip of concern on her shoulder.

"I'm fine," Miriam replied and lighted the hand lantern. "Now stay behind me, out of the light." She moved into the passage that led to the tunnel nexus, and soon she heard a shuffling sound of a single man pacing, jostling pebbles on the hard-packed floor. Glancing back, she caught the sweat-sheen of Ya'el's face as she crowded too close at her shoulder. "Drop back farther," Miriam whispered, waiting until Ya'el withdrew entirely into the shadows.

She turned and continued to where a dim glow grew, and then the passage widened into the gallery chamber. A tremor had coursed through her each time she had entered this place. Seeing her lantern light tremble on the wall, she gripped Zechariah's staff and steadied herself.

The surroundings brightened, and she saw that Hananiah had found the old brackets on the wall and set two fresh torches blazing there. She was too close to mutter another warning, so she prayed Ya'el had slowed to remain in the dark.

"Where's Lady Cleo?" Hananiah asked boldly, his voice ringing off the stone walls like metal on metal.

"I must first see that you have Matthew."

"Is she hiding in the dark?" Hananiah asked, his black eyes gleaming as he peered into the shadows behind Miriam. Then his stare fixed on Miriam.

"I must see Matthew... now," Miriam said as she set down the lantern and took two steps away.

Hananiah pulled a long, broad-bladed knife from the sheath at his waist. Its metal glinted and rippled under the torchlight, and he turned away into the darkness behind him. Shortly there came a rustling noise and a grunt of pain.

Miriam moved toward the sound, thrusting her free hand behind her, palm out, signaling Ya'el not to move.

The slack figure that Hananiah dragged into the rim of the torchlight was semiconscious, the filthy tunic torn and crimson-stained. The left side of his head was caked with what must be blood and half-covered by tangled clotted hair, but Miriam could not see the face. Hananiah effortlessly bore the man's weight with one arm and used the flat of his knife blade to lift the man's chin toward the light.

"Matthew!" Miriam declared, then raised the staff to point the metal ferrule toward the knifemaker.

Hananiah rotated his dagger with a twist of his wrist and pressed the blade into the hollow of Matthew's throat. "Do not be foolish, Miriam... you think that because some old man taught you how to wield a staff, you know how to fight. Send Cleo over here to me... or your brother dies. Then you can go."

Hananiah's tone had a hint of urgency or maybe irritation, and Miriam needed to waste no more time. "Release him!" she cried, preparing to signal Ya'el to strike the instant Hananiah took the blade from Matthew's throat. "Lower your knife, Hananiah... and you will get what you want."

"But you are a liar, Miriam... you mislead and deceive." Hananiah pressed the dagger tight where Matthew's jaw met his neck, and her brother's head lolled to one side. He seemed to be beyond the comprehension of what was happening, but she saw the slow rise and fall of his chest and then saw his eyelids flicker.

"Enough."

Miriam was startled by the voice behind her. Ya'el stepped into the light and moved past her toward Hananiah and Matthew, stopping to set her bow and quiver against the wall beneath one torch.

"Enough...." Ya'el repeated softly and looked back at Miriam. "It's time to do what I must."

Miriam took a step toward her. "Ya'el, don't do this."

"I must."

Miriam went to Ya'el, keeping her eyes on Hananiah. "Then grab his knife arm and pull it down as I attack," she whispered.

"Get Matthew free," Ya'el whispered back, "but let Hananiah take me. It's the only way I'll get revenge—you know what I must do.

Please care for Elian until this all ends." Ya'el turned away and walked to Hananiah.

The knifemaker's sudden blow—a fist to Ya'el's face—sent Ya'el to the ground with Matthew as Hananiah let him fall. After her startle, Miriam started to rush at Hananiah, but an unfamiliar, cruel, commanding voice stopped her in her tracks.

"It seems we have more here than we bargained for, Hananiah," said Gessius Florus as he, Krateros, and two other hulking Thracian mercenaries walked out of the darkness of the Antonia Fortress tunnel to take their quarry.

CLX

Augustus 70 CE

Jerusalem

The Upper City, The Tunnel Nexus

Ya'el sprawled next to Matthew, the taste of blood in her mouth sickeningly familiar as she stared at Gessius Florus for the first time in three years. It did not seem that long ago... and had not been long enough. Dazed by the hit from Hananiah, the accustomed sensations—revulsion and loathing—overwhelmed her. This was not going as expected. Now Miriam and Matthew both were at risk. She watched Hananiah reposition himself one step from Matthew, who lay prone, unmoving, an arm's length from her. Caught in the flare of a torch lighted by one of the brutes with Gessius Florus, Hananiah's eyes widened and then narrowed into their fathomless unblinking stare at the approaching men. *So he, too, is surprised*, she thought.

"You're early, Lord Florus," Hananiah commented.

"And I do not see Lady Cleo." Her husband's squinting eyes swept over her, and Matthew then shifted to Miriam, who stood with staff in one hand and dagger in the other. She realized his eyesight had worsened. *She realized he must think us men*, taking his cue from their clothing.

The largest of Florus's bodyguards gripped a long sword and pulled another large blade from a sheath at his belt. He signaled, and the other two men also drew their swords. All three men wore armor of *lorica hamata*, chain mail, over their upper arms and torsos, and a *galea* of the legionaries protected each one's head. The three approached Hananiah, though one kept his eyes on Miriam until they stopped within sword reach of the knifemaker. Gessius Florus strode forward behind them.

"Which of these is Matthew, and where is Lady Cleo?"

Before Hananiah could reply, a muttered curse came from behind Gessius Florus.

"*Futuo!*" sounded from behind Florus, and Nicanor stepped into the torchlight, planted his feet, and drew his gladius. Next to him, Yosef also gripped a short sword, and his stare went from Miriam to the former Judean Procurator. His scowl joined Nicanor's at the sight of Gessius Florus.

* * *

The sounds of the Thracians' armor had masked Nicanor and Yosef's movements as they followed Florus and his escort from Antonia Fortress. They had crept forward as Florus and his men left the tunnel, keeping pace but well behind them. Then, in this torchlit area, they'd closed with them, and Nicanor had seen two figures on the ground—one must be Cleo.

Once they realized who Florus was there for, they could no longer watch silently to see what happened next. "*Futuo!*" Nicanor cursed again and drew his dagger with his free hand. Gessius Florus was no physical threat, but the three Thracians were as sure as Hades. Even with Yosef's help—lacking armor—Nicanor did not know if he could kill all three. He and Yosef stepped together from the mouth of the tunnel toward the former procurator. "Lord Florus, we will not let you take Lady Cleo," he declared.

Gessius Florus gestured grandly, his jewels glittering in the light of the flickering flames. "So, centurion, I mean tribunus," sneered the former procurator. "You will prevent me? You and the Jew—now called Josephus, I'm told—Titus and his father seem oddly fond of him." Florus motioned toward the Thracians.

Krateros understood and ordered his two men: "Kill them."

Nicanor directed Yosef to put some distance between them, thankful there was room to maneuver in the central area of the nexus but little room in the torchlight. Beyond a dim stretch, the lantern on the stone floor behind Miriam cast a pool of light where she had moved closer to the prostrate form of Cleo and another that must be Matthew. From the corner of his eye, Nicanor saw Yosef remove his cloak and roll his shoulders to loosen them. Nicanor had witnessed little of Yosef's combat skill during the fighting at Yotapta, but he had trained with him in Rome and, in the years since, had had no doubts about his courage. But Nicanor would need to kill his man quickly to help Yosef. While Nicanor had some slight protection from the leather *subarmilis* he wore over his chest, though he regretted having no chain mail over it, Yosef only had the wool of his tunic. And Yosef had only an unfamiliar sword he had taken from the Antonia Fortress armory before entering the tunnel.

Hoping Yosef followed his lead, Nicanor charged at his Thracian. Their only hope was in attack; trying to defend against an armored

Final Siege

fighter meant eventual death. Nicanor had never fought for Rome unarmored but had fought thus for himself and Graius—even for Cleo, in a way—in the arena in Marianum. He had earned money to tend to Graius, or the old gladiator would have died. And were it not for what Graius had taught him, he would not have reached Marcus Otho. But Cleo's brother's short-lived imperial powers died with him before they were of any aid to her. Nicanor knew what he must do, and he prayed Yosef could thwart or dodge the other Thracian while he attempted it.

Nicanor's short sword glinted as it thrust and swung in a series of chopping attacks the Thracian avoided by backing away. Each time the mercenary blocked his blow, the clash sent a shock up Nicanor's arm and into his shoulder. The Thracian counter-thrust and Nicanor spun to avoid it, then struck with his dagger at the mercenary's thick torso as the man half-twisted away from him. Nicanor's blade found an opening, and he leaned into it to punch through the rings of the mail armor. The tip bit into the Thracian's side, but not deep enough. Nicanor tore the weapon free, and his second thrust missed.

A roundhouse strike from the mercenary's fist closed around his dagger and caught Nicanor on the side of the head, and pain shot through his jaw and cheekbone. He spat blood and wished for the reach of Graius's *spatha*. He had left the long sword behind in his tent in favor of the more practical short sword he wore around camp. But he had formed the habit of wearing the back sheath rig Graius had given him between his shoulders. Its width should accept a gladius.

Despite the slippery blood from the ragged cut along his sword arm, he gripped the sword and stepped toward the big Thracian. He wiped his hand on his thigh and re-gripped the sword. With a nod at the mercenary, he rendered the salute Graius had taught him. Then, lifting the sword up and over, he sheathed the blade between his shoulders. He dropped his *pugio* at his feet as he raised his arms and waited.

The Thracian closed on Nicanor. As the man's arm pulled back to begin a disemboweling thrust, Nicanor stepped toward him and twisted at the waist, his arms still raised. He dropped his hand to his shoulder, to the short sword's hilt, and drew it from the sheath. His descending cut tore the helmet from the mercenary's head. Nicanor pivoted to bring the blade around again, the man screaming as the tip sliced into one eye. Nicanor spun again and put all his weight into stabbing his short sword into the side of the man's head, and the

Thracian sank to the ground. Nicanor's kicked the man's twitching leg aside, and he stooped to pick up his dagger.

Risking hurried glances through that skirmish, Nicanor had seen Yosef dodging in and out of the torch's light. Now his friend traded thrust and counter-thrust with his Thracian near where Miriam knelt as if rooted. Nicanor checked the largest mercenary to see him in the same spot, but with his blade leveled at the chest of the man Florus had addressed as Hananiah. That was a name Nicanor recalled from three years before. On his way to Rome for Vespasian, a centurion had told him of a strange Alexandrian knifemaker who had traveled with him and his men to Caesarea. Could this be the man? Did he also work for Florus? Was that why he did not use the knife he held to strike at the huge mercenary threatening him?

Glad that the two men watched each other and not him, Nicanor moved toward Yosef and his attacker. With a flurry of strikes, the Thracian beat Yosef's blade down and swung up his own to gouge a furrow of flesh from Yosef's brow. His friend's chest heaved, and he raised his blade too slowly. The mercenary's fist crashed into Yosef's jaw, and a tree-trunk leg booted him backward into the shadows. With a scream, Miriam finally moved—dropping her staff, she plunged her blade two-handed into the base of the Thracian's skull. The man fell, his dead weight pulling the dagger from her hand.

"Krateros!" Florus called with a panicked order, his voice echoing in the chamber.

Nicanor turned to see the largest of the Thracians turn away from Hananiah and lock eyes with him. He now knew the name of the captain of the mercenaries. With the man's attention diverted, Hananiah raised his knife, and Nicanor saw Matthew struggling to his knees to clutch at Hananiah's leg. Off balance, the knifemaker kneed Matthew in the head. His dagger hand shifted toward Krateros, who jabbed his blade into the meat of Hananiah's shoulder. Hence, he had to sink back into the shadows as Krateros wheeled toward Nicanor, and Matthew fell to the ground again. Nicanor glimpsed Cleo's upturned, blood-smeared face as she shook her head and tried to stand.

"Let's see how you fight, Roman... I've seen you senior officers in the legions... safe in the rear while real men do the fighting," the mercenary captain taunted.

Nicanor met him in the center of the nexus. With the first series of parries, he knew the Thracian was stronger than he was. A dark figure—Miriam?—dashed into the scant light, and a wooden staff struck hard across Krateros's sword arm. Nicanor heard the crack and wondered if the arm or the staff had broken until Krateros's clenching of his arm answered the question. Then a sweeping kick from the staff-wielder sent the Thracian captain's sword skittering into the darkness. Then Miriam—staff in hand—returned to Cleo, who knelt over Matthew.

With a roar, Krateros bull-rushed Nicanor, driving him into the wall. The flat of the Thracian's hand on his chest pressed him back as the man's dagger came up at Nicanor's throat. Nicanor twisted as Krateros's hand slipped on the oil smeared on his leather chest plate. The knife thrust missed its target but still scored a lengthy cut along his neck. Nicanor pulled away from him.

A rumbling sound filled the gallery, and a billow of dirt plumes filled the tunnel to Antonia Fortress. Krateros's eyes jerked toward the sound, then to Gessius Florus—who had backed away from the fighting—as Nicanor's sword arced down and severed the Thracian's tattooed hand at the wrist. The second slash ripped open the man's throat.

"That's how I fight," Nicanor said as he spat on the Thracian and sheathed his sword. Slouching, hands on his knees, he breathed deeply and turned as Yosef came from the shadows to join him. Blood coated one side of Yosef's face from the jagged gash on his brow.

"Where's Florus?" Nicanor asked.

"When that big Thracian fell, he ran that way." Yosef pointed down the tunnel Miriam and the others had come through. He dropped to the ground, his head drooping, chin to his chest.

"And where's Hananiah?" Miriam asked Cleo, who gestured toward another tunnel, and without a word, Miriam raced after him. Nicanor went to Yosef, knelt, and checked his wound. He took his *pugio*, cut off a piece of Yosef's tunic, and handed it to him. "Here, use this to slow the bleeding."

"Help me up," Yosef said as he gripped Nicanor's arm and got to his feet. "Where are Miriam and Cleo?"

"Your sister ran down that tunnel," Nicanor pointed. "Cleo's by your broth—"

Nicanor stopped. Matthew had not moved, but Cleo was gone.

CLXI

Augustus 70 CE

Jerusalem

The Tunnel Beneath the Temple Enclosure

Miriam felt another shudder through the ground as she passed through the tunnel beneath the Temple Enclosure. The collapse of Herod's Tunnel from Antonia Fortress had shaken all the underground passages, and several sealed side chambers had cracked open. She moved cautiously, silently, stopping to listen for Hananiah. But she could not discern the sound of human movement from the settling of dirt and stone. Was the wounded knifemaker hiding, hoping to return and somehow rejoin Florus? Or would he return to the nexus and try to flee back into the city?

A chill shot through her. What if Hananiah knew of the redoubt? What if he had followed them to the bucket-hoist room? Matthew had left the lines rigged so one could climb down into the Great Sea cistern beneath the Temple Enclosure. From there, Hananiah could reach the galleries where Rachel, Leah, and Elian hid. He could then take his revenge or even try to exchange them for Matthew and Cleo!

Miriam decided. She hurried to the passage that descended into the bucket-hoist chamber, but then she slowed, exchanging speed for stealth. She could not be far behind Hananiah and did not want to alert him with any sound, though he might spot the glow of her torch. Several shuffling steps and a stumble—human noises—stopped her momentarily. But they came from behind her. Hananiah had been in one of the side chambers! Her torch revealed one of the newly-opened passages ahead. With the tip of Zechariah's staff, she pushed aside half-dislodged stones to clear her way. She shoved herself inside, tumbling stones and making enough noise to guide her follower. She must lead him away from the passage to the bucket-hoist chamber. She came to a place where the corridor bent northerly, opposite the direction of the Great Sea cistern. *Good*, she thought. *This way*. She watched for an opening, alcove, or other hiding places to spring from and attack Hananiah. She would let him pass and then put herself between him and the way they had come. He would not pass that way again.

Final Siege

* * *

Hananiah had staggered through the darkness to find a safe place to catch his breath and assess his wounds. The stab from the Thracian mercenary captain had gone deep, transfixing his shoulder, and then he had fallen and struck his head. Stunned, he took a few moments to rise to see the huge Thracian confront the almost-as-big Roman. While those two were engaged, he needed a secure place to stop the bleeding and regain his wits. He would return to see if Florus's henchman Krateros had dealt with the big Roman and gotten control of the others. Then he could conclude his dealings with Gessius Florus. But if that big Roman soldier meant more were coming... then Gessius Florus's plan must have failed, and he must find a way out.

Outside the side chamber he hid within, Hananiah heard footsteps on the layer of grit upon the passage floor. He checked the wad of wool he had torn from his tunic and packed it into his shoulder wound, and readied for whoever was outside. The light and the sounds passed, so he crouched and slid into the entry enough to peek out and see who had followed him.

* * *

Miriam had found no alcoves or recesses from which to spring her attack. Her uncanny sense of direction and distance told her that if she were above ground, she would be about a third of the way into the Temple's Outer Courtyard. This broad expanse separated the Temple Sanctuary from Antonia Fortress. She could sense the tunnel widening ahead before the light of her torch revealed an antechamber, its back wall framing a wide entrance to what must be a larger chamber. Again, she visualized her route. Above her was the memorial tomb for King Alexander Yanna'y... the second king of the Hasmonean dynasty. Her father and Yosef had told her stories of that king's wars, the never-ending conflicts to expand his kingdom. She must be standing before where King Herod had ordered his remains be moved when the Temple grounds grew to the north. Dead bodies—unclean—could not be too near the Temple.

Hearing the noises behind her coming closer, Miriam stepped inside, quickly discovering no way out of the chamber. Yosef filled Miriam's thoughts as she held still, recalling his stories of King Alexander. She shook her head as she wedged her torch in a crack above a waist-high ledge carved into one wall, far enough away to leave the entry in shadows. Without thinking, she had rushed to save Yosef and help his Roman friend. Now she was torn between wishing she had left them to their fate and wanting to return and confront her brother. But first, she would make Hananiah pay for his role in Ehud's death, pay for all he had done—so he could never threaten her loved ones again.

Miriam hurried to the darkness surrounding the chamber entrance, pulled both daggers, and waited. The labored steps grew louder, sometimes slipping on the rubble, and the arc of firelight pushed away the shadows at the entry. All she could make out was the hand that held the oil lantern—a man's hand. As he crossed into the chamber, she launched herself, and at her movement, he turned his face toward her.

With a reflexive twist, she struck her forearm into his throat instead of the blade's point. Gagging, still gripping the lantern, the man staggered, then went to his knees.

She looked down at Yosef.

CLXII

Augustus 70 CE

Jerusalem

The Tunnel Beneath the Temple Enclosure

Florus stumbled through the dark and, knees bloodied, reached a dead-end of the tunnel, but in his panicked groping, he found a ladder reaching up the rock wall. Had he missed a side passage that would be more promising than this dead-end? He tried to quiet his breathing and listen for any pursuit, but his ragged gasps still whistled through his teeth. With the Antonia Fortress and the tunnel to his valley encampment both now sealed off, this ladder seemed his only way out. But to where? What part of the city... Roman or rebel-held? He gripped a rung of the ladder and hesitated. Perhaps Krateros had risen and killed that damned Nicanor and the Jew who was Vespasian and Titus's pet. Maybe he should turn back.

"Ya'el... Miriam?" piped a thin whisper in the darkness.

A streamer of sparks caught on a wick that flared and revealed at Florus's feet a boy hunkered down to one side of the ladder. When the light bloomed, the boy shrank from Florus and moved to rise and run, but there was nowhere to go. He grabbed the fabric of the boy's tunic at his shoulder and pulled a jeweled dagger from a sheath at his hip, holding it in front of the wide eyes. "Where does this lead, boy?" He gestured at the ladder.

"Ya'el!" the boy yelled. "It's Lord Florus!"

"Who is this Ya'el you call?" Florus asked, shaking the boy. "Is it one of those with Hananiah... the knifemaker?" Over the beating of his heart, Florus thought he heard the thud of someone approaching from down the tunnel. He hoisted the boy off his feet, then set him down and held the tip of his blade against the smooth, young throat. "Where does the ladder go?" Florus pointed up.

"To the market, in the Upper City."

"Lead me," Florus said as he shoved the boy against the ladder, knocking the lamp from his hand. It broke upon the ground, and the spilled oil formed a pool of fire at his feet. With a curse and quick side-step, he dodged the flames but kept firm hold of the boy. His blade drew a line of blood along the boy's neck, and the terrified youngster began to climb. Florus sheathed his dagger and followed.

* * *

Ya'el heard Elian's cry and began to run. Miriam had taught her how to move quickly through a familiar dark tunnel by brushing one side wall with outstretched fingertips. The touch kept her following the form of the wall and prevented disorientation. But she had to be careful—tunnel walls weren't smooth, and she could easily jam her fingers against an outcrop or wooden shoring post or cut them on the rough stone. Miriam could do it unerringly, almost always without injury. But Ya'e had already gashed the fingers of her right hand.

The passage floor was more littered with small rocks than she recalled from when she had followed Miriam earlier. Rolling an ankle on one, Ya'el fell to her knees, catching herself with one hand and keeping her strung bow high so it didn't slam into the ground. She grabbed her ankle, wincing, then rose to hurry on. Ahead, the vestige of a burning oil patch lighted the ladder as she skidded to a stop. Slinging her bow on her shoulder and securing her quiver, she gripped a rung and headed up.

* * *

THE UPPER CITY, MARKET ALLEY

Gessius Florus still breathed heavily. The boy would have gotten away if he had not snagged his tunic on the brambles outside that screened the trapdoor of the tunnel exit. With one hand grasping the boy and the other holding his dagger at the boy's head, Florus looked down the alley and up the high walls that formed it. He saw no one, but the city echoed with shouts and screams, and clouds of dust and smoke filled the sky.

He slowly dragged the boy out of the alley, where the louder cries were a mix of pleas and prayers from what must be the people of Jerusalem and fainter curses and imprecations from Roman soldiers. Dozens of Jews, some reeling and bloody, poured past them, away from the indistinct rumble of what must be Roman legionaries entering this part of the city. "What is back there that they are running from?" Florus asked.

"The viaduct to the Temple and the Xystus," the boy said with a glare at him

Final Siege

Then the boy's earlier words struck him. "How do you know me?" he asked, and the boy spat at him. Florus knotted his fist into a firmer grip of the boy's tunic and pressed the knife tip to the base of his skull. He pushed out into the street and toward the Romans. His garb and bearing should slow any quick-fingered, ill-tempered soldier. Florus had papers from Tiberius Alexander that would protect him. He was sure he could talk his way to safety, but he kept the boy in front of him.

* * *

Ya'el came out of the alley and turned this way and that, searching for Elian or Florus, guilt-ridden that she yearned more to find the man. Seeing her husband had unleashed a flood of shame and pain Ya'el had not felt since she'd escaped from him in Ptolemais. Her agony had subsided with the exhilaration of being free and relatively safe, then the labor of trying to remain so in Jerusalem. Now the past washed over her again, with all its indignities and achings. She shook as she scanned the street. From the direction of the Temple came the clatter of armored men, the shouting of commands, and the clang of combat. *Florus would run toward the Roman soldiers*, she was sure. She turned and limped that way.

Not many steps ahead... she saw the billowing cloak of a man. Not a soldier, not a Jew, but a finely-dressed man who seemed to almost stumble with something he pushed or bore in front of him. A twisting half-stagger revealed the boy fighting to free himself from Florus. "Elian!" she shouted and ran toward them, ignoring the grinding pain in her ankle.

As Ya'el closed on Elian and his captor, a shield wall of advancing legionaries appeared behind them, spanning the broad street and driving all the citizens before them. She watched as Florus kicked Elian away from him and hurried toward the Roman ranks. Without slowing her limping pursuit, Ya'el slipped the bow from her shoulder and reached with her other hand into the quiver. With bloodied fingertips, she nocked the shaft and held it ready. *Gods and goddesses—Great Diana—please let me get close enough to kill this terrible man. He has hurt so many. And Jehovah, god of the Jews, allow my arrow to pierce your people's worst enemy.*

Florus was only a dozen steps from the ranks of legionaries who had halted. Once they parted their shields to take Florus among them, she would lose her chance. Then Elian rushed at Florus's back, leaping at his cloak, clawing at it to slow him down.

"No!" Ya'el saw the dagger in Forus's hand slash down, cutting Elian across the face. The boy, his face instantly masked in blood, tumbled to one side. The scream that came from Ya'el's mouth was guttural, primal. All the burning, bitter hate for Gessius Florus turned cold as she drew the bowstring back and loosed her last arrow while at a run.

Because Gessius Florus had turned toward her to knife Elian, the arrow struck Florus's left breast at the level of his heart and sank deep, the shaft thrumming with the force of the impact. He stood there, one hand closed around the shaft and the other dropping his knife to the street as he reached to brush his fingertips over the feathers, bright green in the sun. Bright as the blood that frothed on his lips as Ya'el watched him mouth the words: *"That damned bird."* Ya'el lurched to a stop before him., where he had sunk to his knees and gazed up at her.

"Cleo."

"Yes... now die, my husband," she said. Ya'el watched him keel over and suddenly lurched and grunted as the iron-tipped *pilum* struck her, the spear's point buried deep in her upper right chest. She fell next to Gessius Florus, who stared sightlessly at her. She blinked at the shadow that passed over her eyes.

"Elian?" she called quietly. The boy, his face dripping blood, tried to drag her from the approaching soldiers, and she screamed at the pain. "No, Elian!" she said with the last urgency she could muster. "Leave me... run." Her eyes closed.

CLXIII

Augustus 70 CE

Jerusalem

Beneath the Temple Outer Court, King Alexander's Burial Chamber

The lantern, now on its side but still burning, illuminated Yosef's face. Miriam was irritated at his affectations. Familiar features she had loved all her life, now clean-shaven, his Roman clothing starkly wrong.

"You look like a Roman," she said, picking up the lantern. Her blow had dislodged the strip of cloth wound around Yosef's head, and the gash at his brow spilled fresh blood over the dry blood caked on his cheek. "Would that all Romans were bloody and at the feet of the people of Jerusalem." She backed away into the chamber, ordering, "Get up."

Yosef silently followed her, and the entry returned to shadows.

Miriam stopped and turned so abruptly that he almost ran into her. "What are you doing here, and why did you follow me?"

"To make sure you were safe." Yosef shook his head. "And now we must get away from these underground traps."

"What are you talking about?" Miriam asked.

"Smell what's in the air... the Temple is burning above us."

Miriam did not relax her fierce expression, but she caught the first trace of acrid fumes. Still, she glared at him as if he'd said nothing.

"Who are you after, Miriam?" Yosef asked, fumbling with the bandage on his head, his eyes on her. "What are you doing?"

"I don't need you to keep me safe." Miriam scowled, and she knew her months of hunger and worry for the others had carved sharp planes in her face—whatever maidenly beauty she'd once had was now burned away. *So be it*, she thought. "I'm trying to defend my family and to punish those who've hurt them." A wave of dizziness came over her. The hatred that had fed her for so long had burned through her and left her weak. "Those who've hurt me, too...." She tottered and set down the lantern.

"Who has hurt you?" Yosef wiped the remaining blood from his face. "The Romans? What they've done here?"

"Yes... the Romans... and *you*!" The dagger she had returned to her forearm sheath reappeared just as quickly, and she brandished it at Yosef. "You've betrayed our people."

Yosef held both bloodied hands up, palms out. "No, Miriam. I've tried to help our people."

"You had to become a Roman to do that?" Miriam took two steps toward Yosef, who backed away toward the entry.

"I haven't become a Roman."

"Because of the Romans, thousands have died... more are dying now... and mother and father remain imprisoned, and there they suffer... if they have not already perished."

"Yohanan ben Levi has them, not the Romans. You told me that."

"Were it not for the Romans, men like Yohanan ben Levi and Simon bar Giora would not have come to Jerusalem. They would not have taken power and used it to heap even more misery on our people. And now our Temple burns...."

"I tried to get Yohanan ben Levi and his men to leave the Temple," Yosef said. "Titus would have let them—and he was reluctant to bring on a Roman assault. But the Gischalan would not listen... he and his men jeered at me and threatened me. I tried to stop him in Galilee and to convince Jerusalem's leaders not to provoke this war with the Romans."

"Yet when they freed you, you stayed with them."

"Free?" Yosef's harsh laugh echoed through the tunnel. "I'm not free and never will be." He stepped toward her, then back when she raised the knife.

"And never will I be free, either!" Miriam cried, tears channeling down her face as she suddenly felt herself melting. She felt her chin trembling as she said, "Never to be free from the shame of what Romans did to me."

"I believe whatever that disgrace is," the man's voice startled them both, "you deserve it." A dark figure separated from the shadowed entrance and moved upon them. In the moments it took him to close with them, she saw Zechariah's staff in one hand and in his other... a gleaming blade.

***

Yosef didn't see the blow from the staff that felled him. At the same instant, he glanced over his shoulder at the source of the voice; the staff struck the side of his head with a crack. He heard no sound, but his vision filled with jagged sparks as he fell. He felt the man brush past him and toward Miriam.

"You're a liar and a deceiver, Miriam," the man accused her.

Dazed, Yosef rolled to his knees, and a throbbing pain shot through his head so that he had to blink several times. He tried to focus on the man advancing on Miriam as she backed farther into the torchlight. He wondered at the man's words, sharp as the knife in his hand. The man dropped the staff, and his hand went to a pouch tied to his belt.

"I've never been paid... never been asked... to kill a woman. And I wouldn't have accepted that commission... I did not think there'd be any satisfaction in it for me. But for a woman who dresses as a man," he waved the dagger hand back and forth as if slashing her clothing, "it will please me." I've never taken an ear from a woman, either, but I will from you... perhaps even both of them... to add to my collection." The man stopped stroking the bag, and Yosef shuddered to think what must be inside it, and he watched the man draw a second blade from a sheath at his waist. "You lied to me, Miriam."

"To protect my family, I did, Hananiah, and to find out who threatens them and my people. I've done terrible things that have made me feel no better, though I thought they would. Still, they might have helped my people." Miriam's eyes widened as if she realized she had just used Yosef's own words, and she darted a look at him, then back to the man. She said, "Hananiah, you are far worse than me—you are nothing but a Roman tool. You serve Gessius Florus... but for money, not principle."

Miriam backed farther toward the torch, drawing the man with her, then she cried out, "You made me kill Ehud!" She launched at him, her remaining dagger flashing in a glittering horizontal arc.

The man ducked away from Miriam's slashing arm, straightened, and pinned her arm against his side, trapping her knife hand. She raked her fingernails down Hananiah's face, gouging furrows that quickly filled with blood, though she missed his eyes. She spun away from him, sweeping her leg to hook behind his, spilling him to the ground. She leaped upon him, thrusting with her knife. He blocked again, and his free blade cut across her upper chest, making a deep wound. Blood coursed down the front of her tunic. Tumbling away from him, she staggered to her feet.

As Hananiah charged after her, Yosef rolled and grabbed the wooden staff. He stumbled toward the man, raising the staff as Hananiah's over-and-under thrusts with both hands stabbed high and down, low and up, into Miriam's left chest. Impaled on the knives, held upright only by Hananiah's grip on them and on her, Miriam pressed her palm against her blood-soaked tunic. She splayed it flat on Hananiah's chest. "I'm not some woman who dresses as a man... I *am* 'The Hand.'" With what strength she had left, she shoved but could not move him.

Hananiah slid one dagger from Miriam's chest, flattening the blade along the side of her head, under her disheveled hair. "Now, I'll have that ear...."

Yosef brought the staff down hard across Hananiah's wounded shoulder, eliciting a cry as the wood snapped, breaking in half. Yosef grabbed his shoulders with both hands, wrestling him away from Miriam. Both men staggered as Yosef pried Hananiah's knife from his blood-slicked hand and brought the blade up and into Hananiah's throat.

As Hananiah fell, his unblinking eyes locked on Miriam. He tried to speak and choked on blood. His eyes lost their obsidian glint as they widened and dulled. Only then did Miriam collapse. Yosef caught her and lowered her to the ground as a shuddering gasp escaped her. He frantically tried to press his hand over the wounds to slow the blood pumping from her chest.

"No... no...." Miriam stopped him with a hand on his wrist. "Yosef, I cannot be saved... but you must save the others—Ya'el, Leah, Rachel, and a boy—Elian—that Ya'el brought with her to Jerusalem."

Yosef didn't tell her that Ya'el—Cleo—had disappeared. "Where are they?" he asked.

"In the gallery of the Great Sea cistern cavern. Tunnels to the cave... Hinnom Valley. Bucket-hoist chamber... water for the Temple." A spasm of pain shook her.

"The chamber below the end of this passage?"

"You remember." Miriam nodded and smiled weakly.

"Matthew and I went there when we were boys."

"You wouldn't let me...."

"You were too young and small."

"So long... I wish...." Miriam's breathing stuttered. "Leah still loves you... Rachel, too," Miriam rasped. "Save Matthew... find mother and father—save them if they live."

"I will." Yosef took her hand. Her breathing became labored, and her chest lurched with her breaths, not rising and falling smoothly and steadily. His tears fell upon her.

"Why, Yossi... why?" Miriam asked with a gurgling cough, propping herself on her elbow to plead with her eyes.

606

Final Siege

He knew what she meant. "Since my capture, I've done everything possible to stop this war." Yosef paused. There was too much to say and no time to say it. And it no longer mattered. "You told this man what you've done. Why?"

"Two Roman soldiers... raped me... you were in Rome. Almost destroyed me—I broke my betrothal. A good man—that's his staff... he saved me, taught me to defend... to fight. I've killed men who deserved it. And I," she choked on blood, "I killed Ehud—*he* was good!"

Miriam lay back and took two big, shuddering breaths, seeming to compose herself to speak. "Hananiah was a spy for Gessius Florus," she said in a monotone but clearly as if she wanted to make a last testament. "He forced Ehud to help him—threatened his family in Alexandria." Tears ran down Miriam's face as she looked from the ceiling to her brother's eyes. "Ya'el can tell you the story." Miriam exhaled. "I have been lost... so lost. I don't ask for forgiveness for all I've done...." She whispered, then, as if to herself, "Maybe just some understanding... for why I did it."

"That's all I ask, too..." Yosef said as he clasped her hand in his and closed his eyes against the tears that spilled from them. "You did what was right, Miriam. And no matter how much you hate me, I will always love you."

He felt her squeeze his hand.

"Yossi...."

He opened his eyes.

"Now I realize... I never stopped loving you." Another shudder wracked Miriam, and her cough sprayed blood. "Now go. Let me stay here where there are no Romans." A last gurgling breath wheezed from her, and her eyes remained fixed on him, their light gone.

Yosef laid his forehead on her shoulder and wept for all they had lost. After a while, the torch flickered, almost spent. With a deep sigh, he removed the blade from her chest, then carried her body to the ledge cut into the wall beside them and arranged her there. He placed her dagger in her hand and the two halves of the staff beside her. "Rest here, my sister. It is a fitting place for you... where our ancestral king was once laid. Find peace—you are free now."

CLXIV

Augustus 70 CE

Jerusalem

The Upper City, Tunnel Nexus

Nicanor turned toward the sound in the passageway that led toward the Temple Enclosure, still gripping his sword in one hand and a newly burning torch in the other. Yosef appeared in the guttering light of the nearly exhausted torch on the wall, dragging something heavy.

"I was about to search for you," Nicanor said. "I managed to find a new torch—compliments of one of those dead Thracians." Nicanor gestured behind him toward the passage to Antonia Fortress. "That one will take a dozen men a week to clear... if they can."

Then he saw the fresh blood all over Yosef and the grief in his expression—and his eyes went to the burden he was dragging—a body, face-down! "What happened... and who is that?"

Yosef let the leg drop. "The man who killed my sister. I couldn't leave him with her."

"What?" Nicanor went to the body, hooked a toe under it, and rolled it over. "Hananiah... the knifemaker," he said. "I grieve your loss. Miriam was valiant."

I killed him in return." Yosef went to the wall for the torch and held it high as he looked around the nexus. "Where's Matthew?"

"When I came back, he was gone. If you didn't see him... he must have gone that way." He pointed in the direction of the tunnel Gessius Florus had entered.

"He can get back into the Upper City that way," Yosef said, staring hard into the darkness. "Cleo and Florus went that way, too."

"I'm truly sorry about your sister." Nicanor kicked at the corpse. "And I'm also sorry about this... that we can't go after your brother... nor Cleo. Titus is assaulting the Temple as we speak"—he held his palm out and looked up to the rock ceiling. "Then he will move into the Upper City before sweeping through into the Lower City, and Jerusalem will finally fall."

Nicanor paused, then said, "Yosef, we must go," though his heart sank at the thought of abandoning Cleo. "I must make an appearance for Titus, and then, when the fighting lessens, we can search the city." When Yosef did not move, he stepped closer and gripped his shoulder. "There's nothing more we can do here."

"Yes, there is... leave me, and I'll do it alone."

* * *

THE GREAT SEA CISTERN CAVERN

"At least it's cooler here," Nicanor remarked, releasing the rope and rubbing his shoulder, trying to work the ache out of it but failing. He walked to where Yosef had descended first and now stood on the stone walkway bordering the massive water pool. He had drawn a bucket of water and used it to wash the worst of the blood from his face and arms, though there was no help for his tunic. Tucked in the sash at his waist were two new torches they had found above in the bucket-hoist room. Two more were secured at Nicanor's belt. Nicanor rinsed himself a little after taking great gulps of water from the bucket.

Yosef had been quiet since his last words in the tunnel nexus, silently nodding when Nicanor followed him into this place.

"This way," Yosef finally said, leading them with a torch on a circuit to where the stone border met hard-packed earth that bellied into a deep-set gallery. They moved carefully, but every sound was magnified. They paused three times to listen, and, on the third, Nicanor heard the sobbing of a woman. A few steps later, they came around the arc of a natural stone wall and saw ahead the flickering flames of a small fire.

The weeping woman knelt over another who lay beside the fire, and the kneeling woman stifled her sobs in alarm and struggled to her feet. "Elian... is that you... where have you been?" she asked, then drew back with a gasp as her eyes adjusted from the fire's light to stare at their torch.

Yosef lowered the torch from where he held it aloft and illuminated their faces so she could recognize him. "Rachel?" he said.

"Yo... Yosef?!" Rachel stammered, her hand going to her mouth as if to stop from saying his name. Then she wrung her hands, cried out "Yosef!" and rushed forward, stopping short before him.

Yosef put out a cautious hand of greeting with the formality Nicanor knew the Jews observed between men and women, and she, in her fervor, grasped it and held it to her face as she knelt before him. He raised her to her feet, and she reached out a hand to almost touch his smooth cheek, now cleansed of the dried blood.

"It is you," Rachel said in a whisper of unbelief.

"We're here to help you," Yosef said, gesturing toward the figure on the pallet by the fire. "Is that Leah? She sleeps?" He took a step toward the fire.

"She's been sick, Yosef," Rachel said, following him. "So sick." The sobs thickened again in Rachel's voice. "She barely breathes...."

Yosef knelt and touched the blanket. Even in the flickering firelight, he could see how pale Leah was, and she shook with chills, her cheeks sunken below dark-hollowed eyes. Her hands were clutched across her chest, barely moving with her shallow breaths.

"Leah." he leaned closer. "Leah," he whispered near her ear.

Eyelids fluttered, and Yosef heard her breath cross her lips.

"Leah, it's Yosef," he said. He rested his hand on her tightly-clenched fists. Her eyelids fluttered again and opened as her mouth moved, her lips quivering.

"You—you finally came for me." Her smile held for an instant, then faltered. A stronger tremor rippled through her.

Yosef's heart—the heart he thought could break no more—shattered. He dry-swallowed twice and finally mustered the words. "Yes, I finally came for you. I should never have left you to go to the Essenes. Should never have left you with Yonatan while I went to Rome nor when I went to fight in Galilee." The choices of the past cut into him with all their sharp edges and agony-filled consequences. All he had done had not prevented pain, suffering, and tragedy. No matter what he did, this war seemed destined to happen, and leaving the ones he loved to try to prevent it, then to fight in it, had only caused grief.

Leah's shaky hand lifted to touch his chin and caressed his face with her icy fingertips. As he began to sob, she pressed her hand on his. "Shhh... everything is now well," she said. "I got to see you again and to tell you...."

Her hand touching his relaxed.

"To tell you I love you." Her eyelids fluttered and closed. Beneath his hand, he felt her chest go still.

Rachel was beside him then, quietly arranging Leah's body and covering her face with a veil, even as Yosef kept his hand upon hers.

"Yosef," Nicanor called softly. "Yosef...."

Yosef rose from the dark well of his memories and regrets and heard Nicanor calling his name. "Yes."

"We must go now. We'll come back... the fighting will soon be over, and we'll come back."

Final Siege

Yosef looked up and thought about what he must do. He pressed Leah's hand and was about to stand when his fingers caught on a slender length of leather beneath her hand. Gently, he withdrew it until a small coin dangled before him. He knew it well...

"Ya'el returned that to her just before she and Miriam left," Rachel said. "They went to meet someone Miriam said she must settle with to free Matthew. Do you know? Have you seen Miriam and Ya'el... did they?"

CLXV

Augustus 70 CE

Jerusalem

Beneath the Temple Enclosure, The Great Sea Cistern Cavern

Nicanor partly answered when Yosef did not. "We saw them...." He noticed Yosef was absent, staring again at the coin on the cord. He stepped close to Rachel, who flinched from him at first but then took his offered hand to rise to her feet, and he assured her, "I meant what I said. I'm Yosef's friend, trying to help." The young woman nodded, and he continued. "When you heard us, you called out... that's the boy Cleo—Ya'el—brought with her to Jerusalem?"

Rachel said, "Yes. Elian was here when Miriam and Ya'el left... then later, I realized he had gone. Exploring, I think, though he's been warned not to." She looked down at Yosef, still gazing at the coin, and asked, "What's happened, Yosef? Where are Miriam and Ya'el?"

"Miriam's dead, and Ya'el's missing," Yosef said flatly.

"What?" Rachel looked with fright at Nicanor as her hand covered her mouth. Then she looked down at the back of Yosef's head, where he knelt next to Leah's body. "How?"

Yosef shook his head, and his chin dropped to his chest. A single drop of blood dripped from the gash at his brow and fell upon his hand.

Nicanor handed the torch to Rachel and stepped away from the fire, tipping his head back to sniff the air. "That smell is more than burning wood," he said. "The fire must be raging above us, and soon even mortar and bricks will collapse. This cavern could fill with smoke. We must go."

"What fire?" Rachel asked, her eyes filled with tears.

"The Temple burns," Yosef said as he stood at last, wiping at the blood trickling down his cheek.

With his eyes adjusted to the darkness now that Rachel held the torch, Nicanor could see tendrils of smoke wafting from the cistern area on a current of air, then gathering above them. "It will take time, but the air will become bad here." Yosef nodded.

"But," Nicanor pointed at Rachel, "we can't take her back the way we came—we would emerge from the tunnels into the fire and fighting."

Yosef shook his head. "We *must* return that way. I have to search for Matthew."

"The streets will be a chaos of killing, Yosef." Nicanor took a sterner tone. "I won't be able to protect *one* of you, much less two." Nicanor stepped closer to Yosef and said, "You need to get her somewhere safe. Try to find the boy and take them both to that cave in the Hinnom Valley. You said it could be reached from here."

Yosef stood unmoving and asked, "Then you'll come with us, and we can go into the city once Rachel, at least, is safe in the cave?"

"No," said Nicanor. "I'm the only one who can search for Cleo and your brother and have a chance at not getting killed." He paused until Yosef met his gaze. "Not only Romans will try to kill you."

"Can you find your way back?" Yosef asked.

"Yes," Nicanor assured him. "You said that tunnel from the nexus, the one Matthew and Cleo must have taken, leads to another and then into the Upper City?"

"Yes, to an alley within the agora."

Nicanor gripped Yosef's shoulder. "I'll do all I can to find them. And I will meet you at that cave in the Hinnom Valley at sundown tomorrow." Nicanor turned and lit a torch from Rachel's and strode away.

* * *

Yosef stood silent, gazing after Nicanor's torchlight until the growing smell of smoke and renewed sobbing stirred him. Rachel sat next to Leah's body, weeping again. He sat beside her, beginning to plan their way out of the place, waiting for Rachel's questions that were sure to come.

"What happened to Miriam?" Rachel asked, and Yosef knew her tears included mourning for his sister.

"Hananiah, the knifemaker, killed her, but I will not say more. Nicanor is right—we must go. Do you know the way to the passage Miriam used to reach the cave in the Hinnom Valley?"

Rachel nodded, wiping tears from her chin with her wrist. "She showed us." She pointed toward the darkest recess of the gallery.

"Then I'll search for the boy while you gather what food and blankets you have. Thankfully, there's plenty of water." Yosef took a deep breath and released it. "Once I find the boy—if I can do so quickly—you must both go to the cave and wait for Nicanor. You can trust he will keep you safe."

"But Yosef, your Roman friend, is right. You cannot go back to the streets of the city. You'll be killed by our people as easily as by the Romans!"

"I've failed Rachel. Our Temple is burning, Jerusalem is being destroyed, and my family... my family...." Yosef bowed his head into his open hands and murmured, "I should die with our people. I thought our Lord spoke to me, guiding me to save them. But they have not been saved. I must die defending Jerusalem, or they will see me only as a traitor."

Rachel gently pulled his hands from his face. "No, Yosef. No. This war—all that's happened—is not your fault. God's judgment was ordained. He used you to warn our people, just as He used Yirmiyahu and the Babylonians." She pressed Yosef's hand between her own. "You should not choose to die when you have a chance to survive. I am your family, too. I cannot make it alone, and I cannot bear to leave my sister here. Yosef, I need your help. I... I...," she stammered and then steadied her voice. "I love you as Leah loved you. Please don't leave me. Don't cast away your life. You must tell the world what happened here. Only you can do that."

She paused then, momentarily, and looked into his eyes with tears sparkling in hers. "We must hope to live so those we've lost can be remembered. Live that hope with me."

* * *

GAIUS AETERIUS FRONTO'S PRISON CAMP

After she fell, Cleo heard the legionaries joke in surprise after one of them reported he thought the archer was a woman. Another groped her breast to confirm it as he yanked the spear out of her.

But their bravado carried a bit of caution, too. A woman dressed as a man, a fighter, who attacked what seemed to be a Roman nobleman... that had startled them. She lay there praying Elian had gotten away. After a moment, one man shouted at the boy to stop, and then she heard the clank and clatter of an armored soldier running. She smiled—there was no way a man so encumbered would catch the racing, darting Elian. That comforted her despite the torture of the wound ripped open further when the spear was jerked from her chest.

Speak only Aramaic... don't give them an inkling you're Roman, she kept telling herself, willing her mind to control her body, her lips.

Gessius Florus might be dead—he was still sprawled not far from her—but he had men in the legions who served him. How else could he brazenly sneak into a city under siege? Those men might still want to collect the bounty if they could dress his wounds and keep him alive. But she would rather die as Ya'el—as a slave—than be taken as Lady Cleo, the "treasonous" wife of Gessius Florus. She prayed he was a dead man who could not pay the reward.

Then two legionaries pulled her to her feet, and a lightning bolt of pain shot through her chest where torn muscles could not support her, and everything blurred and dimmed. Then went black.

She had awaked here—where... she didn't know—among the sporadic screams and constant crying of hundreds of women. Her head swam, and she vomited, though nothing was in her stomach but bile. Its bitterness gushed and frothed out of her as she turned to spew the poison to one side. It pooled around her head and shoulder, mingling with blood flowing from her side. As she gagged, she kept thinking, *Speak only Aramaic... you're not a Roman, not a Roman.*

She sensed someone leaning over her and opened her eyes. A shape... then it resolved in her vision to a woman with a scattered haystack of hair and a soiled face lined by the tracks of tears. The woman had a small knife, but Cleo could not flinch away from it—her agonized muscles had frozen. The knife bit into her chest, and then she felt a current of air as her tunic was cut open. Then the woman pressed her hand into the center of Cleo's agony, and a scream broke from her lips, and all went black again.

CLXVI

Augustus 70 CE

Jerusalem

Beneath the Temple Enclosure, The Upper City

The smoke got thicker, with the weight of full-bellied rain clouds sinking slowly toward the ground as Nicanor prepared to climb. These gray billows carried the smell of death. He pulled free his undertunic and cut a swath that he wetted in the pool and wrapped around his face covering his nose and mouth. Heat radiated down as he climbed through fumes into the bucket-hoist room. Above him, the hoist was smoldering. Coughing, he moved swiftly across the chamber and up the steps into the passage leading to the nexus. There the air was clearer, and the smoke thinned as it wafted on a current through the tunnel to the agora.

Many minutes later, Nicanor sucked in a deep breath of relatively fresh air. Then cursed the thorns that scratched his arms as he disentangled himself from the bush over the trap door. But a pall of smoke grew overhead here, too, and not just from the burning temple... other parts of the city were also blazing.

Nicanor paused before plunging into the chaos of the city. *I must be crazed*, he thought. *How can I hope to find Cleo... or Matthew?* What could he expect to report to Yosef at sunset the next day? And that assumed some surviving rebels did not come upon him alone and cut him down. Or some anxious legion archer put a shaft or two into him before he could speak.

But he put his head down and struck into the street, pushing aside the other troubling thought—how would he explain his absence to Titus? Still, he could not live with himself if he did not try. He had little hope of finding Yosef's brother... but had sworn to save Cleo. If only he could find her.

* * *

The market was eerily devoid of fighting. Bodies were strewn everywhere, the cries of the wounded, and the coppery odor of fresh-spilled blood evidence that fierce combat had only recently subsided. Many of the dead were legionaries and auxiliaries. *The Jews fight to the end*, he thought as he entered a residential area. He heard farther on the cacophony of active fighting ringing through the far streets deep within Jerusalem's affluent district. He tried to recall where Yosef's family lived. He had been there only once, at the Jewish Passover over four years before, soon after Gessius Florus had become the Procurator of Judea, bringing Cleo with him. And that was just before Florus began the killing that escalated into the war. He cast an eye at the sky, leaden gray with only streaks of blue. *Gods, grant that if I cannot kill him for what he's done... some rebel has found the bastard and cut him down already.*

Nicanor thought he recognized the street of Yosef's family home—the place to try first. Cleo might seek refuge there... or make it her last stand. He hated considering what he might find in that house that had offered him such warm hospitality a few years before. He held back as a group of armored legionaries, heavy infantry, moved into one of the broader avenues. As the sounds of their movement faded, he heard no more belligerent shouts of defiance nor curses at the Roman soldiers. He heard only the screams of pain from the dying and the moans of those whose deaths would come more slowly.

The bodies here numbered far more Jewish than Roman and seemed so odd piled around the entries to the elaborate Jewish homes. It was like a mass of flotsam and jetsam had washed ashore after the storm of the legion passed through. Nicanor saw a fallen man outside one gate whose appearance was unlike the others on either side. Wearing battered armor, the man carried a shield riven nearly in half and still held a notch-bladed sword, though his bare head had been nearly cleaved from his shoulders. Next to him lay a boy.

Nicanor stooped over the body, which was quite still and bore a wicked blood-crusted gash across the face. He seemed tall for the age the boy Elian was supposed to be, but then he would have been thin, too. His tunic and arms were covered in dried blood, and he seemed just another corpse among the piles of corpses. But then Nicanor saw a bit of green at his neck—a twisted cord with green feathers. He squatted to touch the cord and study it more closely.

"Parrot feathers..." he muttered. *What was that damn bird's name...?* The boy's eyes flew open. *"Futuo!"* Nicanor rocked back on his heels.

* * *

The boy leaped up to flee down the street, but Nicanor called out, "Cleo!" and the boy stopped. "Is she safe?" Nicanor asked.

The boy stood trembling, the urge of wild flight still in his eyes.

"I'm her friend—I'm Nicanor," he said. "You are Elian, right?"

Those words brought a smile, and the boy beckoned him inside the home—Nicanor had remembered the right one.

Nicanor had expressed concern over Elian's wound, and the boy soon found a sealed, baked-clay jar of water and a clean cloth he held out to the Roman on the strength of their shared friends. Nicanor tried to be gentle but had little experience tending to a child's injury. Still, the boy stoically withstood the work with the wet cloth to clean his crusted face and not break open the wound. As he finished and had the boy rest against the dusty cushions on a bench, he asked what he knew or remembered about what had happened.

"Some soldiers took Cleo—she is my mother now."

Nicanor's heart lurched at the pitiable confidence of the boy, but still, perhaps there was still a chance...

"They laughed when they saw she was a woman, saying she'd fetch a good price if she lived. One said, 'Fronto's slave camp.' I remembered the name so someone could find her."

"That was good, Elian," Nicanor said. "You took good care—"

"I couldn't save her, though. She made me run—called out to me to run! So I did. I had nowhere else to go and came here to find Eleasar leaving. He was looking for us."

"Eleasar? Who is that?" And then Nicanor, at the sight of the boy knuckling away a tear, asked quietly, "The man outside?"

Elian nodded miserably. "Eleasar ben Ananias was a soldier—a captain—at the Temple. He was Matthew's friend and helped us. When the Romans came on this street, he told me to lie still and pretend to be dead until nightfall. Then try to find a place to hide." The boy's eyes were wide, his face pale but for the dark, bloody wound. "But there's nowhere to hide."

"You will come with me... I'll keep you safe... safe as I can." For nowhere was really safe, and the boy knew it. He handed the boy the rinsed-out cloth and pantomimed that he should wipe the blood from his hair.

"What will we do now?" Elian asked.

"I'm going to save Cleo, too—*we* are." Nicanor smiled to give the little fellow some courage. He needed more than a boy's help but did not know if he would receive it.

CLXVII

Augustus 70 CE

Jerusalem

The Roman Encampment

The camp thrummed like a nest of hornets with an air of victory. Nicanor had caught snatches of men talking about the upcoming release of the legions... since there were no more walls to breach... nor significant strongholds to take. And so many spoils to be found in the Jews' houses in the Upper City! Even the lowest rank soldiers had found bounty.

Only a few men were in the area of the staff officer quarters, and none noticed Nicanor as he led the boy toward his tent, his hand on the scruff of Elian's neck for show. The boy came willingly once he understood he could hide here in the one place Nicanor could keep him safe. Inside the tent, Nicanor rummaged among the stores and then handed Elian a packet of dried fruit and a skin of water. "You must stay here until I return," he said. "If you hear men outside, hide under that cot." He pointed as he went to Yosef's small writing table, took out a sheet of parchment and pen, wrote a rough note, and signed it. "If anyone comes here, this tells them you are my property." At the flash of alarm and anger in the boy's eyes, he held up a hand and said, "I'm saying that to protect you. You're not my slave, Elian. But you must stay here. Understand?"

The boy nodded. Nicanor closed the tent flap behind him. Now he had to convince Titus to grant him a choice of slaves.

* * *

Titus's Command Tent

The aide outside Titus's tent told Nicanor while he awaited admittance that the general had calmed since returning from the temple attack and witnessing its burning. A calm reception would not make Nicanor's request easier, but it did make it more likely to be considered.

"General," Nicanor said, announcing himself rather than beginning a request. He planted himself squarely in front of Titus's campaign desk.

"Tribunus... you saw what happened at the Jews' temple?" A slight frown creased Titus's face, just as Nicanor had seen in Vespasian.

"Yes, General. I was there." *That was true, after all, even if I was underground.*

"I did not want that." Titus shook his head. "Was Yosef with you to see it?"

"Yes, General... it was hard for him."

"Where is he?"

Nicanor carefully drew a deep breath, trying to conceal his need to gain composure. "During the fighting, Yosef spotted a cousin, and I took it upon myself to see her safe. He is with her now." He prayed Titus would not ask more and offered a distraction: "I must congratulate you on this victory, General."

Titus paused, squinting up at him. "There is more to do," he said, glancing at a scroll of vellum he'd spread flat before him. He tapped the lines in its middle. "I've ordered the capture of the two most prominent rebel leaders... Yohanan ben Levi and Simon bar Giora. This Simon, in particular, for his defeat of the 12th Legion at Beth Horon." He paused as if waiting for Nicanor to comment. When he did not, he tapped again. "And now we must take everything of value from this city."

"What then, General... afterward?" Nicanor had heard mutterings of what he would answer, suggestions from Tiberius Alexander. He regretted that it would hurt Yosef further.

"I will level Jerusalem, leaving only a few structures, to show its former scale. Then all will recognize Rome's might in reducing such a city to rubble."

Titus's frown eased as it seemed he had a more pleasant thought. "Then I will return to Rome... and join my father."

It was the right moment. "General," Nicanor said, "with this campaign ending, I wish to retire." His voice was steady. "If I have been of good service to you and your father, I ask a single reward." Nicanor saw a hint of the scowl return but not harden nor linger as Titus nodded.

Good. I have not pushed too far. Not yet.

"You've served Rome, my father, and me well. What do you ask for?"

Some of the tension drained away from Nicanor. "Thank you, General. That one thing... my choice of two persons from the captured who will be sold as slaves. I wish to take them with me into retirement."

Titus studied Nicanor long enough for concern to grip him again. Then the general let the scroll curl back into a cylinder, set it aside, and slid a blank sheet of parchment before him. He reached for a pen and an ink jar and slid closer a small pot of red wax warming in its holder over a tiny flame. "Very well," he said. Titus wrote, signed, and then tipped a blob of wax beneath his signature. He pressed his seal into it. The general studied Nicanor again while he let it set and cool, then handed him the authorization. "You and Yosef join me tomorrow at my evening meal," he said.

"Yes, General." As Nicanor left, he prayed Yosef would be in that cave in the Hinnom Valley tomorrow to meet as planned. He wished he could go straight to Gaius Fronto's prison camp and find Cleo. But it must be first thing in the morning when he was sure Lord Fronto was there to accept the document Titus had just given him. As tired as he was, he knew he would not sleep.

CLXVIII

Augustus 70 CE

Northeast of Jerusalem

Gaius Aeterius Fronto's Prison Camp

When Nicanor arrived at the camp, the sun had just cleared the mountains to the east. He had impatiently watched it rise higher as he waited for the *tesserarius* to return from presenting his authorization from Titus to Gaius Fronto. Yosef had mentioned to Nicanor that the scorching desert winds came with September; he could feel that now. The month would not cool until the beginning of the *Tishri*, the early fall rains. Now that wind was a wave of heat as it lifted, billowed, and twisted Nicanor's cloak. He wished for that rain. After turning his tail into the wind, Albus stood stoically with more patience than Nicanor felt. He patted the horse's neck, wiped sandy grit from his eyes, and sweated. The gusts did little to dry him.

"Tribunus."

Nicanor looked up from shielding his eyes to see the guard sergeant. "Yes?" he said, and the man looked irritated. No doubt, Fronto was not pleased with giving up prisoners that would have brought revenue for the empire and himself. And the nobleman must have made his feelings known by berating the bearer of the order from Titus. Or maybe the man was still angry, with the rest of the 12th Legion, for getting restricted duty as camp guards. There was little reward in that... and the city was now laid bare before them for the looting.

"I'm to escort—"

Nicanor's glower changed his words. "I'm to accompany you while you make your... selection."

"Then take me to the women's section." Nicanor challenged the man's leer with an even fiercer glare.

* * *

"This is the last of them," the *tesserarius* said, waving his hand at a group of about a hundred women, some walking shakily, others kneeling, caring for the women lying on the ground. Nicanor had underestimated how difficult finding Cleo would be. There were thousands of women prisoners, and after a long time searching, he had begun to despair.

Nicanor moved slowly, his gaze sweeping over the faces and forms, studying each woman who flinched and did not meet his probing gaze. Just as his heart fell into the pit of his stomach, he found her. Cleo lay on a thin, soiled blanket that served her little better than the ground. Given her condition, they had not shackled her, and Nicanor was thankful for that. The thought of Cleo in chains had tumbled through his head all night. He had dreaded the idea that that might be his first sight of her. Her eyes were closed, and her face pale with a sweat sheen Nicanor hoped meant any fever had broken. She still wore men's garb though her tunic had been slit open in the front, revealing a band of cloth over her breasts. Someone had pulled aside the tunic to bare her shoulders. Her ribs showed so prominently that he was shocked by the pain of it, more so than at the crude, bloody bandage over her upper chest.

Nicanor waved at the *tesserarius* to step away and knelt beside her. "Ya'el," he whispered and checked the distance to guard. "Cleo..." He touched her hand. Her eyelids fluttered, and her eyes half-opened. A scum of dried spittle separated as her lips parted.

"Nicanor... is it really you?"

Nicanor felt a fist grip his heart. The last time he had been this close to her was in the port taberna in Ptolemais so long ago. Since then, his vision of her had become what he most often saw when he hoped for his life after the legion when he no longer served the empire. Instead, he would serve himself and whomever he chose to be with him. He did not know if Cleo would be that woman or if he could ever ask her to join him. She was a Roman noblewoman, yet she could not return to that life as long as Gessius Florus threatened her. But what Nicanor wanted did not matter. What did Cleo want? He dared not hope...

All that mattered was saving her life. "I'm getting you from here to someplace safe where you'll be taken care of." He got his arms under her and gently lifted, feeling a twinge from the old wound in his thigh. Surprised at how light she was, he ignored the throbbing and willed his knee to hold. He stood, cradling her against his chest. Cleo smothered a cry of pain that hurt him more than did the ache of old wounds.

The guard sergeant watched him, puzzled. "You choose some scrawny, wounded Jewess... when there are others more comely, healthy enough for—" The man stopped at Nicanor's scowl. Instead, he asked: "What about the other—the second slave you are to choose?

"Another day..." Nicanor said, though there never would be another. He never wanted to see the squalor of a prison camp again. He brushed past the guard—he needed to get Cleo to a *medicus* and settled safely with Elian. His document from Titus now protected them both. And then, he must go to the Hinnom Valley for Yosef and return in time to meet Titus.

CLXIX

Augustus 70 CE

Jerusalem

Near the Hinnom Valley

Nicanor stopped at the pool where Celsus Evander's men had stashed the food they had drawn for Yosef's sister when she'd been at the cave in the Hinnom Valley. Rachel would have to remain there alone, hidden until the fighting was over. He could protect only Cleo and Elian, and Yosef must return with him to meet with Titus. Albus shook his head, throwing off wisps of dust from his mane as Nicanor secured the bag of provisions and a large waterskin to his saddle and mounted. "Now, my friend... let's go get Yosef."

As he rode, Nicanor's mind was crowded with worries about Cleo. Returning to the encampment with her, he had found a crusty old infantry cohort medicus nearing retirement. The man nursed a shoulder wound that prevented him from joining the units scouring the city for wounded soldiers to treat—but really for taking their booty. Nicanor sensed the man's frustration was more about missing out on the looting than his desire to be in action.

The medicus had looked at Cleo's unconscious form, shook his head, and turned away. The man changed his mind when Nicanor gripped his bad shoulder—hard—and pulled him back toward Cleo. Persuaded by Nicanor's glare and his ready grip on the blood-crusted pugio sheathed at his waist, the man examined her, particularly the nasty shoulder wound. Further swayed by the coins Nicanor took from a pouch sewn into his broad belt, he treated Cleo more gently as he inspected the work of the blade.

After a few minutes, the medicus wiped his hands on a cloth and turned to him, saying, "I've cleaned the wound, but it's too inflamed and swollen to stitch. It looks like a spear puncture, but whoever pulled it out of her was as savage as the one who threw it. He ripped her a fair gash, for legion spear tips go in easier than they come out. The swelling's got to come down, then you need to get someone to close the wound."

The man eyed the coins in Nicanor's hand and took a stack of strips of folded cloth and a cured-hide bag from the table. "Keep the wound covered with compresses of cool water and vinegar." He shook the bag, and it sloshed. "She's too thin.... I've seen many that thin dead in the city, without a scratch on them, starved to death. Some of the carcasses were cut up like wild boar for the cooking." The man grimaced and shook his head.

Nicanor understood his meaning. He had heard the reports of the weakest becoming food for the starving, who were willing to do anything to live. The medicus blinked as if clearing that vision from his eyes as he took the coins. "If there's more of these," he jingled the coins in his hand, "when the swelling's down, bring her to me, and I'll stitch her up." He took a small packet from the table and handed it to Nicanor. "For pain... but be careful... she's so weak. Too much could kill her. Try to get some food into her."

Nicanor nodded, took the packet and tucked it in his belt, slung the skin bag of vinegar over his shoulder, placed the stack of bandages on Cleo's stomach, her tunic folded over them, and carried her away.

He entered and gently placed Cleo on his cot in his tent. Seeing Elian asleep underneath, he thought, *the boy has his wits about him and feels safer there, probably wise to do.* He woke him and noticed he still clutched a dried fig. The boy's joy at seeing Cleo faded as she feebly muttered, not acknowledging him. Nicanor mixed a small portion of the pain medicine in broth, and Cleo swallowed some. At the small desk, he had added to the note he'd left with Elian that Cleo was also his possession, as decreed by General Titus. He gave Elian some broth and old soldier's biscuits and made him repeat his instructions about the compresses.

"I do not want to leave you and... Ya'el, Elian, but I must. I will return in the evening." He repeated that if anyone came to the tent and found him and Cleo, Elian should show them his note referencing Titus's decree and protection. Nicanor prayed that would be enough.

* * *

OUTSIDE THE CITY WALL, APPROACHING THE ROMAN ENCAMPMENT

With twilight growing, Nicanor had not spent long at the cave in Hinnom Valley. He was thankful that the news about finding Cleo seemed to stir Yosef, who had agreed that keeping Rachel safe meant her staying in the cave and waiting for them to return. Rachel had cleaned Yosef's wound and rinsed the blood from his hair. Nicanor had brought clean clothes for Yosef to make him presentable enough to dine with Titus.

Nicanor would get them back to the tent in camp so he could put on his *tribunus* regalia, perhaps for the last time.

Yosef had been silent behind him on the ride from the cave. Nicanor tried again to lift his friend from his sorrow by speaking practically. He spoke over his shoulder. "While you dressed, I talked with your cousin. She asked me to keep a close eye on you—said you were talking about returning to the city and dying with your people." Nicanor waited for a reply, then continued. "I'm glad you did nothing foolish. I have no idea what I would tell Titus if you didn't return."

"I'm not a fool, Nicanor," Yosef finally spoke.

"I know you're not. But you are grieving and angry, and that can make men do desperate things—make rash decisions. I cannot imagine how you feel, and I'm sorry, my friend, for all that's happened to you and your family. But there is still good you can do."

Yosef shook his head and pointed over Nicanor's shoulder at the macabre forest that had sprung up outside Jerusalem's once mighty walls. Hundreds of cross-beamed wooden shafts rose from the ground. Legionaries and *immunes*, legion workmen, pulled from their wagons the timber they had reclaimed and repurposed from the barrier surrounding and sealing the city. They affixed cross-beams to the long shafts, then took prisoners—defeated men, people of Jerusalem—from a long line and mounted them to the crosses. Some screamed others were silent, either stoic or beyond feeling fresh pain.

"What good can I do, Nicanor?" Yosef asked as they moved through the spreading thicket of suffering men.

Nicanor's eyes swept ahead and noted that some of the workmen, done for the day, had begun to turn toward the city and the encampment. He turned Albus toward a man just ahead, seemingly one of the newest crucifixions. He felt Yosef lower his head, but Nicanor looked up. The man hanging from the cross-beam was silent but alive. His eyes flared with agony and rage as he stared down at them. Nicanor said over his shoulder to Yosef, "Titus told me he did not want your temple burned. I think he regrets that—and all the suffering of your people."

"Why are you telling me this, Nicanor?" Yosef asked, gripping Nicanor's shoulder as if to demand an answer.

"Because I think Titus's feelings can be used. There is more good that you—we—can do." Nicanor gestured and looked up at the man above them. Yosef's eyes followed his.

"Matthew!"

CLXX

Augustus 70 CE

Jerusalem

The Roman Encampment, Titus's Quarters

Titus pushed his plate away and waved the attendants to clear the table. His plate and Nicanor's were mostly empty, but Yosef's was untouched. They had spoken little beyond a greeting when they arrived for the meal. Titus had studied Yosef through the brief meal. *Yes, keep watching him,* Nicanor thought.

At the feet of Matthew on the cross, a frantic Yosef had tried to climb up and release him, but Nicanor had stopped him before the approaching legionaries, swords out, got to the scene. Nicanor had ordered them away, then shook Yosef by the shoulders and made him listen: "You must use your head. Matthew is tied to the cross, not nailed. He'll likely survive another day or more. When we meet with Titus, do not plead with him. Rather, use silence to draw out his thoughts and then use his engagement with you, his concern for you, to persuade him to save your brother."

Nicanor knew Titus's remorse at the despoiling of Jerusalem for the enrichment of the soldiers and the empire might soften him to Yosef's plight. So much gold was being taken from Jerusalem that the glut made it lose half its value with the traders and bankers in Antioch. The value would soon climb again, and Vespasian would be pleased with all that had been added to the empire's coffers. So Titus had done well for the empire. Perhaps now he could do good for one from whom everything had been taken. And both Titus and his father respected Yosef, someone who could write of this rebellion and record the events of father and son—emperor and general—who had won such a victory for Rome.

"In my father's latest letter," Titus said, breaking the quiet, "he asks about you, Yosef. Asks how goes your writing and documenting—"

"Of the siege and the destruction of my city? Does he want to hear that Roman commanders sacrificed to their legion standards in the Temple, in our Holy of Holies, before it was destroyed?"

Final Siege

That's too strong a start, my friend, thought Nicanor, who tried to catch Yosef's eye. The sting of that barb showed in Titus's frown. He said, "Even now, the rebels and your priests refuse to surrender, though I offer to spare their lives. They suffer the consequences of their decision. Still, I did not wish your Temple destroyed, Yosef. Before the fire grew too great, I entered myself and witnessed some of its grandeur. Why would Rome avenge itself on a building? Why destroy a magnificent structure whose presence as part of the empire would accrue glory for Rome? Such a loss...."

Yosef bowed his head, then raised it to meet Titus's gaze. "That is what I will record, Lord Titus... I will write of the opportunities you gave the rebels to surrender and save Jerusalem and its people from all this destruction and suffering. Please tell Emperor Vespasian, Lord Titus, that recording the past—what's happened during this war—is my value for the future." Yosef glanced at the fabric ceiling of the tent and then at Nicanor and said, "What is that Roman saying, Nicanor? *Vae victis*... woe to the vanquished. The conquered are at the mercy of the conquerors." Nicanor nodded his understanding and was relieved to see Titus's expression had eased.

"My father is very interested that the story of this rebellion is told fairly," Titus said and settled back, raising his cup of wine.

Nicanor nodded as Yosef sipped from his cup. There was his opening.

"Speaking of mercy, Lord Titus, Nicanor told you of my cousin he helped save. I ask your favor to grant her an additional kindness... and extend it to other family members I've found. History will speak well of your graciousness."

Titus leaned forward and asked, "Other family... those close to you?"

"My brother is one of the newly crucified. I saw him as I came here this very evening. He is alive... as are some of the others with him. I'd like to save him—and them—from such a death. And, if you allow it, Lord Titus, I'd like your protection to go where the rebel leader Yohanan ben Levi imprisoned my father and mother to see if they live."

"This man, Yohanan ben Levi, confined your parents? Why?"

"Partly because I protested the rebellion and the war, and he was for it all. He made me out to be a traitor to anyone in Jerusalem who would listen. But he did it mostly because I was against him personally. I thought he sought leadership in Galilee to enrich himself... not help Galileans."

Titus sat back and steepled his fingers, resting his fingertips against his chin. "Come to my command tent tomorrow morning, the first hour after dawn. I will let you know my decision."

* * *

Next morning

NEARING TITUS'S COMMAND TENT

Yosef had been alarmed at Cleo's condition when Nicanor let him see her after the meal with Titus. Nicanor must have known he'd have difficulty getting Yosef to the general's tent once Yosef saw how wounded and ill she was, so he sent him on to wait there while he went to the tent to put on his formal clothing.

When they returned to the tent after the dinner, silent in their mutual prayers and hopes that Titus would rule in Matthew's favor, in support of Yosef's search for his parents, Elian had reported that Cleo had not wakened fully in the hours Nicanor was away and had managed to drink only a little water. Nicanor calmed Yosef with assurance of the care she had received and showed him how to apply the vinegar and give her a dose of the medicine.

When he rose at dawn, Yosef had insisted Nicanor stay with Cleo, and he would meet Titus alone. He prayed to Jehovah, who seemed so distant now that the meeting with the general would yield a way to save his family.

He heard cursing and turned to see if the imprecations were intended for him, just as he realized it was only because the siege was over that it was quiet enough in the camp to hear simple curses. The boiling, pent-up tumult of the camp had been released by the ending of the siege. The fighting now moved inside, into the Lower City. Those rebels who did not fight fled to hide in tunnels, sewers, and the ravines of the Tyropeon Valley.

Yosef stood and watched as the four cursing men passed him, struggling to bear the grand menorah from the Temple. Made of 100 pounds of pure gold, the base and lampstand—five feet tall and three feet wide—had been hammered from a single lump of the precious metal. Attached to its shaft were six branches. Seven lamps topped the six branches and main stem, with nine flowers, eleven knobs, and 22 ornamental goblets. The lampstand was first written about in the *Shemot* within the *Torah*, and the Jewish people were forbidden to replicate its design that came directly from Jehovah.

Final Siege

The four men delivered the treasure to Titus's tent just ahead of Yosef, and he followed to the tent that now held the precious thing that his people had lost.

CLXXI

Augustus 70 CE

Jerusalem

The Roman Encampment, Nicanor, and Yosef's Tent

Nicanor stepped from the tent to see who called for him. "Celsus!" he cried, glad to see his friend. "Why are you here?"

The tall commander strode toward him. "I'm to meet with the legion quartermasters to coordinate moving siege equipment to Caesarea. Then we'll send most of it on to Alexandria and Antioch." Celsus gripped Nicanor's hand. "General Titus told me you've requested your retirement!"

"It's time—I have things to do that I cannot do in the legion."

"What things?"

"Come inside," Nicanor waved him into the tent.

"What is this?" Celsus stared at Elian, who was trying to change the compress on Cleo as she tossed fitfully on the cot. "You found her!"

"That is part of what I must do. Cleo and the boy are now my responsibility."

Celsus shook his head, dumbfounded. "I also have a message from Marinus for you."

"Is he still in Caesarea, then? What is the message?"

"Yes, he's on the *Egeria*. He asked me to tell you he has news but must share it in person."

"Is his daughter with him?"

"Yes."

"Then I'll return to Caesarea with you and bring Lady Cleo and the boy. The Lady is not getting better, and Anyte is a skilled healer.

"What will become of Yosef?"

"Titus will protect him... he may even save Yosef's brother. I've done all I can for my friend. I must care for Cleo now... and the boy. Can you settle what you must today and be ready to leave at sunrise tomorrow? I need your help to make it an easy journey for her."

Celsus studied the pale, thin figure breathing shallowly on the cot. Nicanor realized the man found it hard to see the Roman noblewoman she once was. But to Nicanor, Cleo was always as she had been when he first saw her aboard the *Salacia* years before.

"This evening, I'll send a woman to bathe her for you," Celsus said. Nicanor saw in the sad shake of his head and the shifting of his eyes that he doubted Cleo would arrive in Caesarea alive. "I'll prepare a wagon and litter for her and come for you at dawn."

* * *

That evening...

Yosef reported soberly, quietly so as not to waken Cleo, but with deep gratitude, "Titus allowed me to save my brother, and even some of the others crucified with him. He ordered ten heavy infantrymen under the command of one of his guard officers to escort me into the Upper City, to where Yohanan ben Levi held his prisoners. There were dozens of dead inside and several still alive, my mother and father with them, hiding among the dead. One of Yohanan ben Zaccai's followers had stayed and tended to my parents, managing to find water and a little food for them. They are weak but live. I've asked Titus if they could receive his protection, too, and when they are healthy enough... travel to join Yohanan ben Zaccai in Yavneh. He has agreed."

"I am grateful for this news, Yosef, amid so much death and destruction." Nicanor clasped his friend's shoulders. "But I have news that saddens me. I must leave you. I take Cleo and Elian to Caesarea to Anyte, Marinus's daughter, tomorrow morning. I can trust her to save Cleo." He felt a pang at the crestfallen look that spread over Yosef's face and clouded the spark of joy that had been there a moment before. "I will speak with Titus this evening," Nicanor said, "asking for my immediate release from duty pending retirement and telling him I must go. But we will surely see you soon in Caesarea."

CLXII

SEPTEMBER 70 CE

CAESAREA

THE PORT, ONBOARD THE *EGERIA*

Nicanor knocked on the cabin door, and when it opened, he announced, "Yosef is here! I can hear the arrival up there"—he cast his eyes to the ceiling of the cabin below deck. The flash of Cleo's smile, wan as it was, lifted his heart, and he helped her rise and go out to see their friend.

When Anyte first saw Cleo on board the *Egeria*, the healer looked stricken and immediately ordered all she needed to tend to her patient. Saving Cleo had been a close call, for the infection proved stubborn, and Anyte complained that Cleo did not fight to live.

Nicanor had taken charge of Elian, who had recovered quickly, as a child does, with good food. Both man and boy took tender care of Cleo the whole way, but once they'd arrived at the ship and turned Cleo over to Anyte, the boy started chattering and seemed never to come to an end of it. Nicanor's head hurt at all the words—questions about where they would live, plans for things they would do, and food they would eat. And he insisted they get another parrot and tell it about Cicero... whose memory must be honored.

When the boy was occupied with Marinus, learning all the old captain wanted to teach him about the ship, Nicanor took his place by Cleo as she slept. He held her hand and promised he would always protect her. Finally, he told her she must get better soon so that he could keep a last vow in Rome.

Yosef had often told Nicanor that words mattered, so it seemed for Cleo. Care and companionship had helped to kindle the spirit still within her. Anyte's treatment had quelled the infection. She had trimmed the wound's edges—a painful operation—to close it without a terrible scar. Little by little, Cleo stayed awake more, ate soups and broth, and gained strength. She had gained weight and spent part of each day on deck, enjoying the cool breeze on the water. The cargo vessels loaded with siege equipment had sailed—some for Alexandria, others to Antioch—so the port was quiet.

Final Siege

On deck, Marinus's sailors had erected a screen to provide a pleasant place for Cleo—away from the stares of other sailors and wastrels. And there, the sailors were setting out a table laden with food, amphoras of wine, and pitchers of beer—suitable for a celebration. Elian was already at the food as Yosef stood bemused, watching the boy gobble fruit.

"I think he will always be hungry," Cleo remarked as Nicanor brought her to Yosef. She gently pushed Nicanor's supporting arm away and laughed, drawing her robe tighter around her, its hem whipping in the breeze. As with the reappearance of her smile, the return of the song-sound quality of her voice—long lost once she married Gessius Florus—made Nicanor smile.

Nicanor could see some of the terrible weight Yosef had borne for so long lift for a moment. But there were still the vestiges of a haunted look in his eyes despite the smile that broke out as he saw them.

"Cleo... you look well!" He hurried to take her hand and clasped Nicanor hard on the shoulder with his other hand. "You too, my friend!"

Cleo grew serious. "I'm so sorry for your losses, Yosef. Miriam became my best friend, and I will never forget her. She and all your family did so much for Elian and for me. And Leah, too... I know how you loved her and that she loved you as much in return."

In her words, Nicanor detected her fondness for Yosef. But there was no longer the note of love evident in Ptolemais years before, where Yosef had been held after his capture. Long ago, when Emperor Nero had directed Nicanor to show the Judean some of the might of the Roman army, Yosef commented, "Conquest has built your empire." Yosef explained that though he admired much about Rome, "Any war destroys." And Rome had had a hand in many wars. "War brings death—not just to people, but to a people's beliefs, identity and spirit."

The Judean war of rebellion had also destroyed the love once there between his friends. They had changed, and so had he. Nicanor walked to the table, poured a mug of beer, and sat next to Elian, then Cleo and Yosef joined them. "How are Matthew and your parents?" Cleo asked.

"They are better, much stronger. Soon they will be able to join Yohanan ben Zaccai."

"Your letters say that you have become Titus's chief spokesperson with the Jews who remain around Jerusalem and throughout Judea," Nicanor said. "When will Titus leave Judea to its procurator and return to Rome?"

"Likely not for some time," Yosef said with a sigh. "And there will be little left to call my birthplace. Yohanan ben Levi finally climbed out of the sewers. They found Simon bar Giora hiding among thousands of bodies in King Solomon's quarry. He surrendered dressed in robes of white and purple as if he were a ruler of some importance. Titus just ruled they would be sent to Rome to meet their fate. And he ordered what's left of the city razed. Only the towers Phasaelus, Hippicus, and Mariamne will remain. But Titus does not understand that my people will not forget Jerusalem as the heart of their nation even if a thousand years or more were to pass by. Once, long ago, our people went into captivity under another king. One of us wrote a psalm vowing we would never forget, for Jerusalem is our greatest joy."

The sad words hung in the air as a silence grew around them, finally to be broken by the cry of seagulls soaring over. "And what *is* the fate the two rebel leaders who brought so much suffering?" Cleo asked.

"The Gischalan will be imprisoned for life... I don't know where. Maybe in Rome, since Titus has ordered that Simon bar Giora be taken there for execution before the Roman people."

Nicanor grunted. "That's because he led the rebels who defeated us, the 12th Legion, at Beth Heron and stole its *aquila*, not as much for the rebellion in Jerusalem. Rome will have its vengeance on the commander of any enemy that takes the Roman eagle standard from a legion. His execution will become a spectacle for the people of Rome."

"Titus has also ordered the 12th Legion to Armenia Minor, northeast of Antioch," Yosef said.

"Another region of trouble," commented Nicanor, "no easy duty for Commander Galerius Senna and his First Centurion, Tyrannius Priseus. Most men of the 12th don't deserve to be sent to serve in a remote fringe of the empire, but the leaders do."

"The 10th Legion will remain to garrison what's left of Jerusalem," Yosef said. "All that can be identified as rebels have been killed or captured to sell into slavery. Titus freed 40,000 men, women, and children who had been captured since the burning of the Temple. But he ordered the right hands cut off all the males so none could ever raise a sword against Rome again. The 5th and 15th Legions will go with Titus to Alexandria, then he will travel to Rome."

"Will you go with him?" Cleo asked.

Nicanor watched as Yosef searched her face and then sighed. "I don't know. Titus has given me an estate and a stipend, so I can focus solely on writing a war history. Rachel will be with me."

"But if Titus goes to Rome, I hope to go with him. I have too many enemies on both sides in my country, and we will need protection from them."

Nicanor shifted in his chair and nodded soberly. "Vespasian will surely send for you at some point, so you may well travel with Titus when he returns to Rome. He'll want to see what you've written about him and his son." Nicanor gave his empty cup to Elian to fill. The boy, proud of his task, took it with a grin, poured, and handed it back. "How will you treat us—Romans—in your writing?" Nicanor asked, then took a sip, waiting for the answer.

"The Romans are the victors, Nicanor. You know how I must write about them." Yosef shook his head. "Still, I will do my best to show my people's side. Vespasian and Titus, especially, have been merciful to my family, and I'm thankful. What I write of the war must be received favorably so I can write the greater history of my people. As you know, what is not written down... "

"...is forgotten," Nicanor finished for him.

"Yes."

"I will forget none of these past seven years," declared Cleo, her eyes welling with tears. "I will not forget," her voice quavered, "those we've lost." Elian went to her side and patted her hand.

"I miss Sayid," Elian said.

"In Elysium, Sayid smiles upon us," Nicanor said with assurance. "He is glad that we live." He gazed at the sky, a darkening cerulean as the sun dropped. "Graius is with him, and he is pleased, too." Nicanor drained his cup and waved off Elian, who had scrambled to fill it again.

"What will you do now, Nicanor?" Yosef asked.

"I must return to Rome. I promised Graius something that involves Lady Cleo, so I will take her there."

"And afterward?" Yosef asked but looked at Cleo. "Have you heard anything of Gessius Florus? The last we saw of him was when he ran from the tunnel. He could still threaten you, Cleo, especially in Rome. He may still have allies there."

She did not answer, and the moment passed.

"Nicanor," asked Yosef, "what happened to Gessius Florus's treasure ship in Sycaminum?"

"One of Marinus's ships followed the vessel when it sailed northwest into the waters of the *Mare Aegaeum*. They sailed close behind until an early storm nearly wrecked them. He thinks Florus's vessel sank, for when the weather cleared, much debris was strewn on the water along the rocky coast of an island. Marinus said one body was found, a squat broad-shouldered man—head bashed in and bloodied—his giant hands still gripped the tangle of rope that lashed him to piece of decking."

"So, that part of the Temple treasure is lost," Yosef said, "along with the remainder still hidden in Judea. It may never be found without the copper scroll and its key." He rubbed his eyes, reminding them all of his recent journey. "What will you do now, Cleo. After your trip to Rome?"

"I'll find somewhere safe, where Elian and I can be free of the past and live in peace," she replied.

"Will you still sail tomorrow?" Yosef asked, sounding forlorn.

"Marinus says we must," Nicanor said. "The season of storms is near."

CLXXIII

September/October 70 CE

At Sea

The Western Saronic Gulf, The *Egeria*

"We're in the *Saronikós kólpo*s now," Marinus said, pointing at the rugged coastline the ship passed, "and that's the island Kalymnos."

"You tell me this, why?" asked Nicanor, who stood beside him, amidships while Cleo, Anyte, and Elian stood windblown at the bow. "Why are we slowing?"

"This is where Gessius Florus's treasure ship went onto the rocks. Treacherous waters... but I have sponge divers in these islands who could search for the wreck."

Nicanor heard the unasked question in Marinus's words. He shook his head. "*Male parta, male dilabuntur*... what has been wrongfully gained... is wrongly lost. Let Poseidon have it."

***

Rome

Antonia Caenis's Oppian villa, part of the Domus Aurea grounds

Nicanor had been surprised when Marcus Attilius met the *Egeria* in Ostia. "Marinus sent word to Antonia Caenis when to expect you," he explained. "She told me you would come with a woman and a boy." His eyes had turned to Cleo in her plain cloak and a cowl covering her face as if shielding it from the brisk breeze that swirled the harbor. "Is that—"

But Nicanor cut him off. "She is Ya'el—say no more about her." And then he saw the horse Marcus Attilius had brought with him—Carmenta!

It had elated Nicanor that the mare instantly recognized him. Whinnying as he approached, then softly nuzzling him as he rubbed her neck. His fingertips had traced the jagged scar, and the mare had quirked her ears at him. Carmenta must remember Graius, too. When one of Marinus's sailors had unloaded Albus and brought him to Nicanor on the quay, Carmenta had flicked her eyes and tail at the usurper of his attention. The phlegmatic horse's steady eyes studied her, then Nicanor. With a shoulder twitch that seemed a human shrug, Albus had shifted so that Carmenta was closer to Nicanor than he. That satisfied the mare.

In the morning, he had explained to Carmenta that she would carry Cleo, and he would ride Albus. Cleo's soothing voice and neck strokes soon reconciled Carmenta to the arrangement.

On the half-day ride to Rome, with Elian astraddle behind him, Nicanor had only half-listened to Cleo's conversation with Marcus from the evening before. Marcus had told her and Elian tales of his adventures with Nicanor in the taberna. Cleo and the boy seemed to delight in the stories. So he had not asked Marcus to stop until his friend said too much about what Nicanor and Graius went through to reach Cleo's brother Marcus Otho and how Graius had died. The boy had listened, mouth agape. Cleo's gaze had lingered on him when he suggested Marcus save the stories for some another time.

As they mounted their horses that morning, Elian had said to Nicanor, "Last night, you said Marcus Attilius was the best fighter you ever met. Even now, with just one arm?" Nicanor answered the wide-eyed boy, "Even now...."

Marcus had brought them directly to the still-extensive grounds of the Domus Aurea in Rome. They passed through the main palace and up to the villa beyond. There, Emperor Vespasian's consort, Antonia Caenis, had greeted them. Nicanor had introduced Cleo as Ya'el, and her son, Elian. Antonia Caenis's knowing glance and approving nod told Nicanor she knew the woman he had saved. After finding they'd eaten on the road just before Rome, she said, "Bathe and rest tonight. Tomorrow we'll have a dinner to welcome you back."

Nicanor stood on the second-floor balcony overlooking the extensive grounds of Antonia Caenis's villa. He had been at the Domus Aurea last, briefly, years ago, when Emperor Nero's plans for it were nearly fulfilled. Its extravagant cost and Nero's profligacy had emptied the empire's treasury, and large sections had been reclaimed for better purposes since Nero's death. Nicanor had noticed someone had removed the overly ornate and grandiose trappings from the main palace. Surely that was Vespasian's frugal nature at work, converting the unneeded ostentation into badly needed money for the empire.

Still, the rooms—connected by a small central atrium—given to him and Cleo by Antonia Caenis were far more sumptuous than any others he had ever stayed in, even in Alexandria with Vespasian, at the Aegyptus Prefect's palace. Cleo was off bathing with the help of an attendant and then planned to rest after their journey. He wondered what she thought about returning to Rome and to a familiar setting. But she would have only a brief time to enjoy the surroundings. They had timed their arrival for after sundown, and what he needed to accomplish tomorrow would be done quietly and inconspicuously. Dressed far more simply than a Roman noblewoman, Cleo was unlikely to be recognized alone, without attendants and trappings. Still, they must be careful.

Nicanor gave the night view from the balcony a last glimpse and stretched, pressing his hands into the small of his back and feeling the crackle of joints. He turned into his room and went to its adjacent private bathing area. A hot bath, and then maybe he could sleep. The days at sea, not something he had ever enjoyed, had been a pleasure because he was with Cleo. He had watched her grow stronger every day. And he had relaxed for the first time since... since... he could not remember.

But that loosening of tension had reversed, rewinding, as they got closer to Rome. Tomorrow he would deliver on his vow to Graius and to himself. Then he needed to decide on the future. Suddenly, he doubted the bath would help him sleep.

* * *

Next afternoon...

THE TEMPLE OF HERCULES

Nicanor heard Elian's laughter echo through the clearing around the temple. Marcus Attilius, armed with a downed tree branch, parried with Elian, who bore a wooden sword that reminded Nicanor of Graius's *rudis*, the symbol of the old gladiator's freedom. Nicanor knelt in the grass near the temple, set the stone marker into the thin rectangle he'd cut, and peeled away to reveal bare dirt. He had had the marker made in Caesarea, the incised words reading, *Graius: fortissimus amicus... fortissimus ac liber.*

"Champion, friend, free man," Cleo read aloud, tears thickening her voice. "Graius was all that and more."

"He was." Nicanor looked up, moved by the bittersweetness of the moment, remembering his friend. "He told me he loved you as if you were his child...." He gazed upon Cleo then. Dressed in simple robes and a plain cloak, the hood thrown back on her shoulders. Her face turned toward the bright sun that showed cheeks that had regained a little of their fullness. That sight, too, gripped his heart.

While Elian and Marcus were still on their way to join them that morning, Nicanor had taken her to an *argentarii*. Two years before, with Graius's witnessed testament, he had transferred the old gladiator's money into his account. Now he directed the banker to set up an account for Ya'el and moved the old gladiator's untouched portion into it. Not nearly enough for Cleo to replace the wealth she formerly had, but enough for Ya'el to get by for a little while as she decided what to do next. He worried about what that decision might be.

* * *

That evening...

ANTONIA CAENIS'S OPPIAN VILLA

Nicanor did not see any sudden multiplication of servants at the villa nor the appearance of soldiers he would have expected with Vespasian joining them for the evening.

An attendant had cleaned and set out his *tribunus* uniform Nicanor had brought from Caesarea, hoping not to have to wear it again. But dining with the emperor's consort—even without the emperor, it seemed—he should respect her wishes. Just as he finished dressing, a servant said from the doorway, "Dinner, sir."

He had followed the young man and been surprised when he passed by the antechamber to the grand dining area he had seen the night before—it was now empty. But farther on, they entered a smaller chamber with much simpler decorations and a cheering fire next to a doorway to a terrace that overlooked the city. He looked out into the darkness and saw, beyond the terrace, lighted torches, lamps, and lanterns that winked from many buildings and pathways below. The runs of straight lines of lights at equal distances demarked streets, and any sizable radiance with four distinct corners marked courtyards and civic squares. Back inside, he saw the servant had gone, and he was alone where a table had been set with a center lamp, waist-high divans for four on three sides, and chairs for two at the head of the table.

"Hello!" he called out to the empty room. He heard Elian's laughter he'd come to recognize as the boy came into the room from the terrace, giggling, with Marcus Attilius at his side. Both of them were dressed better than Nicanor had ever seen. They grinned at him as they reclined self-consciously on the couches on one side of the table. Then Cleo came in with Antonia Caenis, the hostess striking in a blue robe with the black and gray twist of her hair draping over her shoulder. But Cleo was breathtaking in a silver silken gown that rippled with glints of light from the lamp and fire. Her hair was pulled into a knot fixed at the back of her head, leaving her nape bare. Her lovely face glowed, and her eyes held no shadows. Hers was not the loveliness of youth and innocence as when he had first seen her. For Nicanor, Cleo's beauty came from what she had endured and survived. He could see her strength. Her inner beauty shone through.

She smiled at him as Antonia Caenis settled on the divan on the other side of the table from Marcus Attilius, and Cleo reclined on the couch next to her.

Antonia Caenis gestured to a chair at the head of the table. "Sit, Nicanor."

With a nod, Nicanor pulled the chair out and sat. Just as he did, the doorway to the terrace filled with the figure of the emperor, and Nicanor shot to his feet.

"It's good to see you again, Nicanor," Emperor Vespasian said as he entered the room, carrying a hinged pair of bronze tablets. Nicanor's heart beat heavily, for he knew what the emperor carried. The tablets formed the military diploma that signified a legionary's retirement and the benefits he would receive for long years of service. The full text was engraved on the outer side of *tabula one*, while the outer side of *tabula two* displayed the names of seven witnesses, their seals protected by metal strips. The text of *tabula one* was reproduced on the two inner sides. The plates were then folded shut and sealed so the external inscription would be legible without breaking the seals, the internal inscription serving as the official witnessed copy of the original text. That was the *constitutio* published in the *Tabularium*, the offices where official records were kept in the Roman Forum.

Then Nicanor found his tongue. "Thank you, sire. It's good to see you too." He was amazed when imperial bodyguards did not immediately follow Vespasian into the chamber. But then, Vespasian was not typical of any nobleman he had ever met. Still, the Praetorians were undoubtedly nearby.

The emperor waved him back into his seat and set the hinged tablet on the table before him. His eyes went to Antonia Caenis, who dipped her head in a slight nod to him and then to Cleo. Vespasian nodded with a small smile as if to himself as much as Cleo. He took the other chair at the head of the table.

"You've served Rome well, Nicanor," he said. "More personally, you have better served my family and me. You saved my life during the siege of Yotapta. You've helped Antonia. You and Marcus Attilius saved Domitian. And you have been a sage advisor to Titus. With great pleasure, I bestow this *honesta missio* ...... honorable discharge upon you. And tomorrow, I will see that my *praefecti aerarii militaris* transfer 40,000 sesterces to you from the treasury."

Nicanor gasped. "Sire, that's more than twice what's customary! Even if I had served all my years as a Praetorian."

"You have earned it. The empire and I also wish to grant you land where you may settle. What is your wish?"

"Sire?"

"Where do you wish to settle?"

Surprised at the suddenness of it all, Nicanor shook his head and spoke what he'd thought of often. "Well, the shipowner, Marinus, told me once of a town called Cenchrae, in the province of Achea, in the *Pelopónnēsos*."

Vespasian nodded. "Done," he said and turned to Cleo. "What of you, Lady Cleo? Gessius Florus has disappeared. He has not been seen since the rout of the rebels in Judea. So, I cannot hold him accountable for what's been reported of his plans to steal what rightfully belonged to the empire. And such punishment would protect you from him forever." He nodded at Antonia Caenis. "I'm told that is needed."

Cleo's eyes went to Nicanor and then to the emperor. "I wish to disappear, too, sire."

***

At Sea

Onboard the *Egeria*

Nicanor had never asked the gods for much... but now they had looked down on him in favor. Next to him at the rail of the *Egeria*, Cleo watched the craggy coast they followed to the port of Cenchrae. He thought again of the last night in Rome. After the dinner with Vespasian, he had gone to Cleo and told her: "I hoped to make sure Gessius Florus never hurts you again... though I did not get to kill him myself. I cannot leave you and risk that he's still alive, that he might find you and threaten you."

"Do not worry, Nicanor. He never will again," Cleo had replied.

"How do you know?"

Final Siege

"Because Lady Cleo died in Judea... she no longer exists." Her confident tone—full of iron—then shifted and became brittle. "I am Ya'el now... and do not need protection. But I wish to see what life could be like somewhere safe with someone who cares for me... someone I have come to care for, too."

"Nicanor!" The call came from the ship's stern where Marinus stood, breaking Nicanor's reverie that had strengthened his hope. The shipmaster's voice cut through the sea wind again. "Nicanor..." The former tribunus left Ya'el at the rail to go to Marinus just as Elian joined her and took her hand.

"Are you sure?" Marinus asked as Nicanor got close to him.

"About what?"

Marinus pointed. "A day and a half, maybe two days of sailing east-southeast lies Florus's treasure ship. When winter is over, and the weather's better, we could...."

"No, Marinus." He looked toward Ya'el, who was smiling at Elian, throwing scraps of bread for the gulls cavorting above. The boy's laughter rang out over the water. He smiled at the thought that in the hold below, Albus and Carmenta, with her foal that Antonia Caenis had brought from Tibur, were more than ready for landfall and their new home. "I have all I need."

* * *

"It's late, Nicanor," said Ya'el. "What are you doing still awake? We enter port at dawn." She stood at the door of his small cabin, which she had persuaded him to take.

He closed the wax tablet Anyte had given him. His writing was crude and rough, but he had made a start. As he had watched Yosef do so many times, he would transfer it to ink on parchment once they were settled on land. He turned to her and said, "I'm done... for now."

"For now?" Ya'el said with a smile. "Have you become like Yosef... a scribe?"

"Well, he's right. What's not written is forgotten, and I have much I do not want to forget." Nicanor smiled. *And now, I have much to look forward to....*

CLXXIV

Junius 71 CE

Rome

Nicanor, Marcus Attilius, and Ya'el slowed their horses to a halt on the *via Ostiensis* just outside the Servian Wall at its *Porta Trigemina*. The road from Ostia Antica's port to Rome was heavily traveled. Its triple gateway led straight into the *Forum Boarium* near Rome's first commercial docks on the Tiber. That long waterway ran to the sea southwest of Rome from the *Apenninus* mountains in *Italia's* north. Nicanor sniffed the easterly wind. "I haven't missed that at all." Those unused to the smell of Rome could not ignore the odor of a vast, bustling population.

Ya'el laughed and said to Marcus Attilius, "Nicanor would have preferred to stay and help Anyte and Elian with the birth of Carmenta's second foal."

Marcus's laugh joined hers. "I know well Nicanor's opinion of the center of the empire." He shifted to half-turn in his saddle and studied the retired tribunus. "I was surprised to get your message that you accepted the invitation."

Nicanor grew serious. "Well, when it comes from the emperor, you cannot refuse. Especially since Vespasian has been so gracious to us. So we will watch this Triumph he bestows on Titus."

"Will you see your friend Yosef?"

"Of course," Nicanor said with a nod, then grumbled, "If these gods-cursed people will move along so we can get into the city."

* * *

At Flavius Josephus's Villa

Marcus Attilius had picked them up at the small, plain inn Nicanor had chosen, rejecting Yosef's and Antonia Caenis's offers of hospitality. He greeted them quietly, a little cowed by Ya'el's simple dignity: "My lady...." Marcus had then squinted at Nicanor, whose tasteful yet modest garb, that of a somewhat successful farmer or merchant, was in keeping with Ya'el's. "Yet you look out of place. Despite the clothing of a shopkeeper, you are still a centurion in your bearing... and wearing those." He nodded toward the *pugio,* and *gladius* sheathed at the sides of Nicanor's hips.

"Are there not still murderers and thieves in Rome?" Nicanor had snorted and climbed into the carriage next to Ya'el, who sat with the cowl of her light cloak pulled forward, covering three-quarters of her face. Now the carriage climbed the southern spur of the Esquiline Hill and turned onto a gravel path that led to a sizable-but-not-ostentatious villa built into the shoulder of the hill.

"The villa of Flavius Josephus," Marcus announced, stepping down from the carriage and offering a hand to Ya'el. Nicanor climbed down after her and stood with his hands on his hips. He regarded the domus, but really he was thinking, *Flavius Josephus...* how did his friend feel about that renaming now that it seemed formalized? Nicanor studied the Praetorian Guards who scrutinized them. He knew others were likely at the sides and rear of the villa and patrolled the grounds. *Will my friend ever be truly safe again?* he wondered.

* * *

Nicanor watched the two servants clear the table under Rachel's scrutiny. Yosef introducing her as his wife had surprised Nicanor but not Ya'el. The two women had exchanged a look: he thought it a challenge from Rachel and a deferential acknowledgment from Ya'el. Rachel had recovered from the tribulations of the siege, and she nicely filled out her fine robe, and her eyes sparkled. Her composure occasionally faltered when she darted glances at Yosef, who stood beside her, his right hand absently turning a twined rawhide circlet on his left wrist.

Nicanor raised his full goblet carefully and turned to his friend, who looked like he had endured a personal, private siege since Caesarea. Yosef had lost weight, his features had become more drawn, and, after the initial joy when greeting them, he had smiled little.

"All the talk we heard from Ostia and here in Rome... was of the glorious victory Titus and his father have won," Nicanor commented carefully. He suspected that was the reason for Yosef's somber demeanor.

"It's been that way for months, I'm told," Yosef replied sourly. He hadn't touched his own full cup.

Nicanor hoped to change the tone. "Perhaps it will end after tomorrow's event."

Yosef shook his head. "I do not think so. Emperor Vespasian has at least two monuments planned to memorialize this victory over a 'powerful enemy,' as he calls us."

Nicanor glanced at Ya'el, who had also heard Yosef's bitter emphasis.

"Construction has begun on his *Amphitheatrum Flavium*. It will be the largest arena in the empire." Yosef sighed and took a drink. "He can build it only through the riches taken from Jerusalem."

Nicanor's thoughts flicked to Florus's sunken treasure ship; Yosef knew the ship's supposed fate. Marinus was now confident of the wreck's location—should he tell Yosef? But what good would that information be to Yosef or his people? Would they use the treasure to buy weapons and continue to fight Rome, causing even more death and destruction? *No, there's been enough of that.* It was better to remain silent.

"Also under construction... also paid for by Jewish wealth, is the emperor's *Templum Pacis*, a tribute to his restoring peace to the empire. Vespasian plans to decorate its interior and surrounding buildings with our treasures. Those that have not already been converted into funds to replenish the empire's treasury."

"Antonia Caenis told me the heightened...." Marcus Attilius paused as if finding the right word. "The rampant propaganda was necessary for Vespasian to stabilize the empire. He needed to present a conquest to the citizens of Rome and the provinces. It could not have been a mere campaign to restore order."

"Mere!" Yosef exclaimed, and Nicanor sat forward, ready to intervene. "Mere...." The heat left Yosef's tone as he shook his head. "Before I returned with Titus, the count came in for the siege: over 97,000 of my people enslaved... and hundreds of thousands... or more... dead—across Judea. Tomorrow, hundreds of my people will march in chains in Titus's Triumph... I've heard it will be a parade all of Rome will remember."

* * *

Daybreak...

CAMPUS MARTIUS

Nicanor, Ya'el, Yosef, and Marcus Attilius were grouped with Antonia Caenis in the emperor's entourage on a platform looking down upon the Field of Mars. From there, the *pompa*, the procession, would travel two and a half miles—at a walk, with many stops—to the

Temple of Jupiter Optimus Maximus atop the Capitoline Hill. Below and before them, in a four-horse chariot, Titus waited to join the procession at his assigned place. He was dressed in an all-purple *toga picta*, his resplendent regalia identifying him as a victorious general and near-divine hero of Rome.

Yosef heard Marcus whisper to Nicanor next to him: "Why does Titus not wear the customary laurel crown?"

Yosef answered the question for him. "Titus says the victory is not his alone... but shared with the legions and the people of Rome." Nicanor raised an eyebrow at him. Yosef nodded toward Antonia Caenis, who stood with Vespasian's youngest son, Domitian, behind the Praetorian Guards in ranks surrounding the emperor.

"He was guided by the deft hand of a wise political advisor," Yosef added. Nicanor nodded, his eyes shifting again to Antonia Caenis. Yosef turned back toward the mass queued before them that began to move as the sun climbed over the hills to the east.

First came Simon bar Giora and Yohanan ben Levi, followed by several hundred Jewish prisoners in chains. Some walked steadily, others shakily... still, others were helped by the men beside them. Yosef knew some were destined for execution the next day or for further display—eventual death—in the Games. Their captured weapons and armor were stacked on flatbed wagons trailing them. Next came cartloads of gold, silver, statuary, and other treasures, including the grand menorah he had last seen being delivered to Titus in Jerusalem. Then Rome's senators and magistrates came on foot, followed by the *lictors*, the officials' attendants, and bodyguards in their red robes signifying war.

But nothing in the procession compared to what Yosef witnessed next. Pulled by teams of mules came massive moving stages three or four stories high. Wooden scaffolding supported tapestries interwoven with gold stretched upon a framework of wrought ivory. On these tapestries, the war won by Rome was shown—in many representations, in separate sections—in vivid paintings. Yosef saw first a prosperous land—his country—then its devastation. Mighty walls demolished by siege engines. Strong fortresses overpowered. Cities with well-manned defenses completely mastered and Roman legions pouring through broken ramparts into an area soon deluged with blood. Entire battalions of defenders, the enemy—his people—slaughtered. The hands of those incapable of resistance were raised in supplication, temples were set on fire, and houses pulled down over their owners' heads.

The flood did not nourish cultivated land nor supply drink to man and beast but flowed across a country—his country—in the form of flames. Another tapestry depicted his people in flight from the legions, and still another showed masses led into captivity. The meaning was clear: the Jews were destined to such suffering when they chose war with Rome.

Shocked by the magnificent display of artwork portraying such tragedy, he turned away to look at his friends. The pageantry of pain moved beyond them, and Yosef saw the stunned look on Nicanor and Ya'el's faces and thumbed tears from his own eyes. He turned back to the spectacle and saw the man he knew so well.

General Titus, the *vir triumphalis*, the man of triumph, cracked his whip over the team of horses, and his chariot rolled under the slanting rays of the rising sun. Behind him trailed the two garlanded, flawless white oxen he would sacrifice within the temple at the Triumph's end. Sunlight dazzled off their gilded horns.

* * *

JOSEPHUS'S VILLA

The moon had reached its apex before falling to the west by the time they returned to the villa, though it was clear the city would continue to celebrate throughout the night.

Rachel greeted them with red-rimmed eyes. She had not wanted to witness the Triumph, and there had been no need for her to go. Yosef was glad she had not seen it but wondered why she cried anyway. They settled onto divans and seats on the balcony, appreciating the night breeze that soothed them and dried their sweat-dampened clothing. Rachel handed Yosef a coin that glinted in the torchlight: "One of the servants brought me this," she told him.

On one side was a profile of Vespasian, and on the other, an image of a grieving woman. She clearly symbolized a defeated Judea kneeling beneath a palm tree. Over the woman, standing proudly, was a tall Roman figure, perhaps meant to represent Vespasian or Titus. "*Judea capta*, Judea conquered," muttered Yosef.

"I've seen it before," Nicanor commented, "with Galba, Vitellius, and Otho. Special coins were minted despite their brief reigns. They are a good way to spread a ruler's political message—or show his power—through the money people handle."

"Another is to connect that message to the taxes they pay," Yosef added wryly.

Final Siege

"What do you mean?" Ya'el asked. She had been quiet for most of the day, and Yosef wondered how the Triumph weighed on her thoughts.

"There is now a *fiscius judaicus,* a Jewish tax. So, people of my faith will continue to pay all their lives for choosing to rebel against Rome," Yosef explained. "It will replace the half-shekel—two denarii—tax each Jew donated to Jerusalem's Temple for payment to Rome. Through this new tax, Vespasian's message is that Rome has permanently abolished the Jewish Temple and its worshippers, the core of the Jewish resistance against Rome. The humiliated Jews who wish to continue in their faith—who remain potential enemies of the empire—are obligated to now send that money to the Temple of Jupiter Capitolinus."

Yosef looked at Nicanor and said, "I saw that your friend Marcus wears the fish symbol of the Christians. I asked about it, and he mentioned he took you to where Paul is believed to be buried. Many visit there as the Christian belief spreads, even though it comes with a great risk of persecution. I recall our conversation about Loukas, who wrote of the accounts and teachings of Yeshua ish Natzrat. Are you interested in becoming a follower of his?"

Nicanor shook his head slowly, thoughtfully. "At first, I wasn't. I didn't want to dissent with Rome—I served her too long. But I now find myself agreeing with much of what Paul told me. And from the accounts of Paul's companion Loukas that I could read, I find the Christian messiah and his teachings convincing. Those beliefs make his followers willing to die rather than abandon them. They will not renounce this messiah. I respect that strength. And I don't think they want to challenge Rome's authority."

"Belief like theirs is compelling. My people know this...."

"But such thinking can be dangerous," Nicanor replied.

"They know that, too," Yosef said with a sigh and a weary smile. "Yeshua apparently warned my people: 'All who draw the sword will die by the sword.'"

"Marinus brought us news," Nicanor said, sorry to add more to the grim musings. "There is a rumor of a new siege planned at Masada," Nicanor said.

Yosef nodded, thinking again how apt Yeshua's words were. "Titus spoke of it before we left Caesarea. If the Sicarii in Masada don't surrender, it will happen soon—not this year but next. Titus left orders for the 10th Legion, *Fretenis,* and its 4,800 auxiliaries to prepare."

"How many are at Masada?" Ya'el asked, her low voice tinged with sadness.

"I'm told by some of the captured that it's believed to be several hundred, maybe a thousand men, women, and children," Yosef replied. The room grew still. He broke the silence by asking, "Nicanor, are you sure you will not stay longer? Tomorrow they will execute Simon bar Giora. He was a greater terror to my people than were the Romans and deserves that fate. Do you not want to see the man punished who led the rebels against you at Beth Horon?"

"No. We'll leave tomorrow after paying respects to the emperor. I've seen enough death and punishment in my life. They plan to cast him from the Tarpeian Rock... a fate I was once threatened with. If I had been caught doing what I must for those I... I owed a responsibility to."

Yosef watched as Ya'el shifted on her divan to lean over and grip Nicanor's hand. He saw their eyes meet and felt a pang for Cleo... for Ya'el. *So many things that could have been... were not. So many things in the past and present that should not be so.* Yosef rubbed his eyes; what was done was done. But there was one more thing of the past he had to tell her and Nicanor.

"Ya'el," he said, "two days after I saw you and Nicanor. Before you sailed to Rome, I was with Titus when a report came in of the body of a Roman nobleman found in the Upper City. He had a green-feathered arrow in his heart." He saw Nicanor understood what that meant.

Nicanor looked at Ya'el. "Why didn't you tell me?"

"I feared *anyone* knowing...." She met Nicanor's stare. "I told you Gessius Florus would never threaten me again. And now I know I'm safe... especially so, with you by my side."

Ya'el turned to Yosef and Rachel, saying, "We will be married when we return home." She smiled at Nicanor.

* * *

The next morning...

Yosef watched Nicanor and Ya'el leave and felt Rachel's easing. She had especially welcomed Ya'el's news that she would wed Nicanor. Rachel needed nothing and no one around to remind her of the past. But he would never be free of the past... its presence was part of him and always would be—it was his calling. He again turned the leather cord he'd braided into a band around his wrist. The coin once attached to it—the *kinyan*—had been a token of his and Leah's binding love. He had buried it with her, a return of that eternal gift.

"I'm going to write now," he said, and Rachel squinted at his fingers working the leather circlet, nodded, and left him.

Yosef went to his desk and picked up the letter he had read many times. Each time it both lightened and tore at his heart. Matthew told him that he, Mother, and Father were healthy and thankful to have survived. But Yavneh was no Jerusalem... and no city could ever replace it for their people. Yosef refolded and set it aside. He picked up the bundle that always sat near his hand as he wrote. He unwrapped its leaves of supple leather to reveal a silver *hamsa*, scratched and deeply scored. In Caesarea, Elian handed it to him, explaining that he had hidden it to keep it safe from the Romans. The boy thought he should have it. He turned the *hamsa* over and rubbed his thumb across her name etched on its back. *Oh, Miriam....* He set it down and rewrapped it when it and the ache grew too heavy to bear.

The table next to his desk was stacked with wax tablets. Most of them he had transcribed before leaving Judea, but a few remained, bearing his latest notes. Yosef picked up the most recent that contained his thoughts formed on the ship to Rome from Judea. *Will I ever see what's left of my family and homeland again?* He opened the tablet to his notes on the *shmita*, the *shəvi'it*, the sabbath year of the land. As directed by the Torah, all fields were left fallow every seventh year, and the most recent *shmita* had begun before the siege. Now it seemed it would never end.

He took a deep breath, held it for two heartbeats, and let it go as he set the tablet aside and drew a sheet of blank parchment from a stack. *Even though it is gone... or lost for a thousand years... Jerusalem will always be at the heart of the Jewish people. If I forget you, O Jerusalem, may my right hand forget my skill.* Yosef dipped his pen in ink and began to write.

IF YOU ENJOYED THIS BOOK, PLEASE CONSIDER LEAVING A REVIEW ON AMAZON. THAT'S THE PRIMARY WAY INDEPENDENT AUTHORS GET THEIR WORK NOTICED.

For updates about the author's writing, please visit:

www.CryForJerusalem.com

ABOUT THE AUTHOR

Dr. Ward Sanford is an internationally renowned hydrogeologist who has spent over thirty years studying and writing journal articles on the availability and sustainability of groundwater around the United States and the world. He has given professional advice on several sites across North America, Europe, and the Middle East and undertaken missions with the International Atomic Energy Agency to Thailand and the U. S. State Department to Libya.

More recently, he has developed a keen interest in the first-century history of Israel through the writings of the contemporary historian Flavius Josephus. His desire is now to bring those recorded events to life through dramatization in a series of novels entitled CRY FOR JERUSALEM. Dr. Sanford is a member of the Historical Novel Society of North America. He and his wife, two grown sons, and daughter-in-law live in the Virginia suburbs of Washington, DC.

More From the Author

THE JOSEPHUS PROBLEM: COUNTING IN CIRCLES

When the Romans captured the town after the siege at Yodfat in 67 CE, Josephus and a band of his Jewish soldiers took to a hiding place in a cave beneath the town. They held out for many days but were eventually discovered by the Romans. The Romans made an offer to Josephus that if he surrendered, he would not be harmed. But his soldiers would have none of that. They knew they might end up being crucified, and so they threatened to kill themselves and Josephus if he tried to surrender. So, Josephus had a problem. He thought he could help the Jews and Jerusalem if he was taken captive, for he could negotiate with the Romans, but his soldiers would not permit it.

Josephus tried to persuade his soldiers that suicide was against God's law, but they were not convinced. So, his solution was for them to cast lots to see who would slit the throat of the next one in line. The last two would remain alive to bear witness to what had occurred. In this way, God would choose who would live or die, and also, no one would die by their own hand. The soldiers agreed. As fate would have it, Josephus was the next to the last chosen by lot and survived. Many critics and enemies of Josephus later claimed his story to be totally invented to cover for his own cowardice in surrendering to the Romans when his soldiers perished. But, in his defense, the second survivor was there to bear witness to the story. Emperor Titus was a witness as well when the account was told to Titus's father (General Vespasian) right after Josephus was captured.

Josephus did not give many details as to how the lots were cast, so different individuals have suggested different scenarios. This story has, in fact, led to a formal problem in mathematics known as the "Josephus Problem." Rather than trying to placate suicidal soldiers, the mathematical problem is how to avoid death yourself in this situation. The assumption behind the problem is that a group of people are standing in a circle. Everyone counts off by three, where every third person is to be killed. Given there are many persons in the circle when you reach around to the beginning of the circle, the counting continues around a second time, and then as many times as is needed until only one survivor remains.

The problem to solve is this: If you are a very smart person, where should you stand in the circle to be the survivor? This implies that Josephus might have been a mathematical genius and figured out where to stand so the lot would never fall to him. Even though Josephus does not describe choosing every third or fourth person or them standing in a circle, this mathematical problem has still intrigued mathematicians for centuries. It might not be too hard to figure out the answer by counting if you knew how many were in the circle and at what interval there were to be culled. But the true challenge has been to come up with a general formula that can predict the safe position in which to stand given any number of persons in a circle and for different culling intervals.

For more on this mathematical puzzle, I recommend the reader visit https://en.wikipedia.org/wiki/Josephus_problem.

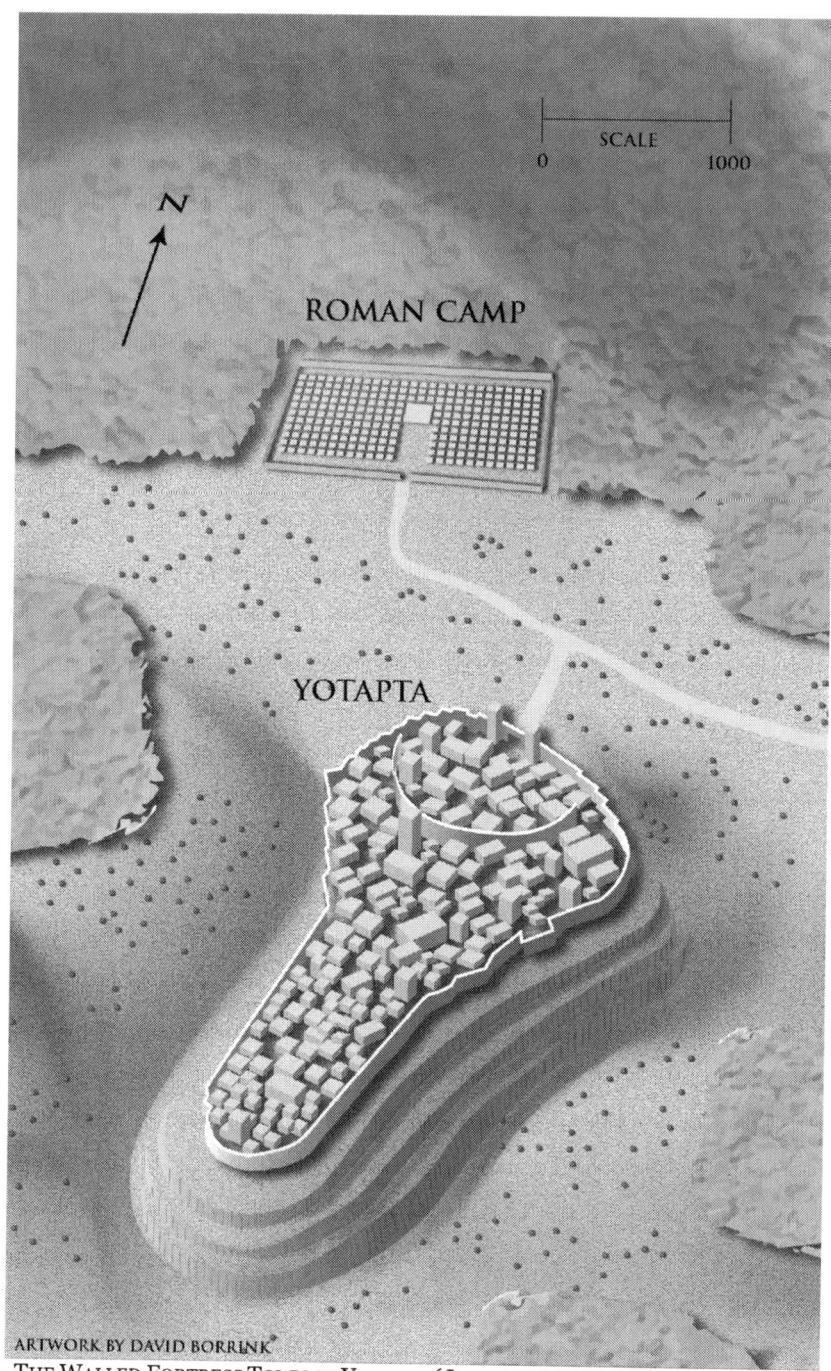

The Walled Fortress Town of Yotapta (Jotapata in Josephus, modern-day Yodfat) in the First Century CE

The Copper Scroll: Map to an Insanely Large Treasure.

Out of all the scrolls found at the Dead Sea Qumran site, one scroll made of copper is the most unique. Unique not only in its composition but also in its content.

Copper was a common metal used during the first century CE for archiving important administrative records. And the Copper Scroll from Qumran appears to be just that, a record of assets, not a literary work of religious nature. Those assets are gold and silver in amounts listed in talents—a talent being about 400 oz of gold or silver—or two and half modern bars of gold that would weigh about 75 pounds. The scroll lists 64 specific sites at which roughly 900 talents of gold are buried, in addition to a similar amount of silver. The gold at today's rate of $2000 per oz would value over two billion dollars!

Several theories have been put forward by scholars as to what this treasure represents: (1) the Essene's personal treasury—although this contradicts the Essenes being ascetic and rejecting personal wealth. (2) Herod's Temple treasure near the time of the Roman siege in 70 AD—although the Romans were known to have confiscated much treasure from that Temple. (3) Treasure from the Babylonian siege in the 6th century BCE, although the writing appears to be from the first century CE, and (4) a total hoax.

Many have found explanation (2) to be the most plausible, and in fact, books and novels have been written following that reasoning. Treasure hunters have dug all over Israel, trying to follow the clues on the scroll, but to no avail.

This has led many to believe that either the Romans or Jews during the 2nd Revolt dug up the treasure. The Romans were known to go to great lengths to extract information that would lead to buried treasure. For most of history, those being conquered would hide their treasures to keep them away from the conquerors.

In our novel series, *Cry For Jerusalem*, we use the plausible explanation that the Jews were trying to keep the Romans from confiscating the treasure. We also postulate that they only hid perhaps half of the treasure because if the Romans found nothing in the Temple, then they would assume it had been hidden and go and look for it. But if they found a lot there, they might think they had found it all. The obsession of our antagonist to obtain this treasure becomes a subplot in the story. Like all subplots in the series, we attempt to use plausible events and explanations as ways to further dramatize the events of the day.

WAS DAVID'S TOMB BOOBY-TRAPPED?

Today "King David's Tomb" is a venerated site in Jerusalem visited by many religious Jews and tourists to this day. But most scholars do not believe that site to be the real location of King David's actual tomb. The site only became famous during the Middle Ages. An actual underground tomb has yet to be discovered, although many have looked for it, lured by the rumors of treasure. What do we actually know about where King David might have been buried? Was treasure buried with him? Did anyone set traps to ensnare potential robbers? Visions from the recent movies "The Mummy" or "The Goonies" bring to mind booby traps set in Egyptian tombs or Pirate caves to protect the hoard. Let's look back at the writings from ancient Jerusalem to see what they can tell us. There are more details there than most people are aware of. The writer of the Book of Kings gives us the first clue:

"So David slept with his fathers and was buried in the city of David." 1 Kings 2:10

Today many dug-out sepulchers can be found around Jerusalem from thousands of years ago. The area is underlain by limestone, which is soft enough for rooms to be easily carved into. In fact, just east of the Old City, many tombs have been uncovered or excavated that were dug into the hillside of the Kidron Valley.

And we have written evidence from the first century CE that the location of David's Tomb was common knowledge. The New Testament writer Luke records a speech of the Apostle Peter speaking t a crown around 33 CE:

"Men and brethren, let me freely speak unto you of the patriarch David, that he is both dead and buried, and his sepulchre is with us unto this day." Acts 2:29

But King David lived at about 1000 BCE, so this is one thousand years later. What else can we find that describes David's Tomb? Amazingly, Josephus gave us very important clues that very few people are aware of. First, he tells us that the tomb was raided 165 years before Peter by the Judean Hasmonean King and High Priest John Hyrcanus:

MORE FROM THE AUTHOR

"But Hyrcanus opened the sepulchre of David, who excelled all other kings in riches, and took out of it three thousand talents (of silver)." Antiquities 13:240

Josephus was reporting that Hyrcanus needed this money to pay off the Seleucid/Greek leader Antiochus VII, who had laid siege to Jerusalem. So apparently, a great deal of treasure was buried with King David. And given that Solomon was later buried in the same place, perhaps much additional treasure was added. But the plot thickens, for Josephus tells us that King Herod the Great was the next one to try to pilfer treasure from the tomb in about 10 BCE:

"As for Herod, he had spent vast sums about the cities, both without and within his own kingdom: and as he had before heard that Hyrcanus, who had been king before him, had opened David's sepulchre, and taken out of it three thousand talents of silver, and that there was a much greater number left behind, and indeed enough to suffice all his wants, he had a great while an intention to make the attempt. And at this time, he opened that sepulchre by night and went into it and endeavored that it should not be at all known in the city but took only his most faithful friends with him. As for any money, he found none, as Hyrcanus had done, but instead, furniture of gold and those precious goods that were laid up there, all of which he took away. However, he had a great desire to make a more diligent search and to go farther in, even as far as the very bodies of David and Solomon, where two of his guards were slain by flame that burst out upon those that were in, as the report was. So he was terribly frightened and went out and built a propitiatory monument of that fright he had been in, and this of white stone, at the mouth of the sepulchre, and that at a great expense also." Antiquities 16:179-182

We find out here that Herod tried to plunder the treasure in secret by night but only partly succeeded. When two of his men were sent deeper in to find more treasure, they were consumed by a fiery explosion. Sounds like a booby trap to me! Herod was so frightened by this he feared he would be punished by God for desecrating the tomb and built a substantial monument at the entrance for penance. Josephus is relating this story from 50 years before he was born, and it sounds like it scared anyone else from reattempting what Herod had tried. Many scholars believe the story was invented for this reason--to keep away thieves. As a hydrogeologist, I have to think there might be a natural explanation for what happened. Most people are aware that explosions can occur in coal mines from leaking methane. But methane can also escape naturally from groundwater and accumulate in poorly aerated caves (or sealed tomb rooms). Thus, Herod's men entering with torches could have ignited the methane, causing the explosion that killed them. It's an interesting hypothesis to consider. Was the story real? If so, was the explosion the result of a natural phenomenon? Or human tampering to protect the site?

THE TEMPLE MOUNT PARADOX: SOLVED

The Temple Mount in Jerusalem stands today with massive retaining walls in a near-rectangle quadrilateral roughly 900-ft wide by 1500-ft long. The wall's lower sections are from the 1st century CE and earlier. Yet no historical writer from that era even once mentions these dimensions—thus the paradox. Instead, they write that the outer Temple Enclosure was square—either 600 feet (according to Josephus) or 750 feet (according to rabbis who wrote the Mishnah and the Talmud). Today the prevailing theory by Israeli historians and archaeologists follows the rabbis and the most popular recreated models *(1)* of Herod's Temple cover all of today's existing rectangular Mount. Solid walls are hard to ignore.

In my blog, I introduce you to Thomas Lewin, the 19th-century London barrister, and Josephus scholar, and discuss some of his conclusions about what was originally beneath the Dome of the Rock. Today I will summarize his landmark, forgotten paper of 1873, which solves the paradox by, as he put it, pitting the landscape and Josephus against each other until they agree. *(2)* Lewin first lays out six careful arguments as to why the Temple Enclosure was indeed 600-ft square and located in the SW corner of the platform (see map below):

1. Josephus states in three separate ways that the Temple area was 600 feet on each side. In one place, he states it was 400 cubits (1.5 ft per cubit). Elsewhere he states it was one stadia—1/8th of a Roman mile (4,800 ft)—also 600 feet. Finally, he states that the southern Royal Stoa had 162 columns extending across the entire enclosure's length. This colonnade had four rows of Corinthian columns with two extra at the western gate. That meant 40 columns per row, and, given the universal distance between such columns was 15 feet, that resulted in a 600-ft distance. If those 40 columns extended over today's 900-ft platform, it would require well over 20 feet between columns, an unprecedented and unstable arrangement.

2. Robinson's Arch is the remnant of the bridge leading to the temple. The center of the bridge would have lined up perfectly—to the nearest foot—with the center aisle of the Royal Collonade. Today's standard model proponents *(1)* agree with this fit. Historians who have long argued against a

temple in Lewin's SW location *(3)* often claim it was disproven by Warren *(4)*. Warren, however, mainly disproved Fergusson's argument (5) that the Dome of the Rock was the site of the original Holy Sepulchre. Fergusson did also suggest exactly Lewin's location for the Temple, shown on the map of Catherwood (6). This SW site was not disproven by evidence but rather disregarded because Warren argued the Temple was somewhere else—at the Dome of the Rock.

3. Josephus describes four gates leaving the Temple's west side (see map below). The third gate from the south lies 600 feet from the southern wall's edge lining up exactly with the northern colonnade. You will notice though, that the fourth gate is north of the 600-ft square. Josephus reported that Herod doubled the original Temple area to extend northward, with the extra space being spanned by one-stadia-long cloisters connecting the NW Temple corner to Fortress Antonia. A section of these cloister/ramparts were cut down fending off the attempted Roman raid of the Temple's gold in 66 CE. When they were burned down during the siege, Josephus bemoaned to the crowd the well-known omen of the time "When square the walls, the Temple falls!" Josephus also states the gate(s) in the southern wall was near (not at) the center of it—the Double Gate fits this description for the 600-ft square Mount—the Double and the Triple Gates do not for today's 900-ft-wide Mount (see map).

4. The Temple needed a water supply to wash away sacrificial blood, and the Mishnah clearly states that large cisterns beneath the Mount were filled via the aqueduct and drawn upon to deliver this need. Most of these caverns are beneath southern part of the Mount, with the largest by far being squarely beneath where the Temple would have stood in Lewin's map. Surveys have found no large cisterns under or close to the Dome of the Rock.

5. King Agrippa was stated to have elevated his bedroom at his palace in the western city so he could see the sacrifices at the Temple altar. The priests responded by raising a counter wall on the western end of the Temple. A straight line of sight connecting the three (palace, altar, and counter wall) only

exists for Lewin's Temple location and not for the Dome of the Rock.

6. The Wailing Wall today lies very close to where the Temple was, according to Lewin's map. For centuries after the second revolt, Jews were only given access one day a year on Tisha B'Av to mourn at the walls of the Temple Mount. They chose one location year after year, presumably where they could be closest to where the Temple had been. They did not forget.

You will also see in Lewin's map the location the former Greek fortress known as the Acra at today's Dome of the Rock site. I will discuss the Acra more later. My final thought here is that Lewin reminded us that Josephus carefully described the perimeter of the outer city walls. The third and northernmost wall also ran south on the western side to connect, not to the Temple, but to the first wall, which itself ended at the "Ophlas" (Ophel) at the SE Temple corner from the east. This helps to solve the paradox—the eastern Temple Mount wall today is not the original Temple wall but the original city wall, with the space in between the two described by Josephus as being the "so-called Cedron Ravine." Josephus says the rebel leader John's followers held the so-called Cedron (Kidron) Ravine and kept the attacking Romans at bay from both there and before the Tombs of King Alexander. The recent Temple Mount Sifting Project results *(7)* support this "ravine" having been an intra-wall zone. The debris from there has yielded items that span centuries, suggesting a landfill slowly filled with debris over many centuries rather than a Herodian-age constructed platform to support the surface we see today.

There are many more details and well-thought-out arguments in Lewin's 45-page paper. I have placed the entire paper on our website for your perusal at www.cryforjerusalem.com/documents.

REFERENCES CITED.

(1) Ritmeyer, Leen (2006) *The Quest—Revealing the Temple Mount in Jerusalem.* Carta, Jerusalem, 440 p.

(2) Lewin, Thomas, Esq., M.A., F.S.A. (1873) Observations on the probable sites of the Jewish Temple and Antonia, and the Acra, with reference to the results of the recent Palestine Explorations. *Archaeologia*, vol. 44, p. 19.

(3) Jacobson, D.M., 2019, George Grove and the establishment of the Palestine Exploration Fund, In, *Exploring the Holy Land, 150 Years of the Palestine Exploration Fund*. Gurevich D, and Kidron, A. Eds., Equinox Publishing Limited, United Kingdom, p. 18.

(4) Warren, Charles (1880) The Temple or the Tomb, Richard Bentley and Son, London, 227 p.

(5) Fergusson, J. (1878) The Temples of the Jews and the Other Buildings in the Haram Area at Jerusalem. John Murray, London.

(6) Fergusson, J. (1847) An essay on the ancient topography of Jerusalem; with restored plans of the Temple, and with plans, sections, and details of the church built by Constantine the Great over the Holy Sepulchre, now known as the Mosque of Omar. John Weale, London, plate IV shows Catherwood's map.

(7) www.tmsifting.org. The Temple Mount Sifting Project.

More from the Author

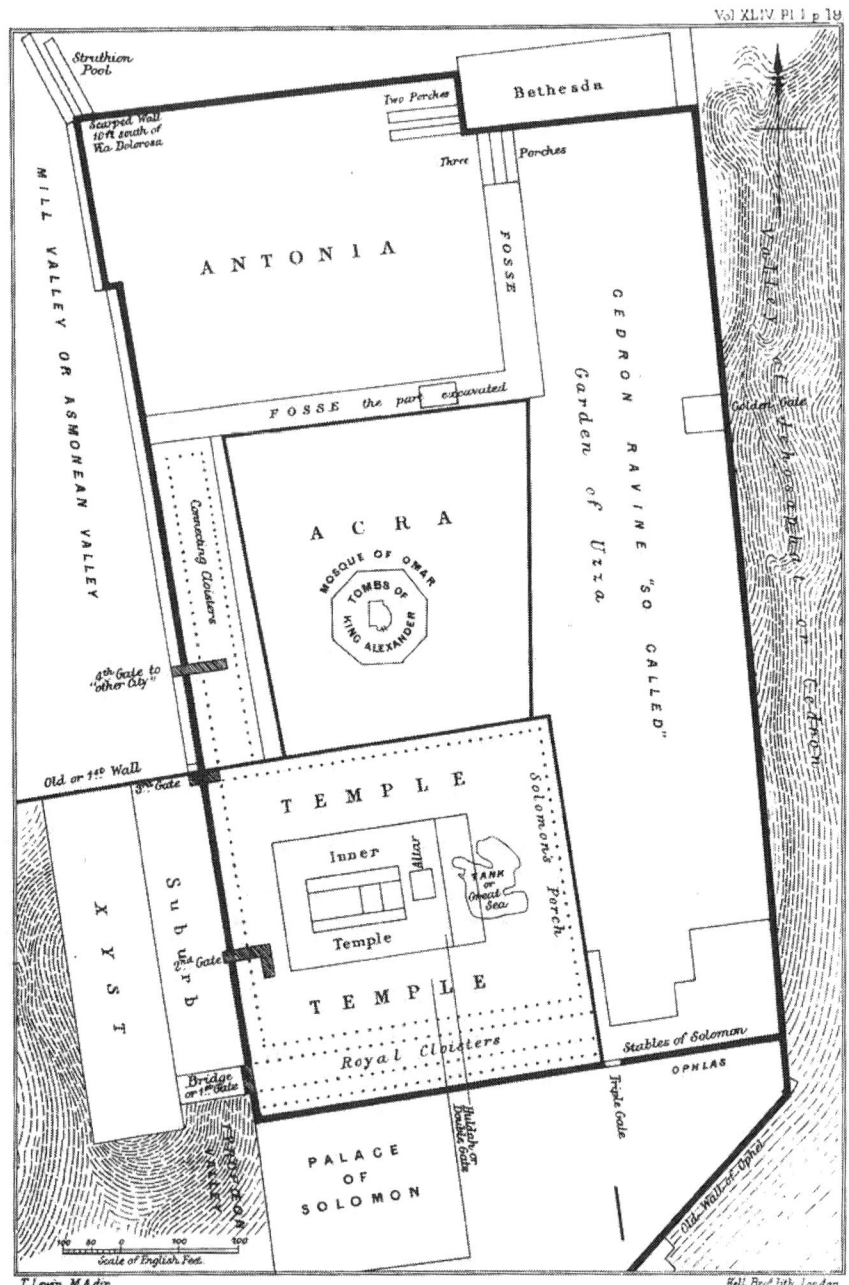

LEWIN'S MAP FROM HIS 1873 ARTICLE IN ARCHAEOLOGIA.

These additional articles and more can be found on the CryForJerusalem.com blog:

The Roman Colosseum: Built with Blood Money

The Well of Souls—What is it? What was it?

Yeshua ben Ananias—The Prophet of Doom

Revelation and the Destruction of Jerusalem

The Jewish Assassins: Who Were the Sicarii?

Water Cisterns on the Temple Mount

Fortress Antonia: The Guardian of Herod's Temple

Tomb of King Alexander

Made in the USA
Middletown, DE
10 June 2023

31991255R00391